GREAT
CRIME
STORIES

GREAT
CRIME
STORIES

CHANCELLOR
PRESS

First published in Great Britain in 1936 by Odhams Press Ltd.

Previously published as
Great Tales of Detection (1991) by Chancellor Press

Reprinted 1992

This 2002 edition published by Chancellor Press, an imprint of
Bounty Books, a division of Octopus Publishing Group,
2-4 Heron Quays, London E14 4JP

ISBN 0 7537 0571 0

Printed in Great Britain by Mackays of Chatham

CONTENTS

AUSTIN FREEMAN. *The Magic Casket.*
An ordinary, and apparently quite valueless metal
casket, but it had a tale to tell—and nearly cost a woman
her life.   11

H. C. BAILEY. *The President of San Jacinto.*
A young man was accused of murder, and an almost
perfect chain of evidence was brought to prove it. He
might have hanged, but for one thing ; he said he didn't
do it, and Mr. Fortune believed him.   33

ANTHONY BERKELEY. *Outside the Law.*
There was the Irishman, the German and the Cockney :
the Cockney was the hardest boiled crook of the lot.
And when they were surrounded by the " busies " the
German tried to justify himself—without much success.   55

THE BARONESS ORCZY. *The Regent's Park Murder.*
A thick fog, a voice that cried for help, a revolver shot,
a reckless and desperate young man tried for murder.
The jury made their decision, but the Old Man in the
Corner ventured to disagree.   66

MARGERY ALLINGHAM. *They Never Get Caught.*
The murder was planned carefully, patiently and carried
out almost stolidly ; the only person who was really
disconcerted was the victim.   79

J. J. CONNINGTON. *Before Insulin.*
He was only a boy still—and he was dying. It was not
only a tragedy, it was a great responsibility for his
trustee ; for he was heir to a fortune, and it was his to
will away—if he lived to attain his majority.   101

STACY AUMONIER. *The Perfect Murder.*
He believed that a perfect murder could be committed.
So he planned it—and it was actually carried out—
but with unexpected results.   110

G. K. CHESTERTON. *The Shadow of the Shark.*
If a murder seems to be committed in a way so unusual
as to be supernatural, it needs imagination to solve it.
That is why the poet could see further into the mystery
than the police.   126

PAGE

O. HENRY. *The Marionettes.*
This is a story of a dying profligate attended by a crook
doctor. Both men, according to the accepted standards,
are " evil doers," yet each has, and maintains his standard
of honour. 147

F. BRITTEN AUSTIN. *Diamond Cut Diamond.*
He insisted that he had murdered his best friend, but
before he gave himself up he wanted to know why he
had done it. 159

AUGUSTUS MUIR. *Murder at the Microphone.*
If the broadcast speech had not been recorded, they
might have hanged the wrong man. 183

MILWARD KENNEDY. *Death in the Kitchen.*
He was a man who was not used to a kitchen—or he
might not have overlooked the thing he did. 197

FREEMAN WILLS CROFTS. *The Vertical Line.*
Inspector French *knew* the man was guilty. Yet his
alibi was perfect and it seemed that he would go free—
until the detective realised the significance of the vertical
line. 201

EDGAR WALLACE. *The Clue of Monday's Settling.*
A man used a simple psychology game to solve a crime. 215

GERARD FAIRLIE. *The Ghost of a Smile.*
If he hadn't seen that faint trace of a smile on her face,
the doctor would never had realised that she was glad
because her husband was dead. 228

BERTRAM ATKEY. *Sons of the Chief Warder.*
They were twins, and so alike to look at that no one
could tell them apart. But only two men realised how
different were their characters. 245

SEAMARK. *Query.*
He had spent the best years of his life trying to work out
the problem. He solved it at last, and gave the legal
profession a bad shock. 267

RALPH STRAUS. *The Room on the Fourth Floor.*
A young English girl with her mother arrives at a Paris
hotel and becomes involved in the most mysterious and
horrible adventure which drives her nearly to the point
of insanity. 278

A. E. W. MASON. *The Wounded God.*
For years the girl had carried with her a secret that had
overshadowed her life. At last she met the one person
who had the right to share it with her. 288

CONTENTS

PAGE

LORD DUNSANY. *The Electric King.*
He had spent years fighting for his sanity, and at last he
had found the one safe way of keeping madness at bay.　309

A. J. ALAN. *Charles.*
They had to agree as to what they would say at the
inquest. Of course, everything was quite a mistake—
and yet if questions had been asked, it might had been
awkward.　328

JOHN METCALFE. *The Funeral March of a Marionette.*
The two boys were out with their guy on a November
afternoon. They had a very realistic guy—too horribly
life-like altogether.　336

W. W. JACOBS. *The Interruption.*
They were both people who wanted peace and the good
things of this life, and they both over-reached themselves
in trying to get what they wanted.　346

C. D. HERIOT. *Nobody at Home.*
He considered that it was rather fine of him to go so far
out of his way to look up an old friend who had not done
so well in life as himself and he was annoyed to receive
no welcome.　358

MRS. BELLOC LOWNDES. *St. Catherine's Eve.*
She was a woman torn between love and duty, and she
chose duty ; but was it destiny, or her mad husband
who meted out a frightful fate to the man she loved ?　362

F. MARION CRAWFORD. *The Screaming Skull.*
The old sea captain would not let himself believe he was
in any way responsible for the death of the woman—
until, at last, conviction was horribly brought home to
him.　389

JOSEPH CONRAD. *The Idiots.*
The tragedy of a Breton peasant farmer who needed
sons to serve the soil as he himself served it—but his
children were not as other men's.　417

SYDNEY HORLER. *The Vampire.*
There were strange stories told about the newcomer to
the district, and his fellow creatures shunned him.
One man was his confidante, and knew his terrible
secret.　440

SAKI (H. H. MUNRO). *The Interlopers.*
They had been sworn enemies for years. In the face of
mutual catastrophe they stopped for the first time, to
consider how useless was their feud. Then a third factor
entered into the story.　446

PAGE

L. P. HARTLEY. *The Travelling Grave.*
As a keen collector, he was naturally anxious to see if his latest acquisition could do all that was claimed for it. To find that out he needed a human being who could disappear without causing comment. 452

E. A. POE. *The Tell-Tale Heart.*
In which the reader enters into the terrible imaginings of a madman's mind. 474

H. SPICER. *The Bird Woman.*
The girl said she had no fear of lunatics or human oddities, but she met with a case that shook even her strong nerve. 479

W. FRYER HARVEY. *The Dabblers.*
Goaded on by something stronger than themselves, terrified schoolboys took part in strange, traditional rites, the meaning and origin of which they did not know. 482

VERNON LEE. *Marsyas in Flanders.*
Strange things happened in the little French church where the miraculous crucifix hung. Those who witnessed them went mad and died. 492

ELEANOR SCOTT. *The Room.*
Four men slept in that room and came out changed persons. A fifth, despite their pleading, insisted on sharing their experience. 504

MARJORIE BOWEN. *Florence Flannery.*
He did not know where she came from or who she was, but he brought her to that desolate dreary house as his bride. When she saw her own name scratched on the window, and heard the strange story of the woman who had borne it before her, she knew that destiny had overtaken her. 521

ERNEST BRAMAH. *The Ghost at Massingham Mansions.*
A blind man cannot see even ghosts ; but that does not mean that he is deceived by their antics. 540

NORMAN MATSON. *The House on Big Faraway.*
The woman had waited for years to redeem her act of cowardice—but it was useless because a man had told too much. 564

NAOMI ROYDE-SMITH. *Madam Julia's Tale.*
She loved life and music, but she was old and very frail. Yet she knew that the life to which she clung so tenaciously was guarded by an angel. 574

CONTENTS

PAGE

OLIVER ONIONS. *The Cigarette Case.*
Roses, wine and lavender—all the scent of a summer
night in Provence clings to this charming story of two
young Englishmen entertained in a foreign land by their
own country-women.   597

SIR ARTHUR QUILLER-COUCH. *A Pair of Hands.*
It was a very gentle and loving little ghost that haunted
the old house on the Cornish coast.   609

ILLUSTRATIONS

" I THOUGHT SO," HE MUTTERED AND TURNED THE BODY OVER. PAGE
BELL GAVE A STIFLED CRY   *by S. A. Field*   51

HE REMEMBERED HIS OWN PENCILLED WORDS, AS IF HE COULD
READ THEM, " MILLIE DEAR, THIS DOES EXPLAIN ITSELF,
DOESN'T IT ? "   *by Ronald Lampitt*   97

THEY LOOKED AT EACH OTHER . . . AND DOWN AT THE BODY
by H. A. Seabright   135

HE DROPPED HIS TEST TUBES AND BEGAN TO SWING ROUND.
BEFORE HE COULD DO SO WILDE FIRED   *by Colin Orme*   207

THE MAN WAS NOT EATING.   HE WAS GAZING INTENTLY AT
EX-661   *by Bertram Prance*   257

I SAW POLYDORE CROMECQ RAISE A GREAT STICK   *by J. Nicolle*   305

THE POLICEMAN'S MANNER HAD GROWN CURIOUS, THEN PUZZLED,
GRAVELY DUBIOUS, SERIOUS FINALLY—AND SOMETHING
ELSE   *by Norman Howard*   343

SHE HAD SCREAMED " ALIVE ! " AND AT ONCE VANISHED BEFORE
HIS EYES   *by Margaret Bradley*   437

" THE FOOT'S INSIDE IT ALL RIGHT," CRIED CURTIS, AND BEGAN
TUGGING AT ONE OF THE SHOES   *by Freeman*   471

A SLOW PROCESSION SINGING—BUT FRIGHTENED, HORRIBLY
FRIGHTENED   *by Cyril Holloway*   489

" HE CAME FLOPPING UP THE STAIRS, HE BROKE THE BOLTS ;
HE JUMPED ON THE BED   *by S. Tresilian*   535

A SECOND BEFORE THE LIFT TOOK HER OUT OF HIS SIGHT, HER
EYES MET HIS   *by H. M. Brock*   593

THE MAGIC CASKET

By

R. AUSTIN FREEMAN

IT was in the near neighbourhood of King's Road, Chelsea, that chance, aided by Thorndyke's sharp and observant eyes, introduced us to the dramatic story of the Magic Casket. Not that there was anything strikingly dramatic in the opening phase of the affair, nor even in the story of the casket itself. It was Thorndyke who added the dramatic touch, and most of the magic, too ; and I record the affair principally as an illustration of his extraordinary capacity for producing odd items of out-of-the-way knowledge and instantly applying them in the most unexpected manner.

Eight o'clock had struck on a misty November night when we turned out of the main road, and, leaving behind the glare of the shop windows, plunged into the maze of dark and narrow streets to the north. The abrupt change impressed us both, and Thorndyke proceeded to moralise on it in his pleasant, reflective fashion.

" London is an inexhaustible place," he mused. " Its variety is infinite. A minute ago we walked in a glare of light, jostled by a multitude. And now look at this little street. It is as dim as a tunnel, and we have got it absolutely to ourselves. Anything might happen in a place like this."

Suddenly he stopped. We were, at the moment, passing a small church or chapel, the west door of which was enclosed in an open porch ; and as my observant friend stepped into the latter and stooped, I perceived, in the deep shadow against the wall, the object which had evidently caught his eye.

" What is it ? " I asked, following him in.

" It is a handbag," he replied ; " and the question is, what is it doing here ? "

He tried the church door, which was obviously locked, and coming out, looked at the windows.

"There are no lights in the church," said he ; "the' place is locked up, and there is nobody in sight. Apparently the bag is derelict. Shall we have a look at it ? "

Without waiting for an answer, he picked it up and brought it out into the mitigated darkness of the street, where we proceeded to inspect it. But at the first glance it told its own tale ; for it had evidently been locked, and it bore unmistakable traces of having been forced open.

"It isn't empty," said Thorndyke. "I think we had better see what is in it. Just catch hold while I get a light."

He handed me the bag while he felt in his pocket for the tiny electric lamp which he made a habit of carrying—and an excellent habit it is. I held the mouth of the bag open while he illuminated the interior, which we then saw to be occupied by several objects neatly wrapped in brown paper. One of these Thorndyke lifted out, and untying the string and removing the paper, displayed a Chinese stoneware jar. Attached to it was a label, bearing the stamp of the Victoria and Albert Museum, on which was written :

"MISS MABEL BONNEY,
168 Willow Walk, Fulham Road, W."

"That tells us all that we want to know," said Thorndyke, re-wrapping the jar and tenderly replacing it in the bag. "We can't do wrong in delivering the things to their owner, especially as the bag itself is evidently her property, too," and he pointed to the gilt initials, "M. B.," stamped on the morocco.

It took us but a few minutes to reach the Fulham Road, but we then had to walk nearly a mile along that thoroughfare before we arrived at Willow Walk—to which an obliging shopkeeper had directed us ; and, naturally, No. 168 was at the farther end.

As we turned into the quiet street we almost collided with two men, who were walking at a rapid pace, but both looking back over their shoulders. I noticed that they were both Japanese—well-dressed, gentlemanly-looking men—but I gave them little attention, being interested, rather, in what they were looking at. This was a taxicab which was dimly visible by the light of a street lamp at the farther end of the "Walk," and from which four persons had just alighted. Two of these had hurried ahead to knock at a door, while the other two walked very slowly across the pavement and up the steps to the threshold. Almost immediately the door was opened ; two of the shadowy figures entered, and the other two returned slowly to the cab ; and as we came nearer, I could see that these latter were policemen in uniform. I had just time to note this fact when they both got into the cab and were forthwith spirited away.

" Looks like a street accident of some kind," I remarked ; and then, as I glanced at the number of the house we were passing, I added : " Now, I wonder if that house happens to be—yes, by Jove ! it is. It is 168 ! Things have been happening, and this bag of ours is one of the dramatis personæ."

The response to our knock was by no means prompt. I was, in fact, in the act of raising my hand to the knocker to repeat the summons when the door opened and revealed an elderly servant-maid, who regarded us inquiringly, and, as I thought, with something approaching alarm.

" Does Miss Mabel Bonney live here ? " Thorndyke asked.

" Yes, sir," was the reply ; " but I am afraid you can't see her just now, unless it is something urgent. She is rather upset, and particularly engaged at present."

" There is no occasion whatever to disturb her," said Thorndyke. " We have merely called to restore this bag, which seemed to have been lost ; " and with this he held it out towards her. She grasped it eagerly, with a cry of surprise, and as the mouth fell open, she peered into it.

" Why," she exclaimed, " they don't seem to have taken anything, after all. Where did you find it, sir ? "

" In the porch of a church in Spelton Street," Thorndyke replied, and was turning away when the servant said earnestly: " Would you kindly give me your name and address, sir ? Miss Bonney will wish to write and thank you."

" There is really no need," said he ; but she interrupted anxiously :

" If you would be so kind, sir. Miss Bonney will be so vexed if she is unable to thank you ; and besides, she may want to ask you some questions about it."

" That is true," said Thorndyke (who was restrained only by good manners from asking one or two questions, himself). He produced his card-case, and having handed one of his cards to the maid, wished her " good-evening " and retired.

" That bag had evidently been pinched," I remarked, as we walked back towards the Fulham Road.

" Evidently," he agreed, and was about to enlarge on the matter when our attention was attracted to a taxi, which was approaching from the direction of the main road. A man's

head was thrust out of the window, and as the vehicle passed a
street lamp, I observed that the head appertained to an elderly
gentleman with very white hair and a very fresh-coloured face.

" Did you see who that was ? " Thorndyke asked.

" It looked like old Brodribb," I replied.

" It did ; very much. I wonder where he is off to."

He turned and followed, with a speculative eye, the receding
taxi, which presently swept alongside the kerb and stopped,
apparently opposite the house from which we had just come.
As the vehicle came to rest, the door flew open and the passenger shot out like an elderly, but agile, Jack-in-the-box, and
bounced up the steps.

" That is Brodribb's knock, sure enough," said I, as the
old-fashioned flourish reverberated up the quiet street. " I
have heard it too often on our own knocker to mistake it. But
we had better not let him see us watching him."

As we went once more on our way, I took a sly glance, now
and again, at my friend, noting with a certain malicious enjoy-
ment his profoundly cogitative air. I knew quite well what
was happening in his mind ; for his mind reacted to observed
facts in an invariable manner. And here was a group of related
facts : the bag, stolen, but deposited intact ; the museum
label ; the injured or sick person—probably Miss Bonney,
herself—brought home under police escort ; and the arrival,
post-haste, of the old lawyer ; a significant group of facts.
And there was Thorndyke, under my amused and attentive
observation, fitting them together in various combinations to see
what general conclusion emerged. Apparently my own mental
state was equally clear to him, for he remarked, presently, as if
replying to an unspoken comment :

" Well, I expect we shall know all about it before many
days have passed if Brodribb sees my card, as he most probably
will. Here comes an omnibus that will suit us. Shall we hop
on ? "

He stood at the kerb and raised his stick ; and as the
accommodation on the omnibus was such that our seats were
separated, there was no opportunity to pursue the subject
further, even if there had been anything to discuss.

But Thorndyke's prediction was justified sooner than I had
expected. For we had not long finished our supper, and had
not yet closed the " oak," when there was heard a mighty
flourish on the knocker of our inner door.

" Brodribb, by Jingo ! " I exclaimed, and hurried across
the room to let him in.

" No, Jervis," he said as I invited him to enter, " I am not
coming in. Don't want to disturb you at this time of night.
I've just called to make an appointment for to-morrow with
a client."

" Is the client's name Bonney ? " I asked.

He started and gazed at me in astonishment. " Gad,
Jervis ! " he exclaimed, " you are getting as bad as Thorndyke.
How the deuce did you know that she was my client ? "

" Never mind how I know. It is our business to know
everything in these chambers. But if your appointment con-
cerns Miss Mabel Bonney, for the Lord's sake come in and
give Thorndyke a chance of a night's rest. At present, he is
on broken bottles, as Mr. Bumble would express it."

On this persuasion, Mr. Brodribb entered, nothing loath
—very much the reverse, in fact—and having bestowed a jovial
greeting on Thorndyke, glanced approvingly round the room.

" Ha ! " said he, " you look very cosy. If you are really
sure I am not—— "

I cut him short by propelling him gently towards the fire,
beside which I deposited him in an easy chair, while Thorndyke
pressed the electric bell which rang up in the laboratory.

" Well," said Brodribb, spreading himself out comfortably
before the fire like a handsome old Tom-cat, " if you are going
to let me give you a few particulars—but perhaps you would
rather that I should not talk shop."

" Now you know perfectly well, Brodribb," said Thorndyke,
" that ' shop ' is the breath of life to us all. Let us have those
particulars."

Brodribb sighed contentedly and placed his toes on the
fender (and at this moment the door opened softly and Polton
looked into the room. He took a single, understanding glance
at our visitor, and withdrew, shutting the door without a
sound).

" I am glad," pursued Brodribb, " to have this opportunity
of a preliminary chat, because there are certain things that one
can say better when the client is not present ; and I am deeply
interested in Miss Bonney's affairs. The crisis in those affairs
which has brought me here is of quite recent date—in fact, it
dates from this evening. But I know your partiality for having
events related in their proper sequence, so I will leave to-day's
happenings for the moment and tell you the story—the whole
of which is material to the case—from the beginning."

Here there was a slight interruption, due to Polton's noiseless entry with a tray on which was a decanter, a biscuit box,

and three port glasses. This he deposited on a small table, which he placed within convenient reach of our guest. Then, with a glance of altruistic satisfaction at our old friend, he stole out like a benevolent ghost.

" Dear, dear ! " exclaimed Brodribb, beaming on the decanter, " this is really too bad. You ought not to indulge me in this way."

" My dear Brodribb," replied Thorndyke, ' you are a benefactor to us. You give us a pretext for taking a glass of port. We can't drink alone, you know."

" I should, if I had a cellar like yours," chuckled Brodribb, sniffing ecstatically at his glass. He took a sip, with his eyes closed, savoured it solemnly, shook his head, and set the glass down on the table.

" To return to our case," he resumed ; " Miss Bonney is the daughter of a solicitor, Harold Bonney—you may remember him. He had offices in Bedford Row ; and there, one morning, a client came to him and asked him to take care of some property while he, the said client, ran over to Paris, where he had some urgent business. The property in question was a collection of pearls of most unusual size and value, forming a great necklace, which had been unstrung for the sake of portability. It is not clear where they came from, but as the transaction occurred soon after the Russian Revolution, we may make a guess. At any rate, there they were, packed loosely in a leather bag, the string of which was sealed with the owner's seal.

" Bonney seems to have been rather casual about the affair. He gave the client a receipt for the bag, stating the nature of the contents, which he had not seen, and deposited it, in the client's presence, in the safe in his private office. Perhaps he intended to take it to the bank or transfer it to his strong-room, but it is evident that he did neither ; for his managing clerk, who kept the second key of the strong-room—without which the room could not be opened—knew nothing of the transaction. When he went home at about seven o'clock, he left Bonney hard at work in his office, and there is no doubt that the pearls were still in the safe.

" That night, at about a quarter to nine, it happened that a couple of C.I.D. officers were walking up Bedford Row when they saw three men come out of one of the houses. Two of them turned up towards Theobald's Road, but the third came south, towards them. As he passed them, they both recognised him as a Japanese named Uyenishi, who was believed to be a member of a cosmopolitan gang and whom the police were keeping under observation. Naturally, their suspicions were aroused. The first two men had hurried round the corner and were out of sight ; and when they turned to look after Uyenishi, he had mended his pace considerably and was looking back at them. Thereupon one of the officers, named Barker, decided to follow the Jap, while the other, Holt, reconnoitred the premises.

" Now, as soon as Barker turned, the Japanese broke into a run. It was just such a night as this : dark and slightly foggy. In order to keep his man in sight, Barker had to run, too ; and he found that he had a sprinter to deal with. From the bottom of Bedford Row, Uyenishi darted across and shot down Hand Court like a lamp-lighter. Barker followed, but at the Holborn end his man was nowhere to be seen. However, he presently learned from a man at a shop door that the fugitive had run past and turned up Brownlow Street, so off he went again in pursuit. But when he got to the top of the street, back in Bedford Row, he was done. There was no sign of the man, and no one about from whom he could make inquiries. All he could do was to cross the road and walk up Bedford Row to see if Holt had made any discoveries.

" As he was trying to identify the house, his colleague came out on to the doorstep and beckoned him in ; and this was the story that he told. He had recognised the house by the big lamp-standard ; and as the place was all dark, he had gone into the entry and tried the office door. Finding it unlocked, he had entered the clerks' office, lit the gas, and tried the door of the private office, but found it locked. He knocked at it, but getting no answer, had a good look round the clerks' office ; and there, presently, on the floor in a dark corner, he found a key. This he tried in the door of the private office, and finding that it fitted, turned it and opened the door. As he did so, the light from the outer office fell on the body of a man lying on the floor just inside.

" A moment's inspection showed that the man had been murdered—first knocked on the head and then finished with a knife. Examination of the pockets showed that the dead man was Harold Bonney, and also that no robbery from the person seemed to have been committed. Nor was there any sign of any other kind of robbery. Nothing seemed to have been disturbed, and the safe had not been broken into, though that was not very conclusive, as the safe key was in the dead man's pocket. However, a murder had been committed, and obviously Uyenishi was either the murderer or an accessory ; so

Holt had, at once, rung up Scotland Yard on the office tele-phone, giving all the particulars.

" I may say at once that Uyenishi disappeared completely and at once. He never went to his lodgings at Limehouse, for the police were there before he could have arrived. A lively hue and cry was kept up. Photographs of the wanted man were posted outside every police-station, and a watch was set at all the ports. But he was never found. He must have got away at once on some outward-bound tramp from the Thames. And there we will leave him for the moment.

" At first it was thought that nothing had been stolen, since the managing clerk could not discover that anything was missing. But a few days later the client returned from Paris, and presenting his receipt, asked for his pearls. But the pearls had vanished. Clearly they had been the object of the crime. The robbers must have known about them and traced them to the office. Of course the safe had been opened with its own key, which was then replaced in the dead man's pocket.

" Now, I was poor Bonney's executor, and in that capacity I denied his liability in respect of the pearls on the ground that he was a gratuitous bailee—there being no evidence that any consideration had been demanded—and that being mur-dered cannot be construed as negligence. But Miss Mabel, who was practically the sole legatee, insisted on accepting liability. She said that the pearls could have been secured in the bank or the strong-room, and that she was morally, if not legally, liable for their loss ; and she insisted on handing to the owner the full amount at which he valued them. It was a wildly foolish proceeding, for he would certainly have accepted half the sum. But still I take my hat off to a person—-man or woman—who can accept poverty in preference to a broken covenant ; " and here Brodribb, being in fact that sort of person himself, had to be consoled with a replenished glass.

" And mind you," he resumed, " when I speak of poverty, I wish to be taken literally. The estimated value of those pearls was fifty thousand pounds—if you can imagine anyone out of Bedlam giving such a sum for a parcel of trash like that ; and when poor Mabel Bonney had paid it, she was left with the prospect of having to spread her butter mighty thin for the rest of her life. As a matter of fact, she has had to sell one after another of her little treasures to pay just her current expenses, and I'm hanged if I can see how she is going to carry on when she has sold the last of them. But there, I mustn't take up your time with her private troubles. Let us return to our muttons.

"First, as to the pearls. They were never traced, and it seems probable that they were never disposed of. For, you see, pearls are different from any other kind of gems. You can cut up a big diamond, but you can't cut up a big pearl. And the great value of this necklace was due not only to the size, the perfect shape and ' orient ' of the separate pearls, but to the fact that the whole set was perfectly matched. To break up the necklace was to destroy a good part of its value.

"And now as to our friend Uyenishi. He disappeared, as I have said ; but he reappeared at Los Angeles, in custody of the police, charged with robbery and murder. He was taken red-handed and was duly convicted and sentenced to death ; but for some reason—or more probably, for no reason, as we should think—the sentence was commuted to imprisonment for life. Under these circumstances, the English police naturally took no action, especially as they really had no evidence against him.

"Now Uyenishi was, by trade, a metal-worker ; a maker of those pretty trifles that are so dear to the artistic Japanese, and when he was in prison he was allowed to set up a little workshop and practise his trade on a small scale. Among other things that he made was a little casket in the form of a seated figure, which he said he wanted to give to his brother as a keepsake. I don't know whether any permission was granted for him to make this gift, but that is of no consequence ; for Uyenishi got influenza and was carried off in a few days by pneumonia ; and the prison authorities learned that his brother had been killed, a week or two previously, in a shooting affair at San Francisco. So the casket remained on their hands.

"About this time, Miss Bonney was invited to accompany an American lady on a visit to California, and accepted gratefully. While she was there she paid a visit to the prison to inquire whether Uyenishi had ever made any kind of statement concerning the missing pearls. Here she heard of Uyenishi's recent death ; and the governor of the prison, as he could not give her any information, handed over to her the casket as a sort of memento. This transaction came to the knowledge of the press, and—well, you know what the Californian press is like. There were ' some comments,' as they would say, and quite an assortment of Japanese, of shady antecedents, applied to the prison to have the casket ' restored ' to them as Uyenishi's heirs. Then Miss Bonney's rooms at the hotel were raided by burglars—but the casket was in the hotel strong-room—and Miss Bonney and her hostess were shadowed by various undesirables in such a disturbing fashion that the two ladies became alarmed and secretly made their way to New York. But there another burglary occurred, with the same unsuccessful result, and the shadowing began again. Finally, Miss Bonney, feeling that her presence was a danger to her friend, decided to return to England, and managed to get on board the ship without letting her departure be known in advance.

" But even in England she has not been left in peace. She has had an uncomfortable feeling of being watched and attended, and has seemed to be constantly meeting Japanese men in the streets, especially in the vicinity of her house. Of course, all the fuss is about this infernal casket ; and when she told me what was happening, I promptly popped the thing in my pocket and took it to my office, where I stowed it in the strong-room. And there, of course, it ought to have remained. But it didn't. One day Miss Bonney told me that she was sending some small things to a loan exhibition of oriental works of art at the South Kensington Museum, and she wished to include the casket. I urged her strongly to do nothing of the kind, but she persisted ; and the end of it was that we went to the museum together, with her pottery and stuff in a hand-bag and the casket in my pocket.

" It was a most imprudent thing to do, for there the beastly casket was, for several months, exposed in a glass case for any-one to see, with her name on the label ; and what was worse, full particulars of the origin of the thing. However, nothing happened while it was there—the museum is not an easy place to steal from—and all went well until it was time to remove the things after the close of the exhibition. Now, to-day was the appointed day, and, as on the previous occasion, she and I went to the museum together. But the unfortunate thing is that we didn't come away together. Her other exhibits were all pottery, and these were dealt with first, so that she had her handbag packed and was ready to go before they had begun on the metal-work cases. As we were not going the same way, it didn't seem necessary for her to wait ; so she went off with her bag and I stayed behind until the casket was released, when I put it in my pocket and went home, where I locked the thing up again in the strong-room.

" It was about seven when I got home. A little after eight I heard the telephone ring down in the office, and down I went, cursing the untimely ringer, who turned out to be a policeman at St. George's Hospital. He said he had found Miss Bonney lying unconscious in the street and had taken her to the hospital, where she had been detained for a while, but she was now recovered and he was taking her home. She would like me, if possible, to go and see her at once. Well, of course, I set off forthwith and got to her house a few minutes after her arrival, and just after you had left.

"She was a good deal upset, so I didn't worry her with many questions, but she gave me a short account of her mis-adventure, which amounted to this : She had started to walk home from the museum along the Brompton Road, and she was passing down a quiet street between that and Fulham Road when she heard soft footsteps behind her. The next moment, a scarf or shawl was thrown over her head and drawn tightly round her neck. At the same moment, the bag was snatched from her hand. That is all that she remembers, for she was half-suffocated and so terrified that she fainted, and knew no more until she found herself in a cab with two policemen, who were taking her to the hospital.

"Now it is obvious that her assailants were in search of that damned casket, for the bag had been broken open and searched, but nothing taken or damaged ; which suggests the Japanese again, for a British thief would have smashed the crockery. I found your card there, and I put it to Miss Bonney that we had better ask you to help us—I told her all about you —and she agreed emphatically. So that is why I am here, drinking your port and robbing you of your night's rest."

"And what do you want me to do ? " Thorndyke asked.

"Whatever you think best," was the cheerful reply. " In the first place, this nuisance must be put a stop to—this shadow-ing and hanging about. But apart from that, you must see that there is something queer about this accursed casket. The beastly thing is of no intrinsic value. The museum man turned up his nose at it. But it evidently has some extrinsic value, and no small value either. If it is good enough for these devils to follow it all the way from the States, as they seem to have done, it is good enough for us to try to find out what its value is. That is where you come in. I propose to bring Miss Bonney to see you to-morrow, and I will bring the infernal casket, too. Then you will ask her a few questions, take a look at the casket —through the microscope, if necessary—and tell us all about it in your usual necromantic way."

Thorndyke laughed as he refilled our friend's glass. " If

faith will move mountains, Brodribb," said he, " you ought to have been a civil engineer. But it is certainly a rather intriguing problem."

" Ha ! " exclaimed the old solicitor ; " then it's all right. I've known you a good many years, but I've never known you to be stumped ; and you are not going to be stumped now. What time shall I bring her ? Afternoon or evening would suit her best."

" Very well," replied Thorndyke ; " bring her to tea—say, five o'clock. How will that do ? "

" Excellently ; and here's good luck to the adventure." He drained his glass, and the decanter being now empty, he rose, shook our hands warmly, and took his departure in high spirits.

It was with a very lively interest that I looked forward to the prospective visit. Like Thorndyke, I found the case rather intriguing. For it was quite clear, as our shrewd old friend had said, that there was something more than met the eye in the matter of this casket. Hence, on the following afternoon, when, on the stroke of five, footsteps became audible on our stairs, I awaited the arrival of our new client with keen curiosity, both as to herself and her mysterious property.

To tell the truth, the lady was better worth looking at than the casket. At the first glance, I was strongly prepossessed in her favour, and so, I think, was Thorndyke. Not that she was a beauty, though comely enough. But she was an example of a type that seems to be growing rarer ; quiet, gentle, soft-spoken, and a lady to her finger-tips ; a little sad-faced and careworn, with a streak or two of white in her prettily-disposed black hair, though she could not have been much over thirty-five. Altogether a very gracious and winning personality.

When we had been presented to her by Brodribb—who treated her as if she had been a royal personage—and had enthroned her in the most comfortable easy-chair, we inquired as to her health, and were duly thanked for the salvage of the bag. Then Polton brought in the tray, with an air that seemed to demand an escort of choristers ; the tea was poured out, and the informal proceedings began.

She had not, however, much to tell ; for she had not seen her assailants, and the essential facts of the case had been fully presented in Brodribb's excellent summary After a very few questions, therefore, we came to the next stage ; which was introduced by Brodribb's taking from his pocket a small parcel which he proceeded to open.

" There," said he, " that is the *fons et origo mali*. Not much to look at, I think you will agree." He set the object down on the table and glared at it malevolently, while Thorndyke and I regarded it with a more impersonal interest. It was not much to look at. Just an ordinary Japanese casket in the form of a squat, shapeless figure with a silly little grinning face, of which the head and shoulders opened on a hinge ; a pleasant enough object, with its quiet, warm colouring, but certainly not a masterpiece of art.

Thorndyke picked it up and turned it over slowly for a preliminary inspection ; then he went on to examine it detail by detail, watched closely, in his turn, by Brodribb and me. Slowly and methodically, his eye—fortified by a watchmaker's eyeglass—travelled over every part of the exterior. Then he opened it, and having examined the inside of the lid, scrutinised the bottom from within, long and attentively. Finally, he turned the casket upside down and examined the bottom from without, giving to it the longest and most rigorous inspection of all—which puzzled me somewhat, for the bottom was absolutely plain. At length, he passed the casket and the eyeglass to me without comment.

" Well," said Brodribb, " what is the verdict ? "

" It is of no value as a work of art," replied Thorndyke. " The body and lid are just castings of common white metal— an antimony alloy, I should say. The bronze colour is lacquer."

" So the museum man remarked," said Brodribb.

" But," continued Thorndyke, " there is one very odd thing about it. The only piece of fine metal in it is in the part which matters least. The bottom is a separate plate of the alloy known to the Japanese as Shakudo—an alloy of copper and gold."

" Yes," said Brodribb, " the museum man noted that, too, and couldn't make out why it had been put there."

" Then," Thorndyke continued, " there is another anomalous feature ; the inside of the bottom is covered with elaborate decoration—just the place where decoration is most inappropriate, since it would be covered up by the contents of the casket. And, again, this decoration is etched ; not engraved or chased. But etching is a very unusual process for this purpose, if it is ever used at all by Japanese metal-workers. My impression is that it is not ; for it is most unsuitable for decorative purposes. That is all that I observe, so far."

" And what do you infer from your observations ? " Brodribb asked.

" I should like to think the matter over," was the reply.

" There is an obvious anomaly, which must have some significance. But I won't embark on speculative opinions at this stage. I should like, however, to take one or two photographs of the casket, for reference ; but that will occupy some time. You will hardly want to wait so long."

" No," said Brodribb. " But Miss Bonney is coming with me to my office to go over some documents and discuss a little business. When we have finished, I will come back and fetch the confounded thing."

" There is no need for that," replied Thorndyke. " As soon as I have done what is necessary, I will bring it up to your place."

To this arrangement Brodribb agreed readily, and he and his client prepared to depart. I rose, too, and as I happened to have a call to make in Old Square, Lincoln's Inn, I asked permission to walk with them.

As we came out into King's Bench Walk I noticed a smallish, gentlemanly-looking man who had just passed our entry and now turned in at the one next door ; and by the light of the lamp in the entry he looked to me like a Japanese. I thought Miss Bonney had observed him, too, but she made no remark, and neither did I. But, passing up Inner Temple Lane, we nearly overtook two other men, who—though I got but a back view of them and the light was feeble enough—aroused my suspicions by their neat, small figures. As we approached, they quickened their pace, and one of them looked back over his shoulder ; and then my suspicions were confirmed, for it was an unmistakable Japanese face that looked round at us. Miss Bonney saw that I had observed the men, for she remarked, as they turned sharply at the Cloisters and entered Pump Court :

" You see, I am still haunted by Japanese."

" I noticed them," said Brodribb. " They are probably law students. But we may as well be companionable " ; and with this, he, too, headed for Pump Court.

We followed our oriental friends across the Lane into Fountain Court, and through that and Devereux Court out to Temple Bar, where we parted from them ; they turning westward and we crossing to Bell Yard, up which we walked, entering New Square by the Carey Street gate. At Brodribb's doorway we halted and looked back, but no one was in sight. I accordingly went my way, promising to return anon to hear Thorndyke's report, and the lawyer and his client disappeared through the portal.

My business occupied me longer than I had expected, but nevertheless, when I arrived at Brodribb's premises—where he lived in chambers over his office—Thorndyke had not yet made his appearance. A quarter of an hour later, however, we heard his brisk step on the stairs, and as Brodribb threw the door open, he entered and produced the casket from his pocket.

" Well," said Brodribb, taking it from him and locking it, for the time being, in a drawer, " has the oracle spoken ; and if so, what did he say ? "

" Oracles," replied Thorndyke, " have a way of being more concise than explicit. Before I attempt to interpret the message, I should like to view the scene of the escape ; to see if there was any intelligible reason why this man Uyenishi should have returned up Brownlow Street into what must have been the danger zone. I think that is a material question."

" Then," said Brodribb, with evident eagerness, " let us all walk up and have a look at the confounded place. It is quite close by."

We all agreed instantly, two of us, at least, being on the tip-toe of expectation. For Thorndyke, who habitually under-stated his results, had virtually admitted that the casket had told him something ; and as we walked up the Square to the gate in Lincoln's Inn Fields, I watched him furtively, trying to gather from his impassive face a hint as to what the something amounted to, and wondering how the movements of the fugitive bore on the solution of the mystery. Brodribb was similarly occupied, and as we crossed from Great Turnstile and took our way up Brownlow Street, I could see that his excitement was approaching bursting-point.

At the top of the street Thorndyke paused and looked up and down the rather dismal thoroughfare which forms a con-tinuation of Bedford Row and bears its name. Then he crossed to the paved island surrounding the pump which stands in the middle of the road, and from thence surveyed the entrances to Brownlow Street and Hand Court ; and then he turned and looked thoughtfully at the pump.

" A quaint old survivor, this," he remarked, tapping the iron shell with his knuckles. " There is a similar one, you may remember, in Queen Square, and another at Aldgate. But that is still in use."

" Yes," Brodribb assented, almost dancing with impatience and inwardly damning the pump, as I could see, " I've noticed it."

" I suppose," Thorndyke proceeded, in a reflective tone,
" they had to remove the handle. But it was rather a pity."

" Perhaps it was," growled Brodribb, whose complexion
was rapidly developing affinities to that of a pickled cabbage,
" but what the d—— "

Here he broke off short and glared silently at Thorndyke,
who had raised his arm and squeezed his hand into the opening
once occupied by the handle. He groped in the interior with
an expression of placid interest, and presently reported : " The
barrel is still there, and so, apparently, is the plunger "—
(Here I heard Brodribb mutter huskily, " Damn the barrel and
the plunger too ! ") " but my hand is rather large for the
exploration. Would you, Miss Bonney, mind slipping your
hand in and telling me if I am right ? "

We all gazed at Thorndyke in dismay, but in a moment
Miss Bonney recovered from her astonishment, and with a
deprecating smile, half shy, half amused, she slipped off her
glove, and reaching up—it was rather high for her—inserted
her hand into the narrow slit. Brodribb glared at her and
gobbled like a turkey-cock, and I watched her with a sudden
suspicion that something was going to happen. Nor was I
mistaken. For, as I looked, the shy, puzzled smile faded from
her face and was succeeded by an expression of incredulous
astonishment. Slowly she withdrew her hand, and as it came
out of the slit it dragged something after it. I started forward,
and by the light of the lamp above the pump I could see that
the object was a leather bag secured by a string from which
hung a broken seal.

" It can't be ! " she gasped as, with trembling fingers, she
untied the string. Then, as she peered into the open mouth,
she uttered a little cry.

" It is ! It is ! It is the necklace ! "

Brodribb was speechless with amazement. So was I ; and
I was still gazing open-mouthed at the bag in Miss Bonney's
hands when I felt Thorndyke touch my arm. I turned quickly
and found him offering me an automatic pistol.

" Stand by, Jervis," he said quietly, looking towards
Gray's Inn.

I looked in the same direction, and then perceived three
men stealing round the corner from Jockey's Fields. Brodribb
saw them, too, and snatching the bag of pearls from his client's
hands, buttoned it into his breast pocket and placed himself
before its owner, grasping his stick with a war-like air. The
three men filed along the pavement until they were opposite

us, when they turned simultaneously and bore down on the pump, each man, as I noticed, holding his right hand behind him. In a moment, Thorndyke's hand, grasping a pistol, flew up—as did mine, also—and he called out sharply :

"Stop ! If any man moves a hand, I fire."

The challenge brought them up short, evidently unprepared for this kind of reception. What would have happened next it is impossible to guess. But at this moment a police whistle sounded and two constables ran out from Hand Court. The whistle was instantly echoed from the direction of Warwick Court, whence two more constabulary figures appeared through the postern gate of Gray's Inn. Our three attendants hesitated but for an instant. Then, with one accord, they turned tail and flew like the wind round into Jockey's Fields, with the whole posse of constables close on their heels.

"Remarkable coincidence," said Brodribb, "that those policemen should happen to be on the look-out. Or isn't it a coincidence ? "

"I telephoned to the station superintendent before I started," replied Thorndyke, "warning him of a possible breach of the peace at this spot."

Brodribb chuckled. "You're a wonderful man, Thorndyke. You think of everything. I wonder if the police will catch those fellows."

"It is no concern of ours," replied Thorndyke. "We've got the pearls, and that finishes the business. There will be no more shadowing, in any case."

Miss Bonney heaved a comfortable little sigh and glanced gratefully at Thorndyke. "You can have no idea what a relief that is ! " she exclaimed ; "to say nothing of the treasure-trove."

We waited some time, but as neither the fugitives nor the constables reappeared, we presently made our way back down Brownlow Street. And there it was that Brodribb had an inspiration.

"I'll tell you what," said he. "I will just pop these things in my strong-room—they will be perfectly safe there until the bank opens to-morrow—and then we'll go and have a nice little dinner. I'll pay the piper."

"Indeed you won't ! " exclaimed Miss Bonney. "This is my thanksgiving festival, and the benevolent wizard shall be the guest of the evening."

"Very well, my dear," agreed Brodribb. "I will pay and charge it to the estate. But I stipulate that the benevolent

wizard shall tell us exactly what the oracle said.   That is essential to the preservation of my sanity."

" You shall have his *ipsissima verba*," Thorndyke promised;
and the resolution was carried, *nem. con.*

An hour and a half later we were seated around a table in a
private room of a café to which Mr. Brodribb had conducted
us.   I may not divulge its whereabouts, though I may, perhaps,
hint that we approached it by way of Wardour Street.   At any
rate, we had dined, even to the fulfilment of Brodribb's ideal,
and coffee and liqueurs furnished a sort of gastronomic doxo-
logy.   Brodribb had lighted a cigar and Thorndyke had produced a vicious-looking little black cheroot, which he regarded
fondly and then returned to its abiding-place as unsuited to
the present company.

" Now," said Brodribb, watching Thorndyke fill his pipe
(as understudy of the cheroot aforesaid), " we are waiting to
hear the words of the oracle."

" You shall hear them." Thorndyke replied.   " There were
only five of them.   But first, there are certain introductory
matters to be disposed of.   The solution of this problem is
based on two well-known physical facts, one metallurgical and
the other optical."

" Ha ! " said Brodribb.   " But you must temper the wind
to the shorn lamb, you know, Thorndyke.   Miss Bonney and
I are not scientists."

" I will put the matter quite simply, but you must have the
facts.   The first relates to the properties of malleable metals
—excepting iron and steel—and especially of copper and its
alloys.   If a plate of such metal or alloy—say, bronze, for
instance—is made red-hot and quenched in water, it becomes
quite soft and flexible—the reverse of what happens in the
case of iron.   Now, if such a plate of softened metal be placed
on a steel anvil and hammered, it becomes extremely hard
and brittle."

" I follow that," said Brodribb.

" Then see what follows.   If, instead of hammering the
soft plate, you put on it the edge of a blunt chisel and strike
on that chisel a sharp blow, you produce an indented line.
Now the plate remains soft ; but the metal forming the indented line has been hammered and has become hard.   There
is now a line of hard metal on the soft plate.   Is that clear ? "

" Perfectly," replied Brodribb ; and Thorndyke accordingly continued :

" The second fact is this : If a beam of light falls on a

polished surface which reflects it, and if that surface is turned through a given angle, the beam of light is deflected through double that angle."

"H'm!" grunted Brodribb. "Yes. No doubt. I hope we are not going to get into any deeper waters, Thorndyke."

"We are not," replied the latter, smiling urbanely. "We are now going to consider the application of these facts. Have you ever seen a Japanese magic mirror?"

"Never; nor even heard of such a thing."

"They are bronze mirrors, just like the ancient Greek or Etruscan mirrors—which are probably 'magic' mirrors, too. A typical specimen consists of a circular or oval plate of bronze, highly polished on the face and decorated on the back with chased ornament—commonly a dragon or some such device—and furnished with a handle. The ornament is, as I have said, chased; that is to say, it is executed in indented lines made with chasing tools, which are, in effect, small chisels, more or less blunt, which are struck with a chasing-hammer.

"Now these mirrors have a very singular property. Although the face is perfectly plain, as a mirror should be, yet, if a beam of sunlight is caught on it and reflected, say, on to a white wall, the round or oval patch of light on the wall is not a plain light patch. It shows quite clearly the ornament on the back of the mirror."

"But how extraordinary!" exclaimed Miss Bonney. "It sounds quite incredible."

"It does," Thorndyke agreed. "And yet the explanation is quite simple. Professor Sylvanus Thompson pointed it out years ago. It is based on the facts which I have just stated to you. The artist who makes one of these mirrors begins, naturally, by annealing the metal until it is quite soft. Then he chases the design on the back, and this design then shows slightly on the face. But he now grinds the face perfectly flat with fine emery and water so that the traces of the design are completely obliterated. Finally, he polishes the face with rouge on a soft buff.

"But now observe that wherever the chasing-tool has made a line, the metal is hardened right through, so that the design is in hard metal on a soft matrix. But the hardened metal resists the wear of the polishing buff more than the soft metal does. The result is that the act of polishing causes the design to appear in faint relief on the face. Its projection is infinitesimal—less than the hundred-thousandth of an inch—and totally invisible to the eye. But, minute as it is, owing to the optical law which I mentioned—which, in effect, doubles the projection—it is enough to influence the reflection of light. As a consequence, every chased line appears on the patch of light as a dark line with a bright border, and so the whole design is visible. I think that is quite clear."

"Perfectly clear," Miss Bonney and Brodribb agreed.

"But now," pursued Thorndyke, "before we come to the casket, there is a very curious corollary which I must mention. Supposing our artist, having finished the mirror, should proceed with a scraper to erase the design from the back; and on the blank, scraped surface to etch a new design. The process of etching does not harden the metal, so the new design does not appear on the reflection. But the old design would. For although it was invisible on the face and had been erased from the back, it would still exist in the substance of the metal and continue to influence the reflection. The odd result would be that the design which would be visible in the patch of light on the wall would be a different one from that on the back of the mirror.

"No doubt, you see what I am leading up to. But I will take the investigation of the casket as it actually occurred. It was obvious, at once, that the value of the thing was extrinsic. It had no intrinsic value, either in material or workmanship. What could that value be? The clear suggestion was that the casket was the vehicle of some secret message or information. It had been made by Uyenishi, who had almost certainly had possession of the missing pearls, and who had been so closely pursued that he never had an opportunity to communicate with his confederates. It was to be given to a man who was almost certainly one of those confederates; and, since the pearls had never been traced, there was a distinct probability that the (presumed) message referred to some hiding-place in which Uyenishi had concealed them during his flight, and where they were probably still hidden.

"With these considerations in my mind, I examined the casket, and this was what I found. The thing, itself, was a common white-metal casting, made presentable by means of lacquer. But the white metal bottom had been cut out and replaced by a plate of fine bronze—Shakudo. The inside of this was covered with an etched design, which immediately aroused my suspicions. Turning it over, I saw that the outside of the bottom was not only smooth and polished; it was a true mirror. It gave a perfectly undistorted reflection of my face. At once, I suspected that the mirror held the secret; that the message, whatever it was, had been chased on the back, had then been scraped away and an etched design worked on it to hide the traces of the scraper.

" As soon as you were gone, I took the casket up to the laboratory and threw a strong beam of parallel light from a condenser on the bottom, catching the reflection on a sheet of white paper. The result was just what I had expected. On the bright oval patch on the paper could be seen the shadowy, but quite distinct, forms of five words in the Japanese character.

" I was in somewhat of a dilemma, for I have no knowledge of Japanese, whereas the circumstances were such as to make it rather unsafe to employ a translator. However, as I do just know the Japanese characters and possess a Japanese dictionary, I determined to make an attempt to fudge out the words myself. If I failed, I could then look for a discreet translator.

" However, it proved to be easier than I had expected, for the words were detached ; they did not form a sentence, and so involved no questions of grammar. I spelt out the first word and then looked it up in the dictionary. The translation was ' pearls.' This looked hopeful, and I went on to the next, of which the translation was ' pump.' The third word floored me. It seemed to be ' jokkis,' or ' jokkish,' but there was no such word in the dictionary ; so I turned to the next word, hoping that it would explain its predecessor. And it did. The fourth word was ' fields,' and the last word was evidently ' London.' So the entire group read : ' Pearls, Pump, Jokkis, Fields, London.'

" Now, there is no pump, so far as I know, in Jockey's Fields, but there is one in Bedford Row close to the corner of the Fields, and exactly opposite the end of Brownlow Street. And by Mr. Brodribb's account, Uyenishi, in his flight, ran down Hand Court and returned up Brownlow Street, as if he were making for the pump. As the latter is disused and the handle-hole is high up, well out of the way of children, it offers quite a good temporary hiding-place, and I had no doubt that the bag of pearls had been poked into it and was probably there still. I was tempted to go at once and explore ; but I was anxious that the discovery should be made by Miss Bonney, herself, and I did not dare to make a preliminary exploration for fear of being shadowed. If I had found the treasure I should have had to take it and give it to her ; which would have been a flat ending to the adventure. So I had to dissemble and be the occasion of much smothered objurgation on the part of my friend Brodribb. And that is the whole story of my interview with the oracle."

Our mantelpiece is becoming a veritable museum of trophies of victory, the gifts of grateful clients. Among them is a squat, shapeless figure of a Japanese gentleman of the old school, with a silly grinning little face—The Magic Casket. But its possession is no longer a menace. Its sting has been drawn ; its magic is exploded ; its secret is exposed, and its glory departed.

THE PRESIDENT OF
SAN JACINTO

By

H. C. BAILEY

MR. REGINALD FORTUNE lay in a long chair. On his right hand a precipice fell to still black water. On his left the mountains rose into a tiara of snow. Far away in front sunlight found the green flood of a glacier. But Mr. Fortune saw none of these things. He was eating strawberries and cream.

The Hon. Sidney Lomas, Chief of the Criminal Investigation Department, disguised as a bloodthirsty fisherman, arrived stiffly but happy, and behind him a large Norwegian bore the corpses of two salmon into the farm-house. " The lord high detective," Reggie murmured. " An allegorical picture, by the late Mr. Watts."

" Great days," Lomas said, and let himself down gingerly into a chair. " Hallo, has there been a post ? " He reached for one of the papers at Reggie's feet. " My country, what of thee ? "

" They're at it again, Lomas. They've murdered a real live lord."

" Thank heaven I'm not there. Who is it ? "

" One Carwell. In the wilds of the Midlands."

" Young Carwell ? He's a blameless youth to slay. What happened ? "

" They found him in his library with his head smashed. Queer case."

Lomas read the report, which had nothing more to tell. " Burglary, I suppose," he pronounced.

" Well, I have an alibi," said Reggie.

Neither the Chief of the Criminal Investigation Department nor his scientific adviser saw any reason to end a good holiday for the sake of avenging Lord Carwell. The policemen who

33

dealt with the affair did not call for help. Mr. Fortune and Mr. Lomas continued to catch the salmon and eat the strawberries of Norway and let the world go by and became happily out of date. It was not till they were on the North Sea that they met the Carwell case again.

The Newcastle packet was rolling in a slow, heavy rhythm. Most of the passengers had succumbed. Lomas and Reggie fitted themselves and two chairs into a corner of the upper deck with all the London newspapers that were waiting for them at Bergen. Lomas, a methodical man, began at the beginning. Reggie worked back from the end. And in a moment, " My only aunt ! " he said softly. " Lomas, old thing, they're doing themselves proud. Who do you think they've taken for that Carwell murder ? The cousin, the heir, one Mark Carwell. This is highly intriguing."

" Good Gad ! "

" As you say," Reggie agreed. " Yes. Public Prosecutor on it. Old Brunker leading for the Crown. Riding pretty hard, too. The man Mark is for it, I fear, Lomas. They do these things quite neatly without us. It's all very disheartening."

" Mark Carwell ? A harum-scarum young ruffian he always was."

" Yes. Have you noticed these little things mean much ? I haven't."

" What's the case ? "

" The second housemaid found Lord Carwell sitting in the library with his head smashed. He was dead. The doctor came up in half an hour, found him cold, and swears he had been dead five or six hours. Cause of death—brain injury from the blow given by some heavy, blunt instrument. No one in the house had heard a sound. No sign of burglary, no weapon. There was a small house-party, the man Mark, the girl Carwell was engaged to, Lady Violet Barclay and her papa and mamma, and Sir Brian Carwell—that's the contractor, some sort of distant cousin. Mark was left with Lord Carwell when the rest of them went to bed. Lady Violet and papa and mamma say they heard a noisy quarrel. Violet says Carwell had told her before that Mark was writing to him for money to get married on, and Carwell didn't approve of the girl."

" I don't fancy Carwell would approve of the kind of girl Mark would want to marry."

" Yes, that's what the fair Violet implies. She seems to be a good hater. She did her little best to hang Mark."

" Why, if he killed her man, can you wonder ? "

" Oh, I don't wonder. But I wouldn't like to get in her way myself. Not really a nice girl. She swore Mark had been threatening Carwell, and Carwell was afraid of him. The prosecution put in a letter of Mark's which talked wild about doing something vague and desperate if Carwell didn't stump up."

" Did Mark go into the box ? "

" Yes. That was his error. I'm afraid he isn't respectable, Lomas. He showed no seemly grief. He made it quite clear that he had no use for Hugo, Lord Carwell. He rather suggested that Hugo had lived to spite him, and got killed to spite him. He admitted all Lady Violet's evidence and underlined it. He said Hugo had been more against him than ever since she came into the family. He owned to the quarrel of Hugo's last night. Only he swore that he left the man alive."

" Well, he did his best to hang himself."

" As you say. A bold, bad fellow. That's all, except that cousin Mark had a big stick, a loaded stick with a knob head, and he took it down to Carwell Hall."

" What's the verdict ? "

" To be continued in our next. The judge was going to sum up in the morning. In the paper we haven't got."

Lomas lay back and watched the grey sea rise into sight as the boat rolled to starboard. " What do you make of it, Fortune ? "

" There's the rudiments of a case," said Reggie. " The Carwell estate is entailed. Mark is the heir. He didn't love the man. The man was going to marry and that would wash out Mark. Mark was the last man with him, unless there is some hard lying. They had a row about money and girls, which are always infuriating, and Mark had a weapon handy which might have killed him. And nobody else had had any motive, there's no evidence of anybody else in the business. Yes, the rudiments of a case."

" I don't see the rudiments of a defence."

" The defence is that Mark says that he didn't."

" Quite, quite," Lomas nodded. " It's not the strongest case in the world, but I have had convictions on worse. The jury will go by what they made of Mark in the box."

" And hang him for his face." Reggie turned over a paper and held out the portrait of a bull-necked, square-headed young man.

" I wouldn't say they'd be wrong," Lomas said. " Who's the judge ? Maine ? He'll keep 'em straight."

" I wonder. What is straight, Lomas ? "

" My dear fellow, it all turns on the way this lad gave his evidence, and that you can't tell from a report."

" He don't conciliate me," Reggie murmured. " Yet I like evidence, Lomas."

" Why, this is adequate, if it's true. And Mark didn't challenge it."

" I know. Adequate is the word. Just enough and nothing more. That's unusual, Lomas. Well, well. What about tea?"

They picked their way over some prostrate bodies to the saloon and again gave up the Carwell case.

But when the boat had made her slow way through the clatter of the Tyne, Reggie was quick to intercept the first customs officer on board. " I say, what was the result of that murder trial ? "

The man laughed. " Thought you wanted the 3.30 winner, you were so keen, sir. Oh, Mark Carwell's guilty, of course. His mother's white-haired boy, he is. Not 'alf."

" The voice of the people," said Lomas, in Reggie's ear.

On the way to London they read the judge's summing up, an oration lucid and fair, but relentless.

" He had no doubt," Reggie said.

" And a good judge too," Lomas tossed the paper aside. " Thank heaven they got it out of the way without bothering me."

" You are an almost perfect official," said Reggie with reverence.

In the morning when Reggie came down to his breakfast in London he was told that some one had rung up to know if he was back in England yet. He was only half-way through his omelet when the name of Miss Joan Amber was brought to him.

Every one who likes to see a beautiful actress act, and many who don't care whether she can act or not, know what Miss Amber looks like, that large young woman with the golden eyes whom Reggie hurried to welcome. He held her hand rather a long while. " The world is very good to-day," he said, and inspected her. " You don't need a holiday, Miss Amber."

" You've had too much, Mr. Fortune."

" Have you been kind enough to want me ? "

" I really meant that you looked—— " she made a large gesture.

" No, no—not fat," Reggie protested. " Only genial. I expand in your presence."

"Well—round," said Miss Amber. "And my presence must be very bad for you."

"No, not bad for me—only crushing."

"Well, I did sometimes notice you were away. And I want you now. For a friend of mine. Will you help her ? "

"When did I ever say ' No ' to you ? "

"Bless you," said Miss Amber. "It's the Carwell case."

"Oh, my prophetic soul," Reggie groaned. "But what in wonder have you to do with the Carwell case ? "

"I know Nan Nest. She's the girl Mark Carwell is going to marry."

"Do you mind if you sit down ? " said Reggie, and wandered away to the window. "You're disturbing to the intellect, Miss Amber. Let us be calm. You shouldn't talk about people marrying people and look like that." Miss Amber smiled at his back. –She has confessed to moments in which she would like to be Reggie Fortune's mother. "Yes. Well now, does Miss Amber happen to know the man Mark ? "

"I've met him. He's not a bad fellow. A first-class fighting-subaltern. That sort of thing."

Reggie nodded. "That's his public form too."

"Oh, Mr. Fortune, he's absolutely straight. Not a very wise youth, of course. You know, I could imagine him killing his cousin, but what I can't imagine is that he would ever say he didn't if he did."

"Yes. There weren't any women on the jury ? "

"Don't sneer."

"I never do when you're listening. That was a scientific statement. Now, what's Miss Nest like ? "

"Like a jolly schoolboy. Or she was, poor child. Oh, they would have been splendidly happy, if that tiresome man had set Mark up somewhere in the country instead of getting himself murdered."

Reggie smiled sadly. "Don't say that to any one but me. Or let her say it. Why did the tiresome man object to her ? I suppose it's true that he did ? "

"Oh, heavens, yes. Because she's on the stage. She plays little parts you know—flappers and such. She's quite good as herself. She can't act."

"What was the late Carwell ? What sort of fellow ? That didn't come out at the trial."

"A priceless prig, Mark says. I suppose he was the last survivor of our ancient aristocracy. Poor Mark ! "

"I wonder," Reggie murmured.

" What ? "

" Well "—he spread out his hands—" everything. You haven't exactly cleared it up, have you ? "

" Mark told Nan he didn't do it," she said quietly, and Reggie looked into her eyes. " Oh, can't you see ? That's to trust to. That's sure." Reggie turned away. " You will help her ? " the low voice came again.

And at last, " My dear, I daren't say so," Reggie said. " You mustn't tell her to hope anything. I'll go over all the case. But the man is condemned."

" Why, but there's a court of appeal."

" Only for something new. And I don't see it."

" Mark didn't kill him ! " she cried.

Reggie spread out his hands. " That's faith."

" Mr. Fortune ! When I said I had come about the Carwell case, you said, ' Oh, my prophetic soul ! ' You don't believe the evidence, then. You never did. You always thought there was something they didn't find out."

" I don't know. I don't know," Reggie said slowly. " That's the last word now. And it may be the last word in the end."

" You ! " she said, and held out her hand.

When she was gone, Reggie stood looking at the place where she had sat. " God help us," he said—rare words on his lips. And the place he went to was Scotland Yard.

Lomas was occupied with other sublime officials. So Superintendent Bell reported. He had also been telephoning for Mr. Fortune. Mr. Fortune was admitted and found himself before a large red truculent man who glared. " Hallo, Finch. Is this a council of war ? " said Mr. Fortune ; for at that date Mr. Montagu Finchampstead was the Public Prosecutor.

" Lomas tells me "—Finchampstead has a bullying manner —" you've formed an opinion on the evidence in the Carwell case."

" Then he knows more than I do. The evidence was all right—what there was of it."

" The chain is complete," Finchampstead announced.

" Yes. Yes. If you don't pull it hard."

" Well, no one did pull it."

" That's what I'm pointing out, Finch," said Reggie sweetly. " Why are you so cross ? "

" The trouble is, Fortune, the Carwell butler's bolted," Lomas said.

Reggie walked across the room and took one of Lomas's

cigars and lit it, and made himself comfortable in his chair.
" That's a new fact," he said softly.

" Nonsense," Finchampstead cried. " It's irrelevant. It
doesn't affect the issue. The verdict stands."

" I noticed you didn't call the butler at the trial," Reggie
murmured.

" Why the devil should we ? He knew nothing."

" Yet he bolts."

Lomas smiled. " The unfortunate thing is, Fortune, he
bolted before the trial was over. At the end of the second day
the local police were told that he had vanished. The news was
passed on to Finchampstead. But the defence was not informed. And it didn't come out at the trial."

" Well, well. I thought you were riding rather hard, Finch.
You were."

" Rubbish. The case was perfectly clear. The disappearance of the butler doesn't affect it—if he has disappeared. The
fellow may very well have gone off on some affair of his own,
and turn up again in a day or two. And if he doesn't, it's
nothing to the purpose. The butler was known to have a
kindness for Mark Carwell. If we never hear of him again I
shall conclude that he had a hand in the murder, and when he
saw the case was going against Mark, thought he had better
vanish."

" Theory number two," Reggie murmured.

" What do you mean ? "

" Your first was that the butler knew nothing. Your second
is that he knows too much. Better choose which leg you'll
stand on in the Court of Appeal."

Finchampstead glared.

" In the meantime, Finch, we'll try to find the butler for
you," said Lomas cheerfully.

" And I think I'll have a look at the evidence," Reggie
murmured.

" There is no flaw in the evidence," Finchampstead
boomed.

" Well, not till you look at it."

Finchampstead with some explosions of digust removed
himself.

" Zeal, all zeal," said Reggie sadly. " Well-meaning man.
Only one idea at a time. And sometimes a wrong un."

" He's a lawyer by nature," Lomas apologized. " You
always rub him up the wrong way. He don't like the scientific
mind. What ? " Bell had come in to give him a visiting card.

He read out, " Sir Brian Carwell." He looked at Reggie. " Now which side is he on ? "

" One moment. Who exactly is he ? Some sort of remote cousin ?"

" Yes. He comes of a younger branch. People say the brains of the Carwell's went to them. His father was the engineer, old Ralph Carwell. This man's an engineering contractor. He made his pile over South American railways."

" You wouldn't say he was passionately interested in the late Lord Carwell or Cousin Mark."

There came in a lean man with an air of decision and authority, but older than his resilient vigour suggested, for his hair was much sprinkled with grey, and in his brown face, about the eyes and mouth, the wrinkles were many. He was exact with the formalities of introduction and greeting, but much at his ease, and then, " I had better explain who I am, Mr. Lomas."

" Oh, we've heard of Sir Brian Carwell."

" Thanks. But I dare say you don't know my private affairs. I'm some sort of fifteenth cousin of these two unfortunate young fellows. And just now I happen to be the acting head of the family. I'm not the next heir, of course. That's old Canon Carwell. But I was on the spot when this thing happened. After his arrest Mark asked me to take charge for him, and the Canon wished me to act. That's my position. Well, I carried on to keep things as they were at the Hall and on the estate. Several of the servants want to quit, of course, but they haven't gone yet. The butler was a special case. He told me he had given Hugo notice some time before. I could find no record, but it was possible enough, and as he only wanted to retire and settle down in the neighbourhood, I made no difficulty. So he set himself up in lodgings in the village. He was looking about for a house, he told me. I suppose he had done pretty well. He had been in service at the Hall thirty or forty years, poor devil. What a life ! He knew Hugo and Mark much better than I do, had known 'em all their young lives. He knew all the family affairs inside and out. One night the people where he was lodging went round to the police to say he'd gone out and not come back. He hasn't come back yet."

" And what do you conclude, Sir Brian ? "

" I'll be damned if I know what I conclude. That's your business, isn't it ? "

" Not without some facts," said Lomas. " When did he leave the Hall ? "

" After Mark was arrested. May 13. And he disappeared on the evening of the second day of the trial."

" That would be when it looked certain that Mark would be found guilty. Why did he wait till then ? "

Sir Brian laughed. " If I knew that, I suppose I shouldn't be here. I'm asking you to find him."

" Quite, quite," Lomas agreed. " The local police knew of his disappearance at once ? "

" I said so. I wish I had known as soon. The police didn't bother to mention it at the trial. It might have made some difference to the verdict, Mr. Lomas."

" That's matter of opinion, of course," said Lomas. " I wasn't in England myself. I needn't tell you that it's open to the defence to appeal against the conviction."

" Is it ? " Sir Brian's shadowed eyes grew smaller. " You don't know Mark, Mr. Lomas. If I were to tell you Mark refuses to make an appeal on this ground because it would be putting the murder on the butler, what would you say ? "

" Good Gad ! " was what Lomas did say. He lay back and put up his eyeglass and looked from Sir Brian to Reggie and back again. " You mean Mark admits he is guilty ? "

" Guilty be damned," said Sir Brian. " No, sir, I mean Mark liked the wretched fellow and won't hear of anything against him. Mark's a fool. But that's not a reason for hanging him. I say you got your conviction by suppressing evidence. It's up to you to review the case."

" Still, Lord Carwell was killed," said Lomas gently, " and somebody killed him. Who was it ? "

" Not Mark. He hasn't got it in him. I suppose he never hit a fellow who couldn't hit back in his life."

" But surely," Lomas purred, " if there was a quarrel, Lord Carwell might—— "

" Hugo was a weed," Sir Brian pronounced. " Mark never touched him, my friend."

" Yes, yes, very natural you should think so." Lomas shifted his papers. " Of course you won't expect me to say anything, Sir Brian. And what exactly is it you want me to do ? "

Sir Brian laughed. " My dear sir, it's not for me to tell you your duty. I put it to you that a man has disappeared, and that his disappearance makes hay of the case on which the Crown convicted a cousin of mine of murder. What you do about it is your affair."

" You may rely upon it, Sir Brian," said Lomas in his most

official manner, " the affair will be thoroughly investigated."

" I expected no less, Mr. Lomas." And Sir Brian ceremoniously but briskly took his leave.

After which, " Good Gad ! " said Lomas again, and stared at Reggie Fortune.

" Nice restful companion, isn't he ? Yes. The sort of fellow that has made Old England great."

" Oh, I don't mind him. He could be dealt with. But he's right, confound him. The case is a most unholy mess."

" Well, well," said Reggie placidly. " You must rub it out, dear, and do it again."

" If everybody had tried to muddle it they couldn't have done worse."

Reggie stared at him. " Yes. Yes, you have your moments, Lomas," he said.

" Suppose the butler did the murder. Why in the world should he wait to run away till Mark was certain to be found guilty ? "

" And suppose he didn't, why did he run away at all ? You can make up quite a lot of riddles in this business. Why should any one but Mark do it ? Why is Mark so mighty tender of the butler's reputation ? Why is anything ? "

" Yes, it's all crazy—except Sir Brian. He's reasonable enough, confound him."

" Yes. Yes, these rational men are a nuisance to the police. Well, well, begin again at the beginning."

" I wish I knew where it did begin."

" My dear fellow ! Are we downhearted ? I'll have a look at the medical evidence. You go over Carwell Hall and the butler's digs with a small tooth comb."

But the first thing which Mr. Fortune did was to send a note to Miss Amber :

MY DEAR CHILD,
   Mark can appeal. The ground for it is the disappearance of the Carwell butler—and a good ground. But he must appeal. Tell Miss Nest.
                                        R.F.

Two days afterwards he went again to Scotland Yard, summoned to a conference of the powers. The public prosecutor's large and florid face had no welcome for him. " Any more new facts, Finch ? " he said cheerfully.

" Mark Carwell has entered an appeal," Mr. Finchampstead boomed. " On the ground of the butler's disappearance."

" Fancy that ! " Reggie murmured, and lit a cigar. " Sir Brian doesn't seem to have been very well informed, Lomas."

" The boy's come to his senses, I suppose. But we haven't found the butler. He left no papers behind him. All he did leave was his clothes and about a hundred pounds in small notes."

" So he didn't take his ready money. That's interesting."

" Well, not all of it. He left another hundred or so in the savings bank, and some small investments in building societies and so forth—a matter of five hundred. Either he didn't mean to vanish, or he was in the deuce of a hurry to go."

" Yes. Yes, there's another little point. Five or six hundred isn't much to retire on. Why was he in such a hurry to retire ? "

" He may have had more than we can trace, of course. He may have gone off with some Carwell property. But there is no evidence of anything being stolen."

" The plain fact is," Finchampstead boomed, " you have found out nothing but that he's gone. We knew that before."

" And it's a pity you kept it dark," said Lomas acidly. ' You wouldn't have had an appeal to fight."

" The case against Mark Carwell is intrinsically as strong as ever," Finchampstead pronounced. " There is no reason whatever to suspect the butler, he had no motive for murder, he gained nothing by it, his disappearance is most naturally accounted for by an accident."

" Yes, you'll have to say all that in the Court of Appeal. I don't think it will cut much ice."

" I am free to admit that his disappearance is an awkward complication in the case," Finchampstead's oratory rolled on. " But surely, Lomas, you have formed some theory in explation ? "

Lomas shook his head.

" We've had too much theory, Finch," said Reggie cheerfully. " Let's try some facts. I want the body exhumed."

The eyes of Mr. Finchampstead goggled. His large jaw fell.

" Good Gad, you don't doubt he's dead ? " Lomas cried.

" Oh, he'll be dead all right. I want to know how he died."

" Are you serious ? " Finchampstead mourned. " Really, Fortune, this is not a matter for frivolity. The poor fellow was found dead with one side of his head beaten in. There can be no dispute how he died. I presume you have taken the trouble to read the medical evidence."

" I have. That's what worries me. I've seen the doctors
you called. Dear old things."

" Very sound men. And of the highest standing," Finchampstead rebuked him.

" As you say. They know a fractured skull when they see
it. They would see everything they looked for. But they
didn't look for what they didn't see."

" May I ask what you mean ? "

" Any other cause of death."

" The cause was perfectly plain. There was nothing else
to look for."

" Yes. Yes." Reggie lay back and blew smoke. " That's
the sort of reasoning that got you this verdict. Look here,
Finch. That smashed head would have killed him all right,
but it shouldn't have killed him so quick. He ought to have
lingered unconscious a long while. And he had been dead
hours when they found him. We have to begin again from the
beginning. I want an order for exhumation."

" Better ask for a subpoena for his soul."

" That's rather good, Finch," Reggie smiled. " You're
beginning to take an interest in the case."

" If you could take the evidence of the murdered," said
Lomas, " a good many convictions for murder would look
rather queer."

Mr. Finchampstead was horrified. " I conceive," he
announced with dignity, " that a trial in an English court is a
practically perfect means of discovering the truth."

Reverently then they watched him go. And when he was
gone, " He's a wonderful man," said Reggie. " He really
believes that."

The next morning saw Mr. Fortune, escorted by Superintendent Bell, arrive at Carwell Hall. It stands in what Mr.
Fortune called a sluggish country, a country of large rolling
fields and slow rivers. The air was heavy and blurred all
colour and form. Mr. Fortune arrived at Carwell Hall feeling
as if he had eaten too much, a sensation rare in him, which he
resented. He was hardly propitiated by the house, though
others have rejoiced in it. It was built under the Tudors out
of the spoils and, they say, with the stones of an abbey. Though
some eighteenth-century ruffian played tricks with it, its mellow
walls still speak of an older, more venturous world. It is a
place of studied charm, gracious and smiling, but in its elabora-
tion of form and ornament offering a thousand things to look
at, denies itself as a whole, evasive and strange.

Reggie got out of the car and stood back to survey it.

" Something of everything, isn't it, Bell ?   Like a Shake-speare play.   Just the place to have a murder in one room with a children's party in the next, and a nice girl making love on the stairs, and father going mad in the attics."

" I rather like Shakespeare myself, sir," said Superintendent Bell.

" You're so tolerant," said Reggie, and went in.

A new butler said that Sir Brian was expecting them.   Sir Brian was brusquely civil.   He was very glad to find that the case was being reopened.   The whole place was at their orders.   Anything he could do——

" I thought I might just look round," Reggie said.   " We are rather after the fair, though."   He did not think it necessary to tell Sir Brian that Lord Carwell's body would be dug up that night.

They were taken across a hall with a noble roof of hammer beams to the place of the murder.   The library was panelled in oak, which at a man's height from the ground flowered into carving.   The ceiling was moulded into a hundred coats of arms, each blazoned with its right device, and the glow and colour of them, scarlet and bright blue and gold, filled the room.   Black presses with vast locks stood here and there.   A stool was on either side of the great open hearth.   By the massive table a stern fifteenth-century chair was set.

Bell gazed about him and breathed heavily.   " Splendid room, sir," he said.   " Quite palatial."

" But it's not what I'd want after dinner myself," Reggie murmured.

" I've no use for the place," said Sir Brian.   " But it suited Hugo.   He would never have a thing changed.   He was really a survival.   Poor old Hugo."

" He was sitting here ? " Reggie touched the chair.

" So they tell me.   I didn't see him till some time after the girl found him.   You'd better hear what she has to say."

A frightened and agitated housemaid testified that his lord-ship had been sitting in that chair bent over the table and his head rested on it, and the left side of his head was all smashed, and on the table was a pool of his blood.   She would never forget it, never.   She became aware of Reggie's deepening frown.   " That's the truth, sir," she cried, " so help me God it is."

" I know, I know," said Reggie.   " No blood anywhere else ?   No other marks in the room ? "

There hadn't been anything. She had cleaned the room herself. And it had been awful. She hadn't slept a night since. And so on till she was got rid of.

" Well ? " said Sir Brian. " What's the expert make of her ? "

Reggie was looking at the table and fingering it. He looked up suddenly. " Oh, she's telling the truth," he said. " And that's that."

The lunch bell was ringing. Sir Brian hoped they would stay at the Hall. They did stay to lunch and talked South America, of which Sir Brian's knowledge was extensive and peculiar. After lunch they smoked on the terrace and contemplated through the haze the Carwell acres. " Yes, it's all Carwell land as far as you see—if you could see anything," Sir Brian laughed. " And nothing to see at that. Flat, arable. I couldn't live in the place. I never feel awake here. But the family's been on the ground four hundred years. They didn't own the estate. The estate owned them. Well, I suppose one life's as good as another if you like it. This isn't mine. Watching Englishmen grow wheat ! My God ! That just suited Hugo. Poor old Hugo ! "

" Had the butler anything against him, sir ? " Bell ventured.

" I can't find it. The butler was just a butler. I never saw a man more so. And Hugo—well, he didn't know servants existed unless they didn't answer the bell. But he was a queer fellow. No notion of anybody having rights against him. He wouldn't let you get near him. I've seen that make quiet men mad."

" Meaning any one in particular, sir ? " Bell said.

" Oh, Lord, no. Speaking generally." He looked at Bell with a shrewd smile. " Haven't you found that in your job ? " And Bell laughed. " Yes, I'm afraid I don't help you much. Are you going to help Mark ? Where is the butler ? "

" Yes. Yes, we are rather wasting time, aren't we ? " Reggie stretched himself. " It's too soothing, Sir Brian. Can we walk across the park ? I hate exercise, but man must live."

" I don't think any one would have to murder me if I stayed here long," Sir Brian started up. " I'll show you the way. We can send your car round to the village."

Over immemorial turf they went their warm way. A herd of deer looked at them critically, and concluded they were of no importance. " Pretty creatures," said Superintendent Bell.

" I'd as soon keep white mice," said Sir Brian, and dis-

coursed of the wilder deer of other lands till he discovered that
Reggie was left behind.

Reggie was wandering off towards a little building away in
a hollow among trees. It was low, it was of unhewn stone
bonded with lines of red tile or brick, only a little above the
moss-grown roof rose a thin square tower. The tiny rounded
windows showed walls of great thickness and over its one door
was a mighty round arch, much wrought.

" Does the old place take your fancy ? " Sir Brian said.

" How did that get here ? " said Reggie.

" Well, you've got me on my blind side," Sir Brian confessed. " We call it the old church. I dare say it's as old as
the Hall."

" The Hall's a baby to it," said Reggie angrily. " The
porch is Norman. There's Saxon work in that tower. And
that tile is Roman."

Sir Brian laughed. " What about the Greeks and the
Hebrews ? Give them a look in." Reggie was not pleased
with him. " Sorry, afraid these things don't mean much to
me. I don't know how it began."

" It may have been a shrine or a chapel over some sacred
place."

" Haven't a notion. They say it used to be the village
church. One of my revered ancestors stopped the right of
way—didn't like the people disturbing his poultry, I suppose
—and built 'em a new church outside the park."

" Priceless," Reggie murmured.

" What, the place or my ancestors ? "

" Well, both, don't you think ? "

For the rest of the way Sir Brian told strange stories of the
past of the family of Carwell.

" He's a good talker, sir," said Superintendent Bell, when
they had left him at the park gate and were in their car. " Very
pleasant company. But you've something on your mind."

" The chair," Reggie mumbled. " Why was the man in
his chair ? "

" Lord Carwell, sir ? " Bell struggled to adjust his mind.
" Well, he was. That girl was telling the truth."

" I know, I know. That's the difficulty. You smash the
side of a man's head in. He won't sit down to think about it."

" Perhaps he was sitting when he was hit."

" Then he'd be knocked over just the same."

" I suppose the murderer might have picked him up."

" He might. But why ? Why ?

Superintendent Bell sighed heavily. " I judge we've some way to go, sir. And we don't seem to get any nearer the butler."

" Your job," said Reggie, and again the Superintendent sighed.

That night through a drizzling rain, lanterns moved in the village churchyard. The vault in which the Carwells of a hundred and fifty years lie crumbling was opened, and out of it a coffin was borne away. One man lingered in the vault holding a lantern high. He moved from one coffin to another. And came up again to the clean air and the rain. " All present and correct," he said. " No deception, Bell."

Superintendent Bell coughed. Sometimes he thinks Mr. Fortune lacking in reverence.

" Division of labour," Reggie sank into the cushions of the car and lit a pipe, " the division of labour is the great principle of civilization. Perhaps you didn't know that ? In the morning I will look at the corpse and you will look for the butler."

" Well, sir, I don't care for my job, but I wouldn't have yours for a hundred pounds."

" Yet it has a certain interest," Reggie murmured, " for that poor devil with the death sentence on him."

To their hotel in Southam Reggie Fortune came back on the next day rather before lunch time. " Finished at the mortuary, sir ? " said Bell. " I thought you looked happy."

" Not happy. Only pleased with myself. A snare, Bell, a snare. Have you found the butler ? "

Bell shook his head. " It's like a fairy tale, sir. He went out on that evening, walked down the village street, and that's the last of him they know. He might have gone to the station, he might have gone on the Southam motor-bus. They can't swear he didn't, but nobody saw him. They've searched the whole country-side and dragged the river. If you'll tell me what to do next, I'll be glad."

" Sir Brian's been asking for me, they say," said Reggie. " I think we'll go and call on Sir Brian."

They took sandwiches and their motor to Carwell Hall. The new butler told them Sir Brian had driven into Southam and was not yet back. " Oh, we've crossed him, I suppose," Reggie said. " We might stroll in the park till he's back. Ah, can we get into the old church ? "

The butler really couldn't say, and remarked that he was new to the place.

" Oh, it's no matter." Reggie took Bell's arm and strolled away.

They wandered down to the little old church. " Makes you feel melancholy, sir, don't it ? " Bell said. " Desolate, as you might say. As if people had got tired of believing in God."

Reggie looked at him a moment and went into the porch and tried the worm-eaten oak door. " We might have a look at the place," he said, and took out of his pocket a flat case like a housewife.

" Good Lord, sir, I wouldn't do that," Bell recoiled. " I mean to say—it's a church after all."

But Reggie was already picking the old lock. The door yielded and he went in. A dank and musty smell met them. The church was all but empty. Dim light fell on a shattered rood screen and stalls, and a bare stone altar. A tomb bore two cadaverous effigies. Reggie moved hither and thither, prying into every corner, and came at last to a broken flight of stairs. " Oh, there's a crypt, is there," he muttered, and went down. " Hallo ! Come on, Bell."

Superintendent Bell, following reluctantly, round him struggling with pieces of timber, relics of stall and bench, which held a door closed. " Give me a hand, man."

" I don't like it, sir, and that's the truth."

" Nor do I," Reggie panted, " not a bit," and dragged the last piece away and pulled the door open. He took out a torch and flashed the light on. They looked into a place supported on low round arches. The beam of the torch moved from coffin to mouldering coffin.

" Good God," Bell gasped, and gripped Reggie's arm.

Reggie drew him in. They came to the body of a man which had no coffin. It lay upon its face. Reggie bent over it, touching gently the back of the neck. " I thought so," he muttered, and turned the body over. Bell gave a stifled cry.

" Quite so, quite—— " he sprang up and made a dash for the door. It was slammed in his face. He flung himself against it, and it yielded a little but held. A dull creaking and groaning told that the timbers were being set again in place. Together they charged the door and were beaten back.

" And that's that, Bell," said Reggie. He flashed his light round the crypt, and it fell again on the corpse. " You and me and the butler."

Bell's hand felt for him. " Mr. Fortune—Mr. Fortune— was he dead when he came here ? "

" Oh, Lord, yes. Sir Brian's quite a humane man. But business is business."

" Sir Brian ? " Bell gasped.

" My dear chap," said Reggie irritably, " don't make conversation." He turned his torch on the grey oak of the door. . . .

It was late in that grim afternoon before they had cut and kicked a hole in it, and Reggie's hand came through and felt for the timbers which held it closed. Twilight was falling when, dirty and reeking, they broke out of the church and made for the Hall.

Sir Brian—the new butler could not conceal his surprise at seeing them—Sir Brian had gone out in the big car. But the butler feared there must be some mistake. He understood that Sir Brian had seen the gentlemen and was to take them with him. Sir Brian had sent the gentlemen's car back to Southam. Sir Brian——

" Where's your telephone ? " said Reggie.

The butler was afraid the telephone was out of order. He had been trying to get——

Reggie went to the receiver. There was no answer. Still listening, he looked at the connexions. A couple of inches of wire were cut out.

Half an hour later two breathless men arrived at the village post office and shut themselves into the telephone call-box.

On the next day Lomas called at Mr. Fortune's house in Wimpole Street and was told that Mr. Fortune was in his bath. A parlourmaid with downcast eyes announced to him a few minutes later that if he would go up Mr. Fortune would be very glad to see him.

" Pardon me," said the pink cherubic face from the water, " I am not clean. I think I shall never be clean again."

" You look like a prawn," said Lomas.

" That's your unscientific mind. Have you got him ? "

Lomas shook his head. " He has been seen in ten places at once. They have arrested a blameless bookmaker at Hull and an Irish cattle-dealer at Birkenhead. As usual. But we ought to have him in time."

" My fault entirely. He is an able fellow. I have underrated these business men, Lomas. My error. Occasionally one has a head. He has."

" These madmen often have."

Reggie wallowed in the water. " Mad ? He's as sane as I am. He's been badly educated, that's all. That's the worst

"*I thought so,*" *he muttered and turned the body over.*
Bell gave a stifled cry.

of business men. They're so ignorant. Just look at it. He killed Hugo by a knife thrust in the vertebrae at the base of the skull. It's a South American fashion, probably indigenous. When I found that wound in the body I was sure of the murderer. I had a notion before from the way he spoke about Hugo and the estate. Probably Hugo was bent over the table and the blow was struck without his knowledge. He would be dead in a moment. But Sir Brian saw that wouldn't do. Too uncommon a murder in England. So he smashed in the skull to make it look like an ordinary crime of violence. Thus ignorance is bliss. He never thought the death wasn't the right kind of death for that. Also it didn't occur to him that a man who is hit on the head hard is knocked down. He don't lay his head on the table to be hammered same like Hugo. I don't fancy Brian meant Mark to be hanged. Possibly he was going to manufacture evidence of burglary when he was interrupted by the butler. Anyhow the butler knew too much and had to be bought off. But I suppose the butler wouldn't stand Mark being hanged. When he found the trial was going dead against Mark he threatened. So he had to be killed too. Say by appointment in the park. Same injury in his body—a stab through the cervical vertebrae. And the corpse was neatly disposed of in the crypt."

" What in the world put you on to the crypt."

" Well, Sir Brian was so anxious not to be interested in the place. And the place was so mighty convenient. And the butler had to be somewhere. Pure reasoning, Lomas, old thing. This is a very rational case all through."

" Rational ! Will you tell me why Sir Brian came to stir us up about the butler and insisted Mark was innocent ? "

" I told you he was an able man. He saw it would have looked very fishy if he didn't. Acting head of the family—he had to act. And also I fancy he liked Mark. If he could get the boy off, he would rather do it than not. And who could suspect the worthy fellow who was so straight and decent ? All very rational."

" Very," said Lomas. " Especially the first murder. Why do you suppose he wanted to kill Hugo ? "

" Well, you'd better look at his papers. He talked about Hugo as if he had a grudge against the way Hugo ran the estate. I wonder if he wanted to develop it—try for minerals perhaps—it's on the edge of the South Midland coal-field—and Hugo wouldn't have it."

" Good Gad ! " Lomas said. " You're an ingenious fellow,

Fortune. He had proposed to Hugo to try for coal, and Hugo turned it down."

Reggie emerged from the bath. " There you have it. He knew if Hugo was out of the way he could do what he wanted. If Mark or the old parson had the place, he could manage them. Very rational crime."

" Rational ! Murder your cousin to make a coal mine ! "

" Business men and business methods. Run away and catch him, Lomas, and hang him to encourage the others."

But in fact Lomas did not catch him. Some years afterwards Mrs. Fortune found her husband on the veranda of an hotel in Italy staring at a Spanish paper. " Don't dream, child," she said. " Run and dress."

" I'm seeing ghosts, Joan," said Mr. Fortune.

She looked over his shoulder. " Who is San Jacinto ? "

" The last new South American republic. Here's His Excellency the President. *Né* Brian Carwell. Observe the smile."

OUTSIDE THE LAW

By

ANTHONY BERKELEY

FOR a moment there was a tense silence in the shabby room.
Very cautiously Smith had drawn the window-curtain a little further aside as he continued to peer out from behind it into the street below. From the seat at the table Pat O'Donnell watched him in silence, his large mouth drooping open. Against the wall, whither he had sprung at the first hint of danger, the lad Muller cowered, his heart beating furiously.

Then O'Donnell spoke. " Well ? "

Smith turned slightly. " It's the busies," he announced, unemotionally. " They've found us."

Muller's heart gave a little jump, and his eyes flew to the pile of silver articles on the table. He knew little English, but already he had gathered that the word " busies " meant the police.

" The divil they have. Would you believe that, now ? " Pat O'Donnell was obviously trying to imitate Smith's calm.

He heaved his big frame out of the chair and crossed to the window. Smith made room for him to peep out.

" See that hound, skulking in the doorway ? He's been there for the last hour or more. He's watching the house. I didn't tell you before because I wasn't sure. Now I am." Smith's pale, almost ascetic face seemed aflame ; behind their pince-nez his slightly prominent, pale-blue eyes gleamed. The man seemed actually elated.

" And what makes ye sure now ? "

" Because he nodded to a couple of the swine that went into the tobacconist's next door. And there's another couple turned up the mews. You can bet some have gone round the back, too. By cripes, there must be a dozen of 'em. We're surrounded."

"Houly Jakers!" O'Donnell's voice had a curious croak in it. "'Tis a bad business altogether."

In spite of his fear of Smith, Muller was unable to restrain the wail of terrified inquiry that rose to his lips. "Surrounded? *Ach, mein Gott, was ist denn los?*"

O'Donnell rounded on him fiercely. "Och, hould that foreign jabber!"

It was the fierceness of fear, but Muller did not know that. The tears started into his eyes. If Pat himself could speak to him like that, he was indeed forsaken.

"A dozen?" O'Donnell was muttering. "Why would they be sending a dozen, Smithy?"

"They know *me*," said Smith, with a curious pride.

"Ah, and me too." O'Donnell's voice seemed to suggest that he got some consolation from the fact. "But sure, 'tis a pity the stuff's here with us. That'll look bad now. We should have left it in the garridge at Aylsham."

"They know all about Aylsham," Smith returned, contemptuously. "They couldn't have traced us here without. You can bet they've got the car identified by now."

O'Donnell stared despondently down into the quiet street. "'Tis a bad look-out, entirely. Sure I don't know what we're to do now at all, the way you say the house is surrounded."

Smith's thin face flamed again. "By cripes, they haven't caught us yet!"

"Arrah, that's the boy. Sure, if anyone can get us out of it at all, it's you're the one with that same headpiece." He looked at the other hopefully.

"Let me think." Smith began to walk slowly up and down the little room, his head dropped on his chest.

From his place by the wall Muller watched him with terrified eyes. He was frightened, of course, of the detectives outside; but by now he was far, far more frightened of Smith. Smith was a devil: a cold, relentless fiend. Even now it made Muller feel quite sick to remember how coolly and readily Smith had shot last night at the man who had tried to bar their way. It was only by the mercy of heaven that the shot had missed and the policeman on that lonely road still lived.

Muller wiped the cold sweat from his forehead, furtively. Why had he ever let himself get entangled with this terrible pair? And was it really only last night that Pat had come up to him in the street and drawn him, half-starved and cold as he was, into the warm public-house, and given him sausages and ham-rolls to eat and beer to drink, while he talked jovially of the fine job he had to offer and all the money that was to be earned for nothing at all, just nothing at all ?

Muller had not understood a quarter of it all, but he had known at once that here was the finest, the noblest, the most wonderful man he had ever met. It had never occurred to him not to trust such a man. Even when, scared and incredulous two hours later, he understood at last the real nature of the job, it had been to Pat's entreaties, not to Smith's threats, that he acceded when, weak with fear, he climbed through the tiny window that would not admit even Smith's lean length, and opened the door from the inside.

That was how that pile of silver came to be lying on the table now. Muller knew that of that pile a certain proportion of the value had already been allotted, by Smith's cold justice, to himself. But he did not want it. He did not want anything now, except to get out of this dreadful house in safety and never to see either Smith or O'Donnell again.

Muller wiped his forehead again, and thought of sunny little Ehrensdorf on the Rhine, and of Lisa, who had so warmly approved his great plan to make his fortune in London. He had been mad to leave them both. London did not want German waiters. Would he ever see them again ? He shivered. Muller was not brave.

Smith and O'Donnell were conferring now in low tones, and Pat was nodding his great head.

" Through the room to the left below," he nodded, " out of the window, drop into the yard, cross that and over the wall to the right into the timber yards, and then out through the main gates as bold as brass. I've got ye, Smithy, me boy. Sure, it's the great lad ye are. I never knew there was that way at all. And meself to go first all the way ? "

" You first, then Muller, and I'll cover the rear. And you're responsible for him as well as yourself."

" Faith, that I'll be. Fritzy knows I wouldn't be leaving him in the lurch, don't ye, Fritzy ? " At the prospect of escape the big man seemed to have thrown off his despondency. He grinned at Muller in quite the old way.

Muller tried to smile back, but his mouth felt stiff.

" Get on then, Pat," Smith said, impatiently.

O'Donnell tiptoed to the door. He opened it softly and peered down the stairs, then nodded over his shoulder. With a frightened glance, Muller obeyed the wave of the revolver which had appeared in Smith's hand, and ranged himself behind Pat. His heart was thumping painfully, but it was with hope now. Smith was infallible : they were all going to escape; and in the confusion it would surely be easy to give the other two the slip, and then an honest job somewhere and no more of these horrors. In front of him, Pat began to creep down the stairs.

Then everything seemed to happen at once.

There was a shout from O'Donnell. " There's one of 'em here. Back—get back ! " He rushed back into the room, sweeping Muller and Smith with him, and slammed the door.

Smith turned on him angrily. " Why didn't you shoot, you fool ? We could have got away. Now they're warned."

" Arrah, don't talk nonsense now," O'Donnell panted. " Wasn't it yourself said the house was surrounded ? "

" We might have shot our way out if you'd had any guts. You've got your barker, haven't you ? " O'Donnell pulled a revolver out of his pocket. " Well, why didn't you use it ? "

" What, on that busy ? "

" Of course on that busy."

" Och ! " O'Donnell laughed uneasily. " Do ye not be talking foolish now, Smithy, boy. Ye know well enough ye'd not have used it yourself. Sure, 'twould be a hanging job for all of us if we did that. It's yerself knows they'd never let up on us if we shot a busy till they had us all hanged. Och, come now, I know what ye mean. 'Tis just frightening them with the barkers ye'd be, the way they'd let us get past and out of the window."

" Not much I wouldn't," Smith snarled. " If I use the barkers on those hounds, I shoot to kill."

O'Donnell's face fell ludicrously. " But 'tis madness. 'Tis hanging all of us ye'll be."

" Afraid, Pat ? " Smith sneered.

" Faith, and 'tis you should know whether I'm afraid or not," O'Donnell answered, hotly. " I'm only telling you, 'tis madness to use the barkers like that. Maybe we'll get away now, or maybe we won't ; but what's a few years out of your life compared with the losing of it altogether ? Have sense, Smithy."

" Well, you can do as you like, but I'm not going to rot in jail." Smith's cold blue eyes were blazing now with the light of the fanatic. " I'll go to hell first—and I'll take a few of those swine with me, too."

O'Donnell turned away. " Ah, 'tis madness," he muttered. " But you'll have sense when it comes to the point."

Muller was crouching on the mattress in the corner of the room, his face stiff and his teeth chattering. The dreadful look on Smith's face would alone have been enough to terrify him ; but in addition, the purport of the conversation he had just heard was only too plain. Smith meant to shoot at the police. If he did that, they would all be hanged. Muller began to pray desperately that somehow, by some miracle, Smith might die himself before he could shoot at the police.

Hardly two minutes had passed since the three of them had tumbled back into the room, but already O'Donnell was looking towards his leader in a pleading way.

"Come on then, Pat," Smith said, with a tight, almost contemptuous little smile. "I'm not done yet. If you're afraid to face up to the busy down there, I've another way over the roof—if you're not afraid of heights."

O'Donnell swallowed the insult without appearing to notice it. "There is ? That's the great boy ye are. Show it me, and I'll hould us both on by the eyebrows, Fritzy and me."

"Come along, Muller," Smith ordered, curtly.

The courage of despair came to Muller's help. "*Nein, nein,*" he muttered brokenly. "*Ich kann nicht. Ich habe furcht.*"

"What's he say ? " queried O'Donnell, suspiciously.

"He doesn't want to come."

"Och, listen now, Fritzy, boy. Sure, I wouldn't be—— "

"Never mind," Smith interrupted, impatiently. "If he won't come, we must leave him. He's had his chance. Come on."

Muller almost sobbed with joy. He was going to be left ! The terrible Smith had relinquished him. Nothing mattered now.

Already the other two were moving towards the door. Smith's hand was actually stretched out towards the handle, when it began to rattle as if of its own accord ; there was a bang on the further side of the door, and a gruff voice shouted:—

"Open this door, in the name of the law."

There was a pause, while both men glided silently back.

Then the handle rattled again without result, for O'Donnell had turned the key in the lock three minutes ago, and the gruff voice repeated its demand.

Smith and O'Donnell looked at each other. Slowly Smith raised the revolver in his hand. Muller cowered on his mattress.

"Don't shoot, Smithy ! " O'Donnell whispered, urgently.

" 'Tis madness. Ye know 'tis madness." But he made no effort to restrain the other by physical means.

Smith called out loudly. " Get away from that door, you, or I'll shoot."

" O'Donnell's face looked ludicrous in its desperate anxiety. " Ye'll hang us all," he muttered. " Smithy ! "

Muller crammed his knuckles into his mouth as he stared at the revolver, now pointing straight at the door. Wild ideas rushed into his mind of throwing himself on Smith ; but the certainty that the revolver would be turned first on himself, kept him shivering, a collapsed heap, on the mattress.

The brief pause seemed to last for hours.

Then the man on the other side of the door spoke again.

" Come on, Smith and O'Donnell. I want you."

Smith's hand made a tiny movement on the revolver. O'Donnell watched it motionless, as if hypnotized. Muller screamed. " *Nicht schiessen—nicht schiessen !* "

Smith fired.

There was a hoarse cry from the other side of the door ; then a series of sickening, dull bumps on the stairs.

" *Du lieber Gott !* " Muller moaned.

O'Donnell's face was twitching. " Mother of God, have mercy on us," he muttered. " Ye've croaked him, Smithy."

" Yeah," Smith agreed, calmly. " I've croaked him. That's the first. By cripes, I'll show the hounds." He walked over to the window and looked out. " Not one of 'em in sight," he announced, with a kind of cold triumph. " That's given 'em something to think about."

" Well, we're in for it now," said O'Donnell, heavily. Neither of them took the least notice of Muller.

There was the sound of heavy footsteps on the stairs.

" Is it croaking they *want* ? " O'Donnell scowled. " Houly Jakers, then 'tis croaking they'll get."

" That's more like what I expected from you, Pat," Smith said, with a short laugh.

There was another bang on the door, another command to open.

" *Weg—weg !* " Muller shouted hysterically. " Go, or ―― " He broke off abruptly as Smith's revolver menaced him, and crammed his knuckles back into his mouth.

" Come on, now. Open this door."

O'Donnell pushed Smith aside with a reckless laugh. " Faith, we can't be worse off than we are. This one's mine."

" *Ach, nein, nein,* " Muller moaned. " *Nicht schiessen !* "

O'Donnell fired all six cartridges, splintering the door in half-a-dozen places. But this time there was no cry.

" He stood aside," said Smith in a low voice.

There was the sound of stealthy footsteps, creeping downstairs.

Smith swore softly. " Out of the way, Pat."

He turned the key in the lock and whipped open the door, leaning round the jamb. Two shots sounded from his revolver. This time there did come a cry, and the sound of a heavy fall. Smith jumped back into the room and slammed the door.

" Got him on the run, the skunk."

" Smithy's the boy ! " shouted O'Donnell, wildly.

" That'll keep 'em quiet for a bit," Smith said calmly.

The two men reloaded their weapons.

Shivering in his corner, Muller watched them. He dared not speak, he hardly dared move. For both the men had gone mad now. They had killed, and the dreadful joy of killing was upon them. Smith, the true criminal, the fanatical enemy of organized society, showed it only by the almost insane light in his blazing, pale-blue eyes. O'Donnell, with his ape-like face and uncouth frame, had simply reverted to the primitive. Smith would kill as precisely and carefully as he brushed the neat blue serge suit he wore. O'Donnell would go ecstatically berserk. But either of them, Muller was convinced, might turn at any moment and put a casual bullet into himself. He crouched in his corner.

O'Donnell waved his re-loaded revolver round his head with a great shout. " What'll we do now, Smithy, boy ? Just say the word. 'Tis aching I am for another shot at the craitures."

" We'll try the roof again," Smith replied.

" The roof it is ! And let them not be trying to stop us this time, or 'twill be the worse for someone. Lead on, boy."

Smith opened the door, and the two men disappeared.

Muller gave a great sob of relief. They had not even glanced at him. They had forgotten all about him. Let them but get on the roof, or anywhere, and he could escape at last. He crept over to the door.

The next instant there came the sound of a shot, and then of several shots. Muller fled back to his corner as Smith and O'Donnell tumbled back into the room and slammed the door.

" Well, and would ye believe the likes of that, now ? " O'Donnell was saying, in high indignation. " Shooting at us, the murdering devils ! 'Tis a dirty thing to do, that, entirely."

Smith was breathing quickly, his eyes blazing.

" By cripes, I'll show them," he panted. " They don't know who they're up against yet. Pat, look after the stairs."

" Sure, I'll shoot the nose off anyone who pokes it round the bend," shouted O'Donnell. He took up his position in the doorway. " What'll ye be after doing, Smithy, me pretty boy ? "

" I'll take on the swine in the street." Smith was crouching by the window, waiting for a target.

For a minute or two there was silence, broken only by O'Donnell's heavy breathing and the shuddering sobs which Muller, for all his efforts, could not suppress. From Smith came no sound or movement. With his revolver-muzzle resting in the two or three inches of space at the bottom of the slightly opened window, he was patiently waiting to kill.

He fired a shot, and swore briefly. " Missed him, by cripes ! "

There was another pause, and then another shot which was followed by the sharp splintering of glass.

" Faith ! " O'Donnell exclaimed. " That was never you, boy ? "

" No. They're firing at us now, from the house opposite."

" Do ye tell me that now ? Let them then, the dirty skunks. And a fine chance they have of hitting us."

" Wait till I see which window they're at," Smith muttered.

Another shot crashed through the glass of the window, causing Muller to duck in his corner with a little cry of terror.

Smith had not flinched, though the bullet passed only just over his head. He fired six shots in quick succession, and there followed them the faint noise of glass tinkling on the pavement.

" Any luck, Smithy ? " O'Donnell asked, eagerly.

" Don't know. I saw which window they're using. There's not much of it left now." Smith's voice was deadly in its level coolness. He dropped his emptied revolver on the floor and took another from his pocket.

" That's the great boy," rejoined O'Donnell with enthusiasm. " Arrah," he shouted down the stairs, " come on, the lot of you. Quit skulking, and let me shoot the noses off your ugly mugs."

A voice answered from the landing below. " Throw that gun away and come down. You've still got a chance, O'Donnell. We know it wasn't you who did the croaking. Better save your neck while you can. We're bound to get you and Smith later or sooner, and this game won't help you much then. Don't be a fool."

" Faith, and 'tis yourself's the fool if it's thinking ye are ye can take me in with that kind of talk," O'Donnell roared. " Just come round the corner and give me the pleasure of shooting the ugly face off ye. That's all I'm wanting."

" You throw that gun down the stairs and follow it yourself, and I'll promise to do my best for you later. That's straight."

O'Donnell winked hugely at Smith. " And will ye do the best ye can for me pal, too ? "

" For Smith ? No, I'm sorry. He's gone too far."

" Has he, then ? Well, listen now, Mr. Skulking Busy. I'm going with him. Ye'll get us both, or ye'll get neither."

This time there was no answer from below.

Smith smiled tightly. " That's the great chap ye are, Pat," he mimicked.

O'Donnell flushed like a girl. " Faith, I wouldn't be giving ye up for the likes of those craitures, Smithy, boy," he mumbled, and to relieve his feelings discharged a volley down the stairs.

Almost at the same moment Smith's revolver cracked.

He laughed shortly. " Made him jump, by cripes. Pat, come here a second."

O'Donnell ran across lightly and crouched by the other.

Smith gestured towards the end of the street. The pride was obvious in his voice. " See that crowd ? There's a dozen busies there and more, not counting the ones we can't see. We're giving the hounds something to think about."

" And we'll give 'em more yet," O'Donnell rejoined, warmly. " Sure, 'tis a great fight." He hurried back to his post.

As he was crossing the room Smith, without turning his head, said :—

" Muller, or whatever your name is, come here and load for me." He pulled a handful of ammunition out of his pocket and dropped it on the floor beside the empty revolver.

On his hands and knees Muller crawled across the room and with shaking fingers began to load.

Smith fired again.

" Got him ! " he exclaimed. " Knocked him clean over in the road. Cripes, he's moving. Try to crawl away, would you ? "

" *Ach, Gott, nein !* " shuddered Muller as Smith, with

deliberate callousness, emptied his revolver at the wounded man below.

His eyes still on the road, Smith stretched out an imperative hand for the other revolver ; but with a convulsive jump Muller leapt backwards and stood upright, clutching it.

" *Nein !* " he cried, wildly. " *Nein*, I give it you not ! "

Smith turned his head and stared at Muller. The boy quailed before the cold ferocity in the blue eyes, but desperation stiffened him. He knew, too, that if he gave the gun back now, its first bullet would be for himself.

Smith rose. " Give me that gun, you little scum, or . . ."

Muller retreated two more steps. The revolver in his hand was pointed at Smith now, waveringly but unmistakably.

" *Nein, ich geb' es nicht*," he sobbed hysterically. " You have killed enough mans. *Nein, zuruck, sonst.* . . . Go away from me, or I shoot you ! "

Smith took a resolute stride. " Give me that gun, or—— "

" *Ich schiesse !* " Muller shrieked. " I shoot ! "

From the doorway O'Donnell watched in amazement.

In spite of himself Smith halted. " Oh, very well," he said, and stooped towards the empty revolver on the floor.

" *Nein !* Leave alone that barker."

Smith looked angrily at O'Donnell. " Plug the little rat."

" No, no ! " said Muller, with a little gasp, " I plug you first, Pat. Please to turn round."

" Faith, I believe he would, too," muttered O'Donnell, and turned half round.

" By cripes, if you're afraid—— "

For an instant the three were motionless, like a waxwork tableau : O'Donnell turned sideways in the doorway, Smith by the window bending a little forward as if to spring, Muller by the further wall, white with terror and desperation, not knowing how to control the situation which he himself had brought about.

For a second they remained so. Then Smith sprang.

There was a shot, and Smith dropped to the floor. How Muller's fingers had tightened on the trigger he hardly knew.

O'Donnell seemed momentarily stupefied. Then he shouted a furious oath. " Houly Jakers ! Ye—ye've croaked him."

" Yes," Muller agreed. " I've croaked him." Curiously, he felt quite calm now, and not at all afraid of O'Donnell. " Now I go, please."

" Ye'll go, ye murdering little spalpeen ? " shouted O'Donnell in rage. " Ye think I'll let ye go, when ye've just croaked
the finest man that ever walked this earth ? I'll show ye."

" Then I croak you too. If you come near to me, I
shoot you. Throw your barker at the floor, please."

For a second O'Donnell struggled with his courage. But
the new resolution which seemed to have taken possession of
Muller decided him. Sullenly he let his revolver drop to
the floor.

" So ! " said Muller, without emotion. " Now go backwards."

O'Donnell, under the muzzle of the gun which had just
killed his leader, backed on to the landing. Muller picked up
the two empty revolvers.

" I throw them out of the window. You have killed enough
mans. You kill no more. Then I go."

" Ah, come now, Fritzy boy, ye wouldn't do a thing like
that," O'Donnell whined. " Do ye not be throwing them
barkers away. Sure, go if ye want to : I wouldn't be stopping
ye. But leave me the barkers, else the busies will get me for
sure."

" *Das ist mir gleich.*" Muller walked to the window.

Something made him glance over his shoulder. O'Donnell
was running silently after him. Without hesitation, Muller
fired.

Muller hardly stopped to glance at O'Donnell's huge body
sprawled across Smith's. His calm had been a false one. Now
that the necessity for it had gone, hysteria rapidly supervened.
His one frantic idea now was to get out of that terrible room.
The smoking revolver still in his hand, he rushed down the
stairs.

His brain, numbed by terror, had hardly registered the fact
that he had killed two men. All he knew was that he was free
again at last : free from Smith, free from the police. For he
had done the job of the police for them. That would show the
police that he was their friend, and they his.

He rushed out on to the front step and exultantly waved
his revolver to his friends the police, to summon them to see
the great thing he had done for them.

The shot took him through the throat.

As he crumpled up, Muller's face took on an expression of
great surprise. Why had his friends the police shot him, after
all he had done for them ?

THE REGENT'S PARK MURDER

By

BARONESS ORCZY

B Y this time Miss Polly Burton had become quite accustomed to her extraordinary *vis-à-vis* in the corner.
He was always there, when she arrived, in the selfsame
corner, dressed in one of his remarkable check tweed suits ; he
seldom said good morning, and invariably when she appeared
he began to fidget with increased nervousness, with some
tattered and knotty piece of string.

" Were you ever interested in the Regent's Park murder ? "
he asked her one day.

Polly replied that she had forgotten most of the particulars
connected with that curious murder, but that she fully remembered the stir and flutter it had caused in a certain section of
London Society.

" The racing and gambling set, particularly, you mean," he
said. " All the persons implicated in the murder, directly or
indirectly, were of the type commonly called ' Society men,' or
' men about town,' whilst the Harewood Club in Hanover
Square, round which centred all the scandal in connection with
the murder, was one of the smartest clubs in London.

" Probably the doings of the Harewood Club, which was
essentially a gambling club, would for ever have remained
' officially ' absent from the knowledge of the police authorities
but for the murder in the Regent's Park and the revelations
which came to light in connection with it.

" I dare say you know the quiet square which lies between
Portland Place and the Regent's Park and is called Park Crescent
at its south end, and subsequently Park Square East and West.
The Marylebone Road, with all its heavy traffic, cuts straight
across the large square and its pretty gardens, but the latter are
connected together by a tunnel under the road ; and of course

you must remember that the new tube station in the south portion of the Square had not yet been planned.

" February 6th, 1907, was a very foggy night, nevertheless Mr. Aaron Cohen, of 30, Park Square West, at two o'clock in the morning, having finally pocketed the heavy winnings which he had just swept off the green table of the Harewood Club, started to walk home alone. An hour later most of the inhabitants of Park Square West were aroused from their peaceful slumbers by the sounds of a violent altercation in the road. A man's angry voice was heard shouting violently for a minute or two, and was followed immediately by frantic screams of ' Police ' and ' Murder.' Then there was the double sharp report of firearms, and nothing more.

" The fog was very dense, and, as you no doubt have experienced yourself, it is very difficult to locate sound in a fog. Nevertheless, not more than a minute or two had elapsed before Constable F 18, the point policeman at the corner of Marylebone Road, arrived on the scene, and, having first of all whistled for any of his comrades on the beat, began to grope his way about in the fog, more confused than effectually assisted by contradictory directions from the inhabitants of the houses close by, who were nearly falling out of the upper windows as they shouted out to the constable.

" ' By the railings, policeman.'

" ' Higher up the road.'

" ' No, lower down.'

" ' It was on this side of the pavement I am sure.'

" ' No, the other.'

" At last it was another policeman, F 22, who, turning into Park Square West from the north side, almost stumbled upon the body of a man lying on the pavement with his head against the railings of the Square. By this time quite a little crowd of people from the different houses in the road had come down, curious to know what had actually happened.

" The policeman turned the strong light of his bull's-eye lantern on the unfortunate man's face.

" ' It looks as if he had been strangled, don't it ? ' he murmured to his comrade.

" And he pointed to the swollen tongue, the eyes half out of their sockets, bloodshot, and congested, the purple, almost black, hue of the face.

" At this point one of the spectators, more callous to horrors, peered curiously into the dead man's face. He uttered an exclamation of astonishment.

" ' Why, surely, it's Mr. Cohen from No. 30 ! '

" The mention of a name familiar down the length of the street had caused two or three other men to come forward and to look more closely into the horribly distorted mask of the murdered man.

" ' Our next-door neighbour, undoubtedly,' asserted Mr. Ellison, a young barrister, residing at No. 31.

" ' What in the world was he doing this foggy night all alone, and on foot ? ' asked somebody else.

" ' He usually came home very late. I fancy he belonged to some gambling club in town. I dare say he couldn't get a cab to bring him out here. Mind you, I don't know much about him. We only knew him to nod to.'

" ' Poor beggar ! it looks almost like an old-fashioned case of garrotting.'

" ' Anyway, the blackguardly murderer, whoever he was, wanted to make sure he had killed his man ! ' added Constable F 18, as he picked up an object from the pavement. ' Here's the revolver, with two cartridges missing. You gentlemen heard the report just now ? '

" ' He don't seem to have hit him though. The poor bloke was strangled, no doubt.'

" ' And tried to shoot at his assailant, obviously,' asserted the young barrister with authority.

" ' If he succeeded in hitting the brute, there might be a chance of tracing the way he went.'

" ' But not in the fog.'

" Soon, however, the appearance of the inspector, detective, and medical officer, who had quickly been informed of the tragedy, put an end to further discussion.

" The bell at No. 30 was rung, and the servants—all four of them women—were asked to look at the body.

" Amidst tears of horror and screams of fright, they all recognised in the murdered man their master, Mr. Aaron Cohen. He was therefore conveyed to his own room pending the coroner's inquest.

" The police had a pretty difficult task, you will admit ; there were so very few indications to go by, and at first literally no clue.

" The inquest revealed practically nothing. Very little was known in the neighbourhood about Mr. Aaron Cohen and his affairs. His female servants did not even know the name or where-about of the various clubs he frequented.

" He had an office in Throgmorton Street and went to

business every day. He dined at home, and sometimes had friends to dinner. When he was alone he invariably went to the club, where he stayed until the small hours of the morning.

"The night of the murder he had gone out at about nine o'clock. That was the last his servants had seen of him. With regard to the revolver, all four servants swore positively that they had never seen it before, and that, unless Mr. Cohen had bought it that very day, it did not belong to their master.

"Beyond that, no trace whatever of the murderer had been found, but on the morning after the crime a couple of keys linked together by a short metal chain were found close to a gate at the opposite end of the Square, that which immediately faced Portland Place. These were proved to be, firstly, Mr. Cohen's latch-key, and, secondly, his gate-key of the Square.

"It was therefore presumed that the murderer, having accomplished his fell design and ransacked his victim's pockets, had found the keys and made good his escape by slipping into the Square, cutting under the tunnel, and out again by the further gate. He then took the precaution not to carry the keys with him any further, but threw them away and disappeared in the fog.

"The jury returned a verdict of wilful murder against some person or persons unknown, and the police were put on their mettle to discover the unknown and daring murderer. The result of their investigations, conducted with marvellous skill by Mr. William Fisher, led, about a week after the crime, to the sensational arrest of one of London's smartest young bucks.

"The case Mr. Fisher had got up against the accused briefly amounted to this :

"On the night of February 6th, soon after midnight, play began to run very high at the Harewood Club, in Hanover Square. Mr. Aaron Cohen held the bank at roulette against some twenty or thirty of his friends, mostly young fellows with no wits and plenty of money. 'The Bank' was winning heavily, and it appears that this was the third consecutive night on which Mr. Aaron Cohen had gone home richer by several hundreds than he had been at the start of play.

"Young John Ashley, who is the son of a very worthy county gentleman who is M.F.H. somewhere in the Midlands, was losing heavily, and in his case also it appears that it was the third consecutive night that Fortune had turned her face against him.

"Remember," continued the man in the corner, "that when I tell you all these details and facts, I am giving you the

combined evidence of several witnesses, which it took many
days to collect and to classify.

" It appears that young Mr. Ashley, though very popular
in society, was generally believed to be in what is vulgarly
termed ' low water ' ; up to his eyes in debt, and mortally
afraid of his dad, whose younger son he was, and who had on
one occasion threatened to ship him off to Australia with a £5
note in his pocket if he made any further extravagant calls upon
his paternal indulgence.

" It was also evident to all John Ashley's many companions
that the worthy M.F.H. held the purse-strings in a very tight
grip. The young man, bitten with the desire to cut a smart
figure in the circles in which he moved, had often recourse to
the varying fortunes which now and again smiled upon him
across the green tables in the Harewood Club.

" Be that as it may, the general consensus of opinion at the
Club was that young Ashley had changed his last ' pony '
before he sat down to a turn of roulette with Aaron Cohen on
that particular night of February 6th.

" It appears that all his friends, conspicuous among whom
was Mr. Walter Hatherell, tried their very best to dissuade him
from pitting his luck against that of Cohen, who had been
having a most unprecedented run of good fortune. But young
Ashley, heated with wine, exasperated at his own bad luck,
would listen to no one ; he tossed one £5 note after another
on the board, he borrowed from those who would lend, then
played on parole for a while. Finally, at half-past one in the
morning, after a run of nineteen on the red, the young man
found himself without a penny in his pockets, and owing a
debt—a gambling debt—a debt of honour of £1,500 to Mr.
Aaron Cohen.

" Now we must render this much maligned gentleman that
justice which was persistently denied to him by press and
public alike ; it was positively asserted by all those present that
Mr. Cohen himself repeatedly tried to induce young Mr.
Ashley to give up playing. He himself was in a delicate position
in the matter, as he was the winner, and once or twice the taunt
had risen to the young man's lips, accusing the holder of the
bank of the wish to retire on a competence before the break in
his luck.

" Mr. Aaron Cohen, smoking the best of Havanas, had
finally shrugged his shoulders and said : ' As you please ! '

" But at half-past one he had had enough of the player who
always lost and never paid—never could pay, so Mr. Cohen

probably believed. He therefore at that hour refused to accept Mr. John Ashley's ' promissory ' stakes any longer. A very few heated words ensued, quickly checked by the management, who are ever on the alert to avoid the least suspicion of scandal.

" In the meanwhile Mr. Hatherell, with great good sense, persuaded young Ashley to leave the Club and all its temptations and go home ; if possible to bed.

" The friendship of the two young men, which was very well known in society, consisted chiefly, it appears, in Walter Hatherell being the willing companion and helpmeet of John Ashley in his mad and extravagant pranks. But to-night the latter, apparently tardily sobered by his terrible and heavy losses, allowed himself to be led away by his friend from the scene of his disasters. It was then about twenty minutes to two.

" Here the situation becomes interesting," continued the man in the corner in his nervous way. " No wonder that the police interrogated at least a dozen witnesses before they were quite satisfied that every statement was conclusively proved.

" Walter Hatherell, after about ten minutes' absence, that is to say at ten minutes to two, returned to the club room. In reply to several inquiries, he said that he had parted with his friend at the corner of New Bond Street, since he seemed anxious to be alone, and that Ashley said he would take a turn down Piccadilly before going home—he thought a walk would do him good.

" At two o'clock or thereabouts Mr. Aaron Cohen, satisfied with his evening's work, gave up his position at the bank and, pocketing his heavy winnings, started on his homeward walk, while Mr. Walter Hatherell left the club half an hour later.

" At three o'clock precisely the cries of ' Murder ' and the report of fire-arms were heard in Park Square West, and Mr. Aaron Cohen was found strangled outside the garden railings.

" Now at first sight the murder in the Regent's Park appeared both to police and public as one of those silly, clumsy crimes, obviously the work of a novice, and absolutely purposeless, seeing that it could but inevitably lead its perpetrators, without any difficulty, to the gallows.

" You see, a motive had been established. ' Seek him whom the crime benefits,' say our French confrères. But there was something more than that.

" ' Constable James Funnell, on his beat, turned from Portland Place into Park Crescent a few minutes after he had heard the clock at Holy Trinity Church, Marylebone, strike half-past two. The fog at that moment was perhaps not quite so dense as it was later on in the morning, and the policeman saw two gentlemen in overcoats and top-hats leaning arm in arm against the railings of the Square, close to the gate. He could not, of course, distinguish their faces because of the fog, but he heard one of them saying to the other :

" ' It is but a question of time, Mr. Cohen. I know my father will pay the money for me, and you will lose nothing by waiting.'

" To this the other apparently made no reply, and the constable passed on ; when he returned to the same spot, after having walked over his beat, the two gentlemen had gone, but later on it was near this very gate that the two keys referred to at the inquest had been found.

" Another interesting fact," added the man in the corner, with one of those sarcastic smiles of his which Polly could not quite explain, " was the finding of the revolver upon the scene of the crime. That revolver, shown to Mr. Ashley's valet, was sworn to by him as being the property of his master.

" All these facts made, of course, a very remarkable, so far quite unbroken, chain of circumstantial evidence against Mr. John Ashley. No wonder, therefore, that the police, thoroughly satisfied with Mr. Fisher's work and their own, applied for a warrant against the young man, and arrested him in his rooms in Clarges Street exactly a week after the committal of the crime.

" As a matter of fact, you know, experience has invariably taught me that when a murderer seems particularly foolish and clumsy, and proofs against him seem particularly damning, that is the time when the police should be most guarded against pitfalls.

" Now in this case, if John Ashley had indeed committed the murder in Regent's Park in the manner suggested by the police, he would have been a criminal in more senses than one, for idiocy of that kind is to my mind worse than many crimes.

" The prosecution brought its witnesses up in triumphal array one after another. There were the members of the Harewood Club—who had seen the prisoner's excited condition after his heavy gambling losses to Mr. Aaron Cohen ; there was Mr. Hatherell, who, in spite of his friendship for Ashley, was bound to admit that he had parted from him at the corner of Bond Street at twenty minutes to two, and had not seen him again till his return home at five a.m.

" Then came the evidence of Arthur Chipps, John Ashley's valet. It proved of a very sensational character.

" He deposed that on the night in question his master came home at about ten minutes to two. Chipps had then not yet gone to bed. Five minutes later Mr. Ashley went out again, telling his valet not to sit up for him. Chipps could not say at what time either of the young gentlemen had come home.

" That short visit home—presumably to fetch the revolver —was thought to be very important, and Mr. John Ashley's friends felt that his case was practically hopeless.

" The valet's evidence and that of James Funnell, the constable, who had overheard the conversation near the park railings, were certainly the two most damning proofs against the accused. I assure you I was having a rare old time that day. There were two faces in court to watch which was the greatest treat I had had for many a day. One of these was Mr. John Ashley's.

" Here's his photo—short, dark, dapper, a little ' racy ' in style, but otherwise he looks a son of a well-to-do farmer. He was very quiet and placid in court, and addressed a few words now and again to his solicitor. He listened gravely, and with an occasional shrug of the shoulders, to the recital of the crime, such as the police had reconstructed it, before an excited and horrified audience.

" Mr. John Ashley, driven to madness and frenzy by terrible financial difficulties, had first of all gone home in search of a weapon, then waylaid Mr. Aaron Cohen somewhere on that gentleman's way home. The young man had begged for delay. Mr. Cohen perhaps was obdurate ; but Ashley followed him with his importunities almost to his door.

" There, seeing his creditor determined at last to cut short the painful interview, he had seized the unfortunate man at an unguarded moment from behind, and strangled him ; then, fearing that his dastardly work was not fully accomplished, he had shot twice at the already dead body, missing it both times from sheer nervous excitement. The murderer then must have emptied his victim's pockets, and, finding the key of the garden, thought that it would be a safe way of evading capture by cutting across the squares, under the tunnel, and so through the more distant gate which faced Portland Place.

" The loss of the revolver was one of those unforeseen accidents which a retributive Providence places in the path of the miscreant, delivering him by his own act of folly into the hands of human justice.

" Mr. John Ashley, however, did not appear the least bit impressed by the recital of his crime. He had not engaged the services of one of the most eminent lawyers, expert at extracting contradictions from witnesses by skilful cross-examinations— oh, dear me, no ! he had been contented with those of a dull, prosy, very second-rate limb of the law, who, as he called his witnesses, was completely innocent of any desire to create a sensation.

" He rose quietly from his seat, and, amidst breathless silence, called the first of three witnesses on behalf of his client. He called three—but he could have produced twelve—gentle-men, members of the Ashton Club in Great Portland Street, all of whom swore that at three o'clock on the morning of February 6th, that is to say, at the very moment when the cries of 'Murder' roused the inhabitants of Park Square West, and the crime was being committed, Mr. John Ashley was sitting quietly in the club-rooms of the Ashton playing bridge with the three wit-nesses. He had come in a few minutes before three—as the hall porter of the Club testified—and stayed for about an hour and a half.

" I need not tell you that this undoubted, this fully proved, *alibi* was a positive bomb-shell in the stronghold of the prosecu-tion. The most accomplished criminal could not possibly be in two places at once, and though the Ashton Club transgresses in many ways against the gambling laws of our very moral country, yet its members belong to the best, most unimpeach-able classes of society. Mr. Ashley had been seen and spoken to at the very moment of the crime by at least a dozen gentlemen whose testimony was absolutely above suspicion.

" Mr. John Ashley's conduct throughout this astonishing phase of the inquiry remained perfectly calm and correct. It was no doubt the consciousness of being able to prove his inno-cence with such absolute conclusion that had steadied his nerves throughout the proceedings.

" His answers to the magistrate were clear and simple, even on the ticklish subject of the revolver.

" ' I left the club, sir,' he explained, ' fully determined to speak with Mr. Cohen alone in order to ask him for a delay in the settlement of my debt to him. You will understand that I should not care to do this in the presence of other gentlemen. I went home for a minute or two—not in order to fetch a revolver, as the police assert, for I always carry a revolver about with me in foggy weather—but in order to see if a very impor-tant business letter had come for me in my absence.

"' Then I went out again, and met Mr. Aaron Cohen not far from the Harewood Club. I walked the greater part of the way with him, and our conversation was of the most amicable character. We parted at the top of Portland Place, near the gate of the Square, where the policeman saw us. Mr. Cohen then had the intention of cutting across the Square, as being a shorter way to his own house. I thought the Square looked dark and dangerous in the fog, especially as Mr. Cohen was carrying a large sum of money.

"' We had a short discussion on the subject, and finally I persuaded him to take my revolver, as I was going home only through very frequented streets, and moreover carried nothing that was worth stealing. After a little demur Mr. Cohen accepted the loan of my revolver, and that is how it came to be found on the actual scene of the crime ; finally I parted from Mr. Cohen a very few minutes after I had heard the church clock striking a quarter before three. I was at the Oxford Street end of Great Portland Street at five minutes to three, and it takes at least ten minutes to walk from where I was to the Ashton Club.'

" This explanation was all the more credible, mind you, because the question of the revolver had never been very satisfactorily explained by the prosecution. A man who has effectually strangled his victim would not discharge two shots of his revolver for, apparently, no other purpose than that of rousing the attention of the nearest passer-by. It was far more likely that it was Mr. Cohen who shot—perhaps wildly into the air, when suddenly attacked from behind. Mr. Ashley's explanation therefore was not only plausible, it was the only possible one.

" You will understand therefore how it was that, after nearly half an hour's examination, the magistrate, the police, and the public were alike pleased to proclaim that the accused left the court without a stain upon his character."

" Yes," interrupted Polly eagerly, since, for once, her acumen had been at least as sharp as his, " but suspicion of that horrible crime only shifted its taint from one friend to another, and, of course, I know—— "

" But that's just it," he quietly interrupted, " you don't know—Mr. Walter Hatherell, of course, you mean. So did every one else at once. The friend, weak and willing, committing a crime on behalf of his cowardly, yet more assertive friend who had tempted him to evil. It was a good theory ; and was held pretty generally, I fancy, even by the police.

" I say ' even ' because they worked really hard in order to build up a case against young Hatherell, but the great difficulty was that of time. At the hour when the policeman had seen the two men outside Park Square together, Walter Hatherell was still sitting in the Harewood Club, which he never left until twenty minutes to two. Had he wished to waylay and rob Aaron Cohen he would not have waited surely till the time when presumably the latter would already have reached home.

" Moreover, twenty minutes was an incredibly short time in which to walk from Hanover Square to Regent's Park without the chance of cutting across the squares, to look for a man, whose whereabouts you could not determine to within twenty yards or so, to have an argument with him, murder him, and ransack his pockets. And then there was the total absence of motive."

" But—— " said Polly meditatively, for she remembered now that the Regent's Park murder, as it had been popularly called, was one of those which had remained as impenetrable a mystery as any other crime had ever been in the annals of the police.

The man in the corner cocked his funny bird-like head well on one side and looked at her, highly amused evidently at her perplexity.

" You do not see how that murder was committed ? " he asked with a grin.

Polly was bound to admit that she did not.

" If you had happened to have been in Mr. John Ashley's predicament," he persisted, " you do not see how you could conveniently have done away with Mr. Aaron Cohen, pocketed his winnings, and then led the police of your country entirely by the nose, by proving an indisputable *alibi* ? "

" I could not arrange conveniently," she retorted, " to be in two different places half a mile apart at one and the same time."

" No ! I quite admit that you could not do this unless you also had a friend—— "

" A friend ? But you say—— "

" I say that I admired Mr. John Ashley, for his was the head which planned the whole thing, but he could not have accomplished the fascinating and terrible drama without the help of willing and able hands."

" Even then—— " she protested.

"Point number one," he began excitedly, fidgeting with his inevitable piece of string. "John Ashley and his friend Walter Hatherell leave the club together, and together decide on the plan of campaign. Hatherell returns to the club, and Ashley goes to fetch the revolver—the revolver which played such an important part in the drama, but not the part assigned to it by the police. Now try to follow Ashley closely, as he dogs Aaron Cohen's footsteps. Do you believe that he entered into conversation with him ? That he walked by his side ? That he asked for delay ? No ! He sneaked behind him and caught him by the throat, as the garrotters used to do in the fog. Cohen was apoplectic, and Ashley is young and powerful. Moreover, he meant to kill—— "

"But the two men talked together outside the Square gates," protested Polly, "one of whom was Cohen, and the other Ashley."

"Pardon me," he said, jumping up in his seat like a monkey on a stick, "there were not two men talking outside the Square gates. According to the testimony of James Funnell, the constable, two men were leaning arm in arm against the railings and *one* man was talking."

"Then you think that—— "

"At the hour when James Funnell heard Holy Trinity clock striking half-past two Aaron Cohen was already dead. Look how simple the whole thing is," he added eagerly, "and how easy after that—easy, but oh, dear me ! how wonderfully, how stupendously clever. As soon as James Funnell has passed on, John Ashley, having opened the gate, lifts the body of Aaron Cohen in his arms and carries him across the Square. The Square is deserted, of course, but the way is easy enough, and we must presume that Ashley had been in it before. Anyway, there was no fear of meeting any one.

"In the meantime Hatherell has left the club : as fast as his athletic legs can carry him he rushes along Oxford Street and Portland Place. It had been arranged between the two miscreants that the Square gate should be left on the latch.

"Close on Ashley's heels now, Hatherell too cuts across the Square, and reaches the further gate in good time to give his confederate a hand in disposing the body against the railings. Then, without another instant's delay, Ashley runs back across the gardens, straight to the Ashton Club, throwing away the keys of the dead man, on the very spot where he had made it a point of being seen and heard by a passer-by.

"Hatherell gives his friend six or seven minutes' start, then he begins the altercation which lasts two or three minutes, and finally rouses the neighbourhood with cries of ' Murder ' and report of pistol in order to establish that the crime was committed at the hour when its perpetrator has already made out an indisputable *alibi*.

" I don't know what you think of it all, of course," added the funny creature as he fumbled for his coat and his gloves, " but I call the planning of that murder—on the part of novices, mind you—one of the cleverest pieces of strategy I have ever come across. It is one of those cases where there is no possibility whatever now of bringing the crime home to its perpetrator or his abettor. They have not left a single proof behind them ; they foresaw everything, and each acted his part with a coolness and courage which, applied to a great and good cause, would have made fine statesmen of them both.

" As it is, I fear, they are just a pair of young blackguards, who have escaped human justice, and have only deserved the full and ungrudging admiration of yours very sincerely."

He had gone. Polly wanted to call him back, but his meagre person was no longer visible through the glass door. There were many things she would have wished to ask of him—what were his proofs, his facts ? His were theories, after all, and yet, somehow, she felt that he had solved once again one of the darkest mysteries of great criminal London.

THEY NEVER GET CAUGHT

By

MARGERY ALLINGHAM

" *ILLIE dear, this does explain itself, doesn't it ? Henry.*"
Mr. Henry Brownrigg signed his name on the back of
the little blue bill with a flourish.   Then he set the
scrap of paper carefully in the exact centre of the imperfectly
scoured developing bath, and, leaving the offending utensil on
the kitchen table for his wife to find when she came in, he
stalked back to the shop, feeling that he had administered the
rebuke surely and at the same time gracefully.

In fifteen years Mr. Brownrigg felt that he had mastered
the art of teaching his wife her job.   Not that he had taught
her.   That, Mr. Brownrigg felt, with a woman of Millie's
staggering obtuseness was past praying for.   But now, after
long practice, he could deliver the snub or administer the
punishing word in a way which would penetrate her placid
dullness.

Within half an hour after she had returned from shopping
and before lunch was set upon the table, he knew the bath
would be back in the dark-room, bright and pristine as when it
was new, and nothing more would be said about it.   Millie
would be a little more ineffectually anxious to please at lunch,
perhaps, but that was all.

Mr. Brownrigg passed behind the counter and flicked a
speck of dust off the dummy cartons of face-cream.   It was
twelve twenty-five and a half.   In four and a half minutes
Phyllis Bell would leave her office further down the High
Street, and in seven and a half minutes she would come in
through that narrow, sunlit doorway to the cool, drug-scented
shop.

On that patch of floor where the sunlight lay blue and
yellow, since it had found its way in through the enormous

79

glass vases in the window which were the emblem of his trade, she would stand and look at him, her blue eyes limpid and her small mouth pursed and adorable.

The chemist took up one of the ebony-backed hand mirrors exposed on the counter for sale and glanced at himself in it. He was not altogether a prepossessing person. Never a tall man, at forty-two his wide, stocky figure showed a definite tendency to become fleshy, but there was strength and virility in his thick shoulders, while his clean-shaven face and broad neck were short and bull-like and his lips were full.

Phyllis liked his eyes. They held her, she said, and most of the other young women who bought their cosmetics at the corner shop and chatted with Mr. Brownrigg across the counter might have been inclined to agree with her.

Over-dark, round, hot eyes had Mr. Brownrigg ; not at all the sort of eyes for a little, plump, middle-aged chemist with a placid wife like Millie.

But Mr. Brownrigg did not contemplate his own eyes. He smoothed his hair, wiped his lips, and then, realising that Phyllis was almost due, he disappeared behind the dispensing desk. It was as well, he always thought, not to appear too eager.

He was watching the door, though, when she came in. He saw the flicker of her green skirt as she hesitated on the step and saw her half-eager, half apprehensive expression as she glanced towards the counter.

He was glad she had not come in when a customer was there. Phyllis was different from any of the others whose little histories stretched back through the past fourteen years. When Phyllis was in the shop Mr. Brownrigg found he was liable to make mistakes, liable to drop things and fluff the change.

He came out from his obscurity eager in spite of himself, and drew the little golden-haired girl sharply towards him over that part of the counter which was lowest and which he purposely kept uncluttered.

He kissed her and the sudden hungry force of the movement betrayed him utterly. He heard her quick intake of breath before she released herself and stepped back.

" You—you shouldn't," she said, nervously tugging her hat back into position.

She was barely twenty, small and young looking for her years, with yellow hair and a pleasant, quiet style. Her blue eyes were frightened and a little disgusted now, as though she found herself caught up in an emotion which her instincts considered not quite nice.

Henry Brownrigg recognised the expression. He had seen it before in other eyes, but whereas on past occasions he had been able to be tolerantly amused and therefore comforting and glibly reassuring, in Phyllis it irritated and almost frightened him.

" Why not ? " he demanded sharply, too sharply he knew immediately, and the blood rushed into his face.

Phyllis took a deep breath.

" I came to tell you," she said jerkily, like a child saying its piece, " I've been thinking things over. I can't go on with all this. You're married. I want to be married some day. I —I shan't come in again."

" You haven't been talking to someone ? " he demanded, suddenly cold.

" About you ? Good heavens, no ! "

Her vehemence was convincing, and because of that he shut his mind to its uncomplimentary inference and experienced only relief.

" You love me," said Henry Brownrigg. " I love you and you love me. You know that."

He spoke without intentional histrionics, but adopted a curious monotone which, some actors have discovered, is one of the most convincing methods of conveying deep sincerity.

Phyllis nodded miserably and then seemed oddly embarassed. Wistfully her eyes wandered to the sunlit street and back again.

" Good-bye," she said huskily and fled.

He saw her speeding past the window, almost running.

For some time Henry Brownrigg remained looking down at the patch of blue sunlight where she had stood. Finally he raised his eyes and smiled with conscious wryness. She would come back. To-morrow, or in a week, or in ten days perhaps, she would come back. But the obstacle, the unsurmountable obstacle would arise again, in time it would defeat him and he would lose her.

Phyllis was different from the others. He would lose her. Unless that obstacle were removed.

Henry Brownrigg frowned.

There were other considerations too. The old, mottled ledger told those only too clearly.

If the obstacle were removed it would automatically wipe

away those difficulties also, for was there not the insurance
and that small income Millie's father had left so securely tied,
as though the old man had divined his daughter would grow
up a fool ?

Mr. Brownrigg's eyes rested upon the little drawer under
the counter marked : " Prescriptions : private." It was locked
and not even young Perry, his errand boy and general assistant,
who poked his nose into most things, guessed that under the
pile of slips within was a packet of letters scrawled in Phyllis's
childish hand.

He turned away abruptly. His breath was hard to draw
and he was trembling. The time had come.

Some months previously Henry Brownrigg had decided
that he must become a widower before the end of the year,
but the interview of the morning had convinced him that he
must hurry.

At this moment Millie, her face still pink with shame at the
recollection of the affair of the ill-washed bath, put her head
round the inner door.

" Lunch is on the table, Henry," she said, and added with
that stupidity which had annoyed him ever since it had ceased
to please him by making him feel superior, " Well, you do
look serious. Oh, Henry, you haven't made a mistake and
given somebody a wrong bottle ? "

" No, my dear Millie," said her husband, surveying her
coldly and speaking with heavy sarcasm. " That is the peculiar
sort of idiot mistake I have yet to make. I haven't reached my
wife's level yet."

And as he followed her uncomplaining figure to the little
room behind the shop a word echoed rhythmically in the back
of his mind and kept time with the beating of his heart.
" Hurry ! Hurry ! Hurry ! "

" Henry, dear," said Millie Brownrigg, turning a troubled
face towards her husband, " why Doctor Crupiner ? He's so
expensive and so old."

She was standing in front of the dressing-table in the big
front bedroom above the shop, brushing her brown, grey
streaked hair before she plaited it and coiled it round her head.

Henry Brownrigg, lying awake in his bed on the far side of
the room, did not answer her.

Millie went on talking. She was used to Henry's silence.
Henry was so clever. Most of his time was spent in thought.
" I've heard all sorts of odd things about Doctor Crupiner,"

she remarked. "They say he's so old he forgets. Why shouldn't we go to Mother's man ? She swears by him."

"Unfortunately for your mother she has your intelligence, without a man to look after her, poor woman," said Henry Brownrigg.

Mille made no comment.

"Crupiner," continued Henry Brownrigg, "may not be much good as a general practitioner, but there is one subject on which he is a master. I want him to see you. I want to get you well, old dear."

Millie's gentle, expressionless face flushed and her blue eyes looked moist and foolish in the mirror. Henry could see her reflection in the glass and he turned away. There were moments when, by her obvious gratitude for a kind word from him, Millie made him feel a certain distaste for his project. He wished to God she would go away and leave him his last few moments in bed to think of Phyllis in peace.

"You know, Henry," said Mrs. Brownrigg suddenly, "I don't feel ill. Those things you're giving me are doing me good, I'm sure. I don't feel nearly so tired at the end of the day now. Can't you treat me yourself ? "

The man in the bed stiffened. Any compunction he may have felt vanished and he became wary.

"Of course they're doing you good," he said with the satisfaction of knowing that he was telling the truth up to a point, or at least of knowing that he was doing nothing reprehensible—yet.

"I don't believe in patent medicines as a rule, but Fender's Pills are good. They're a well known formula, and they certainly do pick one up. But I just want to make sure that you're organically sound. I don't like you getting breathless when you hurry, and the colour of your lips isn't good, you know."

Plump, foolish Millie looked in the mirror and nervously ran her forefinger over her mouth.

Like many women of her age she had lost much of her colour, and there certainly was a faint, very faint, blue streak round the edge of her lips.

The chemist was heavily reassuring.

"Nothing to worry about, I'm sure, but I think we'll go down and see Crupiner this evening," he said, and added adroitly, "we want to be on the safe side, don't we ? "

Millie nodded, her mouth trembling.

"Yes, dear," she said, and paused, adding afterwards in that insufferable way of hers, "I suppose so."

When she had gone downstairs to attend to breakfast Henry Brownrigg rose with his own last phrase still on his lips. He repeated it thoughtfully.

" The safe side." That was right. The safe side. No ghastly hash of it for Henry Brownrigg.

Only fools made a hash of things. Only fools got caught. This was almost too easy. Millie was so simple-minded, so utterly unsuspecting.

By the end of the day Mr. Brownrigg was nervy. The boy Perry had reported innocently enough that he had seen young Hill in his new car going down Acacia Road at something over sixty, and had added casually that he had had the Bell girl with him. The youngest one. Phyllis. Did Mr. Brownrigg remember her ? She was rather pretty.

For a moment Henry Brownrigg was in terror lest the boy had discovered his secret and was wounding him maliciously. But, having convinced himself that this was not so, the fact and the sting remained.

Young Hill was handsome and a bachelor. Phyllis was young and impressionable. The chemist imagined them pulling up in some shady copse outside the town, holding hands, perhaps even kissing, and the heart which could remain steady while Millie's stupid eyes met his anxiously as she spoke of her illness turned over painfully in Henry Brownrigg's side at the thought of that embrace.

" Hurry." The word formed itself again in the back of his mind. Hurry . . . hurry.

Millie was breathless when they arrived at Doctor Crupiner's old-fashioned house. Henry had been self-absorbed and had walked very fast.

Doctor Crupiner saw them immediately. He was a vast, dusty old man. Privately Millie thought she would like to take a good stiff broom to him, and the picture the idea conjured in her mind was so ridiculous that she giggled nervously and Henry had to shake his head at her warningly.

She flushed painfully, and the old, stupid expression settled down over her face again.

Henry explained her symptoms to the doctor and Millie looked surprised and gratified at the anxiety he betrayed. Henry had evidently noticed her little wearinesses much more often than she had supposed.

When he had finished his recital of her small ills, none of them alarming in themselves but piling up in total to a rather terrifying sum of evidence, Doctor Crupiner turned his eyes, which were small and greasy, with red veins in their whites, on to Millie, and his old lips, which were mottled like Henry's ledger, moved for a fraction of a second before his voice came, wheezy and sepulchral.

"Well, madam," he said, "your husband here seems worried about you. Let's have a look at you."

Millie trembled. She was getting breathless again from sheer apprehension. Once or twice lately it had occurred to her that the Fender's Pills made her feel breathless, even while they bucked her up in other ways, but she had not liked to mention this to Henry.

Doctor Crupiner came close to her, breathing heavily through his nose in an effort of concentration. He thrust a stubby, unsteady finger into her eye socket, dragging down the skin so that he could peer short-sightedly at her eyeball. He thumped her half-heartedly on the back and felt the palms of her hands.

Mr. Brownrigg, who watched all this somewhat meaningless ritual, his round eyes thoughtful and uneasy, suddenly took the doctor on one side, and the two men had a muttered conversation at the far end of the long room.

Millie could not help overhearing some of it, because Doctor Crupiner was deaf these days and Henry was anxious to make himself understood.

"Twenty years ago," she heard. "Very sudden." And then, after a pause, the awful word " hereditary."

Millie's trembling fit increased in intensity and her broad, stupid face looked frightened. They were talking about her poor papa. He had died very suddenly of heart disease.

Her own heart jumped painfully. So that was why Henry seemed so anxious.

Doctor Crupiner came back to her. She had to undo her dress and Doctor Crupiner listened to her heart with an ancient stethoscope. Millie, already trembling, began to breathe with difficulty as her alarm became unbearable.

At last the old man finished with her. He stared at her unwinkingly for some seconds and finally turned to Henry, and together they went back to the far end of the room.

Millie strained her ears and heard the old man's rumbling voice.

"A certain irregularity. Nothing very alarming. Bring her to see me again."

Then there was a question from Henry which she could not catch, but afterwards, as the doctor seemed to be fumbling in

his mind for a reply, the chemist remarked in an ordinary tone :
" I've been giving her Fender's pills."

" Fender's pills ? " Doctor Crupiner echoed the words with
relief. " Excellent. Excellent. You chemists like patent
medicines, I know, and I don't want to encourage you, but that's
a well-known formula and will save you mixing up my prescription. Carry on with those for a while. Very good things ; I
often recommend them. Take them in moderation, of course."

" Oh, of course," said Henry. " But do you think I'm
doing right, Doctor ? "

Millie looked pleased and startled at the earnestness of
Henry's tone.

" Oh, without doubt, Mr. Brownrigg, without doubt."
Doctor Crupiner repeated the words again as he came back to
Millie. " There, Mrs. Brownrigg," he said with spurious
jollity, " you take care of yourself and do what your husband
says. Come to see me again in a week or so and you'll be as
right as ninepence. Off you go. Oh, but Mrs. Brownrigg, no
shocks, mind. No excitements. No little upsets. And don't
over-tire yourself."

He shook hands perfunctorily, and, while Henry was helping
Millie to collect her things with a solicitude quite unusual in
him, the old man took down a large, dusty book from the
shelves.

Just before they left he peered at Henry over his spectacles.
" Those Fender's pills are quite a good idea," he remarked
in a tone quite different from his professional rumble. " Just
the things. They contain a small percentage of digitalin."

One of Mr. Brownrigg's least attractive habits was his
method of spending Saturday nights.

At half-past seven the patient but silently disapproving
Millie would clear away the remains of the final meal of the
day and place one glass and an unopened bottle of whisky and
a siphon of soda on the green serge tablecloth.

This done, she would retire to the kitchen, wash up, and
complete the week's ironing. She usually left this job until
then, because it was a longish business, with frequent pauses
for minor repairs to Henry's shirts and her own underclothing,
and she knew she had plenty of undisturbed time on her hands.

She had, in fact, until midnight. When the kitchen clock
wheezed twelve Millie folded her ironing board and turned up
the irons on the stove to cool.

Then she went into the living-room and took away the glass

and the empty bottle, so that the daily help should not see them in the morning. She also picked up the papers and straightened the room.

Finally, when the gas fire had been extinguished, she attended to Henry.

A fortnight and three days after her first visit to Doctor Crupiner—the doctor, at Henry's suggestion, had increased her dose of Fender's pills from three to five a day—she went through her Saturday ritual as usual.

For a man engaged in Mr. Brownrigg's particular programme to get hopelessly and incapably drunk once, much less once a week, might well have been suicidal lunacy.

One small glass of whisky reduced him to taciturnity. Twelve large glasses of whisky, or one bottle, made of him a limp, silent sack of humanity, incapable of movement or speech, but, quite remarkably, not a senseless creature.

It might well have occurred to Millie to wonder why her husband should choose to transform himself into a Therese Raquin paralytic once every week in his life, but in spite of her awful stupidity she was a tolerant woman and honestly believed that men were odd, privileged creatures who took delight in strange perversions. So she humoured him and kept his weakness secret even from her mother.

Oddly enough, Henry Brownrigg enjoyed his periodical orgy. He did not drink during the week, and his Saturday experience was at once an adventure and a habit. At the outset of his present project he had thought of foregoing it until his plan was completed, but he realised the absolute necessity of adhering rigidly to his normal course of life, so that there could be no hook, however small, on which the garment of suspicion could catch and take hold.

On this particular evening Millie quite exhausted herself getting him upstairs and into bed. She was so tired when it was all over that she sat on the edge of her couch and breathed hard, quite unable to pull herself together sufficiently to undress.

So exhausted was she that she forgot to take the two Fender's pills that Henry had left on the dressing-table for her, and once in bed she could not persuade herself to get out again for them.

In the morning Henry found them still in the little box. He listened to her startled explanations in silence and then, as she added apology to apology, suddenly became himself again.

" Dear Millie," he said in the old exasperated tone she knew

so well, " isn't it enough for me to do all I can to get you well
without you hampering me at every turn ? "

Millie bent low over the stove and, as if he felt she might be
hiding sudden tears, his manner became more conciliatory.

" Don't you like them ? " he inquired softly. " Don't you
like the taste of them ? Perhaps they're too big ? Look here,
old dear, I'll put them up in an easier form. You shall have
them in jelly cases. Leave it to me. There, there, don't worry.
But you must take your medicine, you know."

He patted her plump shoulder awkwardly and hurried
upstairs to dress.

Millie became thoughtful. Henry was clearly very worried
about her indeed, or he would never be so nice about her
silly mistake.

Young Bill Perry, Brownrigg's errand boy assistant, was
at the awkward stage, if indeed he would ever grow out of it.

He was scrawny, red headed, with a tendency to acne, and
great raw, scarlet wrists. Mr. Brownrigg he loathed as only
the young can loathe the possessor of a sarcastic tongue, but
Millie he liked, and his pale, sandy-fringed eyes twinkled
kindly when she spoke to him.

Young Perry did not think Millie was half so daft as the
Old Man made out.

If only because she was kind to him, young Perry was
interested in the state of Millie's health.

On the Monday night young Perry saw Mr. Brownrigg
putting up the contents of the Fender's pills in jelly cases and
he inquired about them.

Mr. Brownrigg was unusually communicative. He told
young Perry in strict confidence that Mrs. Brownrigg was far
from well and that Doctor Crupiner was worried about her.

Mr. Brownrigg also intimated that he and Doctor Crupiner
were, as professional men, agreed that if complete freedom
from care and Fender's pills could not save Mrs. Brownrigg,
nothing could.

" Do you mean she might die ? " said young Perry, aghast.
" Suddenly, I mean, sir ? "

He was sorry as soon as he had spoken, because Mr. Brownrigg's hand trembled so much that he dropped one of the jelly
cases and young Perry realised that the Old Man was really
wild about the Old Girl after all, and that his bullyragging her
was all a sham to hide his feelings.

At that moment young Perry's sentimental, impressionable

heart went out to Mr. Brownrigg, and he generously forgave him for his observation that young Perry was patently cut out for the diplomatic service, since his tact and delicacy were so great.

The stores arrived. Bill Perry unpacked the two big cases ; the smaller case he opened, but left the unpacking to his employer.

Mr. Brownrigg finished his pill making, although he was keeping the boy waiting, rinsed his hands and got down to work with his usual deliberation.

There were not a great many packages in the case and young Perry, who had taken a peep at the mottled ledger some time before, thought he knew why. The Old Man was riding close to the edge. Bills and receipts had to be juggled very carefully these days.

The boy read the invoice from the wholesaler's, and Mr. Brownrigg put the drugs away.

" Sodii Bicarbonas, Magnesia Levis," he read, stumbling over the difficult words. " Iodine, Quininæ Hydrochloridum, Tincture Digitalin . . . that must be it, Mr. Brownrigg. There, in the biggish packet."

Bill Perry knew he read badly and was only trying to be helpful when he indicated the parcel, but Mr. Brownrigg shot a truly terrifying glance in his direction as he literally snatched up the package and carried it off to the drug cabinet.

Young Perry was dismayed. He was late and he wanted to go. In his panic he floundered on, making matters worse.

" I'm sorry, sir," he said. " I was only trying to help. I thought you might be—er—thinking of something else and got a bit muddled."

" Oh," said Mr. Brownrigg slowly, fixing him with those hot, round eyes in a way which was oddly disturbing. " And of what should I be thinking when I am doing my work, boy ? "

" Of—of Mrs. Brownrigg, sir," stammered the wretched Perry helplessly.

Henry Brownrigg froze. The blood congealed in his face and his eyes seemed to sink into his head.

Young Perry, who realised he had said the wrong thing, and who had a natural delicacy which revolted at prying into another's sorrow, mistook his employer's symptoms for acute embarrassment.

" I'm sorry," he said again. " I was really trying to help. I'm a bit—er—windy myself, sir. Mrs. Brownrigg's been very kind to me. I'm sorry she's so ill."

A great sigh escaped Henry Brownrigg.

" That's all right, my boy," he said, with a gentleness his assistant had never before heard in his tone. " I'm a bit rattled myself, too. You can go now. I'll see to these few things."

Young Perry sped off, happy to be free on such a sunny evening, but also a little awe-stricken by the revelation of this tragedy of married love.

Phyllis hurried down Coe's Lane, which was a short cut between her own road and Priory Avenue. It was a narrow, paper-baggy little thoroughfare, with a dusty hedge on one side and high tarred fence on the other.

On this occasion Coe's Lane appeared to be deserted, but when Phyllis reached the stunted may tree half-way down the hedge a figure stepped out and came to meet her.

The girl stopped abruptly in the middle of the path. Her cheeks were patched with pink and white and she caught her breath sharply as though afraid of herself.

Henry Brownrigg himself was unprepared for the savagery of the sudden pain in his breast when he saw her, and the writhing, vicious, mindless passion which checked his breathing and made his eyelids feel sticky and his mouth dry, frightened him a little also.

They were alone in the lane and he kissed her, putting into his hunched shoulders and greedy lips all the insufferable, senseless longing of the past eighteen days.

When he released her she was crying. The big, bright tears which filled her eyes brimmed over on to her cheeks and made her mouth look hot and wet and feverish.

" Go away," she said and her tone was husky and imploring. " Oh, go away—please, please ! "

After the kiss Henry Brownrigg was human again and no longer the fiend-possessed soul in torment he had been while waiting in the lane. Now he could behave normally, for a time at least.

" All right," he said, and added so lightly that she was deceived, " going out with Peter Hill again this afternoon ? "

The girl's lips trembled and her eyes were pleading.

" I'm trying to get free," she said. " Don't you see I'm trying to get free from you ? It's not easy."

Henry Brownrigg stared at her inquisitively for a full minute. Then he laughed shortly and explosively and strode away back down the lane at a great pace.

Henry Brownrigg went home. He walked very fast, his

round eyes introspective but his step light and purposeful. His thoughts were pleasant. So Phyllis was there when he wanted her, there for the taking when the obstacle was once removed. That had been his only doubt. Now he was certain of it. The practical part of his project alone remained.

Small, relatively unimportant things like the new story the mottled ledger would have to tell when the insurance money was in the bank and Millie's small income was realised and reinvested crowded into his mind, but he brushed them aside impatiently. This afternoon he must be grimly practical. There was delicate work to do.

When he reached home Millie had gone over to her mother's.

It was also early-closing day and young Perry was far away, bowling wides for the St. Anne's parish cricket club.

Mr. Brownrigg went round the house carefully and made sure that all the doors were locked. The shop shutters were up too, and he knew from careful observation that they permitted no light from within to escape.

He removed his jacket and donned his working overall, switched on the lights, locked the door between the shop and the living-room, and set to work.

He knew exactly what he had to do. Millie had been taking five Fender's pills regularly now for eight days. Each pill contained $\frac{1}{16}$ gr. Nativelle's Digitalin, and the stuff was cumulative. No wonder she had been complaining of biliousness and headaches lately ! Millie was a hopeless fool.

He took out the bottle of Tincturæ Digitalin, which had come when young Perry had given him such a scare, and looked at it. He wished he had risked it and bought the Quevenne's, or the freshly powdered leaves. He wouldn't have had all this trouble now.

Still, he hadn't taken the chance, and on second thoughts he was glad. As it was, the wholesalers couldn't possibly notice anything unusual in his order. There could be no inquiry : it meant he need never worry—afterwards.

He worked feverishly as his thoughts raced on. He knew the dose. All that had been worked out months before when the idea had first occurred to him, and he had gone over this part of the proceedings again and again in his mind so that there could be no mistake, no slip.

Nine drachms of the tincture had killed a patient with no digitalin already in the system. But then the tincture was notoriously liable to deteriorate. Still, this stuff was fresh ;

barely six days old if the wholesalers could be trusted. He had thought of that.

He prepared his burner and the evaporator. It took a long time. Although he was so practised, his hands were unsteady and clumsy, and the irritant fumes got into his eyes.

Suddenly he discovered that it was nearly four o'clock. He was panic-stricken. Only two hours and Millie would come back, and there was a lot to be done.

As the burner did its work his mind moved rapidly. Digitalin was so difficult to trace afterwards ; that was the beauty of it. Even the great Tardieu had been unable to state positively if it was digitalin that had been used in the Pommeraise case, and that after the most exhaustive P.M. and tests on frogs and all that sort of thing.

Henry Brownrigg's face split into the semblance of a smile. Old Crupiner was no Tardieu. Crupiner would not advise a P.M. if he could possibly avoid it. He'd give the certificate all right ; his mind was prepared for it. Probably he wouldn't even come and look at the body.

Millie's stupid, placid body. Henry Brownrigg put the thought from him. No use getting nervy now.

A shattering peal on the back door startled him so much that he nearly upset his paraphernalia. For a moment he stood breathing wildly, like a trapped animal, but he pulled himself together in the end, and, changing into his coat, went down to answer the summons.

He locked the shop door behind him, smoothed his hair, and opened the back door confident that he looked normal, even ordinary.

But the small boy with the evening paper did not wait for his Saturday's sixpence but rushed away after a single glance at Mr. Brownrigg's face. He was a timid twelve-year-old, however, who often imagined things, and his employer, an older boy, cuffed him for the story and made a mental note to call for the money himself on the Monday night.

The effect of the incident on Henry Brownrigg was considerable. He went back to his work like a man in a nightmare, and for the rest of the proceedings he kept his mind resolutely on the physical task.

At last it was done.

He turned out the burner, scoured the evaporator, measured the toxic dose carefully, adding to it considerably to be on the safe side. After all, one could hardly overdo it ; that was the charm of this stuff.

Then he effectively disposed of the residue and felt much better.

He had locked the door and changed his coat again before he noticed the awful thing. A layer of fine dust on the top of one of the bottles first attracted his attention. He removed it with fastidious care. He hated a frowsy shop.

He had replaced his handkerchief before he saw the show-case ledge and the first glimmering of the dreadful truth percolated his startled mind.

From the ledge his eyes travelled to the counter top, to the dummy cartoons, to the bottles and jars, to the window shutters, to the very floor.

Great drops appeared on Henry Brownrigg's forehead. There was not an inch of surface in the whole shop that was innocent of the thinnest, faintest coat of yellowish dust.

Digitalin ! Digitalin over the whole shop ! Digitalin over the whole world ! The evidence of his guilt everywhere, damning, unescapable, clear to the first intelligent observer.

Henry Brownrigg stood very still.

Gradually his brain, cool at the bidding of the instinct of self-preservation, began to work again. Delay. That was the all-important note. Millie must not take the capsule to-night as he had planned. Not to-night, nor to-morrow. Millie must not die until every trace of that yellow dust had been driven from the shop.

Swiftly he rearranged his plan. To-night he must behave as usual and to-morrow, when Millie went to church, he must clear off the worst of the stuff before young Perry noticed anything.

Then on Monday he would make an excuse and have the vacuum cleaning people in. They came with a great machine and put pipes in through the window. He had often said he would have it done.

They worked quickly ; so on Tuesday . . .

Meanwhile, normality. That was the main thing. He must do nothing to alarm Millie or excite her curiosity.

It did not occur to him that there would be a grim irony in getting Millie to help him dust the shop that evening. But he dismissed the idea. They'd never do it thoroughly in the time.

He washed in the kitchen and went back into the hall. A step on the stairs above him brought a scream to his throat which he only just succeeded in stifling.

It was Millie. She had come in the back way without him hearing her, heaven knew how long before.

" I've borrowed a portière curtain from Mother for your
bedroom door, Henry," she said mildly. " You won't be
troubled by the draught up there any more. It's such a
good thick one. I've just been fixing it up. It looks very nice."

Henry Brownrigg made a noise which might have meant
anything. His nerves had gone to pieces.

Her next remark was reassuring, however ; so reassuring
that he almost laughed aloud.

" Oh, Henry," she said, " you only gave me four of those
pills to-day, dear. You won't forget the other one, will you ? "

" Cold ham from the cooked meat shop, cold tinned peas,
potato salad and Worcester sauce. What a cook ! What a
cook I've married, my dear Millie."

Henry Brownrigg derived a vicious pleasure from the
clumsy sarcasm, and when Millie's pale face became wooden
he was gratified.

As he sat at the small table and looked at her he was aware
of a curious phenomenon. The woman stood out from the
rest of the room's contents as though she alone was in relief.
He saw every line of her features, every fold of her dark cotton
foulard dress, as though they were drawn with a thick black
pencil.

Millie was silent. Even her usual flow of banality had dried
up, and he was glad of it.

He found himself regarding her dispassionately, as though
she had been a stranger. He did not hate her, he decided. On
the contrary, he was prepared to believe that she was quite an
estimable, practicable person in her own limited fashion. But
she was in the way.

This plump, fatuous creature, not even different in her very
obtuseness from many of the other matrons in the town, had
committed the crowning impudence of getting in the way of
Henry Brownrigg. She, this ridiculous, lowly woman, actually
stood between Henry Brownrigg and the inmost desires of his
heart.

It was an insight into the state of the chemist's mind that
at that moment nothing impressed him so forcibly as her
remarkable audacity.

Monday, he thought. Monday, and possibly Tuesday,
and then . . .

Millie cleared away.

Mr. Brownrigg drank his first glass of whisky and soda
with a relish he did not often experience. For him the pleasure

of his Saturday night libations lay in the odd sensation he experienced when really drunk.

When Henry Brownrigg was a sack of limp, uninviting humanity to his wife and the rest of the world, to himself he was a quiet, all-powerful ghost, seated, comfortable and protected, in the shell of his body, able to see and comprehend everything, but too mighty and too important to direct any of the drivelling little matters which made up his immediate world.

On these occasions Henry Brownrigg tasted godhead.

The evening began like all the others, and by the time there was but an inch of amber elixir in the square bottle, Millie and the dust in the shop and Doctor Crupiner had become in his mind as ants and ant burdens, while he towered above them, a colossus in mind and power.

When the final inch had dwindled to a yellow stain in the bottom of the white glass bottle Mr. Brownrigg sat very still. In a few minutes now he would attain the peak of that ascendancy over his fellow mortals when the body, so important to them, was for him literally nothing ; not even a dull encumbrance, not even a nerveless covering but a nothingness an unimportant, unnoticed element.

When Millie came in at last a pin could have been thrust deep into Mr. Brownrigg's flesh and he would not have noticed it.

It was when he was in bed, his useless body clad in clean pyjamas, that he noticed that Millie was not behaving quite as usual. She had folded his clothes neatly on the chair at the end of the bed when he saw her peering at something intently.

He followed her eyes and saw for the first time the new portière curtain. It certainly was a fine affair, a great, thick, heavy plush thing that looked as though it would stop any draught there ever had been.

He remembered clearly losing his temper with Millie in front of young Perry one day, and, searching in his mind for a suitable excuse, had invented this draught beneath his bedroom door. And there wasn't one, his ghost remembered ; that was the beauty of it. The door fitted tightly in the jamb. But it gave Millie something to worry about.

Millie went out of the room without extinguishing the lights. He tried to call out to her and only then realised the disadvantages of being a disembodied spirit. He could not speak, of course.

He was lying puzzled at this obvious flaw in his omnipotence when he heard her go downstairs instead of crossing into her room. He was suddenly furious and would have risen, had it been possible. But in the midst of his anger he remembered something amusing and lay still, inwardly convulsed with secret laughter.

Soon Millie would be dead. Dead—dead—dead.

Millie would be stupid no longer. Millie would appal him by her awful mindlessness no more. Millie would be dead.

She came up again and stepped softly into the room.

The alcohol was beginning to take its full effect now and he could not move his head. Soon oblivion would come and he would leave his body and rush off into the exciting darkness, not to return until the dawn.

He saw only Millie's head and shoulders when she came into his line of vision. He was annoyed. She still had those thick black lines round her, and there was an absorbed expression upon her face which he remembered seeing before when she was engrossed in some particularly difficult household task.

She switched out the light and then went over to the far window. He was interested now, and saw her pull up the blinds.

Then to his astonishment he heard the crackle of paper ; not an ordinary crackle, but something familiar, something he had heard hundreds of times before.

He placed it suddenly. Sticky paper. His own reel of sticky paper from the shop.

He was so cross with her for touching it that for some moments he did not wonder what she was doing with it, and it was not until he saw her silhouetted against the second row of panes that he guessed. She was sticking up the window cracks.

His ghost laughed again. The draught. Silly, stupid Millie trying to stop the draught.

She pulled down the blinds and turned on the light again. Her face was mild and expressionless as ever, her blue eyes vacant and foolish.

He saw her go to the dressing-table, still moving briskly, as she always did when working about the house.

Once again the phenomenon he had noticed at the evening meal became startlingly apparent. He saw her hand and its contents positively glowing because of its black outline, thrown up in high relief against the white table cover.

Millie was putting two pieces of paper there : one white with a deckle edge, one blue and familiar.

He remembered his own pencilled words, as if he could read them
" Millie dear, this does explain itself, doesn't it ? "

Henry Brownrigg's ghost yammered in its prison. His body ceased to be negligible : it became a coffin, a sealed, leaden coffin suffocating him in its senseless shell. He fought to free himself, to stir that mighty weight, to move.

Millie knew.

The white paper with the deckle edge was a letter from Phyllis out of the drawer in the shop, and the blue paper—he remembered it now—the blue paper he had left in the dirty developing bath.

He re-read his own pencilled words as clearly as if his eye had become possessed of telescopic sight :

" *Millie dear, this does explain itself, doesn't it ?* "

And then his name, signed with a flourish. He had been so pleased with himself when he had written it.

He fought wildly. The coffin was made of glass now, thick, heavy glass which would not respond to his greatest effort.

Millie was hesitating. She had picked up Phyllis's letter. Now she was reading it again.

He saw her frown and tear the paper into shreds, thrusting the pieces into the pocket of her cardigan.

Henry Brownrigg, understood. Millie was sorry for Phyllis. For all her obtuseness she had guessed at some of the girl's piteous infatuation and had decided to keep her out of it.

What then ? Henry Brownrigg writhed inside his inanimate body.

Millie was back at the table now. She was putting something else there. What was it ? Oh, what was it ?

The ledger ! He saw it plainly, the old mottled ledger, whose story was plain for any fool coroner to read and misunderstand.

Millie had turned away now. He hardly noticed her pause before the fire-place. She did not stoop. Her felt-shod slipper flipped the gas tap over.

Then she passed out of the door, extinguishing the light as she went. He heard the rustle of the thick curtain as she drew the wood close. There was an infinitesimal pause and then the key turned in the lock.

She had behaved throughout the whole proceeding as though she had been getting dinner or tidying the spare room.

In his prison Henry Brownrigg's impotent ghost listened. There was a hissing from the far end of the room.

In the attic, although he could not possibly hear it, he knew the meter ticked every two or three seconds.

Henry Brownrigg saw in a vision the scene in the morning.

Every room in the house had the same key, so Millie would have no difficulty in explaining that on awakening she had noticed the smell of gas and, on finding her husband's door locked, had opened it with her own key.

The ghost stirred in its shell. Once again the earth and earthly incidents looked small and negligible. The oblivion was coming, the darkness was waiting ; only now it was no longer exciting darkness.

The shell moved. He felt it writhe and choke. It was fighting—fighting—fighting.

The darkness drew him. He was no longer conscious of the shell now. It had been beaten. It had given up the fight.

The streak of light beneath the blind where the street lamp shone was fading. Fading. Now it was gone.

As Henry Brownrigg's ghost crept out into the cold a whisper came to it, ghastly in its conviction :

" They never get caught, that kind. They're too dull, too practical, too unimaginative. They never get caught."

BEFORE INSULIN

By

J. J. CONNINGTON

" I'D more than the fishing in my mind when I asked you over for the week-end," Wendover confessed. " Fact is, Clinton, something's turned up and I'd like your advice."

Sir Clinton Driffield, Chief Constable of the county, glanced quizzically at his old friend.

" If you've murdered anyone, Squire, my advice is : Keep it dark and leave the country. If it's merely breach of promise, or anything of that sort, I'm at your disposal."

" It's not breach of promise," Wendover assured him with the complacency of a hardened bachelor. " It's a matter of an estate for which I happen to be sole trustee, worse luck. The other two have died since the will was made. I'll tell you about it."

Wendover prided himself on his power of lucid exposition. He settled himself in his chair and began.

" You've heard me speak of old John Ashby, the iron-master ? He died fifteen years back, worth £53,000 ; and he made his son, his daughter-in-law, and myself executors of his will. The son, James Ashby, was to have the life-rent of the estate ; and on his death the capital was to be handed over to his offspring when the youngest of them came of age. As it happened, there was only one child, young Robin Ashby. James Ashby and his wife were killed in a railway accident some years ago ; so the whole £53,000, less two estate duties, was secured to young Robin if he lived to come of age."

" And if he didn't ? " queried Sir Clinton.

" Then the money went to a lot of charities," Wendover explained. " That's just the trouble, as you'll see. Three years ago, young Robin took diabetes, a bad case, poor fellow. We did what we could for him, naturally. All the specialists had a turn, without improvement. Then we sent him over to Neuenahr, to some institute run by a German who specialised in diabetes. No good. I went over to see the poor boy, and he was worn to a shadow, simply skin and bone and hardly able to walk with weakness. Obviously it was a mere matter of time."

" Hard lines on the youngster," Sir Clinton commented soberly.

" Very hard," said Wendover with a gesture of pity. "Now as it happened, at Neuenahr he scraped acquaintance with a French doctor. I saw him when I was there : about thirty, black torpedo beard, very brisk and well-got-up, with any amount of belief in himself. He spoke English fluently, which gave him a pull with Robin, out there among foreigners ; and he persuaded the boy that he could cure him if he would put himself in his charge. Well, by that time, it seemed that any chance was worth taking, so I agreed. After all, the boy was dying by inches. So off he went to the south of France, where this man—Prevost, his name was—had a nursing home of his own. I saw the place : well-kept affair though small. And he had an English nurse, which was lucky for Robin. Pretty girl she was : chestnut hair, creamy skin, supple figure, neat hands and feet. A lady, too."

" Oh, any pretty girl can get round you," interjected Sir Clinton. " Get on with the tale."

" Well, it was all no good," Wendover went on, hastily. " The poor boy went down hill in spite of all the Frenchman's talk ; and, to cut a long story short, he died a fortnight ago, on the very day when he came of age."

" Oh, so he lived long enough to inherit ? "

" By the skin of his teeth," Wendover agreed. " That's where the trouble begins. Before that day, of course, he could make no valid will. But now a claimant, a man Sydney Eastcote, turns up with the claim that Robin made a will the morning of the day he died and by this will this Eastcote fellow scoops the whole estate. All I know of it is from a letter this Eastcote man wrote to me giving the facts. I referred him to the lawyer for the estate and told the lawyer—Harringay's his name—to bring the claimant here this afternoon. They're due now. I'd like you to look him over, Clinton. I'm not quite satisfied about this will."

The Chief Constable pondered for a moment or two.

" Very well," he agreed. " But you'd better not introduce me as Sir Clinton Driffield, Chief Constable, etc. I'd better be Mr. Clinton, I think. It sounds better for a private confabulation."

"Very well," Wendover conceded. "There's a car on the drive. It must be they, I suppose."

In a few moments the door opened and the visitors were ushered in. Surprised himself, the Chief Constable was still able to enjoy the astonishment of his friend ; for instead of the expected man, a pretty chestnut-haired girl, dressed in mourning, was shown into the room along with the solicitor, and it was plain enough that Wendover recognised her.

"You seem surprised, Mr. Wendover," the girl began, evidently somewhat taken aback by Wendover's expression. Then she smiled as though an explanation occurred to her. "Of course, it's my name again. People always forget that Sydney's a girl's name as well as a man's. But you remember me, don't you ? I met you when you visited poor Robin."

"Of course I remember you, Nurse," Wendover declared, recovering from his surprise. "But I never heard you called anything but ' Nurse ' and didn't even hear your surname ; so naturally I didn't associate you with the letter I got about poor Robin's will."

"Oh, I see," answered the girl. "That accounts for it."

She looked inquiringly towards the Chief Constable, and Wendover recovered his presence of mind.

"This is a friend of mine, Mr. Clinton," he explained. "Miss Eastcote. Mr. Harringay. Won't you sit down ? I must admit your letter took me completely by surprise, Miss Eastcote."

Wendover was getting over his initial astonishment at the identity of the claimant, and when they had all seated themselves, he took the lead.

"I've seen a copy of Robin's death certificate," he began slowly. "He died in the afternoon of September 21st, the day he came of age, so he was quite competent to make a will. I suppose he was mentally fit to make one ? "

"Dr. Prevost will certify that if necessary," the nurse affirmed quietly.

"I noticed that he didn't die in Dr. Prevost's Institute," Wendover continued. "At some local hotel, wasn't it ? "

"Yes," Nurse Eastcote confirmed. "A patient died in the Institute about that time and poor Robin hated the place on that account. It depressed him, and he insisted on moving to the hotel for a time."

"He must have been at death's door then, poor fellow," Wendover commented.

"Yes," the nurse admitted, sadly. "He was very far through. He had lapses of consciousness, the usual diabetic coma. But while he was awake he was perfectly sound mentally, if that's what you mean."

Wendover nodded as though this satisfied him completely.

"Tell me about this will," he asked. "It's come as something of a surprise to me, not unnaturally."

Nurse Eastcote hesitated for a moment. Her lip quivered and her eyes filled with tears as she drew from her bag an envelope of thin foreign paper. From this she extracted a sheet of foreign note-paper which she passed across to Wendover.

"I can't grumble if you're surprised at his leaving me this money," she said, at last. "I didn't expect anything of the kind myself. But the fact is . . . he fell in love with me, poor boy, while he was under my charge. You see, except for Dr. Prevost, I was the only one who could speak English with him, and that meant much to him at that time when he was so lonely. Of course he was much younger that I am ; I'm twenty-seven. I suppose I ought to have checked him when I saw how things were. But I hadn't the heart to do it. It was something that gave him just the necessary spur to keep him going, and of course I knew that marriage would never come into it. It did no harm to let him fall in love ; and I really did my very best to make him happy, in these last weeks. I was so sorry for him, you know."

This put the matter in a fresh light for Wendover, and he grew more sympathetic in his manner.

"I can understand," he said gently. "You didn't care for him, of course. . . ."

"Not in that way. But I was very very sorry for him, and I'd have done anything to make him feel happier. It was so dreadful to see him going out into the dark before he'd really started in life."

Wendover cleared his throat, evidently conscious that the talk was hardly on the businesslike lines which he had planned. He unfolded the thin sheet of note-paper and glanced over the writing.

"This seems explicit enough. ' I leave all that I have to Nurse Sydney Eastcote, residing at Dr. Prevost's medical Institute.' I recognise the handwriting as Robin's, and the date is in the same writing. Who are the witnesses, by the way ? "

" Two of the waiters at the hotel, I believe," Nurse Eastcote explained.

Wendover turned to the flimsy foreign envelope and examined the address.

" Addressed by himself to you at the institute, I see. And the postmark is 21st September. That's quite good confirmatory evidence, if anything of the sort were needed."

He passed the two papers to Sir Clinton. The Chief Constable seemed to find the light insufficient where he was sitting, for he rose and walked over to a window to examine the documents. This brought him slightly behind Nurse Eastcote. Wendover noted idly that Sir Clinton stood sideways to the light while he inspected the papers in his hand.

" Now just one point," Wendover continued. " I'd like to know something about Robin's mental condition towards the end. Did he read to pass the time, newspapers and things like that ? "

Nurse Eastcote shook her head.

" No, he read nothing. He was too exhausted, poor boy. I used to sit by him and try to interest him in talk. But if you have any doubt about his mind at that time—I mean whether he was fit to make a will—I'm sure Dr. Prevost will give a certificate that he was in full possession of his faculties and knew what he was doing."

Sir Clinton came forward with the papers in his hand.

" These are very important documents," he pointed out, addressing the nurse. " It's not safe for you to be carrying them about in your bag as you've been doing. Leave them with us. Mr. Wendover will give you a receipt and take good care of them. And to make sure there's no mistake, I think you'd better write your name in the corner of each of them so as to identify them. Mr. Harringay will agree with me that we mustn't leave any loophole for doubt in a case like this."

The lawyer nodded. He was a taciturn man by nature, and his pride had been slightly ruffled by the way in which he had been ignored in the conference. Nurse Eastcote, with Wendover's fountain pen, wrote her signature on a free space of each paper. Wendover offered his guests tea before they departed, but he turned the talk into general channels and avoided any further reference to business topics.

When the lawyer and the girl had left the house, Wendover turned to Sir Clinton.

" It seems straight enough to me," he said, " but I could

see from the look you gave me behind her back when you were
at the window that you aren't satisfied. What's wrong ? "

    " If you want my opinion," the Chief Constable answered,
" it's a fake from start to finish. Certainly you can't risk handing over a penny on that evidence. If you want it proved up
to the hilt, I can do it for you, but it'll cost something for
inquiries and expert assistance. That ought to come out of
the estate, and it'll be cheaper than an action at law. Besides,"
he added with a smile, " I don't suppose you want to put that
girl in gaol. She's probably only a tool in the hands of a
cleverer person."

    Wendover was staggered by the Chief Constable's tone of
certainty. The girl, of course, had made no pretence that she
was in love with Robin Ashby ; but her story had been told as
though she herself believed it.

    " Make your inquiries, certainly, " he consented. " Still,
on the face of it the thing sounds likely enough."

    " I'll give you definite proof in a fortnight or so. Better
make a further appointment with that girl in, say, three weeks.
But don't drag the lawyer into it this time. It may savour too
much of compounding a felony for his taste. I'll need these
papers."

                *   *   *   *   *   *

    " Here's the concrete evidence," said the Chief Constable,
three weeks later. " I may as well show it to you before she
arrives, and you can amuse yourself with turning it over in
the meanwhile."

    He produced the will, the envelope, and two photographs
from his pocket-book as he spoke and laid them on the table,
opening out the will as he put it down.

    " Now first of all, notice that the will and envelope are of
very thin paper, the foreign correspondence stuff. Second,
observe that the envelope is of the exact size to hold that sheet
of paper if it's folded in four—I mean folded in half and then
doubled over. The sheet's about quarto size, ten inches by
eight. Now look here. There's an extra fold in the paper.
It's been folded in four and then it's been folded across once
more. That struck me as soon as I had it in my hand. Why
the extra fold, since it would fit into the envelope without that?"

    Wendover inspected the sheet carefully and looked rather
perplexed.

    " You're quite right," he said, " but you can't upset a
will on the strength of a fold in it. She may have doubled it
up herself, after she got it."

"Not when it was in the envelope that fitted it," Sir Clinton pointed out. "There's no corresponding doubling of the envelope. However, let's go on. Here's a photograph of the envelope, taken with the light falling sideways. You see the postal erasing stamp has made an impression?"

"Yes, I can read it, and the date's 21st September right enough." He paused for a moment and then added in surprise, "But where's the postage stamp? It hasn't come out in the photo."

"No, because that's a photo of the impression on the back half of the envelope. The stamp came down hard and not only cancelled the stamp but impressed the second side of the envelope as well. The impression comes out quite clearly when it's illuminated from the side. That's worth thinking over. And, finally, here's another print. It was made, before the envelope was slit to get at the stamp impression. All we did was to put the envelope into a printing-frame with a bit of photographic printing paper behind it and expose it to light for a while. Now you'll notice that the gummed portions of the envelope show up in white, like a sort of St. Andrew's Cross. But if you look carefully, you'll see a couple of darker patches on the part of the white strip which corresponds to the flap of the envelope that one sticks down. Just think out what they imply, Squire. There are the facts for you, and it's not too difficult to put an interpretation on them if you think for a minute or two. And I'll add just one further bit of information. The two waiters who acted as witnesses to that will were given tickets for South America, and a certain sum of money each to keep them from feeling homesick. . . . But here's your visitor."

Rather to Wendover's surprise, Sir Clinton took the lead in the conversation as soon as the girl arrived.

"Before we turn to business, Miss Eastcote," he said, "I'd like to tell you a little anecdote. It may be of use to you. May I?"

Nurse Eastcote nodded politely and Wendover, looking her over, noticed a ring on her engagement finger which he had not seen on her last visit.

"This is a case which came to my knowledge lately," Sir Clinton went on, "and it resembles your own so closely that I'm sure it will suggest something. A young man of twenty, in an almost dying state, was induced to enter a nursing home by the doctor in charge. If he lived to come of age, he could make a will and leave a very large fortune to anyone he choose ·

but it was the merest gamble whether he would live to come of age."

Nurse Eastcote's figure stiffened and her eyes widened at this beginning, but she merely nodded as though asking Sir Clinton to continue.

" The boy fell in love with one of the nurses, who happened to be under the influence of the doctor," Sir Clinton went on. " If he lived to make a will, there was little doubt that he would leave the fortune to the nurse. A considerable temptation for any girl, I think you'll agree.

" The boy's birthday was very near, only a few days off ; but it looked as though he would not live to see it. He was very far gone. He had no interest in the newspapers and he had long lapses of unconsciousness, so that he had no idea of what the actual date was. It was easy enough to tell him, on a given day, that he had come of age, though actually two days were still to run. Misled by the doctor, he imagined that he could make a valid will, being now twenty-one ; and he wrote with his own hand a short document leaving everything to the nurse."

Miss Eastcote cleared her throat with an effort.

" Yes ? " she said.

" This fraudulent will," Sir Clinton continued, " was witnessed by two waiters of the hotel to which the boy had been removed ; and soon after, these waiters were packed off abroad and provided with some cash in addition to their fares. Then it occurred to the doctor that an extra bit of confirmatory evidence might be supplied. The boy had put the will into an envelope which he had addressed to the nurse. While the gum was still wet, the doctor opened the flap and took out the ' will,' which he then folded smaller in order to get the paper into an ordinary business-size envelope. He then addressed this to the nurse and posted the will to her in it. The original large envelope, addressed by the boy, he retained. But in pulling it open, the doctor had slightly torn the inner side of the flap where the gum lies ; and that little defect shows up when one exposes the envelope over a sheet of photographic paper. Here's an example of what I mean."

He passed over to Nurse Eastcote the print which he had shown Wendover and drew her attention to the spots on the St. Andrew's Cross.

" As it chanced, the boy died next morning, a day before he came of age. The doctor concealed the death for a day, which was easy enough in the circumstances. Then, on the afternoon of the crucial date—did I mention that it was September 21st ?—he closed the empty envelope, stamped it, and put it into the post, thus securing a post-mark of the proper date. Unfortunately for this plan, the defacement stamp of the post office came down hard enough to impress its image on *both* the sheets of the thin paper envelope, so that by opening up the envelope and photographing it by a sideways illumination the embossing of the stamp showed up—like this."

He handed the girl the second photograph.

" Now if the ' will ' had been in that envelope, the ' will ' itself would have borne that stamp. But it did not ; and that proves that the ' will ' was not in the envelope when it passed through the post. A clever woman like yourself, Miss Eastcote, will see the point at once."

" And what happened after that ? " asked the girl huskily.

" It's difficult to tell you," Sir Clinton pursued. " If it had come before me officially—I'm Chief Constable of the county, you know—I should probably have had to prosecute that unfortunate nurse for attempted fraud ; and I've not the slightest doubt that we'd have proved the case up to the hilt. It would have meant a year or two in gaol, I expect.

" I forgot to mention that the nurse was secretly engaged to the doctor all this while. And, by the way, that's a very pretty ring you're wearing, Miss Eastcote. That, of course, accounted for the way in which the doctor managed to get her to play her part in the little scheme. I think, if I were you, Miss Eastcote, I'd go back to France as soon as possible and tell Dr. Prevost that. . . . Well, it hasn't come off."

THE PERFECT MURDER

By

STACY AUMONIER

ONE evening in November two brothers were seated in a little *café* in the Rue de la Roquette discussing murders. The evening papers lay in front of them, and they all contained a lurid account of a shocking affair in the Landes district, where a charcoal-burner had killed his wife and two children with a hatchet. From discussing this murder in particular they went on to discussing murder in general.

" I've never yet read a murder case without being impressed by the extraordinary clumsiness of it," remarked Paul, the younger brother. " Here's this fellow murders his victims with his own hatchet, leaves his hat behind in the shed, and arrives at a village hard by with blood on his boots."

" They lose their heads," said Henri, the elder. " In cases like that they are mentally unbalanced, hardly responsible for their actions."

" Yes," replied Paul, " but what impresses me is—what a lot of murders must be done by people who take trouble, who leave not a trace behind."

Henri shrugged his shoulders. " I shouldn't think it was so easy, old boy ; there's always something that crops up."

" Nonsense ! I'll guarantee there are thousands done every year. If you are living with anyone, for instance, it must be the easiest thing in the world to murder them."

" How ? "

" Oh, some kind of accident—and then you go screaming into the street, ' Oh, my poor wife ! Help ! ' You burst into tears, and everyone consoles you. I read of a woman somewhere who murdered her husband by leaving the window near the bed open at night when he was suffering from pneumonia. Who's going to suspect a case like that ? Instead of that, people must always select revolvers, or knives, or go and buy poison at the chemist's across the way."

" It sounds as though you were contemplating a murder yourself," laughed Henri.

" Well, you never know," answered Paul ; " circumstances might arise when a murder would be the only way out of a difficulty. If ever my time comes I shall take a lot of trouble about it. I promise you I shall leave no trace behind."

As Henri glanced at his brother making this remark he was struck by the fact that there was indeed nothing irreconcilable between the idea of a murder and the idea of Paul doing it. He was a big, saturnine-looking gentleman with a sallow, dissolute face, framed in a black square beard and swathes of untidy grey hair. His profession was that of a traveller in cheap jewellery, and his business dealings were not always of the straightest. Henri shuddered. With his own puny physique, bad health, and vacillating will, he was always dominated by his younger brother. He himself was a clerk in a drapery store, and he had a wife and three children. Paul was unmarried.

The brothers saw a good deal of each other, and were very intimate. But the word friendship would be an extravagant term to apply to their relationship. They were both always hard up, and they borrowed money from each other when every other source failed.

They had no other relatives except a very old uncle and aunt who lived at Chantilly. This uncle and aunt, whose name was Taillandier, were fairly well off, but they would have little to do with the two nephews. They were occasionally invited there to dinner, but neither Paul nor Henri ever succeeded in extracting a franc out of Uncle Robert. He was a very religious man, hard-fisted, cantankerous, and intolerant. His wife was a little more pliable. She was in effect an eccentric. She had spasms of generosity, during which periods both the brothers had at times managed to get money out of her. But these were rare occasions. Moreover, the old man kept her so short of cash that she found it difficult to help her nephews even if she desired to.

As stated, the discussion between the two brothers occurred in November. It was presumably forgotten by both of them immediately afterwards. And indeed there is no reason to believe that it would ever have recurred, except for certain events which followed the sudden death of Uncle Robert in the February of the following year.

In the meantime the affairs of both Paul and Henri had

gone disastrously. Paul had been detected in a dishonest transaction over a paste trinket, and had just been released from a period of imprisonment. The knowledge of this had not reached his uncle before his death. Henri's wife had had another baby, and had been very ill. He was more in debt than ever.

The news of the uncle's death came as a gleam of hope in the darkness of despair. What kind of will had he left ? Knowing their uncle, each was convinced that, however it was framed, there was likely to be little or nothing for them. However, the old villain might have left them a thousand or two. And in any case, if the money was all left to the wife, here was a possible field of plunder. It need hardly be said that they repaired with all haste to the funeral, and even with greater alacrity to the lawyer's reading of the will.

The will contained surprises both encouraging and discouraging. In the first place the old man left a considerably larger fortune than anyone could have anticipated. In the second place all the money and securities were carefully tied up, and placed under the control of trustees. There were large bequests to religious charities, whilst the residue was held in trust for his wife. But so far as the brothers were concerned the surprise came at the end. On her death this residue was still to be held in trust, but a portion of the interest was to be divided between Henri and Paul, and on their death to go to the Church. The old man had recognised a certain call of the blood after all !

They both behaved with tact and discretion at the funeral, and were extremely sympathetic and solicitous towards Aunt Rosalie, who was too absorbed with her own trouble to take much notice of them. It was only when it came to the reading of the will that their avidity and interest outraged perhaps the strict canons of good taste. It was Paul who managed to get it clear from the notary what the exact amount would probably be. Making allowances for fluctuations, accidents, and acts of God, on the death of Mme. Taillandier the two brothers would inherit something between eight and ten thousand francs a year each. She was now eighty-two and very frail.

The brothers celebrated the good news with a carouse up in Montmartre. Naturally their chief topic of conversation was how long the old bird would keep on her perch. In any case, it could not be many years. With any luck it might be only a few weeks. The fortune seemed blinding. It would mean comfort and security to the end of their days. The rejoicings were mixed with recriminations against the old man for his stinginess. Why couldn't he have left them a lump sum down now ? Why did he want to waste all this good gold on the Church ? Why all this trustee business ?

There was little they could do but await developments. Except that in the meantime—after a decent interval—they might try and touch the old lady for a bit. They parted, and the next day set about their business in cheerier spirits.

For a time they were extremely tactful. They made formal calls on Aunt Rosalie, inquiring after her health, and offering their services in any capacity whatsoever. But at the end of a month Henri called hurriedly one morning, and after the usual professions of solicitude asked his aunt if she could possibly lend him one hundred and twenty francs to pay the doctor who had attended his wife and baby. She lent him forty, grumbling at his foolishness at having children he could not afford to keep. A week later came Paul with a story about being robbed by a client. He wanted a hundred. She lent him ten.

When these appeals had been repeated three or four times, and received similar treatment—and sometimes no treatment at all—the old lady began to get annoyed. She was becoming more and more eccentric. She now had a companion, an angular, middle-aged woman named Mme. Chavanne, who appeared like a protecting goddess. Sometimes when the brothers called Mme. Chavanne would say that Mme. Taillandier was too unwell to see anyone. If this news had been true it would have been good news indeed, but the brothers suspected that it was all prearranged. Two years went by, and they both began to despair.

" She may live to a hundred," said Paul.

" We shall die of old age, first," grumbled Henri.

It was difficult to borrow money on the strength of the will. In the first place their friends were more of the borrowing than the lending class. And anyone who had a little was suspicious of the story, and wanted all kinds of securities. It was Paul who first thought of going to an insurance company to try to raise money on the reversionary interest. They did succeed in the end in getting an insurance company to advance them two thousand francs each, but the negotiations took five months to complete, and by the time they had insured their lives, paid the lawyer's fees and paid for the various deeds and stamps, and signed some thirty or forty forms, each man only received a little over a thousand francs, which was quickly lost in paying accrued debts and squandering the remainder. Their hopes were raised by the dismissal of Mme. Chavanne, only to be lowered again by the arrival of an even more aggressive companion. The companions came and went with startling rapidity. None of them could stand for any time the old lady's eccentricity and ill-temper. The whole of the staff was always being changed. The only one who remained loyal all through was the portly cook, Ernestine. Even this may have been due to the fact that she never came in touch with her mistress. She was an excellent cook, and she never moved from the kitchen. Moreover, the cooking required by Mme. Taillandier was of the simplest nature, and she seldom entertained. And she hardly ever left her apartment. Any complaints that were made were made through the housekeeper, and the complaints and their retaliations became mellowed in the process ; for Ernestine also had a temper of her own.

Nearly another year passed before what appeared to Paul to be a mild stroke of good fortune came his way. Things had been going from bad to worse. Neither of the brothers was in a position to lend a sou to the other. Henri's family was becoming a greater drag, and people were not buying Paul's trinkets.

One day, during an interview with his aunt—he had been trying to borrow more money—he fainted in her presence. It is difficult to know what it was about this act which affected the old lady, but she ordered him to be put to bed in one of the rooms of the villa. Possibly she jumped to the conclusion that he had fainted from lack of food—which was not true—Paul never went without food and drink—and she suddenly realised that after all he was her husband's sister's son. He must certainly have looked pathetic, this white-faced man, well past middle age, and broken in life. Whatever it was, she showed a broad streak of compassion for him. She ordered her servants to look after him, and to allow him to remain until she countermanded the order.

Paul, who had certainly felt faint, but quickly seized the occasion to make it as dramatic as possible, saw in this an opportunity to wheedle his way into his aunt's favours. His behaviour was exemplary. The next morning, looking very white and shaky, he visited her, and asked her to allow him to go, as he had no idea of abusing her hospitality. If he had taken up the opposite attitude she would probably have turned him out, but because he suggested going she ordered him to stop. During the daytime he went about his dubious business, but he continued to return there at night to sleep, and to enjoy a good dinner cooked by the admirable Ernestine. He was in clover.

Henri was naturally envious when he heard of his brother's good fortune. And Paul was fearful that Henri would spoil the whole game by going and throwing a fit himself in the presence of the aunt. But this, of course, would have been too obvious and foolish for even Henri to consider seriously. And he racked his brains for some means of inveigling the old lady. Every plan he put forth, however, Paul sat upon. He was quite comfortable himself, and he didn't see the point of his brother butting in.

" Besides," he said, " she may turn me out any day. Then you can have your shot."

They quarrelled about this, and did not see each other for some time. One would have thought that Henri's appeal to Mme. Taillandier would have been stronger than Paul's. He was a struggling individual, with a wife and four children. Paul was a notorious ne'er-do-well, and he had no attachments. Nevertheless the old lady continued to support Paul. Perhaps it was because he was a big man, and she liked big men. Her husband had been a man of fine physique. Henri was puny, and she despised him. She had never had children of her own, and she disliked children. She was always upbraiding Henri and his wife for their fecundity. Any attempt to pander to her emotions through the sentiment of childhood failed. She would not have the children in her house. And any small acts of charity which she bestowed upon them seemed to be done more with the idea of giving her an opportunity to inflict her sarcasm and venom upon them than out of kindness of heart.

In Paul, on the other hand, she seemed to find something slightly attractive. She sometimes sent for him, and he, all agog—expecting to get his notice to quit—would be agreeably surprised to find that, on the contrary, she had some little commission she wished him to execute. And you may rest assured that he never failed to make a few francs out of all these occasions. The notice to quit did not come. It may be—poor deluded woman !—that she regarded him as some kind of protection. He was in any case the only " man " who slept under her roof.

At first she seldom spoke to him, but as time went on she would sometimes send for him to relieve her loneliness. Nothing could have been more ingratiating than Paul's manners in these circumstances. He talked expansively about politics, knowing beforehand his aunt's views, and just what she would like him to say. Her eyesight was very bad, and he would read her the news of the day, and tell her what was happening in Paris. He humoured her every whim. He was astute enough to see that it would be foolish and dangerous to attempt to borrow money for the moment. He was biding his time, and trying to think out the most profitable plan of campaign. There was no immediate hurry. His bed was comfortable, and Ernestine's cooking was excellent.

In another year's time he had established himself as quite one of the permanent household. He was consulted about the servants, and the doctors, and the management of the house, everything except the control of money, which was jealously guarded by a firm of lawyers. Many a time he would curse his uncle's foresight. The old man's spirit seemed to be hovering in the dim recesses of the over-crowded rooms, mocking him. For the old lady, eccentric and foolish in many ways, kept a strict check upon her dividends. It was her absorbing interest in life, that and an old grey perroquet, which she treated like a child. Its name was Anna, and it used to walk up and down her table at meal-times and feed off her own plate. Finding himself so firmly entrenched Paul's assurance gradually increased. He began to treat his aunt as an equal, and sometimes even to contradict her, and she did not seem to resent it.

In the meantime Henri was eating his heart out with jealousy and sullen rage. The whole thing was unfair. He occasionally saw Paul, who boasted openly of his strong position in the Taillandier household, and he would not believe that Paul was not getting money out of the old lady as well as board and lodging. With no additional expenses Paul was better dressed than he used to be, and he looked fatter and better in health. All—or nearly all—of Henri's appeals, although pitched in a most pathetic key, were rebuffed. He felt a bitter hatred against his aunt, his brother, and life in general. If only she would die ! What was the good of life to a woman at eighty-five or six ? And there was he—four young children, clamouring for food, and clothes, and the ordinary decent comforts. And there was Paul, idling his days away at *cafés* and his nights at cabarets—nothing to do, and no responsibilities.

Meeting Paul one day he said :

" I say, old boy, couldn't you spring me a hundred francs ? I haven't the money to pay my rent next week."

" She gives me nothing," replied Paul.

Henri did not believe this, but it would be undiplomatic to quarrel. He said :

" Aren't there—isn't there some little thing lying about the villa you could slip in your pocket ? We could sell it, see ? Go shares. I'm desperately pushed."

Paul looked down his nose. Name of a pig ! did Henri think he had never thought of that ? Many and many a time the temptation had come to him. But no ; every few months people came from the lawyer's office, and the inventory of the whole household was checked. The servants could not be suspected. They were not selected without irreproachable characters. If he were suspected—well, all kinds of unpleasant things might crop up. Oh, no, he was too well off where he was. The game was to lie in wait. The old lady simply must die soon. She had even been complaining of her chest that morning. She was always playing with the perroquet. Somehow this bird got on Paul's nerves. He wanted to wring its neck. He imitated the way she would say : "There's a pretty lady ! Oh, my sweet ! Another nice grape for my little one. There's a pretty lady ! " He told Henri all about this, and the elder brother went on his way with a grunt that only conveyed doubt and suspicion.

In view of this position it seemed strange that in the end it was Paul who was directly responsible for the *dénouement* in the Taillandier household. His success went to his rather weak head like wine. He began to swagger and bluster and abuse his aunt's hospitality. And, curiously enough, the more he advanced the further she withdrew. The eccentric old lady seemed to be losing her powers of resistance so far as he was concerned. And he began to borrow small sums of money from her, and, as she acquiesced so readily, to increase his demands. He let his travelling business go, and sometimes he would get lost for days at a time. He would spend his time at the races, and drinking with doubtful acquaintances in obscure *cafés*. Sometimes he won, but in the majority of cases he lost. He ran up bills and got into debt. By cajoling small sums out of his aunt he kept his debtors at bay for nearly nine months.

But one evening he came to see Henri in a great state of distress. His face, which had taken on a healthier glow when he first went to live with his aunt, had become puffy and livid. His eyes were bloodshot.

" Old boy," he said, " I'm at my wits' end. I've got to find seven thousand francs by the twenty-first of the month.

or they're going to foreclose. How do you stand ? I'll pay you back."

To try to borrow money from Henri was like appealing to the desert for a cooling draught. He also had to find money by the twenty-first, and he was overdrawn at the bank. They exchanged confidences, and in their mutual distress they felt sorry for each other and for themselves. It was a November evening, and the rain was driving along the boulevards in fitful gusts. After trudging a long way they turned into a little *café* in the Rue de la Roquette, and sat down and ordered two cognacs. The *café* was almost deserted. A few men in mackintoshes were scattered around reading the evening papers. They sat at a marble table in the corner and tried to think of ways and means. But after a time a silence fell between them. There seemed nothing more to suggest. They could hear the rain beating on the skylight. An old man four tables away was poring over *La Patrie*.

Suddenly Henri looked furtively around the room and clutched his brother's arm.

" Paul ! " he whispered.

" What is it ? "

" Do you remember—it has all come back to me—suddenly—one night, a night something like this—it must be five or six years ago—we were seated here in this same *café*—do you remember ? "

" No. I don't remember. What was it ? "

" It was the night of that murder in the Landes district. We got talking about—don't you remember ? "

Paul scratched his temple and sipped the cognac. Henri leant closer to him.

" You said—you said that if you lived with anyone, it was the easiest thing in the world to murder them. An accident, you know. And you go screaming into the street—— "

Paul started, and stared at his brother, who continued :

" You said that if ever you—you had to do it, you would guarantee that you would take every trouble. You wouldn't leave a trace behind."

Paul was acting. He pretended to half remember, to half understand. But his eyes narrowed. Imbecile ! Hadn't he been through it all in imagination a hundred times ? Hadn't he already been planning and scheming an act for which his brother would reap half the benefit ? Nevertheless he was staggered. He never imagined that the suggestion would come from Henri. He was secretly relieved. If Henri was to receive half the benefit, let him also share half the responsibilities. The risk in any case would be wholly his. He grinned enigmatically, and they put their heads together. And so in that dim corner of the *café* was planned the perfect murder.

Coming up against the actual proposition, Paul had long since realised that the affair was not so easy of accomplishment as he had so airily suggested. For the thing must be done without violence, without clues, without trace. Such ideas as leaving the window open at night were out of the question, as the companion slept in the same room. Moreover, the old lady was quite capable of getting out of bed and shutting it herself if she felt a draught. Some kind of accident ? Yes, but what ? Suppose she slipped and broke her neck when Paul was in the room. It would be altogether too suspicious. Besides, she would probably only partially break her neck. She would regain sufficient consciousness to tell. To drown her in her bath ? The door was always locked or the companion hovering around.

" You've always got to remember," whispered Paul, " if any suspicion falls on me, there's the motive. There's a strong motive why I should—it's got to be absolutely untraceable. I don't care if some people do suspect afterwards—when we've got the money."

" What about her food ? "

" The food is cooked by Ernestine, and the companion serves it. Besides, suppose I got a chance to tamper with the food, how am I going to get hold of—you know ? "

" Weed-killer ? "

" Yes, I should be in a pretty position if they traced the fact that I had bought weed-killer. *You* might buy some an let me have a little on the quiet.

Henri turned pale. " No, no ; the motive applies to me too. They'd get us both."

When the two pleasant gentlemen parted at midnight their plans were still very immature, but they arranged to meet the following evening. It was the thirteenth of the month. To save the situation the deed must be accomplished within eight days. Of course they wouldn't get the money at once, but, knowing the circumstances, creditors would be willing to wait. When they met the following evening in the Café des Sentiers, Paul appeared flushed and excited, and Henri was pale and on edge. He hadn't slept. He wanted to wash the whole thing out.

" And sell up your home, I suppose ? " sneered Paul.

" Listen, my little cabbage. I've got it. Don't distress yourself. You proposed this last night. I've been thinking about
it and watching for months. Ernestine is a good cook, and very
methodical. Oh, very methodical ! She does everything every
day in the same way exactly to schedule. My apartment is on
the same floor, so I am able to appreciate her punctuality and
exactness. The old woman eats sparingly and according to
routine. One night she has fish. The next night she has a
soufflé made with two eggs. Fish, soufflé, fish, soufflé, regular
as the beat of a clock. Now listen. After lunch every day
Ernestine washes up the plates and pans. After that she prepares roughly the evening meal. If it is a fish night, she
prepares the fish ready to pop into the pan. If it is a soufflé
night, she beats up two eggs and puts them ready in a basin.
Having done that, she changes her frock, powders her nose,
and goes over to the convent to see her sister who is working
there. She is away an hour and a half. She returns punctually
at four o'clock. You could set your watch by her movements."
    " Yes, but—— "
    " It is difficult to insert what I propose in fish, but I don't
see any difficulty in dropping it into two beaten-up eggs, and
giving an extra twist to the egg-whisk, or whatever they call it."
    Henri's face was quite grey.
    " But—but—Paul, how are you going to get hold of the
—poison ? "
    " Who said anything about poison ? "
    " Well, but what ? "
    " That's where *you* come in."
    " I ! "
    " Yes, you're in it too, aren't you ? You get half the spoils,
don't you ? Why shouldn't you—some time to-morrow when
your wife's out—— "
    " What ? "
    " Just grind up a piece of glass."
    " Glass ! "
    " Yes, you've heard of glass, haven't you ? An ordinary
piece of broken wineglass will do. Grind it up as fine as a
powder, the finer the better, the finer the more—effective."
    Henri gasped. No, no, he couldn't do this thing. Very
well, then ; if he was such a coward Paul would have to do it
himself. And perhaps when the time came Henri would also
be too frightened to draw his dividends. Perhaps he would
like to make them over to his dear brother Paul ? Come, it
was only a little thing to do. Eight days to the twenty-first.

To-morrow, fish day, but Wednesday would be soufflé. So easy, so untraceable, so safe.

" But you," whined Henri, " they will suspect you."

" Even if they do they can prove nothing. But in order to avoid this unpleasantness I propose to leave home soon after breakfast. I shall return at a quarter-past three, letting myself in through the stable yard. The stables, as you know, are not used. There is no one else on that floor. Ernestine is upstairs. She only comes down to answer the front-door bell. I shall be in and out of the house within five minutes, and I shan't return till late at night, when perhaps—I may be too late to render assistance."

Henri was terribly agitated. On one hand was—just murder, a thing he had never connected himself with in his life. On the other hand was comfort for himself and his family, an experience he had given up hoping for. It was in any case not exactly murder on his part. It was Paul's murder. At the same time, knowing all about it, being an accessory before the fact, it would seem contemptible to a degree to put the whole onus on Paul. Grinding up a piece of glass was such a little thing. It couldn't possibly incriminate him. Nobody could ever prove that he'd done it. But it was a terrible step to take.

" Have another cognac, my little cabbage."

It was Paul's voice that jerked him back to actuality. He said : " All right, yes, yes," but whether this referred to the cognac or to the act of grinding up a piece of glass he hardly knew himself.

From that moment to twenty-four hours later, when he handed over a white packet to his brother across the same table at the Café des Sentiers, Henri seemed to be in a nightmarish dream. He had no recollection of how he had passed the time. He seemed to pass from that last cognac to this one, and the interval was a blank.

" Fish to-day, soufflé to-morrow," he heard Paul chuckling. " Brother, you have done your work well."

When Paul went he wanted to call after him to come back, but he was frightened of the sound of his own voice. He was terribly frightened. He went to bed very late and could not sleep. The next morning he awoke with a headache, and he got his wife to telegraph to the office to say that he was too ill to come. He lay in bed all day, visualising over and over and over again the possible events of the evening.

Paul would be caught. Someone would catch him actually
putting the powder into the eggs. He would be arrested.
Paul would give *him* away. Why did Paul say it was so easy
to murder anyone if you lived with them ? It wasn't easy at
all. The whole thing was chock-a-block with dangers and
pitfalls. Pitfalls ! At half-past three he started up in bed. He
had a vision of himself and Paul being guillotined side by side !
He must stop it at any cost. He began to get up. Then he
realised that it was already too late. The deed had been done.
Paul had said that he would be in and out of the house within
five minutes at three-fifteen—a quarter of an hour ago ! Where
was Paul ? Would he be coming to see him ? He was going
to spend the evening out somewhere, " returning late at night."
He dressed feverishly. There was still time. He could call
at his aunt's. Rush down to the kitchen, seize the basin of
beaten-up eggs, and throw them away. But where ? how ?
By the time he got there Ernestine would have returned. She
would want to know all about it. The egg mixture would be
examined, analysed. God in Heaven ! it was too late ! The
thing would have to go on, and he suffer and wait.
    Having dressed, he went out after saying to his wife :
" It's all right. It's going to be all right," not exactly
knowing what he meant. He walked rapidly along the streets,
with no fixed destination in his mind. He found himself in
the *café* in the Rue de la Roquette, where the idea was first
conceived, where he had reminded his brother.
    He sat there drinking, waiting for the hours to pass.
    Soufflé day, and the old lady dined at seven ! It was now
not quite five. He hoped Paul would turn up. A stranger
tried to engage him in conversation. The stranger apparently
had some grievance against a railway company. He wanted to
tell him all the details about a contract for rivets, over which he
had been disappointed. Henri didn't understand a word he
was talking about. He didn't listen. He wanted the stranger
to drop down dead, or vanish into thin air. At last he called the
waiter and paid for his reckoning, indicated by a small pile of
saucers. From there he walked rapidly to the Café des Sentiers,
looking for Paul. He was not there. Six o'clock. One hour
more. He could not keep still. He paid and went on again,
calling at *café* after *café*. A quarter to seven. Pray God that
she threw it away. Had he ground it fine enough ?
    Five minutes to seven. Seven o'clock. Now. He picked
up his hat and went again. The brandy had gone to his head.
At half-past seven he laughed recklessly. After all, what was

the good of life to this old woman of eighty-six ? He tried to
convince himself that he had done it for the sake of his wife
and children. He tried to concentrate on the future, how he
could manage on eight or ten thousand francs a year. He
would give notice at the office, be rude to people who had been
bullying him for years—that old blackguard Mocquin !

At ten o'clock he was drunk, torpid, and indifferent. The
whole thing was over for good or ill. What did it matter ?
He terribly wanted to see Paul, but he was too tired to care
very much. The irrevocable step had been taken. He went
home to bed and fell into a heavy drunken sleep.

" Henri ! Henri ! Wake up ! What is the matter with
you ? "

His wife was shaking him. He blinked his way into a
partial condition of consciousness. November sunlight was
pouring into the room.

" It's late, isn't it ? " he said, involuntarily.

" It's past eight. You'll be late at the office. You didn't
go yesterday. If you go on like this you'll get the sack, and
then what shall we do ? "

Slowly the recollection of last night's events came back
to him.

" There's nothing to worry about," he said. " I'm too ill
to go to-day. Send them another telegram. It'll be all right."

His wife looked at him searchingly. " You've been
drinking," she said. " Oh, you men ! God knows what will
become of us."

She appeared to be weeping in her apron. It·struck him
forcibly at that instant how provoking and small women are.
Here was Jeannette crying over her petty troubles. Whereas
he——

The whole thing was becoming vivid again. Where was
Paul ? What had happened ? Was it at all likely that he could
go down to an office on a day like this, a day that was to decide
his fate ?

He groaned, and elaborated rather pathetically his imaginary
ailments, anything to keep this woman quiet. She left him at
last, and he lay there waiting for something to happen. The
hours passed. What would be the first intimation ? Paul or
the gendarmes ? Thoughts of the latter stirred him to a state
of fevered activity. About midday he arose, dressed, and went
out. He told his wife he was going to the office, but he had
no intention of doing so. He went and drank coffee at a place

up in the Marais. He was terrified of his old haunts. He wandered from place to place, uncertain how to act. Late in the afternoon he entered a *café* in the Rue Alibert. At a kiosk outside he bought a late edition of an afternoon newspaper. He sat down, ordered a drink and opened the newspaper. He glanced at the central news page, and as his eye absorbed one paragraph he unconsciously uttered a low scream. The paragraph was as follows :

MYSTERIOUS AFFAIR AT CHANTILLY

A mysterious affair occurred at Chantilly this morning. A middle-aged man, named Paul Denoyel, complained of pains in the stomach after eating an omelette. He died soon after in great agony. He was staying with his aunt, Mme. Taillandier. No other members of the household were affected. The matter is to be inquired into.

The rest was a dream. He was only vaguely conscious of the events which followed. He wandered through it all, the instinct of self-preservation bidding him hold his tongue in all circumstances. He knew nothing. He had seen nothing. He had a visionary recollection of a plump, weeping Ernestine, at the inquest, enlarging upon the eccentricities of her mistress. A queer woman, who would brook no contradiction. He heard a lot about the fish day and the soufflé day, and how the old lady insisted that this was a fish day, and that she had had a soufflé the day before. You could not argue with her when she was like that. And Ernestine had beaten up the eggs all ready for the soufflé—most provoking ! But Ernestine was a good cook, of method and economy. She wasted nothing. What should she do with the eggs ? Why, of course, Mr. Paul, who since he had come to live there was never content with a *café complet*. He must have a breakfast, like these English and other foreigners do. She made him an omelette, which he ate heartily.

Then the beaten-up eggs with their deadly mixture were intended for Mme. Taillandier ? But who was responsible for this ? Ernestine ? But there was no motive here. Ernestine gained nothing by her mistress's death. Indeed she only stood to lose her situation. Motive ? Was it possible that the deceased—— The inquiry went on a long while. Henri himself was conscious of being in the witness-box. He knew nothing He couldn't understand it. His brother would not be likely to do that. He himself was prostrate with grief. He loved his brother.

There was nothing to do but return an open verdict. shadowy figures passed before his mind's eye—shadowy figures and shadowy realisations. He had perfectly murdered his brother. The whole of the dividends of the estate would one day be his, and his wife's and children's. Eighteen thousand francs a year ! One day——

One vision more vivid than the rest—the old lady on the day following the inquest, seated bolt upright at her table, like a figure of perpetuity, playing with the old grey perroquet, stroking its mangy neck.

" There's a pretty lady ! Oh, my sweet ! Another nice grape for my little one. There's a pretty lady ! "

THE SHADOW OF THE SHARK

By

G. K. CHESTERTON

IT is notable that the late Mr. Sherlock Holmes, in the course
of those inspiring investigations for which we can never be
sufficiently grateful to their ingenious author, seems only
twice to have ruled out an explanation as intrinsically impossible.
And it is curious to notice that in both cases the distinguished
author himself has since come to regard that impossible thing
as possible, and even as positively true. In the first case the
great detective declared that he never knew a crime committed
by a flying creature. Since the development of aviation, and
especially the development of German aviation, Sir Arthur
Conan Doyle, patriot and war historian, has seen a good many
crimes committed by flying creatures. And in the other case
the detective implied that no deed need be attributed to spirits or
supernatural beings ; in short, to any of the agencies to which
Sir Arthur is now the most positive and even passionate witness.
Presumably, in his present mood and philosophy, the Hound
of the Baskervilles might well have been a really ghostly hound ;
at least, if the optimism which seems to go with spiritualism
would permit him to believe in such a thing as a hell-hound.
It may be worth while to note this coincidence, however, in
telling a tale in which both these explanations necessarily
played a part. The scientists were anxious to attribute it to
aviation, and the spiritualists to attribute it to spirits ; though
it might be questioned whether either the spirit or the flying-
man should be congratulated on his utility as an assassin.

A mystery which may yet linger as a memory, but which
was in its time a sensation, revolved round the death of a certain
Sir Owen Cram, a wealthy eccentric, chiefly known as a patron
of learning and the arts. And the peculiarity of the case was
that he was found stabbed in the middle of a great stretch of

yielding sand by the sea-shore, on which there was absolutely no trace of any foot-prints but his own. It was admitted that the wound could not have been self-inflicted ; and it grew more and more difficult even to suggest how it could have been inflicted at all. Many theories were suggested, ranging, as we have said, from that of the enthusiasts for aviation to that of the enthusiasts for psychical research ; it being evidently regarded as a feather in the cap either of science or spiritualism to have effected so neat an operation. The true story of this strange business has never been told ; it certainly contained elements which, if not supernatural, were at least supernormal. But to make it clear, we must go back to the scene with which it began ; the scene on the lawn of Sir Owen's seaside residence, where the old gentleman acted as a sort of affable umpire in the disputes of the young students who were his favourite company ; the scene which led up to the singular silence and isolation, and ultimately to the rather eccentric exit of Mr. Amos Boon.

Mr. Amos Boon had been a missionary, and still dressed like one ; at any rate, he dressed like nothing else. His sturdy, full-bearded figure carried a broad-brimmed hat combined with a frock-coat ; which gave him an air at once outlandish and dowdy. Though he was no longer a missionary, he was still a traveller. His face was brown and his long beard was black ; there was a furrow of thought in his brow and a rather strained look in his eyes, one of which sometimes looked a little larger than the other, giving a sinister touch to what was in some ways so commonplace. He had ceased to be a missionary through what he himself would have called the broadening of his mind. Some said there had been a broadening of his morals as well as of his mind ; and that the South Sea Islands, where he had lived, had seen not a little of such ethical emancipation. But this was possibly a malicious misrepresentation of his very human curiosity and sympathy in the matter of the customs of the savages ; which to the ordinary prejudice was indistinguishable from a white man going *fantee*. Anyhow, travelling about alone with nothing but a big Bible, he had learned to study it minutely, first for oracles and commandments, and afterwards for errors and contradictions ; for the Bible-smasher is only the Bible-worshipper turned upside down. He pursued the not very arduous task of proving that David and Saul did not on all occasions merit the Divine favour; and always concluded by roundly declaring that he preferred

the Philistines.   Boon and his Philistines were already a byword
of some levity among the young men who, at that moment,
were arguing and joking around him.

At that moment Sir Owen Cram was playfully presiding
over a dispute between two or three of his young friends about
science and poetry.   Sir Owen was a little restless man, with a
large head, a bristly grey moustache, and a grey fan of hair
like the crest of a cockatoo.   There was something sprawling
and splayfooted about his continuous movement which was
compared by thoughtless youth to that of a crab ; and it corresponded to a certain universal eagerness which was really ready
to turn in all directions.   He was a typical amateur, taking up
hobby after hobby with equal inconsistency and intensity.   He
had impetuously left all his money to a museum of natural
history, only to become immediately swallowed up in the single
pursuit of landscape painting ; and the groups around him
largely represented the stages of his varied career.   At the
moment a young painter, who was also by way of being a poet,
was defending some highly poetical notions against the
smiling resistance of a rising doctor, whose hobby was biology.
The data of agreement would have been difficult to find,
and few save Sir Owen could have claimed any common
basis of sympathy ; but the important matter just then was
the curious effect of the young men's controversy upon
Mr. Boon.

" The subject of flowers is hackneyed, but the flowers are
not," the poet was insisting.   " Tennyson was right about the
flower in the crannied wall ; but most people don't look at
flowers in a wall, but only in a wall-paper.   If you generalize
them, they are dull, but if you simply see them they are always
startling.   If there's a special providence in a falling star, there's
more in a rising star ; and a live star at that."

" Well, I can't see it," said the man of science, good-
humouredly ; he was a red-haired, keen-faced youth in pince-
nez, by the name of Wilkes.   " I'm afraid we fellows grow out
of the way of seeing it like that.   You see, a flower is only a
growth like any other, with organs and all that ; and its inside
isn't any prettier or uglier than an animal's.   An insect is much
the same pattern of rings and radiations.   I'm interested in it
as I am in an octopus or any sea-beast you would think a
monster."

" But why should you put it that way round ? " retorted
the poet.   " Why isn't it quite as logical the other way round ?
Why not say the octopus is as wonderful as the flower, instead

of the flower as ordinary as the octopus ? Why not say that crackens and cuttles and all the sea-monsters are themselves flowers ; fearful and wonderful flowers in that terrible twilight garden of God. I do not doubt that God can be as fond of a shark as I am of a buttercup."

" As to God, my dear Gale," began the other quietly, and then he seemed to change his form of words. " Well, I am only a man—nay, only a scientific man, which you may think lower than a sea-beast. And the only interest I have in a shark is to cut him up ; always on the preliminary supposition that I have prevented him from cutting me up."

" Have you ever met a shark ? " asked Amos Boon, intervening suddenly.

" Not in society," replied the poet with a certain polite discomposure, looking round with something like a flush under his fair hair ; he was a long, loose-limbed man named Gabriel Gale, whose pictures were more widely known than his poems.

" You've seen them in the tanks, I suppose," said Boon ; " but I've seen them in the sea. I've seen them where they are lords of the sea, and worshipped by the people as great gods. I'd as soon worship those gods as any other."

Gale the poet was silent, for his mind always moved in a sort of sympathy with merely imaginative pictures ; and he instantly saw, as in a vision, boiling purple seas and plunging monsters. But another young man standing near him, who had hitherto been rather primly silent, cut in quietly ; a theological student, named Simon, the deposit of some epoch of faith in Sir Owen's stratified past. He was a slim man with sleek, dark hair and darting, mobile eyes, in spite of his compressed lips. Whether in caution or contempt, he had left the attack on medical materialism to the poet, who was always ready to plunge into an endless argument with anybody. Now he intervened merely to say :

" Do they only worship a shark ? It seems rather a limited sort of religion."

" Religion ! " repeated Amos Boon, rudely ; " what do you people know about religion ? You pass the plate round, and when Sir Owen puts a penny in it, you put up a shed where a curate can talk to a congregation of maiden aunts. These people have got something like a religion. They sacrifice things to it—their beasts, their babies, their lives. I reckon you'd turn green with fear if you'd ever so much as caught a glimpse of Religion. Oh, it's not just a fish in the sea ; rather it's the sea round a fish. The sea is the blue cloud he moves in,

or the green veil or curtain hung about him, the skirts of which
trail with thunder."

All faces were turned towards him, for there was something
about him beyond his speech. Twilight was spreading over
the garden, which lay near the edge of a chalk cliff above the
shore, but the last light of sunset still lay on a part of the lawn,
painting it yellow rather than green, and glowing almost like
gold against the last line of the sea, which was a sombre indigo
and violet, changing nearer land to a lurid, pale green. A long
cloud of a jagged shape happened to be trailing across the sun ;
and the broad-hatted, hairy man from the South Seas suddenly
pointed at it.

" I know where the shape of that cloud would be called the
shadow of the shark," he cried, " and a thousand men would
fall on their faces ready to fast or fight, or die. Don't you see
the great black dorsal fin, like the peak of a moving mountain ?
And then you lads discuss him as if he were a stroke at golf ;
and one of you says he would cut him up like birthday cake ;
and the other says your Jewish Jehovah would condescend
to pat him like a pet rabbit."

" Come, come," said Sir Owen, with a rather nervous
waggishness, " we mustn't have any of your broad-minded
blasphemies."

Boon turned on him a baneful eye ; literally an eye, for
one of his eyes grew larger till it glowed like the eye of the
Cyclops. His figure was black against the fiery turf, and they
could almost hear his beard bristling.

" Blasphemy ! " he cried in a new voice, with a crack in it.
" Take care it is not you who blaspheme."

And then, before anyone could move, the black figure
against the patch of gold had swung round and was walking
away from the house, so impetuously that they had a momentary fear that he would walk over the cliff. However, he found
the little wooden gate that led to a flight of wooden steps ; and
they heard him stumbling down the path to the fishing village
below.

Sir Owen seemed suddenly to shake off a paralysis like a
fit of slumber. " My old friend is a little eccentric," he said.
" Don't go, gentlemen ; don't let him break up the party.
It is early yet."

But growing darkness and a certain social discomfort had
already begun to dissolve the group on the lawn ; and the host
was soon left with a few of the most intimate of his guests.
Simon and Gale, and his late antagonist, Dr. Wilkes, were

staying to dinner ; the darkness drove them indoors, and eventually found them sitting round a flask of green Chartreuse on the table ; for Sir Owen had his expensive conventions as well as his expensive eccentricities. The talkative poet, however, had fallen silent, and was staring at the green liquid in his glass as if it were the green depth of the sea. His host attacked with animation the other ordinary topics of the day.

" I bet I'm the most industrious of the lot of you," he said. " I've been at my easel on the beach all day, trying to paint this blessed cliff, and make it look like chalk and not cheese."

" I saw you, but I didn't like to disturb you," said Wilkes. " I generally try to put in an hour or so looking for specimens at high tide : I suppose most people think I'm shrimping or only paddling and doing it for my health. But I've got a pretty good nucleus of that museum we were talking about, or at least the aquarium part of it. I put in most of the rest of the time arranging the exhibits ; so I deny the implication of idleness. Gale was on the sea-shore, too. He was doing nothing as usual ; and now he's saying nothing, which is much more uncommon."

" I have been writing letters," said Simon, in his precise way, " but letters are not always trivial. Sometimes they are rather tremendous."

Sir Owen glanced at him for a moment, and a silence followed, which was broken by a thud and a rattle of glasses as Gale brought his fist down on the table like a man who had thought of something suddenly.

" Dagon ! " he cried, in a sort of ecstasy.

Most of the company seemed but little enlightened ; perhaps they thought that saying " Dagon " was his poetical and professional fashion of saying " Damn." But the dark eyes of Simon brightened, and he nodded quickly.

" Why, of course you're right," he said. " That must be why Mr. Boon is so fond of the Philistines."

In answer to a general stare of inquiry, he said smoothly : " The Philistines were a people from Crete, probably of Hellenic origin, who settled on the coast of Palestine, carrying with them a worship which may very well have been that of Poseidon, but which their enemies, the Israelites, described as that of Dagon. The relevant matter here is that the carved or painted symbol of the god seems always to have been a fish."

The mention of the new matter seemed to reawaken the tendency of the talk to turn into a wrangle between the poet and the professional scientist.

" From my point of view," said the latter. " I must confess myself somewhat disappointed with your friend Mr. Boon. He represented himself as a rationalist like myself, and seemed to have made some scientific studies of folk-lore in the South Seas. But he seemed a little unbalanced ; and surely he made a curious fuss about some sort of a fetish, considering it was only a fish."

" No, no, no ! " cried Gale, almost with passion. " Better make a fetish of the fish. Better sacrifice yourself and everybody else on the horrible huge altar of the fish. Better do anything than utter the star-blasting blasphemy of saying it is *only* a fish. It's as bad as saying the other thing is only a flower."

" All the same, it *is* only a flower," answered Wilkes, " and the advantage of looking at these things in a cool and rational way from the outside is that you can—— "

He stopped a moment and remained quite still, as if he were watching something. Some even fancied that his pale, aquiline face looked paler as well as sharper.

" What was that at the window ? " he asked. " Is anybody outside this house ? "

" What's the matter ? What did you see ? " asked his host, in abrupt agitation.

" Only a face," replied the doctor, " but it was not—it was not like a man's face. Let's get outside and look into this."

Gabriel Gale was only a moment behind the doctor, who had impetuously dashed out of the room. Despite his lounging demeanour, the poet had already leapt to his feet with his hand on the back of the chair, when he stiffened where he stood ; for he had seen it. The faces of the others showed that they had seen it too.

Pressed against the dark window-pane, but only wanly luminous as it protruded out of the darkness, was a large face looking at first rather like a green goblin mask in a pantomime. Yet it was in no sense human ; its eyes were set in large circles, rather in the fashion of an owl. But the glimmering covering that faintly showed on it was not of feathers, but of scales.

The next moment it had vanished. The mind of the poet, which made images as rapidly as a cinema, even in a crisis of action, had already imagined a string of fancies about the sort of creature he saw it to be. He had thought involuntarily of some great flying fish winging its way across the foam, and the flat sand and the spire and roofs of the fishing village. He had half-imagined the moist sea air thickening in some strange way to a greener and more liquid atmosphere in which the marine monsters could swim about in the streets. He had entertained the fancy that the house itself stood in the depths of the sea, and that the great goblin-headed fishes were nosing round it, as round the cabin windows of a wreck.

At that moment a loud voice was heard outside crying in distinct accents :

" The fish has legs."

For that instant, it seemed to give the last touch to the monstrosity. But the meaning of it came back to them, a returning reality, with the laughing face of Dr. Wilkes as he reappeared in the doorway, panting.

" Our fish had two legs, and used them," he said. " He ran like a hare when he saw me coming ; but I could see plainly enough it was a man, playing you a trick of some sort. So much for that psychic phenomenon."

He paused and looked at Sir Owen Cram with a smile that was keen and almost suspicious.

" One thing is very clear to me," he said. " You have an enemy."

The mystery of the human fish, however, did not long remain even a primary topic of conversation in a social group that had so many topics of conversation. They continued to pursue their hobbies and pelt each other with their opinions ; even the smooth and silent Simon being gradually drawn into the discussions, in which he showed a dry and somewhat cynical dexterity. Sir Owen continued to paint with all the passion of an amateur. Gale continued to neglect to paint, with all the nonchalance of a painter. Mr. Boon was presumably still as busy with his wicked Bible and his good Philistines as Dr. Wilkes with his museum and his microscopic marine animals, when the little seaside town was shaken as by an earthquake with the incomprehensible calamity which spread its name over all the newspapers of the country.

Gabriel Gale was scaling the splendid swell of turf that terminated in the great chalk cliff above the shore, in a mood consonant to the sunrise that was storming the skies above him. Clouds haloed with sunshine were already sailing over his head as if sent flying from a flaming wheel ; and when he came to the brow of the cliff he saw one of those rare revelations when the sun does not seem to be merely the most luminous object in a luminous landscape, but itself the solitary focus and streaming fountain of all light. The tide was at the ebb, and the sea was only a strip of delicate turquoise over which rose the tremendous irradiation. Next to the strip of turquoise was a strip of orange sand, still wet, and nearer the sand was a desert of a more dead yellow or brown, growing paler in the increasing light. And as he looked down from the precipice upon that plain of pale gold, he saw two black objects lying in the middle of it. One was a small easel, still standing, with a camp-stool fallen beside it ; the other was the flat and sprawling figure of a man.

The figure did not move, but as he stared he became conscious that another human figure was moving, was walking over the flat sands towards it from under the shadow of the cliff. Looking at it steadily, he saw that it was the man called Simon ; and in an instant he seemed to realize that the motionless figure was that of Sir Owen Cram. He hastened to the stairway down the cliff and so to the sands ; and soon stood face to face with Simon ; for they both looked at each other for a moment before they both looked down at the body. The conviction was already cold in his heart that it was a dead body. Nevertheless, he said sharply : " We must have a doctor ; where is Dr. Wilkes ? "

" It is no good, I fear," said Simon, looking away at the sea.

" Wilkes may only confirm our fears that he is dead," said Gale, " but he may have something to say about how he died."

" True," said the other, " I will go for him myself." And he walked back rapidly towards the cliff in the track of his own foot-prints.

Indeed, it was at the foot-prints that Gale was gazing in a bemused fashion at that moment. The tracks of his own coming were clear enough, and the tracks of Simon's coming and going ; and the third rather more rambling track of the unmistakable boots of the unfortunate Sir Owen, leading up to the spot where his easel was planted. And that was all. The sand was soft, so that the lightest foot would disturb it ; it was well above the tides ; and there was not the faintest trace of any other human being having been near the body. Yet the body had a deep wound under the angle of the jaw ; and there was no sign of any weapon of suicide.

Gabriel Gale was a believer in common-sense, in theory if not always in practice. He told himself repeatedly that these things were the practical clues in such a case ; the wound, the weapon or absence of weapon, the foot-prints or absence of foot-prints. But there was also a part of his mind which was always escaping from his control and playing tricks ; fixing

They looked at each other. . . and down at the body

on his memory meaningless things as if they were symbols, and then haunting him with them as mysteries. He made no point of it ; it was rather sub-conscious than self-conscious ; but the parts of any living picture that he saw were seldom those that others saw, or that it seemed sensible to see. And there were one or two details in the tragedy before him that haunted him then and long afterwards. Cram had fallen backwards in a rather twisted fashion, with his feet towards the shore ; and a few inches from the left foot lay a starfish. He could not say whether it was merely the bright orange colour of the creature that irrationally rivetted his eye, or merely some obscure fancy of repetition, in that the human figure was itself spread and sprawling flat like a starfish, with four limbs instead of five. Nor did he attempt to analyse this æsthetic antic of his psychology ; it was a suppressed part of his mind which still repeated that the mystery of the untrodden sands would turn out to be something quite simple ; but that the starfish possessed the secret.

He looked up to see Simon returning with the doctor, indeed with two doctors ; for there was more than one medical representative in the mob of Sir Owen's varied interests. The other was a Dr. Garth, a little man with an angular and humorous face ; he was an old friend of Gale's, but the poet's greeting was rather. *distrait.* Garth and his colleagues, however, got to work on a preliminary examination, which made further talk needless. It could not be a full examination till the arrival of the police, but it was sufficient to extinguish any hope of life, if any such had lingered. Garth, who was bent over the body in a crouching posture, spoke to his fellow physician without raising his head.

" There seems to be something rather odd about this wound. It goes almost straight upwards, as if it was struck from below. But Sir Owen was a very small man ; and it seems queer that he should be stabbed by somebody smaller still."

Gale's sub-consciousness exploded with a strange note of harsh mockery.

" What," he cried, " you don't think the starfish jumped up and killed him ? "

" No, of course not," said Garth, with his gruff good humour. " What on earth is the matter with you ? "

" Lunacy, I think," said the poet, and began to walk slowly towards the shore.

As time went on he almost felt disposed to fancy that he had correctly diagnosed his own complaint. The image began to figure even in his dreams, but not merely as a natural nightmare about the body on the sea-shore. The significant sea creature seemed more vivid even than the body. As he had originally seen the corpse from above, spread flat out beneath him, he saw it in his visions as something standing, as if propped against a wall or even merely drawn or graven on a wall. Sometimes the sandy ground had become a ground of old gold in some decoration of the Dark Ages, with the figure in the stiff agonies of a martyr, but the red star always showed like a lamp by his feet. Sometimes it was a hieroglyphic of a more Eastern sort, as of some stone god rigidly dancing ; but the five-pointed star was always in the same place below. Sometimes it seemed a rude, red-sandstone sort of drawing ; yet more archaic ; but the star was always the reddest spot in it. Now and again, while the human figure was as dry and dark as a mummy, the star would seem to be literally alive, waving its flaming fingers as if it were trying to tell him something. Now and then even the whole figure was upside down, as if to restore the star to its proper place in the skies.

" I told Wilkes that a flower was a living star," he said to himself. " A starfish is more literally a living star. But this is like going crazy. And if there is one thing I strongly object to, it is going crazy. What use should I be to all my brother lunatics, if I once really lost my balance on the tight-rope over the abyss ? "

He sat staring into vacancy for some time, trying to fit in this small and stubborn fancy with a much steadier stream of much deeper thoughts that were already driving in a certain direction. At last, the light of a possibility began to dawn in his eyes ; and it was evidently something very simple when it was realized ; something which he felt he ought to have thought of before ; for he laughed shortly and scornfully at himself as he rose to his feet.

" If Boon goes about everywhere introducing his shark and I go into society always attended by my starfish," he murmured to himself, " we shall turn the world into an aquarium bigger and better than Dr. Wilkes is fixing up. I'm going down to make some inquiries in the village."

Returning thence across the sands at evening, after several conversations with skippers and fishermen, he wore a more satisfied expression.

" I always did believe," he reflected, " that the foot-print business would be the simplest thing in the affair. But there are some things in it that are by no means simple."

Then he looked up, and saw far off on the sands, lonely and dark against the level evening light, the strange hat and stumpy figure of Amos Boon.

He seemed to consider for a moment the advisability of a meeting ; then he turned away and moved towards the stairway up the cliff. Mr. Boon was apparently occupied in idly drawing lines on the sand with his shabby umbrella ; like one drawing plans for a child's sand-castle, but apparently without any such intelligent object or excuse. Gale had often seen the man mooning about with equally meaningless and automatic gestures ; but as the poet mounted the rocky steps, climbing higher and higher, he had a return of the irrational feeling of a visionary vertigo. He told himself again, as if in warning, that it was his whole duty in life to walk on a tight-rope above a void in which many imaginative men were swallowed up. Then he looked down again at the drop of the dizzy cliffs to the flats that seemed to be swimming below him like a sea. And he saw the long, loose lines drawn in the sand unified into a shape, as flat as a picture on a wall. He had often seen a child, in the same fashion, draw on the sand a pig as large as a house. But in this case he could not shake off his former feeling of something archaic, like a palæolithic drawing, about the scratching of the brown sand. And Mr. Boon had not drawn a pig, but a shark ; conspicuous with its jagged teeth and fin like a horn exalted.

But he was not the only person overlooking this singular decorative scheme. When he came to the short railings along the brow of the cliff in which the stairway terminated, he found three figures leaning on it and looking down ; and instantly realized how the case was closing in. For even in their outlines against the sky he had recognized the two doctors and an inspector of police.

" Hullo, Gale," observed Wilkes, " may I present you to Inspector Davies ; a very active and successful officer."

Garth nodded. " I understand the inspector will soon make an arrest," he said.

" The inspector must be getting back to his work and not talking about it," said that official good-humouredly. " I'm going down to the village. Anybody coming my way ? "

Dr. Wilkes assented and followed him, but Dr. Garth stopped a moment, being detained by the poet, who caught hold of his sleeve with unusual earnestness.

" Garth," he said, " I want to apologise. I'm afraid I was wool-gathering when we met the other day, and didn't hail you as I ought to hail an old friend. You and I have been in one or two queer affairs together, and I want to talk to you about this one. Shall we sit down on that seat over there ? ''

They seated themselves on an iron seat set up on the picturesque headland ; and Gale added, " I wish you could tell me roughly how you got as far as you seem to have got.''

Garth gazed silently out to sea, and said at last :

" Do you know that man Simon ? ''

" Yes,'' replied the poet, " that's the way it works is it ? ''

" Well, the investigation soon began to show that Simon knew rather more than he said. He was on the spot before you ; and for some time he wouldn't admit what it was he saw before you turned up. We guessed it was because he was afraid to tell the truth ; and in one sense he was.''

" Simon doesn't talk enough,'' said Gale thoughtfully. " He doesn't talk about himself enough ; so he thinks about himself too much. A man like that always gets secretive ; not necessarily in the sense of being criminal, or even of being malicious, but merely of being morbid. He is the sort that is ill-treated at school and never says so. As long as a thing terrified him, he couldn't talk about it.''

" I don't know how you guessed it,'' said Garth, " but that is something like the line of discoveries. At first they thought that Simon's silence was guilt, but it was only a fear of something more than guilt ; of some diabolic destiny and entanglement. The truth is, that when he went up before you to the cliff-head at daybreak, he saw something that hag-rode his morbid spirit ever since. He saw the figure of this man Boon poised on the brink of the precipice, black against the dawn, and waving his arms in some unearthly fashion as if he were going to fly. Simon thought the man was talking to himself, and perhaps even singing. Then the strange creature passed on towards the village and was lost in the twilight ; but when Simon came to the edge of the cliff he saw Sir Owen lying dead far out on the sands below, beside his easel.''

" And ever since, I suppose,'' observed Gale, " Simon has seen sharks everywhere.''

" You are right again,'' said the doctor. " He has admitted since that a shadow on the blind or a cloud on the moon would have the unmistakable shape of the fish with the fin erect. But, in fact, it is a very mistakable shape ; anything with a triangular top to it would suggest it to a man in his state of nerves. But the truth is that so long as he thought Boon had dealt death from a distance by some sort of curse or spell, we could get nothing out of him. Our only chance was to show him that Boon might have done it even by natural means. And we did show it, after all."

" What is your theory, then ? " asked the other.

" It is too general to be called a theory yet," replied the doctor ; " but, honestly, I do not think it at all impossible that Boon might have killed a man on the sands from the top of a cliff, without falling back on any supernatural stuff. You've got to consider it like this : Boon has been very deep in the secrets of savages, especially in that litter of islands that lie away towards Australia. Now, we know that such savages, for all they are called ignorant, have developed many dexterities and many unique tools. They have blow-pipes that kill at a considerable distance ; they harpoon and lasso things, and draw them in on a line. Above all, the Australian savages have discovered the boomerang that actually returns to the hand. Is it quite so inconceivable that Boon might know some way of sending a penetrating projectile from a distance, and even possibly of recovering it in some way ? Dr. Wilkes and I, on examining the wound, found it a very curious one : it was made by some tapering, pointed tool, with a slight curve ; and it not only curved upwards, but even slightly outwards, as if the curve were returning on itself. Does not that suggest to you some outlandish weapon of a strange shape, and possibly with strange properties ? And always remember that such an explanation would explain something else as well, which is generally regarded as the riddle. It would explain why the murderer left no foot-prints round the body."

Gale gazed out to sea in silence, as if considering ; then he said simply :

" An extremely shrewd argument. But I know why he left no foot-prints. It is a much simpler explanation than that."

Garth stared at him for a few moments ; and then observed gravely :

" May I then ask, in return, what is your theory ? "

" My theory will seem a maze of theories, and nothing else," said Gale. " It is, as many would say, of such stuff as dreams are made of. Most modern people have a curious contradiction ; they abound in theories, yet they never see the part that theories play in practical life. They are always talking about temperament and circumstances and accident ; but most men are what their theories make them ; most men go in for murder or marriage, or mere lounging because of some theory of life, asserted or assumed. So I can never manage to begin my

explanations in that brisk, pointed, practical way that you
doctors and detectives do. I see a man's mind first, sometimes
almost without any particular man attached to it. I could only
begin this business by describing a mental state—which can't
be described. Our murderer or maniac, or whatever you call
him, is certainly affected by some of the elements attributed to
him. His view has reached an insane degree of simplicity, and
in that sense of savagery. But I doubt whether he would
necessarily transfer the savagery from the end to the means.
In one sense, indeed, his view might be compared to the
barbaric. He saw every creature and even every object naked.
He did not understand that what clothes a thing is sometimes
the most real part of it. Have you ever noticed how true is
that old phrase, ' clothed and in his right mind ' ? Man is not
in his right mind when he is not clothed with the symbols of
his social dignity. Humanity is not even human when it is
naked. But in a lower sense it is so of lesser things, even of
lifeless things. A lot of nonsense is talked about auras ; but
this is the truth behind it. Everything has a halo. Everything
has a sort of atmosphere of what it signifies, which makes it
sacred. Even the little creatures he studied had each of them
its halo ; but he would not see it."

"But what little creatures did Boon study ? " asked Garth
in some wonder. "Do you mean the cannibals ? "

" I was not thinking about Boon," replied Gabriel Gale.

" What do you mean ?." cried the other, in sudden excitement. " Why, Boon is almost in the hands of the police."

" Boon is a good man," said Gale, calmly ; " he is very
stupid ; that is why he is an atheist. There are intelligent
atheists, as we shall see presently ; but that stunted, stupid sort
is much commoner, and much nicer. But he is a good man ;
his motive is good ; he originally talked all that tosh of the
superiority of the savage because he thought he was the under-
dog. He may be a trifle cracked, by now, about sharks and
other things ; but that's only because his travels have been too
much for his intellect. They say travel broadens the mind ;
but you must have the mind. He had a mind for a suburban
chapel, and there passed before it all the panorama of gilded
nature-worship and purple sacrifice. He doesn't know if he's
on his head or his heels, any more than a good many others.
But I shouldn't wonder if heaven is largely populated with
atheists of that sort, scratching their heads and wondering
where they are.

" But Boon is a parenthesis ; that is all he is. The man I

am talking about is very much the point, and a sharp one at that. He dealt in something very different from muddled mysticism about human sacrifice. Human sacrifice is quite a human weakness. He dealt in assassination ; direct, secret, straight from a head as inhuman as hell. And I knew it when I first talked to him over the tea-cups and he said he saw nothing pretty in a flower."

" My dear fellow ! " remonstrated Dr. Garth.

" I don't mean that a man merely dissecting a daisy must be on the road to the gallows," conceded the poet, magnanimously, " but I do say that to mean it as he meant it is to be on a straight road of logic that leads there if he chooses to follow it. God is inside everything. But this man wanted to be outside everything ; to see everything hung in a vacuum, simply its own dead self. It's not only not the same, it's almost the opposite of scepticism in the sense of Boon or the Book of Job. That's a man overwhelmed by the mysteries ; but this man denies that there are any mysteries. It's not, in the ordinary sense, a matter of theology, but psychology. Most good pagans and pantheists might talk of the miracles of nature ; but this man denies that there are any miracles, even in the sense of marvels. Don't you see that dreadful dry light shed on things must at last wither up the moral mysteries as illusions, respect for age, respect for property, and that the sanctity of life will be a superstition ? The men in the street are only organisms, with their organs more or less displayed. For such a one there is no longer any terror in the touch of human flesh, nor does he see God watching him out of the eyes of a man."

" He may not believe in miracles, but he seems to work them," remarked the doctor. " What else was he doing, when he struck a man down on the sand without leaving a mark to show where he stood ? "

" He was paddling," answered Gale.

" As high up on the shore as that ? " inquired the other.

Gale nodded. " That was what puzzled me ; till something I saw on the sand started a train of thought that led to my asking the seafaring people about the tides. It's very simple ; the night before we found the body was a flood-tide, and the sea came up higher than usual ; not quite to where Cram was sitting, but pretty near. So that was the way that the real human fish came out of the sea. That was the way the divine shark really devoured the sacrifice. The man came paddling in the foam, like a child on a holiday."

"Who came ? " asked Garth ; but he shuddered.

"Who did go dredging for sea-beasts with a sort of shrimp-ing-net along the shore every evening ? Who did inherit the money of the old man for his ambitious museum and his scientific career ? Who did tell me in the garden that a cowslip was only a growth like a cancer ? "

"I am compelled to understand you," said the doctor gloomily. "You mean that very able young man named Wilkes ? "

"To understand Wilkes you must understand a good deal," continued his friend. "You must reconstruct the crime, as they say. Look out over that long line of darkening sea and sand, where the last light runs red as blood ; that is where he came dredging every day, in the same bloodshot dusk, looking for big beasts and small ; and in a true sense everything was fish that came to his net. He was constructing his museum as a sort of cosmos ; with everything traced from the fossil to the flying fish. He had spent enormous sums on it, and had got quite disinterestedly into debt ; for instance he had had magnificent models made, in wax or papier maché, of small fish magnified, or extinct fish restored ; things that South Kensington cannot afford, and certainly Wilkes could not afford. But he had persuaded Cram to leave his money to the museum, as you know ; and for him Cram was simply a silly old fool, who painted pictures he couldn't paint, and talked of sciences he didn't understand ; and whose only natural func-tion was to die and save the museum. Well, when every morning Wilkes had done polishing the glass cases of his masks and models, he came round by the cliff and took a turn at the fossils in the chalk with his geological hammer ; then he put it back in that great canvas bag of his, and unslung his long shrimping net and began to wade. This is where I want you to look at that dark red sand and see the picture ; one never understands anything till one sees the picture. He went for miles along the shallows of that desolate shore, long inured to seeing one queer creature or another stranded on the sand ; here a sea-hedgehog, and there a starfish, and then a crab, and then another creature. I have told you he had reached a stage when he would have looked at an angel with the eye of an ornithologist. What would he think of a man, and a man looking like that ? Don't you see that poor Cram must have looked like a crab or a sea-urchin ; his dwarfed, hunched figure seen from behind, with his fan of bristling whiskers, his straggling bow legs and restless twisting feet all tangled up with the three legs of his stool ; making him look as if he had five limbs like a starfish ? Don't you see he looked like a Common Object of the Seashore ? And Wilkes had only to collect this specimen, and all his other specimens were safe. Everything was fish that came to his net, and . . .

"He stretched out the long pole in his hand to its full extent, and drew the net over the old man's head as if he were catching a great grey moth. He plucked him backwards off his stool so that he lay kicking on his back on the sand ; and doubtless looking more like a large insect than ever. Then the murderer bent forward, propped by one hand upon his pole, and the other armed with his geological hammer. With the pick at the back of that instrument he struck in what he well knew to be a vital spot. The curve you noticed in the wound is due to that sharp side of the hammer being shaped like a pickaxe. But the unusual position of it, and the puzzle of how such a blow could be struck upwards, was due to the queer posture of the two figures. The murderer struck at a head that was upside down. It could only occur as a rule if the victim were standing on his head, a posture in which few persons await the assassin. But with the flourish and sweep of the great net, I fancy a starfish caught in it fell out of it, just beyond the dead man's foot. At any rate, it was that starfish and the accident of its flying so high on the shore, that set my mind drifting in the general direction of tides ; and the possibility of the murderer having been moving about in the water. If he made any prints the breakers washed them out ; and I should never have begun to think of it but for that red five-fingered little monster."

" Then do you mean to tell me," demanded Garth, " that all this business about the shadow of the shark had nothing to do with it ? "

" The shadow of the shark had everything to do with it," replied Gale. " The murderer hid in the shadow of the shark, and struck from under the shadow of the shark. I doubt if he would have struck at all, if he had not had the shadow of that fantastic fin in which to hide. And the proof is that he himself took the trouble to emphasize and exaggerate the legend of poor Boon dancing before Dagon. Do you remember that queer incident of the fish's face at the window ? How did anybody merely playing a practical joke get hold of a fish's face ? It was very life-like ; for it was one of the masks modelled for the Wilkes museum ; and Wilkes had left it in the hall in his great canvas bag. It seems simple, doesn't it, for a man to raise an alarm inside a house, walk out to see, and instantly put on a mask and look in at a window ? That's all he did ; and you can see his idea, from the fact that he proceeded to warn Sir Owen of an enemy. He wanted all this idolatrous and mystical murder business worked for all it was worth, that his own highly reasonable murder might not be noticed. And you see he has succeeded. You tell me that Boon is in the hands of the police."

Garth sprang to his feet. " What is to be done ? " he said.

" You will know what to do," said the poet. " You are a good and just man, and a practical man, too. I am not a practical man." He rose with a certain air of apology. " You see, you want an unpractical man for finding out this sort of thing."

And once more he gazed down from the precipice into the abysses below.

THE MARIONETTES

By

O. HENRY

THE policeman was standing at the corner of Twenty-fourth Street and a prodigiously dark alley near where the elevated railroad crosses the street. The time was two o'clock in the morning ; the outlook a stretch of cold, drizzling, unsociable blackness until the dawn.

A man, wearing a long overcoat, with his hat tilted down in front, and carrying something in one hand, walked softly but rapidly out of the black alley. The policeman accosted him civilly, but with the assured air that is linked with conscious authority. The hour, the alley's musty reputation, the pedestrian's haste, the burden he carried—these easily combined into the " suspicious circumstances " that required illumination at the officer's hands.

The " suspect " halted readily and tilted back his hat, exposing, in the flicker of the electric lights, an emotionless, smooth countenance with a rather long nose and steady dark eyes. Thrusting his gloved hand into a side pocket of his overcoat, he drew out a card and handed it to the policeman. Holding it to catch the uncertain light, the officer read the name " Charles Spencer James, M.D." The street and number of the address were of a neighbourhood so solid and respectable as to subdue even curiosity. The policeman's downward glance at the article carried in the doctor's hand—a handsome medicine case of black leather, with small silver mountings—further endorsed the guarantee of the card.

" All right, doctor," said the officer, stepping aside, with an air of bulky affability. " Orders are to be extra careful. Good many burglars and hold-ups lately. Bad night to be out. Not so cold, but—clammy."

With a formal inclination of his head, and a word or two

corroborative of the officer's estimate of the weather, Doctor James continued his somewhat rapid progress. Three times that night had a patrolman accepted his professional card and the sight of his paragon of a medicine case as vouchers for his honesty of person and purpose. Had any one of those officers seen fit, on the morrow, to test the evidence of that card he would have found it borne out by the doctor's name on a handsome door-plate, his presence, calm and well dressed, in his well-equipped office—provided it were not too early, Doctor James being a late riser—and the testimony of the neighbourhood to his good citizenship, his devotion to his family, and his success as a practitioner the two years he had lived among them.

Therefore, it would have much surprised any one of those zealous guardians of the peace could they have taken a peep into that immaculate medicine case. Upon opening it, the first article to be seen would have been an elegant set of the latest conceived tools used by the " box man," as the ingenious safe burglar now denominates himself. Specially designed and constructed were the implements—the short but powerful " jimmy," the collection of curiously fashioned keys, the blued drills and punches of the finest temper—capable of eating their way into chilled steel as a mouse eats into a cheese, and the clamps that fasten like a leech to the polished door of a safe and pull out the combination knob as a dentist extracts a tooth. In a little pouch in the inner side of the " medicine " case was a four-ounce vial of nitroglycerine, now half empty. Underneath the tools was a mass of crumpled banknotes and a few handfuls of gold coin, the money, altogether, amounting to eight hundred and thirty dollars.

To a very limited circle of friends Doctor James was known as " The Swell ' Greek.' " Half of the mysterious term was a tribute to his cool and gentlemanlike manners ; the other half denoted, in the argot of the brotherhood, the leader, the planner, the one who, by the power and prestige of his address and position, secured the information upon which they based their plans and desperate enterprises.

Of this elect circle the other members were Skitsie Morgan and Gum Decker, expert " box men," and Leopold Pretzfelder, a jeweller downtown, who manipulated the " sparklers " and other ornaments collected by the working trio. All good and loyal men as loose-tongued as Memnon and as fickle as the North Star.

That night's work had not been considered by the firm to

have yielded more than a moderate repayal for their pains. An old-style two-story side-bolt safe in the dingy office of a very wealthy old-style dry-goods firm on a Saturday night should have excreted more than twenty-five hundred dollars. But that was all they found, and they had divided it, the three of them, into equal shares upon the spot, as was their custom. Ten or twelve thousand was what they expected. But one of the proprietors had proved to be just a trifle too old-style. Just after dark he had carried home in a shirt box most of the funds on hand.

Doctor James proceeded up Twenty-fourth Street, which was, to all appearance, depopulated. Even the theatrical folk —who affect this district as a place of residence, were long since abed. The drizzle had accumulated upon the street ; puddles of it among the stones received the fire of the arc lights, and returned it, shattered into a myriad liquid spangles. A captious wind, shower-soaked and chilling, coughed from the laryngeal flues between the houses.

As the practitioner's foot struck even with the corner of a tall brick residence of more pretension than its fellows the front door popped open, and a bawling negress clattered down the steps to the pavement. Some medley of words came from her mouth, addressed, like as not, to herself—the recourse of her race when alone and beset by evil. She looked to be one of that old vassal class of the South—voluble, familiar, loyal, irrepressible ; her person pictured it—fat, neat, aproned, kerchiefed.

This sudden apparition, spewed from the silent house, reached the bottom of the steps as Doctor James came opposite. Her brain transferring its energies from sound to sight, she ceased her clamor and fixed her pop-eyes upon the case the doctor carried.

" Bress de Lawd ! " was the benison the sight drew from her. " Is you a doctor, suh ? "

" Yes, I am a physician," said Doctor James, pausing.

" Den fo' God's sake come and see Mister Chandler, suh. He done had a fit or sump'n. He layin' jist like he wuz dead. Miss Amy sont me to git a doctor. Lawd knows whar old Cindy'd a skeared one up from, if you, suh, hadn't come along. Ef old Mars' knowed one ten-hundredth part of dese doin's dey'd be shootin' gwine on, suh—pistol shootin'—leb'm feet marked off on de ground, and ev'ybody a-duellin'. And dat po' lamb, Miss Amy—— "

" Lead the way," said Doctor James, setting his foot upon

the step, " if you want me as a doctor. As an auditor I'm not open to engagements."

The negress preceded him into the house and up a flight of thickly carpeted stairs. Twice they came to dimly lighted branching hallways. At the second one the now panting conductress turned down a hall, stopping at a door and opening it.

" I done brought de doctor, Miss Amy."

Doctor James entered the room, and bowed slightly to a young lady standing by the side of a bed. He set his medicine case upon a chair, removed his overcoat, throwing it over the case and the back of the chair, and advanced with quiet self-possession to the bedside.

There lay a man, sprawling as he had fallen—a man dressed richly in the prevailing mode, with only his shoes removed ; lying relaxed, and as still as the dead.

There emanated from Doctor James an aura of calm force and reserve strength that was as manna in the desert to the weak and desolate among his patrons. Always had women, especially, been attracted by something in his sick-room manner. It was not the indulgent suavity of the fashionable healer but a manner of poise, of sureness, of ability to overcome fate, of deference and protection and devotion. There was an exploring magnetism in his steadfast, luminous brown eyes ; a latent authority in the impassive, even priestly, tranquillity of his smooth countenance that outwardly fitted him for the part of confidant and consoler. Sometimes, at his first professional visit, women would tell him where they hid their diamonds at night from the burglars.

With the ease of much practice, Doctor James's unroving eyes estimated the order and quality of the room's furnishings. The appointments were rich and costly. The same glance had secured cognizance of the lady's appearance. She was small and scarcely past twenty. Her face possessed the title to a winsome prettiness, now obscured by (you would say) rather a fixed melancholy than the more violent imprint of a sudden sorrow. Upon her forehead, above one eyebrow, was a livid bruise, suffered, the physician's eye told him, within the past six hours.

Doctor James's fingers went to the man's wrist. His almost vocal eyes questioned the lady.

" I am Mrs. Chandler," she responded, speaking with the plaintive Southern slur and intonation. " My husband was taken suddenly ill about ten minutes before you came. He has had attacks of heart trouble before—some of them were very bad." His clothed state and the late hour seemed to prompt her to further explanation. "He had been out late ; to—a supper, I believe."

Doctor James now turned his attention to his patient. In whichever of his " professions " he happened to be engaged he was wont to honor the " case " or the " job " with his whole interest.

The sick man appeared to be about thirty. His countenance bore a look of boldness and dissipation, but was not without a symmetry of feature and the fine lines drawn by a taste and indulgence in humor that gave the redeeming touch. There was an odor of spilled wine about his clothes.

The physician laid back his outer garments, and then, with a penknife, slit the shirt-front from collar to waist. The obstacles cleared, he laid his ear to the heart and listened intently.

" Mitral regurgitation ? " he said, softly, when he rose. The words ended with the rising inflection of uncertainty. Again he listened long ; and this time he said, " Mitral insufficiency," with the accent of an assured diagnosis.

" Madam," he began, in the reassuring tones that had so often allayed anxiety, " there is a probability—— " As he slowly turned his head to face the lady, he saw her fall, white and swooning, into the arms of the old negress.

" Po' lamb ! po' lamb ! Has dey done killed Aunt Cindy's own blessed child ? May de Lawd 'stroy wid his wrath dem what stole her away ; what break dat angel heart ; what left—— "

" Lift her feet," said Doctor James, assisting to support the drooping form. " Where is her room ? She must be put to bed."

" In here, suh." The woman nodded her kerchiefed head towards a door. " Dat's Miss Amy's room."

They carried her in there, and laid her on the bed. Her pulse was faint, but regular. She passed from the swoon, without recovering consciousness, into a profound slumber.

" She is quite exhausted," said the physician. " Sleep is a good remedy. When she wakes, give her a toddy—with an egg in it, if she can take it. How did she get that bruise upon her forehead ? "

" She done got a lick there, suh. De po' lamb fell—No, suh "—the old woman's racial mutability swept her into a sudden flare of indignation—" old Cindy ain't gwineter lie for dat debble. He done it, suh. May de Lawd wither de hand what—dar now ! Cindy promise her sweet lamb she ain't gwine tell. Miss Amy got hurt, suh, on de head."

Doctor James stepped to a stand where a handsome lamp burned, and turned the flame low.

" Stay here with your mistress," he ordered, " and keep quiet so she will sleep. If she wakes, give her the toddy. If she grows any weaker let me know. There is something strange about it."

" Dar's mo' strange t'ings dan dat' round here," began the negress, but the physician hushed her in a seldom-employed peremptory, concentrated voice with which he had often allayed hysteria itself. He returned to the other room, closing the door softly behind him. The man on the bed had not moved, but his eyes were open. His lips seem to form words. Doctor James bent his head to listen. " The money ! the money ! " was what they were whispering.

" Can you understand what I say ? " asked the doctor, speaking low, but distinctly.

The head nodded slightly.

" I am a physician, sent for by your wife. You are Mr. Chandler, I am told. You are quite ill. You must not excite or distress yourself at all."

The patient's eye seemed to beckon to him. The doctor stooped to catch the same faint words.

" The money—the twenty thousand dollars."

" Where is this money ?—in the bank ? "

The eyes expressed a negative. " Tell her "—the whisper was growing fainter—" the twenty thousand dollars—her money "—his eyes wandered about the room.

" You have placed this money somewhere ? "—Doctor James's voice was toiling like a siren's to conjure the secret from the man's failing intelligence—" Is it in this room ? "

He thought he saw a fluttering assent in the dimming eyes. The pulse under his fingers was as fine and small as a silk thread.

There arose in Doctor James's brain and heart the instincts of his other profession. Promptly, as he acted in everything, he decided to learn the whereabouts of this money and at the calculated and certain cost of a human life.

Drawing from his pocket a little pad of prescription blanks, he scribbled upon one of them a formula suited, according to the best practice, to the needs of the sufferer. Going to the door of the inner room, he softly called the old woman, gave

her the prescription, and bade her take it to some drug store
and fetch the medicine.

When she had gone, muttering to herself, the doctor stepped
to the bedside of the lady. She still slept soundly ; her pulse
was a little stronger ; her forehead was cool, save where the
inflammation of the bruise extended, and a slight moisture
covered it. Unless disturbed, she would yet sleep for hours.
He found the key in the door, and locked it after him when he
returned.

Doctor James looked at his watch. He could call half an
hour his own, since before that time the old woman could
scarcely return from her mission. Then he sought and found
water in a pitcher and a glass tumbler. Opening his medicine
case he took out the vial containing the nitroglycerine—" the
oil," as his brethren of the brace-and-bit term it.

One drop of the faint yellow, thickish liquid he let fall in
the tumbler. He took out his silver hypodermic syringe case,
and screwed the needle into its place. Carefully measuring each
modicum of water in the graduated glass barrel of the syringe,
he diluted the one drop with nearly half a tumbler of water.

Two hours earlier that night Doctor James had, with that
syringe, injected the undiluted liquid into a hole drilled in the
lock of a safe, and had destroyed, with one dull explosion, the
machinery that controlled the movement of the bolts. He now
purposed, with the same means, to shiver the prime machinery
of a human being—to rend its heart—and each shock was for
the sake of the money to follow.

The same means, but in a different guise. Whereas, that
was the giant in its rude, primary dynamic strength, this was
the courtier, whose no less deadly arms were concealed by
velvet and lace. For the liquid in the tumbler and in the
syringe that the physician carefully filled was now a solution of
glonoin, the most powerful heart stimulant known to medical
science. Two ounces had riven the solid door of the iron safe ;
with one fiftieth part of a minim he was now about to still
forever the intricate mechanism of a human life.

But not immediately. It was not so intended. First there
would be a quick increase of vitality ; a powerful impetus given
to every organ and faculty. The heart would respond bravely
to the fatal spur ; the blood in the veins return more rapidly
to its source.

But, as Doctor James well knew, over-stimulation in this
form of heart disease means death, as sure as by a rifle shot.
When the clogged arteries should suffer congestion from the

increased flow of blood pumped into them by the power of the burglar's " oil," they would rapidly become " no thoroughfare," and the fountain of life would cease to flow.

The physician bared the chest of the unconscious Chandler. Easily and skilfully he injected, subcutaneously, the contents of the syringe into the muscles of the region over the heart. True to his neat habits in both professions, he next carefully dried his needle and re-inserted the fine wire that threaded it when not in use.

In three minutes Chandler opened his eyes, and spoke, in a voice faint but audible, inquiring who attended upon him. Doctor James again explained his presence there.

" Where is my wife ? " asked the patient.

" She is asleep—from exhaustion and worry," said the doctor. " I would not awaken her, unless—— "

" It isn't—necessary." Chandler spoke with spaces between his words caused by his short breath that some demon was driving too fast. " She wouldn't—thank you to disturb her—on my—account."

Doctor James drew a chair to the bedside. Conversation must not be squandered.

" A few minutes ago," he began, in the grave, candid tones of his other profession, " you were trying to tell me something regarding some money. I do not seek your confidence, but it it my duty to advise you that anxiety and worry will work against your recovery. If you have any communication to make about this—to relieve your mind about this—twenty thousand dollars, I think was the amount you mentioned—you would better do so."

Chandler could not turn his head, but he rolled his eyes in the direction of the speaker.

" Did I—say where this—money is ? "

" No," answered the physician. " I only inferred, from your scarcely intelligible words, that you felt a solicitude concerning its safety. If it is in this room—— "

Doctor James paused. Did he only seem to perceive a flicker of understanding, a gleam of suspicion upon the ironical features of his patient ? Had he seemed too eager ? Had he said too much ? Chandler's next words restored his confidence.

" Where—should it be," he gasped, " but in—the safe—there ? "

With his eyes he indicated a corner of the room, where now, for the first time, the doctor perceived a small iron safe, half-concealed by the trailing end of a window curtain.

Rising, he took the sick man's wrist. His pulse was beating in great throbs, with ominous intervals between.

" Lift your arm," said Doctor James.

" You know—I can't move, Doctor."

The physician stepped swiftly to the hall door, opened it, and listened. All was still. Without further circumvention he went to the safe, and examined it. Of a primitive make and simple design, it afforded little more security than protection against light-fingered servants. To his skill it was a mere toy, a thing of straw and pasteboard. The money was as good as in his hands. With his clamps he could draw the knob, punch the tumblers and open the door in two minutes. Perhaps, in another way, he might open it in one.

Kneeling upon the floor, he laid his ear to the combination plate, and slowly turned the knob. As he had surmised, it was locked at only a " day com."—upon one number. His keen ear caught the faint warning click as the tumbler was disturbed; he used the clue—the handle turned. He swung the door wide open.

The interior of the safe was bare—not even a scrap of paper rested within the hollow iron cube.

Doctor James rose to his feet and walked back to the bed.

A thick dew had formed upon the dying man's brow, but there was a mocking, grim smile on his lips and in his eyes.

" I never—saw it before," he said, painfully, " medicine and—burglary wedded ! Do you—make the—combination pay—dear Doctor ? "

Than that situation afforded, there was never a more rigorous test of Doctor James's greatness. Trapped by the diabolic humor of his victim into a position both ridiculous and unsafe, he maintained his dignity as well as his presence of mind. Taking out his watch, he waited for the man to die.

" You were—just a shade—too—anxious—about that money. But it never was—in any danger—from you, dear doctor. It's safe. Perfectly safe. It's all—in the hands—of the bookmakers. Twenty—thousand—Amy's money. I played it at the races—lost every—cent of it. I've been a pretty bad boy, Burglar—excuse me—Doctor, but I've been a square sport. I don't think—I ever met—such an—eighteen-carat rascal as you are, Doctor—excuse me—Burglar, in all my rounds. Is it contrary—to the ethics—of your—gang, Burglar, to give a victim—excuse me—patient, a drink of water ? "

Doctor James brought him a drink. He could scarcely swallow it. The reaction from the powerful drug was coming in regular, intensifying waves. But his moribund fancy must have one more grating fling.

" Gambler—drunkard—spendthrift—I've been those, but —a doctor-burglar ! "

The physician indulged himself to but one reply to the other's caustic taunts. Bending low to catch Chandler's fast crystallizing gaze, he pointed to the sleeping lady's door with a gesture so stern and significant that the prostrate man half-lifted his head, with his remaining strength, to see. He saw nothing ; but he caught the cold words of the doctor—the last sounds he was to hear :

" I never yet—struck a woman."

It were vain to attempt to con such men. There is no curriculum that can reckon with them in its ken. They are offshoots from the types whereof men say, " He will do this," or " He will do that." We only know that they exist ; and that we can observe them, and tell one another of their bare performances, as children watch and speak of the marionettes.

Yet, it were a droll study in egoism to consider these two— one an assassin and a robber, standing above his victim ; the other baser in his offences, if a lesser law-breaker, lying, abhorred, in the house of the wife he had persecuted, spoiled, and smitten, one a tiger, the other a dog-wolf—to consider each of them sickening at the foulness of the other ; and each flourishing out of the mire of his manifest guilt his own immaculate standard—of conduct, if not of honor.

The one retort of Doctor James must have struck home to the other's remaining shreds of shame and manhood, for it proved the *coup de grâce*. A deep blush suffused his face—an ignominious *rosa mortis* ; the respiration ceased, and, with scarcely a tremor, Chandler expired.

Close following upon his last breath came the negress, bringing the medicine. With a hand gently pressing upon the closed eyelids, Doctor James told her of the end. Not grief, but a hereditary *rapprochement* with death in the abstract, moved her to a dismal watery snuffling, accompanied by her usual jeremiad.

" Dar now ! It's in de Lawd's hands. He am de jedge ob de transgressor, and de suppo't of dem in distress. He gwine hab suppo't us now. Cindy done paid out de last quarter fer dis bottle of physic, and it nebber come to no use."

" Do I understand," asked Doctor James, " that Mrs. Chandler has no money ? "

" Money, suh ? You know what make Miss Amy fall down,

and so weak ? Stahvation, suh. Nothin' to eat in dis house but some crumbly crackers in three days. Dat angel sell her finger rings and watch mont's ago. Dis fine house, suh, wid de red cyarpets and shiny bureaus, it's all hired ; and de man talkin' scan'lous about de rent. Dat debble—'scuse me, Lawd —he done in Yo' hands fer jedgment, now—he made way wid everything."

The physician's silence encouraged her to continue. The history that he gleaned from Cindy's disordered monologue was an old one, of illusion, wilfulness, disaster, cruelty and pride. Standing out from the blurred panorama of her gabble were little clear pictures—an ideal home in the far South ; a quickly repented marriage ; an unhappy season, full of wrongs and abuse, and, of late, an inheritance of money that promised deliverance ; its seizure and waste by the dog-wolf during a two months' absence, and his return in the midst of a scandalous carouse. Unobtruded, but visible between every line, ran a pure white thread through the smudged warp of the story— the simple, all-enduring, sublime love of the old negress, following her mistress unswervingly through everything to the end.

When at last she paused, the physician spoke, asking if the house contained whiskey or liquor of any sort. There was, the old woman informed him, half a bottle of brandy left in the sideboard by the dog-wolf.

" Prepare a toddy as I told you," said Doctor James. " Wake your mistress ; have her drink it, and tell her what has happened."

Some ten minutes afterward, Mrs. Chandler entered, supported by old Cindy's arm. She appeared to be a little stronger since her sleep and the stimulant she had taken. Doctor James had covered with a sheet, the form upon the bed.

The lady turned her mournful eyes once, with a half-frightened look, toward it, and pressed closer to her loyal protector. Her eyes were dry and bright. Sorrow seemed to have done its utmost with her. The fount of tears was dried ; feeling itself paralyzed.

Doctor James was standing near the table, his overcoat donned, his hat and medicine case in his hand. His face was calm and impassive—practice had inured him to the sight of human suffering. His lambent brown eyes alone expressed a discreet professional sympanthy.

He spoke kindly and briefly, stating that, as the hour was late, and assistance, no doubt, difficult to procure, he would himself send the proper persons to attend to the necessary finalities.

" One matter, in conclusion," said the doctor, pointing to the safe with its still wide-open door. " Your husband, Mrs. Chandler, toward the end, felt that he could not live ; and directed me to open that safe, giving me the number upon which the combination is set. In case you may need to use it, you will remember that the number is forty-one. Turn several times to the right ; then to the left once ; stop at forty-one. He would not permit me to waken you, though he knew the end was near.

" In that safe he said he had placed a sum of money—not large—but enough to enable you to carry out his last request. That was that you should return to your old home, and, in after days, when time shall have made it easier, forgive his many sins against you."

He pointed to the table, where lay an orderly pile of bank-notes, surmounted by two stacks of gold coins.

" The money is there—as he described it—eight hundred and thirty dollars. I beg to leave my card with you, in case I can be of any service later on."

So, he had thought of her—and kindly—at the last ! So late ! And yet the lie fanned into life one last spark of tender-ness where she had thought all was turned to ashes and dust. She cried aloud, " Rob ! Rob ! " She turned, and, upon the ready bosom of her true servitor, diluted her grief in relieving tears. It is well to think, also, that in the years to follow, the murderer's falsehood shone like a little star above the grave of love, comforting her, and gaining the forgiveness that is good in itself, whether asked for or no.

Hushed and soothed upon the dark bosom, like a child, by a crooning, babbling sympathy, at last she raised her head—but the doctor was gone.

DIAMOND CUT DIAMOND

By

F. BRITTEN AUSTIN

"THIS will be the last cigar I shall smoke as a free man, Quayne," said Sir Humphrey Maule, quietly, as he reached for the matches.

Q.Q. raised his eyebrows.

" Going back into harness ? I thought the Indian Government would be after you again. Moscow is getting far too much of a run for its money south of the Himalayas."

Our visitor was Sir Humphrey Maule, who had retired a few months back after a career in India that had remained unknown to the general public until the chorus of Press encomiums at its conclusion made it aware that yet another great servant of the Empire had finished his day's work. Head of a special branch of the Political Department, I remembered.

He sat now, big and impressive, in the chair by Q.Q.'s desk, lighting his cigar.

" No," he said. " I'm on my way to give myself up to the police."

Q.Q.'s quick glance challenged his seriousness.

" Income-tax returns—and a tender conscience ? " He smiled quizzically at him.

Sir Humphrey finished his long puff of cigar-smoke.

" Murder." He sat back in his chair, grimly stolid.

I have rarely seen Q.Q. startled—but he was startled then —startled and instantaneously incredulous.

" You're joking, Maule ? "

" Not in the least."

" My dear chap ! *Murder ?* " Q.Q. puzzled at him.

" Murder."

" But whom ? Some would-be assassin ? "

" Jimmy Loftus."

" Good God ! "

" Yes—my best pal."

Q.Q. stared at him, frankly bewildered.

" *Jimmy Loftus* ! But—in the name of everything—why ? "

" I wish I knew."

" *How*—then ? "

Sir Humphrey looked at him, spoke slowly and deliberately.

" I know—and yet I don't know."

The Chief's hand tapped in exasperation on his desk.

" You are talking in riddles, Maule."

" It is a riddle to me—the whole business. That's why I've come to you, Quayne. I did it—I must have done it—I somehow know I did it, can give you a story of the occurrence, although another part of me is, so to speak, loud in indignant denial—and the circumstantial evidence is beyond doubt. I don't envy my counsel his job of defending me. He hasn't a shred of a case. As an honest man, I should have to say I was guilty if I were asked. It's Jack Ketch for me all right. But —although I shouldn't dream for a moment of putting in the plea—I'd rather have a quick finish than a living death—I'd just like to know for my own personal satisfaction whether it oughtn't to be Broadmoor." He spoke with a grim succinctness, knocked off a little ash from his cigar, and looked straight at Q.Q. " You've solved some pretty queer mysteries, Quayne —we've solved some of them together—as a personal favour, the last probably I shall ask of you, I want you to solve this one for me. When Jack Ketch pulls the drop from under me, I want to go into the next world knowing *why* I did it."

" H'm ! When and where do you say this occurrence happened ? "

" In my rooms—last night."

" And where is—— " Q.Q. hesitated, delicately, " Loftus —now ? "

" In my sitting-room. Behind a locked door. I sent my man off for the day. He doesn't sleep on the premises, you know."

" H'm ! No immediate hurry for the police, then. You ask me if you are sane. You appear sane enough to me. But any of us, given the circumstances, may develop hallucinations that have all the force of reality. You may be under a hallucination now. On what evidence do you think you killed Jimmy Loftus ? "

Sir Humphrey smiled again, grimly.

" On the evidence of all my senses, Quayne. There is no

hallucination about this. I woke up at seven o'clock this morning to find myself in my own sitting-room still in my dress-clothes, and to see Jimmy Loftus, also in his evening kit, sitting crumpled in a chair with a bullet-wound in his head. My own revolver was lying on the floor, one chamber recently discharged. I had a smear of burnt powder on the fingers of my right hand. More than that, I had suddenly an overpowering conviction—I had a queer vivid mental picture of the act, as though someone were calling it up in me—that I had myself shot him."

" Without a motive ? " Q.Q. interjected the question.

" Without the slightest motive. Jimmy and I were the closest pals—the nearest thing I ever had to a brother. You can guess my horror at what I saw." Sir Humphrey's grim mouth clenched tight again for a moment. " The only explanation that I can give myself is that—although I've never had the slightest symptom of epilepsy—I did it in a sort of epileptic fit."

" H'm ! If you had done it in an epileptic fit you would probably have remembered nothing at all about it when you woke up—and you *do* remember, you say ? "

" Yes—in a queer sort of way. I remember it as one remembers a somnambulistic act performed in a dream—like something divorced from one's real self. Half of me protests violently that I did not, could not do it. Yet if I were challenged I could not help but say, with full conviction, automatically— ghastly and motiveless as the thing is—' Yes, I did it.' In fact, there's an immense and curious impulse in me—the usual murderer's impulse, I suppose—to rush out and proclaim the fact."

" That was why you were going to the police-station ? "

Sir Humphrey shrugged his shoulders.

" You can't expect a man of my stamp to give himself the ignominy of dodging the police. There's the fact. I must take the consequences. I prefer to go half-way to meet them. It leaves me some personal dignity, at any rate."

" Why was Jimmy Loftus in your rooms last night ? "

" We'd had a little dinner-party."

" A party ? There were others, then ? "

" Two. But they left soon after eleven."

" Who were they ? "

" A Russian refugee aristocrat—Count Murovieff—and his daughter, Countess Stravinsky."

" Indeed ! " Q.Q. leaned back in his chair, tapped his finger-tips together. " Let's have the whole yarn, Maule.

Why did you have those three people to dinner last night ? It must have been something important to have brought Loftus out."

Sir Humphrey paused to revive the glow of his cigar, to collect his thoughts for a commencement. " There's something in your guess about the Indian Government, Quayne. I *have* been approached—I'd more than half promised to go out again, in fact. Naturally, I began to sit up and take a little notice of things Indian again, to scrounge around for scraps of useful information. About ten days ago I met a couple of very interesting people—met them at my sister's house—this Count Murovieff and his daughter, regular *ancien régime*, red-hot anti-Bolshie. It was the lady I got into conversation with first—fascinating creature, beautiful—and she did me the honour of knowing my name. A compliment rare enough to be appreciated." He smiled grimly. " She asked me if I were going back to India. I have a non-committal sort of answer— as you know, I'm not the sort that unbosoms himself to casual ladies. And then I had a shock. ' Because if you are, Sir Humphrey,' she said, ' I can give you some information that will be of the greatest use to you. Would you like to put your finger on Tretiakeff ? ' You can guess I sat up pretty sharply and took quite a lot of notice at that. Only the very inner circles know even the name of Tretiakeff—a most elusive bird and the hidden manipulator of all the Soviet intrigues in India. At that moment her father came up—a white-haired intellectual-looking little dwarf of a man, more like a professor than an aristocrat. She introduced us—and then my sister swooped down on us—mustn't have any interesting conversation in her drawing-room, you know—against the usages of polite society —one has to ' mix '—that's her word—talk meaningless ape-chatter with the entire cageful."

He paused for another pull at his cigar. Q.Q. made no comment.

Sir Humphrey resumed.

" Anyway, they managed to give me an invitation to visit them at their flat in Mount Street. I went—the next day. And I got quite a lot of information—highly secret information which—as it happened to be already in our possession—I could check. They hated the Bolshie *régime* quite thoroughly, father and daughter alike—and no wonder, if their story was even half true. A story of torture, robbery, and murder of pretty near their entire family that would have been a gold nugget to a

Riga special correspondent. I went several times, and each time I got something more—with a hint of something really big if—and they made this proviso—I were really going out to India again. Finally, I put my cards on the table, told them I was. And then the rabbit came out of the hat. It seems the lady has a cousin—real name Baron Raschevsky, but known to the Communists as Stapouloff. To save his skin he took service under the Soviet Government—won their confidence—and is now second in command under Tretiakeff in India, at the very centre of all their underground intrigues. If they are to be believed, Mr. Stapouloff is consumed by an undying secret hatred of his employers and is only waiting for a chance to play them a thoroughly dirty trick—to blow the entire Soviet organisation in India sky-high, in fact. The long and the short of it was that they promised to put me into touch with this very interesting gentleman."

Once more Sir Humphrey paused for a puff or two at his cigar.

" Of course, that isn't the kind of information that can be ignored," he went on. " I thought the best thing to do was to go and tell Loftus about it—it's down his street, as you know. I did so—and he was quite considerably interested. Naturally, he was very curious to meet my Russian friends. He asked me to invite them to dinner—and not to mention that he would be present."

" And last night was the dinner ? " said Q.Q.

" Yes. We had a very pleasant evening. Of course, I had said nothing about Loftus coming along. He turned up about five minutes after they did, and he was the best of company—really brilliant—you know what he could be when he was in the mood. They all got on splendidly together."

" No sign of recognition on either side ? "

Sir Humphrey shook his head.

" No. Not the least. Of course, I didn't get a chance to talk to Loftus."

" And then what happened ? "

" At a little after eleven the Russians went away. I accompanied them downstairs, saw them into a taxi. I went up again to my rooms, where Loftus was sitting waiting for me—and then—that's the confoundedly queer part about it, Quayne—I can't really remember *with my whole self* what happened."

" Tell me what the part of yourself that remembers or seems to remember most has to say."

" I've got a sort of dream-knowledge—a conviction rather than a memory—of having gone straight to the drawer of my desk where I keep a revolver, taken out the weapon, and deliberately shot Loftus—without any reason whatever—as he sat there in the chair. And then I can't remember anything at all, until I woke up this morning, found myself lying on the carpet, and saw Jimmy sitting there dead in the chair, with the revolver on the floor between me and him."

" And the other part of you—what does that remember ? "

" Nothing at all. It's a blank from the time I saw those people disappearing down the street in their taxi—until the moment that I woke up this morning."

" H'm ! " Q.Q. sat with closely-pressed lips. " What are your domestic arrangements, Maule ? "

" It's a service-flat. The management sent up the dinner from the restaurant and did the waiting. Cleared up after we had finished, while we were in the sitting-room. They do all the work of the place, you know—except my sitting-room. I don't like unknown people messing about with my papers. My man does that."

" He doesn't sleep on the premises, you said. Was he there last night ? "

" I let him off before ten o'clock—when he had brought in the whisky decanter and a couple of siphons. As I told you, I sent him off for the day directly he arrived at seven-thirty this morning. My sitting-room is just as it was last night, with poor Jimmy sitting in that chair—behind a locked door."

Q.Q. pondered for a moment.

" You say you saw your guests depart in their taxi. How did you get back into your rooms ? Did you let yourself in with a key—or did you leave the door open ? "

" I went up in the lift—by Jove, yes, it comes back to me now—I found my door shut, and when I felt for my bunch of keys I found I must have left them inside—I had to ring the bell."

" Who opened the door ? "

" Jimmy, of course—yes, I remember that—besides, there was no one else in the flat."

" Was he quite normal ? "

" Well, we'd had a good dinner—and one or two whiskies—and—sodas afterwards—and, yes, we were a bit cheerful, I suppose."

" And now can you remember anything else at all after Loftus let you into your rooms—apart from your dream-conviction that then or subsequently you shot him ? "

Sir Humphrey shook his head.

"Nothing at all—other than that, it is a blank. But, I say, Quayne!" a sudden excitement came into his voice, "it's a funny thing about those keys! I could swear I hadn't got them in my pocket when I rang at that door—I remember ringing and ringing—Jimmy was slow in tumbling to what had happened—yet I certainly had them in my trouser-pocket when I woke up this morning. I remember turning them out quite normally with all my other things when I changed out of my dress-kit. Here they are." He fished out a bunch of keys from his pocket, held them up. "It's an action so automatic to shift them from one kit to another that I hadn't given them a thought. But I certainly didn't have them last night—unless I was far more drunk than I thought."

"That, of course, is a possibility," said Q.Q. quietly. "I'd like to know a little more about these guests of yours. Can you describe the lady?"

"Tall, slim, raven-black hair, wonderful large grey eyes—beautiful as a goddess—gives you a thrill to look at her."

"H'm!" commented Q.Q., grimly; "enthusiasm is not description. You were more definitely helpful about her father. Wait a moment." He got up, went across to a large cabinet index-file on the farther wall of the room, returned with a couple of "jackets." He sat down again, opened the dossiers, took out three or four photographs from each, spread them on his desk.

"Are these your friends, Maule?"

Sir Humphrey looked at the photographs, uttered a sharp exclamation.

"By Jove, yes! Both of them!" Q.Q. smiled in quiet satisfaction.

"I thought I was guessing right," he said. "But I am surprised that Loftus didn't tell you anything about those people when you rejoined him. He had a quite special interest in them both—and he certainly recognised them. The father's real name—he has, of course, many *aliases*—is Dr. Hugo Weidmann. He was at one time a well-known psycho-analyst in Vienna. Then he got into an unpleasant scandal, cleared out of Austria, and went into German Secret Service, a line of business in which his professional experience was extremely useful. Over here, during the war, he posed as a Russian reformer, who had fled from the Czarist police prior to 1914—and he brought off one or two really big *coups* before our people got on his track and he vanished into thin air."

"Good Lord!" exclaimed Sir Humphrey. "You're making me feel an awful fool, Quayne!"

"The daughter's name," continued Q.Q., imperturbably, "is Clara Weidmann—originally, that is to say ; the names she has given herself would fill a page of *Who's Who*. She was certainly one of the most efficient spies we ever had to deal with. And she got clear away—but not before she had murdered, in very mysterious circumstances, one of Loftus's best men. Jimmy swore he would get her sooner or later—that was why, evidently, half-recognising both from your description, he asked you to arrange a little *dîner intime* so that he could put the matter beyond doubt. You, of course, serving in India all your life, would know nothing of either of them." He leaned back in his chair, finger-tips together. "I'm beginning to see a little daylight in this, Maule."

"I'm damned if I am," replied Sir Humphrey. "With all that. Who are these people working for now?"

"For the Soviet Government, evidently. They knew or guessed that you might be going back to India. You're a formidable adversary, Maule—on your own ground. They did the clever thing—nobbled you from the start. If you had taken all their information seriously—naturally they saw to it that all you could check should be genuine—and had put yourself in the hands of Mr. Stapouloff, you'd have got yourself into a pretty mess."

"Well, that's out of the question now, anyway. I don't go to India—I go to the Old Bailey and to a nasty little ceremony in a prison-yard early one morning. For there's no doubt about it—mad or not—I shot poor Loftus."

Q.Q. looked at him.

"Doesn't it occur to you, Maule, how extremely convenient it is to these two people that Loftus—they certainly recognised him, as he recognised them—should be dead, and you completely out of the way?"

"Yes—but——" Sir Humphrey frowned in a desperation of thought. "It can't be more than a coincidence. I saw them go—I'm certain of that. How could they have got back, killed Loftus, and—this is the vital point, given me the conviction that I had done it myself ? *How could they ?*"

"That, Maule," said Q.Q. caressing his chin, " we're going to try to find out."

Sir Humphrey leaned forward in a sudden hypothesis.

"They couldn't have drugged me—*made* me murder Jimmy, could they ?" he asked, desperately. " It wouldn't go down with a jury, I know, but it means a lot to *me*. It isn't possible—just wildly possible—is it ? Queer things happen in India, you know."

Q.Q. shrugged his shoulders.

" They are very clever people," he said, as he took a sheet of note-paper and commenced to write. He wrote only a few quick words, folded the paper, reached for an envelope, put in the note, stuck it down and addressed it. " What number in Mount Street ? " Sir Humphrey told him. He added it, looked across to me. " A little job for you, Mr. Creighton. Take this note to the Countess Stravinsky and give it to her personally." He glanced at his watch. " It is now just eleven o'clock. You will probably find her at home. She may have something to say to you. Stay and listen to it—stay just as long as she likes to keep you—make the lady's acquaintance, in fact." He smiled at me. " But when you do leave, rejoin us at Sir Humphrey's rooms. Give him the address, Maule."

Sir Humphrey gave me his card, and a few minutes later I was in a taxi speeding towards Mount Street.

A prim, foreign-looking maid led me into a large drawing-room, furnished with an exotic and bizarre luxury, a room of rich Chinese blues touched with vivid greens, where gilt Buddhas and grotesque Hindu gods niched themselves against a simplicity of wall.

" Vait 'ere," said the maid. " I vill tell ze Countess."

I stood there, feeling my heart thump, and waited. And I craved for my automatic, so thoughtlessly left behind. The atmosphere of that room seemed pregnant with something mysteriously sinister. What drama was going to be precipitated by the sealed thin note I fingered ?

I turned from an absent-minded stare at a squat white-jade Chinese idol to see the Countess standing in the room, the door-curtain just falling behind her.

She was beautiful—beautiful, I can only reiterate the word —with such a purity of beauty, such a grave perfection of Madonna-like loveliness, that her presence set me quivering in a surge of awe that overwhelmed the cynicism of reason. Her large, clear grey eyes—wonderful under the raven-black hair, smoothed with the slightest ripple back from her brows— rested upon me in mute inquiry.

" The Countess Stravinsky ? " I said.

" Yes." Her voice, in the utterance of that one syllable, was surprisingly musical on a rich, deep, vibrant note.

I held out the envelope.

She took it, tore it open, read the missive. I saw a sudden hardness come into her beautiful face. Once more the wonderful grey eyes were resting on me.

" You know what is in this note ? "

" No, madame."

The hardness vanished from her face—vanished so that a moment later one could not recall what it had been. She smiled—a sudden opening of dazzling fascination.

" You are a—— " she hesitated, " an *employé* of Mr. Quentin Quayne ? "

I had no cue for my answer. I risked the truth.

" Yes, madame."

Her eyes ranged over me, summed me up.

" You seem to be a gentleman," she said.

I bowed.

" Were you told to bring back an answer to this ? " She indicated the sheet of paper in her hand.

" I was told merely to hand it to you personally, madame." Confound Q.Q. ! Why the devil hadn't he told me what was in that letter ? I should have had at least some idea of what to do or say.

The large grey eyes rested on me again. She pondered something I could not guess at. Then again she smiled.

" Will you not sit down, Mr.—Mr.—— ? " she finished on a note of interrogation.

" Creighton," I said.

I took the soft armchair to which she gestured. She sat down opposite me on a settee. Our eyes met. A part of me reminded me insistently that she was a spy, a murderess. Another part of me, deep down, elemental, blindly instinctive, rose in revolt against an accusation that seemed patently absurd. Q.Q.—Sir Humphrey—both might have been mistaken. Photographs are the most deceptive of evidence. These thoughts flashed through me in a matter of seconds. She was pondering again—pondering, perhaps, what was required of her ? What the devil was in that note ?

Suddenly she smiled once more, stretched out her slim white arm to a cigarette-box on a little table, held it out to me.

" Will you smoke, Mr. Creighton ? " she asked, in that rich, deep voice.

I accepted. She took one herself, reached for the matches, struck a light, held it to my cigarette—her large grey eyes close to mine evoked a peculiar intimate start deep down in me,

sudden surge and tumult of blood, over which I set my teeth
—lit her own. She dropped the still-lighted match into an
antique bronze tripod brazier—Chinese and grotesque—which
stood close to my right hand.

" You are going straight back to Mr. Quayne when you
leave here ? "

" Yes, madame."

" You are not in a hurry ? '

" No, madame."

A quick look came from those clear grey eyes, large under
the raven-black hair, a look that shot through me like a search-
light. It was instantly veiled, replaced by a smile that was
languorously serene.

I sat, my heart thumping, waiting for her next words. I
heard the faint ticking of a clock across the room. And, as I
waited, I became gradually conscious of a subtle incense-like
perfume filling the atmosphere, a diffusion of cloying aromatic
sweetness, semi-pungent to my nostrils, that made me automatically take a deep breath. It filled my lungs, seemed to
mount to my head. I pulled myself out of a momentary
dizziness, glanced round at the brazier into which she had
thrown her match. A slender stem of grey smoke ascended
from the bowl, coiled into a lazy spiral at its summit. Was this
some sinister trick ? No !—impossible !—fantastic ! My
suspicions were running away with me. Yet I dared not—
dumb in the awe she inspired in me—break her silence. She
remained immobile, lost in thoughts, her face a miracle of calm
beauty.

I resigned myself. That slender stem of grey smoke continued to ascend, and with that subtly pervasive aromatic odour
I inhaled at every breath, a numbness in myself—imperceptible
at first—crept over me. My brain dulled. I relaxed, luxuri-
ously, languorously, carelessly scornful of the vigilant alertness
to which a moment before I had endeavoured to hold fast. I
lost the clear sense of my identity. And in place of my normal
self, obscure primitive impulses stirred in me. They frightened
me. I found myself yearning for a mad kiss from that exquisite
mouth. My arms ached to enfold that lithe slender figure, to
crush it frenziedly in an embrace that would enforce reciproca-
tion. My brain whirled at the thought of it—it seemed that
the next moment I should spring forward, hot-breathed upon
her—flung from my seat by an impulse beyond civilised
volition. Yet I did not move. I felt something hurt the fingers

of my right hand on my knee. It was my cigarette, forgotten, which had burnt down to them. With an immense muscular effort I tossed the stump into the brazier whence the grey smoke ascended. In that last flicker of normal consciousness, I glanced at the watch upon my wrist. To my surprise, it marked only half-past eleven.

The silence had lasted a time beyond my computation. She turned her large clear eyes upon me, smiled. I perceived her with a vision that was blurred, heard her—deep-toned, thrillingly sonorous—with a dizzy brain.

" You are thinking things about me—unpleasant things ? "

" Madame—I—I—— " My own voice sounded strange to me.

She leaned forward, exquisitely seductive. Again I felt that primitive reckless urge, almost irresistible, electric, spontaneous, in every fibre of me, repressed it with a last spasm of will.

" I want you to look in my eyes—and see if you can believe them."

The eyes came close, wide open, eyes of a strange clear grey, the pupils peculiarly fascinating, seeking mine.

" Madame—I—I—— " That direct gaze was insupportable. I dropped my own—gasped in a suffocation, my brain in a dizzy whirl.

" Look !   Keep on looking ! "

I looked into those eyes that focussed themselves on mine —looked—kept on looking—saw nothing but those eyes— looked into them for an endless time where I lost perception of all else but those two clear grey eyes holding mine until I could no longer turn away my gaze. My arm jerked of itself—went stiff. An immense fatigue weighed heavy on my shoulders.

" *Lean back !* "   A last flicker of resistance leaped up in me. No ! no !—I—I musn't.   " Lean back ! " I ceded, relaxed, felt suddenly comfortable.

It might have been æons after, I saw, mistily, vaguely, as through my eyelashes, the Countess standing tall above me. By her side was a sharp-faced, white-haired, intellectual-looking little dwarf of a man, peering eagerly at me.

" Yes—I think so."   Her voice came through—through cotton-wool—to my dulled senses. I could not move—had no will to move. I leaned back, locked in a complete passivity I accepted with a last tiny fragment of my consciousness.

" Answer me, Mr. Creighton."

" Yes."   I heard myself answer—a voice that was far away

from me—a voice that spoke with surprising (only I had lost the capacity for surprise) promptness of obedience.

And then—and then—I remember nothing more, until—I cannot say to this day how—I found myself in a taxi, speeding through the London traffic, and knowing quite clearly that I was on my way to Q.Q. at Sir Humphrey Maule's rooms. What had happened in that flat? How did I get into that taxi? I could not remember. I could only remember, very clearly that I was on my way to Q.Q.—that I *must* get to Q.Q.—for a reason still obscure to me—with the minimum of delay. And then another alarm shot into my mind. Was I really going to Sir Humphrey's flat—or was the taxi-driver taking me, under sinister orders, to some other destination? I had not the least recollection of giving him the address. I had scarce grappled with this sudden panic when the cab stopped, in the quiet street off St. James's where Sir Humphrey lived, at the number given on the card I took, for verification, from my pocket. I got out.

"Who gave you this address?" I said.

The taxi-driver stared at me.

"You did, sir," he said.

I hurried into the building, cursing at the exhibition I had made of myself. The lift shot me up to the floor occupied by Sir Humphrey. I rang. Sir Humphrey himself opened the door.

I followed him along a short passage, into an unfamiliar sitting-room adorned with Indian trophies. A white sheet was thrown over something shapeless in a chair near the table. In another chair, near a writing-desk, Q.Q. was sitting. He smiled at me.

I stopped. What was it I had to do when I saw Q.Q.? What was the obscure impulse which surged up in me, which made my fingers work nervously of themselves? A cloud was over my brain. I felt my muscles go spontaneously rigid. Q.Q. still smiled.

"A knife, Mr. Creighton?" he said, blandly—held out an ivory paper-knife.

I took it automatically, felt my fingers clench tightly over it without my volition—and then, as though a trigger were pulled inside me that discharged a sudden nervous force, with no clear consciousness of what I was doing, but under an impulse that filled me suddenly to the exclusion of all else, I sprang at him, stabbed straight at his chest with the paper-knife. And even as I delivered the blow, I had an obscure half-knowledge that it was all right, that it was only harmless make-believe—a complaisance that reconciled conflicting compulsions.

Sir Humphrey leaped forward with a startled cry, clutched my wrist.

Q.Q. smiled. He had sat motionless, without a tremor.

"Let him go. The wrong knife, Mr. Creighton. Give him that Indian dagger, Maule."

Sir Humphrey hesitated.

"Give it to him."

He obeyed. With obvious reluctance he handed me an Indian dagger in place of the paper-knife he had wrenched from my grasp. I stood quivering, in a peculiar suspension of thought, of all volition. It was as though I was under a spell.

"Obey the command given you, Mr. Creighton," said Q.Q., quietly.

At the words once more I sprang—and as I did so I realised with an overwhelming shock what it was I had in my hand, what it was I had been commanded to do—*murder !—murder* Q.Q.! That realisation checked me like a bullet striking me in mid-course. In an immense revulsion of all myself, a violent, spontaneous, shattering recoil from the atrocity I was about to commit, I stopped dead, flung the dagger from me. My brain suddenly cleared. I stood trembling, dazed, bewildered, ready to drop with humiliation. Good God! What would Q.Q. think of me? I could have burst into hysterical tears.

"My God, sir!" I stammered. "What—what's the matter with me? Am I mad?—or—or——?" I had no explanation to offer, even to myself. The lack of it terrified me. I looked at that dagger lying on the floor, and felt suddenly physically sick. I swayed on my feet.

Q.Q. rose quietly from his chair, put his hand on my shoulder.

"All right, Mr. Creighton." His eyes looked into mine, sent reassurance into me, braced me to command of myself. "You've been making yourself useful for once—that's all." He smiled. "Sit down in that chair—and pull yourself together." Once more his eyes looked straight, compellingly, into mine. "You are quite normal again—*quite*—you understand that?"

"Yes, sir." I gasped, and subsided weakly into the chair.

"Well, Maule, do you see the point of that little experiment?"

"I'm damned if I do!" Sir Humphrey looked utterly mystified.

"Then I'll tell you. I sent Mr. Creighton round to your lady-friend of last night—she's the more dangerous of the pair—with a note he was instructed to deliver only into the Countess Stravinsky's own hand. I've no doubt he did so. That note was as follows"—Q.Q. smiled grimly as he paused—"'On behalf of Mr. James Loftus, Mr. Quentin Quayne presents his compliments to Fräulein Clara Weidmann.' Rather a shock to the lady, I'm afraid." He smiled again. "Now do you begin to see?"

"Not in the least."

Q.Q. turned to me.

"What happened in the flat at Mount Street, Mr. Creighton?"

I tried with all my might to remember—found myself baffled with an absolute blankness. It exasperated me, humiliated me anew.

"I—I'm sorry, sir," I stammered. "I don't know what's the matter with me—I can't remember anything about it."

Q.Q. nodded. His voice was kindly as he spoke.

"Never mind. I can guess." He turned again to Sir Humphrey. "Put yourself in the lady's place. Last night she meets Jimmy Loftus, realises that she is recognised, and eliminates him very cleverly. This morning she learns not only that Quentin Quayne is aware of her identity, but that Quentin Quayne holds her responsible for Loftus's death. Obviously, Quentin Quayne also must be eliminated at once. How is she to do it? One method, at least, particularly after last night, would instantly suggest itself to her—a temptation I dangled in front of her, in fact. You will remember that I carefully told Mr. Creighton not to hurry away. I put an opportunity into her hands."

"Opportunity?" queried Sir Humphrey, still puzzled.

"Hypnosis," said Q.Q. succinctly. "You forget her father was professor of psychiatry in Vienna—and she was an apt pupil. She undoubtedly hypnotised Creighton, and gave him the post-hypnotic suggestion, with the safeguard that his memory should be an absolute blank on the matter, that he should stab me directly he saw me. I noticed his fingers working the moment he came into the room. You saw for yourself what happened."

" Good God ! " groaned Sir Humphrey, in a sudden anguish. " And they must have hypnotised *me* also !—made me kill poor Jimmy ! I really did it, then ! That proves it ! "

" It proves nothing of the sort. It proves just the opposite. One of my reasons for making this somewhat dangerous experiment was to establish beyond doubt whether it is or is not possible to hypnotise a subject into committing a genuine murder. It is easy enough to make him act a dummy one— but it is a hotly-disputed point whether he will or will not obey a suggestion to do the real thing. Your lady-friend was doubtless quite aware of this—but the case was urgent with her— she had to take a long chance if she was to do anything at all. She took it—after all, the possibility has never been definitely disproved. And I took a chance that, being quite ready for him, I might be quicker than Mr. Creighton if he meant business with a real knife in his hand. You saw the difference in his behaviour when he had the paper-knife and when he had the real thing. No, Maule," he concluded, decisively, " my experiment proved beyond doubt that whatever hypnotic suggestion was given you last night—your drinks were drugged, of course—you did *not* murder Jimmy Loftus. If the thing can be done at all it could be done with Creighton. She tried. It can *not* be done."

Sir Humphrey mopped his brow.

" You're sure ! "

" Quite sure ! "

The big man stared at him.

" Thank God ! " he ejaculated. " But how do you account for my instinctive conviction that I *did* do it ? "

Q.Q. smiled.

" It is quite easy under hypnosis to make a man wake up with the belief that he has committed a murder—especially if you arrange the circumstantial evidence convincingly. May I use your telephone ? "

" Yes—yes—of course." Sir Humphrey was still bewildered. " What are you going to do ? "

" I'm going to get your friends round here. Very clever people "—Q.Q. smiled again as he picked up the telephone— " but I think they'll find this is a case of diamond cut diamond. Hallo ! Are you there ? " He gave a number, waited. "Hullo! Is that Sebright ? Oh, Sebright, a murder was committed last night at Sir Humphrey Maule's flat—yes, St. James's—I'll give you the details presently. Yes—I want you to come round —but on your way I want you to call at No. 504, Mount Street and bring along a couple of Russian people, Count Murovieff and his daughter, the Countess Stravinsky. Listen—and I'll explain. These two people were guests of Sir Humphrey Maule last night. They left soon after eleven. The murder was committed after that hour. Precisely. They have an alibi. Now, I want you to explain to them that their presence is necessary to verify whether the room is or is not as they left it at eleven. You can tell them, if you like, that the murderer is known. I think you'll have no difficulty in persuading them to come along—they cannot refuse their assistance in eluci-dating the circumstances of the crime. But it is most important that they should accompany you—and, by the way, don't mention my name. Good. You'll find me in Sir Humphrey's flat expecting you."

He hung up the receiver, turned to us with a smile. " Now we'll soon clear up all this little business."

Sir Humphrey had been pacing up and down the room. He swung round to Q.Q.

" I'm still bewildered, Quayne. What really happened in this room last night ? "

Q.Q. smiled at him.

" You've heard of dhatura, Maule ? "

" Of course I have. Favourite drug of the Indian criminal. Seeds rather like capsicum. Usually administered chopped up. Leaves no trace in the human body. Sends the victim into insensibility, and if he doesn't die he wakes up minus his memory—can't remember a thing about it."

" Precisely. Your two pseudo-Russian friends are, how-ever, a little more refined in their methods than the ordinary Indian criminal. They didn't want the police to find you and Loftus lying dead here, and they themselves naturally under suspicion. They wanted Loftus dead and you self-accused of the murder. So they put into your whiskies and sodas a little —not crude dhatura, but a scientific preparation of the drug which is considerably more subtle in its effects—it leaves the victim extremely susceptible to hypnotic influence at the same time that it embroils his memory and paralyses him into a semi-insensible immobility. A drop or two would suffice, and it would take about ten minutes to have its effect. They did this just before they left. You accompanied them downstairs. On the way they picked your pocket of your keys. You came back, found the door shut, and—you remember—it was some little time before you could get Loftus to open it. The drug was already working in him, of course. You thought that both he and you had had a little too much to drink. You both went back into the sitting-room—not very steadily, I expect—and sat down. *You were both sitting there quite helpless*, when at a time convenient to your departed friends—perhaps two hours later, when everybody in the place had gone to bed—they returned, let themselves in at the outer door, and then this door with your keys, and found you nicely ready for them."

" Good God!" exclaimed Sir Humphrey. "And then——?"

" And then they hunted for your revolver, found it, shot Loftus as he sat paralysed in his chair, put the revolver on the floor after smearing your finger with the burnt powder which had escaped from its not very closely-fitting barrel, put the keys back in your pocket, and gave you a detailed hypnotic suggestion that you had done the whole business yourself, that you would sleep till the morning, and wake up with such a full conviction of your guilt that you would surrender yourself to the police. Very neat, I think."

" *Phew !* " Sir Humphrey whistled. He was still only half-convinced, however, and showed it. " All this is damned difficult to prove in a court of law, Quayne. What do you propose to do when you get these people here ? "

Q.Q. smiled again.

" I told you this was a case of diamond cut diamond. You'll see. They should be here in a minute or two now."

We sat and waited, we three—and that sheeted something in the armchair, which, in my state of broken nerve, I was grateful not to see uncovered. The minutes dragged. The ringing of the door-bell—when it came—was almost a relief.

" You go, Maule," said Q.Q.

Sir Humphrey went to open to the new arrivals. Q.Q. turned to the chair by the table, carefully withdrew that shapelessly humped covering, revealed a good-looking man crumpled in the seat, his head forward on his chest, dried blood plastered on his face from a wound in the temple. I gripped myself in a sudden sickening, sat short-breathed in suspense.

The next moment Sir Humphrey was again at the door, speaking to those who followed him.

" In here," he said. He made way politely for the lady.

She entered. I can't describe what sprang up in me at the sight once more of that quiet, Madonna-like beauty. Behind her was the little, intellectual-faced, white-headed dwarf of a man. And behind him was Sebright.

She took a step or two into the room, saw the corpse in the

chair, and then her eyes switched to Q.Q. standing impassively close to it—from Q.Q. to me, fascinated where I sat. She must have recognised him as she recognised me—recognised also, in a flash, that her plan had failed. Q.Q. was still alive—grimly smiling.

She swayed, went deathly pale, jerked out her hand for support at the table.

The little white-haired old man sprang forward, caught her in his arms.

" Poor lady ! Too much of a shock to her seeing that in the chair, Quayne," said Sebright, with reproof in his voice.

But Q.Q. ignored him. He also had sprung forward, caught at the lady, seemed to be mixed up in almost a struggle with the little man as he took her into his own stronger arms.

" All right," he said. " Let me have her. She'll be all right in a minute. Brandy, Maule."

He deposited her carefully in an armchair, turned to take the brandy-decanter Sir Humphrey held out to him.

" A glass ? " Q.Q.'s eyes ranged round the room. " Ah, there's one ! " He went across to a side-table, poured out a stiff peg of brandy, took it back to the woman. She waved it away. " I insist ! " he said, firmly but not unkindly, held it to her mouth, poured some, whether she willed or no, down her throat. She gasped and choked with it.

Sir Humphrey was explaining to Sebright what he knew of the crime.

" I woke up at seven o'clock this morning in this room to —to see that ! " he said, gesturing to the corpse in the chair.

" Good God ! " exclaimed Sebright. " *Loftus !* But who could have done it ? "

" I did ! "

I jumped with the surprise of it. It was Sir Humphrey who had spoken—automatically—with full conviction.

Sebright also had jumped.

" *You?* " he cried. " *You*, Sir Humphrey ? "

Sir Humphrey stood confused.

" I—I really don't know why I said that ! " he stammered. " It—it was like something saying it for me."

Sebright gave him a glance of keen suspicion. Q.Q. interposed.

" All right, Sebright. He didn't meant it. He didn't do it. You'll understand presently."

Sebright looked altogether unconvinced. He turned to the little white-haired man.

" You left Sir Humphrey alone with Mr. Loftus last night, I understand, Count ? " he said, professionally sharp-voiced.

" Yes. At five minutes past eleven. Sir Humphrey accompanied us to the street, put us in a taxi. Is not that so, Sir Humphrey ? " The little old man was suave, pleasantly soft in his tones—a little nervous, however, for he took a white silk handkerchief from his pocket, wiped his mouth in a finically dandified gesture.

" Yes," said Sir Humphrey. I saw the sweat pearling on his forehead. " Yes—that's quite right."

" No one else was in the flat, apparently," continued Sebright, severely. " Your position requires a considerable amount of explanation, Sir Humphrey."

Sir Humphrey stammered.

" I—I—— " He looked helplessly towards Q.Q.

At that moment I uttered a startled cry. A peculiar expression had come over the face of the beautiful woman in the chair. She leaned back limply, stared in front of her with eyes that one guessed saw nothing—seemed as if in a trance.

The little white-haired old man jumped forward again. Q.Q. restrained him.

" All right, Count. Please do not interfere. This is a most fortunate little accident, I think." He smiled pleasantly as he quietly pushed the little old man back. " I had an intuition from the moment I saw your daughter that she was clairvoyant. As you see, she has gone into a trance—quite harmless—overcome perhaps by the sinister influences with which this room must still be soaked. Let us avail ourselves of it—in the interests of justice." He smiled again. " Your daughter will perhaps be able to show us precisely what happened in this room last night."

A frightened look had come into the little old man's eyes.

" I—I protest ! " he said, sharply, making an effort to assert a personal dignity. " I protest against your trying possibly dangerous and certainly quite illegal experiments with my daughter ! "

Q.Q. smiled at him.

" I am afraid, with all due apology, that I must ignore your protests, Count. A murder was committed in this room last night by very clever and quite unscrupulous people. We cannot afford a too scrupulous legality in dealing with them. A case of diamond cut diamond, in fact." He smiled again, turned to Sebright. His manner suddenly changed. " Will you please see that this man does not interfere, Sebright ? I give him formally into your charge as Dr. Hugo Weidmann, against whom there is a warrant as accessory to the murder of Henry Paulin, Mr. Loftus's chief assistant, in January, 1917."

" It's false ! " screamed the little man.

" It is true," replied Q.Q. imperturbably. " Quick, Sebright. Hold him—before he tries any tricks !—and gag him if he begins to utter a word ! "

Sebright, after one quick stare of amazement, leaped to the emergency. In a moment he was by the side of the white-faced little old man, held him fast.

" And now," continued Q.Q. with a grimly bland smile, " we will proceed with the experiment." He turned to Sir Humphrey. " Pull up the chair from which you found this morning you had fallen, Maule, into precisely the position of last night. Sit down in it and do not move. You were drugged, remember. Behave as if you were still drugged."

Sir Humphrey did as he was told, pulled up the chair, sat down in it, facing that dead body gruesomely motionless at the end of the table. His blanched countenance looked almost drugged, in fact, in the tension of the moment.

Q.Q. reverted to the lady. He lifted her hand. It lay limp in his.

" Fräulein Clara Weidmann ! " he said, in a voice of quiet authority. " You will respond to my commands, and to my commands only ! Look into my eyes ! "

The woman sighed. She moved her head slightly, looked into Q.Q.'s eyes, remained looking into them without a blink.

Q.Q. went on :

" You will hear my voice when I speak to you, and only when I speak to you. You will hear no one else. You will see no one in this room except Sir Humphrey Maule and Mr. Loftus. Any other individuals will make no impression whatever on your consciousness. It will seem to you that they are not present. Last night you and your father left these rooms soon after eleven o'clock. It will seem to you that you are back at that hour, that you are living over again whatever happened after it." He turned to Sebright. " You will note, Sebright, that I am giving the lady no specific suggestions of what *did* happen."

The little old man wriggled half-out of Sebright's grasp.

" Clara ! " he cried, gaspingly, " Clara ! Listen to my voice ! Clara ! *You will obey me—me only !* "

" Gag him, Sebright ! " said Q.Q. Sebright clapped a big hand over the man's mouth.

The woman in the chair, however, seemed not to have heard his voice. She remained immobile.

"Now, then, Fräulein Weidmann—*stand up* !" Q.Q. spoke quietly, but authoritatively.

She stood up.

"You have said ' Good night ' to Sir Humphrey and Mr. Loftus. Where are you ? "

"In the taxi." She spoke in a far-away but distinct voice. "I cannot stand in it."

"Sit down, then." She sat on the arm of the chair. "Talk as you talked then."

"*Du hast die Schlussel?* " The words came automatically, spontaneously, a look of eager cunning suddenly vivid in her beautiful face. "*Famos!* " She gabbled quick German I could not catch. "*Ja—ja. Swei Stunden—ja—sicher!* "

"Two hours," said Q.Q. "Those two hours have now passed. It is a quarter-past one. Where are you now ? "

"Here." She stood up, like one in a trance.

"How did you get here ? "

"We let outselves in with the keys we took from Sir Humphrey's pocket." She spoke like one who answers questions in her sleep.

"You are living through that experience again. It *is*, to your consciousness, a quarter-past one. Where did you stand when the clock marked that hour ? "

"We were just coming in the door."

Q.Q. led her—almost pathetically somnambulistic—to the door, released her.

"Behave just as you did then. It is real to you—the experience all over again."

Once more she came suddenly to an uncannily vivid life. She crept forward stealthily from the door, turned to glance over her shoulder as at someone following her, made a beckoning gesture. She whispered swift foreign words—I caught the German for " Yes—yes. Helpless—both of them. Quick !"

Q.Q. and I stood back with Sebright and his still silently struggling prisoner, left the centre of the room clear save for the two figures of Loftus and Sir Humphrey sitting motionless in their chairs. We watched her come across the room, as though watching a drama on the stage.

She went to the writing-desk, pulled open first one drawer and then another in a hurried search for something, uttered a little low cry of satisfaction, turned from it. In her hand was a revolver, Sir Humphrey's own revolver (Q.Q., I remembered, had carefully inquired after its normal resting place, put it back during the time we waited). She held in out to someone invisible.

" Here it is ! " she said, in rapid, low-voiced German, her whole being keyed to a breathless tension. " Quick ! You do it ! "

She released her hold upon the weapon and it dropped upon the floor. But to her it must have seemed that that invisible person had taken it. She gave a little involuntary jump—uncannily dramatic in that silence—as though at a detonation.

" *Gott !* " she whispered, in German. " What a noise ! " Then she sprang towards that collapsed figure of Loftus in his chair, peered at it closely, nodded her head quickly in reassurance. " *Todt !* "

She looked round, looked at Sir Humphrey, his eyes staring and breathing deeply as he sat in his chair. She went across to him, took up his hand, spoke in English.

" You hear me ? " she said, sharply.

" Yes." Sir Humphrey gasped as he looked at her.

" Look into my eyes ! "

He looked, kept staring at them for a minute or two of silence in which she fixed her gaze on his.

" When you wake up you will *know* that you killed your friend Loftus. I tell you how it happened. After putting us in the taxi, you came back here, went straight to your desk, took out your revolver, and shot him where he sat. You will not wake until seven o'clock. You will remember nothing about us except seeing our taxi go away down the street. But you will be so sure that you shot Loftus that you will give yourself up to the police to-morrow morning, and whenever the crime is mentioned you will accuse yourself. You understand ? "

" Yes." Sir Humphrey's voice came from far away.

" Good God ! " exclaimed Sebright.

Fascinated by the drama he was watching, he must for the moment have relaxed his grasp upon his prisoner. I saw the little man wriggle—and the next moment there was a deafening detonation, a faint film of smoke. The woman staggered, went head-long to the floor.

Q.Q. jumped to her, twisted her over, shook his head.

" Through the heart," he said.

I turned with him, to look at the little old man from whom, at that moment, Sebright was wrenching a small automatic pistol. Dr. Hugo Weidmann snarled at us.

" Better for her than your English law," he said. He relapsed suddenly into cool cynicism. " All right, Mr. Quayne. You've won. We did it. But before I go with this gentleman," he jerked his head towards Sebright, " I'd like to know—professionally—what spell you put on my daughter."

Q.Q. smiled at him.

" Simple, my dear sir. When we were both assisting her in her sudden and not unnatural faintness, I picked your pocket of the little phial I guessed you carried there for emergencies "—he held it up—" the stuff with which you drugged Loftus and Maule last night. And I gave her a good stiff dose of it in her brandy. As I have already remarked—diamond cut diamond, eh ? " He ignored the little old man's savage curse, turned to Sir Humphrey, sitting there strangely stiff in his chair, shook him by the shoulder. " Wake up, Maule ! " he said, jocularly, " Seven o'clock ! "

Sir Humphrey stirred, looked about him, jumped up with a sudden horror on his feautres. His eyes met Sebright's.

" All right, Sir Humphrey," said Sebright. " We know now who killed poor Mr. Loftus."

Sir Humphrey stood like one dazed.

" Yes," he said. " God forgive me—I did—I know I did ! Though I don't know why ! Take me in charge ! "

We all stared.

" Good Lord ! " said Q.Q. " I believe she's hypnotised him again ! "

Sebright looked not only bewildered but bad-tempered.

" All this," he grumbled, " is going to sound fantastic in a court of law, Quayne."

" Never mind, Inspector," said a gasping, croaking voice, " it won't come to a court of law." It was the little old man who spoke. His face was livid, dreadful, with foam at the corners of his mouth. " When I first came in—saw Quayne—I—I—guessed—it was—hands up. Took—precautions—— " he grinned horribly, " little glass capsule—held in mouth—too—too clever for you—— " He wilted suddenly in Sebright's strong grasp—went down, lifeless, upon the floor when that grasp was released.

MURDER AT THE MICROPHONE

By

AUGUSTUS MUIR

IT wasn't until the thing actually happened that I recalled
Dr. Louis Raphael's remark.

" When we take an evening off, Meredith," he said with
a smile as we drove away to attend the annual dinner of the
British African Society at the Sutherland Rooms, " when we
take an evening off like this, something always seems to go
wrong." But little did either of us dream how prophetic the
words were to prove. . . .

The dinner itself was a pleasant affair—a reunion of old
friends. Raphael had been a member of the society for years :
no doubt his interest in the Dark Continent arose from the
fact that most of his early life had been spent in North Africa.
Quite a couple of hundred must have been present, men from
the Cape and the Transvaal and Rhodesia, from Uganda and
Kenya and Somaliland, from the Gold Coast, Nigeria, and
the Egyptian Sudan, and a sprinkling of senior Army officers
home on leave.

The guest of honour was Paul Tarland, the young explorer
who had just arrived back in England after leading an expedition into the mountains of Southern Tanganyika. His prospective father-in-law, Henry Skene, the little grey-faced acid-
voiced financier, had put up the money for the expedition ;
and Skene himself sat at the chairman's table looking bored
and disgruntled, as usual, though he was no doubt inwardly
gloating over the fact that he and not Tarland was the real
hero of the evening.

When Paul Tarland rose to make his speech he got a great
ovation. He was slightly-built, but looked as tough as steel-
wire, with a rather ugly but not unpleasant face and a brown
scar on his cheek-bone. His engagement to Skene's adopted

daughter on the eve of setting out for East Africa had added a touch of romance to the affair, and the Press had given him a lot of publicity since his return on the previous Tuesday. It was whispered that he had discovered a valuable platinum-field, which would double if not treble the vast fortune which old Skene had already taken out of Africa. But Tarland had had the sense to be reticent ; and indeed his speech at the Sutherland Rooms (which was to be broadcast) was his first public announcement about his trip into the wilds.

Paul Tarland began his speech well. He spoke in a quiet conversational tone, his hands in the pockets of his dinner-jacket, and the microphone on the table did not seem to worry him. He did not strike me as a particularly modest man, but at least he had the wit to see that any oratorical flourish would have been out of place.

Next to him sat Henry Skene himself, scowling at the table-cloth, and Skene's other neighbour was Charles Fairley, the old man's friend and solicitor. Now and then, the rotund and ruddy-faced Fairley leant towards Skene and whispered a comment, which was seldom so much as acknowledged. Dr. Raphael and I were about half a dozen yards away, and I noticed that my employer seemed to be more interested in old Henry Skene than in the speech of the evening.

It was when a sudden burst of applause died down that a strange thing happened. The lights in the big banqueting-room went out.

Paul Tarland stopped talking. The darkness had come like a sudden thunderclap, and exclamations of surprise arose from all over the room. The chairman, Lord Whitburn, soon gave up the attempt to restore silence, and there was a burst of amused laughter from a distant table. I wondered how the B.B.C. people were coping with the unexpected interruption. Waiters bustled here and there, colliding with each other, and then a voice rang out above the din—a voice that was full of terror :

" The lights, for God's sake ! Something's happened—— "

The words brought sudden silence. When some waiter dropped a tray the metallic clatter seemed to penetrate into every corner of the banqueting-room.

" Lights—quick ! " This time it was a different voice, and I recognised it as Tarland's. As if in obedience to his order, the lights went on again.

Paul Tarland still stood stiffly erect, his hands in the pockets of his dinner-jacket. Two places away sat Charles

Fairley, the solicitor, his face white and horror-struck. Between them was the crumpled and motionless figure of Henry Skene with the haft of a knife jutting out above a crimson stain on his shirt-front.

*   *   *   *   *   *

The man was dead : there was no doubt about that. Raphael was the first doctor to reach his side, and they carried the body of the financier to a couch in the ante-room.

" Lock all the doors and let nobody leave the place—telephone Scotland Yard." Raphael gave rapid instructions to the manager, then called him back : " Ask for Inspector Hanson—if he's on duty, tell him I'm here.   Raphael's my name."

Through the heavy curtains, I could hear the chairman requesting the diners to resume their seats, and a subdued hum of talk rose in the air.

Charles Fairley's lips were twitching as he looked down on the dead face of his friend. " Can nothing be done ? "

Raphael shook his head. " The blade has pierced the heart. It must have been struck over his right shoulder. You were next to him, Mr. Fairley—did you hear any sound ? "

" I heard nothing—until he gave a queer gasp," replied the solicitor. " When I touched him, I felt there was something wrong, so I gave the alarm."

Paul Tarland was standing beside the couch, his mouth twitching. " Did *you* hear anything ? " Raphael asked him.

" Yes—it was like somebody bringing down his fist on the table. I thought nothing of it until Mr. Fairley called out. God, this is horrible ! Dead—who could have done this thing ? . . ." He dropped into a chair, his face between his hands.

" Pull yourself together, Tarland," said the solicitor, touching the younger man on the shoulder. " It's up to us to help the police—they'll be here in a few minutes."

" The police ! " Tarland looked up quickly. " Yes, of course. . . . After the lights went out, I thought I heard footsteps behind me—it may have been a waiter. . . ."

" Or one of the diners ! " added Raphael sharply, and turned to the solicitor. " I think perhaps you should get Mr. Skene's car round to the side door."

Charles Fairley nodded. " I'll see to it myself." Then he hesitated. " Mr. Skene sent his car home half way through dinner. A waiter came with a message that his chauffeur was feeling ill, and I heard him say he'd go home by taxi-cab."

" No matter," returned Raphael. " The police can arrange about the body."

Less than ten minutes later, Inspector Hanson arrived, followed by two other plain-clothes men, and in a few sentences Raphael told them the bare facts. Hanson rapidly examined the body of the dead financier, then hurried through into the banqueting-room.

" There's no need for anyone to wait now," he said on his return. " We've got the printed list of everyone present, and my men are taking the name and address of every waiter in the building." He drew Raphael aside. " Looks to me as if this was going to be a first-class sensation, doctor. That broadcast speech being interrupted by a murder—it'll be meat and drink for the newspapers. Well, I reckon we Yard people have got our work cut out. . . . There must have been two men on the job—one to work the lights. They were switched out in a cupboard along the passage, and the door locked."

" Isn't there another banquet going on upstairs ? " said Raphael. " That means dozens of temporary waiters. It would be easy for a stranger to move about."

" That's why I say we've got our work cut out, doctor ! I've arranged for an ambulance to take the body home. Could I have a statement from you two gentlemen ? " He stepped over to Paul Tarland and Mr. Fairley, who were talking together.

But they could throw no further light upon the tragedy, and Inspector Hanson fingered his moustache.

" Could I see you two gentlemen a little later to-night ? " he asked. " I want to make a further examination of the banqueting-room, and some points may arise. Could we meet in three-quarters of an hour at Mr. Skene's house ? "

" By all means," said Charles Fairley. " You've got the address, Inspector. It's 15 Burgrave Street, Regent's Park. This dreadful thing throws a lot of responsibility on my shoulders—I'm Mr. Skene's solicitor." He turned to Paul Tarland. " Hadn't you better go and break the news to Miss Bryant ? I believe she's dining out with friends to-night."

" Yes ; I know where to find her," said Tarland. " It'll be a horrible blow for poor Enid."

The two men hurried off, and we went back into the banqueting-room. No one could have called the dead financier a well-loved figure, but he had wealth and fame, and you could see from the faces of the departing members of the British

African Society that the tragedy had left them silent with dismay. Two or three pressmen who had been at the dinner were talking in subdued voices—they had already been in touch with their news-editors—and the B.B.C. engineers were removing the microphone which had transmitted the interrupted speech of the young explorer.

Dr. Raphael sat down in the chair which the dead man had occupied, and remained for several minutes with his eyes half-closed in thought, while Inspector Hanson was busy examining the floor.

" There's nothing to be found here, doctor," said the Scotland Yard man at length. " The murder must have been carefully planned—and by some devilishly clever brain."

" Never mind about the clever brain, Hanson," murmured Raphael. " What I'm wondering is why Henry Skene was murdered here, in this chair—to-night ! "

" Old Skene had his enemies," said Hanson.

" No doubt. But why should he have been killed in this room ? Was there some good reason why he should not leave this building alive ? We must find where he intended to go to-night—and whom he intended to meet. Until we know that, we're working in the dark."

But the contents of the dead man's pockets gave us no help ; and after the ambulance arrived for the body, we got into Raphael's motor-car, and I drove towards Regent's Park.

Hanson had already informed the butler of the tragedy by telephone, and the man still seemed a little dazed as he led us across Henry Skene's big luxuriously-furnished hall and switched on the lights in the library.

" The ambulance will be along presently," said the Inspector, and gave some instructions to the butler. " Have Mr. Tarland and Miss Bryant arrived yet ? "

" Not yet, sir."

He had hardly closed the door behind him when an exclamation burst from Raphael's lips, and he pointed to the desk in the corner of the room. Several of the drawers were open. Raphael stepped quickly to the curtains and swept them aside. The French window beyond was ajar.

" Someone's been here," he said rapidly, pulling out the top drawer of the desk. " Look—disorder ! Surely, Skene never left a desk in this state in his life."

Inspector Hanson gave a low whistle, and hurried forward. Raphael already had his magnifying-glass out, and was carefully running over the front of the desk.

"Whoever has been here," he said at last, "had the sense to wear gloves." He paused, and then peered into the top drawer. "What's this?" he muttered, picking something out and placing it carefully on the palm of his hand. It was a tiny piece of thin broken glass.

"How the devil did that get in there?" He looked at it for several moments through his magnifying-glass; then, folding it up in a sheet of paper, he placed it in his pocket, and began to close the drawers of the desk.

"If you take my advice, Hanson," he remarked, "you'll say nothing about this item to anybody—not even to Paul Tarland."

"Perhaps you're right, doctor," nodded the Inspector, who had turned to examine the French window. "What was that you said about Mr. Skene's chauffeur coming home early because he was ill?"

"Maybe the butler can give us further information," said Raphael, and was about to touch the bell when the library door was opened, and Mr. Charles Fairley was shown in.

"Has Tarland not turned up yet?" asked the solicitor in surprise, glancing at his watch. "It's a quarter to eleven now—he left the Sutherland Rooms at ten, the same time as I did," He lowered his voice and came nearer. "Well, I may as well take the chance while I've got it, Dr. Raphael. There's something I couldn't tell you while others were present. It's about the murder—Henry Skene was killed to-night by accident."

"By accident?" cried Inspector Hanson incredulously.

"Yes; I'm confident that I'm right. The murderer made a mistake in the darkness. The knife that killed my friend Skene was meant for me!"

Hanson was staring at the solicitor in surprise. "How do you make out that, sir?"

Charles Fairley drew in a long breath. "I don't mind telling you, Inspector, I've been a pretty scared man the last month or two. I was mixed up in an ugly case last December, and I was responsible for a tough called Lees getting seven years for blackmail. I had an anonymous warning from his friends to drop the case or I'd suffer for it, but I went on—and afterwards, I got a second message telling me to look out. I think Lees was connected with the Mutrie gang—and the Mutrie gang, well, you know what they are! I may be wrong, Inspector, but I believe I've given you the situation in a nutshell."

" You should have asked for police protection, sir ! " burst out Hanson. " This—this might never have occurred."

Fairley bowed his head. " Little did I think they meant to go to the length of murder ! But I should have known the Mutrie gang wouldn't stop short of that. However, it's too late to reproach myself now." His grey eyes flashed with sudden anger, and the good-natured lips were set. " If it *was* the Mutrie crowd, by God, I'll hunt them down, though it costs me every penny I possess . . ." His voice broke, and he turned away.

" We were talking about the chauffeur before you came in," said Raphael. " Do you happen to know anything about him ? "

" Nothing at all."

" It seems that he sent in a message to Mr. Skene at dinner that he was ill and would have to go home."

Mr. Fairley nodded.

" I heard a waiter deliver the message."

" Ring for the butler, Hanson," said Raphael. " Perhaps he can tell us something about the man."

The butler replied to Raphael's questions with some reluctance. " Cheston's only been with Mr. Skene for a few weeks, sir, and he's under notice to go. Rather a surly kind of man. The master didn't seem to take to him."

" He came away early from the Sutherland Rooms to-night,"-said Raphael. " Apparently he was feeling ill."

The butler looked surprised. " I didn't know that, sir ! He lives over the garage at the foot of the garden——"

" Then I'd like to see this man," returned Raphael quickly. " Can we go to him now ? "

" Certainly, sir, if you will kindly come this way."

We crossed the hall, and the butler led us through the back garden by the light of Inspector Hanson's pocket-torch, then knocked on a door at the top of an outside stair.

The door was opened by a thin sallow-faced man, whose small startled eyes stared at Raphael suspiciously as we stepped into the room.

" What time did you leave the Sutherland Rooms, Cheston ? "

The chauffeur hesitated, and his glance fastened for a moment on Inspector Hanson's face. " About nine, sir—I was feeling bad. Mr. Skene gave me permission——"

" What was wrong with you ? ' demanded Raphael.

" A splitting headache, sir, and feeling sick," muttered the man. " I think I got a chill. . . ."

" Then why aren't you in bed ? " Raphael put out his
hand to the man's pulse. " No chill about it ! Are you aware
your master was murdered to-night at the Sutherland Rooms
at twenty minutes past nine ? "

The trembling hand of the chauffeur went to his lips, and
with a gasp he fell back a couple of paces. " Good God . . ."

" Did you come straight back here ? "

The chauffeur found his voice. " Straight back—I swear
it ! This ain't . . ."

Raphael turned away. " Let's get back to the house, Mr.
Fairley." But as we were going down the stair, I heard him
whisper to Inspector Hanson : " Detail a man to watch him.
Get him out of the place to-morrow morning, and search his
room."

Paul Tarland had arrive in our absence, and with him was
Enid Bryant, fair-haired and slender. Her beautiful face was
tear-stained, but she spoke in a low restrained voice which was
now under remarkable control.

Tarland put his hand affectionately on his fiancée's shoulder.
" Enid's been very brave—they were like father and daughter
in many ways."

" We expected you a little earlier," remarked Raphael, looking at the clock, which showed that the hour was now eleven.

" Paul didn't come for me until a quarter of an hour ago,"
said the girl.

" Earlier—surely," he protested.

" No, Paul, it was a quarter to eleven ! "

Tarland brushed his hand across his eyes. " Perhaps
you're right. Yes, I—I remember now. I went to my rooms
in Jermyn Street first."

" Why, if I may ask ? " Raphael shot him à quick glance.

Paul Tarland shrugged his shoulders. " I felt rather
knocked out with the whole affair—I wanted a drink."

Raphael's eyes met Hanson's for an instant, and the
Inspector took a step forward.

" How long were you at your rooms, Mr. Tarland ? " he
inquired.

" Can't remember—oh, ten or twenty minutes. . . . ' And
then Tarland's eyes narrowed. " What the devil are you
driving at ? " he demanded angrily.

" You'll forgive me, Mr. Tarland, but I'm entitled to ask
anything that might help us in our investigation."

" Then get on quickly with your investigation," retorted
Tarland. " Any more questions ? "

"Just one, sir," said Hanson promptly. "Have your relations with the dead man always been cordial ? "

"Always."

The look on Enid Bryan's face was not lost upon the Inspector, and Tarland intercepted the glance. He made haste to correct himself.

"Well, to be frank, Mr. Skene was sometimes a difficult man to get on with. Ask Miss Bryant—she knew him better than anyone in the world."

Skene's adopted daughter nodded. "Yes, he was difficult —often."

We left the house ten minutes later, and the moment we got home Raphael went straight into his laboratory, where he unrolled a sheet of notepaper he took from his pocket, and picked up with a pair of forceps the tiny piece of glass he had found in the dead man's desk.

"Go to bed, Meredith," he said wearily. "I've got a couple of hours' work ahead of me."

How long he worked in his laboratory I do not know, but evidently the murder of Henry Skene had given him food for deep thought, for I could still hear the soft music of his piano when I awoke a little before dawn.

*   *   *   *   *   *

My employer did not appear for breakfast, and afterwards I was working quietly in the library when he strolled in.

"Ring up Charles Fairley's office in Lincoln's Inn Fields," he said, " and find out if he's arrived yet. I think he may be able to give us some further information."

I was switched through to the solicitor himself, and he told us to come right along at once.

"Good morning, Dr. Raphael," he said when we were shown into his big pleasant room overlooking the lawns and tennis-courts in the middle of the square. "I was hoping to see you to-day. The position of that chauffeur fellow puzzles me."

Raphael nodded. "Supposing he's connected with the Mutrie gang, and they were planning to pay off an old score with you—it's strange he should have taken employment with Henry Skene."

"Perhaps I'm mistaken about the Mutrie gang being responsible for the murder," admitted the solicitor, " yet I can't get the idea out of my head," He looked pale and a little haggard. " But if the wrong man *was* killed last night, Dr.

Raphael, then I'm in a devilish unpleasant position—and I'll be glad of all the police protection I can get. I hope to heaven I'm mistaken about it ! . . . Have you seen Tarland?"

" Not yet," replied Raphael. " I was wondering if you could tell me a little about him—confidentially, of course."

The solicitor pursed his lips. " I hope you'll be discreet, Dr. Raphael. You see, Tarland and I are joint-trustees of the estate under Henry Skene's will, and obviously it's important we don't fall out." Fairley gave a tired smile. " Last night he told you the old man was sometimes a little difficult to get on with, but I think I can mention another—Tarland himself ! No doubt this expedition has put him on the map as an explorer, but it's a good job he had a wealthy man like Henry Skene at his back. As far as money goes he's absolutely reckless, and there was some trouble between them over the expenses of the expedition. In fact, I think even bigger trouble was blowing up."

" Bigger trouble ? " repeated Raphael.

" Well, I know for a fact he borrowed a cool thousand from the old man two days ago." The solicitor hesitated. " I hope you'll keep your thumb on this, Dr. Raphael—it's a breach of confidence on my part. However, I suppose Tarland's all right now—his prospective wife comes into half a million under Skene's will. . . . I'm sorry for that poor girl —she's horribly cut up, though she doesn't show it. . . . What's your next step to be ? "

" I'm going to have another chat with the chauffeur," said Raphael quietly, and after a few minutes' further conversation we took our leave.

" Drive to Broadcasting House, Meredith," said my employer as we stepped into the car. " I learned this morning they took a Nestorphone record of Tarland's speech last night, and they've promised to run it over for me."

* * * * * *

Inspector Hanson was waiting for us in the vestibule of the building in Portland Place, and we were taken upstairs in the lift to a small room, with some electrical mechanism in a neat cabinet in the corner, and a small loud-speaker above it. There were few formalities, and little was said.

We took our seats, the instrument was started, and the voice of Tarland filled the room, talking in slow deliberate tones. Patiently we waited for the climax, when his voice stopped abruptly, and the loud buzz of conversation in the banquetting-room could be clearly heard. The chairman's voice called for silence, then tailed away, and presently above the hum of excited talk there was the faint sound of a thud and a low gasp, Raphael nodded, then sat upright in his chair. " What was the crackling noise," he exclaimed. " Run over that bit again, please."

Once more we heard the gentle thud, followed by the crackling to which Raphael had referred, and then there was a gentle tinkle, as if a wine-glass had been knocked over and broken against the edge of a plate. With Charles Fairley's anxious cry, and Paul Tarland's voice calling out " Lights—quick ! " the record came to an end.

Raphael rose to his feet.

" Immediately after the blow was struck," he said thoughtfully, " some papers were taken from Henry Skene's pocket. Mr. Fairley was wrong, Hanson. If the Mutrie gang had anything to do with this, I'll retire to the country and feed chickens ! "

Raphael's fingers were slowly tapping on the edge of the table, and then he looked towards the engineer who was stooping over the cabinet.

" Can you get permission to move this apparatus to the Sutherland Rooms to-night ? Very good. Have it there by eight o'clock—and bring the record of Mr. Paul Tarland's speech ! "

* * * * * *

I drove alone to Raphael's house on the Embankment, for he went off with Inspector Hanson ; and I sat at my typewriter in the library until six o'clock, when my employer rang me up on the telephone.

" Have your dinner early, Meredith," he said ; " I want you at the Sutherland Rooms by eight o'clock. . . ."

Without another word, he rang off, and I was left with no inkling of his intentions. Since he had not even given me a hint about the line his investigations might be taking in the afternoon, I turned up at the Sutherland Rooms a few minutes before eight o'clock in a state of puzzled suspense.

A uniformed policeman stood at the door of the ante-room, and it wasn't until he had referred to a list of names on a sheet of paper that he allowed me to pass through.

To my surprise, about a dozen men stood in groups, and I recognised them as those who had occupied the top table at dinner the previous night. Standing by himself in a corner was a sullen-faced man—Cheston, the chauffeur.

Raphael himself was talking to Inspector Hanson and Mr. Fairley, and a couple of plain-clothes men were at the curtains which had been drawn across the opening that led into the banqueting-room.

With a final word to the solicitor, Dr. Raphael stepped forward and spoke in a loud clear tone :

" Gentlemen, I would like to thank you for coming here to-night—at the request of Scotland Yard. The investigation of the death of the late Henry Skene has taken a turn that made your presence here necessary. I hope we won't detain you very long. Will you kindly take your places at the dinner table—the same places that you occupied last night."

The curtains were drawn aside, and the little company filed into the hall. Paul Tarland was the last to enter ; he walked slowly, his body held erect, his arms stiffly at his side.

When everyone was seated, Raphael ordered the chauffeur to take up his position near one of the doors ; and behind Lord Whitburn—who had been chairman on the previous night— a couple of B.B.C. men stood beside the cabinet I had seen at Broadcasting House.

A slight shiver ran down my spine as I looked around me. The appearance of the crowded banqueting-room last evening was a strange contrast to the present scene. A white cloth had been laid on the top table, but the others were bare, with chairs piled on them in long rows. It somehow reminded me of a house that had been dismantled after the funeral of its owner, and the empty chair of the dead man intensified the grim illusion.

I took up my position beside Raphael at the end of the table as he spoke again :

" Gentlemen, we are here to reconstruct the crime that was committed in this room last night. On the instrument behind you, there is a record of Mr. Tarland's speech, or as much of it as he delivered. At the appropriate point, the lights will be put out, and the room will remain in darkness for exactly three minutes."

He paused, and a gripping silence fell. A row of white strained faces were staring at him as he continued :

" You will hear from the record that the microphone picked up several sounds that might have escaped a human ear. For one thing, gentlemen, you will hear—perhaps faintly —the sound of papers being taken from the dead man's pocket immediately after the murder. If you listen carefully, you will also hear the noise of a wine-glass being broken, due to the murderer's haste." His voice dropped to a deliberate whisper. " *The gentleman who drank a liqueur called Kirsch-wasser after dinner last night will know exactly what I mean !* For the murderer of Henry Skene is among us. . . . Are you all ready ? Please stand up, Mr. Tarland ; your speech is about to be transmitted."

He snapped his fingers. Beside the cabinet, the engineer made a movement, and from the loud-speaker the voice of Paul Tarland was sent out across the banqueting-room. Everyone sat rigid in their places, some looking fixedly at Dr. Raphael, others with averted eyes. The air felt electric, and the strain grew almost intolerable. But the voice from the loud-speaker had barely uttered half a dozen sentences, when I caught my breath. For the room was suddenly plunged into complete darkness.

" What's gone wrong ? " It was Raphael's voice, and it rang out anxiously above the tones of the loud-speaker. The engineer at the cabinet switched off the record, and there was a momentary silence, which was broken by quick exclamations. " What's happened ? " cried Raphael. " Put up the lights. . . ."

He must have moved from my side, for I could hear nothing more except the mutter of voices at the table and the sound of chairs being hurriedly pushed back. Then there followed the sound of a blow, and one long gasping cry.

At last a dim light was switched on. Everyone had risen to his feet, and was staring about in consternation—everyone except Raphael himself. And he sat in the dead man's chair, his head sagging forward, the handle of a knife protruding from his crimson shirt-front.

For one horrible moment, the blood seemed to go icy in my veins. There was a long and breathless stillness, and then Raphael rose slowly to his feet, and flung down the handle of a knife on the table.

" That is all, gentlemen," he said quietly—" except the last step. . . ."

He turned slowly, his dark penetrating eyes fixed upon the deathly face of Charles Fairley at his side. " Except the last step ! " he repeated, and put out his hand.

But with a low cry, the solicitor pitched forward across the table in a dead faint. When he recovered his senses, there were manacles upon his wrists.

*   *   *   *   *   *

" I thought his nerve wouldn't stand the strain," said

Raphael to Paul Tarland and Enid Bryant when they called
the following afternoon. " My first idea was to reconstruct
the crime exactly, but I decided that an element of surprise—
with a slight touch of the dramatic—would have the desired
result: You see, our evidence against him was so slender,
it was necessary to catch him out—to make him commit himself. . . . How much do you say he had embezzled from Henry
Skene ? "

" We can trace about eleven thousand," replied Tarland,
" but we haven't had time to go through all the securities yet.
Mr. Skene must have had his suspicions, because Charles
Fairley was to have come to the old man's house after the
dinner and give a full explanation of a report he had sent in
the day before about some securities he'd been handling—
a report that must have been pretty unsatisfactory. That's
why he went through the old man's desk immediately after
the dinner and took everything that might have incriminated
him."

Raphael nodded. " And for the same reason, he removed
a sheaf of pencilled notes from Mr. Skene's pockets during
the few seconds after the murder. Charles Fairley left no
stone unturned to hide his guilt—just as he's now whining
for mercy. Well, if it hadn't been for a chip of his broken
wine-glass which I suppose must have lodged between his
cuff and sleeve—anyhow it dropped into the desk—he might
never have been detected. I fancy it was my reference to
Kirschwasser that broke his nerve."

Raphael held out his hand. In the centre of his palm lay
a tiny piece of crystal. " It was the most difficult piece of
analysis I have ever done in my life." He laughed. " Have
you ever tasted Kirschwasser, Mr. Tarland ? Never ? Nor
have I ! " He pointed to a bottle, newly uncorked, which stood
on a tray. " Then I suggest that we repair the omission ! "

DEATH IN THE KITCHEN

By

MILWARD KENNEDY

RUPERT MORRISON straightened himself, drawing a deep
breath. He glanced round the little kitchen, deliberately
looking at the figure which lay huddled on the floor ;
huddled, but yet in an attitude which Morrison hoped was as
natural as its unnatural circumstances would permit. For the
head was inside the oven of the rusty-looking gas-stove.

He wondered whether the cushion on which the head
rested was a natural or an unnatural touch. He decided that if
he were committing suicide, he would try to make even a
gas-oven as comfortable as possible.

He walked silently (for he was in stockinged feet) into the
passage, and so to the sitting-room. The curtains he had
drawn so carefully that he had had no hesitation in leaving on
the lights. Quickly but methodically he set to work. Nothing
must be left which connected him in any way with George
Manning. In any way ? Well, how about that package addressed not to Manning but to himself from the local grocer ?
Probably it had been delivered in error. Still, he must take
no chances. He put it aside for future attention.

Where did Manning keep his papers ? He was a careless
devil, not likely to hide them securely or ingeniously. No, here
they were in the writing-table. Only six that concerned
Rupert Morrison ; was that really all ? He untied the packet
and read each of the six. His cheeks reddened as he read ;
they were certainly damning. What a fool he had been in
those days ; still, he had been wise enough to remember it
when Manning turned up out of the blue (he could not have
spent *all* the interval in gaol ?) and started his blackmail.
George Manning on the other hand had grown foolish, for he
had not troubled to discover whether his victim had changed.

Morrison's clumsy gloved hands thrust the packet into his breast pocket. He considered. He had plenty of time. Manning, he knew, lived alone in the cottage, and had few friends, certainly none who were likely to call on him ; his domestic staff was limited to an old woman from the distant village who came in for part of the day.

The important thing was to be thorough. He had no alibi, and knew that it would be folly to fake one. Provided that there was nothing to show that he had a motive for wanting Manning dead, he would not have to account for his own whereabouts ; his tale of a country tramp across the fields and through the woods would not even be wanted. Outside the cottage there was, he knew, nothing to suggest any relationship between Manning and himself save such as might exist between two men, friends long ago in schooldays, who had drifted apart, and then by chance met again : the one respected and prosperous, the other—George Manning.

At last he was satisfied with the sitting-room, but there were still the two bedrooms. Bare, shabby rooms they were, and they did not keep him long. Down to the " parlour " once more. He was reluctant to leave it, for there, if anywhere, he would leave behind a key to the truth.

But he could think of nothing more, except the tumblers on the table and the grocer's package.

There must be only one glass, of course ; one must be washed and put away in the kitchen. The other ? It, too, must be washed, for when it was found there must be no trace of anything more deadly in it than whisky. Of course, he could wash it and provide fresh prints of Manning's fingers.

He had to make two journeys to the kitchen with the " properties " for the scene which he must set.

Soon one tumbler was back in the cupboard ; the other, on which, after he had washed it, he had carefully pressed Manning's limp hand, stood on the table, a trace of neat whisky in it. Beside it the bottle, nearly empty ; Manning certainly had been putting it away. That, no doubt, was why he had been so unnoticing when Morrison (none too neatly) had emptied his little flask into the tumbler. He gave a worried glance at the body ; if the dose had been too strong the whole plan might go astray. But that was absurd—he had felt the pulse only a minute ago.

And now the last detail—to put that half-sheet of paper on the table. He placed it to look as if it had been folded to catch the eye ; he dared not forge a superscription to the coroner.

He smiled ; it was a bit of luck that those words had so exactly filled a half-sheet in Manning's letter. Directly he had received it, months ago, he had seen its possible value. " I am tired of it all. Who can blame me for taking the easiest way ? So take it smiling—as I propose to do.—GEORGE MANNING." But it was cash that Manning had meant to take with a smile—not coal-gas.

There. And the window tight shut. Now to turn on the gas, leave the electric light burning, and be gone. Footprints ? No, his stockinged feet had left none, he was sure. Boots on. Quietly out by the back door, with nothing to carry but a walking-stick and that grocer's packet. . . .

Not a soul did Morrison meet on his way home, and when he had emptied the packet of sugar down the wash basin, and in the same way disposed of the ashes of its cover and of those six letters he took another deep breath—of relief this time. . . .

Naturally the police would come to him, for he was a man of standing and he was known to be on terms of acquaintance with Manning. He would be able to tell them that the " poor chap " had seemed very neurotic. . . . His " Good morning " smile as the sergeant was shown in was at these thoughts as well as a matter of policy.

" Yes, sergeant, I know him slightly." By Jove ! As nearly as no matter he had said " knew " ; he must watch his tongue.

" D'you recognise this, sir ? "

Good God ! What was the man holding up ? A pocket-book, dark blue, with a monogram. He put his hand to his breast pocket. No—could he—— He had an appalling memory of pushing those papers into his pocket. His gloved fingers had felt so clumsy. *Could* he have pulled it out and left it lying on the carpet—there ?

He put out his hand ; his power of speech seemed to have vanished. He took the pocket-book, half surprised that the sergeant allowed him to do so, and turned it over and over, and stared at it. What use was a denial ?

The sergeant was speaking. Was he warning him that anything he might say . . . ?

" That's the boy from Bayley's, the grocer, sir. Seems he delivered the wrong parcel—one for you, it was. Left it last evening at the cottage. Went first thing to get it back. Couldn't get a reply and the front door was locked, so he went round to the back. It seems the back door was open—of course, sir, he hadn't no right to go in, but . . ."

Why *would* the fool bother about that ?   Go on, man.   My
heart won't stand this.
   " Electric light burning in the kitchen and this Manning
lying with his head inside the oven.   Gave the boy a shock, so
he says, but if you ask me . . .   Anyways, he came along on
his bike to me—I found the pocket-book, sir, in the sitting-
room.   I thought I'd have a word with you.   You see, this
Mr. Manning—well—sir, there's a police record."
   Why must he pause ?   Did he expect an answer ?   Morrison
could only stare, his lips trembling.
   " Course, sir.   You may have given it to him.   Or it may
just have been an accident. . . ."
   What was " it " ?   Even if he could have spoken, Morrison
would have refused now.
   " But apart from that, sir—his record and that, I mean—it
struck me there was something queer about Manning.   And I
thought maybe you could help me.   That gas-oven, sir, that
looks like suicide, doesn't it, sir ? "
   " Yes—I suppose so."
   Was that really his voice ?
   " There was a bottle of whisky on the table—that came from
Bayley's yesterday afternoon, too, and it was empty all but a
drain this morning.   Maybe it was that that did it. . . ."
   What *had* gone wrong ?   How had this local bumpkin
stumbled on the truth ?
   " At any rate, sir, whisky or lunacy, would you have thought
anyone, drunk or sober, could put his head in a gas-oven and
turn the tap—and forget the gas was cut off because he hadn't
paid the bill ?   I can understand how it is he's forgotten every
blamed thing about what happened last night, but—Hallo, sir,
what's up ? "
   Rupert Morrison was lying at the sergeant's feet.

THE VERTICAL LINE

By

FREEMAN WILLS CROFTS

THE sweat was running down Arnold Wilde's forehead as from his sitting-room window he watched Chief Inspector French and Sergeant Carter leave his house. It had been a bad half hour, that which was just over, the worst he had ever known in his life. For French was close to the truth, hideously, damnably close, and it had taken all Wilde's brains and skill to preserve his secret intact.

But he had preserved it! That was the great outstanding fact : the only fact which really mattered. French could guess and suspect as much as he liked, but he could *prove* nothing. He, Wilde, had been too clever for him. He had been too clever for any detective who could be put on the job His scheme was without a flaw and he had carried it out with absolute precision.

For Wilde was a criminal. He had just committed a murder—and he was getting away with it.

Arnold Wilde was a technical assistant in the firm of Scott & Son, analytical chemists, of Barchester in Wiltshire. In skill, knowledge and ingenuity he was quite first class, and would quickly have risen in his profession had it not been for a certain impatience or recklessness which made him quick to meet an emergency, but intolerant of humdrum or routine work.

It was this very quality of impatience, coupled with a healthy but uncontrolled love of adventure, which led him into the mad break from which all his later troubles had come.

He had fallen in love and he had not money enough to carry on the courtship as he desired. He could not take Alys Deane to theatres and on week-end excursions, nor give her the continuous presents she so obviously considered her due. He was desperately in love, and he was desperately afraid of losing her. Then the chance of helping himself to the firm's money had come, and with his fatal desire for short cuts and immediate results, he had taken advantage of it.

Though Wilde had never allowed himself to be bound by moral scruples, it was the first time he had gone in for theft on a large scale, and five minutes had not passed before he bitterly regretted his action. But it was then too late. The opportunity of replacement had passed. Restitution would have involved confession, and whatever confession would have meant, it would have included the loss of Alys Deane. Instead he set himself to cover up what he had done, managing to divert suspicion from himself by inventing a mythical individual, traces of whose forced entry to the principal's room he carefully provided.

His scheme had succeeded to the extent of taking in his principals and the local inspector of police who was sent to investigate the theft. After a few days of sharp anxiety Wilde began to breathe more freely. But he had exulted too soon.

On the third evening he was called mysteriously aside by one of the laboratory assistants, a man named Hubbard. Hubbard was indirect in everything he did and it was some time before Wilde realised the significance of what he was hearing. But when he did so, the knowledge was like a blow between the eyes.

Hubbard knew the truth. He had seen Wilde arrange the evidence of the mythical thief.

At first Wilde pictured immediate ruin : dismissal, the police court, prison. . . . But he soon learned that this was not Hubbard's idea. Hubbard was on to a good thing and he was going to make the most of it. In short, his knowledge was a marketable asset, at the disposal of Wilde—for a consideration.

Wilde had paid—he could not help himself. Then like others before him he had discovered that his payment was only temporarily effective. A further payment was required. And still another. . . .

After a year Wilde found himself being slowly bled to death. Most of the money he had stolen had by this time found its way into Hubbard's pockets. Alys had not, it was true, formally broken with him. But he had not improved his position with her, and he was under no misapprehension as to how the present state of affairs would end.

And now Hubbard had made a further demand for a slice

of Wilde's pay. It was a demand which, if admitted, would definitely bring the Alys Deane affair to an end. Wilde swore bitter oaths to himself that nothing would induce him to submit to it.

But what could he do ?

He knew what he could do. All those months of thrawldom had not passed in vain. They had bred a Plan. Yes, he knew what he could do.

Very carefully he worked out the details. His former scheme of the Mythical Thief had been a brilliant success. He would try it again. He would create a Mythical Murderer !

He temporised with Hubbard. He could not pay during the present month : he had spent too much of his salary. He would begin with his next month's cheque.

Hubbard was taken in. He agreed ; and Wilde began the carrying out of the Plan.

First he disguised himself : not ignorantly with a wig and false moustache, but skilfully with glasses, different clothes, a cap instead of his usual hat, and small pieces of rubber in his cheeks. In London he bought an airgun. It was a toy in a sense : scarcely a serious weapon. But Wilde was going to fire into Hubbard's head from only a couple of inches away and he knew it would kill. At shops in different areas he bought also a pair of rubber gloves, a small crowbar, and a second-hand pair of hobnailed shoes, two sizes too big for him, " to help a chap I know to get a job."

The laboratory in which the two men and three other workers were employed was to be the scene of the crime. It was a large ground floor room overlooking the garden of the suburban house used by the firm. The garden was hidden by trees from the observation of neighbours, and Wilde was sure that if the house itself were empty, he could approach and leave the window unseen.

The room was furnished with the usual apparatus for four working chemists. Of these Wilde was one, and Hubbard was assistant to the four. Hamilton, the senior, who over-looked the others' work, had in addition a large roll topped desk. This desk was placed with its back against the wall, and beside it on the right was the sink, bench and stink cupboard Hamilton used. The stink cupboard was in the corner of the room, and close by in the wall at right angles was a window. The top of the desk bore a heterogenious collection of personal treasures, which Hamilton guarded as the apple of his eye. Besides the telephone there was a curiously marked piece of

feldspar which he had picked up on the slopes of the Matter-
horn, a rain gauge which he had said for months he was going
to set up in the garden, a large barograph whose records he
carefully studied week by week, a bottle of Dead Sea water
whose purpose no one had ever been able to discover, and
another bottle containing the vertebrae of a snake which he
had killed in the Pyrenees.

Work normally stopped at half past five, but it any of the
men were in the middle of a test at quitting time, they usually
waited to complete it. Hubbard seldom got away till after the
others, as it was his business to clean up and put away the
apparatus they had used.

With the plea ready of extra work in case he should be
observed, Wilde on several nights returned late to the laboratory to test out the Plan. He went over its every detail till he
was absolutely satisfied it would not fail him. Then he began
to watch for an evening to put it into operation.

The conditions were simple. All that was necessary was
that he and Hubbard should be alone in the building. He
made it his business to learn his companions' plans, so as to be
sure that when they had once left for home, they would not
return.

A suitable evening soon came and Wilde seized the opportunity. He delayed over his work till the others had gone,
pretending that a series of tests had run out longer than he had
anticipated. Surreptitiously he watched Hubbard moving
about the laboratory, collecting test tubes and other dirty
apparatus and carrying them to the sink beside Hamilton's
desk, where he would presently wash them.

Except for occasional distressing qualms, Wilde had up to
this been cool enough about his terrible undertaking. But now
that the moment was upon him he realised what it was he was
doing and grew almost sick with fear and horror. However he
had provided against this also. From his pocket he took a
bottle of brandy and fortified himself with a good nip. It
pulled him together and he became once more his own man.

With the feeling that the action constituted a burning of
his boats, a making irrevocable of his dreadful intention, he
heaved an audible sigh and exclaimed : " There, thank the
Lord that's done ! " going on presently : " I've got a few test
tubes for you, Hubbard. I'll bring 'em across."

Hubbard, his head bent over the sink, grunted. Wilde
seized his airgun, which he had hidden in his locker, and
walked boldly across the room. Hubbard did not look up.

Wilde presented the muzzle of the gun to the back of the man's neck. It was almost touching, and as the head was bent down, the bullet would certainly penetrate to the brain.

Suddenly suspicion seemed to arise in the assistant's mind. He dropped his test tubes and began to swing round. But before he could do so Wilde fired. The report was negligible. Hubbard hung for a moment motionless. Then with a soft choking cry he fell sideways on to Hamilton's desk and from there slid slowly down to the floor. A convulsive tremour passed over his body and lay still.

In spite of the brandy Wilde grew cold and faint. Then once again he pulled himself together. Now was the time for care and coolness ! If he made a mistake now, he was lost.

Quickly he began to work. And first as to the position of the body. A glance told him it was satisfactory. Anyone could see that the man had been working at the sink when he was hit, and as the question of powder blackening did not arise, anyone might suppose that he had been shot through the window. So far, so good.

The next thing was to supply the traces of the assailant. Putting on his rubber gloves and taking the crowbar and shoes, Wilde let himself into the garden. It was almost, but not quite dark : just light enough to see what he was doing, just dark enough to be practically safe from observation. Keeping on the hard walks he went to a small gate leading in from the lane behind the houses. He let himself out with the communal office key, locked the gate behind him, and with the bar forced the lock from the outside. Then he put on the nailed shoes and again went through the motions of forcing the gate, for though the ground at the place was hard, he thought the nails might show. He walked out along the comparatively soft lane till he reached hard road, then returned, taking care not to tread on any of his outward bound footsteps.

Continuing on to the window, which, being normally open at the top, was unlatched, he pushed up the lower sash while standing on the rather untidy flower bed alongside the house. Then he entered, stepped beside the body, and knelt down as if to search it. He straightened himself up again, climbed out of the window, and leaving the lower sash fully up, walked back to the gate. This time he was careful to tread on at least one of his previous prints. At the gate he changed his shoes once again, and carrying the nailed pair, he returned over hard walks to the laboratory.

Here was the trail of the Mythical Murderer, to provide

which was the second part of his Plan. But there was still a third. There must be proof that the Mythical Murderer was not himself.

Retaining his rubber gloves, he quickly reconstructed the apparatus with which he had so carefully experimented. Taking from his pocket a piece of fine thread with the ends knotted together to form a loop, and which at one point he had frayed half-through, he put it over the telephone hook. He saw that the frayed part was just on the hook. Then he got a large beaker or glass jar and placed it in the sink adjoining. He fixed it so that it leant inwards at an angle of forty-five degrees, its base standing across the angle between the side and bottom of the sink. It was just balanced, but to make sure it remained in position he slipped the loop of thread round it close to its top. He had made the loop just large enough to fit tightly. The beaker was thus, as it were, supported by the loop of thread from the telephone hook.

Wilde then removed the telephone receiver. This he could do without calling up the exchange, as the thread loop kept the hook down. Stretching the flex to its fullest extent, he seized Hubbard's right hand and closed it on the receiver. The hand would not of course remain gripped, so Wilde let it fall to its former position. The receiver he left swinging on its flex.

Wilde now had a good look round the room to see that he had forgotten nothing. Then having fastened previously prepared weights to the nailed shoes and the gloves, he put these in his pockets, hid the airgun and bar under his jacket and down his trouser leg, and covered all with an overcoat.

There remained but one further detail. Just before leaving Wilde turned on slightly the water-tap at Hamilton's sink. He had placed the beaker with its top beneath the tap. In from twenty minutes to half an hour the glass would fill sufficiently to overturn. The thread would break, the telephone hook would rise, and a call would be made at the exchange. This would fix the hour of the tragedy. At that hour he, Wilde, would be dining with a number of friends at a small club he frequented.

Wilde was well pleased with his scheme. It contained nothing that could possibly give him away. The upturned beaker and the dripping tap would suggest only that Hubbard was actually at work when he was shot—which would be the truth. The thread was of the kind continuously in use in the laboratory and its presence would therefore be normal and

He dropped his test tubes and began to swing round. Before he could do so Wilde fired.

unsuspicious. Moreover it could not draw attention to the telephone, as the position of the frayed portion would insure that it would break over, and come clear away from, the hook.

Close to the house ran the deep river on which the town was built. It was crossed by a footbridge but little frequented after dark. Wilde ran out on to the bridge and threw the air-gun, bar, shoes and gloves into the black water, as far down stream as he could. They disappeared with hollow splashes. Ten minutes later he was in his club and with an innocent but carefully thought out remark had called the attention of his companions to the time.

The next day or two had been a ghastly ordeal, but as time passed Wilde grew reassured. He was safe. No one could know what he had done.

But at this last interview with French and Carter his confidence had been rudely shattered. French's questions had been terribly disquieting. It seemed certain that he suspected the truth. He had at all events discovered the trick of the alibi. Wilde struggled to hide the panic he felt creeping over him. Again and again he told himself that French could guess and suspect as much as he liked, but he could *prove* nothing. And as long as French could *prove* nothing, he, Wilde, was safe.

All the same as he watched French and Carter going away down the street, he sweated with real fear.

A little later Chief Inspector French and Sergeant Carter were back for the *n*th time in the laboratory. French was looking worried.

" That blighter's going to get away with it," he growled. " He's as guilty as sin, but his counsel would work that telephone stunt with the jury and get him off."

Carter mumbled an unwilling agreement.

" We must get him, no matter what it costs us," French went on. " Just let's go over the blessed case again. Perhaps one of us may see something we've overlooked. I'll put it to you and it may help us both."

French began pacing slowly backwards and forwards as he talked.

What struck us first was the receiver lying off the telephone. Owing to the disappearance of the gun the case was an obvious murder, and the idea suggested was clearly that the deceased saw his danger and was about to call for help, but that before he could do so, he was shot."

Carter nodded, a wary eye on his chief.

" But," went on French, " can you or anyone else imagine the murderer leaving the receiver off ? As long as it remains off it is a signal to the exchange that something is wrong. It's at least on the cards that they may ring up someone close by to have a look. If—as actually happened in this case—one of the partners rang up Hubbard to give him some altered instructions for the next day, he would be told something was wrong. He was told in this case and the tragedy was discovered. Now the murderer would not want that discovery to be made till the last possible moment.

" On the other hand, if the receiver is replaced on the hook, it only means that it was lifted in error. Surely if Hubbard had really tried to phone, the murderer's first act would have been to replace the receiver ? "

Carter nodded more appreciatively.

" This is of course a purely speculative point which proves nothing whatever, but it does suggest that this telephone signal *may* have been a plant, probably intended to fix an erroneous hour for the crime."

" That's right, sir." Carter agreed heavily.

" We test the receiver for finger prints and what do we find ? Again something suggestive, though inconclusive. We find that if the deceased picked up the receiver, he gripped it in a particularly awkward way : diagonally across his hand, too far from the wrist opposite the thumb, too near it opposite the little finger. He *might* in his hurry have so grasped it, but it's unlikely. Again there's the suggestion of a plant."

French turned towards the sink. " Here in the sink we find an assortment of objects. A dripping tap ; a large beaker lying on its side beneath it ; under the beaker a broken loop of thread, partially frayed at the break. Nothing suspicious there—at first."

" That's where the value of routine work comes in, sir," Carter said with slightly exaggerated innocence.

French glanced at him keenly. " Yes, I have pointed that out, haven't I ? " he returned drily. " And I was right this time—if never before." He glared and Carter's manner grew less assured. " Routine work told us that none of the men in that room had used either a beaker or a piece of thread of that length that day."

" Pretty neat, sir," Carter remarked ingratiatingly.

" Incidentally, though we didn't suspect Wilde so far, that's where he made a bad mistake. He should have been able to prove that he had used both. However he didn't twig that till too late."

" The beaker, the thread, the telephone," Carter murmured. " Something fishy about all three."

" Quite : it's easy to repeat a well-known argument. Was there a connection ? Not easy to see one. Then at long last the position of the thread under the beaker and the length of its broken ends does suggest something. We find if the beaker was partially raised, the loop would just go over the telephone hook. We get another thread and reconstruct. Then we turn on the tap and watch what happens. We see the beaker slowly filling till it turns over and snaps the thread and releases the hook. That takes about twenty minutes. The beaker and thread fall where they were found. So there is no longer any doubt."

" But we can't prove it, sir."

" Ah, Carter, how wise you are ! We can't. However, to continue. Routine work again tells us the time at which each member of the staff left the place, and we learn that Wilde was the last to go. We ask him what time he left and he tells us six o'clock. We have no reason to doubt it. But the telephone rings at 6.20, and we note that that was just twenty minutes later. At that hour, 6.20, all the members of the staff, including Wilde, have watertight alibis. We wonder if one of them arranged the time plant. If so, it could only have been Wilde, as he was the last to leave."

" It's a good case, sir, if you ask me."

" I don't ask you," French returned, " because I know you're wrong. We then look for motive. Who could have desired this man's death ? And here at last our excellent routine work gets something more encouraging.

" The deceased was undoubtedly living beyond his income. From some unknown source he was getting cash. Where was it coming from ?

" More routine work. Was anyone else concerned living below his income ? Great trouble to find this out. A week's work for half a dozen of us. But worth it when we get the answer. Wilde had a decent salary, but lived as if he was chronically hard up. And he had saved nothing."

" We can't prove the money passed from Wilde to the deceased."

" No. Neither can we prove blackmail, though our present line of enquiries may tell us that. Then there was the question of the footprints."

" The best bit of work I ever heard of."

" I admit it wasn't too bad," French said with more complaisance. " The length of the pace was small for the size of the shoes. That set us thinking. And we found that the length of the pace, and more important still, the angle at which the toes were turned out, were precisely those of Wilde's normal walk. Practically conclusive to you or me, but still not good enough for court."

French had continued to pace the room, but now he pulled up at the desk. " The position of the body showed that it hit the desk in falling. Let's move the desk a bit. Something might have rolled underneath it."

They pushed the desk sideways. It clung to the oilcloth, then slid with a sudden jerk. Both men searched the floor. There was nothing.

" I didn't expect anything," French admitted, " because though I hadn't moved it, I had already looked below it. Let's have it back again."

But instead of pushing it back, French stood rooted to the ground, staring straight before him with excitement growing in his eyes. Then like a madman he began striking the desk, with his shoulder, with his fist, while still he gazed. " Carter," he gasped, " have we got that blighter after all ? Show me the photographs."

Carter took from a despatch case prints of the photographs which had been taken first thing on the arrival of the police, some hour after the crime. French hurriedly turned them over and selected a large detailed view of the front of the desk, showing everything in and upon it with great clearness. He whipped out a lens. A glance through it was evidently sufficient. He smote his thigh a mighty blow.

" We've got him, Carter ! We've got him ! Proof, absolute and complete and as neat as we could wish ! Come one : we'll go and see him again."

Wilde had sweated after his ordeal as he had watched French and Carter leave his rooms. He grew positively sick with terror when he saw them coming back. If all were well, why should they come back ? Hurriedly he crossed to a cupboard and took out his bottle of brandy.

" Just another question or two, Mr. Wilde," French said gravely when they were seated. " But first I'm bound to warn you again that whatever you say will be taken down and may be used in evidence. Also that you need not answer my questions unless you like. But you said you wished to make a statement and did so. Are you willing to add to that statement ? "

Momentarily Wilde hesitated. " I've nothing to hide," he said with an assumption of ease. " I'll answer your further questions if I can."

French immediately began. But he surprised Wilde. He repeated questions which he had already asked, inoffensive questions, irrelevent questions even. Wilde began to breathe more freely. There was nothing to be alarmed about. It was simply a case of official stupidity.

" You stated that you were alone in the laboratory with the deceased from about half past five, when the others left, to about six, when you left yourself. Do you stick to that statement ? "

" Certainly."

" Where were you working ? "

" At my bench, as I said." Relief was growing in Wilde's mind and was reflected in the tone of his replies.

" From your bench you could see Mr. Hamilton's desk ? "

" Yes, it was straight in front of me."

" Now during that half hour did anything heavy strike the desk ? "

Wilde's relief suddenly evaporated. With terrible clarity he saw in his mind's eye the body growing limp, crashing against the desk, and from it to the floor. Why had French asked this question ? Could it be—that he knew ? And what should he, Wilde, answer ? If yes, what could he say had fallen ? If no, would he give himself away ?

With a dreadful feeling of misgiving he realised that he was delaying his reply. Delay would be fatal. He plunged. Nothing had struck the desk.

" I want to be absolutely certain about that, Mr. Wilde," French went on with relentless insistance. " Your definite statement is that while you were in the room between half past five and six, the desk was not struck a heavy blow ? Is that correct ? Think carefully before you speak ? "

Wilde, terror stricken lest a trap should lurk in the question, now wished he had said he had himself fallen against the desk. But it was too late. He dare not reverse his statement.

" I have already said," he declared, striving desperately for composure, " and I now repeat, that nothing struck the desk while I was in the room."

French nodded, paused, and then gathered himself with

something suggestive of an animal crouching to spring. " I told you that we had discovered the plan by which the telephone call might have been given some twenty minutes after the murderer had left the room : the beaker and thread and so on ? "

" Yes, but that has nothing to do with me," Wilde murmured through dry lips.

" Let me finish," French persisted. " The medical evidence indicates that the deceased struck the desk in his fall. The only question then is, When did he fall ? "

Panic was closing down on Wilde. He could not see where this was leading, but there was something utterly terrifying in French's manner. He nodded without speaking. He could not speak.

" Let me tell you what happened just now," French went on. " We, Sergeant Carter and I, had occasion to move the desk. It stuck to the oilcloth, then came free suddenly. The effect on the desk was a sudden shock, much the same as if a body fell on it."

Wilde could only stare helplessly.

" Do you know what happened as a result of that shock ? Well, I'll tell you. The pen of the barograph vibrated. It recorded a tiny vertical line across its ordinary trace. You see ? " French paused, then took the photograph from his case and with a lens handed it across. " Now here," he went on, " is a photo taken about seven on the evening of the crime. Let us look at the trace of the barograph. What do we find ? We find the pen pointing to seven o'clock with the trace leading back from it, every hour being shown on the scale. Across that trace is a vertical line—one vertical line. Since there is only one, it must represent the fall of the body. Now do you see the hour ? That line was drawn at just a quarter before six."

There came a slight sound in the ensuing silence. Wilde had fainted.

THE CLUE OF MONDAY'S SETTLING

By

EDGAR WALLACE

I T did not seem possible to May Antrim that such things could happen in an ordered world. She paced the terrace of the big house overlooking the most beautiful vale in Somerset, her hands clasped behind her, her pretty head bent, a frown of perplexity upon her pretty face.

Everything must go . . . Sommercourt . . . the home farms . . . the house in Curzon Street . . . her horses . . . she checked a sob and was angry with herself that it needed the check.

And why ?

Because John Antrim had signed a paper—she thought such things only happened in romances. Her father's stability she had never questioned. She knew, as all the county knew, that he was a wealthy man beyond fear of disaster. And out of the blue had come this shattering bolt. It was incredible. Then she caught a glimpse of him. He was sitting in his favourite seat at the far end of the terrace, and at the sight of that dejected figure, she quickened her pace.

He looked up with a faint smile as she came up to him, dropping her hand on his shoulder.

" Well, May ? Thinking things out, too ? "

" I'm trying to," she said, " but I find it difficult to make a start. You see, dear, I don't understand business . . ."

" Sit down."

He made a place for her by his side.

" I'm going to tell you a story. Sounds formidable, eh ? It begins on the 18th of March when the steamship *Phœnician Prince* left New York for Southampton. She is a vessel of 18,000 tons, one of two, the property of the Balte Brothers, Septimus Balte and Francis Balte being the partners who control the stock."

" Our Francis ? " asked the girl in surprise.

" Our Francis," repeated John Antrim grimly.

He went on :

" On board were five million in British, French, and Italian notes, which had been redeemed from the American money market, and were being consigned to the Anglo-American Bank of London. These were packed in six tin cases, soldered air and water tight, and enclosed in stout wooden boxes. They were deposited in the strong-room, which is on the port side of G Deck. Its door opens into a cabin which is occupied in extraordinary circumstances by a quartermaster.

" On this occasion one of the owners was on board, Mr. Francis Balte, and because of the importance of the consignment he had the quartermaster's cabin fitted up for his own use. During the day, and when Mr. Balte was absent from the cabin, it was occupied by his personal steward, Deverly.

" Francis kept the key of the strong-room in his possession. It never left him day or night. On the night of the 26th, the purser went to Francis with certain documents relating to the money. Francis opened the doors of the strong-room and the purser checked the packages ; the door was closed and locked. There was no bathroom attached to the cabin, and Balte used an ordinary sponge bath which was brought in by the steward, together with a dozen small towels. These were used to lay on the floor, with the idea of saving the carpet, which had been newly laid—in fact, especially for Mr. Balte's comfort. The steward went in later, took away the bath and six towels, the other six being unused."

, May frowned again. What had the towels to do with the narrative ?

He must have interpreted her thoughts.

" I have interviewed the steward," he said, " and the loss of the towels seemed to him to be the queerest part of the whole proceedings. The next morning, as the ship approached the Needles, the purser came down, accompanied by half a dozen seamen. Balte was asleep, but he got up and handed the key of the strong-room to the purser, who opened the doors, to find—nothing."

He groaned.

" I should never have underwritten such a vast amount."

" You underwrite ! " she gasped. " Is that why . . . you are responsible for the money ? "

He nodded.

" It was stark madness," he said bitterly. " Ordinarily I should only have been saddled with a small proportion of the loss. But in a moment of insanity I accepted the whole risk. That is the story.

" The ship was searched from end to end—every inch of it. The steward was on duty in the alleyway outside—he sat with his back to the door, dozing, he admits. It was impossible for anybody to get through the porthole, supposing, as was the first theory of the police, that a man let himself down over the side and scrambled through the port. The steward was full of the mystery of the towels—six towels and six boxes of notes ! But in one respect he was very informative. He distinctly heard in the middle of the night a sound like that of a watch or clock being wound up. ' Creak, creak, creak '—he gave me a wonderful imitation."

" What on earth was it ? "

" He heard it six times faintly but distinctly. He says so now, but he also says that he thought it might have been the creaking of gear—one hears strange noises on board ship. And we come again to the fact that six towels were missing. To my mind that is significant. The boxes were very heavy, by the way, many of the notes were of small denomination and had been subjected to hydraulic pressure in the packing to get them into as small a compass as possible. Roughly each box weighed 140 pounds with its iron clamps and bands."

May was interested.

" I never realised that paper money had weight," she said. " How many five pound notes could an ordinary man carry ? "

" A strong man could carry £100,000 worth," replied Antrim, " but he would not care to carry that amount very far. So there it is, my dear. Somewhere in the world is a clever thief in the possession of nearly a third of a ton of negotiable paper. And I am responsible."

They sat in silence until——

" Daddy . . . why don't you see Bennett Audain ? "

" Bennett ? " he was startled, and then a smile played at the corner of his lips. " Bennett came to me just before I left town. He had heard from somebody that I was involved and, like the good fellow that he is, offered to help with . . . with money. I had an idea that I would see Francis."

She pursed her lips thoughtfully. Francis Balte she knew and did not dislike. She had met him at the house in town—a vague, cheery man, full of commonplace phrases.

" You mean that I should let Bennett take the case in

hand ? " asked John Antrim, with a little grimace. " I mistrust amateur detectives, and although I admit your cousin is clever —he is also the veriest amateur. Curiously enough the loss of the towels interested him more than the loss of the money."

Her mind was made up.

" You are to telephone Bennett that we are dining with him to-night," she said determinedly.

" My dear—— "

" Daddy, you must do it—I feel that Bennett is the one man who can help."

*   *   *   *   *   *

The real seven ages of man's conscious existence may be divided into the periods when he wishes to drive a locomotive, when he wants to be a detective, an Adonis, a soldier (or sailor), a millionaire, a prime minister, and a boy.

Bennett Audain never got beyond the second period, but realised some of the others, for he had been a soldier, he was undoubtedly good-looking, and as unquestionably rich.

The right kind of obsession is an invaluable asset for a young man of great possessions, and to current crime he devoted the passionate interest of the enthusiast. He was both student and worker ; he had as great a knowledge of the science which is loosely described as " criminology " as men who had gained fame in its exposition ; he certainly understood the psychology of the criminal mind better than any police officer that ever came from Scotland Yard—an institution which has produced a thousand capable men, but never a genius. Indefatigable, patient, scientific in the sense that science is the " fanaticism for veracity," which is the scientist's basic quality.

" It is queer that a fellow like you should take up psychoanalysis. I should have thought it was just a little off your beat." John Antrim looked critically through his glass of port.

" There are queerer things," said Bennett, with an amused glance at the girl. " It is queer, for example, that having taken a hundred-mile journey to consult me about the strongroom robbery, you haven't yet mentioned it."

The girl smiled, but the frown on her father's face deepened.

" Don't sneer at psycho-analysis, Daddy," she warned him. " Bennett will give us a demonstration—won't you, Bennett ? "

They were dining together at Bennett Audain's house in Park Lane. The big room was dark save for the shaded lamps on the table and the soft glow that flushed the Persian rug before a dying fire.

Bennett had a nervous smile, charming in its diffidence.

"That is a popular label for a queer new system of mind-probing," he said. "I am not accepting or rejecting the Freudian philosophy, and I'm not enough of a doctor to understand his theory of neuroses. I merely say that those responsible for the detection and prevention of crime might, with profit, employ the theory of idea-association."

A gust of wind blew a pattering of rain against the curtained window.

"Humph!" said John Antrim, and looked at his watch.

Bennett laughed softly.

"I knew you would look at your watch when you heard the rain," he said, and the other stared.

"Why?"

"Association of ideas," said the other calmly. "You told me when you came that you thought of leaving May in London and driving back alone to Sommercourt. Uncle John," he leant across, coming from the dusk of shadow into the yellow light, "if I could get the right man to question I would save you exactly a million!"

Antrim frowned horribly.

"I doubt it," he said, in his gruffest tone. "I have been caught. But I was a fool to underwrite the whole consignment —a mad fool. You can do nothing; the best and cleverest police officers are working on the case. What could you do— by psycho-analysis?"

He leant back with a sigh.

"Who is the right man?" asked May eagerly.

Bennett, his eyes fixed on vacancy, did not answer at once.

"Where is Francis?"

The girl started, as well she might, for the question was shot at him with unexpected violence.

"I'm sorry—only I had an idea"—Bennett Audain was apologetic to a point of panic. "I—I get a little explosive at times, which is terribly unscientific——"

"But is human," smiled the other.

John Antrim got up.

"I wonder if he is at the Elysium Club——"

"There is a 'phone over there." Bennett pointed to the shadows. "It is rather late, but perhaps he'll come round."

Antrim hesitated. Before he could make up his mind what to do, May was 'phoning.

Apparently Balte was at the club.

" He's on his way," she smiled ; " poor soul, he was most embarrassed to hear my voice."

May returned to the table.

" Heavens, what a night ! You can't return to Sommercourt, Daddy."

The rain was swishing savagely at the windows, the ceaseless broom-like sweep of it across the panes, the faint tick of the enamel clock on the high mantelpiece, and the wheezy breathing of Bennett's old terrier, stretched before the fire, were the only sounds in the room until Balte came with a clatter.

He was a stout man of thirty-five, fair and ruddy of face, and he brought into the shadowy room something of his own inexhaustible vitality.

" Glad to come, Miss Antrim." He stopped dead at the sight of John Antrim. " Pretty wild night, eh—I'm blessed if it has stopped blowing since I arrived. Old Sep writes that he was in Torquay yesterday, and the sea was absolutely breaking over the front—tramcars drenched and wrecked. Funny, being wrecked in a tramcar."

He put his red hands to the blaze and rattled on.

" Dreadful thing, eh, Miss Antrim ? What's the use of the police—eh ? What's the use of 'em ? Want men like Audain, full of up-to-date ideas. Wish it had been anybody but you, Antrim," He shook his head mournfully.

" Ever heard of Freud ? " asked Bennett, his chin on his clasped hands, his absent gaze on the fire.

" Freud—no. German, isn't he ? Nothing to do with the Germans, old boy, after that beastly war. They sunk three of our ships, by gad ! Who is he, anyway ? "

" A professor," said Bennett lazily, " and an authority on the mind. Why don't you sit down, Balte ? "

" Prefer standing, old boy. Stand and grow better—eh, Miss Antrim ? What about this Hun ? "

" He interprets dreams—— "

" Ought to be in the Police, that's where he ought to be—interpreting some of those pipe-dreams they have," he chuckled.

" I will tell you what I am getting at," said Bennett and explained.

May held her breath, sensing the deadliness of the play.

Mr. Balte was amused.

" You say one word and I'll tell you a word it suggests ? " he said. " That's a kid's game—used to play it when I was so high. You say ' sugar,' I say ' sweet ' ; next fellow says ' orange,' and so forth."

" You see, Mr. Balte," interrupted May, " Bennett thinks he can get at your sub-conscious mind. He believes that he can even tell what happened when you were asleep."

Mr. Balte pulled at his nose and looked down. He was thinking. He wondered if Bennett Audain could get at his mind about May Antrim, and could put into words all that he had dreamed yet had not dared to say, all that he had schemed for. The thought caught his breath. He loved her so, this girl whose beautiful face had never left his vision ; he had dared so much for her and she never knew. To her he was one of the thousands who served as a background of life.

" Try, old boy," he said huskily ; " I don't believe in it, but if you can get hold of any information that will help Mr. Antrim—you don't know how I feel about that—go ahead."

" Sit down."

Mr. Balte obeyed. His china-blue eyes were fixed on his interrogator.

" Ground," said Bennett unexpectedly.

" Eh—er—er—earth," responded the other.

" Dig."

" Garden."

" Hole."

. " Er—I nearly said ' devil,' " chuckled Mr. Balte. " This is funny—like a game ! "

But it was an earnest game with Bennett Audain. Presently :

" Shares," he said.

" Slump," it came promptly, one word suggested by the other. Balte added : " Everything is slumping just now, you know . . ."

They went on quickly. Bennett recited the days of the week.

" Monday ? "

A grimace—the faintest—from Balte.

" Er—— Unpleasant—starting the week, y'know."

Bennett shot out the days.

" Friday ? "

" Calendar—thinking of a calendar, y'know."

" Key ? "

" Wi——door."

He got up.

" A silly game, Audain." He shook his head reproachfully. " Admit it. I can't play games—too worried. Poor old Sep is half off his head, too."

" Where is Septimus ? " asked Bennett.

" At Slapton—pike-fishing. Rum how people can sit in a punt all day . . . fishing. Well, what are you going to do, Audain ? Can you help us ? The police—pshaw ! "

" Will you tell me this ? " asked Bennett. " Are you a heavy sleeper ? "

The stout man shook his head.

" Do you sleep late in the mornings ? "

" No ; up at six, bright and jolly." He paused. " Now I come to think of it, I was very sleepy *that* morning. Drugs, eh . . . do you think I was drugged—chloroform and that sort of thing ? "

" No," said Bennett, and let him go.

" Well ? " asked the girl when the door had closed upon the visitor.

" Stay in town for a day or two," said Bennett Audain.

At seven o'clock the next morning he called a justly annoyed police inspector from his bed. Fortunately Bennett knew him very well.

" Yes, Mr. Audain ; his trunks were searched. Mr. Balte insisted."

" How many trunks had he in the cabin ? "

The inspector, cursing such matutinal inquisitiveness, answered :

" Four."

" Four ? Big ones ? "

" Yes, sir ; pretty big and half empty."

" Did you smell anything peculiar about them ? "

The inspector wagged his head impatiently. His legs were getting cold and the bed he had left was entrancingly warm.

" No, sir, I did *not* smell them."

" Good," said Bennett's cheerful voice.

" The worst of these amateur detectives is that they jump all ways at once," said the inspector as he shuddered back to bed.

" M'm," said his wife, on the border-line of wakefulness.

Bennett, at his end of the wire, gloomed out of the window into the grey moist morning on to the stark, uneasy branches of park trees.

The hour was 7.5. Essential people had not yet turned in their beds ; even the serving-maids and men-servants had scarcely blinked at the toilsome day. Bennett Audain went

back to the remains of his breakfast and wished, when he had
had Francis Balte under examination, he had said, " Paint."
Mr. Balte would surely have responded " See."

Mr. Balte had a large house at Wimbledon.   He was a
bachelor, as was his brother.   He was a simple man, as also
was his brother.   They had inherited considerable property at
a time—the last year of the war—when property had a fictitious
value.   The cream of their father's estate had been swallowed
by the Treasury in the shape of death duties.   Their skimmed
milk was very thin and blue in the days of the great slump.
Stockholders in Balte Brothers Incorporated Shippers—and
they were many—watched the shrinking of profits indignantly.
The last general meeting of the Company had been a noisy
one.   There was one fellow in particular, a bald man with
spectacles, Francis had noted miserably from his place on the
platform—a violent, intemperate man, who had talked of a
change of directors, and he had received more " hear-hears "
than had Francis when he had expressed the pious hope that
trade would improve and shipping return to its old prosperity.

It was Sunday morning, and Francis sat in his library.   It
was a room containing many shelves of books which he had
never read, but the bindings of which were in the best taste.
His elbows were on the table, his fingers in his untidy hair,
and he was reading.   Not the Sunday newspapers, his usual
Sunday's occupation.   These were stacked, unopened, on the
little table by the easy-chair.   It was a book, commonly and
commercially bound, and the more he read the more bewildered he grew.   A little shocked also, for this volume was
embarrassingly intimate.

Thus his brother found him.   Septimus, lank and bent
and short-sighted, glared through his powerful glasses at the
studious figure and sniffed.

" Got it ? " he asked.

Francis closed the book with a bang.

" It is all medical stuff," he said. " Audain is a bit cranky.
Going ? "

The question was unnecessary.   Septimus was muffled to
the chin, his fur gloves were under his arm, and his big racing
car was visible from the library window.

" If there is anything in this Audain stuff, let me know.
I've read something about psycho-analysis—I thought it was
for shell-shocked people.   So long."

" When will you be back ? "

" Tuesday night.   I've written the letter."

" Oh."

Francis stirred the fire thoughtfully.

" Create a bit of a stir your resigning from the Board," he said ; " wish . . ."

" Yes ? "

" No, I don't. I was going to say that I wished it was me. Better you. Everybody knows you're in bad health. . . Warm enough ? "

" Ay," said his brother, and went out pulling on his gloves. Francis did not go to the window to see him off. He bent over the fire uncomfortably, jabbing it unreasonably.

It occurred to him after a long time that his brother had not gone. He put down the poker and shuffled across to the window—he was wearing slippers. There were two cars in the road, bonnet to bonnet, and a man was standing by the seated Septimus. They were talking.

" Audain," said Francis, and meditated, biting his lip. Presently Septimus went off and Bennett Audain came briskly up the path. Francis admitted him.

" Energetic fellow ! " he cried. His voice was an octave higher than it had been when he spoke to his brother, his manner more virile and masterful. He was good cheer and complacency personified. " Come in, come in. You saw old Sep ? Poor old chap ! "

" He tells me that he is resigning from the shipping business." Bennett was warming his hands.

" Yes ; he's going to the south of France, old Sep. Going to buy property. Queer bird, Sep. But he was always a land man—farms, houses . . . anything to do with land . . . very shrewd."

Bennett glanced at the table, and the other anticipated.

" *Interpretation of Dreams*—eh ? " he chuckled. " You've got me going on Freud. Don't understand it. Of course I understand what he says about dreaming and all that . . . but that game of yours . . . eh ? "

Bennett changed the subject, Francis wondering.

" Yes, it is not a bad house," he agreed amiably. " A bit bourgeoise, but we're that kind. Quaintly constructed— would you like to see over it ? "

A home and its attractions can be a man's weakness. In a woman, its appointments are the dominating values ; architecture means no more than convenience. And Bradderly Manor was a source of satisfaction to Francis. They reached the wind-swept grounds in time, because there was a workshop in which old Sep laboured.   It was to him what laboratory, studio, music-room, model dairy, and incubatory are to other men.   It was a workshop, its walls lined with tool cabinets. There was a bench, an electric lathe, vices, drills . . . an oak panel with its unfinished cupids and foliage testified to the artistry and workmanship of Septimus Balte.

" Always was a wonderful workman, old Sep," said Francis in admiration.   " Do you know, he was the inventor of a new depth charge that would have made his name if the war hadn't finished—— "

" That's it, is it ? "

Francis looked round.

Bennett had taken from a shelf a large paint can.   It had not been opened.   The manufacturer's red label pasted on the top of the sunken lid was unbroken

" That's what ? "

Bennett held the can for a second and replaced it.

" Luminous paint," he said.   " Lefvre's—he's the best maker, isn't he ? "

Francis Balte said nothing.   All the way back to the house he said nothing.   Bennett followed him into the library and watched him as he filled a pipe from a jar which he took from the mantelpiece.

" Well ? " he said miserably.   Bennett saw tears in his eyes.

" The two things I am not sure about are," Bennett ticked them off on his fingers :   " One, was John Steele the cause ? Two, why the towels ? "

The stout man puffed furiously and all the time his eyes went blink, blink, blink.

" Friday—Calendar ; that's how you knew.   You wouldn't think I'd fall so easily.   But you must have known all about it or why should you know I meant the *Racing Calendar* ? "

" I guessed.   I did not know that you and your brother had a stud of horses and raced them in the name of John Steele.   That was easy to discover.   When I decided that it was the *Racing Calendar* you meant, the official journal of the Jockey Club, I went to the publishers and got the register of assumed names."

The pipe puffed agitatedly.

" No . . . we lost money on racing, but that wasn't it ; bad business . . . over-valuation of assets.   I wonder what she will think about me. . . ."

He sank down in a chair, the pipe dropped from his mouth, and he wept into his big red hands.

" I have no interest in punishment," said Bennett Audain, and May Antrim, watching the pain in his delicate face, nodded. She was beginning to understand Bennett Audain.

" In solutions of curious human puzzles, yes," said Bennett, as he sipped his tea and noted joyously the first splashes of green that had come to the park trees in one night, " but not in punishment. If you like to put it that way, I am unmoral. Your father received his money ? "

" Of course he did, Bennett—the six boxes arrived at his office yesterday morning."

Bennett laughed very softly.

" It 'is good to be alive when the buds are breaking, May. I feel a very happy man. Suppose you wanted a clockwork contrivance made, where would you go to get the work done ? Look up the Classified Directory. No mention of clockwork-makers or makers of mechanical toys. Yet there are ten people in London who do nothing else. There is a man named Collett in Highbury who made a sort of time-bomb during the war. I went to him after I had learnt that Septimus Balte was working on war inventions. I found that by patient inquiry. It is queer how soon people have forgotten all things pertaining to the war."

" But why did you inquire about clockwork at all ? " asked the girl.

" Creak ! " mocked Bennett. " Did your father tell you how the steward had heard a noise, six noises, as of a watch being wound ? Well, I found Mr. Collett a secretive, furtive man, but reasonable. He had made a simple water-tight machine. It operated a large spool which was held in position by a catch and released three hours after it had been set. Is that clear ? "

May nodded.

" Why water-tight ? " asked Bennett. " The spool itself was outside, and presumably was designed to work in the water. Attached to the steel box containing the mechanism were two iron bolts, one at the top above the spool, one at the bottom. Now what was attached to the spool ? Nothing but ten fathoms of stout light cord, a double length of it. Now do you see ? "

" No," admitted the puzzled girl.

" Then I will explain further. At the end of the cord was a small cork buoy, probably covered with canvas and certainly treated with luminous paint. The towels—— " he laughed, " I ought to have thought of the use to which they would be

put, but I had not seen the cabin.   And the strange thing is
that when I put myself in the place of Francis, it never occurred
to me that if boxes weighing 140 pounds and clamped with
iron were pushed through a porthole, the brass casings of the
port would be scratched—unless the boxes were wrapped in
cloth of some kind."

"Then he threw the boxes into the sea!" gasped May,
sitting back.

Bennett nodded.

"First he took the buoys and attachments from his trunks,
then he wound up the mechanism, threw that and the buoy
out of the porthole—the buoy being attached by a short
length of chain to the under-bolt of the clockwork case—then
he heaved up the money-box and pushed that after.   They
sank immediately.   No belated passenger leaning over the rail
would see a luminous buoy floating back.   Nobody saw those
buoys but Septimus, waiting in his motor-boat twelve miles
south of Slapton Sands.   And he did not see them until the
three hours passed and, the spools releasing the buoys, they
came to the surface.   Then he fastened a stouter rope to one
of the double cords and rove it through the bolt. . . .   He
salvaged all six boxes in an hour, which isn't bad for a sick
man."

She shook her head helplessly.

"How . . . why . . . did you guess ? "

"Guess ? " Bennett's eyebrows rose.   "It wasn't a guess.
Who else would have stolen the boxes ?   In fiction the thief
is the last man you suspect.   In fact, the thief is the last man
you'd acquit.   The police always suspect the man who was
last seen near the scene of the crime, and the police are generally right.   I knew half the Balte secret when the word ' key '
suggested ' wind ' and ' Monday '—the day racing men settle
their bets—suggested ' unpleasant.' "

He looked at his watch.

"Francis and ' poor old Sep ' should at this moment be
boarding the *Rotterdam* at Plymouth," he said.

"But why . . . he had heavy losses, but he would not have
been ruined.   Did he want the money so badly—— "

"There is a woman in the case," said Bennett gravely.
" Somebody he dreamt about and planned for."

"Poor man ! " said May softly.   There were tears in her
eyes, he noticed, and remembered Francis Balte's words : " I
wonder what she will think about me ? "

THE GHOST OF A SMILE

By

GERARD FAIRLIE

MY nerves are on edge to-night.
To-morrow at break of day a woman is to pay the
extreme penalty for murder. This, an unusual event
enough, thank God, in any country, has come about largely
through me.

There is still time for a reprieve ; but I am told on the
best authority that in this case it is not coming. Jackson tells
me this, and Jackson, after all, should know, for he is very
high up at Scotland Yard. It was Jackson's idea that brought
about this strange conviction, and he, I happen to know, is
going to a theatre to-night with some friends.

I know nothing about the justice of the death penalty,
the ethics of a life for a life. But I do know that I could not
go to the theatre to-night. I would not see the players on the
stage. I would only sit and visualise a haggard, white face
and a pair of sleepless eyes staring from within the condemned
cell into what is left of the future—and hoping against hope
for that reprieve which I know, and everyone else knows, is
not to come.

I must do something. I think I'll write down the events
as they occurred, make a narrative of it. The facts are known
to a few ; others may be interested.

It was in January that Philip Forbes first came to see me,
with a letter of introduction from a local doctor at Torquay.
This good man and I had been students at the hospital together
but had not met much since. He had made straight for Devon,
whereas I had remained to prosper in Harley Street as a heart
specialist. This doctor explained his view of the case, and
handed over Philip Forbes and his weak heart to me.

I made my examination. As the letter had warned me,

228

Forbes was undoubtedly in a bad way, but as far as I could tell there was no reason why, with reasonable care, he should not last for many years yet. I was just about to put this tactfully into words when he stopped me.

" Would you mind if my wife came in and heard what you have to say ? " he asked. " She's outside in the waiting-room."

" Why, of course."

I rang the bell on my desk and sent for the lady.

There was something about Mrs. Forbes as she came in that I did not like—nothing tangible, nothing that I could put my finger on and say : " Now I don't like you for that." It was, I suppose, just a general clashing of personalities, which was all the odder because she was undoubtedly attractive —very fair hair, very slim figure and particularly well dressed. I drew forward a chair for her, and she sat down.

" Let me say at the outset, Mr. Forbes," I remarked with the cheerful smile I have to assume in such circumstances, " that although it is no good blinding ourselves to the fact that your heart is not all that it should be, this should cause you little inconvenience provided you are prepared to take reasonable care of yourself."

" What precisely do you mean by inconvenience ? "

" Are you engaged in any business ? " I asked.

" I am the managing director of a large company," he said.

" Well," I remarked, " I should cease to manage it, if I were you. By all means continue your interest in the business, but you must refrain from anything in the nature of hard work, either mental or physical. That, I think, is your golden rule—no exertion. If you obey that I see no great reason for anxiety."

Mrs. Forbes looked at her husband.

" What did I tell you, Philip ? " she said.

He laughed.

" She's been trying to make me drop my work for some time," he said. " As a matter of fact, that is one of the reasons why we have come to London to live. Up here I shall only have to attend necessary board meetings and so on—which I presume do not come under your ban. Up to now I have been trying to manage the Torquay branch as well as all my duties in London, but my living here will alter all that."

" That sounds admirable," I agreed.

" There is one thing, doctor," suddenly said Mrs. Forbes. " We have taken a flat which is on the third floor. There is a lift, but lifts sometimes break down. Would the stairs be all right for Philip ? "

I hesitated.

" Well, Mrs. Forbes, stairs are bad. There's no getting away from that, but if there's a lift, well and good. You must use it, Forbes, always ; but remember if you do ever have to walk up there is much less strain on the heart if you go up slowly one step at a time, and backwards."

" Backwards ? " repeated Mrs. Forbes incredulously.

I laughed.

" I know it sounds rather odd," I said, " but I assure you it is so. When you come to think it out, it stands to reason. From the knee the leg bends naturally in a backward position, and there is, therefore, far less effort required than for mounting steps forward."

The interview ended.

I did not see Philip Forbes again for about two months, and then, since he had asked me to act as his regular medical adviser, I sent him a note reminding him that I should like to see him from time to time just to keep my eye on his heart. The following day my secretary informed me that he had made an appointment.

I was rather shocked at the sight of him. Even so short a time ago as two months he had, though he had certainly been a little flabby and florid, shown none of the usual pronounced signs whereby a doctor can tell heart trouble almost at sight. Now, however, he fairly radiated all the signs.

I made a very thorough examination of him that morning, and when I had finished I think he realised that I was worried.

" Well, doctor ? "

I looked him straight in the eyes.

" It's no good beating about the bush," I said. " You are worse, very much worse. What on earth have you been doing to yourself ? "

Forbes smiled wanly.

" As I told you the last time I saw you," he said, " I came up to London with the idea of doing much less work, but when you've been working all your life and have risen to a very important position, it is hard to throw off habits that you have formed. I'm afraid I have been overworking rather."

I leaned forward across my desk and spoke in my most serious manner.

" Look here, Mr. Forbes," I said deliberately, " you must do no work whatsoever. You must give up smoking and you must give up drinking. You must eat very, very moderately. You have got to be really careful with yourself, and you must have a great deal of rest, with only a little, very gentle exercise every day. Otherwise I cannot answer for the consequences."

It is a very unpleasant thing for any doctor to have to say such words even to a man whom he does not know very well. In my heart, too, I knew I was letting him down gently. Forbes was a very ill man. At the most he could only last a few months longer.

Then a thought struck me.

" What about that flat ? "

Forbes looked at me in mild surprise.

" What about it ? It's quite comfortable."

" Does the lift always work ? " I said, smiling.

." Oh, I see. Yes, always. It's an admirable lift."

" But no lift is infallible," I said shortly. " Remember what I told you about going upstairs if it ever does go out of action."

" I won't forget."

He went away convinced, as I hoped, of the gravity of his position and of the urgent necessity for caution in his way of living, and I am afraid that in the rush of my large practice I forgot all about him for the next few days.

About a fortnight later I received a letter from him. He told me that his firm were anxious to give a farewell lunch to mark his retirement, and he wanted me to raise my ban on plain food and water, just for this one occasion. I replied saying I thought he might attend the function, but warning him again to eat and drink in strict moderation.

A few days after that, just as I was settling down to my work again after lunch, the telephone-bell rang imperatively. I lifted the receiver.

" Dr. Carlton speaking."

" Doctor, for God's sake come at once ! "

The voice was strange to me, but there was no mistaking the urgency of the tone.

" Who are you ? " I said quickly.

" Mrs. Forbes. My husband has collapsed and I can't bring him round."

" Right. I'll be round at once."

Hastily I put into a bag the few things I knew I should want. I rushed into the street, cursing myself for having sent my car away after lunch, and hailed a taxi. In a very few minutes I was at the big block of flats where the Forbeses lived.

Calling to the driver of the taxi to wait for me, I hurried into the main entrance and made for the lift. The commissionaire, I think, realised who I was, for it was hardly necessary for me to give the number of the flat. He shut me into the lift and said, " Third floor, sir." I pressed the appropriate button.

A servant with panic in her face opened the door to me and led me straight to the bedroom where poor Philip Forbes had been carried. I realised at the very first glance that there was no hope. The man was dead.

I made the necessary examination. As I turned from the bed I caught sight of Mrs. Forbes standing at the door. The moment she knew I had seen her she advanced into the room, but not before I had surprised on her face an expression which set me wondering. For one instant as I had looked at her I had caught the faintest flicker of what had seemed to me a smile. Yet, I told myself, the idea was preposterous, incredible. Here was a woman standing on the threshold of the room where lay her husband dead less than an hour since. No, I thought, it must be some trick of my imagination or of the light. Yet the impression returned to me again and again. I was puzzled. I could have sworn that I had seen about her lips the ghost of a smile, born and dead, when my back had been turned towards her.

She looked at me inquiringly.

I shook my head.

" I'm afraid I'm too late. He's dead."

She took me into the drawing-room.

" How did it happen ? " I asked, as the door closed behind me.

" He had been out to that wretched lunch," she said— " that wretched farewell affair. I knew he ought not to go. I told him so, but he would go. He was so wrapped up in the firm, you know. They all admired him so much. He always went to all the functions, and he would have hated to miss this one. . . . "

She spoke rapidly, nervously, I thought, and I could not help wondering at this flood of irrelevant words. I contrasted this overwrought manner with her unnatural calm in the bedroom only a few moments ago. It has been my unhappy lot to be the witness of many people suddenly bereaved in this manner, and I have learnt to sum up the sincerity of the grief. Generally I have found that it is the dry-eyed, silent woman who suffers the most. People react differently to the shock of grief. I knew all this, and yet I could not reconcile such a strange mixture of emotions as this woman's curious quietude of a few minutes back, and the mood, almost of hysteria, which was now upon her. Try as I might I could not rid myself of the notion that she was acting to me.

" I happened to be coming out of the flat just as he came into the building . . . " she ran on. " I saw him coming up the stairs instead of taking the lift. I knew what a risk it was and, what was still worse, he wasn't even coming up slowly. He was taking the stairs in the ordinary way, and seemed in a great hurry. I started to call out to him, but before I could do so he had commenced running up the remaining stairs. As he reached me he tried to tell me something, but before he could utter a word he had collapsed at my feet. Oh, doctor, it was awful ! "

" But what could have induced him to rush upstairs like that, after all my warnings ? "

" I haven't the slightest idea. I was always urging him to be careful. I've racked my brains."

There was nothing more to be said. I did not like to suggest to her that her husband might possibly have had too much to drink at the lunch. Anyway, the harm was done now and it was no good upsetting her unnecessarily.

I went back to my house in Harley Street, and found that that afternoon I had a crowded appointments book and was fully occupied until late in the evening. Alone during dinner, however, there came repeatedly before my eyes a vision of poor Philip Forbes running up those stairs as Mrs. Forbes had described, and with it there ever recurred the thought of that fleeting glimpse I had caught of Mrs. Forbes when, standing in the doorway of her husband's room of death, she had—smiled. For the more I considered it the more certain I became that I had not been mistaken, and that what I had seen had been the lingering shade of a smile—whether of triumph, or malice, or satisfaction, or simply the twisted smile of hysteria, who could tell ? Certainly not I.

I decided to dismiss the matter from my mind, but in spite of all my efforts my thoughts constantly reverted to it. For the life of me I could find no adequate reason for finding myself so taken up with this matter. True it was sad that Forbes had one so suddenly, but after all it was no more than I had expected, and the case was only one of the kind with which I constantly came into contact in the course of my practice.

Nevertheless, the thing remained with me and continually obtruded itself upon my consciousness during my ordinary duties of the next few days. Indeed, I began to feel seriously annoyed with myself and to fear that I had got some foolish and meaningless obsession about the affair.

But when a few more days had passed and it was still haunting my thoughts at every turn, I decided that in the hope of ridding myself of this bogey I would go round and see Mrs. Forbes and try to find out something more about it all.

Accordingly, that evening I walked down to the Forbeses' flat after my work was over, ostensibly to offer her my respects and see how things were going with her.

I rang the bell and the same maid opened the door. I asked for Mrs. Forbes and, after a certain hesitation, was admitted to the drawing-room, where I had last seen her.

It was with a feeling of some surprise that I became aware of the figure of a man seated in an arm-chair by the fire. His general attitude had an indefinable air of being entirely at home and at ease. Evidently he was no casual acquaintance. I was introduced to Oliver Barrett.

Mrs. Forbes was looking her most attractive. Instead of, as I had expected, a woman somewhat subdued by recent grief, perhaps in deep mourning, sitting here with her sorrow, I found a beautiful creature, slim and flushed, glowing with happiness and obviously pleased with her life and her surroundings. She wore black, it is true, but it was so skilfully softened with some filmy whiteness, so exquisitely cut, and worn with such chic, that it gave her rather the appearance of being decked for joyousness than of being clothed darkly for mourning. Black so perfectly becomes a woman of her fairness.

She welcomed me with every appearance of pleasure yet I could not help feeling that I was intruding upon an intimate *tête-à-tête*, and I wished that the maid had had the sense to tell me Mrs. Forbes was entertaining a visitor.

" You'll have a cocktail, doctor ? "

" Thanks, I will," I said.

She turned casually to Barrett.

" Will you mix them, Oliver ? "

Barrett at once rose to his feet and moved over to a cupboard in the far corner of the room, from which he produced the various ingredients. I could not help noticing how familiar he seemed with everything in the room.

I stayed just long enough to finish my drink. Then, still

with the same sensation of being *de trop*, I decided that I could take my leave without being impolite.

Mrs. Forbes saw me to the door. She acknowledged my few words quite naturally.

I did not ring for the lift but went down the stairs thoughtfully, stopping for a moment, before going into the street, to light a cigarette.

" Good evening, sir."

I looked up.

The commissionaire who had been so helpful to me the afternoon of the tragedy, touched his cap.

" A very cold night, sir."

I acknowledged the truth of his remark.

" Sad about poor Mr. Forbes, wasn't it ? "

I concurred.

" A very nice gentleman he was, too, sir. We all liked him very much. You were the medical gentleman who came to see him, weren't you, sir ? "

" I was."

" That was a terrible day for me, sir. Funny how, when things go wrong, they all go wrong at once. First there was that Mrs. Forbes coming down and sending me off on her messages just when I was back from my lunch. There's always lots of things to do down here between half-past two and three, sir, you'd be surprised. About a quarter to three it was when I went out, sir, and it was a good long message. Then when I come back there was that awful tragedy of poor Mr. Forbes dying, all while I'd been out. Then down comes Mr. Dixon from number twenty-three, grumbling about my lift being out of order, which it wasn't, sir, because I always keep it running very smooth and regular. Anyway, he swears there was a label on it saying ' Out of Order.' If there was, I never put it there, and it wasn't there when I came back. I can't understand it at all."

I looked at him sharply. What was this about the lift ? Was I on the verge of discovering the reason why Philip Forbes had taken that mad risk the day he died ?

" The lift was out of order, you say ? "

" No, sir, it was not. It was only Mr. Dixon who said it was."

" Well, he must have had some reason for saying so."

" He said there was that notice, sir, but I say if it was there it wasn't put there by me, and I'm the only one that has any right to put up a notice like that. When I come back from

my errand I was called up at once about poor Mr. Forbes,
and when I come down I know it was working all right because
I saw Mr. Pearson of number fifty-three going up in it."

I came to a decision. Murmuring that I had left something in Mrs. Forbes's flat, I turned and went up the stairs
again until I came to Mr. Dixon's flat. I rang the bell and was
informed that Mr. Dixon was at home. I was shown into a
small sitting-room, and was very soon joined by a middle-aged
man with a kindly face, whom I liked at sight.

" Dr. Carlton ? " he queried.

I rose as he entered.

" I'm terribly sorry," I said, " for butting in in this way,
but I was Mr. Forbes's medical adviser and I was naturally
interested in the reason that induced him to walk upstairs
when the lift was available, especially as I had so often warned
him that just such a proceeding might prove fatal. The
commissionaire has now told me that immediately before the
time of the tragedy you found the lift out of order, but he, on
the other hand, is certain that it was in perfect running order
all day. I came up really to ask you to confirm this statement,
as it seems rather a curious circumstance."

" I am sure I was right," at once replied Dixon. " As I
came into the building I saw a notice stuck on the door of the
lift, saying ' Out of Order,' so I had to walk up—a process to
which I object most strongly at my time of life," he added
with a smile.

" May I ask what time it was when you came up ? " I said.

After a moment's thought he replied :

" About two-forty-five, I should think. I can't swear to
the minute, of course, but it must have been just about that."

I thanked him and, with renewed apologies for having
bothered him, I took my leave.

I walked back to my home, all the time turning over in my
mind this strange new information. By now I was really
interested, and was thankful that I had acted on my impulse
to go and visit Mrs. Forbes.

But I did not like the way my thoughts were leading me.
I dined alone that night, and all the time I was trying to make
up my mind that I was allowing my imagination to run riot
without a shade of justification. But I failed to convince
myself, and by the time I had finished my lonely meal I had
decided upon a course of action. There remained one possible
source of information. I went to the telephone in my study
and rang up a man I knew who was one of poor Forbes's

business associates. Very soon I heard his voice over the wire.

"Look here, Rendall," I said, "were you at that farewell lunch which was given to Forbes?"

"What, the poor fellow who died? Yes, I was."

"Tell me, did he by any chance have a little too much to drink that day?"

There was a moment's silence, and I thought he was perhaps hesitating to give Forbes away.

"Don't answer if you don't want to," I said, "but I assure you this is no impertinent question. You may or may not know that I was his doctor, and I have a good reason for asking."

I heard Rendall laugh.

"My dear fellow," he said, "I'm not hesitating. I'm only trying to remember the circumstances, and I do remember now that he didn't drink too much. In fact he drank practically nothing at all. I distinctly remember his saying he wasn't allowed to, by doctor's orders."

"Thank you," I said, and rang off.

I sat down in a big arm-chair by the fire and with deliberation filled and lit my pipe, but all the time my mind was actively turning over the situation in its new light. It was certain that Forbes had not taken too much to drink that day. All at once I made up my mind. I went over to the telephone again and asked for a number. Someone answered me.

"Hallo," I said. "Is that Inspector Jackson?"

"Speaking," came a voice.

"Ah, Jackson. I did not recognise your voice. Are you busy this evening?"

I spoke rapidly so that he should have no chance of making an excuse.

"I wish you'd come in for a drink and a chat, if you don't mind. I have rather an interesting story I should like to tell you."

Not so very long before I had been useful to Jackson and Scotland Yard in an important case of theirs, and he and I had struck up a friendship. I was not surprised, therefore, when he said he would come at once.

Twenty minutes later, when I had Inspector Jackson comfortably seated in an arm-chair with a drink on a small table and a cigar in his mouth, I told him my tale.

I warned him at the very start that all I was going to say might easily be the result of a distorted imagination, coupled with my instinctive dislike of Mrs. Forbes.

"Well," I began, "this patient of mine, Forbes, had a very bad heart indeed, and I had constantly warned him not to do anything foolish. Particularly had I said he should not use the stairs to his flat unless he was absolutely compelled to do so. This I told him in the presence of his wife.

"I have since found out that on the day he died the lift was in perfect running order at two-thirty, at which time the commissionaire had returned from lunch and had occasion to use it ; that at or about two-forty-five the commissionaire was sent out on an errand by Mrs. Forbes, which took him just over a quarter of an hour ; that at or about the same time a Mr. Dixon, the occupant of one of the flats, came in and saw a notice on the lift to the effect that it was out of order. He walked up. While the commissionaire was out Forbes arrived, and according to the story told to me by Mrs. Forbes he at once started to walk up the stairs. He was obviously in a hurry, and before she could call out to him, as she had intended to do, he began to run up the remaining steps and collapsed at her feet. When the commissionaire returned to the flats, at about three o'clock, he was called up to the Forbeses' flat and took the lift. When he came down again he saw another resident of the flats, Mr. Pearson, take the lift and ascend to his flat. And now comes the part of my story which you may tell me is sheer imagination. All the same, I am convinced that when I was summoned by Mrs. Forbes to see the dead man, she was acting to me, and this within half an hour of her husband's death. I hardly like to tell you, Jackson, but I am morally certain that as she stood looking at me while I bent over the poor chap, she was smiling with something that seemed to me very like triumph. I am quite prepared for you to pooh-pooh this idea. For some time I was not sure myself. Nevertheless, I cannot shake off the idea that when I turned round to meet her there was on her face what is best termed as the ghost of a smile. After the funeral I still thought of all this, and at last I decided to go and see how Mrs. Forbes was getting on and see if everything seemed all right. When I got there I found her with an attractive young man, who obviously knew his way about and was entirely at ease in her society. They were sitting there together in the firelight over tea, and though I was greeted with every apparent feeling of welcome I could not get rid of the feeling that I was interrupting a *tête-à-tête*. I didn't stay long. The whole incident has remained in my memory and I am not satisfied, not satisfied that that poor fellow did not meet his death by some foul means.

That's why I have asked you to come along. I feel sure you will be able to help me."

After I had finished there was a silence that lasted several minutes.

I watched Jackson narrowly and saw that he was staring at the fire, puffing vigorously at his cigar and evidently turning over the factors of my story in his mind.

Suddenly he looked up.

" You may be right, Dr. Carlton. If a murder has been committed I should think there is only one person who could have done it—and that is his wife. But "—he paused again and took a drink—" I say this between these four walls, of course, that old saying ' Murder will out ' is not so true as people think. There are many murders done every year which simply cannot, for lack of sound proof, be brought home to the murderers. This looks like being one of them—if murder it is at all. However, thank you very much for telling me, doctor. I'll go into it and let you know what I find out."

Shortly after that he left me and it so happened that for the next week or so I had one of the busiest times of my life. Having told Jackson all I knew and suspected, I seemed more able to shake the whole matter off my mind, and I gave very little thought to it.

It must have been about ten days later that Jackson rang me up and asked me if he might come round to see me.

That evening found him once again in my study arm-chair close to a warm, bright fire.

" Well, Dr. Carlton," he said. " I have discovered three things. One, that Mrs. Forbes has for some time been obviously desirous of getting rid of her husband, and that once she was even so indiscreet as to utter this wish in public. Two, that you were quite right in assuming young Barrett knew his way about the flat a bit too well. He had been constantly associating with her for at least six months before her husband died, and—and here is my third discovery—they have made arrangements to be married very shortly."

He paused for a moment and then went on.

" We certainly have no concrete evidence to go on. All we can do is to point to certain events and say : ' Well, that was strange.' All the same, taking into consideration what you have told me, combined with my own discoveries, I am absolutely convinced in my own mind that Mrs. Forbes was her husband's murderer."

I looked at him, and marvelled at the calm with which he

made this statement. Then, just for a second, I was vouch-safed some insight into his real feelings, for he suddenly turned to me, and in a voice of suppressed feeling, said :
" By God ! If it is humanly possible I'm going to bring it home to her, though. A murder of sudden passion I can understand, but a premeditated killing in cold blood such as this, is simply dastardly."

I waited for a second to see what he would say next, but he relapsed into silence.

" How on earth can you do it ? " I asked at last. He looked up at me and smiled and I caught the excitement of the hunter in his eyes.

" I have an idea," he said. " It's based on the French method of reconstructing the crime in front of the suspected person."

Then, lowering his voice as if he were fearful of being overheard, he told me of his plans.

*   *   *   *   *   *

It was over a month later that I next heard from Jackson. Then he rang up to tell me that all was fixed and that I was to be in readiness to answer a call from him at any time.

I spent the next day or two in a state of mingled apprehension and anticipation ; so much so that I found it difficult to carry on with the ordinary routine of my work. At last it came—another telephone call from Jackson asking me to go at once to an address which I knew to be the block where the Forbeses' flat was. The number of the flat given was that immediately below it.

I summoned my secretary ; told her I should be away for the rest of the day, and leapt into a taxi. In a very short time I was ringing the bell. Jackson himself opened the door to me and took me into a room which was evidently under the drawing-room of the Forbeses' flat above. Here he introduced me to a tall, distinguished-looking man, with slightly greying hair.

" Dr. Carlton—Mr. John Royd."

I recognised the name as that of a well-known author and writer of short stories, whose work I had often read in the magazines.

Here was another proof that Jackson was really on the warpath. He had influential friends in all quarters who could help him. I turned to him.

" Has everything gone according to plan ? " I asked.

Jackson smiled, the smile of a very satisfied man.

"Thanks to Mr. Royd here, and some very acceptable help from the commissionaire downstairs, everything is working out perfectly. I took the facts to Mr. Royd and he's written one of the best stories I've ever read in my life. It's the case complete, as you presented it to me, only the woman in the story is an avowed murderess. It came out in to-day's *Echo*, which I sent round to young Barrett about half an hour ago. If he reacts to it as I expect him to, he ought to be round here very shortly. The only thing is he may not read the story at once, but I've marked it up very heavily and common curiosity should do the trick. All we've got to do now is to stay here and listen."

He pointed to a small wireless set on the table nearby. It was provided with three sets of ear-phones.

Suddenly he laughed.

"Although I says it myself, I think it's a neat little idea to have a microphone upstairs."

"Of course," I said, rather hesitantly, "the only flaw in this neat scheme of yours is that, after all, we've only got verbal evidence."

"You wait, my friend," he said, "there's something else upstairs as well as the microphone. I'm out for a confession."

For a short time we sat silent, all rather apprehensive lest the scheme, so far successful, might after all miscarry in some way at the last moment.

The door opened and the commissionaire put his head around it. He whispered in a husky voice :

"Mr. Barrett's gone upstairs, sir."

"Ah !" said Jackson, with an air of utter satisfaction.

We all three made a rush for the ear-phones and putting them on sat down at the table.

It was an eerie sensation, sitting there listening to the faint buzz which comes from a " live " wireless, and, try as I would, I could not rid myself of the idea that I was eavesdropping. But I reassured myself with the thought that, though this might be an unusual way of obtaining information, we were acting on the side of law and order and for the common good.

So suddenly that the sound almost made me jump, I heard a door being opened and slammed to again.

"Oliver ! What on earth's the matter ? You look like death."

Mrs. Forbes's voice, even over the instrument, sounded thoroughly strained and startled.

" I feel like it ! Read that ! "

A wealth of suppressed emotion could be sensed in the man's reply.

There followed a long silence. Evidently Mrs. Forbes was reading the story. In imagination I saw her face as the meaning of the tale was gradually borne in upon her. We sat there, tense with excitement and longing for the end of this interval of suspense.

But the silence held. Instead of the garbled explanations born of her fear, which I had half expected to hear from the woman, there came only the sound of a faint thud. She had doubtless fainted. Then Barrett's voice came again.

" Julie, my darling. It's all right."

Then his footsteps crossed the floor and in my mind's eye I saw him, as I had seen him on that other occasion, make straight for the cupboard in the corner.

" Here, drink this," his voice went on.

There came a faint little moan. Julia Forbes was evidently coming to.

The man's voice came again, insistent, loving.

" My dearest, don't be so terribly upset. I don't care if you did do it. It doesn't make any difference to me what you've done so long as we have each other. Only it all seemed so queer. My getting that story sent to me marked like that. But do tell me the truth, darling. I don't care a bit what it is, but I simply must know."

" Oliver," she moaned. " Yes, I did do it. But I did it for you. Don't be angry with me, darling. It was such hell dragging on week after week without you. And Philip was bound to die very soon, anyway," she added with a spurt of defiance.

" But is this story true, then ? " The man sounded bewildered. " Did you really do what it says here ? "

" Yes, I did," she answered. " I sent the commissionaire out for me, just when I knew Philip was coming home. Dr. Carlton had told him not to walk upstairs if he could help it, and if he did to go up backwards. So I put the notice on the lift. I wrote it with a pencil off the mantlepiece. Then I crept out and hung it on the lift gate. How anyone found out I can't imagine. Then I waited and watched, and at last I saw Philip. I saw him go to the gate and read the notice. Then he came to the bottom of the stairs and turned his back to me, just as the doctor had told him to do. Very carefully he started up the stairs, one at a time, slow and steady.

Suddenly I gave a terrified scream. I shouted to him : ' Oh, Philip, come quickly ! ' He turned round at once, instinctively facing upwards like any ordinary person, and began to run. When he had just got to the top he fell down—and died. So that's what happened. And I'm glad I did it, glad—glad."

She ended in a burst of uncontrollable weeping.

" Oh, my dear. I wish you hadn't done this awful thing for my sake. But I love you for it more than ever," he said, an immense tenderness in his voice. " But we're in the devil of a fix now," he went on hurriedly. " Obviously somebody knows, or this story would never have been written. We must clear out at once. Come on now, quickly. Just pack something and we'll get away at once. We'll get married right away and then p'raps they'll forget about it. My God ! What a ghastly hole to be in ! "

So engrossed was I in the drama that was being enacted overhead that I had almost forgotten where we were until I heard Jackson's voice—quiet, triumphant, almost gloating. I remember thinking how strangely insensitive were these official sleuths. They seemed quite to forget the human side of the story in their hunter's zeal. For me, I almost felt like backing young Barrett and letting them get away together.

" No you don't, young feller-me-lad," Jackson was saying. " You're too late now." He gathered us with his glance. " Well, gentlemen, shall we go up and witness the end of this little play ? "

Without a word we followed him to the door, but as he opened it and before he went upstairs he beckoned to two men in plain clothes who were standing in the hall.

They followed us.

Jackson rapped imperatively on the door of Mrs. Forbes's flat. For a few moments nothing happened. Then the door was partially opened by Oliver Barrett himself.

Jackson did not stand on ceremony. He pushed the door wide open in Barrett's face and walked straight through, with Royd, myself and the others in close attendance.

" I am Detective-Inspector Jackson of Scotland Yard," he said shortly. " I have a warrant for the arrest of Julia Forbes on a charge of murder."

For a moment I thought Barrett would leap at him, but he was saved, I think, by Julia Forbes herself, who then appeared at the door of the drawing-room.

" What is the meaning of this intrusion ? "

Her voice was as cold as ice, as hard as steel.

In that moment, when she must have known that the game
was up, I could not help but admire her.

Jackson whipped round and faced her.

" May I have a word with you, madam ? "

She threw open the drawing-room door and we followed
her in.   Seating herself gracefully in an arm-chair by the fire,
she motioned towards the other chairs about the room.

" Please be seated."

Jackson answered for us.

" I would rather not, madam.   I have come here to arrest
you on a charge of murdering your husband."

I thought I saw a faint tremor of her eyes, but she
answered boldly enough.

" How ridiculous ; what on earth do you mean ?   What
possible ground can you have for such an accusation ? "

I was looking at Jackson and I saw the faintest suggestion
of a smile on his lips.

He did not answer her in words but moved over to a curtain
by the window and drew it aside.   On the window-sill was a
small wooden box which had an open front of wire gauze.
With deft movements Jackson removed the lid and set the
machinery in motion.   Turning to her he said :

" Dictaphones are useful little things at times."

Into the silence fell uncannily the mechanical voice of the
dictaphone, grinding out the words of that very conversation
between Julia Forbes and Oliver Barrett to which we had just
been listening.

Suddenly Julia Forbes lost all control and leapt to her
feet.

" Stop it ! " she screamed, " for God's sake stop it ! Yes,
I killed Philip, if that's what you want. . . . "

*   *   *   *   *   *

It took me till nearly five this morning to write this.   Now
it is after nine.   In the interval I have been to the prison and
have seen that slip of paper posted on the gate.   Just a certificate
of a sentence duly carried out for the good of the community,
and signed by the prison governor.

I looked uneasily at the little knot of people that curiosity
had drawn to the spot.   I felt that all eyes were focused upon
me ; that each one there in the early day was marking me out
as a . . . killer.

But I must not get morbid.   I shall ring up Jackson and
ask him to lunch.

THE SONS
OF THE CHIEF WARDER

By

BERTRAM ATKEY

IN their boyhood their father had been Chief Warder of
Brandmoor Prison, so that the twin brothers, John and
James Smith, had gradually and unconsciously acquired a
complete knowledge of that great grim tomb. They had been
reared in the shadow of its grey and haunted walls, and, in a
small way, had been one of the chief local curiosities—for they
were physically more alike than two new pennies stamped one
after the other from the same die.

That—in those days—had been most entertaining and, to a
limited extent, productive of coppers and various attractive
edibles from people who, seeking amusement in a place where
amusement was scarce, were glad to teach them small mischiefs
based on their amazing likeness.

Only the schoolmaster—an oldish man who drank—ever
suggested that in character they were totally unlike.

" Jackie's the dull bone handle of the knife, Jimmy's the
sharp steel blade ! " he used to say. But nobody ever cared
about that—least of all that " dull " Jackie.

For he adored his brother above all people and above all
things.

Their mother had died when they were born, their father
lived long enough in his Chief Wardership to see them both
started in life, John entering the police force with a view later
to transfer into the prison service as a warder who should in
due time duplicate his father's success, and James going to
London as a clerk in an insurance office.

Only John was present when the old Chief Warder died—
James, for some reason, telegraphed by a friend, obscurely
worded and a little difficult to understand, could not arrive for

another two days. So it was to John only that the old Chief
Warder spoke of their future.

" You're all right, Jack—well settled in a good job. You'll
get on—you're like me, slow but sure. You'll be Chief Warder
here one of these days if you keep trying for it. I can see you
succeeding in life, my boy—steady, slow but sure. Yes. You'll
be all right. You've been a good boy—make a good man.
. . . Credit."

There had been a pause.

" Jim—Jimmy. I wish he could have been here. I—I've
been wondering about Jimmy. He's different from you . . .
inside. Outside I could never tell you apart. But inside he's
different—too reckless, too confident. Sharp . . . too sharp.
I seem to have a fancy that he'll get himself into trouble one of
these fine days. Maybe not—maybe not. Stick to him, Jack,
if he does. You've got something steady in you that he hasn't
got. He's—easy led—and crafty . . . Looking so much alike
. . . You'll do that, Jack . . . stick to Jimmy . . . he's too artful
by half . . . always was . . . Promise that . . . Should like
my boys to be as successful as their old dad . . . successful . . ."

It had begun to get rambling then.

But John had never forgotten—though he had never acquired what he considered the presumption to attempt to
advise his brother. John rarely saw him, but he gleaned from
occasional letters that Jimmy, in the succeeding years, became
brilliantly successful. He left the insurance and went on the
stage, left the stage just when (John understood) he was beginning to make some small reputation as an actor, and became
" something in the City." Later he forsook the City and was
associated with " something new " in connection with racing.

So the years flickered by.

John had been a warder at Brandmoor Prison for five years,
and he was thirty-seven years old, when, among his duties one
day was included that of escorting the only convict arriving
that day, to take the prison bath—a man booked in under the
surname Berris.

But it was his brother, Jimmy. . . . And he was sentenced
for life.

He was sentenced for life not for the intricacy of fraudulence
and blackmail proved against him during his trial, but for the
killing of one of his criminal associates. Only the fact that the
dead man had attacked him first had saved him from the
gallows.

" A lot of it wasn't true, Jack. Tenbold—the Scotland

Yard man—worked me up to it in the end. He was always badgering me. They knew I was always haunted and superstitious about Tenbold. That man I killed was impersonating Tenbold—blackmailing me ! I oughtn't to have got a lifer for him ! Life ! Life ! Do your best for me, Jack," the convict had muttered as he stripped.

" I will—I swear I—— " The white-faced warder broke off then at the sound of a step in the stone passage outside. " Stop that talking—get in ! " he added harshly.

The Chief Warder looked in, ran his eye over the stripped convict, said nothing and moved on, busy on his sombre affairs, rapt in his thoughts.

It may have occurred to him that Warder Smith looked extraordinarily pale—but it is certain that it did not occur to him that Warder Smith and Convict 661 were astonishingly alike. For the eyes of a convict do not look out from their sockets with the same expression as those of a free man, and the poise and air and balance of a prison guard in uniform with a good record behind him are far otherwise than the poise and air and balance of a naked and shivering convict with his haunted eyes fixed on the appalling years to come.

II

IT was nearly a year before Convict 661 completed telling the story of a career that had ended at Brandmoor. The only chances they had of talking occurred when the warder was on night duty. For, in those already distant pre-war days, there was a more stringent discipline in the places where the dangerous men, the cunning ones and the nuisances are buried alive. A jail is always a place of eyes and whispers and strange treacheries ; of curious and patient intrigues and deep strategies ; singular traffics that would seem petty to free men but are almost vital to prisoners and, sometimes, to the guards.

The story lost nothing in the telling—and gained much, for 661 was one with the glib, ready and practised tongue of the confidence-trick man. He had, too, a sense of drama—and years ago he had exactly appraised his brother's mentality. . . . He had become, moreover, a bad, callous and utterly treacherous blackguard. He was in the right place for the right number of years.

Free, he was a menace and a pest. Jailed, he was one dangerous nuisance the less to war on a community already over-afflicted with a huge variety of preventable nuisances.

But the warder did not know that. Nor would he have
believed it if anyone had told him the truth. He had always
loved Jimmy, and admired him. He had always believed Jimmy
to be his superior—whereas by every standard 661 knew his
brother was a plain fool.

Yet he was honest and, hitherto, had done his duty well and
steadily, though not brilliantly. But brilliancy is not required
in a long-term prison guard—a habit of unsleeping watchful-
ness is of more value in a place where a " lifer " working with
a heavy implement may, in an instant, go " cafard " or mad
and wheel on a careless guard with an unreasoning lust to use
his implement as a club.

661 was patient and cunning.

" Think it over, Jack, and tell me next chance what father
said when he died. I couldn't come—it broke my heart . . .
I'd like to hear about that," he said once.

In the interval Jack had time to relive that death-bed
scene, and to describe it to his brother.

" 'Thank God the dear old man was dead before ever I was
hunted into this place ! " said 661 with a dry, indrawn gasp.
" It would have killed him, Jack ! "

" Through no real fault of mine ! Tenbold, the man who
sent me here, would have been the guilty one—morally,
Detective-Inspector Tenbold ! . . . He hazed me ! Never haze
one of us poor devils, Jack. You don't know what we suffer.
He frightened me—he was always like a big black thunder-
cloud hanging over me. .... I had been a young fool—too
reckless—you know how I always was—and I admit I'd done
one or two silly things. This chap, this bullying wolf Tenbold,
got hold of those things in a way and set out to ' keep an eye '
on me, as the saying goes. He made my life a hell, Jack, a
hell—— "

Here some small event would interrupt and he might not
have a chance to continue. He did not mind much, for he had
made his plan and he was working for a great stake.

The terrible secret envy of the prisoner for the free man in
authority had long turned his former easy, condescending,
almost contemptuous liking for his brother into a cold hatred.

" To see that stupid fool going around like a kind of god
while I'm rotting here ! " he would sometimes mutter under
his breath in his cell, even as he chewed a bit of the forbidden
tobacco smuggled in to him by his brother. Then he would
control himself, and sit silently, planning, planning. . . .

He was prepared to spend years, if necessary, in perfecting

his desperate plan of carefully directing his brother's mind towards the idea that it was entirely possible to change places occasionally.

He intended to lead Jack's mentality, slowly, patiently and inexorably to a point where the warder's affection and pity for his brother, manipulated with eternal patience, great skill and minute care, would render such an exchange possible. It was his scheme to time this thing so that it coincided with one of the warder's annual leaves—a fortnight. . . .

He would sit in his cell, hunched-up a little, thinking, planning, his eyes gleaming, his body taut and very still— waiting as some great spider waits, motionless but watchful for the fly that buzzes heedlessly within a millimetre of the silky death-web spread for it.

But his chance came much more quickly and dramatically than he expected.

An old " lifer "—an ignorant, brutal and utterly bestial old savage, who had spent almost the whole of his adult life in serving sentences for the shameful crime in which he specialized, and with a record that, in a more enlightened age, would long since have qualified him for the lethal chamber—went " mad " or, as the saying loosely goes, " saw red."

They were doing heavy work at the quarries when quite suddenly and in full view of the convict gang and half-a-dozen warders this gorilla-man attacked, with a heavy pickaxe, the nearest warder. It chanced to be Warder John Smith. The convict missed his swing—probably he was half-blinded by some strange red murder-mist before his eyes and enveiling his soul. He had intended to bury the iron beak of his pickaxe in the warder's brain—but the warder ducked, and the heavy haft of the big tool smashed on to his shoulder, beating him to the ground.

Then Convict 661 leaped like a pouncing cat on to the back of the murderer who had swung up his pick for a surer blow, and clamped his calloused hands round the killer's throat as both of them fell forward. Three seconds later four of the other warders had the maniac safe.

It was perhaps generous to represent to the authorities, as the Governor did, that Convict 661 had saved the life of Warder Smith. But he had come near to that, and his sentence was remitted to fifteen years.

He took the news with an air of profound and humble gratitude. But there was no suggestion either of humility or gratitude in the cold glare of triumph in his eyes when later he sat alone, planning and carefully examining his plans through the lens of a mind which the approach of success had whetted to a keenness that was formidable.

III

SIX-SIXTY-ONE'S hour came shortly after when his brother told him he was due to take a fortnight's leave in three weeks' time.

"You deserve it, Jack," he whispered rapidly, gripping his brother's hand. "But me—I shall either be dead or mad by the time you get back!"

"Eh?" Jack stared.

"I can't stand any more of it, old man," came the convict's swift and ready whisper. "Been brooding too long. That time I saved your life I banked on getting let out at once—total remission.... Built on it! It broke my heart to get five years of freedom—if I live long enough—in return for a man's life. That wasn't fair, Jack, was it? I ask you. But for me you'd be dead and buried.... And, as it is, you're going on a fortnight's holiday—and *I'm* buried!"

He gripped his brother's sleeve with hungry hands.

"And I'll be dead by the time you get back—dead or mad—dead or mad! If only *I* could be the one to have a fortnight out—a fortnight—it'd save *my* life!"

Warder Smith was distressed.

"Good God, don't talk like that, Jim—it half kills me. What can I do? I did my best about that other—went to the Governor myself and begged for total remission for you—— "

His face was wrung and tormented. 661 saw that his moment was here.

"You can do one thing to save me—as I saved you, Jack. Give me your fortnight—in exchange for the life I gave you! Change places—so that I can breathe free man's air for just fourteen days!"

He listened. He was far calmer than his brother.

"Go now—think it over. It's easy. Think it over!"

He half-pushed his brother to the cell door, which a moment later shut upon him.

The warder resumed night patrol, staring before him down the grim corridors like a man who sees an apparition and cannot satisfy himself whether it is that of an angel or a devil.

" It isn't possible," he muttered under his breath as he went his round.

" But it *is* . . . Jim's right—you could do it for him if you meant what you said. A fortnight for a life . . . only fourteen days—for Jimmy, and never a soul would be the wiser ! "

The voice of the old Chief Warder, his father, seemed continually to come back to him now, insistently, like the voice of his own conscience.

" Stick to him, Jack . . . if ever he gets into trouble. You'll do that ? Stand by Jimmy ! " . . .

His face began to clear and his eyes to brighten as he paced the corridors. And he had made his decision and taken his resolution with the grim and almost fanatic stubbornness of his slow type of mind by the time he went off duty at dawn.

IV

ODDLY, it was the convict rather than the warder who was most patient and meticulous.

" It isn't just the question of changing clothes one night, Jack—there's more to it than that. I've thought it out. Can't afford mistakes ! Be guided by me, for God's sake, Jack ! "

Long before the vital day 661 had made it clear that no preventable mistakes should happen. He had thought of everything. The length of their hair, the condition of their teeth, and hands, the exact tint of their dark complexions— he had been working with the outdoor gang, so that there was little difficulty about this—bit by bit, trifle by trifle, he matched his brother to himself. He went without food for three days because he fancied he was just a shade fatter in the face than his brother. Minutely, subtly, infinitesimally, microscopically he matched them, till even the warder was amazed at the patient mastery of detail and fertility of resource the convict possessed.

So, in the end, they were ready. Luck favoured them also to the extent that the warder was on duty the night before his leave started. That simplified several important risks— eliminating as it did the necessity for the convict to act as warder in his brother's place for, possibly, several days.

He could have done this—but it was great good fortune that he would not need to do it.

The convict smiled tensely as he sat in his cell running over every little point, making sure that nothing was forgotten.

" It's fool-proof," he said at last. " What with this bit of night-duty luck. Yes, fool-proof. Night after next, just before Jack goes off, he slips in, changes clothes, and *I* step out and go off duty—and away, my God ! *Away !* Nothing to hinder—not a chance of coming back—not a risk "—his face shadowed—" except two ! Just those two—the finger-prints and Tenbold ! . . . If Jack gets tired and gives it away and proves it with his finger-prints ! And if that bloodhound Tenbold gets on to me. . . ."

He drew in his breath.

" He'll get me . . . if ever he starts for me. He always will ! " It was the first hint of nervousness he had shown even when alone.

For Detective-Inspector Tenbold was a terror and an obsession ; he was Fate to James Smith, alias Berris ; he was something surer and more inexorable than a cherished superstition, for he was an incubus, something that rode the soul of 661—feared above all things. Even as the smallest weasel trailing the biggest rabbit can paralyse the doomed animal into a trance of fear that halts it rigid, to await the death stroke, so in a lesser degree Tenbold could scare 661 into nerveless panic. Yet in all else 661 was bold, crafty and dangerous. He knew it—he told himself so, and so at last contrived to control himself. For he said that Tenbold could never know—even if Jack got tired and confessed, Tenbold would never know till he, 661, was thousands of miles from England.

All was well. . . .

There was nothing except lack of nerve to prevent things from going well.

At five o'clock in the morning—one hour before he would go " off duty " for a fortnight—he stepped into his brother's cell. Jimmy was waiting there for him, stripped. In his turn, the warder stripped, exchanged clothing ; then both men redressed in silence and desperate haste.

Jack was far from being the clever actor that his brother was, but there was no need.

The man who, a few moments later, sat on the cell-pallet, clad in the shocking arrow-marked garb of those days, was as blatantly a convict as the man in the blue uniform who faced him was a warder—steady, honest, not too intelligent, but reliable !

There was no time to linger, for a prison is full of fox-keen listening ears.

But even ex-661 gasped as his keen eyes took in his brother.

" Thanks, Jack ! " he whispered. " Don't fret ! "

The ex-warder's eyes were suddenly full of tears.

" Have a good time, Jimmy . . . I can stand it all right,
Jimmy. There's forty pounds in the top left-hand drawer of
my chest of drawers in my room. 'Tis all I got. Take it—
and have a good holiday."

" Thanks—thanks, old man. Don't worry. I'll be back.
Don't fret if I'm not to time for a day or two, it'll all depend
on the night duty detail. You understand about that ? As
soon as I can ! "

There was a noise of sorts far down the corridor, and hastily
he offered his hand.

" So long, old man ! "

" So long, Jimmy—good luck ! Have a good time ! "

They exchanged a grip. That of Judas was the more convincing. It always is.

The cell-door closed, and " Warder " Smith went angrily
down the corridor to deal with the convict who was making
forbidden noises. . . .

His heart stood still when he went off duty, for it chanced
that the Chief Warder was present. And this one's heavy-
lidded glance dwelled on him for a few seconds.

" You don't look quite yourself, Smith," he said. " Time
you had a bit of leave."

Ex-661 pressed his hand to his stomach, and half-groaned
as he answered :

" I've been suffering here, sir, last few days—something I
et "—(Jack would have said " et ")—" It'll be all right, sir !
Didn't want to spoil my leave going sick ! "

The Chief Warder nodded, and ex-661 left the prison,
walking tranquilly, without haste. He was entirely confident,
and his plans were perfect. It was a little annoying that Jack
had only managed to save a miserable forty pounds—a man
in a steady job such as the warder's had been should have
accumulated at least a hundred pounds, more if he had been
careful. Still, forty pounds was better than nothing. He could
have a fairly thrilling three days in London for about fifteen
pounds, and the balance would get him well out of the country
by the time the fortnight's leave was up. He smiled and hummed a tune as he ransacked at his leisure his brother's quarters.
If there was any cloud on his horizon it seemed in that moment
of triumph to be so small that it was hardly a shadow—the
shadow of Detective-Inspector Tenbold. . . .

At mid-day he took the train to London.

V

Ex-661—or as he now called himself, John Wilson—proceeded to enjoy himself in London. He avoided his old haunts but not his old extravagances. The unaccustomed alcohol, in various forms, the richer food ; certain joyous feminine society ; the unlimited cigarettes, the comfort of good clothes and the suave luxury of very good underclothing—all these things had their almost instant effect. He had left the prison keen-witted, clear-minded, completely unscrupulous—wary as a wolf, cunning as a fox.

But a week's wallowing in the sheer gratification of his sensual needs had its effect both on his mind—and his money.

He lost a good deal of self-control—though he never became reckless. He drank far too much—but never enough to render him foolish. He talked freely with the two or three of the sort of acquaintances a man apparently with money to spend may pick up easily enough in town—but he never confided in them anything that mattered.

At the end of ten days he was reduced to his last five pounds. That meant he must work his way out of England and see about it next day. That did not worry him much. He had worked his way on ships before—and he believed that Jack would not panic if he did not put in an appearance promptly.

" Still, I must get a move on," he told himself. " One more decent dinner to-night, now, and I'll get to work."

He turned into a large, rather garish and noisy second-rate restaurant, found a table and settled down to his last few pounds' worth of luxury. The bottle of champagne he ordered charmed him into a mood of purring satisfaction. Except occasionally to regret that his brother had not saved a little more money, he had not a doubt nor a care in the world, for, as he said, he " knew his way about."

Halfway through his meal it occurred remotely to his wine-lulled instincts of caution that something was wrong. It was purely animal reaction—the instinct of a creature accustomed to be hunted.

Ex-661 went a little rigid. He did not know why. He put down, untouched, the third glass of wine he had been raising, and quietly continued his meal. But now he began to look about him, very carefully, with gentle movements of the head, and slow-moving indifferent eyes.

He dropped a hand casually to the pocket in which lay the

weapòn which, if worst came to worst, would save him from return to Brandmoor.

A few minutes of stealthy scrutiny of the people at neighbouring tables satisfied him that no danger threatened from them. Yet, by now, alarum bells were clanging in his very soul.

He searched the many wall-mirrors about him, and at last understood the subtle panic that had gripped him. Some distance away, behind him and to his right, was a small table for two, set near a big pillar. The heavy, whitish face of a man was visible from behind this pillar.

This man was not eating. Instead, he was staring intently, with odd, rather close-set, curiously colourless eyes, at ex-661.

And suddenly the veins of ex-661 were choked with ice—for these were the eyes of his incubus, Detective-Inspector Tenbold!

And Tenbold knew him.

Ex-661 sensed it instantly . . . and as instantly was again the desperately wary and dangerously-cunning wolf he had been on the day he left Brandmoor.

Carelessly he allowed his glance to wander across the face of the mirror, then quietly he turned to the dish the waiter had just brought him. . . .

It was desperately difficult, but he succeeded in refraining from looking at Tenbold again. And he ate his meal with every appearance of tranquillity to the very end, lingered a little over a cigarette, made a small joke when he paid the waiter, and presently strolled to the cloak room.

Twice as he made his way out to the busy crowded entrance of the restaurant Tenbold met him full face, crossed glances, and passed on.

He hesitated on the pavement outside, like a man who does not quite know what to do to amuse himself for the evening, then he strolled away through the busier parts of the West End. . . . Within half-an-hour he knew he was being shadowed.

Presently he yawned like a man bored and tired, and turned back to the house in which he had a room. He knew himself tracked almost to the doorstep. Yet he knew also that for an hour or so he was safe from interruption, for he judged correctly that Tenbold was doing even as he would have done himself, namely, telephoning to Brandmoor to ask if the convict Berris was safely in his cell.

He was quite cool now, for he knew what Brandmoor would say to that.

Nevertheless, he believed himself in danger, for he knew something of the extraordinary tenacity and intuition of Tenbold. In the same way that a good reporter has a curious instinct for " news," so did Tenbold have an instinct for secret crime—an instinct that had made him one of the most feared men in the Metropolitan Police. Tenbold had told him so, even boasted of it, just after he had arrested him for the crime which had sent him to Brandmoor. No matter how promptly and adequately Brandmoor answered Tenbold's inquiry, ex-661 sensed that he would be shadowed for a time. Tenbold would want to know something about a man who looked so exactly like one who should be in jail for many years to come—and, with next to no money, ex-661 knew that he was going to find it difficult to avoid the detective long.

He sat down, rigidly steady now, and desperately cool, and began to think things out. . . .

When presently he went to bed his plans were complete— and as cruel and cold-blooded as they were complete.

VI

SIX-SIXTY-ONE rose at dawn and wiped everything he had touched in that room carefully with a handkerchief soaked in whisky. He had not taken off his gloves from the moment he had left the restaurant overnight—and he had been careful to smear every implement of cutlery and glass he had touched which must remain on the table when he left it. He knew that Tenbold would need only one glance at any clear fingerprint of his to spring on him like a tiger.

Then he had breakfast in his room, paid his bill, and left. . . .

It took him an hour to shake off his shadow in the confusion of a big crowd at a sale at one of the huge West End emporiums. Then he headed for Brandmoor, travelling partly by train, partly by motor-bus, partly on foot. He called in at a dentist's and a chemist's as he passed through a small town. . . .

" So far, so good," he said, and made himself some tea. No more whisky for him—till Jack was dead and buried.

He reported for duty sharp on time.

" Been in the wars, haven't you ? " said the Chief Warder, eyeing the gap created by two missing upper-teeth.

" Yes, sir—a pickpocket in London. I grabbed him—a shrimp of a chap—but he must have been a light-weight

The man was not eating.   He was gazing intently at ex-661.

bruiser or something, for he hit like the kick of a mule, sir.
As quick as lightning ! Got these teeth and cut my cheek
to the bone ! ”

The Chief Warder eyed the big criss-cross of sticking
plaster.

“ Huh ! Bad cut ? ”

“ The doctor said he reckoned I was scarred for life, sir ! ”

“ Pity,” said the Chief Warder. “ You ought to have been
a bit smarter, Smith. Man get away ? ”

“ Yes, sir.”

“ Huh ! You want to wake your ideas up next time
you go to town, Smith ! ” he said impassionately, and passed
on.

Ex-661 grinned deep down in his soul. He had hated
savagely the necessity of having those teeth out and of incising
that two-inch gash under the plaster, but it was worth it. . . .

He was on night duty a few nights later, and stole a minute
with Jack.

The significance of the new marks did not occur at once
to the pseudo-convict. But ex-661 pointed them out softly,
in a tone of bitter regret.

Then Jack saw, and he stared at his brother, horrified.

“ But, Jim—Jim—how am I going to get back ? ” he asked.
“ I can’t take on the uniform without a scar and two teeth
missing—and you can’t take on the prison clothes with a scar
and two teeth missing ! What—what is there to do ? For
God’s sake, Jim—I couldn’t stand much more of this—
coming from warder to convict. It’s awful, Jim. I never
believed——”

661 slid a blue-clad arm round his brother’s shoulder.

“ Easy, boy, easy. Keep your head. I’ll fix up something.
Give me a few days—a week or two. . . . False teeth. . . .
Let the cut heal a bit, and have an accident to your cheek
in the quarry. I’ll manage all right, Jimmy—stick it, boy,
for a little bit longer. I’m working for you. . . .”

Jimmy nodded, staring dully, and the “ Warder ” went
out, marvelling that so far his brother had not thought of the
obvious thing—the finger-prints.

That was what he feared—the finger-prints ! The finger-
prints—they haunted his evil soul by day, by night. If Jimmy
thought of that, and, getting unbearably tired, requested an
interview with the prison governor, told the truth, and
demanded a comparison of finger-prints, what would happen ?
He would lose—he was lost. Twins or no twins, the finger-

prints—— He stopped short in the corridor at an idea that electrified him.

But—were their finger-prints different ? Are the finger-prints of twins different ? He did not know, but, by God, he would soon find out !

If they were alike, all was well. He would remain free, resign as soon as he could lay up enough money, and clear out of the country, leaving Jack to convince the Governor if he could.

If the finger-prints were not alike—why, so much the worse for Jack. For he, ex-661, was quite prepared to kill Jack, to kill anybody—even in the last resort, himself—rather than return to the tomb from which, by a miracle of good fortune, he had contrived to resurrect himself.

His plastered face white and bitterly resolute, " Warder " James Smith prowled the corridors of Brandmoor like a beast of prey. . . . In his cell " Convict 661 " sat staring, wide-eyed and frightened, at the stone floor.

VII

Ex-661 was ingenious with the cruel and implacable in- genuity of desperation. He reminded his brother, who was growing thinner and more lined, that if worst came to worst the finger-prints would always be ample proof.

" That is, if they are different—as they're bound to be. I suppose even twins' prints *are* different. But we'd better make sure ! "

He got out the things he had in readiness, took a quick impression of Jack's fingers, and hurried out of the cell.

At the next visit—a week later—he took with him two sets of his own, in duplicate, on one of which he had written " Jacks," on the other, " Jim's." One eager glance through the magnifying-glass showed Jack that the sets were exactly identical. He stared at his brother, a sudden real terror in his eyes.

" But, good God, Jim, I'm done for ! If my prints are the same as yours, registered at Scotland Yard, and if anything happened to you, I'm here for nearly fifteen years ! "

There was fear and horror in his voice.

" That won't happen, Jack," said ex-661 smoothly. " If they don't believe you—they'll believe me when I confess ! "

But Jack was not so sure.

" You'll have to be quick, then, Jim. We're getting more and more unlike every day—you're getting fatter I'm getting thinner—and there's the scar, and the teeth ! "

" I'll fix all that, Jack ; those things won't matter when I explain that they happened *after* we exchanged. Leave it to me, old man. Be patient. You shall be *set free*, I promise that, if necessary. But I've got a better idea. I'm working it out. Hang on a little longer—just a little longer—I can fix it so that neither of us ever sees the cell again. If you *escape*—ssh !—I'm fixing it—— "

He listened, feigned to hear a sound, and went out.

Escape ! The word electrified the trapped man.

He slumped on to his bed, thinking, his eyes bright with hope. Nobody knew better than he the incredible difficulty of escaping which the average convict in Brandmoor must overcome. Unaided, it was, for such a convict, practically impossible. But with a warder helping him—a warder as sharp-witted and clever as his brother Jim—that altered things.

And he knew the moor by heart. Nobody in the world knew the moor better than he—not even the moormen themselves. As a boy he had learned it for miles around—every nook and crevice and cranny of those grey rocks that encrust it. And he had good friends on and about the moor—old friends who had known him and his brother as boys and who would understand quite easily the extraordinary situation. They would help him if necessary.

Yes . . . escape. . . . That was the solution. There were great tears of relief rolling unnoticed down his flushed cheeks as he sat there thinking.

And because he was a man of simple heart he was faintly conscious of a sense of guilt—for once or twice there had flickered in on his consciousness a suspicion, ugly as the flickering tongue of a snake, that his brother intended to leave him where he was.

He was ashamed of that now. He ought to have known better. Jimmy had been in for life—but he had saved his, Jack's, life at the risk of his own, and even the authorities had rewarded him with five years' freedom—five years off the life sentence which, normally, would have been about twenty years. If those aloof, far-off, god-like people, the authorities, did not grudge five years reward to one who had saved one of their servants—what sort of a man was that servant who could not endure a few months of torment so that his saviour and brother should breathe free air again for those brief months?

The " convict " crouched abashed and ashamed, adoring his brother—that brother of the clever brain and generous heart, who was prowling the midnight corridors planning his perfect infamy. . . .

Escape !

The word beat on the " convict's " brain like the slow strokes of a bell. Once on the moor, dressed in the clothes that Jim would hide for him, and he would be safe. For the moor and the mists of the moor, the rocks and valleys, the secret places of his youth, would enfold and shelter him as forests receive and shelter hunted deer.

And the old friends—the moormen—who would understand this terrible thing.

" Warder " Smith's eye at the spyhole, a little later, saw nothing more than the man called 661 kneeling like a child at his pallet.

Six weeks later ex-661 conveyed to his brother the information that all was ready—except the opportunity.

" You understand now, Jack—when the chance comes I'll tell you in plain words—no signs. It will be when I'm nearest to you. When I say ' Go for it,' don't wait, but *go*. Make for the five rocks they used to call the Monks in the Mist. Remember 'em ? "

" Yes, yes ! "

" Under the middle one will be lying the remains of a dead sheep. Drag it away, and you'll find a few bits of wood over a hole. Drag those away, and you'll find a suit of clothes wrapped in a waterproof sheet. Tourists' clothes—suit, mackintosh, stick, gloves and all complete. You'll have start enough to get 'em on—then roll up the prison suit, put it in the hole, cover it with the wood and the dead sheep, and make for old Tom Penellen's farm. It's only a couple of miles. Young Tom—the old man's dead—will give you some money and run you over to Exeter in his car. There he'll hand you over to a man named Munstone with a big car, who will drive right away to Birmingham. He'll drop you at a quiet little pub, the Guinea Fowl, kept by a man with a black moustache, called Murch. Murch'll go with you to Liverpool and fix everything for you so that within a fortnight you'll be in Canada. Go right through to Vancouver—you'll have enough money—and get a job there. Call yourself Simms— Robert Simms. I'll join you there sooner or later. Repeat that, Jack—quick—quick—— "

His slow wits electrified by this concrete and vital plan, the " convict " repeated the string of lies without error.

" Keep saying it over and over again. . . . I'll check you when I get a chance, Jack—and *be ready*. It may come to-morrow—and it mayn't come for a year. But keep ready ! All right ? "

" Yes, yes ! "

" Here, take this ! "

A lump of tobacco slid into John Smith's trembling fingers.

" So long, boy ! "

The " warder " was gone like a blue phantom.

VIII

IT was eleven months later, and mid-winter, when two convicts in charge of one warder were ordered out to clear a drain that was choked with an accumulation of semi-frozen snow-water.

It was a short and simple job, some three wide fields away from the prison, near a dip in the main road, over which the diverted water was forming a slippery film.

" Warder " Smith was instructed to take Convicts 661 and 727 to do the work.

He marched his two men out ahead of him across the dazzling fields, heavily cloaked in newly-fallen snow. Once as he followed them, like doom, he slid back the bolt of his rifle and noted the brass rim, the copper cap, of the cartridge snug in the breech. He shot home the oily, smooth bolt.

They came to the choked drain.

" Get to the lower end, 727," ordered the " warder."
" Cut the snow out towards you and shovel it on the bank ! . . . You take the top end, 661 ! "

He peered at the lower end.

" Get a move on, 727—sooner it's done the sooner you'll be in out of this weather ! "

727 began to dig.

" Warder " James Smith slid his rifle " safe " off, and stepped back. He was on the knife-edge of freedom—and knew it.

" 661 " waited—he, too, was on the knife-edge of freedom. Then the Judas whisper came like the hiss of a snake.

" *Now, Jack—go for it !* "

" 661 " dropped his shovel and ran, crouching a little as he ran. Without a sound the " warder " half-wheeled, throwing his rifle to his shoulder. . . . Now—through the heart.

But he slipped in the deceptive snow as he turned, slithered, lost his balance, and rolled, arms whirling, down the slight bank on which he had been standing. But he kept his grip on the rifle and he was up like a cat.

The running " convict " was still an easy mark. "Warder" Smith dropped on one knee to make quite sure.

He did not hurry. He aimed steadily. Through the open sights the back of his brother looked as broad as a barn-door. But the " warder " was searching for a heart shot.

He aimed with confident but extreme care. He was on it . . . no . . . yes . . . yes . . . *yes* !

His sights dead on his brother's heart, he pressed the trigger, for freedom.

Freedom it was. The rifle burst, for its barrel was choked with snow, and the heavy bolt was driven clean out from its oily grooves straight through the eye of the man who fired, and the vile brain behind his eye.

With half his head blown away, " Warder " Smith slumped into the snow—and the freedom of death.

727 straightened up with a cry of horror. . . . Warders poured out of the great grey prison. And " 661 " ran for the Monks in the Mist.

Panting, he gained that place, made for the tall middle rock, and—there was no sheep's body there, no fleece, no wood, nothing but the solid earth at the foot of each of those natural monoliths. He hacked in frenzy with his heels at the ground at the base of each rock, realized that there never had been a hollow at either place, and so understood his brother at last. He groaned and faced the moor, plunging almost at random through the snow-drifts.

There was no chance at all for him. Twenty minutes later he found himself staring at the muzzles of the rifles of two mounted warders.

" All right," he said dully. " I'm not going to try anything. . . . Only, I'm Warder John Smith ! Listen, Hayler and Moon—you know me, only you don't know you know me. I want to see the Governor."

The warders were grim.

" Get on ! You'll see him fast enough ! " they said.

The Governor of Brandmoor was, necessarily, a man of great patience, extreme acumen, and enormous experience.

" Jimmy will tell you it's the truth, sir ! Send for Jimmy —my brother—in charge of the party I escaped from. He's my brother—my twin brother, sir ! " implored " 661."

But the Governor sent instead for certain old warders, long since pensioned, and, dismissing " 661 " temporarily, questioned them and other people about the past in the neighbourhood of the prison, for a long time.

When he sent them away he was convinced that many years ago there had been twin sons of a long-dead Chief Warder.

He had not forgotten an unusual night-call received a long time ago from a detective at Scotland Yard.

Now he, too, in his turn, telephoned Scotland Yard, and then recalled " 661."

" Your story will be considered," he said. " And the finger-prints will show whether it is a true story. You understand that, 661 ? If your finger-prints are identical with those of the man booked in here and numbered 661—I warn you that almost certainly you will be assumed to be that man and will serve your term plus your punishment for an attempt to escape!

" But they are, sir ! They're alike—Jim—my brother told me so ! "

The Governor's face was entirely impassive. He made a sign to the Chief Warder—who moved to the desk.

" Steady, 661 ! Just do as you're told ! Press your fingers here—yes—now here ! Not too hard, man ! Good. . . . *Attention !* "

" But if you had Jimmy—Warder Smith—in, sir," begged " 661," " he could prove it."

" Warder Smith is *dead* ! " said the Governor. " But his finger-prints, too, have been taken. You have nothing to fear —if you are telling the truth ! "

It was all very simple to Detective-Inspector Tenbold, that tenacious man who arrived next day. He studied the finger-prints of the dead " warder." They matched microscopically with those of the man Berris and with those of the real 661.

Those of John Smith were totally unlike those of the real convict.

" There's no question about it, sir," Tenbold told the Governor, presently, " the man's telling the truth. . . . I ought to have known it without the finger-prints—if I'd had real confidence in myself. . . . When I saw him in town that time I *knew* him. Even went so far as to put a man on him. . . . Well, sir, there it is."

In the end and after many days the Governor sent for John Smith.

He dismissed the Chief Warder and gave Smith a seat.

" Well, Smith," he said, " I have done my best for you . . . and you are free.

" I suppose there are penalties prescribed somewhere for what you did—but nobody in authority seems anxious to enforce them. . . . No. . . . So you are free."

The Governor stood up and, stiffly, John Smith rose, facing him.

" There's this . . ." said the Governor. " Don't be bitter about it, Smith. It was a unique thing. You did well—speaking as one man to another. Yet you were victimised and all but doomed. It's the way of things. Yet in the end all's well. I am not allowed to keep you here as warder any longer—you wouldn't care for that, in any case. If I can help you at any time, let me know. I'll do my best for you—you see, I understand. I, too, have had a brother. . . . Well, good luck to you ! "

The Governor offered his hand—and then John Smith walked out of the prison quietly, unhurrying, unescorted, in the manner of a private citizen.

He went on like a man in a dream. But the dream was not intolerably unpleasant—and already his slow mind was beginning to plan, rather humbly, some sort of a future.

QUERY

By

"SEAMARK"

THOMAS MASTERICK looked dully at the little square of grey sky behind his cell window. He had come to regard it as something of an entity, something almost possessing life. It had a unique talent. It was the only thing in his cell that ever changed. It was a tiny, slow-moving picture in a world that was fixed and motionless. He talked to it in a low, uncomplaining monotone that was cow-like in its contemplative absence of expression. For fifteen years he had been talking to various objects in his cell, reasoning with them vaguely on his one cankering grievance against life.

Not that it was a grievance in the ordinary sense of the word, for there was not a scrap of resentment in the soul of Thomas Masterick. Only a dim perplexity, a puzzlement that refused to submit to elucidation no matter how earnestly he tried to think it out. All he asked of life was an explanation, a reason for the rather unfair thing life had done to him. And he could never quite get down to that explanation. It eluded him persistently. A thousand times he had tried to think down to the real reason. And he had overdone it. Later he came to realize that that was probably why he could no longer think as easily as he used to.

" The trouble is," he admitted to the grey square, " I've been thinking too much. I've had too many thinks. A lot too many thinks. I know I have ; because now when I try to have a real good think all I get is a bad dizzy. And these dizzies make my head ache. I've been having too many of them dizzies lately.

" But They can say what They like," he added moodily. " They can say what They like, but They can't say I killed Fred Smith. They can say and say and say. But that don't make out I killed him."

He sat on the edge of his stool and fretfully fingered the leaves of the Bible on the white-scrubbed table.

"Of course the other trouble is," he said. "They think I did. And that's where They've got me. That's what makes it more awkward. It's not much use me saying I didn't, if all the time They tell me I did. They don't believe me any more than I believe Them. They're the most awful crowd of liars I ever met.

"That long, lanky chap in the black gown—he was the worst of the lot. And he was the start of it. Never heard such a lying devil in all my life. Stood up in the middle of the court he did—in the middle of the court, mind you—and deliberately argued that I killed Fred Smith. And there was a hell of a crowd of people there. All listening. They must have heard it. Couldn't have done otherwise.

"And how could *he* know ? " he asked with placid wonderment. "Eh ? How *could* he know. He wasn't there. He admitted he'd never seen Fred Smith in his life. And he laughed when I asked him. I didn't like that laugh. So stinkin' cocky it was. He admitted he'd never seen me, not till that day They put me in court. So how could *he* know. Yet he stood in the very middle of that court and deliberately made out to the judge how I did it. Stuck at it for four days he did. He was a marvel of a chap. He proved I did do it ! Actually proved it. He was a marvel of a chap. Proved it as plain as plain. An absolute marvel of a chap. But the most God-forsaken liar I ever came across in my life.

"And the questions he asked ! Couh ! You'd have thought he'd known Smithy all his life. Long, lanky devil, he had me tied up all ways. Couldn't move a hand's turn. A fair knockout. He proved me a liar. And a perjurer. And a thief. And then he went and proved I killed Fred Smith. And that was where I had him. Because I never killed Fred Smith. I never saw Fred Smith that day. And if ever I get out of this I'll tell him so, too. Never such a chap in all my born days. Simply wouldn't listen to reason. And now it's raining like the very devil.

"I never told him any lies. I never told him any perjury. And I never nicked anything in my life. Well, not since I left school, anyway. And then for him to stand up in the middle of that court and say the things he did—well ! It beats me. Beats me flat.

"And then the judge told me he was going to hang me. I wish to Gord he had now. I wouldn't have been stuck here all this time. Can't make out why he didn't. They was so damn cock-sure I'd done it. If I did, why didn't he hang me ? If I'd done it, he ought to have hung me, and none of these half-larks. If I didn't do it, then They got no right to have me hung. And They haven't hung me. Looks precious much to me as if They ain't sure I did do it, after all.

"I knew it was going to rain. I knew it this morning. And I said so to Four-eighty-four out in the exercise. ' Ginger,' I said, ' it's going to rain.' ' I don't care a damn,' says Ginger. ' Before dinner,' I said. ' Will it,' says Ginger. ' I'll bet you three hundred thousand pounds it don't.'

"Well, I've got that to come, anyway. That ought to set me up a bit when I get outside. But I don't suppose I'll get it. He won't pay up. He never does. I don't believe he's got three hundred thousand pounds. He's a fly devil is Ginger. Different as anything from Southampton Jack. Southampton Jack betted me a bread ration that I couldn't get him the result of the Derby before supper-time. Of course I could get him the result of the Derby before supper-time. I know the ropes. After all the years I've been here I ought to know the ropes. People who don't know how to get hold of the ropes never ought to go to prison.

"But Ginger don't even pay up on a bread ration. He betted me a bread ration last Sunday that the chaplain would give out hymn number four-eighty-four in the evening. And he didn't. The biggest number he gave out was three hundred and eight. But that only shows how much Ginger knows about religion. Hymn number four-eighty-four is a Christmas hymn. And this ain't Christmas. Not by a long chalk. But he never paid up.

"Southampton Jack paid up next morning. Chucked it in my cell as he was passin' through to the exercise. That's the best of sailors. They're only fly devils sometimes. Mostly they're all right. He's here because he sold a lot of cargo. He says he'd go dotty if they put him in prison without him selling some cargo first. I'm here because I never killed Fred Smith. If I had of killed Fred Smith They'd have hung me.

"Southampton Jack don't believe I killed Fred Smith. Don't believe a word of it. ' What ? You ? ' he said. ' You killed Fred Smith ? Not you, my cocker,' he said. ' You ain't got the guts to kill Fred Smith.' Which was quite right then. But ain't now. I wouldn't think twice about having a lam at that long, lanky devil who stood up in the middle of

that court and spouted about me the way he did. It was him
that got me lagged, I reckon.

" Sometimes I used to think I'd go dotty when They put
me in here without me first killing Fred Smith. But I don't
get that way now. All I get is the dizzies. And only when
I'm having too many thinks.

" It's funny old Ginger letting himself get caught over his
own hymn number. You'd reckon they'd all know their own
hymn numbers by the time they've been here a lot of years.
When all you've got to read is that Bible and hymn-book,
it makes you study 'em a bit. I must have read that Bible
down a hundred times. And I'm hanged if I can see what
there is in it for people to go raving crazy about. A finer pack
of lies I never did see. Nor a bigger lot of twaddle. Unless it
was the lot that long lanky devil said about me in that
court.

" Most of us know where we are in the hymn-book. Joe
Bennett is a Holy Baptism and Tim Cheyne is a 'Piphany.
There's a couple of Trinity Sundays down there past the wash-
house and all of 'em up there on the top landing are Lents.
Me and the lags either side is Ember Days. I've been here
years and years and I've never been sung yet. Dan Rafferty
gets sung most. He's a Times of Trouble. But the best one
is old Three-fifty-one. He's a Matrimony and he's in for a
lot of bigamy. I reckon that's damn funny. Thinking about
that has got me out a dizzy many a time. Southampton Jack
is a Harvest Festival and Tom Earle, who used to be a warder
here once, is the only Rogation Day in this block. The other
Rogation cells are full of scrubbing gear.

" In my honest opinion I don't believe Fred Smith ever
was killed. I believe he took ship that day. It's just the sort
of thing he would do. It would be just his delight to land me
in the soup. He always said he would. And, my God, he
did ! Not half he didn't. He always went on sailing ships.
And if he suddenly went off on one of those damn long Mel-
bourne cruises of his, he wouldn't be heard of for months
and months. More especially if he got bad winds. It would
have been all over before he made land. All over and done
with. And I'd have been put away prop'ly.

" Southampton Jack might know. He's been to sea long
enough. Running east, too. He would tell me if he's heard
anything about Smithy since I've been here. If he has, then
all I've got to do is to wait till my time's up and go and find
him. If I did find him I wouldn't half be able to take the mike

out of that cocksure crowd in that court. I'd give 'em a shock all right. I'd make 'em think a bit too, I'll lay.

"And I don't believe that body they had up on that slab was old Freddy Smith at all. Smithy never wore a wristwatch. He was a sailor. A blue water sailor. And I doubt if his eyesight was good enough to see the time by a wristwatch. And I'm dead sure he never wore brown boots in his life. I've told the Governor that. And the Chaplain. And the Visiting Justices. But, you see, they didn't know Fred Smith. So they couldn't say. And they wouldn't believe me much, anyway—not after what that long, lanky devil said about me.

Rubber-shod feet and a jingle of steel went past his door and up the stairs of the main hall.

"That's old Neversweat," he observed. "Going up to start opening all the doors for dinner. Mutton broth and jackety spuds it'll be to-day. And no duff. Because there's bread. That ought to be all right. And after that we'll all have a bath. And after that Six-thirty-one will scrape the hide off our faces with that razor of his. And then we'll all be all right for Sunday. Six-thirty-one tries to make out he was a real barber before he came here. Couh! I pity his customers. Southampton Jack reckons his customers must have got him put away—if he really was a barber outside. Jack only let him shave him once. Then he put in to be allowed to grow a beard. The Governor laughed like hell when old Neversweat told him why."

The wards of the lock clanged solidly back to the thrust of a ponderous key.

"Basins," said the cookhouse orderly in front of an adequate warder.

Thomas Masterick received his dinner, and the warder poked his head into his cell.

"Number Three-five-four," he said, "you won't go through to exercise after dinner. You'll remain in your cell till the chaplain comes. He will see you this afternoon."

"Will he, sir? All right. Thank you."

The warder looked at him oddly. "You feeling unwell?" he snapped.

"No sir. I'm all right. Only I think I've got one of my dizzies coming on. I'll be all right, sir, after this bit of broth."

"Well, take my tip when the chaplain comes, and look better than you do now. Or he will be having you trotted along to the infirmary. And you don't want that, do you?"

Masterick looked at him with a childlike incredulity. Of

all the desirable heavens in the world of the penal prison the infirmary was the sweetest and best.

" I wouldn't mind going to the infirmary, sir," he said bleakly. " It's very nice in the infirmary."

Regardless of the din of impatient basins and spoons lower down the corridor, the warder stepped right into the cell.

" Say, Three-fifty-four, don't you know what he is going to see you for ? " he asked.

Masterick looked up with a spot of fear in his eyes.

" You're going out to-morrow, Three-fifty-four. Didn't you know ? Oh, you poor devil ! "

That last was because Thomas Masterick had trembled a little, grinned a little, and slid down to the floor with the mutton broth spreading all over his chest.

" My Gawd ! " said the warder in the mess-room half an hour later. " Now what the devil was that Number Three-fifty-four living for ? Eh ? What was he looking forward to ? He wasn't even keeping tally of his time. He's the first one I've ever known who couldn't tell you to a second how many *hours* he still had to do—at any time of the day or night."

" Well, you see," Thomas Masterick was informing his basin at that moment, " when I was a Feast and Thanksgiving down there by the doctor's shop, I had it all written up in the whitewash. Got a splinter off the floor boards, I did. And scratched 'em all up in the white-wash. All in bundles of ten. And I scratched one out at each breakfast. Five thousand four hundred and eighty days. That's what they give you for a lifer. And I had 'em all written up.

" The first time I lost count was years and years ago. While we were out in the exercise the maintenance party came round and put fresh whitewash up in the cells. And when I tried to think down to how many I'd done and how many I still had to do, I got a dizzy. And then, just when I had it nearly all put to rights again by licking off a lot of the new whitewash, they went and changed my cell and made me an Ember Day."

*   *   *   *   *   *

When the chaplain came he found Masterick very quiet and subdued.

" How are you, Number Three-fifty-four ? " he asked with kindly austerity. " Well, I hope ?—and prepared for your big adventure to-morrow ?—I really and sincerely trust we shall never see you again ? "

Masterick turned his eyes to the window-patch.

" Well, sir that all depends on how *They* look at it," he said, a little distantly. " I never quite know what They're going to do with me next. You never ought to have seen me to start with. Not really. Because I never killed Fred Smith. But you know that, don't you ? I told you."

" Yes ; but I want to know what you are going to do. I can probably help you with your arrangements and help you to get settled down again. Have you any people living to whom you can definitely go ? "

" That I can't say, sir. You see, I've been here a tidy long while. And most likely all the people I used to know have died. Perhaps even Fred Smith has died too. A tidy long while I've been here. There's been a war finished and done with since I've been here. And you see that little flag-pole against my bit of window ? Well, I always thought that was a flag-pole from the day it first went up, five months back. But that ain't a flag-pole. It's a wireless. So Southampton Jack tells me. I'll have to step very quiet till I pick up that lot of ropes outside again."

" Yes, quite. H'm ! A great pity you haven't somewhere definite to go—something definite to do. Perhaps I may be able to exert——"

" Oh, I've got something definite to do all right, sir."

" Oh, you have. Oh, well, of course, that's splendid. Regular employment, is it ? "

" Pretty regular, maybe. I want to take the mike out of that cocksure crowd in the court. Because, you see, sir, I never killed Fred Smith."

* * * * * *

The chaplain who had heard that curiously uncomplaining fact reiterated with such steady persistence that he had almost come to believe it himself, made a mental note that Thomas Masterick was a case which would have to be watched pretty closely when he got clear of the prison.

But he needn't have worried. The authorities admitted two months later that their suspicions about Masterick were groundless, and They called off the System. He had harboured no dark animosity against those connected with his trial—a trial which, except for the fact that Thomas Masterick did not kill Fred Smith, was perfectly honest and fair. In fact, he made what they called " quite a good recovery." He picked into the old ruts with deliberate, if painful, endeavour. He got a job down about the docks and set about his task of climbing back into civilization again with calm stolidity. In his case They did not fear for the recidivist.

And yet, a month after that, they freely admitted that it would have been far better for them and for the pomp and vanity of all the legal world if Thomas Masterick had gone straight out, bought a gun and kicked up ten different hells according to his own half-burned-out lights. For the problem that Thomas Masterick flung at them with cold and calculated deliberation when the time was ripe shook the law-officers of the Crown to their finger-tips. He knocked the Law clean out. He left it flat and gasping. He sent every legal mind in the country hectically scampering through old and ancient tomes for light and guidance. But there was no light and guidance. Thomas Masterick had floored them utterly and completely, ludicrously and horribly.

For, three months after his release from prison, and quite by accident, he met the long, lanky devil in the black gown. Counsel for the Crown was also wearing a Knighthood and a K.C. Thomas Masterick was not to know that. Not that it would have mattered to that numb, pulseless soul, even if he had know it.

It was by the " Griffin," where Fleet Street melts into the Strand, and he walked up to him, and he said :

" Hey, mister—you know all that lot of stuff you said about me ? "

The K.C. looked down at him shrewdly, and paused for a moment.

" No," he said evenly. " I don't think I do."

" Yes, you remember—that lot of stuff you said about me in the court. To the judge."

The K.C.'s eyes contracted ever so slightly. Somewhere, right away in the back blocks of memory there came a tiny, fleeting picture—a glimpse.

" Oh, yes—I believe I do," he said. " Let me see, now—er —wasn't it—er——"

" Yes, mister ; that's what it was. And it was all wrong. All the whole lot of it. I said so at the time, didn't I ? And I'm saying so again. I never killed Fred Smith. Not in spite of all what you said. Honest I didn't. And one of these days I'll prove it to you. I'll give you the surprise of your life. And that surprise of everybody else's life who was in that court."

The K.C. drew in a long breath, slowly.

" Ye gods ! " he breathed, almost too low to be heard. " So you—you have only just come out, have you ? "

" Yes, mister. A couple of months ago."

" Are you working ? I mean, have you got anything to do ? "

" Yes, mister. Got a regular job. Wapping to Convent Garden. I'm often along here."

" That's a good man." The K.C. slipped a fiver into his hand. " Get yourself a nice new Sunday suit," he said, with a pat on his shoulder.

" Thank you very much, mister." Thomas Masterick pocketed the fiver and hung around. After a moment he said :

" Could you—would you give me a word of advice, too, sir ? "

" Certainly, certainly. What's the trouble ? "

" Well, supposing I ever found that Fred Smith you said I killed. See, just supposing. How would I have to go about it ? "

The K.C. whistled under his breath. " Well ! " he said, " that would be a poser. Perhaps the best thing you could do would be to come along and see me—here in my chambers. Any of the bobbies here will show you—just here in the Inner Temple."

" Because down in my lodging-house there's a White Star man says he's seen Fred Smith—that's since you said I killed him. It was in 'Frisco, he said, and Fred was running grain in the hog-backs. Got tired o' sail, he did."

" Well, look here, old man, if ever you do manage to get hold of him, you come along and see me. I'll do all I can to help you."

" I wouldn't half be able to take the mike out of that cocky lot of devils, wouldn't I ? "

" You would what ? "

" Prove 'em a lot of unholy liars."

" You certainly would."

" Not 'arf, I wouldn't," said Thomas Masterick tonelessly. " I'd do more than that, too ! "

The K.C. nodded genially and went off with a little pity and a lot of amusement in his heart. He was a good soul in his way, was the K.C., but the acid of the Law ran tart in his veins. His perceptions were too subservient to the dictates of logic.

But it happened that he heard from Thomas Masterick again. On a most propitious day, too. The K.C. was lunching a few legal friends in his chambers. There were three other K.C.'s, a former Chancellor, and two judges of the High Court among them.

The K.C.'s secretary entered and slipped behind his chair.
" There's a very persistent fellow outside, sir—a man who calls
himself Thomas Masterick. He says you wouldn't turn him
away for anything. That it's very important. And that he's
got Fred Smith with him ! "

" Good God ! " said the K.C., swinging round. " Here ?
He's got Smith here."

" There is another man with him, sir, yes—frightened-
looking man."

" Goodness gracious me ! " The K.C. turned to his lunch-
party with wild excitement in his eyes.

" Well, if that isn't the most amazing thing ! " he cried.
" Listen here, you fellows. I've got the most unique course
just coming in you've ever sampled in your lives. This is a
lunch you'll remember and talk about for years. A real tit-
bit. Do you—do you remember that dock murder fifteen
years or so ago ? Feller named Masterick killed a chap called
Fred Smith. I was conducting for the Crown. You, Rumbold,
you were judge at the time. He got the black cap—obvious
from the first ; but the Home Sec. commuted. That, too,
was obvious. He——"

Rumbold nodded and the others all intimated their precise
memory of the case.

" Well, Masterick is here and Smith is here ! " cut in the
K.C. with a rush. In a few words he outlined the details of
the case to them and the history of his last meeting with Thomas
Masterick in Fleet-street.

" Show them in, Plender," he said. And the two men came
in—Masterick calm and a little bit suspicious ; Fred Smith
openly scared.

" Who's all this lot ? " demanded Masterick, nodding once
at the guests.

" Friends of mine, old chap. Friends who are, I am sure,
quite as eager to hear you and help you as I am myself. I
doubt if any man in the world ever had such an array of legal
talent—ha, ha, that's one for you, Rumbold—to help him as
you."

" I don't want any help," said Masterick flatly. He dragged
Smith farther into the room. " I've had a hell of a hunt to
find him," he announced. " And when I did find him he
wouldn't come along—not till I told him about you, mister.
I ain't got much to say—I'm afraid I've got a dizzy coming
on ; that's what comes of trying to think too hard. But the
way I look at it is this. You were a cocksure crowd of devils

in that court, weren't you ? Wouldn't listen to reason, no ways. I told you a hundred times I never killed Fred Smith, but you wouldn't have it ; you was that damned cocky about it. You lagged me for fifteen years for murdering that swipe there. And I hadn't done it. But I've done the punishment for it, blast you !

"And now "—he suddenly pulled out a gun and shot Fred Smith clean through the heart where he stood—" *now I've done the murder for which I've already been punished*," he thundered. " And what the hell are you going to do about it ? "

THE ROOM
ON THE FOURTH FLOOR

By

RALPH STRAUS

JOHN CHESTER ought never to have gone in for politics.
I am quite certain that he should have sat down at a desk
and written romances, and become a " best-seller," and
built himself a marble house, and married a wife, and hired a
press-agent. Instead, as everybody knows, he elected to be
returned to Parliament twenty-five years ago, and there he
has remained ever since, always upon the fringe of the Government, though never actually entering those extraordinary
precincts.

Probably succeeding Premiers have considered that
Chester's duties as a raconteur at fashionable dinner-tables
must for ever preclude him from undertaking anything else,
though, I dare say, he has refused office on his own account.
He is just the kind of man to do such a thing—a man too keen
about other people to look properly after his own interests.

His appearance, as you know, is military. That white
moustache suggests the field-marshal, and his clothes are
obviously of the dragoon cut. Also, he has a figure which,
to my knowledge has changed not an inch in the last twenty
years. Some people call him a phenomenon and expect you
to know exactly what they mean, and somehow you do. He
knows everyone and goes everywhere. He has more friends
than any other man in Europe. And he is the kind of man to
whom people, even the discreet people, tell things, which
possibly accounts for his amazing stock of stories.

I was dining with him a week or two ago at the House of
Commons. A world-famous ex-Minister was sitting in solitary
state at the next table. Chester had been unusually silent,
and I wondered what was troubling him ; but when the great
statesman hurried away, my host gave the peculiar chuckle

which, with him, is the invariable introduction to some yarn or other.

" The most remarkable man in England," he began, looking in the direction of the now empty table.

" So I am given to understand."

" He is the only man who guessed the Farringham riddle, you know. Guessed it at once, too. Most remarkable man. Yes. And yet . . ."

He paused and looked at me as though I had contradicted him.

" Sometimes," he continued, twirling the white moustache, " I wonder whether he knew more about the affair than he pretended. He *might* have heard of it, of course, in his official capacity."

" You mean when he was Prime Minister ? "

" Precisely."

" You pique my curiosity," said I.

John Chester emptied his glass. " You have never heard of the Farringham case, then ? No, well, in the ordinary way you wouldn't. So many of these things have to be hushed up. Besides, it is thirty years old now."

I lit a cigar and prepared for one of Chester's inimitable yarns.

*   *   *   *   *   *

" Yes," he began, " Mrs. Farringham was a beautiful widow with a passion for travelling in unusual places. She had plenty of money, and she moved from one continent to the next as you or I drive to our clubs. She never took a maid with her ; but her daughter, I suppose, did much to fill the maid's place. I met them first in Florence, I remember. The girl must have been about twenty then, Mrs. Farringham nearly forty, though she scarcely looked older than her daughter.

" She was entertaining some Italian prince who wanted to become her son-in-law or her husband—I couldn't make up my mind which, and didn't like to ask—and I was invited to call at her London house. I fully intended to go as soon as I returned home, but—well, you shall hear why I never had the opportunity.

" It was in the year of the great Exhibition in Paris—1900. The Farringhams had been travelling in Russia and Turkey. They had spent a week in Constantinople—a detestable place —and had decided to make a tour through Asia Minor. But apparently for no reason at all Mrs. Farringham suddenly took it into her head that she would like to buy new carpets for her

London house, and the Asia Minor trip was indefinitely post-
poned.

" The ladies visited Thomas Cook, and Thomas Cook in
his best English told them how to reach home in the most
comfortable manner. Incidentally, he advised a night or two
in Paris. The Exhibition had just opened its gates. Now I
don't suppose for one moment that Mrs. Farringham cared
in the least whether she saw the Exhibition or not, but her
daughter had not seen so much of the world as her indefatigable
mother, and it was decided that twenty-four hours in Paris
would make a pleasant break in a tiresome journey.

" And so it happened that three days later the two ladies,
rather tired and rather irritable, arrived at the Paris terminus.
It was just eight o'clock in the evening. They had already
dined in the train. A porter found their baggage—three large
trunks and a green bag which had accompanied Mrs. Farringham from the time she had first crossed the Channel—and,
with the help of a cabman, succeeded in placing the four pieces
on the roof of the cab. Before driving off, however, the cabman
altered the position of the green bag. Apparently he had got
it into his head that the green bag was the last straw to break
his conveyance, and he put it beneath his feet on the box.

" When they arrived at one of the big hotels—I forgot for
the moment which it was—the ladies asked for two adjoining
rooms.

" The politest of hotel managers shrugged his shoulders
many times. ' Paris,' said he, ' is full. It flows over with *tout
le monde*. It is beyond me to give madame and mam'selle two
rooms in the closest adjoinment. But if madame will take an
apartment on the fourth floor, and mam'selle an apartment
on the fifth floor—of the extreme comfort—it will be well.'
His manner implied that only madame's beauty had made such
a favour possible.

" The ladies agreed, and signed their names in the visitor's
book. One of the hotel porters took charge of the trunks, and
a chambermaid showed the visitors to their rooms. Mrs.
Farringham's bedroom was not very large, but it looked comfortable. Her daughter's room was exactly above it.

" The porter unstrapped Mrs. Farringham's trunks, and in
the politest possible way hoped that the ladies would enjoy
their visit to Paris. Then he received a small coin and disappeared. The chambermaid uttered a similar sentiment and
followed his example. Mother and daughter were left alone.
You follow so far ? "

" Perfectly," said I.

John Chester looked up at the ceiling. " Very well, then. Here you have two estimable ladies arriving one evening in a Paris hotel of unimpeachable respectability and being given rooms one over the other. Good.

" For a short while Miss Farringham stayed with her mother and helped her to unpack a few things. Then, feeling tired, she suggested that they should both go to bed.

" ' Immediately ? ' asked her mother. ' It is not yet nine o'clock.'

" ' Very well,' said the girl, ' I will lie down for half an hour or so in my own room and then come down to help you undress.'

" And she went to her room on the fifth floor.

" She was feeling particularly drowsy. Nearly two days in a continental train is enough to make anyone drowsy. She just lay down on her bed, dressed as she was, and in a minute or two was asleep."

Again my host paused this time to refill his glass. " Quite an ordinary story, isn't it ? " he asked, with a twinkle in his eye.

I knew better than to utter a word.

" Yes," he went on, " the girl lay on her bed and fell asleep. When she awoke it was ten minutes before midnight. She went down to the fourth floor and knocked on the door of her mother's room. There was no answer. She went in. The room was dark. She turned on the electric light. The bed was empty. Indeed, the room was obviously untenanted. It was awaiting the arrival of some visitor.

" Of course she must have made some mistake. She went out into the passage. Her mother's room would be an adjoining one. But on one side of the empty room was a bathroom, and outside the door of the other stood two unmistakably masculine boots. Added to which she was almost certain that she recalled the correct number. She rang for the chambermaid.

" ' I am afraid I have made some mistake,' she said. ' I thought this was my mother's room, but—this is the fourth floor, by the way, isn't it ? '

" The maid looked at her curiously. ' Yes, mam'selle, this is indeed the fourth floor, but what does mam'selle mean ? No lady accompanied mam'selle to the hotel. Mam'selle travelled with herself ! ' "

* * * * * *

John Chester looked at me across the table in much the

same way as I imagined the chambermaid had stared at Miss Farringham. It was almost a minute before he spoke again. I had no notion what was coming, but already felt in some vague way that I was no longer sitting in the dining-room of the House of Commons. I leant forward over the table. " Go on, dear man, please ! "

" ' Mam'selle travelled with herself,' " he repeated. " Yes, that is what the chambermaid said, and Miss Farringham stared at her. ' You are making a very stupid mistake,' she said. ' Why, surely it was you who took in my mother's bag—a large green bag. We came together, about half-past eight.'

" The maid seemed completely bewildered. ' Shall I ring for the porter ? ' she asked, more or less mechanically.

" Miss Farringham nodded. A feeling of uneasiness had suddenly come over her.

" The porter came up, and the girl recognized him. She repeated her question. The porter allowed his mouth to open to its widest extent, which happened to be his method of expressing the completest surprise. No madame, said he, had arrived with mam'selle. He had certainly taken mam'selle's two trunks to a room on the fifth floor, but what did she mean ?

" And then, I fancy, a tiny pang must have touched Miss Farringham's heart. Yet, obviously, this could only be an absurd mistake. In another moment she would be laughing with her mother. She looked hard at the two servants standing there in foolish bewilderment. ' Call the manager, please,' she said.

" They brought the manager to her. He was, as always, vaguely apologetic. Mam'selle was not comfortable in her room ? Was there anything he could do ? She had not supped ? Some refreshment in her room ?

" The girl explained. Her mother had been given a room on the fourth floor. Apparently this had been changed. Where was she now ? She asked the questions quite calmly, but her heart was beating at a greater rate than was good for it. On a sudden it seemed to her that something was horribly, immeasurably wrong. You are probably familiar with that feeling yourself.

" The manager's manner changed ever so slightly. His tones were still suave, but a note of incredulity would not be hidden. It was as though he were angry at being summoned to the fourth floor by a possibly mad Englishwoman for no reason at all. ' Mam'selle is joking ? ' he asked almost coldly.

" It was then that the girl realized how frightened she was. Wherever her mother might be, even though no more than a single wall was separating them, she was at that moment alone in Paris with strangers who were obviously in no mood to believe what she said. ' But my mother and I, we drove from the station. You gave us the rooms yourself. Yes, and you said how sorry you were that we could not have adjoining rooms because the hotel was full. And then—of course, you remember—we wrote our names in the visitor's book.'

" The manager retained his professional politeness. That is the first necessity in a hotel manager. ' I cannot understand mam'selle,' he said quietly. Then he turned to the porter. ' Bring up the visitor's book,' he ordered.

" The visitor's book was produced. You can imagine how eagerly Miss Farringham examined it. Yes, there, four or five names from the bottom of the last page, was her own ; but it was sandwiched in between a vicomte and an English baronet. Her mother's name was not there.

" You can picture her dismay.

" ' Perhaps mam'selle is tired, and over-wrought after her journey,' suggested the polite manager. English girls, he knew, were often peculiar, and Miss Farringham was undoubtedly pretty.

" ' But—my mother ! ' stammered the girl. ' What does it all mean ? I don't understand—— '

" ' There is a doctor in the hotel if mam'selle—— '

" She interrupted him. ' Oh, you think I am ill. But I am not. We must search the hotel. Perhaps my mother has found a friend ; or she may be in the drawing-room. I am horribly nervous. You must help me.'

" The manager shrugged his apologetic shoulders.

" They searched the hotel."

John Chester handed me his cigarette-case. " Yes," he repeated, " they searched the hotel."

" And they found—— "

" Everyone but the mother. In an hour's time, as you can imagine, Miss Farringham had become frantic. The manager did everything he could. As a final recourse he despatched the porter to look for the cabman who had driven the girl from the station. It was a rather forlorn hope, but the girl seemed eager to see him. She was in that state of mind in which things are no longer ordinary or extraordinary, but merely hopeful or hopeless. Fortunately the cabman was found. He was still on duty, as a matter of fact, at the terminus.

And at two o'clock in the morning he was standing, hat in hand, in the foyer of the hotel."

" It was the same cabman ? " I asked.

" Miss Farringham recognized him instantly. ' You remember me ? ' she asked eagerly.

" ' But yes, mam'selle. You arrived at eight-ten—alone. I drove you to this hotel. Two trunks.'

" ' No, no. My mother was with me. There were three trunks and a large green bag.'

" The cabman looked stupidly at her.

" ' And don't you remember, you changed the position of the bag as we drove off. Perhaps you thought that it was unsafe on the roof. You put it beneath your feet on the box. Oh, you must remember, you must remember ! '

" The cabman was obviously astonished. ' But there was no green bag,' said he. ' I remember precisely. The young lady, I think, must be American or English, or she would not be travelling with herself.'

" Miss Farringham stared wildly about her and fell down in a faint.

" They got her to bed and promised to send a telegram to England. Early next morning she crossed the Channel, just dazed. And she was met at Charing Cross by friends just as mystified as herself. That night she was seriously ill. Brain fever."

" But the mother ? " I asked.

" Nothing more," said John Chester, " was ever heard of the mother."

The division bell was ringing, and my host excused himself. " I must vote," he explained. " I shall be back in ten minutes, which will give you just sixty times as long as the ex-Prime Minister took to solve the riddle." He nodded, and hurried away.

I tried to exercise those faculties which the detective of fiction finds so useful. Either Mrs. Farringham had arrived at the hotel in Paris, I argued, or she had not. John Chester had stated distinctly that she had arrived, and therefore. . . .

*   *   *   *   *   *

My host had returned. " A pretty problem ? " said he. " Confess yourself completely at sea."

" Completely," said I.

" Come along to the terrace, then, ' and we walked out and stood looking over the Thames. It was not a warm night, and we were coatless.

" I have often wondered," he began at last, " why Mrs. Farringham had that sudden desire to buy carpets for her London house."

I hurriedly sought for a clue in the carpets, but found none.

" Perhaps," he continued, " it was an excuse. Perhaps she shared in common with most of her sex the desire to practice the gentle art of self-deception. It is just possible, that is to say, that Mrs. Farringham gave up the proposed trip through Asia Minor because she was not in her usual health."

He was silent for so long that I drew his attention to the low temperature.

" Then I'll explain," he said, with a smile. " It is all quite simple, and depends on one little fact which may or may not have escaped your notice. In France they have a peculiar way of doing things. A logical way, I admit, but sometimes peculiar. Consequently things happen in France, and particularly in Paris, which could not possibly happen anywhere else. The Farringham affair is a case in point. I will tell you exactly what happened, and then you shall come inside to hear the debate.

" Well, then, here, as I said before, you have the fact of two ladies arriving one evening in a Paris hotel. There is no question about that : they both arrived, and Mrs. Farringham was given a room on the fourth floor, the actual room which her daughter found untenanted at midnight. Now I will say at once that there was nothing peculiar about this room ; it was just an ordinary bedroom in a big hotel. What was peculiar was the fact that while Mrs. Farringham had been in the room at half-past eight, she was not there, nor indeed anywhere in the hotel, at midnight. Consequently, at some period between these two hours she went out, or was taken out."

" But the manager and the porter . . ."

" I see you will not let me tell the story in my own way," smiled John Chester. " I was going to show you how you might have solved the riddle. No matter. You shall have the plain sequence of things at once. A few minutes after Mrs. Farringham had been shown to her room her daughter had gone up to the fifth floor and she was alone. Ten minutes later the bell in the room rang. The chambermaid appeared, and to her dismay found madame lying motionless on the floor. She rang for the porter, and the porter, hardly less frightened than herself, fetched the manager. The manager called for a doctor. Fortunately there was one in the hotel. The doctor appeared and made his examination. Mrs. Farringham was dead."

" Dead ! " I repeated.

" Dead," said John Chester. " Now the death of a lady in a large hotel is an unpleasant event at all times, but in this case there was something so peculiarly unpleasant that the doctor, instead of notifying the police, called up one of the Government offices on the telephone, and was lucky enough to find a high official still at his post.

" What followed you may think extraordinary, and extraordinary it certainly must have been. In less than an hour's time there had arrived at the hotel a small army of men. Some seemed to be visitors, others workmen. If you had watched them at all, you might have come to the conclusion that a large quantity of furniture was being removed. As a matter of fact it was. In particular, an ottoman might have been seen being carried downstairs and placed in a furniture van, which drove rapidly away. If you had waited about the fourth floor, you might further have seen new furniture brought into the room which Mrs. Farringham had occupied, and you might have been puzzled at a peculiar odour until the manager, whom you would have met casually on the stairs, informed you that a clumsy servant had upset a case of drugs destined for the exhibition.

" At the same time, if you had been allowed into the manager's own sanctum downstairs you would have seen three or four gentlemen talking earnestly to a chambermaid and a porter, and, at a later hour, to a cabman who happened to have taken up his stand outside the hotel. The porter and the chambermaid incidentally received large sums of money, and the cabman, similarly enriched, was bidden to await instructions. Also several lessons in the art of acting had been given."

" I am more bewildered than ever."

" And yet," said John Chester, " two words whispered over the telephone had been sufficient to cause all these curious events to take place ! "

Once again he paused. " Mrs. Farringham had been travelling in the East. Doesn't that suggest something to you ? "

" You mean——" I was beginning ; but he interrupted me.

" *Bubonic plague !* "

" But I don't see——"

" At headquarters they were obliged to come to a speedy decision. In the interests of the community, my dear fellow, it was decided—the Government, that is to say, decided—

that Mrs. Farringham *had never arrived in Paris.* Further they were not concerned. That was the only vital point."

" But even then——"

" Do you suppose," asked John Chester, " that anybody would have visited Paris if a case of bubonic plague had been reported? Even if there was no more than a rumour that ——"

" No, but——"

" It was a case of one against the many. The Government, being Republican, and also patriotic, made its choice for the many. Also, being French, it did not lack the artistic temperament."

" It's ghastly ! " I murmured.

" It was Exhibition year," said my host. " But you are quite right," he added ; " it is very cold. Let us go in."

I do not remember what question was being debated that evening.

THE WOUNDED GOD

By

A. E. W. MASON

THERE were only two really young people in Mrs. Maine's drawing-room that evening and naturally enough they sat apart talking to each other. At least that is how Cynthia Maine would have put it. The young man in fact was dutifully listening and Cynthia was in full flight. The eager thrill of her voice, her face a-quiver, the sparkling intensity of her charming and charmingly dressed person, all suggested that she was satisfactorily solving one of the world's great problems. But she was not. She was debating with her beau—as Cynthia understood debate—where they should go and dance the night away as soon as these tiresome elders had trailed off to their beds. Should it be the Fifty-Fifty, or the Embassy, or the Café de Paris ? But before the momentous decision was reached, Cynthia suddenly gave up. She leaned back in her chair and her hands dropped over the arms.

"I have been fighting against it all the evening, but I'm beaten," she said moodily. Then she rose abruptly and slipped out between the curtains on to the balcony.

Her bewildered companion found her there. She was leaning, her elbows propped upon the red cushion which stretched along the top of the balcony's parapet, and her hands pressed tightly over her eyes in a vain endeavour to shut out some vision which obsessed her.

"Cynthia, what in the world have I done to hurt you ? " the youth asked remorsefully.

Cynthia lifted her face up and stared at him. She found his quite natural question utterly inexplicable.

"You, Jim ? Why, nothing of course."

She looked out over the Green Park, and threw up her head as though she was bathing her forehead and her throat in its cool fresh darkness ; and drew from it some balm for her agitation.

" This is one of Mummy's parties, ' she said. " There are people here whom I don't know. People she met this spring when I wasn't with her, at Cairo, or Tunis, or Algiers, or somewhere. So I can't tell which of them is doing it. Can I ? "

" No, you certainly can't," Jim asserted stoutly.

Cynthia swerved like a filly when a sheet of paper blows across the road in front of her, and with a frown wrinkling her pretty forehead, surveyed through the gaps between the curtains her mother's guests. Jim looked over her shoulder, frowning still more portentously, and forgot his manners.

" They look as commonplace a crowd as I ever saw gathered together in my life. Not one of them has got anything on you," he said.

" Yes, but there is one of them who isn't commonplace at all," returned Cynthia with conviction. " One of them is doing it."

Jim was half inclined to jest and sing, " Everybody's doing it." But tact was his strong suit on this summer night.

" Doing what, Cynthia ? " he asked gently.

" Hush ! "

An appealing hand was thrust under his arm and pressed into his coat-sleeve. Cynthia wanted companionship, not conversation.

" I shall have an awful night, Jim, unless we put up a barrage."

Cynthia was very miserable. Jim turned back his hand and got hold of Cynthia's.

" I know. We'll slip out now and get away. I have got my little car at the door."

Cynthia, however, shook her head.

" It wouldn't be fair on Mummy. We must wait. They'll all go very soon. Besides, it is important to me to find out which of them it is who's doing it. Then I can make sure that whoever it is never comes to this house again."

It was an appalling threat, but Jim recognized that it was just. People had no right to do things to Cynthia which would give her an awful night, even across a drawing-room. They must be black-balled thoroughly. Then a dreadful explanation of Cynthia's misery smote him.

" My dear, you are not a natural medium, are you ? " he asked in a voice of awe. He turned her towards him and contemplated her with pleasure. He looked her up and down from her neatly shingled fair brown hair to her shining feet. She was a slim, long-legged, slinky creature. All that he had ever heard about mediums led him to believe that as a rule they ran to breadth and flesh. He drew a breath of relief, but Cynthia looked at him very curiously.

" No," she answered after a moment's reflection. " It's just this one thing. I am not odd in any other way. And this one thing isn't my fault either. And there's a very good real reason for it too." She broke off to ask anxiously, " I don't seem to you to be incoherent at all, do I, Jim ? "

Jim firmly reassured her.

" No one could be more lucid."

Cynthia breathed her relief.

" Thank you. You are a comfort, Jim. I'll tell you something more now. This thing—somebody in that drawing-room knows about it—has been thinking about it all the evening— has been making me think about it—has come here to-night to make me think about it. And it's a horror ! "

And she suddenly swept her arm out across the expanse of the Green Park, from Piccadilly on the north to Buckingham Palace on the south.

" Yes, it's a horror," she repeated in a low voice.

She was watching a dreadful procession go by, endlessly and always from north to south. It moved not in the darkness, but along a straight white riband of road under a hot sun, between pleasant and sunny fields, but in a choking mist of yellow dust. There was a herd of white oxen at one point of the procession, and here a troop of goats and there a flock of bleating sheep. But the bulk of it was made up of old clumsy heavy carts, drawn by old, old horses, and accompanied by old, old men, and piled up with mattresses and stores and utensils, on the top of which lurched and clung old, old women and very young children. It was the age of all, men and beasts, who were taking part in this stupendous migration which gave to it its horror. These were no pioneers. It was a flight. There was one particularly dreadful spectacle, an old man without cart or horse who carried upon his bent back like a sack a still older woman. All through the day, dipping down from the northern horizon and rising to the edge of the southern, the procession streamed slowly by. At nightfall it just stopped ; at daybreak it resumed. There would come a moment, Cynthia knew well—it always did come—but after she was asleep—when the procession would begin to race, when the old men and the old horses would begin to leap and jump, grotesquely with stiff limbs, like marionettes—and that was much more horrible. For some of them would fall and be trampled under foot, and no one would mind. But that moment was not yet.

There was a stir in the drawing-room behind her.

" They are going," she said.

Both of these young people turned to the window, and Cynthia laid her hand again on Jim's arm and detained him.

" Wait ! Wait ! " she whispered eagerly. " I believe we shall find out which of them it is."

They watched through the gap between the curtains all the preliminary movements of a general and on the whole eagerly welcomed retreat, the guests rising as one person, the hostess with just a little less but not much less alacrity and murmurs about a delightful evening coming as if from the mouths of a succession of polite automata. They saw Mrs. Maine turn her head towards a picture on the wall. They heard her say :

" That ? Yes, it is quite lovely, isn't it ? Let us look at it."

Both Cynthia and Jim fixed their eyes upon the particular guest who had called Mrs. Maine's attention to the picture and now crossed the room with her. A woman, if anything a little below the average height, of an indeterminate age somewhere between thirty-six and fifty, she had no distinctive personality. She was dark, neither ugly nor beautiful. There was even something ungraceful in her walk.

" She is as commonplace as a sheep," said Jim, meaning that it could not possibly be she who had so disturbed and controlled the shining young creature just in front of him.

" Wait ! " Cynthia advised. " Were you introduced to her, Jim ? "

" No."

" I suppose that Mummy introduced me to her. But I don't remember anything about her. She was at the other end of the dinner table too."

" It can't be her," said Jim.

Mrs. Maine led her visitor to the picture, a sketch of an old French château glowing in a blaze of sunlight. A great lawn, smooth and green as an emerald and set in a wide border of flowers, spread in front of a building at once elegant and solid ; and a wide stream with a glint of silver, bathed the edge of the lawn in front. At the sides of the château, tall chestnut trees made an avenue and behind the château rose a high bare hill.

" Many years ago, my husband and I saw that house when we were touring in France," Mrs. Maine explained. " I fell in love with it and he bought it for me. We spent four months a year there. After my husband died, I still went back to it, but five years ago Cynthia―― "

" Your daughter ? " interrupted the stranger.

" Yes, my daughter took a distaste for it. So I sold it to a Monsieur Franchard. He made a great fortune out of the War and is very fond of it, I am told.

" That's the woman, Jim," said Cynthia with a little shake in her voice.

But the woman in question showed no further interest in the picture. Jim had a fear lest the very intensity of Cynthia's regard, the concentration of all her senses, should draw that strange woman's eyes to the curtain behind which the pair of them stood concealed. But not a bit of it ! The strange woman smiled, thanked her hostess for her evening, shook her hand and waddled―the word was in Jim's thoughts―waddled out of the room. Nothing could have been more banal than her exit.

As soon as she had gone Cynthia slipped back between the curtains and took her place by her mother's side.

" Who was it who was talking to you about the Château Doré, Mummy ? " she asked in an interval between shaking hands with departing guests.

" A Madame D'Estourie," replied her mother. " She was kind to me in Algiers. She came to London a week ago and called upon me. So I asked her to dinner."

" Algiers ! " Cynthia repeated with a start, and to herself she said : " I was right. She must never come to the house any more. I'll speak to Mummy to-morrow."

The room was now empty except for her mother, herself and Jim.

" We are going off now to dance," she said.

Cynthia's mother smiled.

" You have got your latchkey ? "

" Yes."

Mrs. Maine turned to the young man.

" And. Jim, don't let her stay up too late. She's going to dance again to-morrow. Good night, my dear."

At the door of the drawing-room Cynthia said :

" Jim, I am going to run up for a cloak and you can start your old car and wait for me in the hall."

She ran upstairs, through her little sitting-room and into

her bedroom beyond it. Whilst she was getting her cloak out of the cupboard, it seemed to her that she heard a slight movement in her sitting-room. When she re-entered that room she saw that the door on to the staircase was closed ; and that Madame D'Estourie was sitting in a chair, waiting for her.

But Madame D'Estourie was no longer insignificant.

II

"I THOUGHT that you had gone," Cynthia stammered. Madame D'Estourie smiled at so childish a notion and by her smile made Cynthia feel a child and rather a helpless child—a sensation which she very much disliked.

"I knew of course that you were behind the curtains on the balcony," Madame D'Estourie explained quite calmly. "I slipped into the dark room at the side of the drawing-room and watched for you. I saw you run upstairs. I followed you."

Cynthia was troubled and exasperated. She did something she hated herself for even whilst she was doing it. She became impudent.

"Do you think it's decent manners to come to Mummy's dinner-party in order to spy and intrude on me ?" she asked, haughtily lifting her pretty face above the ermine collar of her coat and stamping her foot.

"I didn't give my manners a thought," Madame D'Estourie replied calmly. "I have been searching for you for years. I got this spring the first hint that it was you I was searching for. I became certain to-night. I couldn't let you go for the sake of my good manners."

Cynthia did not pretend any bewilderment as to the object of Madame D'Estourie's persistence.

"I have never spoken about it to anyone, not even to Mummy," she said, yielding a little in spite of herself.

"In that you are to blame," Madame D'Estourie returned relentlessly.

Cynthia's face had lost its resentment. She was on weak ground here. She had no sharp words of rejoinder.

"I hate thinking about it at all," she said in excuse.

"Yet you do think about it."

"At times. I can't help it " ; and Cynthia shivered and clasped her cloak about her.

"When you have talked about it, you won't have to think about it. You will be freed from the tyranny of your memories."

Cynthia looked curiously, almost hopefully, at Madame D'Estourie.

" I wonder," she said.

It might be possible that all these recurring nightmares, these obsessions by day were warnings that she should speak, and punishments because she did not. She tried one final evasion.

" I'll come and talk to you one day, Madame D'Estourie, and quite, quite soon. I have to go out to-night."

Madame D'Estourie shook her head, and for the first time in that interview a smile of humour softened the set of her lips.

" It will take you five minutes to tell your story, and the young gentleman in the hall has before now no doubt waited for ten."

Cynthia was no match for her unwelcome visitor. Madame D'Estourie was as undistinguished as Jim had declared. But she had the tremendous power conferred by a single purpose never forgotten for an hour during ten long years. The young girl, gracious, independent, exquisite and finished from the points of her toes to the top of her head, in spite of her belief that the world belonged exclusively to the young, sat obediently down in face of her commonplace and rather dowdy companion and recited her story. Recited is the only suitable word : her recollections were so continuous and so clear.

III

" I was nine years old that July. On the fifteenth of the month I crossed from England with my governess, passed through Paris and out by the Eastern Railway to Neuilly-sur-Morin, which was the station for the Château Doré. Mummy was in London and meant to join me in August. So, you see, my governess and I were caught at the Château Doré. Even in Paris, on the Friday nothing definite was known and then at midday on Saturday the Eastern Railway was taken over by the Army. There we were, fifty miles from Paris. Our two motors, every horse under twenty years old, and the farm carts were commandeered the next day. No one could get to us, we could not get away and no letters or telegrams arrived —not even a newspaper. You can understand that a little girl of nine thoroughly enjoyed it. I was reading with my governess Jules Verne's *Career of a Comet*, and I used to play at imagining that we had been carried away into space like the soldiers in the garrison. We were indeed just as isolated—except for the

noise of the great trains which thundered by to the East at the
back of the hill all day and all night.

"Thrilling things too happened in our little village. One
morning I found the old schoolmaster and Polydore Cromecq,
the Mayor who kept the little estaminet, driving two great
posts into the road and closing it with a heavy chain.

"'Now let the spies come!' cried Polydore Cromecq.
'Ah, les salauds! We shall be ready for them.'

"He took a great pull at a bock of beer and explained to
the little Miss as he called me that night and day there was to
be a guard upon the chain and no one was to pass without
papers.

"Polydore fascinated me at that time tremendously. He
was short and squat and swarthy; he had a great rumbling
laugh and great hands and feet to match the laugh; and he
had an enormous walrusy black moustache, which I adored.
For it used to get all covered with the froth of the beer and
then there would be little bubbles winking and breaking all
over it, until after a time he would put a huge tongue out and
lick it all off. He knew how I adored this and used to make
quite a performance of it. I watched him now and clapped
my hands when he had finished. Polydore burst out laughing.

"'Good little Miss! Sleep in your bed without fear!
No one shall pass. Courage! Courage!'

"Polydore in those days was always shouting 'Courage!'
though why I could not imagine. We knew of course that
leagues and leagues away soldiers were fighting, but it wasn't
real to any of us—yet. Our village was not even on the main
road which ran east and west at the back of the hill close to the
railway. It was tucked into its own little corner at a bend of the
Morin and the by-road which led to it led to nowhere else.

"For three weeks then our village slept in the sunlight, and
Polydore shouted, 'Courage! Courage! We shall get them.'
Then Polydore shouted no more, and he went about heavy and
sour and if he saw me he shrugged his shoulders and said
bitterly, 'Of course, it's only France'; as if, because I wasn't
French, I had scored some mean advantage over France. For
the carts of the refugees began to rumble all day on the road
on the other side of the hill, and we heard each day a little
nearer the boom and reverberation of the heavy guns, and my
governess set to work to install the château as a hospital. Then
one night, the last night I slept in the Château Doré, I heard
suddenly in the middle of a deadly stillness a quite new strange
sound. It was as though a boy was running along a path and

drawing, as he ran, a stick across a paling of iron rails. It was
the first time I had ever heard a machine-gun.

" The next morning, immediately after breakfast, I ran
down to the village. The whole of the village council was
assembled in the Mayor's office, and the remaining inhabitants
were standing silent and crowded together outside watching
through the windows the progress of the debate. A rumour
had spread that we were surrounded by Uhlans. Everybody
believed it. Uhlans ! There were peasants who remembered
1870. The mere name carried with it panic and despair. So
overwhelming was the dread that when a party of four men in
uniform came out from a little wood, at the end of the village,
the women and even some of the men began to scream, ' The
Uhlans ! The Uhlans ! '

" The village council broke up in a hurry and rushed into
the street, Polydore wiping his forehead with a great coloured
handkerchief, and cursing under his breath. The old schoolmaster was the first to recall everybody to reason.

" ' These are French uniforms,' he cried. ' They are
Zouaves ' ; and everybody began to pelt along the streets
towards them, cheering at the tops of their voices in their
relief. But the cheers dropped as we got nearer. For we saw
that three of the Zouaves were supporting and almost carrying
the fourth. He was a young lieutenant, almost a boy, and very
handsome. He was as white as a sheet of paper, and there
was a dreadful look of pain in his eyes, though his lips smiled
at us. The blood was bubbling out of his coat at the breast.
He seemed to me a young wounded god.

" I forced my way through the crowd and said :

" ' He must be taken to the château. There we will look
after him.'

" But one of the soldiers shook his head and smiled
gratefully.

" ' No, Miss. We must leave him here at the first house.
If the bleeding is stopped and he can lie quiet, he may recover.
Many do. Besides, we have to find our own company.'

" The first house in the village was a small general store
and sweet-shop kept by a Mademoiselle Cromecq, a withered
old spinster and a sister of the Mayor.

" ' But he will spoil my furniture,' she cried, standing in
her shop door and barring the way.

" A storm of protests rose from the throats of all the other
villagers who didn't have to have their furniture spoiled. On
all sides I heard :

" ' Did you ever hear anything like it ? '

" ' There's a Frenchwoman for you ! '

" ' A dirty vixen ! '

" Fists were shaken, mouths spat. The only good-humoured people were the soldiers.

" ' Come, Mother,' said the one who had smiled at me. ' Imagine for a moment that this fine lad's your son.'

" They pushed her good-humouredly out of the way and carried the boy into a room at the side of the shop and laid him very gently on a couch. Then the leader of them—he wore a sergeant's stripes—came out again and, walking straight up to me, saluted.

." ' Mademoiselle,' he said, ' at your château you have bandages and someone who can nurse. He is a good boy, our young officer. I leave him to you. For us, we have been separated from our battalion—a glass of wine in a hurry—what ?—and we go back.'

" Somehow, in the presence of this cheerful—what shall I say ?—adequate soldier who knew exactly what he wanted, we all felt emboldened. Polydore ran to his estaminet half-way down the small village street for a jug of wine and some glasses. Meanwhile I—you must remember that I was a child of nine—I ran home as fast as my legs would carry me, my heart swelling with pride. The smiling soldier had singled me out, had confided the young wounded god to my care. Fast as I ran, however, I had not reached the house before I heard a great sound of cheering and looking down from the slope leading up to the château, I saw the three remaining soldiers waving their kepis as they hurried back into the wood. I burst into the house with my story and in a minute, my governess with Honorine, one of the servants, and myself at her heels, all of us laden with lint and cotton-wool and bottles of disinfectant, and a suit of pyjamas, were racing back to the little general store.

" The village was still massed outside the shop, still on fire with loyalty. We were welcomed with a torrent of cheers.

" ' Ah, the English women ! The English women ! ' some of them cried—we were popular in France in those days except with Polydore. And an old man of eighty looked at me with a chuckle.

" ' The little one ! I wish I had her legs—that's all ! '

" ' Yes, she has the legs, the little foreigner,' Polydore added sourly. ' She will be able to run.'

" My governess would not allow me to follow them into the house. So I remained outside, hopping from one foot on

to the other in my anxiety, wondering what they were doing
to my young wounded god, and praying with all my heart that
they would not hurt him. Meanwhile the villagers drifted
away. It was summer. The crops had to be got in, the vines
to be tended, and there were no young men to help. I was glad
when they went. I didn't want them to hear a groan or even
a sign of pain from my young god, lest they should remember
it and thereafter think the less of him. But not a sound came
through the open window. And all my pride in him was
changed into a dreadful fear lest he should have died.

" I remember shutting my eyes and clenching my fists in a
refusal to believe it, when I heard Polydore Cromecq grumbling
behind me.

" ' It is true, you know. The old one will have her furniture spoilt. All that blood ! And who will pay for it ? The
Government ? I don't think ! '

" It was the grocer who replied, a little ferrety man :

" ' Yes, they should have taken him to the château. What
does it matter to the rich ones at the château if some of their
fine sheets are ruined ? They can afford it. He will die ?
But this is war and he is a soldier.'

" ' It is worse than war,' cried Polydore Cromecq with an
oath. ' This is 1870 over again.'

" Suddenly they became silent and I had a conviction that
one of them was nudging the other in the ribs and pointing
towards me.

" The silence was broken by a new-comer to that group—
my old friend, the schoolmaster.

" ' Monsieur le Maire,' he said, addressing Polydore
Cromecq in the formal tones which he kept for authority, ' I
think that if a wounded officer is brought into this village the
enemy must be very near. We hear no good accounts of them
from the refugees. I put it to you, Monsieur le Maire, that
the women should be ordered to leave.'

" The old schoolmaster was the only man in the village
with a cool head upon his shoulders. Polydore Cromecq and
the little grocer Gavroche had been occupied by their own little
grievances and meannesses. We had lost our hearts and our
senses in our enthusiasm over our wounded hero. The
proximity of the enemy had been overlooked. Even the
Uhlans had been forgotten during the last hour.

" Polydore ran off to make out an order for the evacuation
of the village and at the same time my governess called to me
from the window of the cottage.

" ' He wants to thank you.'

" I went into the room on tiptoe. The young Zouave was lying in a bed made up on a great couch. His wound had been staunched, he had been washed and dressed in the pyjamas we had brought from the château.

" ' You need not speak, Monsieur Henri,' said my governess. He was already ' Monsieur Henri ' to them—in his full title the ♦Lieutenant Henri Flavelle of the 6th Regiment of Zouaves.

" ' He has been shot through the lung, but the wound is clean and, if he is sensible, he will get well.'

" The Zouave smiled at me. He was easier now. The look of pain had gone from his eyes. He beckoned me with a little movement of his fingers and I sat down—oh, so gently !—on the side of his bed so as not to shake him.

" ' You wanted to take me into your château,' he whispered. ' I thank you, little friend. No, you mustn't cry. You heard what Mademoiselle said. I am going to get well.' Then he laughed a little, in spite of a warning shake of the fingers from my governess. ' When I am well and you are grown up, will you marry me, little friend ? '

" I clasped my hands together with a gasp. Oh, wouldn't I just !

" ' Good ! Then that's settled,' he said, his eyes twinkling with fun, and then he became serious. ' Now listen, all of you ! You must leave this village to-night. You have bicycles? Good ! Take what money you have and leave secretly after dark. Countries at war are not very safe for young women with no men to protect them. Travel by the by-roads as fast as you can and not towards Paris. Go south.'

" ' But we can't leave you here like this,' I cried, and he shook his head reproachfully.

" ' What sort of dog's life shall we lead when we are married, if you refuse my first prayer. Promise ! '

" Before I could promise, a boy covered with dust and panting for breath burst into the room.

" ' I was sent here from the château. It is Mees Lovetear.'

" We were all accustomed to hearing Miss Lowther addressed in that way. My governess held out her hand, and the boy put his hand into his blouse and drew forth a letter. It was from Mummy.

" ' I have got to Barbizon, but cannot get nearer. Come at once on your bicycles. The boy will show you the way.'

" 'You see,' said the Zouave. ' To-night you will go ? '

" We promised. The boy had come on a bicycle from Barbizon, and had been two days upon the journey. We sent him off to the château to get some food. My governess put a jug of water by the Zouave's bed, gave him some opium tablets, and paid some money to Mademoiselle Cromecq for his nourishment. Then we left him.

" It was a day of events. Opposite the little ' Mairie ' I saw our old bearded forest-guardian, Papa François, ta king to Polydore Cromecq and Gavroche, and the tears were rolling down his face. He was blubbering like a child as he talked. . . . It was horrible to see. . . . And it frightened me. But the moment we got near, Polydore cried ' Chut ! Chut ! ' in a savage undertone and the old forester stopped at once. That frightened me still more. I had a feeling that something horrible was growing and growing in the village, some idea which was monstrous. I returned to the château and whilst we ate a meal and waited for darkness my uneasiness grew until I burst out sobbing as if my heart would break. My governess put my outburst down to terror at our position, to fear for myself. But I wasn't afraid for myself. I hadn't realized that we were in any danger.

" ' It's getting dark already, Cynthia,' she said to comfort me. ' We'll be off in a few minutes' ; and she went upstairs to put a few things together.

" I was left alone in the great dining-room. The shadows were deepening in every corner every second. I ran into the kitchen. All the servants had gone already. Only the boy who was to guide us was there finishing his meal.

" ' Gilbert,' I asked, ' which way do we go ? '

" ' Over the little bridge at the back of the village, across the Morin, then by the cart-track through Jouy-le-Chatel, Mademoiselle.'

" ' Good ! You must take my bicycle with you, Gilbert. I will meet you and Mademoiselle at the gate where the cart-track begins. Tell Mademoiselle and wait for me there.'

" I gave him no time to answer me. I left him gaping at me with his mouth open. I was terrified lest my governess should come down whilst I was still in the house. I ran out by the kitchen and down the avenue of trees. In the village there was only one light burning and that came through the open door of Cromecq's estaminet and lay like a broad yellow blade across the street. I crept to the edge of it and then raced across. But no one had seen me. No one called. I ran on to the cottage at the end of the village. That was in darkness too.

I stopped under the window where the Zouave lay and listened. I couldn't even hear him breathing. I raised my hand to tap upon the window-pane. But the window was open. I stood upon tiptoe with my fingers on the sill and could just look in. It was all black—yes, even where the white sheets of his bed should have glimmered.

" ' Henri,' I whispered. ' Monsieur Henri ! ' But not even a sigh answered me.

" I felt sure that he was dead. I heard myself sobbing. But I had got to make sure. I tried the door. It was locked. I knocked upon it gently at first, then in a fury. There wasn't a sound. The house was empty—empty of all perhaps but the young Zouave. I found a pail, by chance. I turned it upside down and standing on it climbed into the room through the open window.

" ' Monsieur Henri,' I whispered. I was terribly afraid, but I had got to make sure. There was no one on the couch at all. The very sheets had been taken away. I crept over to the corner where I had seen his uniform folded. That too had disappeared. So had his sword which had been leaning against the corner of the wall. There was no longer a trace of him at all. I was seized with a panic as I stood in that dark empty room. I ran to the window and tumbled out of it—somehow. As I reached the ground I upset the pail. The clattering of it sounded to me like a peal of thunder. I turned to run and someone grasped and held my arm. I gave a gasp and should have fainted, but a rough friendly voice spoke to me.

" ' You, Mademoiselle ! What are you doing here ? You should have gone with the rest. All the women have gone. There is an order. Don't you know that ? ' and he shook my arm chidingly. ' My word, how you frightened me ! It is not right to frighten an old man like that ! '

" ' We are going to-night, Papa François,' I answered. ' We are going to Barbizon. But I wanted to say good-bye to the Zouave and make sure that he was comfortable. And he has gone, Papa François.'

" ' But of course he has gone. Don't you know ? Haven't you heard ? They will occupy the village to-morrow morning.' I did not have to ask whom he meant by ' they.' ' They caught me in the forest and sent me back with a message for the Mayor. If a French soldier, a French weapon, even a French uniform is found in Neuilly-sur-Morin, they will burn every house to the ground. We could not leave an officer at the very first house they will come to—the house of Mademois-

elle Cromecq too.　You see that, little Miss ? '　Poor Papa
François was torn between terror for his village and pity for
the young officer.　Remorsefully he pleaded his necessity.
' The house of the sister of the Mayor.　No, then, for sure,
everything would be destroyed.　So we moved him—but very
tenderly.　There is a stretcher, you know.　We did not hurt
him—oh, no.'

"' And where is he now, Papa François ? ' I broke in.

" The old man hesitated and blundered.　Oh, it took ages
to get the truth out of him, as he grumbled and quavered and
whispered in that dark street.

"' It is the only place. . . .　He is safe there. . . .　The
village too.　And after all it is not so bad.　Bah !　He is a
soldier.　He has slept in many worse places this last month. . . .'

"' Where ?　Where ? ' I insisted.

"' It is in the Fire-shed.　But it is only for an hour or two.
To-night Monsieur le Maire and Gavroche will carry him
across the Morin and hide him safely in a farm—— '

" But I did not wait to hear more excuses.　I tore my arm
free from Papa François and darted across the street.　Yes,
we had a Fire-shed at the back of the estaminet, on the river
bank—a miserable little hut filled up with our little hand-drawn
fire-engine, and with a mud floor.　Oh, I was not afraid any
longer.　I was mad with passion, the passion of a little girl
nine years old for a young god, in a uniform too, dropped out
of the clouds, wounded—a young god who had asked her to
marry him.　And they treated him like that !　Once more I
hadn't a doubt who ' they ' were—Polydore Cromecq, and his
sister whose furniture would be spoilt by a bleeding man, and
little Gavroche, the grocer !

" Skimming along in the darkness, with my heart all upside
down, I nearly ran headlong into the vine-covered trellis work
which stretched out into the road on each side of the estaminet
and made a shelter for the little tables.　I pulled up in time,
however, and the next moment I was crouching against the
vine-leaves, holding my breath, listening—that is, listening as
well as the beating of my heart would allow me.

" For just on the other side of the trellis, seated at a little
table in the corner where the light from the open door could not
reach, there were Polydore and Gavroche, drinking.　They
must have heard me, I was convinced, but they had not, and
immediately I learnt why.

" The neck of a bottle rattled on the rim of a glass and
Polydore in a thick wheedling voice said :

" ' Another glass, old comrade ! I do not bring out such brandy as this for every client. No ! '

" ' It is good,' answered Gavroche. ' We need such drink for our work. To save this little corner of France, eh, my friend.'

" They were both of them half drunk. I did not trouble my head about what they were saying. They talked of France, they thought of themselves. But they had not yet carried my wounded god across the river. I slipped by the side of the house through the grass to the little Fire-shed. It was very dark that night, but I had the eyes of a cat and I could see the triangle of the roof against the sky. The door was unlocked. I pulled it open.

" ' Monsieur Henri,' I said in a low voice, and he answered from my feet. There was just room for him to lie across the shed between the engine and the door, and they had laid his stretcher there on the mud floor.

" ' You little angel ! ' he whispered in a startled tone. ' What are you doing here ? You should have gone hours ago.'

" I dropped down on my knees beside him. He was shivering with cold.

" ' The brutes ! The brutes ! '

" He lifted a hand and laid it over my lips.

" ' Listen, little one ! Before you go. You must never mention to anyone, not even to your mother, one word about what has happened to-night. Promise me ? For the honour of France ! '

" ' I don't understand,' I sobbed.

" ' But you will, dear. Kiss me once ! Thank you ! Remember ! For the honour of France ! Now go ! ' and since I did not move, his voice strengthened suddenly. " Then I shall sit up and that will kill me.'

" ' No, no ! ' I prayed, and I sprang to my feet—and through the open door we both heard the Mayor and Gavroche encouraging one another drunkenly as they stumbled through the grass.

" ' Look quickly ! Do they carry a lantern ? ' Henri asked. He was frightened now—since the morning of that day I have never been able to mistake the sound of fear in a man's voice— but frightened for me.

" ' No, they have no lantern.'

The Zouave drew a breath of relief.

" ' Then run ! Run, little betrothed one, as fast as you can, as silently as you can. Oh, whilst there's time, my dear.' His head fell back upon the pillow. ' You see I can do nothing ! '

"There was such an agony of appeal in his voice that I slipped round the side of the shed at once. I hid behind a bush on the river bank and I heard Polydore utter a startled oath as his hand knocked against the open door of the shed.

" ' So you have had a visitor, my Lieutenant,' he said, and I never heard geniality ring with so false a note.

" ' I ? ' replied Henri, and he spoke as loudly, as warningly as he could. ' I was stifled in here. I pushed the door open with the one hand I could use.'

" ' Yes, it is bad,' Gavroche agreed. " But all that are left in the village are asleep now. We can carry you, my Lieutenant, to a place where no one can betray you. Gently ! Gently ! So ! '

"The two men moved away from the shed with the stretcher between them. Yes, but they didn't carry it eastwards towards the bridge but westwards where there was no bridge at all. They were drunk—that was what I thought—they had mistaken their way. I ran out from the hedge—I was on the point of calling to them—when I heard an oath and one of them stumbled—or seemed to stumble. I heard a loud splash, I saw in the darkness a sudden swirl of white as the river broke into foam, and above the sound of the splash a cry rose in a clear young vibrating voice :

" ' Run ! Run ! '

"A cry to me ! But I was paralysed by the horror of the accident. For a moment I couldn't run. Then I did—towards the spot where the accident had happened. I was close to them when a dreadful thing happened. The wounded Zouave's head rose above the water, his hands clutched at the bank, and I saw Polydore Cromecq raise a great stick and beat with all his strength upon the knuckles. A groan answered the blows, and the Zouave with a groan sank again beneath the water.

"The two men remained kneeling upon the bank, peering into the darkness, listening. Polydore said :

" ' It is over now.'

"And Gavroche replied :

" ' Yes, it is over. We had to think of our village, hadn't we ? Yes, yes, we had to think of France.'

"Then they stood up and saw me just behind them. Now, indeed, I ran, with both of them at my heels, in and out amongst the bushes along the river bank, towards the bridge. Polydore Cromecq had grudged me my young legs that afternoon. He

I saw Polydore (Cromecq) raise a great stick.

grudged me them still more during these minutes. I heard the two men crushing through the grass after me, panting, swaying, but I gained on them. Then Polydore raised his voice :

" ' Little Miss, wait for me ! Come back to the estaminet and wish us good-bye ! You shall see me drink a bock and the little bubbles wink on my big moustache. That will be amusing—what ? For the last time, eh ? It is good to part with a laugh.'

" But I ran the faster. I crossed the bridge. My governess and the boy were waiting with the bicycles at the gate.

" ' Quick, please, quick,' I cried. ' I will tell you afterwards.'

" My governess was the woman for an emergency. We were off down the cart-track on our bicycles when Polydore and Gavroche crossed the bridge.

" ' Little Miss ! Little Miss ! '

" The cry rang out, once, twice, and each time fainter. Then we heard it no more. I never did tell my governess afterwards of the crime which was committed that night—no, nor anyone, since my Zouave had forbidden me. But I have broken my promise to him to-night. The cruel thing is that ' they ' never did enter the village. For they began their retreat the next morning."

IV

CYNTHIA ended her story. For a minute the middle-aged woman and the girl stared into the unlit grate. Then Madame D'Estourie said slowly :

" For the honour of France, he said."

" Yes. I didn't understand what he ment. I do now, of course. It's better that nothing should be said. War makes some men monsters."

Madame D'Estourie stood up.

" And many women, childless," she added.

Cynthia looked quickly at her.

" But Madame D'Estourie," she began, and her visitor interrupted her.

" I was Madame Flavelle, before I was Madame D'Estourie. Your wounded Zouave was my boy. For six years I have been searching why he died and meaning to exact justice to the uttermost farthing. But—for the honour of France—he said"; and she let her arms drop against her sides in resignation. She turned her eyes to Cynthia. They were wells of pain.

" I may kiss you ? " she asked. She held the girl tight to her breast. " Thank you ! Thank you ! " she whispered in a breaking voice. She let her go and wrapped her cloak about her throat.

" Now," she said in a cheerful voice. " We shall go downstairs together."

But Cynthia drew back. Madame D'Estourie, however, would have none of it.

" No, no, that won't do," she cried. " That poor young man has been waiting in the hall more than his ten minutes. Let us go to him. And I think that old misery, now that you have told it to me, will not haunt you any more."

She put her arm tenderly about Cynthia's waist and they went down the stairs. But half-way down Madame D'Estourie ran forward with a little sob, as though her self-restraint at last was failing her. When Cynthia reached the floor, she found Jim seated patiently on a hall-chair, exchanging consolatory phrases with a no less patient butler.

It did not occur to Jim to complain, nor on the other hand did it occur to Cynthia to apologize. She said :

" Oh, Jim, I don't want to dance to-night. Be an angel, will you ? Drive me down the Portsmouth road as far as Ripley and back, will you ? "

Jim's face lit up with a smile.

" Cynthia," he said, " there are bright moments in your young life which give me hopes for your future " ; and he went outside and cranked up his car.

THE ELECTRIC KING

By

LORD DUNSANY

THIS is a story Jorkens told me one day. It goes to prove that he does not talk always of himself, as some of the members of our club have chosen to assert ; and, since there is no personal motive to be served by any inaccuracy, I see no reason for doubting it. And if this story of his be true, why not his other ones ? That is the way I look at it, without any wish whatever to interfere with the judgment of others.

He had fallen asleep after a somewhat heavy meal, and all the other members but I had left : some had business to attend to, while others were irritated by Jorkens' snoring, though I couldn't see what harm his snores were doing ; or what good their business did, if you come to that. And presently one of Jorkens' snores turned to a gurgle, which seemed for a moment to be going to choke him ; and that woke him up ; and, being all alone with him ; I made the remark, " I suppose you have seen some pretty queer things in your time."

" And people," said Jorkens. And very soon he was well started, wonderfully refreshed by his sleep, and by whatever he may have had with his lunch. And this is the tale. He was in America, knocking about in New England, and chancing to be somewhat out of funds. And he had taken up reporting for a paper, and interviewing, whenever he could get a scrap of work to do, in order to get on to what he called a financial footing ; which I expect meant money enough to get back to England third class. And one day they had sent him to see Makins, the millionaire, who had been having a good deal of publicity lately, and to get an interview from him. In case the name of Makins conveys little, he was better known as the Electric King ; and his publicity had come from the interest that had been taken in the case to prove that he was capable of administering his own affairs. That he was so capable had been triumphantly proved by his lawyer, chiefly by full details of the organizing, the working, the tending, even the very oiling, of the giant dynamos that were watched and directed personally by Makins himself for fourteen hours out of every twenty-four, the whole year round, year after year. What the dynamos were used for was a point that was brushed aside with such consummate brilliance that unless my reader be thoroughly trained in the law he would never be able to appreciate it. These were the dynamos that Jorkens saw when he went to interview Makins.

Jorkens would never have had the job if it had been an easy one, and yet he got the man's whole story. There was something about him that Makins had liked, even if it was only that " he took his wine like a man," to use Makins' own words, and so he had got his story. Jorkens had congratulated him on the news with which the world was ringing, that he had just been proved capable of controlling his own affairs, and Makins had said, " Isn't it just marvellous ? " And then he had been silent for a quarter of an hour, sitting, sometimes shaking his head, in a large carved chair, till he suddenly muttered, and soon his voice gained strength, and he told Jorkens this story.

" I had the idea of busting the whole electric light of America and then gathering it all up again into my own hands: one company to illuminate every city of the United States. We should have been a power, at the lowest computation, equal to the full moon. I had it all clear in my head, and I could have done it—I can't give you the details : it isn't clear now : but it was in those days ; clear to the last cent. You might have asked me any question about the minutest part of the scheme, and I could have answered at once in those days.

" I should have controlled all that light ; think of it. As much as the full moon sheds on the North American continent. Then my leisure went. I suddenly lost my leisure. A slight attack, the doctor called it. But it wasn't an attack : I was perfectly well in body. And it certainly wasn't my mind : that was clearer than ever, too clear in fact ; my thoughts were crystal-clear, but too many of them. I simply lost my leisure. It takes a good deal of work, a good deal of thought, for one man to control big business ; and when I stopped to breathe at the summit of my career, on a pinnacle higher than I had ever dreamed of, my thoughts ran on. They would not stop, and so I lost my leisure. Well, I didn't mind at first : they all went into the business. But when I found that the most trivial thoughts began to run through my head, like a mob of dirty children in a great ballroom, thoughts too trivial and silly and irrelevant even to mention, and no keeping them out, why then I began to panic, and went to a doctor, and said to him, ' What about it ? ' And he said, ' Sea voyage.' And I sailed from New York for Bombay.

" Well, I found the sea voyage was not doing me any good, and I did some thinking then ; I was always thinking ; and I figured it out then that what I wanted was not a doctor, but one who dealt with the terrors of the soul. Yes, I don't exaggerate : I was pretty well frightened by then : I began to see that those thoughts were hunting my reason : Noses down, tails up, ears flapping, that's what they were after, as surely as hounds a long way behind a fox. Well, there were one or two priests on board, of various denominations, and I talked to them a good deal, walking round the decks in the evening with one or other of them, and putting my case to him as soon as he began to listen. But they mostly talked to me about going to Heaven, and I figured that their advice was too like my doctor's, who had sent me to Bombay ; not that Bombay's like heaven, in the hot weather not at all. And besides, I knew their talk pretty well already ; and my thoughts went racing on.

" And then I remembered that I had heard that there were a good many religions in India, some with idols and some without ; it was all one to me ; I was being hunted over a precipice and was anxious to clutch at anything. I mean any prejudice I may have had against idols seemed now merely absurd : you mayn't like brambles, but you'd grab them going over an edge and to such a drop as I saw. Yes, sir, my wits were tottering. And that thought went on hunting them.

" It had come down chiefly to one thought now. It was something about a rat that I had once thrown a stone at. That was the nearest one, the leading one of the pack : night and day you know, and of course no sleep to speak of.

" I got to know a man on board who had been in India a good deal. I guessed it by his face and began to talk to him. And in a day or two I had put my whole case before him, as near as I dared, for I daren't speak of the rat in those days. Ebblit his name was, and he told me about the Ganges. Our acquaintance began in the Mediterranean ; we used to play chess at first, and sit and talk when the game was over. But he never really spoke out, never told me all he felt, or half he knew, till we turned that corner where de Lesseps stands, with one bronze hand held out to the eastern gate of the world ; and the corrupt city of Port Said drops astern, a cluster of white domes in the evening, the sort of thing an angel might dream on waking ; just leaving it behind him, you know, as we were. And Ebblit soon after that began to talk of the East, as though it were really there, and there were nothing odd about it ; while the West and its ways seemed to drop further and further away from him, till he seemed no longer intimidated by its prejudices and customs. And then he spoke of the beauty of that river. He did not seem to know whether the calm of its beauty moulded the thoughts of those people, soothing and lulling them to an undreamed content, or whether it was the thoughts of generations of people that had given the river that surpassing sanctity. But I began to see there was ease to be found on the Ganges ; and rest, as I dared to hope, for my hunted wits. And I asked him what part of the river was best to go to ; and he thought for a little while and answered, ' Benares.'

" I had a long way yet to go, and that rat with its wounded tail was terribly close. I forgot to tell you that its tail was broken. Gosh, I'm a tough man ! I've known hundreds of men right through, their little minds clear as glass to me, and I don't know one of them, not one, that would have held out against that rat through the Red Sea.

" They had a large tank on board rigged up as a swimming bath, and I used to get some coolness there after sunset, floating on the water and looking up at the stars and thinking of the rat.

" And then I used to go and talk to Ebblit. Every bit of information I could get from him I used to collect like a stamp collector—the name of the best hotel, the best part of the river to sit at, the priests, the temples, the legends—everything I could get from him while we walked up and down in the heat. And one day I very nearly mentioned the rat to him. Not quite, but I think he saw it coming. After that I found it more difficult to get him to have a talk with me, especially when alone.

" I was practically all alone with the rat after that.

" And at last we reached Bombay.

" Of course there are things to see in India between Bombay and Benares, quite a lot in fact. The eighth wonder of the world is at Agra, and the earthly paradise in the old palace at Delhi, not to mention the marvels of history which are the equals of legend in other lands. There's a lot to look at beyond the pinnacles of the Western Ghats. But by now I could see nothing but the slow blood oozing from the battered bruise in the tail. So I hurried on to Benares.

"There was a man outside the Cow Temple who would help me, Ebblit had told me, at the right-hand side of the door. He was there three years ago, Ebblit had said, and would probably still be there. And I mustn't mind him being rather dirty, very dirty in fact. I would have laughed at the idea if I'd been able to laugh in those days. Dirty, indeed! What was dirt to that rat?

"I went to that temple in terror. What if the man had gone? Three years seemed a long time to me. But it wasn't long to him, just as Ebblit had said. He was there right enough, at the right-hand side of the door that leads to the Cow Temple; loin-cloth, bare skin, and dirt; sitting upon the ground with a bowl beside him. So I found an interpreter and went back to the dirty man and put my case to him at once, before I had even gone to my hotel. Of course I didn't tell him about the rat; perhaps I might have done so had he been cleaner; but I said that I was a business man much troubled by business worries, and that other thoughts intruded themselves on me too. He seemed to pay little attention, and when my interpreter and I had done, he merely replied, 'Speak openly.'

"You may guess that I didn't like being spoken to in such a way by a man like that, and I was silent a moment. And then in my utter despair I mentioned the rat. And the instant I mentioned it the whole thing poured out : I had never spoken of it before. Its eyes, its whiskers, its fur, I described it all to him, from its eager nose to the mangled bend in its tail.

"And he said to me, if the interpreter got it right, 'The River Ganges is beautiful beyond the conception of man, and beyond the capacity of any mind to estimate. In the contemplation of this beauty is complete fulfilment of all desire. No ambition transcends it. Nothing even hoped for can surpass it. It is the fitting occupation of any lifetime. Go, and sit by it until the picture of the river dwells in your innermost mind, as it does with me, more near than the hands and feet. Sit by it, if needs be, all your days. The reward hereafter is infinite ; and for the seekers, like yourself, for immediate gain, even for these it is adequate.'

"It's odd, but it seemed to me that the man was talking sense. The rat was still there, but a ray of faint hope had shone

from beyond the sound of his voice. I felt like some wayfarer
lost and terribly hunted, who suddenly hears in the darkness
a music of bells, and beyond the bells at last some cottager's
light. That was no mad fancy, but only came from the stress
of weeks without sleep.

" Well, I went to the Ganges. Boys, it's a jewel ! I went
down to it about sunset, and it lay there like a vast piece of a
semi-precious stone, one of those very pale beryls or aqua-
marines. I realised at once it was no use just looking at it ; I
wasn't a sightseer now, but a fugitive from a terror greater
than any of those that ever hunt the body : I would cheerfully have sat and played with a tiger, to get away from that
rat.

" Suicide may be suggesting itself to you as an obvious
remedy. But I wouldn't do that, because I felt that the rat
was after my reason, and I wanted to save it from him with
all its power, not to throw it away. So I had gone to the
Ganges, not to gaze at it, but to let it sink into my soul, to
contemplate its beauty as I had been told, till it became more
to me than my hands and feet, and nothing else should matter,
not even the rat.

" It seemed the world's end, that river; so many steps led
down to it. It was not like tracks that run down to a ford
and go onward the other side, or paths that lead to a ferry,
to wait a while ; these steps thronged down to the water's
edge and ceased, the end of the journeys of pilgrims living or
dead. I sat down on one of the steps near a tiny temple and
watched the day fading, and the more it faded the more easy
I found it to take·my first lesson in the lore that should save
me from the rat. And the beauty of the river began sinking
into me, as easily as if I'd been there for years and years.
Pilgrims came down the steps by twos and threes ; pigeons
came to the little temple beside me, dropping down to their
rest among the tiny domes, and the colour went out of things
with the loss of the sun, all but the river, which seemed to
keep a light of its own. Now for the first time I noticed the
fires of death, flickering up from the burning ghats. Sometimes
a ship with great sails stole down the river, with never a ripple
upon that wondrous calm, so that it seemed that the ship was
a ship of ghosts or the river something from dreamland,
something far out among dreams, a long long way from waking.
Now I saw vividly a slanting moon, young in the west like a
horn, over the little temple. And, as the moon brightened and
the fires of death grew stronger, the colour that had faded out

of the sky with sunset began to return with the afterglow, coming back more gorgeous than it had been before, like a traveller returning to some rural home clad in the silks and splendours of wonderful lands. It increased and increased, till the luminous river seemed dark, beside the astonishing glow of it."

As Makins spoke of the Ganges he talked very fast, gazing straight in front of him over Jorkens' head, without a thought of his scurrying pencil. Jorkens was writing shorthand and even then scarcely kept up. It wasn't so much the beauty of the Ganges that was entrancing him, Jorkens thinks, as the first escape, of a kind, that he had ever had from the rat ; though he hadn't really got away from it. As he put it himself, " Masses of twilight seemed to be descending rapidly, draping the holy city with all their glory : you know how pieces of evening, slabs of light, seem to fall between you and buildings at this enchanted hour, buildings on solid earth, and sky between you and them. It was like that with me and the rat. There was something at last, at last, between me and him. The beauty of the Ganges. It could not overcome him, the thing was too strong for that. But the rat was now on the far side of the river.

" A most intense beauty filled the sky with the deep colours of India, a hush hung heavily at the brink of the river, a hush as though the world had ceased its spinning to watch for the first star : the door of the little temple opened noiselessly, showing all dark within, and the hush deepened over all the river. ·And suddenly bells at the very water's edge sent up a melody clanging across the hush ; wide windows opened in the dark far up above me, from which poured sudden music of instruments utterly strange to us ; drums beat unseen from the little temple near ; the rapidly darkening air throbbed to a strange rhythm, that boomed and resounded among the walls of Benares ; that was their way of worship ; they were giving praise to the river. You'll excuse me a moment, won't you ? " And Makins rose and went to a little shutter, a sliding panel in the library where they were sitting, and moved the panel aside. And at once a great purr filled the room, the voice of a hundred dynamos. Jorkens had heard the murmur of them before, all the time that Makins was talking about the Ganges, but now the roar of their purring filled all the room, and he could see the rows of them, like a vast stable of elephants. What stupendous energies that iron multitude was unloosing Jorkens did not then know, only that a vast power was going invisibly forth. They were looking down on the hall of the dynamos from the height of one story, and men were going about amongst the dark rounded shapes, oiling machinery. " My dynamos are being fed," said Makins. Jorkens said nothing ; the hugeness of the power so near to him, the humble service these monsters were giving to man, and the incompatibility between the organized might of science and the devoted worship of an Indian river seem to have taken his breath away. And Makins continued :

" I stayed there for three days. The rat was now, as I said, on the far side of the river ; but it went no further away. In the gloom of thought I could see its whiskers twitching whenever it sniffed, and I knew whom it was sniffing for. So I went back to the dirty man and told him all about it. And he said, ' The Ganges flows from a hill too high for our feet. And on that hill is a city of pure gold. Everything there is gold, pavement and houses : even the shops are gold. And all the people that dwell in it are Hindus.' When he spoke of the beauty of the river he had me beat ; that was a thing he understood ; but when it came to a definite fact of geography, that set me arguing. ' How did he know,' I asked, ' that the golden city was there ? ' ' I have seen it,' he said. ' I walked for months up the river, walking in my youth, great distances every day ; and I came to the hill, and it was all white, and there was no city there. I was young and had not the faith. And I stayed there looking at it for seven days, fasting and sometimes praying to those to whom prayer is due. And at the end of the seventh day I thought I noticed a change. And the sun set, and there was no change. And all the hill grew dull. And I was faint with fasting. And all of a sudden the golden city came ; street upon street of it straggling along the hill ; and domes and walls and towers all twinkling and shining ; a city of purest gold, as the Brahmins teach.'

" ' Should I see it ? ' I asked.

" ' Not yet,' he said.

" ' When should I see it ? " I asked him.

" ' Stay for three months upon the bank in Benares,' he told me. Well, it seemed a long time, but I did as the dirty man said. And the rat stayed all that time on the far side of the river, and I had some sleep at nights, yet things got no better than that ; I could still see the country of madness too near to my borders, the edges of my imagination almost touched it.

" One day at the very end of the three months, as I sat

watching the pilgrims, it suddenly occurred to me that it was not my river ; that I should never believe the story of the golden city, and its gods could never be my gods. I made up my mind suddenly. I never even told the dirty man. I suppose he is sitting there now by the door of the Cow Temple, with the cows and peacocks strolling about inside, and the worshippers tolling a bell whenever they pray, so that their god shall hear them. I left at once. I suppose I valued too lightly the rest I had had from the rat, or thought that the respite would last. The moment I left the Ganges he crossed the river, and was back again as close as ever he was. He might have driven me back to Benares, but I knew by now that the Ganges could never get rid of him : the holy river was only a palliation, and I had a hope of shaking him off altogether. You see, from the first I thought religion could do it. I am pretty shrewd as men go and make up my mind quickly, and from the very first I had spotted that that rat was one of the terrors of the soul. So that spiritual help was what I needed, if I could only find a religion that had a priest that was ready to fight the rat. And I had not given up hope. The greatest religions, I said, have always come out of deserts. And it must be so : for before a man can even look at the verities, let alone ponder and value them, he must clear off the dust of all the things that don't matter ; like to-day's news, to-day's opinions, to-day's fashions ; yesterday's customs, and to-morrow's fears. So I left the opalescent city of Benares, travelling in search of a desert. And the rat travelled with me.

" I took a train for Delhi to begin with. There I intended to inquire my way to a desert, and in the desert I hoped to find some holy man who might have found enough wisdom, out of the way of cities, to be able to solve the terrific problem I brought him. Well, I was sitting in my railway carriage towards evening, thinking of the rat, when all of a sudden, pale and clear on my right, I saw a range of mountains that I did not know was there.

" While we waited at the next station I asked the station-master about them, and he told me they were the Himalayas. The Himalayas ! Imagine seeing a waterfall and asking its name, and being told that it was Niagara ; or entering a church by chance, and finding it was Westminster Abbey. So I came to the Himalayas.

" The station-master told me the names of the peaks, pale mauve a long way off. I've always found you English very obliging. And then I asked him the name of a white one, all alone over the rest, and he answered as though it were not there at all, or at any rate need not be bothered about.

" ' Oh, that's in Tibet,' he said. Isn't that like you ? You're nearly all like that. It was outside the British Empire, and so it didn't count."

Of course Jorkens said that that wasn't so at all. That we thought rather more of a foreign country if anything than of our own, and would do anything rather than show we thought it was foreign. So a few moments passed over international courtesies, meaningless and polite, while the dynamos purred on faintly the other side of the shutter. And then Makins continued, " I hadn't been looking at them for long when I said to myself, Mountains. Mountains, I said : they're every bit as good as deserts ; and I've heard strange tales of Tibet. On a mountain a man may do as much thinking as he could down on the sand, provided he goes high enough ; all the silly little phrases that buzz round thought and obscure it wouldn't get far up a mountain. I'll go there, I said ; and I decided at once ; at the next stop from that I got out. And the rat hopped out with me.

" I hired a motor in course of time ; you can do anything in time in the East ; and we started straight for those mountains. I was getting no sleep now at all and I made the chauffeur do sixty. We startled the little tree-rats as we shot past. Wonderful little animals. How I wished it were one of them that was after my reason, instead of the foul brute that I knew. Or even a monkey. But I suppose a man can't choose what terror will hunt his soul. And looking at it reasonably, as one always should at anything, I suppose one curse is as bad as another ; only I couldn't think so then.

" Well, we motored on towards the mountains in the afternoon, the afternoon of the day following my talk with the station-master, until what had been patches of blue laid upon lilac began to be great ravines rent in the slope of the mountain. Tibet by now no longer peered down on one, but was hidden by this huge wall, shutting it off from the world.

" We did a lot of mileage that day, till we came to a place where the chauffeur said the car could go no farther. Not that I bothered about that, for I had had from him the rumour of a monastery fifty miles or so farther on, the very thing I was looking for ; and I would gladly have walked without food or rest, with that ahead of me and the rat behind.

"As it turned out I didn't have to walk, and as it turned out it was a lot more than fifty miles ; but we got hold of a bullock cart at a village, a thing they call a tonga : two bullocks drag it, and they can go anywhere. I don't say it was comfortable, but comfort had gone from me since the coming of the rat, and I found bodily discomfort rather pleasant than otherwise : I had come to that pass long ago. We were travelling in the bed of a great river, the man that was driving the oxen, and I, and of course the rat. Our wheels were going over white sand and boulders, everything perfectly dry, except for long narrow pools of shallow water, lying like shreds torn out from a mountain-oread's dress. The sambhur came out of the forest to gaze at us, not the least afraid of the bullock-cart. So thick was the forest all along the dry river that we seldom saw the mountains : when we did see them their imminence was tremendous ; we were all among them now, as though we had strayed unannounced into the assembly of giants, ancient ones of the earth, deputed by Nature to deliberate on her plans. Now night began to fall, and the man halted his oxen and built a little circle of fires for the night, to keep away tigers. I kicked one of his little fires all golden into the darkness. ' Will that keep it off, do you think ? ' I blurted out at him. But he was thinking only of tigers.

" I regretted my violence almost immediately. ' You must forgive me,' I said, ' I can't sleep.' But he understood never a word, and it mattered not what I said to him.

" One tiger came very near ; I heard his whispering footfall above the thought of the rat. The night passed, like all sleepless nights, in about a year ; and dawn came suddenly. We made some tea, and the man ate some food he had brought, and we pushed on for Tibet. We went on all that day, our wheels climbing over the boulders and dropping down with a crash on the other side. But none of these jolts could shake the rat away.

" We made our little bivouac that night far up the slope in the cold with only one fire, above the fear of tigers. Not that I feared tigers. I had only one fear now, and my reason was tottering before it. Another sleepless night dragged by like a long chapter of history ; and in the golden morning my driver pointed ; and there, far enough off, but shining bright as the morning, there on a mountain was the monastery I sought. By noon we were as far as the bullocks could go ; the rest of the way was sheer mountain. We had already changed bullocks twice, and done over sixty of the fifty miles

that they had said it was to the monastery. I found that
distances in India were often like that. But here was the
monastery at last in sight. I was able to get more men to
carry my kit from the tonga, and I pushed on ahead of them
up the mountain. A tiny little path went winding away over
what was otherwise nearly precipice : by the look of it they
didn't often go from that monastery, whoever they were, and
few seemed to go to them. A bell sounded as I climbed up
to them, but there was hardly a welcome in the sound, as you
might expect in this voice from the lonely mountain ; it was
too unearthly for that, too little concerned, so it seemed,
with any cares we know. The way to the door seemed almost
quite untrodden. By the door a bell-handle in bronze, shaped
like a dragon, hung from a light chain. I went up and pulled
the handle, and an astonishing din reverberated through the
monastery. By some system of pulleys the chain that I pulled
so easily must have swung a bell weighing little under a ton.
And out came a wizened man in a monkish robe, and to him
I tried to explain what I wanted without an interpreter, and
without knowing a word of his language, or he knowing any
of mine. But I think he must have guessed from some look
of fear in my eyes, for he led me in ; and presently the men
came up with my baggage, and it was easier to explain more
about myself by pointing to that. Had I come with less kit,
and perhaps bare-footed, they might have sent me on sooner.
As it was, I sent one of the men who brought my baggage to
go and get an interpreter, and it took him a week to find one.
And all this time they housed me and gave me their queer
food, and a small stone cell to sleep in. And when the interpreter came I had a talk with a younger monk, telling him all
my case ; and he told me to ask the interpreter to come back
in a year ; and that at the end of that time I should have
prepared myself by suitable meditation to have speech with
their Lama.

    " That was an unthinkable year. The rat gnawing through
my thoughts and working into my reason and they would
not even let me ask for the cure. A year of horror. A year
of the pit. I will not speak of it. They kept the rat from
doing its worst, I will say that for them ; they knew of exer-
cises, exorcisms and spells, fastings and meditations that kept
up the walls of the soul and kept the powers of night from
actually taking the citadel ; but I was beleaguered by terrors
all that year, and they would not even let me ask for help. A
ghastly, unspeakable year, and the rat so close that were it not

for their bell, were it not for their bell, I don't know what would have happened.

"It came to an end at last. At last they sent for me and said that their Lama would see me ; and they had the interpreter all ready.

"I was shown into his cell ; a man in a yellow robe, with a flat-topped head ; sitting calm at a table, and eyes like the scrutiny of the entire night, like the whole night solving a riddle, unravelling the mystery of courses of worlds that were older than ours. I spoke to him through my interpreter, but he did not speak to me. When I had spoken he merely pointed upwards, not to the sky but up the slope of the mountain, then he sat motionless with his gaze before him and his hands stretched out on the table. I saw that it was time to go, and I bowed to him and left the room, and soon afterwards left the monastery, and started, where he had pointed, up the mountain, where as I was told by one of the younger monks I should find another monastery before nightfall. Something in the reverence with which he spoke of it, something in the awe with which they watched me set forth, gave a fresh hope to my hard-hunted soul. It was in the early morning, and I climbed all day. No track whatever led up from the monastery I left : late in the afternoon I met a track arising out of nowhere and winding upwards. They didn't seem to call on each other much. I could not see the monastery to which I was going, but they had pointed out the direction, and I had no doubt that this insufficient track was the road of the people I looked for. The heat and fatigue were nothing to me, for without the protection, such as it was, that I had had from the monks of the lower monastery, the rat was hunting me sorely. And before the sun set I heard a bell above me ; but so faint it sounded, lonely and lost on the mountain, and so very strange were its notes, so aloof from our joys or troubles, that it hardly seemed to ring from a habitation of men.

"I had brought my interpreter with me, a Hindu from near Naini Tal ; that is to say he had left the lower monastery with me ; but I had let him follow at leisure, not being driven, as I was, over the rocks by the pursuit of the rat. But besides the interpreter I brought nobody ; nobody to carry my kit, and no kit to carry. I had an idea that it might be better to arrive like that this time. They don't set store by the things that we set store by.

"Over a rise the track I was following rambled, leading down to a little valley, and on the far side of the valley the upper monastery stood, with the little rocky valley to look out on, and the mountain going up like a sheer wall behind it. The sun set then, and a queer glow over everything added a mystery to the house I approached. By the door hung a bell-handle of silver, obviously shaped as a symbol, but a symbol of something of which I was utterly ignorant. I pulled the bell-handle, and a gentle note turned all the air of the monastery to music. And presently I heard monkish feet coming slowly down a passage, and the door opened. I had picked up some words of their language in the year at the other monastery, but not enough in which to speak of the terrors of the soul, the soul's affairs being so far more intricate than are those of the body. So I asked him for lodging, trusting to these people's hospitality, and told him that I had come from the lower monastery, and that my interpreter would soon arrive. When I spoke of the lower monastery, looking in his face, I might have been speaking of another world, so little it seemed to mean to him. I hoped from that. I hoped that they had some wisdom here of which they knew nothing below.

" To their hospitality I had not trusted in vain : he took me in at once ; and as soon as the interpreter arrived I went with him to the cell of one of the monks and told over in all its terror my old story. Well, they certainly had spells : they used to chant them round my bed at evening, spells in no language I knew, not even the language that they usually spoke on this mountain and of which I had picked up scraps. They were only like reinforcements on tottering ramparts : they kept the rat away while I got some sleep ; but I was nearing my end now, and palliatives like this could not postpone it much longer—the end was near, and the rat would get my reason. They occupied my day by reading runes to me that were all of them greater than curses, if you could get the right rune against the right curse. But I had a feeling that the rat was winning. And you'd think that when he was winning he'd be all the neater and sleeker ; you'd think that his fur would be smooth and shiny, and the rat in fine condition. It was just the other way about. His fur was like dead fur ; his lower jaw was drooping, his lips were shrunken, his sides were sinking in, and the wound in his tail was rawer and more revolting. Everything was shabby and mildewed about him except his eyes, and they were as keen and penetrating as ever.

" About a month went by. And then one day their Lama

sent for me. I went in terror, for it seemed like my last chance. But all the monks smiled at me, telling me that all would be well. We were shown in, the interpreter and I, to the dim room in which the Lama was sitting, in a yellow robe, at a table of red lacquer. Nothing spoke but his eyes when we came in. And then I told my story. The interpreter knew the grim details of that tale of mine now, and told every terrible sentence after me rapidly. At the end, in the silence, the Lama spoke one word. I could not believe it. One word to my interpreter, and then that empty look upon his face that shows one that the interview is over.

" I looked at the interpreter, but he rose to go. And so I left in despair, having only got one word.

" ' What did he say ? ' I asked, as much out of curiosity as anything.

" ' Prayer,' said the interpreter.

" But prayer ? What prayer ? Did he think I hadn't prayed ? As well advise a hunted fox to run. What did it mean, this one word that he spoke to me, I asked monk after monk ? And they all of them said the same, they did not know; I must go farther up the mountain.

" ' Another monastery ? ' I asked.

" Yes, one more, they said ; a monastery at the top of the mountain. I calculated that that was another two thousand feet, and pretty steep ; but I could not miss my way, it was right at the top of the peak. And so I started, though it was late in the afternoon, and soon night fell on my climbing. But I didn't mind that ; it was better than lying awake on sleepless beds, with the sly rat in the dark, gnawing and gnawing its way through thought to my reason. I climbed all night, letting the interpreter come on when he would, and in the heat of the day I dropped at their door and rested. Here at least they could send me no higher. And after a while I got up and pulled a plain iron bell-handle, and a bell like a cow-bell clanged in the monastery, and a smiling Buddhist with a friendly face opened the door for me, and I staggered in. And for a while I said nothing. And then I said, ' Prayer, Prayer,' using the word that the Lama had said to me, and stumbled through some words of their language, trying to tell of my stress and the near approach of the rat ; but I did not know enough of the language for that, yet he seemed to understand, and took me in and fed me. Then he took me to a cool room, where there was a bed, and gave me a pitcher of water, and there I slept for some hours. When I awoke the interpreter had arrived, and I wanted to tell my terrible story at once ; but some of the monks quieted me, and I rested for some while longer. And when I woke again in the cool evening they seemed to know my story already ; I suppose the interpreter had told them.

"And an older monk came in, and gave me a small square of paper with red writing upon it ; and smiled, and said, ' The prayer.'

" I grasped it, and he went out of the room. But it was all in Tibetan. What was I to do ?

" They did not leave me in perplexity long. The monk who had taken me in at the door came back with a tiny wheel, which he gave to me. Then he slipped the prayer into a catch in the wheel and showed me how to turn it. One did not pray orally, but turned the wheel.

" He went away and left me with my prayer, and I began to turn it. Oh, man, it was the right prayer !

" It .was the right prayer at last. Imagine a man cold, weary, bitterly cold, taken instantly from the uphill road he is trudging to a soft chair by a fire in a warm room, instantly, without troubling to walk to it ; or a man lost in a desert without water suddenly finding it is not true, suddenly finding himself safe at home ; even so the rat faded.

" Well, I needn't tell you that I turned that wheel all day and far into the night. It was the first real rest I'd had for what seemed ages and ages. The only trouble was that the moment I tried to get to sleep, and stopped turning the wheel, the rat came back. Not that I minded that much at the time : it was such a relief to be able to keep that rat away that I turned the wheel till morning and troubled no more about sleep.

" Bright morning poured into my room, and I rose and looked from the window on a land more full of mountain-tops than any field is of ant heaps, always turning my wheel. A bell tolled, I did not know whether for breakfast or prayer, but it showed that the monks were about, so I went down and met them walking in one of the wide corridors. They greeted me and asked me if I had slept well, and then I explained my difficulty.

" A cheery laugh went up when I came to the difficulty about sleeping, as soon as I made myself clear. There was no difficulty in that, they said ; and they sent for the inter-preter, and when he had come they explained that they had little water-wheels all along a mountain-stream for several yards, that turned prayers night and day, and they said they would put one of these at my disposal. A kinder act I never knew ; it meant rest by day, sleep by night ; it meant at last a safe retreat from the rat.

" So two or three of them came down to the stream with me, and it was my turn to laugh when I saw their little wheels. Very crude compared to anything we can do over here. And one thing I didn't quite like about them was that they went slower than the one that you turned by hand. Too slow won't do, you know. It gives the rat time to slip in between thoughts. However, I said nothing of that at the time : I was too grateful to them to risk hurting their feelings. And they showed me the wheel I might use, and I slid my prayer into it. And though thoughts of the rat slipped in at the far end of the revolutions, just before the prayer got round to its starting-point, they were gone too soon to be able to keep me from sleep.

" A few days in that bright crystalline air, with regular sleep every night, and my prayer-wheel turning, and the company of these men, keen as pioneers, giving all their days to extend the limits of human thought, did wonders for me. I put on weight rapidly, and my face began to get some like-ness again to the face that my friends would have recognized. And as my health came back my keenness came with it, my old capacity began to return, my grip of business and industry. And one day I went to one of those monks and said to him, ' See here. You want to let me move those prayer-wheels fifty yards lower down. It will give you a fall of another fifty feet. Or let me move them a hundred yards, and you'll have another twenty feet on to that, seventy feet in all, which will about double your power. And what's more, you've another stream, just as good, quite close, and a hundred men could dig a connecting trench in a day ; or say ten days, working as the people you're likely to get will work ; and that will double your power again. See ? '

" I was speaking as much by signs as by the interpreter. The thing was such obvious sense there was nothing to argue about. But would they do it ? They wouldn't even think about it. They wouldn't turn it over in their minds. Instead of thinking, they said it had always been like that. Instead of improving it, they said it was good enough for their fathers.

" I grant you the wisdom of the East : it had saved my reason. But when it comes to organization, you have to go a long way West for it. God's own country every time. And back to it I returned very soon after that. It wasn't that I was ungrateful, I owed them more than ever I can repay, but I couldn't stand their lack of horse sense. You know, a man may have the wisdom of the ages, and yet be unable to put gasoline into his car if his chauffeur isn't with him. It was the same with these people. I did all I could to teach them, but in the end I had to leave them alone to go their own way. It wasn't that I was ungrateful, and it wasn't that I was not happy there, but those absurd little prayer-wheels were more than I could stand. Why, they had the water-power for ten times the speed they were doing, and I could have quadrupled it in a day or two. But I told you that. And, mind you, all the time the rat was gaining on the wheel. Very slowly, but gaining. And they stood helpless, and letting nobody help them, because it had been good enough for their fathers. So that, even if I had been able to stand their obsolete ways of doing things, the rat would have got me in the end, slipping in between thoughts a little bit quicker than the wheel, just before it completed its lazy revolution. So I came home to these dynamos. I took the little prayer-wheel with me and left them. I tried to get the monk that gave it me to come out here, to see what these dynamos could do. I wanted to pay his way across the world. But he wouldn't come, and so we parted forever ; some slight regret on his part, as I always like to think ; and I in tears.

" In three days I was out of the mountains, and in a few more down to the coast, twiddling my prayer-wheel day and night all the way. You'll wonder how I slept all the way from Bombay to London. That was a very small piece of inventiveness for a man who has controlled the business I have controlled. I fixed my prayer to the electric fan in my state-room.

" And now you see these dynamos. All of them work to turn one wheel. And it's doing nine thousand revolutions a minute. My prayer is on that wheel.

" Not much chance for the rat. Not much chance for him to slip in a thought between one turn and the next. My prayer is down on him before he can dodge it.

" He may try to slip in sometimes. If I have been talking too much of him, as I have to-night, or remembering my time in India ; then when my thoughts are all leaning his way he may make a grab at one of them before the wheel comes round, but he has to be mighty quick. And on just such a night as this, with all that talk about him, and calling to mind those days on the jewel-like Ganges and with the monks in the mountains, he might well be likely to try. But I take no chances. Smedgers," he called through the shutter. " Is Mr. Smedgers there ? " And the man answered from the far end of the stable of those mighty dynamos.

" Accelerate," said Makins.

At once the drone of the dynamos rose to a wail, nearly drowning Makins' voice when he spoke again. " Get them up to twelve thousand," he shouted. Smedgers nodded. " For half an hour," Makins called down to him.

" Right, sir," shouted Smedgers.

" That will stop him," said the Electric King.

This is the story as Jorkens took it down, word for word, in shorthand, and it would have been printed years ago but for some doubt there chanced to be raised at the time as to whether or not the interview was authentic.

CHARLES

By

A. J. ALAN

I EXPECT most of you know Piccadilly Circus. Well, I was walking through it one night, after the theatre, and in the middle there was a taxi with a crowd of people round it. Apparently a perfectly good accident.

I was just making up my mind whether to go and have a look or not, when a tall man came barging out of the crowd, dragging a half-fainting woman after him. When he got nearer I saw he was a man I knew called Charles —— well, Charles.

The moment he spotted me, he said : " Saints alive ! it's A. J. What wonderful luck. Will you look after Margaret and take her home ? " He told me that they were in the taxi and that they'd just run over a woman. She might be dead, and he'd got to stay and see to things.

Anyway, he heaved " Margaret " at me and plunged back into the crowd again. Margaret, I may tell you, was very smart and very pretty.

I supported the good lady across the pavement and propped her up against the wall of the " Criterion." She was shaking all over and sagging at the knees, and looked like doing a complete flop at any moment.

She kept on moaning : " Poor thing, I'm sure we've killed her." And I kept on saying : " Come, come, there, there, it was only an accident ; and in any case you weren't driving." But she was rather a job.

However, after two or three minutes she began to pull herself together, and I said : " What about a taxi, so that I can take you home ? " And she said : " My God, no, I shall never get into a taxi again after this."

Still, she told me that she lived quite near, and where it was, so we decided to walk.

I was rather glad it *was* so near because, frankly, it wasn't the sort of address I should have liked to give a taximan at that time of night.

By the by, before we left the scene of the accident I forced my way into the crowd to inquire after the victim.

Luckily, she'd not been really hurt at all. She was standing up between two bobbies, with her hat on one side, telling everyone why she'd wanted to cross the road. And no one wanted to know, because she was no chicken.

I rejoined Margaret on the pavement, and we started off along Coventry Street. On the way she told me her name, and then I remembered who she was.

She was married to a Polish violinist of the name of Javorsky, and they didn't hit it off very well. I also remembered that she'd once been pointed out to me as a friend of Charles. Anyway, they are married now and live very happily out in New Zealand.

Mind you, I didn't know Charles at all well and I hadn't seen him for ages. He was the sort of man one loses sight of altogether for years at a time, but who crops up again.

Anyhow, at this time Margaret was still Mrs. Javorsky, and she took a lot of trouble to explain how Charles happened to be driving her home.

Incidentally her story didn't quite fit because, if they'd been coming from where she said they'd been, they wouldn't have been where they were when they'd knocked the unfortunate woman over. By unfortunate I mean unlucky, of course.

Personally, I didn't care two hoots where they'd been, but one couldn't help wondering what Mr. Javorsky would say about it all.

I should have to go in and meet him, because the young woman wasn't in a fit state to leave on the mat. One couldn't just ring the bell and run away.

I did ask if her husband knew about Charles—about her being out with him, I mean—and she said he did, but that the two had never actually met.

Well, we eventually reached her abode. It was on the fourth floor of a block of flats in Charing Cross Road.

There wasn't a lift, and she nearly wanted carrying. However, we got to the top, but when she opened the front door of the flat we found the chain was on.

She said: " There now, wouldn't he choose to-night to go to bed and forget I was out ! " It occurred to me that he might have chosen the same night to want to know what time she came in.

As it happened we were both wrong. He hadn't gone to bed, and he didn't care when she came in.

In fact, when he appeared, which he did after we'd rung and knocked for about ten minutes, he didn't even know who she was. We had to tell him—several times.

In other words, Mr. Javorsky was rather blindino. We managed to persuade him to take the chain off and let us in.

He had on a brown velvet smoking-coat—very greasy and moth-eaten.

He couldn't ever have been much to look at. Rather the monkey type, but with a nose like a parrot. It seemed a little strange that any Englishwoman could have married him. It must have been his music.

When we got inside he insisted that I was Charles, and there was a proper row. It was largely lost on me because it was all in Polish. There was a word he kept calling me, oh, a terrible word—he seemed to change gear twice in the middle— and it apparently meant a sort of Don Juan.

She was very indignant about this, also in Polish, and she made him substitute another word, with three changes of gear in it, which suggested a man more like Don Quixote—but I know which of the two I would rather be.

But when he grasped the fact that I was not Charles, he became quite amiable, not to say effusive. He dragged me through into the sitting-room and poured me out a drink that would have lifted the roof off—if I'd touched it. It consisted chiefly of brandy and absinthe.

Now, I don't draw the line at many things, but I *do* draw it at absinthe—just as I do at jazz, thick ankles, and fish—so I gave this precious cocktail a miss. He didn't. He quaffed his in about two goes, and mixed himself another. When he'd necked that, he said : " Now I play to you." And he went to a sort of baby's coffin on four legs and produced a fiddle.

He played steadily, or rather unsteadily, for three-quarters of an hour, and very wonderful it was, too, especially when he had hold of the right end of the bow.

By this time it was after one, and I was trying to think of an excuse to get away, but it was a little bit difficult.

He was in just that state that if anything upset him he would probably turn exceedingly nasty.

If I got up to go he might make out that I didn't like his playing and cut up rough, and she'd get the full benefit after I'd gone. It was a service flat, and no servants sleeping in it.

Then, again, you can hardly tell a man in his own home that he mustn't have any more to drink, when you're a complete stranger and he's doing his best to entertain you. At least, one could, I suppose, if his wife gave one any kind of lead. But she didn't. She just lay back in her chair with her eyes half-shut and watched him.

I know it sounds callous, but I thought : " If he has one more of those poisonous drinks it's bound to knock him endways, and then it will be a case of helping her put him to bed and slipping quietly away."

Well, he *had* another, and about two minutes afterwards Nature took her revenge. He suddenly went chalk-white, dropped his bow and fiddle, and crumpled up in a heap on the floor. I thought : " Oh, well, that's that."

Fortunately, it was a thick carpet and the fiddle wasn't hurt. I put it back in its case (it *was* an Amati), and then went to him and straightened him out a bit. Mrs. Javorsky got up out of her chair and knelt by him, too.

It struck me that he was looking pretty rotten, and I asked her—I said : " Is he often taken like this ? " She said : " Oh, yes, fairly often ; he'll be all right in the morning. He'd better have one of his capsules."

So she went and got one, and we broke it in a handkerchief and held it under his nose. There was a perfectly frantic smell of pear-drops, which told me that it was amyl nitrite. I only knew it because I once used some to stick a patch of celluloid on an old accumulator. It makes you crimson in the face and gives you a beastly headache if you breathe much of it.

However, it didn't seem to be having the slightest effect on Javorsky. His face was still dead white at the end of several minutes.

I said : " That's no good—what's the next move ? " So she produced a medicine glass from the next room with a little liquid in it. I happened to notice that there was distinctly more in the glass than the ordinary dose of, say, ammoniated quinine. In other words, there was more than a teaspoonful of this stuff, whatever it was.

She gave him that, and we waited a bit, but nothing happened, and I began to get rather worried.

I said : " He's jolly bad. He doesn't seem to be breathing at all." And he wasn't. I listened to his heart, too, and there wasn't a sound. In fact, to all intents and purposes, Mr. Javorsky was dead, and I said as much.

The next thing, of course, was to get hold of his doctor. She gave me the telephone number, and I got through. Then came snag number one.

The doctor's secretary answered me. I said I was speaking for Mrs. Javorsky, and asked if Dr. Jones could come at once, and explained what had happened.

She, the secretary, then told me that Dr. Jones had been taken suddenly ill with appendicitis only an hour before. They'd whisked him off to a nursing-home in an ambulance, and at that very moment he was being operated on, like anything.

I said that in that case I wouldn't disturb him, but what did she suggest? However, she was full of ideas. She told me that Dr. Jones had a partner—a Dr. Swallow—or was it Sparrow—some sort of bird, anyway—and he hung out fairly near. She'd get hold of him and send him along. I thanked her very much.

When I got back to the sitting-room Mrs. Javorsky was very anxious to know whether I'd said anything to the doctor about Charles, and I told her I hadn't.

Then she said : " Well, promise me that you won't mention him (Charles, that is)—it's most important that his name should be kept out of all this."

Perhaps it was understandable that she didn't want him dragged in. Anyway, I promised, but I did wish that Charles could manage his own *affaire* without dragging me in.

All the same it struck me that we oughtn't just to wait for the doctor and do nothing else, so I suggested trying artificial respiration. She didn't seem to care much either way, so I gave him some for a few minutes.

While I was doing this I asked her, by way of making conversation, whether he did anything for a living besides playing the fiddle. She then told me that the music was only a blind.

His real job was with a certain undesirable foreign institution in the City. So I gave up the artificial respiration. Not that it was doing him any good—but you never know. It didn't seem patriotic to go on.

Well, the doctor man turned up just before two, and not a bit annoyed at being fetched out of bed.

It didn't take him ten seconds to decide that Javorsky was quite dead, and then he asked us what we'd done. We told him we'd first of all tried the amyl capsule, and when that was no go we'd given him some of the medicine.

He had a look at the prescription which she found for him,

and then he said : " Hum, yes—liquor trini trini. I expect you gave him the full three minims ? " She said : " Yes."

I frankly confess that at that moment I wasn't entirely clear as to how much a minim was. I knew, of course, that four crotchets make a mimim, and two minims make a semibreve, but that didn't seem to get one anywhere.

Then came snag number two. The doctor said he was very sorry but he couldn't possibly give a death certificate. The fact that his partner had been attending the patient wasn't enough. He, himself, had never set eyes on him before, and the law was very strict on the subject—there'd have to be an inquest.

Of course, this cheered me up no end. I don't like inquests and never did, and this looked like being one of the very last kind one would care to be mixed up in.

It was almost certain to get into the papers. There would be posters and headlines—" Tragedy in West End Flat " —like there always are, and people would want to know what I was doing there.

And it wasn't going to be so easy to explain, because this wretched woman again made me promise to keep Charles's name out of it. But what could one do ?

She told me that she and Charles had always meant to get married if anything happened to her husband—this was after the doctor had gone, naturally—and she was afraid people might say things if he appeared on the scene too soon.

She was so insistent about it that I just began to wonder whether there mightn't be some more important reason. Still, I agreed to do my best.

Oh, yes, and then there was the business of finding somewhere for her to go for the rest of the night. She obviously couldn't stay in the flat, and I finally carted her right up to Brondesbury and dumped her down on a married sister of hers who, incidentally, wasn't any too pleased to see her, and there it was.

I got home at twenty past five, which, between you and me, was considered late. By the by, in view of Mr. Javorsky's politics I undressed on · a sheet and stepped off it into an extraordinarily cold bath.

During breakfast, later in the day—much later in the day— I was thinking things over when I remembered that I didn't know how much a minim was.

If you remember, the doctor had said that three minims of the liquor trini trini was the full dose. So I hunted it up in

an encyclopædia and discovered, with some misgiving, that a
minim is a drop.

Now, a drug which ought to be given by the drop probably
has a certain potency when given in bulk. So as we'd given
Javorsky getting on for a dessert spoonful, I measured a dessert
spoon and found it held a hundred and fifty drops.

Ergo ! he'd had something like fifty times the safe dose,
and apparently in pharmacopœia it doesn't necessarily follow
that fifty times the safe dose is fifty times as safe as the safe
dose. In fact, the evidence is all the other way—it's fifty times
as dangerous.

You can quite see that this overdose question made things
slightly less simple, the point being : had she meant to give
it him, or hadn't she ? Not that it mattered either way with a
man like that, so long as he got it, but if I was to corroborate
her story at the inquest I did rather want to know how much of
it was true. The worst of it was, it was going to be a bit
difficult to find out.

One couldn't very well ask her straight out whether she'd
meant to kill her husband, for fear of offending her—you know
how touchy people are.

Anyhow, I had to go up and see her to arrange a few details
about our evidence—how long we'd known each other ; where
we'd spent the evening ; or, rather, where we hadn't spent it ;
and, finally, how much medicine had been given.

These were all questions which some idiot might get up and
ask, and we should look so stupid if our answers didn't agree.

It was rather funny about the medicine. She had the nerve
to tell me that he'd only had three drops, and that she'd measured them most carefully. This put me in a slightly awkward
position, because I jolly well knew she hadn't and yet it was
too late to back out.

So we left it that I hadn't actually seen that bit, and I
managed to persuade her not to be too definite about the
quantity in case the post-mortem didn't bear her out. I said :
" Be a bit vague—and mind you bow to the coroner."

Well, we got our formal notices to attend the inquest, and
duly turned up three days later.

Mrs. Javorsky was called first. They wouldn't let me go
in and hear her evidence, which was rather a nuisance. They
do that to lessen the chance of collusion between witnesses.
Quite right, too.

At all events, they fetched me in a few minutes, and I was
sworn, and so on.

They asked me my name and occupation, and I told them, and no one seemed to mind.

Then the coroner asked me a few questions. He said : " I believe you had been to the Criterion Theatre ? " And I said : " Yes." After all that *was* true. We *had* leant against the wall. Then he just took me quickly through the various events. It was clear he was only checking over his notes of what Mrs. Javorsky had already said. All quite harmless.

Then, just as I was going to leave the box, a mouldy-looking individual got up and said *he* wanted to put a few questions.

He was supposed to be instructed by some of Javorsky's Polish relations, but there was no doubt in my mind that he was really acting for the undesirable foreign institution Javorsky'd worked for. This person looked dirty enough for anything. I took him for an unfrocked barrister.

He started off by wanting to know what medical knowledge I had. I said : " None. Why ? " Then he began about chemistry, and I thought : " Now for it—that last dose of medicine is coming up again." However, I stoutly denied all knowledge of chemistry.

Then he began to get a bit warm. Hadn't Mrs. Javorsky any friend who might want her husband out of the way, and if so, whether *he* had any medical knowledge ?

The coroner chipped in then, and asked him what he was driving at. He said he was instructed that there was such a person, and that there was a strong possibility of foul play.

The coroner promptly shut him up, and said that before grave charges of that kind were made it would be as well to hear the medical evidence.

So the two doctors who had done the post-mortem went into the box, one after the other, and made it perfectly clear that Javorsky had died of angina pectoris. In other words, a painfully natural death.

They went even further. They said he was probably dead before he touched the floor.

This was a distinct relief to me because I thought things were beginning to get a bit too near the bone, especially as Charles was a ship's doctor.

FUNERAL MARCH OF A MARIONETTE

By

JOHN METCALFE

ALF and little George had chosen Millbank and the western sweep of river past the Tate for a variety of reasons. First, since their expedition had demanded secrecy, it was essential to select a route where Mother wouldn't think of following them ; second, the competition in this district promised to be slight and coppers plentiful ; third, and most cogent, they had never been along that way before.

" Not furver than the bridge at anyrate," said little George. " Past there I seen the 'ouses all 'ave steps wiv lions on."

And at the crowded crossing by St. Stephen's Green he had exhaled a sudden breath of wonderment that hung like smoke upon the chilly air. " Gawd, wotcher fink them bobbies gits to eat makes 'em so big ? Three feeds a day, they 'as. . . . I'm tellin' yer—an' rumsteak every time."

Alf was a head and shoulders taller than his brother, more raw-boned, lanker, but with the same snub nose, pale, rather wizened face, and crop of gingerish hair.

" Come orn," he now adjured contemptuously, " an' don't stan' gassin' like a silly kid. Nex' thing you know you'll 'ave us all upset." Against the soap-box trolley which he pushed were nailed at a slight slope two wooden battens. These, though intended primarily to serve as shafts, were at this juncture better used as handles, since George could thus assist more easily by pulling on the rope in front.

Alf was relieved when they had passed the burly figures of the constables. One of them, stamping a sullen foot upon the snow, had, so he fancied, eyed them suspiciously, inimically, and it was foolish to invite enquiry by lingering. Though he himself had thought out this excursion, he could not quite dispel a faint uneasiness. . . .

But in their veins excitement threaded tinglingly like fire, elation, and an exhilarated sense of mystery, adventure. It was an hour ago that, stealing noiselessly, with beating hearts, they had crept out through the back gate, along the mews, and made their way conspiratorially toward the river-front. George, shivering a little in his father's cut-down trousers, had wanted instantly to break into a run, but Alf, more cautious, had restrained him. Despite the cold he had a notion that to be seen running would attract attention. Safer to amble nonchalantly for a bit. Now, halting for a moment beneath Cœur de Lion, he blew upon numbed finger-tips.

" Oo-oo . . ." said little George, slapping his arms from side to side and staring shrewdly upwards at the statue, " Wouldn' arf tip '*im* fer the Derby, Elf, wiv 'is ole sword an' iron gloves an' fings. *Ih.* . . . Gee up, Steve ! "

They stood a minute longer in the wintry stillness. Faces of passers-by were rouged with cold, their footfalls hushed. The November air was raw, and in a greasy, leaden-coloured sky a few fat, smudgy flakes of snow were drifting here and there uncertainly. Already it was growing dark. Beyond them, somewhere, in the Victoria Tower Gardens, came a faint crackle and a spurt of flame.

" Huh ! " uttered Alf, " see that ? That wuz a firework. We best be gittin' on."

Down Millbank they proceeded at a trot, skirting the kerb. Before the front of the art gallery they paused once more. Big Ben, behind them, solemnly boomed half-past three. Upon the river, over silent streets, a greenish dusk was settling. Millais, enveloped in a fleece of dirty snow, loomed with a vague benevolence, though spectrally. Closer, and intermittently illumining the murk with changing gleams, a roman candle popped up emerald and ruby balls.

" Silly young tykes ! " said Alf. " *I* wouldn' let off fizzworks on the fourth ! "

George moved impatiently upon his toes. " Now," he suggested, " Now ! "

Alf looked at him and at the trolley. For a soap-box it was rather longer than usual, and had been fitted carefully with what had once been perambulator wheels. One of them still retained its rubber tyre. Part of the space between the "shafts" was boarded in so as to form a sloping, couch-like back. Something covered loosely with rags and sacking occupied the whole interior and extended for some distance up the slant.

" All right," said Alf. As he unwound the sacking little

338 JOHN METCALFE

George capered excitedly about him. " Good ole Gus ! Elf,
you weren't arf a nut, you weren't, to fink of it. I'm goin' ter
spend my share o' wot 'e gits on fireworks, I am. . . ."
Free of its shrouding rags a curious object lay revealed.
Upon the incline of the, wooden chariot rested, it seemed, the
head and tiny shoulders of a man. But, though the huddled
torso might conform to standards human or half-human, the
face above gave hasty judgment pause. It was rosy, doll-like,
and from beneath a crownless bowler hat surveyed the brothers
with a vacant stare. In the fast-falling dusk its eyes were
blank, expressionless as coals or pools of soot. The hair, black
too, was long, and, at about the level of the ears, grotesquely
" bobbed."
George gave the battered bowler an affectionate pat. "Don't
the ole man look sarsy, Elfy, eh ? But 'e's ter larn 'ow ter
be'ave issef, 'e 'as. None o' yer larks ternight, ole Gus, you
'ear ? Else yer won' git no supper wen we're 'ome."
Alf, from inside his jacket, had produced a square of
cardboard provided with a string. This he hung carefully
round " Gus's " neck, removing for a moment the mis-shapen
hat to do so. Upon the placard ran a legend in block capitals :
" PLEASE SPARE A COPPER FOR THE GI ! "
Out of the sullen sky the flakes came hurrying now more
thickly, steadily. George, who had ceased his hopping to
admire his brother's handiwork, took up his rope again.
" Which way ? " he said. " We better start afore it comes on
'ard. Besides, jes' 'ark at that ! You 'ear jes' then ? Don'
wonner git mixed up wiv *them* ! "
As they set off once more the significance of his words
became apparent. Voices raised in a broken, singsong chant
pursued them distantly. " Please spare a copper . . . a copper
for the Guy . . . ! " Little George, with shoulders braced and
chest thrown out, bristled indignantly. " Some 'opes them
ornerary lot 'as got ! Bet yer they don' make more'n a tanner
altogever. Not arf as much as us at anyrate ! "
But it was not until they had proceeded for ten minutes on
their way that the first penny fell into the cap which Alf had
taken from his own red-tousled head and placed conspicuously
in Gus's lap. A sailor, issuing with boon-companions from a
suddenly illumined doorway, spat copiously, and, having
thrown the copper, mingled abashed profanity with charity.
What did that matter, since the coin was there ? And, after
this, good fortune seemed to follow them. An old gentleman,
peering benevolently through spectacles, contributed another

penny, and a young lady, fashionably dressed in furs, presented Alf with a whole sixpenny piece, her smile next moment fading curiously, instantaneously away. Finally a short, top-hatted man with an umbrella stooped to place twopence in the cap, then raised himself abruptly. He had, Alf fancied, been about to speak, but, as they hurried off, had to content himself with gazing after them inquisitively.

" Tenpence a'ready ! " exclaimed George delightedly. " Didn' I tell yer, Elfy ? *Good* ole Gus ! "

They turned from the river-front up a long street in which a lamplighter had just begun his round. It was colder now, the air sharper, and the snow falling thicker, more continuously. Encircling every light as it sprang up appeared a sudden, haloing swirl of white, but from below, against the yellow radiance of the lamp, each tumbling flake looked black. Alf, with anxiety, noted the growing clearness of the trolley's wheel-tracks and of the prints of little George's feet.

" Better git somewhere where there's people quick," he counselled frowning. " Or else they'll all be gorn indoors afore we're there."

For a while, it seemed, their run of luck had ceased, but presently, as they approached the lights and bustling movement of a more populous shopping district, fate smiled on them again. Windows, behind the seething, ever-falling curtain of the snow, were gaily decked, shone dazzlingly upon a white, a madcap world. Faces were eager, tingling, and from open mouths puffed out great clouds of breath like steam. Voices rang suddenly from nowhere, were the next instant lost and muffled, sinking curiously away. Strange, striding forms, illumined momently, shook tinsel drops from hats and overcoats, then vanished utterly. From somewhere down a side-street came the damp fizz and splutter of a firework, its final smothered and half-hearted *pop* greeted by piercing screams and whoops of joy.

Copper by copper Gus's hoard had mounted steadily. Pennies and halfpennies were flung into the cap or pressed into Alf's hand by people who, half blinded, seldom paused to look more closely at the trolley and its occupant. Little George, his head held high, strutted majestically, sumptuously before, crying, in tones which triumph and excitement rendered gruff, the words upon the placard. Until the opening of the saloons at six it would, Alf thought, be more remunerative as well as pleasanter to keep upon the move than to stand cold and shivering upon a " pitch."

Once, however, they stopped for a few moments by a railway arch where an old man with a wooden leg was playing an accordion. At first, considering probably that their presence would divert the pity of the passers-by and spoil his trade, he eyed them sourly, going so far, when his malevolent looks had no effect, as to grimace and threaten them with oaths. But a little later the expression on his face had changed. He had stumped off, hawking his throat and playing vigorously, then, after he had got a yard or two away, turned back and put a penny in the cap.

On and on, through seething eddies, wildly wreathing clouds of giddying white. Flocking and scurrying, dancing and madly scampering, the icy flakes swept stinging in their eyes, crept in a chilly prickle down their necks. George was elated still, and shouting, but Alf behind him plodded silently. Something was singing in his ears, making his feet feel tired. Within his brain, perpetually, the dizzy helter-skelter of the snow went to a kind of silly, jigging tune. It was the same that the old wooden-legged man had played, and, though he tried to banish it by stamping, blowing on his hands, it sounded numbly yet.

Somewhere between Belgravia and Pimlico they ran into a crowd of urchins pulling or pushing little trolleys like themselves. George's refrain was echoed now competitively on every side, for there were at the least a dozen children "working" the neighbourhood in company. " Please spare a copper . . . a copper for the Guy . . . ! " The downfall for a space had slightly moderated, sufficiently to permit of fireworks being kindled under shelter of a cap or outspread coat. The changing flare of green and crimson lights fell suddenly upon rogue-faces, lolling and grimacing heads. . . . Masks with long noses, grinning red-lipped mouths, protruding tongues, moved in grotesque procession through the night. Once, in a shower of sparks, a squib dropped hissing into Gus's lap, exploded there, and singed the sacking covers. And the next moment a large snowball thudded on Alf's cheek.

" Oo-oo . . . " said little George. " Wot say we jine in wiv this lot—an' git some fizz-works too ? "

But Alf at this suggestion shook his head. " Come orn," he said. " Let's git away from 'ere. We'll 'ave all ours tomorrer on the proper day."

He was tired, all at once dispirited, he could not have said why. His eyes were hot and heavy, dazzled by the light upon the snow, and in his ears the tune that the old man had played

was dinning giddily. A distant clock chimed six. " Now all
the pubs are openin' we'll git a plenty more," said little George.
" We kin jes' stan' arahnd ahtside the door, an' then——Why,
Elf," he suddenly broke off, " Wot's up wiv yer ? "

" Nothin'," said Alf. " Only I guess we oughter think o'
gittin' back . . . "

" Wot, git back 'ome ? Wot for ? " George's voice was blank.

" Yus. I'm a-goin' anyway. I'm cold, I tells yer . . ."
But even to himself he was unable to explain what troubled
him. He leaned forward to brush the snow out of the top of
Gus's hat and from the coverings about his arms and chest.
This office they had halted to perform at intervals upon their
wonderings. Now, as his hands explored the shrunken contours underneath the sacking, a chill more than physical crept
up his spine.

" Git orn," he repeated roughly. " Can't yer 'ear wot I
say ? " Little George, grumbling, picked up the rope which,
in the course of this discussion, he had dropped, and, sullenly,
turned back along the road by which they came.

They made their way, jog-trotting silently, down streets
which were alternately deserted, ghost-like and forlorn, or gay
and glittering with the lights of shops. George, no longer
crying his refrain, was sobered, and, beneath this unnatural
taciturnity, resentful too. In the inviting brilliance streaming
from saloon or window-front he would attempt from time to
time to slacken speed, but, at Alf's instant sharp command,
would hurry on again. They proceeded in this manner for
perhaps half an hour till the riverside was reached.

And here at last they halted to take breath.

The snow was hardly falling now. Only a fitful, wandering
flake or two came feathering down. The sky was even clear
enough for them to see the stars, and, on their right, the river
ran like steel.

Little George was glum and querulous. " Lemme push
now," he said, " an' you kin' take the rope. I've got fed up
wiv pullin' all the time."

Hereabouts it was darkish, but, in the pale reflected glimmer
of the snow, he could make out his brother's face. Its set and
strained expression frightened him.

" Elfy, wot's up ? Wot makes yer look so queer ? " He
paused, then added in a whisper, " Is it 'im ? "

" 'Im ? Nah, of course not. Why should it be 'im ? You
make me tired, silly things you say. We gotter git back 'ome
afore they starts a-missin' 'im, that's all. Come orn ! "

Alf set his hands peremptorily upon the shafts, and George, with a half-discontented, half-submissive sigh, began once more to pull. They had, however, got no farther than a dozen paces when, as by common instinct, they stopped suddenly again. Something was happening in the trolley. Their glances met one instant in a frozen stare, then lowered slowly.

Under the rags and sacking a faint twitching movement was apparent. Gus's head rose slightly from its wooden rest. A curious sound like a thin hiccough was repeated thrice, then ceased.

" Elfy, 'e must a' taken ill, ole Gussy must. 'E was that way las' time afore 'e went into the 'orspital. Elfy, why don't yer speak ? "

But Alf made no reply. It was not he but little George who pulled the trolley onwards to the nearest lamp. " Elfy," he called again more urgently. " Be quick. 'E's bin took bad, I say. Let's git 'im 'ome." He had reached out a timid hand to Gus's shoulder, but, at that instant, started and drew back, staring alarmedly across the shadowed road. " Quick," he repeated in a warning whisper. " I kin 'ear somebody a-comin', see 'im, too." Then, in a desperate undertone, he added : " It's a cop ! "

The policeman who, patrolling stolidly his cheerless beat, had marked the trio underneath the lamp, was moved, in fact, by little more than idle curiosity. Less from suspicion as to what they were about than to relieve monotony he had drawn near. His attitude, when he had strode majestically into the circle of the light, was rather condescendingly benevolent than menacing.

Alf, hanging back, and following slightly in the rear, stopped now a pace or two away. He could see little George stiffen defensively before his natural enemy, could see the Jove-like form above stoop ponderously, with slow, enquiring dignity. . . .

Yet he himself stood fixed and motionless. A strange inertia held him as a dream. For a little while the presence of the constable was even reassuring and consoling. Not that they would escape a beating when they all got home. They would get thrashed for certain if old Gus were really ill and had to go to hospital again. It was his fault. Dully he wondered what would happen to the money in the cap. . . .

But as at length he roused himself and walked reluctantly toward the light, a vague misgiving haunted him again, a dark uncertainty. The policeman's manner was no longer jocular,

*The policeman's manner had grown curious, then puzzled,
gravely dubious, serious finally—and something else.*

amused. His expression had grown curious, then puzzled, gravely dubious ; serious finally—and something else.

Alf, with a sudden terror dragging at his limbs, ran forwards. He caught his brother's arm, and, as he did so, tears of which he could not tell the meaning started in his eyes.

By this time little George, though still uncomprehendingly, was crying, too.

THE INTERRUPTION

By

W. W. JACOBS

THE last of the funeral guests had gone, and Spencer Goddard, in decent black, sat alone in his small, well-furnished study. There was a queer sense of freedom in the house since the coffin had left it ; the coffin which was now hidden in its solitary grave beneath the yellow earth. The air, which for the last three days had seemed stale and contaminated, now smelt fresh and clean. He went to the open window and, looking into the fading light of the autumn day, took a deep breath.

He closed the window and, stooping down, put a match to the fire, and, dropping into his easy chair, sat listening to the cheery crackle of the wood. At the age of thirty-eight he had turned over a fresh page. Life, free and unencumbered, was before him. His dead wife's money was at last his, to spend as he pleased instead of being doled out in reluctant driblets.

He turned at a step at the door, and his face assumed the appearance of gravity and sadness it had worn for the last four days. The cook, with the same air of decorous grief, entered the room quietly and, crossing to the mantelpiece, placed upon it a photograph.

" I thought you'd like to have it, sir," she said, in a low voice, " to remind you."

Goddard thanked her, and, rising, took it in his hand and stood regarding it. He noticed with satisfaction that his hand was absolutely steady.

" It is a very good likeness—till she was taken ill," continued the woman. " I never saw anybody change so sudden."

" The nature of her disease, Hannah," said her master.

The woman nodded, and, dabbing at her eyes with her handkerchief, stood regarding him.

" Is there anything you want ? " he inquired, after a time.

She shook her head. " I can't believe she's gone," she said, in a low voice. " Every now and then I have a queer feeling that she's still here—— "

" It's your nerves," said her master sharply.

" ——and wanting to tell me something."

By a great effort Goddard refrained from looking at her.

" Nerves," he said again. " Perhaps you ought to have a little holiday. It has been a great strain upon you."

" You, too, sir," said the woman respectfully. " Waiting on her hand and foot as you have done, I can't think how you stood it. If you'd only had a nurse—— "

" I preferred to do it myself, Hannah," said her master. " If I had had a nurse it would have alarmed her."

The woman assented. " And they are always peeking and prying into what doesn't concern them," she added. " Always think they know more than the doctors do."

Goddard turned a slow look upon her. The tall, angular figure was standing in an attitude of respectful attention ; the cold, slaty-brown eyes were cast down, the sullen face expressionless.

" She couldn't have had a better doctor," he said, looking at the fire again. " No man could have done more for her."

" And nobody could have done more for her than you did, sir," was the reply. " There's few husbands that would have done what you did."

Goddard stiffened in his chair. " That will do, Hannah," he said curtly.

" Or done it so well," said the woman, with measured slowness.

With a strange, sinking sensation, her master paused to regain his control. Then he turned and eyed her steadily. " Thank you," he said slowly ; " you mean well, but at present I cannot discuss it."

For some time after the door had closed behind her he sat in deep thought. The feeling of well-being of a few minutes before had vanished, leaving in its place an apprehension which he refused to consider, but which would not be allayed He thought over his actions of the last few weeks, carefully, and could remember no flaw. His wife's illness, the doctor's diagnosis, his own solicitous care, were all in keeping with the ordinary. He tried to remember the woman's exact words— her manner. Something had shown him Fear. What ?

He could have laughed at his fears next morning. The

dining-room was full of sunshine and the fragrance of coffee and bacon was in the air. Better still, a worried and commonplace Hannah. Worried over two eggs with false birthcertificates, over the vendor of which she became almost lyrical.

" The bacon is excellent," said her smiling master, " so is the coffee ; but your coffee always is."

Hannah smiled in return, and, taking fresh eggs from a rosy-cheeked maid, put them before him.

A pipe, followed by a brisk walk, cheered him still further. He came home glowing with exercise and again possessed with that sense of freedom and freshness. He went into the garden —now his own—and planned alterations.

After lunch he went over the house. The windows of his wife's bedroom were open and the room neat and airy. His glance wandered from the made-up bed to the brightly-polished furniture. Then he went to the dressing-table and opened the drawers, searching each in turn. With the exception of a few odds and ends they were empty. He went out on to the landing and called for Hannah.

" Do you know whether your mistress locked up any of her things ? " he inquired.

" What things ? " said the woman.

" Well, her jewellery mostly."

" Oh ! " Hannah smiled. " She gave it all to me," she said quietly.

Goddard checked an exclamation. His heart was beating nervously, but he spoke sternly.

" When ? "

" Just before she died—of gastro-enteritis," said the woman.

There was a long silence. He turned and with great care mechanically closed the drawers of the dressing-table. The tilted glass showed him the pallor of his face, and he spoke without turning round.

" That is all right, then," he said huskily. " I only wanted to know what had become of it. I thought, perhaps, Milly —— "

Hannah shook her head. " Milly's all right," she said, with a strange smile. " She's as honest as we are. Is there anything more you want, sir ? "

She closed the door behind her with the quietness of the well-trained servant ; Goddard, steadying himself with his hand on the rail of the bed, stood looking into the future.

II

THE days passed monotonously, as they pass with a man in prison. Gone was the sense of freedom and the idea of a wider life. Instead of a cell, a house with ten rooms—but Hannah, the jailer, guarding each one. Respectful and attentive, the model servant, he saw in every word a threat against his liberty—his life. In the sullen face and cold eyes he saw her knowledge of power ; in her solicitude for his comfort and approval, a sardonic jest. It was the master playing at being the servant. The years of unwilling servitude were over, but she felt her way carefully with infinite zest in the game. Warped and bitter, with a cleverness which had never before had scope, she had entered into her kingdom. She took it little by little, savouring every morsel.

" I hope I've done right, sir," she said one morning. " I have given Milly notice."

Goddard looked up from his paper. " Isn't she satisfactory ? " he inquired.

" Not to my thinking, sir," said the woman. " And she says she is coming to see you about it. I told her that would be no good."

" I had better see her and hear what she has to say," said her master.

" Of course, if you wish to," said Hannah ; " only, after giving her notice, if she doesn't go I shall. I should be sorry to go—I've been very comfortable here—but it's either her or me."

" I should be sorry to lose you," said Goddard in a hopeless voice.

" Thank you, sir," said Hannah. " I'm sure I've tried to do my best. I've been with you some time now—and I know all your little ways. I expect I understand you better than anybody else would. I do all I can to make you comfortable."

" Very well, I leave it to you," said Goddard in a voice which strove to be brisk and commanding. " You have my permission to dismiss her."

" There's another thing I wanted to see you about," said Hannah ; " my wages. I was going to ask for a rise, seeing that I'm really housekeeper here now."

" Certainly," said her master, considering, " that only seems fair. Let me see—what are you getting ? "

" Thirty-six."

Goddard reflected for a moment, and then turned with a benevolent smile. " Very well," he said cordially, " I'll make it forty-two. That's ten shillings a month more."

" I was thinking of a hundred," said Hannah dryly.

The significance of the demand appalled him. " Rather a big jump," he said at last. " I really don't know that I——"

" It doesn't matter," said Hannah. " I thought I was worth it—to you—that's all. You know best. Some people might think I was worth *two* hundred. That's a bigger jump, but after all a big jump is better than—— "

She broke off and tittered. Goddard eyed her.

" ——than a big drop," she concluded.

Her master's face set. The lips almost disappeared and something came into the pale eyes that was revolting. Still eyeing her, he rose and approached her. She stood her ground and met him eye to eye.

" You are jocular," he said at last.

" Short life and a merry one," said the woman.

" Mine or yours ? "

" Both, perhaps," was the reply.

" If—if I give you a hundred," said Goddard, moistening his lips, " that ought to make your life merrier, at any rate."

Hannah nodded. " Merry and long, perhaps," she said slowly. " I'm careful, you know—very careful."

" I am sure you are," said Goddard, his face relaxing.

" Careful what I eat and drink, I mean," said the woman eyeing him steadily.

" That is wise," he said slowly. " I am myself—that is why I am paying a good cook a large salary. But don't overdo things, Hannah ; don't kill the goose that lays the golden eggs."

" I am not likely to do that," she said coldly. " Live and let live ; that is my motto. Some people have different ones. But I'm careful ; nobody won't catch me napping. I've left a letter with my sister, in case."

Goddard turned slowly and in a casual fashion put the flowers straight in a bowl on the table, and, wandering to the window, looked out. His face was white again and his hands trembled.

" To be opened after my death," continued Hannah. " I don't believe in doctors—not after what I've seen of them—I don't think they know enough ; so if I die I shall be examined. I've given good reasons."

" And suppose," said Goddard, coming from the window, " suppose she is curious, and opens it before you die ? "

" We must chance that," said Hannah, shrugging her shoulders ; " but I don't think she will. I sealed it up with sealing-wax, with a mark on it."

" She might open it and say nothing about it," persisted her master.

An unwholesome grin spread slowly over Hannah's features. " I should know it soon enough," she declared boisterously, " and so would other people. Lord ! there would be an upset ! Chidham would have something to talk about for once. We should be in the paper—both of us."

Goddard forced a smile. " Dear me ! " he said gently. " Your pen seems to be a dangerous weapon, Hannah, but I hope that the need to open it will not happen for another fifty years. You look well and strong."

The woman nodded. " I don't take up my troubles before they come," she said, with a satisfied air ; " but there's no harm in trying to prevent them coming. Prevention is better than cure."

" Exactly," said her master ; " and, by the way, there's no need for this little financial arrangement to be known by anybody else. I might become unpopular with my neighbours for setting a bad example. Of course, I am giving you this sum because I really think you are worth it."

" I'm sure you do," said Hannah. " I'm not sure I ain't worth more, but this'll do to go on with. I shall get a girl for less than we are paying Milly, and that'll be another little bit extra for me."

" Certainly," said Goddard, and smiled again.

" Come to think of it," said Hannah, pausing at the door, " I ain't sure I shall get anybody else ; then there'll be more than ever for me. If I do the work I might as well have the money."

Her master nodded, and, left to himself, sat down to think out a position which was as intolerable as it was dangerous. At a great risk he had escaped from the dominion of one woman only to fall, bound and helpless, into the hands of another. However vague and unconvincing the suspicions of Hannah might be, they would be sufficient. Evidence could be unearthed. Cold with fear one moment, and hot with fury the next, he sought in vain for some avenue of escape. It was his brain against that of a cunning, illiterate fool ; a fool whose malicious stupidity only added to his danger. And she drank.

352

W. W. JACOBS

With largely increased wages she would drink more and his very life might depend upon a hiccuped boast. It was clear that she was enjoying her supremacy; later on her vanity would urge her to display it before others. He might have to obey the crack of her whip before witnesses, and that would cut off all possibility of escape.

He sat with his head in his hands. There must be a way out and he must find it. Soon. He must find it before gossip began; before the changed position of master and servant lent colour to her story when that story became known. Shaking with fury, he thought of her lean, ugly throat and the joy of choking her life out with his fingers. He started suddenly, and took a quick breath. No, not fingers—a rope.

III

BRIGHT and cheerful outside and with his friends, in the house he was quiet and submissive. Milly had gone, and, if the service was poorer and the rooms neglected, he gave no sign. If a bell remained unanswered he made no complaint, and to studied insolence turned the other cheek of politeness. When at this tribute to her power the woman smiled, he smiled in return. A smile which, for all its disarming softness, left her vaguely uneasy.

"I'm not afraid of you," she said once, with a menacing air.

"I hope not," said Goddard in a slightly surprised voice.

"Some people might be, but I'm not," she declared. "If anything happened to me—"

"Nothing could happen to such a careful woman as you are," he said, smiling again. "You ought to live to ninety—with luck."

It was clear to him that the situation was getting on his nerves. Unremembered but terrible dreams haunted his sleep. Dreams in which some great, inevitable disaster was always pressing upon him, although he could never discover what it was. Each morning he awoke unrefreshed to face another day of torment. He could not meet the woman's eyes for fear of revealing the threat that was in his own.

Delay was dangerous and foolish. He had thought out every move in that contest of wits which was to remove the shadow of the rope from his own neck and place it about that of the woman. There was a little risk, but the stake was a big one. He had but to set the ball rolling and others would keep it on its course. It was time to act.

He came in a little jaded from his afternoon walk, and left his tea untouched. He ate but little dinner, and, sitting hunched up over the fire, told the woman that he had taken a slight chill. Her concern, he felt grimly, might have been greater if she had known the cause.

He was no better next day, and after lunch called in to consult his doctor. He left with a clean bill of health except for a slight digestive derangement, the remedy for which he took away with him in a bottle. For two days he swallowed one tablespoonful three times a day in water, without result, then he took to his bed.

" A day or two in bed won't hurt you," said the doctor. " Show me that tongue of yours again."

" But what is the matter with me, Roberts ? " inquired the patient.

The doctor pondered. " Nothing to trouble about—nerves a bit wrong—digestion a little bit impaired. You'll be all right in a day or two."

Goddard nodded. So far, so good ; Roberts had not out-lived his usefulness. He smiled grimly after the doctor had left at the surprise he was preparing for him. A little rough on Roberts and his professional reputation, perhaps, but these things could not be avoided.

He lay back and visualised the programme. A day or two longer, getting gradually worse, then a little sickness. After that a nervous, somewhat shamefaced patient hinting at things. His food had a queer taste—he felt worse after taking it ; he knew it was ridiculous, still—there was some of his beef-tea he had put aside, perhaps the doctor would like to examine it ? and the medicine ? Secretions, too ; perhaps he would like to see those ?

Propped on his elbow, he stared fixedly at the wall. There would be a trace—a faint trace—of arsenic in the secretions. There would be more than a trace in the other things. An attempt to poison him would be clearly indicated, and—his wife's symptoms had resembled his own—let Hannah get out of the web he was spinning if she could. As for the letter she had threatened him with, let her produce it ; it could only recoil upon herself. Fifty letters could not save her from the doom he was preparing for her. It was her life or his, and he would show no mercy. For three days he doctored himself with sedulous care, watching himself anxiously the while. His nerve was going and he knew it. Before him was the strain of the discovery, the arrest, and the trial. The gruesome business of his wife's death. A long business. He would wait no longer, and he would open the proceedings with dramatic suddenness.

It was between nine and ten o'clock at night when he rang his bell, and it was not until he had rung four times that he heard the heavy steps of Hannah mounting the stairs.

" What d'you want ? " she demanded, standing in the doorway.

" I'm very ill," he said, gasping. " Run for the doctor. Quick ! "

The woman stared at him in genuine amazement. " What, at this time o' night ? " she exclaimed. " Not likely."

" I'm dying ! " said Goddard in a broken voice.

" Not you," she said roughly. " You'll be better in the morning."

" I'm dying," he repeated. " Go—for—the—doctor."

The woman hesitated. The rain beat in heavy squalls against the window, and the doctor's house was a mile distant on the lonely road. She glanced at the figure on the bed.

" I should catch my death o' cold," she grumbled.

She stood sullenly regarding him. He certainly looked very ill, and his death would by no means benefit her. She listened, scowling, to the wind and the rain.

" All right," she said at last, and went noisily from the room.

His face set in a mirthless smile, he heard her bustling about below. The front-door slammed violently and he was alone.

He waited for a few minutes and then, getting out of bed, put on his dressing-gown and set about his preparations. With a steady hand he added a little white powder to the remains of his beef-tea and to the contents of his bottle of medicine. He stood listening a moment at some faint sound from below, and, having satisfied himself, lit a candle and made his way to Hannah's room. For a space he stood irresolute, looking about him. Then he opened one of the drawers and, placing the broken packet of powder under a pile of clothing at the back, made his way back to bed.

He was disturbed to find that he was trembling with excitement and nervousness. He longed for tobacco, but that was impossible. To reassure himself he began to rehearse his conversation with the doctor, and again he thought over every possible complication. The scene with the woman would be

terrible ; he would have to be too ill to take any part in it.
The less he said the better. Others would do all that was
necessary.

He lay for a long time listening to the sound of the wind
and the rain. Inside, the house seemed unusually quiet, and
with an odd sensation he suddenly realised that it was the
first time he had been alone in it since his wife's death. He
remembered that she would have to be disturbed. The thought
was unwelcome. He did not want her to be disturbed. Let
the dead sleep.

He sat up in bed and drew his watch from beneath the
pillow. Hannah ought to have been back before ; in any case
she could not be long now. At any moment he might hear
her key in the lock. He lay down again and reminded himself
that things were shaping well. He had shaped them, and
some of the satisfaction of the artist was his.

The silence was oppressive. The house seemed to be
listening, waiting. He looked at his watch again and wondered, with a curse, what had happened to the woman. It was
clear that the doctor must be out, but that was no reason for
her delay. It was close on midnight, and the atmosphere of
the house seemed in some strange fashion to be brooding and
hostile.

In a lull in the wind he thought he heard footsteps outside,
and his face cleared as he sat up listening for the sound of the
key in the door below. In another moment the woman would
be in the house and the fears engendered by a disordered fancy
would have flown. The sound of the steps had ceased, but
he could hear no sound of entrance. Until all hope had gone,
he sat listening. He was certain he had heard footsteps.
Whose ?

Trembling, and haggard he sat waiting, assailed by a
crowd of murmuring fears. One whispered that he had failed
and would have to pay the penalty of failing ; that he had
gambled with Death and lost.

By a strong effort he fought down these fancies and, closing
his eyes, tried to compose himself to rest. It was evident
now that the doctor was out and that Hannah was waiting to
return with him in his car. He was frightening himself for
nothing. At any moment he might hear the sound of their
arrival.

He heard something else, and, sitting up suddenly, tried
to think what it was and what had caused it. It was a very
faint sound—stealthy. Holding his breath, he waited for it

to be repeated. He heard it again, the mere ghost of a sound
—the whisper of a sound, but significant as most whispers
are.

He wiped his brow with his sleeve and told himself firmly
that it was nerves, and nothing but nerves ; but, against his
will, he still listened. He fancied now that the sound came
from his wife's room, the other side of the landing. It increased in loudness and became more insistent, but with his
eyes fixed on the door of his room he still kept himself in hand,
and tried to listen instead to the wind and the rain.

For a time he heard nothing but that. Then there came
a scraping, scurrying noise from his wife's room, and a sudden,
terrific crash.

With a loud scream his nerve broke, and springing from
the bed he sped downstairs and, flinging open the front-door,
dashed into the night. The door, caught by the wind, slammed
behind him.

With his hand holding the garden gate open, ready for
further flight, he stood sobbing for breath. His bare feet were
bruised and the rain was very cold, but he took no heed. Then
he ran a little way along the road and stood for some time,
hoping and listening.

He came back slowly. The wind was bitter and he was
soaked to the skin. The garden was black and forbidding, and
unspeakable horror might be lurking in the bushes. He went
up the road again, trembling with cold. Then, in desperation,
he passed through the terrors of the garden to the house, only
to find the door closed. The porch gave a little protection
from the icy rain, but none from the wind, and, shaking in
every limb, he leaned in abject misery against the door. He
pulled himself together after a time and stumbled round to
the back-door. Locked ! And all the lower windows were
shuttered. He made his way back to the porch, and, crouching
there in hopeless misery, waited for the woman to return.

IV

HE had a dim memory when he awoke of somebody questioning him and then of being half pushed, half carried
upstairs to bed. There was something wrong with his head
and his chest, and he was trembling violently, and very cold.
Somebody was speaking.

" You must have taken leave of your senses," said the voice
of Hannah. " I thought you were dead."

He forced his eyes to open. " Doctor," he muttered, " doctor."

" Out on a bad case," said Hannah. " I waited till I was tired of waiting, and then came along. Good thing for you I did. He'll be round first thing this morning. He ought to be here now."

She bustled about, tidying up the room, his leaden eyes following her as she collected the beef-tea and other things on a tray and carried them out.

" Nice thing I did yesterday," she remarked, as she came back. " Left the missus's bedroom window open. When I opened the door this morning I found that beautiful Chippidale glass of hers had blown off the table and, smashed to pieces. Did your hear it ? "

Goddard made no reply. In a confused fashion he was trying to think. Accident or not, the fall of the glass had served its purpose. Were there such things as accidents ? Or was Life a puzzle—a puzzle into which every piece was made to fit ? Fear and the wind . . . no : conscience and the wind . . . had saved the woman. He must get the powder back from her drawer . . . before she discovered it and denounced him. The medicine . . . he must remember not to take it. . . .

He was very ill, seriously ill. He must have taken a chill owing to that panic flight into the garden. Why didn't the doctor come ? He had come . . . at last . . . he was doing something to his chest . . . it was cold.

Again . . . the doctor . . . there was something he wanted to tell him . . . Hannah and a powder . . . what was it ?

Later on he remembered, together with other things that he had hoped to forget. He lay watching an endless procession of memories, broken at times by a glance at the doctor, the nurse, and Hannah, who were all standing near the bed regarding him. They had been there a long time, and they were all very quiet. The last time he looked at Hannah was the first time for months that he had looked at her without loathing and hatred. Then he knew that he was dying.

NOBODY AT HOME

By

CHARLES D. HERIOT

MAURICE had not asked him to come. The idea of visiting him had sprung out of his own subconscious—a desire to recapture some trace of emotions that belonged, by rights, to a section of his life that had passed forever. The desire was not, however, deliberate on his part ; indeed, Maurice had not entered his thoughts for more years than he cared, with an evanescent shame, to remember. But he was in the country, and a chance association of place-names recalled the fact of his friend's existence. Seven miles seemed a pleasant distance to walk if at the end he was to be warmed at a fire struck from those flinty years of neglect by the sharp contact of unexpected reunion.

He had neglected Maurice. After Oxford they had corresponded, dined at stated periods together and, twice, spent holidays linked by ropes on the Dolomites. Then, as a result of unanswered letters, marriage, and divergence of occupation and ideas a silence had fallen between them. He, Frank Hardwick, was aware that Maurice Sault was now a widower living alone in the country, that he was poor and wrote for his living ; but the man's life, aspirations, achievements and philosophy were unknown entities invisibly assembled round the bare fact of his address.

Frank, himself, had not even bothered to excuse himself. Success, even of the comparatively unimportant order to which his belonged, inevitably altered one's life and with it, one's friends. Friendship is static ; and unless on the same planes of space and time, vanishes as completely as into another dimension if deliberate (and, in a way, unnatural) efforts are not made to co-ordinate it with one's own progress. So Maurice had vanished until this morning when Frank had conjured up his expression of pleased amazement at receiving a surprise visit.

He had been told that Maurice lived in a schoolhouse. He visualized one of those sturdy, flint buildings erected in the forties for the education of a rural population that now existed no longer. His road took him up into the wooded hills further and further away from the railway, the telegraph and the village.

Did this symbolise Maurice's life, he thought. Poverty was bearable—could even be pleasant—in the country, but this deliberate withdrawal from the amenities of life seemed to indicate a retrogressive state of mind. Maurice would never be successful as he was successful. On the other hand, he had heard that " literary people " were absurdly sensitive to noise. But that was in itself a weakness. Life is a noisy business, nowadays, and those who flinch and evade its inevitable concomitants are as anti-progress as any conservative or crank pining for the Good Old Days. Besides, no really successful writer that he had heard of ever buried himself in this way. Did Priestley, or Bennett, or for that matter did Shakespeare himself, who, he seemed to remember, racketed around London with the best of them. No ! Shakespeare certainly did not appear to have minded noise. Look at some of those plays of his. . . .

He came to a gate. The road had dwindled, after the last farm, to a grassy track. Beyond the gate a path led through a plantation of firs and larches to Maurice's house. As he had expected, it was a gloomy building of brownish flints with square small windows, lattice-paned. It stood in a clearing with trees close behind rising up the hillside. It had a solitary, sulky appearance, and though there were no unnecessary details about its architecture it looked at once mean and affected. Frank decided that Maurice must not only be poor, but mad. He wondered what sort of books Maurice wrote. At Oxford, he remembered, there were poems—not easy to understand ; and after that a biography of someone or other that he had meant to get from the library but which had slipped his memory. It did not matter. He would say : " How's writing ? " or something vague like that and trust to obliquity for information. He felt sure that Maurice would be far too excited by this unexpected glimpse of the past to care about discussing the present.

He knocked. The door needed painting. He pressed three blisters round the centre panel and watched the dry fragments whirl on to the step before he knocked again. The noise was muffled. The house at least was furnished. An empty house echoed in an unpleasant manner. Damn Maurice! Why didn't he come? Frank discovered how eagerly he had walked through the wood. He had expected, had decided on a welcome. Instead this blank-fronted house remained unresponsive. He turned round on the step. In front of him was the untidy garden with a rusty, close-meshed fence as protection more against the wood than the rabbits. Thunder was hinted at by the dove-coloured sky. The path whence he had arrived looked more pleasant, this way. But to retrace his steps without achieving his purpose, to walk back through the trees with the house pursing its lips sardonically at his back . . . Maurice *must* be in!

He knocked again, sharply.

Empty houses develop a personality of their own, like servants who listen, without understanding, to an order, and whose stupid silence appears, after a while, to be inimical. This house was not empty—he could feel that. True, the uncurtained windows gazed straight before them with irritating blankness, but the echo of his summons was full of mocking suggestion.

He knocked with his ear pressed close to the door. Each sound held promise of responsive movement within. Surely that was a step? Surely a door opened? He became impatient with the birds whose tumult might conceal the first sound of Maurice's arrival. The sun itself shone down too brightly, causing a confusion of scent and light to deaden his other sense.

He became angry with Maurice and with his house. Why should he, Frank, have come all this way on a hot day to be confronted by the shell of a life, not empty—definitely not that, he was sure—but in a state of suspended animation? He pictured a snoring figure upstairs. Maurice asleep? He should not remain so long. Not he! He saw the figure on the bed upstairs turn uneasily, burrowing its head in a hot, soft pillow to escape from the noise. He became a missionary, spreading the gospel of the World Today confronted by a stubborn heretic. But he would conquer. Noise would win, would batter down the walls of resistant sleep and force Maurice to surrender. The other possibility taunted him to a momentary frenzy, and, with the fury of his repeated knockings, he surrounded himself with a nimbus of dust and paint fragments like the materialization of his rage.

He stepped back and gazed sternly at the upper windows. As this had no effect, he walked round the house.

Each side presented a different aspect of the wood and garden. On the west a grove of lilac concealed a vegetable garden, but the lettuce had grown into tall bitter weeds, and carrots, onions and potatoes luxuriated in an unwonted freedom, lashing like a tide the wire netting that restrained their dissolution in the wood. On the north young larches leaned toward him waving their plumes through which he glimpsed the steep, needle-covered hillside. As he turned to the east he saw the back door and a view. Down through a clearing lit by the western sun lay the valley from which he had climbed. A wide arc of sky stippled with pale pink cirrus dwarfed the earth to the minute clearness of a vista seen through the wrong end of a telescope. Frank stood looking at the view before his attention came back to the other door.

He perceived that, like a fool, he had come the longest way. A path led from this door straight down the hill, down into the view. It was obviously the way used by the villagers, and to bear this out there was a slit for letters in the door and beside it a milk can hanging from a hook.

Frank beat with his fist with a despairing realization of defeat. Then he examined the can. The milk was warm and sour. All day it must have hung there under the morning sun and the thunderous afternoon. The house, for all its hints and secrecy, had lied. There was nobody at home.

This definite conclusion was soothing. His anger subsided. He looked at his watch and estimated the time it would take to get back. The clouds had been strained away to the zenith leaving the clear liquid light of a sun about to set. It would be a calm evening, after all. The walk down would be charming through the dew-cooled trees.

Almost jovially he slapped the door for the last time, then stooped to peer through the letter slit, thrusting back its lid.

The spring flew down and nipped his fingers as he withdrew them, but he was not conscious of scraped joints or blackened nails. Through the narrow aperture he had looked into the scullery. Opposite was the door to the kitchen and the rest of the house, and in front of it his eyes had met those of Maurice enlarged in a startled stare. From the mouth an inflamed and discoloured tongue protruded with an expression of ultimate mockery. The head hung to one side, revealing the double coil of clothes-rope which suspended the body from a hook above the door.

No. There was nobody at home, now.

ST. CATHERINE'S EVE

By

MRS. BELLOC LOWNDES

" IN this matter of the railway, James Mottram has proved a false friend, indeed a very traitor to me."

Charles Nagle's brown eyes shone with anger ; he looked loweringly at his companions, and they, a beautiful young woman, and an old man dressed in the sober garb of a Catholic ecclesiastic of that day, glanced at one another apprehensively.

All England was then sharply divided into two camps, the one composed of those who welcomed with enthusiasm the wonderful new invention which obliterated space, the other of those who dreaded and abhorred the coming of the railroads.

Charles Nagle walked to the end of the terrace. He stared down into the wooded combe, or ravine, below, and noted with sullen anger the signs of stir and activity in the narrow strip of wood which till a few weeks before had been so still, so entirely remote from even the quiet human activities of 1835.

At last he turned round, pirouetting on his heel with a quick movement, and his good looks impressed anew each of the two who sat there with him. Eighty years ago beauty of line and colour were allowed to tell in masculine apparel, and this young Dorset squire delighted in fine clothes. Though November was far advanced, it was a mild day, and Charles Nagle wore a bright blue coat, cut, as was then the fashion, to show off the points of his elegant figure—of his slender waist and his broad shoulders ; as for the elaborately frilled waist-coat, it terminated in an India muslin stock, wound many times round his neck. He looked a foppish Londoner rather than what he was—an honest country gentleman who had not journeyed to the capital for some six years, and then only to see a great physician.

" 'Twas a most unneighbourly act on the part of James—
he knows it well enough, for we hardly see him now."

He addressed his words more particularly to his wife, and
he spoke more gently than before.

The old priest—his name was Dorriforth—looked uneasily
from his host to his hostess. He felt that both these young
people, whom he had known from childhood, and whom he
loved well, had altered during the few weeks which had gone
by since he had last seen them. Rather—he mentally corrected
himself—it was the wife, Catherine, who was changed. Charles
Nagle was much the same ; poor Charles would never be other,
for he belonged to the mysterious company of those who,
physically sound, are mentally infirm, and shunned by their
more fortunate fellows.

But Charles Nagle's wife, the sweet young woman who for
so long had been content, nay glad, to share his pitiful exile,
seemed now to have escaped, if not in body then in mind, from
the place where her sad, monotonous duty lay.

She did not at once answer her husband ; but she looked
at him fixedly, her hand smoothing nervously the skirt of her
pretty gown.

Mrs. Nagle's dress also showed a care and research unusual
in that of the country lady of those days. This was partly no
doubt owing to her French blood—her grandparents had been
émigrés---and to the fact that Charles liked to see her in light
colours. The gown she was now wearing on this mild November day was a Lyons flowered silk, the spoil of a smuggler who
pursued his profitable calling on the coast hard by. The short,
high bodice and puffed sleeves were draped with a scarf of
Buckinghamshire lace which left, as was the fashion of those
days, the wearer's lovely shoulders bare.

" James Mottram," she said at last, and with a heightened
colour, " believes in progress, Charles. It is the one thing
concerning which you and your friend will never agree."

" Friend ? " he repeated moodily. " Friend ! James
Mottram has shown himself no friend of ours. And then I
had rights in this matter—am I not his heir-at-law ? I could
prevent my cousin from touching a stone, or felling a tree, at
the Eype. But 'tis his indifference to my feelings that angers
me so. Why, I trusted the fellow as if he had been my brother."

" And James Mottram," said the old priest authoritatively,
" has always felt the same to you, Charles. Never forget that !
In all but name you are brothers. Were you not brought up
together ? Had I not the schooling of you both as lads ? "

He spoke with a good deal of feeling ; he had noticed— and the fact disturbed him—that Charles Nagle spoke in the past tense when referring to his affection for the absent man.

" But surely, sir, you cannot approve that this iron monster should invade our quiet neighbourhood ? " exclaimed Charles impatiently.

Mrs. Nagle looked at the priest entreatingly. Did she by any chance suppose that he would be able to modify her husband's violent feeling. He feared so.

" If I am to say the truth, Charles," said Mr. Dorriforth mildly, " and you would not have me conceal my sentiments, then I believe the time will come when even you will be reconciled to this marvellous invention. Those who surely know declare that, thanks to these railroads, our beloved country will soon be cultivated as is a garden. Nay, perhaps others of our Faith, strangers, will settle here—— "

" Strangers ? " repeated Charles Nagle sombrely, " I wish no strangers here. Even now there are too many strangers about." He looked round as if he expected those strangers of whom the priest had spoken to appear suddenly from behind the yew hedges which stretched away, enclosing Catherine Nagle's charming pleasaunce, to the left of the plateau on which stood the old manor-house.

" Nay, nay," he repeated, returning to his grievance, " never had I expected to find James Mottram a traitor to his order. As for the folk about here, they're bewitched. They believe that this puffing devil will make them all rich. I could tell them different ; but, as you know, there are reasons why I should not."

The priest bent his head gravely. The Catholic gentry of those days were not on comfortable terms with their neighbours. In spite of the fact that legally they were now " emancipated," any malicious person could still make life intolerable to them. The railway mania was at its beginnings, and it would have been especially dangerous for Charles Nagle to take, in an active sense, the unpopular side.

In other parts of England, far from this Dorset countryside, railroads had brought with them a revival of trade. It was hoped that the same result would follow here, and a long strip of James Mottram's estate had been selected as being peculiarly suitable for the laying down of the iron track which was to connect the nearest town with the sea.

Unfortunately the land in question consisted of a wood which formed the boundary-line where Charles Nagle's property marched with that of his kinsman and co-religionist, James Mottram ; and Nagle had taken the matter very ill indeed. He was now still suffering, in a physical sense, from the effects of the violent fit of passion which the matter had induced, and which even his wife, Catherine, had not been able to allay. . . .

As he started walking up and down with caged, impatient steps, she watched him with an uneasy, anxious glance. He kept shaking his head with a nervous movement, and he stared angrily across the ravine to the opposite hill, where against the skyline the large mass of Eype Castle, James Mottram's dwelling-place, stood four-square to the high winds which swept up from the sea.

Suddenly he again strode over to the edge of the terrace : " I think I'll go down and have a talk to those railroad fellows," he muttered uncertainly.

Charles knew well that this was among the forbidden things —the things he must not do ; yet occasionally Catherine, who was, as the poor fellow dimly realized, his mentor and guardian, as well as his outwardly submissive wife, would allow him to do that which was forbidden.

But to-day such was not her humour. " Oh, no, Charles," she said decidedly, " you cannot go down to the wood. You must stay here and talk to Mr. Dorriforth."

" They were making hellish noises all last night ; I had no rest at all," Nagle went on inconsequently. " They were running their puffing devil up and down, ' The Bridport Wonder '—that's what they call it, reverend sir," and he turned to the priest.

Catherine again looked up at her husband, and their old friend saw that she bit her lip, as if checking herself in impatient speech. Was she losing the sweetness of her temper, the evenness of disposition the priest had ever admired in her, and even reverenced ?

Mrs. Nagle knew that the steam-engine had been run over the line for the first time the night before, for James Mottram and she had arranged that the trial should take place then, rather than in the daytime. She also knew that Charles had slept through the long dark hours, those hours during which she had lain wide awake by his side listening to the strange new sounds made by the Bridport Wonder. Doubtless one of the servants had spoken of the matter in his hearing.

She frowned, then felt ashamed. " Charles," she said gently, " would it not be well for me to go down to the wood and discover when these railroad men are going away ? They say in the village that their work is now done."

" Yes," he cried eagerly. " A good idea, my love ! And if they're going off at once, you might order that a barrel of good ale be sent down to them. I'm informed that that's what James has had done this very day. Now I've no wish that James should appear more generous than I."

Catherine Nagle smiled, the indulgent kindly smile which a woman bestows on a loved child who suddenly betrays a touch of that vanity which is, in a child, so pardonable.

She went into the house, and in a few moments returned with a pink scarf wound about her soft dark hair—hair dressed high, turned back from her forehead in the old pre-Revolution French mode, and not, as was then the fashion, arranged in stiff curls.

The two men watched her walking swiftly along the terrace till she sank out of their sight, for a row of stone steps led down to an orchard planted with now leafless pear and apple trees, and surrounded with a quickset hedge. A wooden gate, with a strong lock to it, was set in this closely clipped hedge. It opened on a steep path which, after traversing two fields, terminated in the beech-wood where now ran the iron track of the new railroad.

Catherine Nagle unlocked the orchard gate, and went through on to the field path. And then she slackened her steps.

For hours, nay, for days, she had been longing for solitude, and now, for a brief space, solitude was hers. But, instead of bringing her peace, this respite from the companionship of Charles and of Mr. Dorriforth brought increased tumult and revolt.

She had ardently desired the visit of the old priest, but his presence had bestowed, instead of solace, fret and discomfort. When he fixed on her his mild, penetrating eyes, she felt as if he were dragging into the light certain secret things which had been so far closely hidden within her heart, and concerning which she had successfully dulled her once sensitive conscience.

The waking hours of the last two days had each been veined with torment. Her soul sickened as she thought of the morrow, St. Catherine's Day, that is, her feast-day. The *émigrés*, Mrs. Nagle's own people, had in exile jealously kept up their own customs, and to Charles Nagle's wife the twenty-fifth day of November had always been a day of days, what her birthday is to a happy Englishwoman. Even Charles always remembered the date, and in concert with his faithful man-servant, Collins, sent to London each year for a pretty jewel. The housefolk, all of whom had learnt to love their mistress, and who helped her loyally in her difficult, sometimes perilous, task, also made of the feast a holiday.

But now, on this St. Catherine's Eve, Mrs. Nagle told herself that she was at the end of her strength. And yet only a month ago—so she now reminded herself piteously—all had been well with her ; she had been strangely, pathetically happy a month since ; content with all the conditions of her singular and unnatural life. . . .

Suddenly she stopped walking. As if in answer to a word spoken by an invisible companion she turned aside and, stooping, picked a weed growing by the path. She held it up for a moment to her cheek, and then spoke aloud. " Were it not for James Mottram," she said slowly, and very clearly, " I too, should become mad."

Then she looked round in sudden fear. Catherine Nagle had never before uttered, or permitted another to utter aloud in her presence, that awful word. But she knew that their neighbours were not so scrupulous. One cruel enemy, and, what was especially untoward, a close relation, Mrs. Felwake, own sister to Charles Nagle's dead father, often uttered it. This lady desired her son to reign at Edgecombe ; it was she who in the last few years had spread abroad the notion that Charles Nagle, in the public interest, should be asylumed.

In his own house, and among his own tenants, the slander was angrily denied. When Charles was stranger, more suspicious, moodier than usual, those about him would tell one another that " the squire was ill to-day," or that " the master was ailing." That he had a mysterious illness was admitted. Had not a famous London doctor persuaded Mr. Nagle that it would be dangerous for him to ride, even to walk outside the boundary of his small estate,—in brief, to run any risks which might affect his heart ? He had now got out of the way of wishing to go far afield ; contentedly he would pace up and down for hours on the long terrace which overhung the wood —talking, talking, talking, with Catherine on his arm.

But he was unselfish—sometimes. " Take a walk, dear heart, with James," he would say, and then Catherine Nagle and James Mottram would make their way to some lonely farmhouse or cottage where Mottram had estate business. Yet during these expeditions they never forgot Charles, so Catherine now reminded herself sorely,—nay, it was then that they talked of him the most, discussing him kindly, tenderly, as they went. . . .

Catherine walked quickly on, her eyes on the ground. With a feeling of oppressed pain she recalled the last time she and Mottram had been alone together. Bound for a distant spot on the coast, they had gone on and on for miles, almost up to the cliffs below which lay the sea. Ah, how happy, how innocent, she had felt that day !

Then they had come to a stile—Mottram had helped her up, helped her down, and for a moment her hand had lain and fluttered in his hand. . . .

During the long walk back, each had been very silent ; and Catherine—she could not answer for her companion—when she had seen Charles waiting for her patiently, had felt a pained, shamed beat of the heart. As for James Mottram, he had gone home at once, scarce waiting for good-nights.

That evening—Catherine remembered it now with a certain comfort—she had been very kind to Charles ; she was ever kind, but she had then been kinder than usual, and he had responded by becoming suddenly clearer in mind than she had known him to be for a long time. For some days he had been the old Charles—tender, whimsical, gallant, the Charles with whom, at a time when every girl is in love with love, she had alack ! fallen in love. Then once more the cloud had come down, shadowing a dreary waste of days—dark days of oppression and of silence, alternating with sudden bursts of unreasonable and unreasoning rage.

James Mottram had come, and come frequently, during that time of misery. But his manner had changed. He had become restrained, as if watchful of himself ; he was no longer the free, the happy, the lively companion, he had used to be. Catherine scarcely saw him out of Charles's presence, and when they were by chance alone they talked of Charles, only of Charles and of his unhappy condition, and of what could be done to better it.

And now James Mottram had given up coming to Edgecombe in the old familiar way ; or rather—and this galled Catherine shrewdly—he came only sufficiently often not to rouse remark among their servants and humble neighbours.

Catherine Nagle was now on the edge of the wood, and looking about her she saw with surprise that the railway men she had come down to see had finished work for the day. There were signs of their immediate occupation, a fire was still smouldering, and the door of one of the shanties they had occupied was open. But complete stillness reigned in this kingdom of high trees. To the right and left, as far as she could see, stretched the twin lines of rude iron rails laid down along what had been a cart-track, as well as a short cut between Edgecombe Manor and Eype Castle. A dun drift, to-day's harvest of dead leaves, had settled on the rails ; even now it was difficult to follow their course.

As she stood there, about to turn and retrace her steps, Catherine suddenly saw James Mottram advancing quickly towards her, and the mingled revolt and sadness which had so wholly possessed her gave way to a sudden, overwhelming feeling of security and joy.

She moved from behind the little hut near which she had been standing, and a moment later they stood face to face.

James Mottram was as unlike Charles Nagle as two men of the same age, of the same breed, and of the same breeding could well be. He was shorter, and of sturdier build, than his cousin ; and he was plain, whereas Charles Nagle was strikingly handsome. Also his face was tanned by constant exposure to sun, salt-wind, and rain ; his hair was cut short, his face shaven.

The very clothes James Mottram wore were in almost ludicrous contrast to those which Charles Nagle affected, for Mottram's were always of serviceable homespun. But for the fact that they and he were scrupulously clean, the man now walking by Catherine Nagle's side might have been a prosperous farmer or bailiff, instead of the owner of such large property in those parts as made him, in spite of his unpopular faith, lord of the little world about him.

On his plain face and strong, sturdy figure Catherine's beautiful eyes dwelt with unconscious relief. She was so weary of Charles's absorption in his apparel, and of his interest in the hundred and one fal-lals which then delighted the cosmopolitan men of fashion.

A simple almost childish gladness filled her heart. Conscience, but just now so insistent and disturbing a familiar, vanished for a space ; nay more, assumed the garb of a meddling busybody who seeks to discover harm where no harm is.

Was not James Mottram Charles's friend, almost, as the old priest had said, Charles's brother ? Had she not herself deliberately chosen Charles in place of James when both young men had been in ardent pursuit of her—James's pursuit almost wordless, Charles's conducted with all the eloquence of the poet he had then set out to be ?

Mottram, seeing her in the wood, uttered a word of surprise, and she explained her presence there. Their hands scarce touched in greeting, and then they started walking side by side up the field path.

Mottram carried a stout ash stick. Had the priest been there he would perchance have noticed that the man's hand twitched and moved restlessly as he swung his stick about ; but Catherine only became aware that her companion was preoccupied and uneasy after they had gone some way.

When, however, the fact of his unease seemed forced upon her notice, she felt suddenly angered. There was a quality in Mrs. Nagle that made her ever ready to rise to meet and conquer circumstance. She told herself, with heightened colour, that James Mottram should and must return to his old ways— to his old familiar footing with her. Anything else would be, nay was, intolerable.

" James,"—she turned to him frankly—" why have you not come over to see us lately as often as you did ? Charles misses you sadly, and so do I. Prepare to find him in a bad mood to-day. Just now he distressed Mr. Dorriforth by his unreasonableness touching the railroad."

She smiled and went on lightly, " He said that you were a false friend to him—a traitor."

And then Catherine Nagle stopped and caught her breath. God ! Why had she said that ? But Mottram had evidently not caught the sinister word, and Catherine in haste drove back conscience into the lair whence conscience had leapt so suddenly to her side.

" Maybe I ought, in this matter of the railroad," he said musingly, " to have humoured Charles. I am now sorry I did not do so. After all, Charles may be right—and all we others wrong. The railroad may not bring us lasting good."

Catherine looked at him, surprised. James Mottram had always been so sure of himself in this matter ; but now there was dejection, weariness, in his voice ; and he was walking quickly, more quickly up the steep incline than Mrs. Nagle found agreeable. But she also hastened her steps, telling herself, with wondering pain, that he was evidently in no mood for her company.

" Mr. Dorriforth has already been here two days," she observed irrelevantly.

" Aye, I know that. It was to see him I came to-day ;
and I will ask you to spare him to me for two or three hours
Indeed, I propose that he should walk back with me to the
Eype. I wish him to witness my new will. And then I may
as well go to confession, for it is well to be shriven before a
journey, though for my part I feel ever safer on sea than land."

Mottram had looked straight before him as he had spoken
those words.

" A journey ? "

Catherine repeated the words in a low, questioning tone.
There had come across her heart a feeling of such anguish that
it was as though her body, instead of her soul, were being
wrenched asunder. In her extremity she called on pride—and
pride, ever woman's most loyal friend, flew to her aid.

" Yes," he answered, still staring straight in front of him,
" I leave to-morrow for Plymouth. I have had letters from my
agent in Jamaica which make it desirable that I should hasten
there without delay," and he dug his stick into the soft
earth.

James Mottram was absorbed in himself, and in his desire
to carry himself well in his fierce determination to avoid betray-
ing what he believed to be his secret.

They had come to a steep part of the incline, and Catherine
suddenly quickened her steps and passed him, so making it
impossible that he could see her face. Then she tried to speak,
but the commonplace words she desired to say were strangled,
at birth, in her throat.

" Charles will not mind ; he will not miss me as he would
have missed me before this unhappy business of the railroad
came between us," Mottram said lamely.

She still made no answer ; instead she shook her head
with an impatient gesture. Her silence made him sorry. After
all, he had been a good friend to Catherine Nagle—so much he
could tell himself without shame. He stepped aside on to the
grass, and striding forward turned round and faced her.

The tears were rolling down her cheeks ; but she threw
back her head and met his gaze with a cold, almost a defiant,
look. " You startled me greatly," she said breathlessly, " and
took me so by surprise, James. I am grieved to think how
Charles—nay, how we shall both—miss you. It is of Charles
I think, James ; it is for Charles I weep."

As she uttered the lying words, she still looked proudly
into his face as if daring him to doubt her.

" But I shall never forget—I shall ever think with gratitude

of your great goodness to my poor Charles. Two years out of
your life—that's what it's been, James. Too much—too much
by far ! "

She had regained control over her quivering heart, and it
was with a wan smile that she added, " But we shall miss
you, my dear, kind friend."

Her smile stung him. " Catherine," he said sternly, " I
go because I must—because I dare not stay. You are a woman
and a saint, I a man and a sinner. I've been a fool, and worse
than a fool. You say that Charles to-day called me false
friend, traitor. Catherine—Charles spoke more truly than he
knew."

His burning eyes held her fascinated. The tears had dried
on her cheeks. She was thirstily absorbing the words as they
fell now slowly, now quickly, from his lips.

But what was this he was saying ?

" Catherine, do you wish me to go on ? "

Oh, cruel ! Cruel to put this further weight on her conscience. But she made a scarcely perceptible movement of
assent—and again he spoke.

" Years ago I thought I loved you. I went away, as you
know well, because of that love. You had chosen Charles—
Charles in many ways the better fellow of the two. I went
away thinking myself sick with love of you, but it was false—
only my pride had been hurt. I did not love you as I loved
myself. And when I got clear away, in a new place, among
new people "—he hesitated, and reddened darkly—" I forgot
you. I vow that when I came back I was cured—cured if ever
a man was ! It was of Charles, not of you, Catherine, that
I thought on my way home. To me Charles and you had
become one. I swear it."

He repeated : " To me you and Charles were one."

He waited a long moment, and then, more slowly, he went
on, as if pleading with himself, with her : " You know what
I found here in place of what I had left ? I found Charles
had become a——— "

Catherine Nagle shrank back. She put up her right hand
to ward off the word, and Mottram, seizing her hand, held it
in his with a convulsive clasp.

" 'Twas not the old feeling that came back to me—that I
again swear, Catherine. 'Twas something different, something
infinitely stronger, something that at first I believed to be
all noble."

He stopped speaking, and Catherine Nagle uttered one

word—a curious word. "When?" she asked, and more urgently again she whispered, "When?"

"Long before I knew!" he cried hoarsely. "At first I called the passion that possessed me by the false name of 'friendship.' But that poor hypocrisy soon left me. A month ago, Catherine, I found myself wishing—I'll say this for myself, it was for the first time—that Charles was dead. And then I knew for sure what I had already long suspected, that the time had come for me to go."

He dropped her hand, and stood before her, abased in his own eyes, but one who, if a criminal, had had the strength to be his own judge and pass heavy sentence on himself.

"And now, Catherine, now that you understand why I go, you will surely bid me God-speed. Nay, more "—he looked at her, and smiled wryly—" if you are kind, as I know you to be kind, you will pray for me, for I go from you a melancholy, as well as a foolish, man."

She smiled a strange little wavering smile, and Mottram felt deeply moved. How gently, how kindly, Catherine Nagle had listened to his story. He had been prepared for an averted glance, for words of cold rebuke—such words as his own long-dead mother would surely have uttered to a man who had come to her with such a tale.

They walked on for a while, and Catherine again broke the silence by a question which disturbed her companion. "Then your agent's letter was not really urgent, James?"

"The letters of an honest agent always call for the owner," he muttered evasively.

They reached the orchard gate. Catherine held the key in her hand, but she did not place it in the lock—instead she paused awhile. "Then there is no special urgency?" she repeated. "And James, forgive me for asking it, are you, indeed, leaving England because of this—this matter of which you have just told me?"

He bent his head in answer.

Then she said deliberately: "Your conscience, James, is too scrupulous. I do not think that there is any reason why you should not stay."

She went on in a toneless, monotonous, voice, "When Charles and I were in Italy, I met some of those young noblemen who in times of pestilence go disguised to nurse the sick and bury the dead. It is that work of charity, dear friend, which you have been performing in our unhappy house. You

have been nursing the sick—nay, more, you have been tending "
—she waited, then in a low voice she added—" the dead.
The dead that are yet alive."

Mottram's soul leapt into his eyes.

" Then you bid me stay ? " he asked.

" For the present," she answered, " I beg you to stay.
But only so if it is indeed true that your presence is not really
required in Jamaica."

" I swear, Catherine, that all goes sufficiently well there."

Again he fixed his honest, ardent eyes on her face.

And now James Mottram was filled with a great exultation
of spirit. He felt that Catherine's soul, incapable of even the
thought of evil, shamed and made unreal the temptation which
had seemed till just now one which could only be resisted by
flight. Catherine Nagle, without doubt, was right ; he had
been over scrupulous.

There was proof of it in the blessed fact that even now,
already, the poison which had seemed to possess him, that
terrible longing for another man's wife, had left him, vanishing
in that same wife's pure presence. It was when he was alone
—alone in his great house on the hill, that the devil entered into
him, whispering that it was an awful thing such a woman as
was this woman, sensitive, intelligent, and in her beauty so
appealing, should be tied to such a being as was Charles Nagle
—poor Charles, whom every one, excepting his wife and one
loyal kinsman, called mad. And yet now it was for this very
Charles that Catherine asked him to stay, for the sake of that
unhappy, distraught man to whom he, James Mottram,
recognized the duty of a brother.

" We will both forget what you have just told me," she
said quietly, and he bowed his head in reverence.

They were now on the last step of the stone stairway
leading to the terrace.

Mrs. Nagle turned to her companion ; he saw that her eyes
were very bright, and that the rose-red colour in her cheeks had
deepened as if she had been standing before a great fire.

As they came within sight of Charles Nagle and of the old
priest, Catherine put out her hand. She touched Mottram on
the arm—it was a fleeting touch, but it brought them both,
with beating hearts, to a stand.

" James," she said, and then she stopped for a moment—a
moment that seemed to contain æons of mingled rapture and
pain—" one word about Mr. Dorriforth."

The commonplace words dropped them back to earth.

" Did you wish him to stay with you till to-morrow ? That will scarcely be possible, as to-morrow is St. Catherine's Day."

" Why, no," he said quickly. " I will not take him home with me to-night. All my plans are now changed. My will can wait "—he smiled at her—" and so can my confession."

" No, no ! " she cried almost violently. " Your confession must not wait, James—— "

" Aye, but it must," he said, and again he smiled. " I am in no mood for confession, Catherine." He added in a lower tone, " you've purged me of my sin, my dear—I feel already shriven."

Shame of a very poignant quality suddenly seared Catherine Nagle's soul. " Go on, you," she said breathlessly, though to his ears she seemed to speak in her usual controlled and quiet tones, " I have some orders to give in the house. Join Charles and Mr. Dorriforth. I will come out presently."

James Mottram obeyed her. He walked quickly forward. " Good news, Charles," he cried. " These railway men whose presence so offends you go for good to-morrow ! " And then, " Reverend sir, accept my hearty greeting."

Catherine Nagle turned to the right and went into the house. She hastened through the rooms in which, year in and year out, she spent her life, with Charles as her perpetual, her insistent, companion. She now longed for a time of recollection and secret communion, and so she instinctively made for the one place where no one, not even Charles, would come and disturb her.

Walking across the square hall, she ran up the broad staircase leading to the gallery, out of which opened the doors of her bedroom and of her husband's dressing-room. But she went swiftly past these two closed doors, and made her way along a short passage which terminated abruptly with a faded red baize door giving access to the chapel.

Long, low-ceilinged and windowless, the chapel of Edgecombe Manor had remained unaltered since the time when there were heavy penalties attached both to the celebration of the sacred rites, and to the hearing of Mass. The chapel depended for what fresh air it had on a narrow door opening straight on to ladder-like stairs leading down directly and out on to the terrace below. It was by this way that the small and scattered congregation gained access to the chapel when the presence of a priest permitted of Mass being celebrated there.

Catherine went up close to the altar rails, and sat down on

the arm-chair placed there for her sole use. She felt that now, when about to wrestle with her soul, she could not kneel and pray. Since she had been last in the chapel, acting sacristan that same morning, life had taken a great stride forward, dragging her along in its triumphant wake, a cruel and yet a magnificent conqueror.

Hiding her face in her hands, she lived again each agonized and exquisite moment she had lived through as there had fallen on her ears the words of James Mottram's shamed confession. Once more her heart was moved to an exultant sense of happiness that he should have said these things to her—of happiness and shrinking shame. . . .

But soon other thoughts, other and sterner memories were thrust upon her. She told herself the bitter truth. Not only had she led James Mottram into temptation, but she had put all her woman's wit to the task of keeping him there. It was her woman's wit—but Catherine Nagle called it by a harsher name—which had enabled her to make that perilous rock on which she and James Mottram now stood heart to heart together, appear, to him at least, a spot of sanctity and safety. It was she, not the man who had gazed at her with so ardent a belief in her purity and honour, who was playing traitor—and traitor to one at once confiding and defenceless. . . .

Then, strangely, this evocation of Charles brought her burdened conscience relief. Catherine found sudden comfort in remembering her care, her tenderness, for Charles. She reminded herself fiercely that never had she allowed anything to interfere with her wifely duty. Never ? Alas ! she remembered that there had come a day, at a time when James Mottram's sudden defection had filled her heart with pain, when she had been unkind to Charles. She recalled his look of bewildered surprise, and how he, poor fellow, had tried to sulk—only a few hours later to come to her, as might have done a repentant child, with the words, " Have I offended you, dear love ? " And she who now avoided his caresses had kissed him of her own accord with tears, and cried, " No, no, Charles, you never offend me—you are always good to me ! "

There had been a moment to-day, just before she had taunted James Mottram with being over-scrupulous, when she had told herself that she could be loyal to both of these men she loved and who loved her, giving to each a different part of her heart.

But that bargain with conscience had never been struck, tho' while considering it she had found herself longing for some convulsion of the earth which should throw her and Mottram in each other's arms.

James Mottram traitor ? That was what she was about to make him be. Catherine forced herself to face the remorse, the horror, the loathing of himself which would ensue.

It was for Mottram's sake, far more than in response to the command laid on her by her own soul, that Catherine Nagle finally determined on the act of renunciation which she knew was being immediately required of her.

When Mrs. Nagle came out on the terrace the three men rose ceremoniously. She glanced at Charles, even now her first thought and her first care. His handsome face was over-cast with the look of gloomy preoccupation which she had learnt to fear, though she knew that in truth it signified but little. At James Mottram she did not look, for she wished to husband her strength for what she was about to do.

Making a sign to the others to sit down, she herself remained standing behind Charles's chair. It was from there that she at last spoke, instinctively addressing her words to the old priest.

" I wonder," she said, " if James has told you of his approaching departure ? He has heard from his agent in Jamaica that his presence is urgently required there."

Charles Nagle looked up eagerly. " This is news indeed ! " he exclaimed. " Lucky fellow ! Why, you'll escape all the trouble that you've put on us with regard to that puffing devil."

Mr. Dorriforth glanced for a moment up at Catherine's face. Then quickly he averted his eyes.

James Mottram rose to his feet. His limbs seemed to have aged. He gave Catherine a long, probing look.

" Forgive me," he said deliberately. " You mistook my meaning. The matter is not as urgent, Catherine, as you thought."

He turned to Charles, " I will not desert my friends—at any rate not for the present. I'll face the puffing devil with those to whom I have helped to acquaint him ! "

But Mrs. Nagle and the priest both knew that the brave words were a vain boast. Charles alone was deceived ; and he showed no pleasure in the thought that the man who had been to him so kind and so patient a comrade and so trusty a friend was after all not leaving England immediately.

" I must be going back to the Eype now." Mottram spoke heavily ; again he looked at Mrs. Nagle with a strangely probing, pleading look. " But I'll come over to-morrow morning—to Mass. I've not forgotten that to-morrow is St. Catherine's Day, and that this is St. Catherine's Eve."

Charles seemed to wake out of a deep abstraction. " Yes, yes," he said heartily. " To-morrow is the great day. And then, after we've had breakfast I shall be able to consult you, James, about a very important matter, that new well they're plaguing me to sink in the village."

For the moment the cloud had again lifted ; Nagle looked at his cousin with all his old confidence and affection, and in response James Mottram's face worked with sudden emotion.

" I'll be quite at your service, Charles," he exclaimed, " quite at your service, dear fellow."

Catherine stood by. " I will let you out by the orchard gate," she said. " No need for you to go round by the road."

They walked, silently, side by side, along the terrace and down the stone steps. When in the leafless orchard, and close to where they were to part, he spoke :

" You bid me go—at once ? "

Mottram asked the question in a low, even tone ; but he did not look at Catherine, instead his eyes seemed to be following the movements of the stick he was digging into the ground at their feet.

" I think, James, that would be best."

Even to herself the words Mrs. Nagle had just uttered sounded very cold.

" Best for me ? " he asked. Then he looked up, and with sudden passion, " Catherine ! " he cried. " Believe me, I know that I can stay. Forget the wild and foolish things I said. No thought of mine shall wrong Charles—I swear it solemnly. Catherine !—do not bid me leave you. Cannot you trust my honour ? "

His eyes held hers, by turns they seemed to become beseeching and imperious.

Catherine Nagle suddenly threw out her hands with a piteous gesture. "Ah ! James," she said, " I cannot trust my own——"

And as she thus made surrender of her two most cherished possessions, her pride and her womanly reserve, Mottram's face—the plain-featured face which was now so exquisitely dear to her—became transfigured. He said no word, he made no step forward, and yet Catherine felt as if the whole of his being was calling her, drawing her to him. . . .

Suddenly there rang through the still air a discordant cry : " Catherine ! Catherine ! "

She sighed, a long convulsive sigh. It was as though a deep pit had opened between herself and her companion.

" That was Charles," she whispered, " poor Charles calling me. I must not keep him waiting."

" God forgive me," Mottram said huskily, " and bless you, Catherine, for all your goodness to me."

He took her hand in farewell, and she felt the firm, kind grasp to be that of the kinsman and friend, not that of the lover.

Then came over her a sense of measureless and most woeful loss. She realized for the first time all that his going away would mean to her—of all that it would leave her bereft. He had been the one human being to whom she had been able to bring herself to speak freely. Charles had been their common charge, the link, as well as the barrier, between them.

" You'll come to-morrow morning ? " she said, and she tried to withdraw her hand from his. His impersonal touch hurt her.

" I'll come to-morrow, and rather early, Catherine. Then I'll be able to confess before Mass."

He was speaking in his usual voice, but he still held her hand, and she felt his grip on it tightening, bringing welcome hurt.

" And you'll leave—— ? "

" For Plymouth to-morrow afternoon," he said briefly.

He dropped her hand, which now felt numbed and maimed, and passed through the gate without looking back.

She stood a moment watching him as he strode down the field path. It had suddenly become, from day, night,—high time for Charles to be indoors.

Forgetting to lock the gate, she turned and retraced her steps through the orchard, and so made her way up to where her husband and the old priest were standing awaiting her.

As she approached them, she became aware that something going on in the valley below was absorbing their close attention. She felt glad that this was so.

" There it is ! " cried Charles Nagle angrily. " I told you that they'd begin their damned practice again to-night."

Slowly through the stretch of open country which lay spread to their right, the Bridport Wonder went puffing its way. Lanterns had been hung in front of the engine, and as it crawled sinuously along it looked like some huge monster with myriad eyes. As it entered the wood below, the dark barrel-like body of the engine seemed to give a bound, a lurch forward, and the men that manned it laughed out suddenly and loudly. The sound of their uncouth mirth floated upwards through the twilight.

"James's ale has made them merry ! " exclaimed Charles, wagging his head. " And he, going through the wood, will just have met the puffing devil. I wish him the joy of the meeting ! "

II

IT was five hours later. Mrs. Nagle had bidden her reverend guest good night, and she was now moving about her large, barely furnished bedchamber, waiting for her husband to come upstairs.

The hours which had followed James Mottram's departure had seemed intolerably long. Catherine felt as if she had gone through some terrible physical exertion which had left her worn out—stupefied. And yet she could not rest. Even now her day was not over ; Charles often grew restless and talkative at night. He and Mr. Dorriforth were no doubt still sitting talking together downstairs.

Mrs. Nagle could hear her husband's man-servant moving about in the next room, and his proximity disturbed her.

She waited awhile, and then went and opened the door of the dressing-room. " You need not sit up, Collins," she said.

" I fear that Mr. Nagle, madam, has gone out of doors," he said.

Catherine felt dismayed. The winter before Charles had once stayed out nearly all night.

" Go you to bed, Collins," she said. " I will wait up till Mr. Nagle comes in, and I will make it right with him."

He looked at her doubtingly. Was it possible that Mrs. Nagle was unaware of how much worse than usual his master had been the last few days ?

" I fear Mr. Nagle is not well to-day," he ventured. " He seemed much disturbed to-night."

" Your master is disturbed because Mr. Mottram is again leaving England for the Indies."

Catherine forced herself to say the words. She was dully surprised to see how quietly news so momentous to her was received by this faithful servant.

" That may be it," said the man consideringly, " but I can't help thinking that the master is still much concerned about the railroad. I fear that he has gone down to the wood to-night."

Catherine was startled. " Oh, surely he would not do that,

Collins ? " She added in a lower tone, " I myself locked the orchard gate."

" If that is so," he answered, obviously relieved, " then with your leave, madam, I'll be off to bed."

Mrs. Nagle went back into her room, and sat down by the fire, and then, sooner than she had expected to do so, she heard a familiar sound. It came from the chapel, for Charles was fond of using that little used and secret entry into his house.

She got up and quietly opened her bedroom door.

From the hall below was cast up the dim light of the oil-lamp which always burnt there at night, and suddenly Catherine saw her husband emerge from the chapel passage, and begin walking slowly round the opposite side of the gallery.

She watched him with languid curiosity.

Charles Nagle was treading softly, his head bent as if in thought. Suddenly he stayed his steps by a half-moon table on which stood a large Chinese bowl filled with pot-pourri ; and into this he plunged his hands, seeming to lave them in the dry rose-leaves. Catherine felt no surprise, she was so used to his strange ways ; and more than once he had hidden things—magpie fashion—in that great bowl. She turned and closed her door noiselessly ; Charles much disliked being spied on.

At last she heard him go into his dressing-room. Then came the sounds of cupboard doors being flung open, and the hurried pouring out of water. . . . But long before he could have had time to undress, she heard the familiar knock.

She said feebly, " Come in," and the door opened.

It was as she had feared ; her husband had no thought, no intention, of going yet to bed. Not only was he fully dressed, but the white evening waistcoat he had been wearing had been changed by him within the last few moments for a waistcoat she had not seen before, though she had heard of its arrival from London. It was of cashmere, the latest freak of fashion. She also saw with surprise that his nankeen trousers were stained, as if he had been kneeling on damp ground. He looked very hot, his wavy hair lay damply on his brow, and he appeared excited, oppressively alive.

" Catherine ! " he exclaimed, hurrying up to the place where she was standing near the fire. " You will bear witness that I was always and most positively averse to the railroad being brought here ? "

He did not wait for her to answer him. " Did I not always

say that trouble would come of it—trouble to us all ? Yet sometimes it's an ill thing to be proved right."

" Indeed it is, Charles," she answered gently. " But let us talk of this to-morrow. It's time for bed, my dear, and I am very weary."

He was now standing by her, staring down into the fire.

Suddenly he turned and seized her left arm. He brought her unresisting across the room, then dragged aside the heavy yellow curtains which had been drawn before the central window.

" Look over there, Catherine," he said meaningly. " Can you see the Eype ? The moon gives but little light to-night, but the stars are bright. I can see a glimmer at yon window. They must be still waiting for James to come home."

" I see the glimmer you mean," she said dully. " No doubt they leave a lamp burning all night, as we do. James must have got home hours ago, Charles."

She saw that the cuff of her husband's coat was also covered with dark, damp stains, and again she wondered uneasily what he had been doing out of doors.

" Catherine ? "

Charles Nagle turned her round ungently, and forced her to look up into his face. " Have you ever thought what 'twould be like to live at the Eype ? "

The question startled her. She roused herself to refute what she felt to be an unworthy accusation. " No, Charles," she said, looking at him steadily. " God is my witness that at no time did I think of living at the Eype. Such a wish never came to me—— "

" Nor to me ! " he cried, " nor to me, Catherine ! All the long years that James Mottram was in Jamaica the thought never once came to me that he might die, and I survive him. After all we were much of an age, he had but two years the advantage of me. I always thought that the boy—my aunt's son, curse him !—would get it all. Then, had I thought of it, and I swear I never did think of it, I should have told myself that any day James might bring a wife to the Eype—— "

He was staring through the leaded panes with an intent, eager gaze. " It is a fine house, Catherine, and commodious. Larger, airier than ours—though perhaps colder," he added thoughtfully. " Cold I always found it in winter when I used to stay there as a boy—colder than this house. You prefer Edgecombe, Catherine ? If you were given a choice, is it here that you would live ? "

He looked at her, as if impatient for an answer.

" Every stone of Edgecombe, our home, is dear to me," she said solemnly. " I have never admired the Eype. It is too large, too cold for my taste. It stands too much exposed to the wind."

" It does ! it does ! "

There was a note of regret in his voice. He let the curtain fall, and looked about him rather wildly.

" And now, Charles," she said, " shall we not say our prayers and retire to rest ? "

" If I had only thought of it," he said, " I might have said my prayers in the chapel. But there was much to do. I thought of calling you, Catherine, for you make a better sacristan than I. Then I remembered Boney—poor little Boney crushed by the miller's dray—and how you cried all night, and that though I promised you a far finer, cleverer dog than that poor old friend had ever been. Collins said, ' Why, sir, you should have hid the old dog's death from the mistress till the morning.' A worthy fellow, Collins. He meant no disrespect to me. At that time, d'you remember, Collins had only been in my service a few months ? "

It was an hour later. From where she lay in bed, Catherine Nagle with dry, aching eyes stared into the fire, watching the wood embers turn from red to grey. By her side, his hand in hers, Charles slept the dreamless heavy slumber of a child.

Scarcely breathing, in her anxiety lest he should wake, she loosened her hand, and with a quick movement slipped out of bed. The fire was burning low, but Catherine saw everything in the room very clearly, and she threw over her night-dress a long cloak, and wound about her head the scarf which she had worn during her walk to the wood.

It was not the first time Mrs. Nagle had risen thus in the still night and sought refuge from herself and from her thoughts in the chapel ; and her husband had never missed her from his side.

As she crept round the dimly lit gallery she passed by the great bowl of pot-pourri by which Charles Nagle had lingered, and there came to her the thought that it might perchance be well for her to discover, before the servants should have a chance of doing so, what he had doubtless hidden there.

Catherine plunged both her hands into the scented rose-leaves, and she gave a sudden cry of pain—for her fingers had closed on the sharp edge of a steel blade. Then she drew out a narrow damascened knife, one which her husband, taken by its elegant shape, had purchased long before in Italy.

Mrs. Nagle's brow furrowed in vexation—Collins should have put the dangerous toy out of his master's reach. Slipping the knife into the deep pocket of her cloak, she hurried on into the unlit passage leading to the chapel.

Save for the hanging lamp, which since Mr. Dorriforth had said Mass there that morning signified the presence of the Blessed Sacrament, the chapel should have been in darkness. But as Catherine passed through the door she saw, with sudden, uneasy amazement, the farther end of the chapel in a haze of brightness.

Below the altar, striking upwards from the floor of the sanctuary, gleamed a corona of light. Charles—she could not for a moment doubt that it was Charles's doing—had moved the six high, heavy silver candlesticks which always stood on either side of the altar, and had placed them on the ground.

There, in a circle, the wax candles blazed, standing sentinel-wise about a dark, round object which was propped up on a pile of altar-linen carefully arranged to support it.

Fear clutched at Catherine's heart—such fear as even in the early days of Charles's madness had never clutched it. She was filled with a horrible dread, and a wild, incredulous dismay.

What was the Thing, at once so familiar and so terribly strange, that Charles had brought out of the darkness of the night and placed with so much care below the altar ?

But the thin flames of the candles, now shooting up, now guttering low, blown on by some invisible current of strong air, gave no steady light.

Staying still close to the door, she sank down on her knees, and desiring to shut out, obliterate, the awful sight confronting her, she pressed both her hands to her eyes. But that availed her nothing.

Suddenly there rose up before Catherine Nagle a dreadful scene of that great Revolution drama of which she had been so often told as a child. She saw, with terrible distinctness, the severed heads of men and women borne high on iron pikes, and one of these blood-streaked, livid faces was that of James Mottram—the wide-open, sightless eyes were his eyes. . . .

There also came back to her as she knelt there, shivering with cold and anguish, the story of a French girl of noble birth who, having bought her lover's head from the executioner, had walked with it in her arms to the village near Paris where stood his deserted château.

Slowly she rose from her knees, and with her hands thrown out before her, she groped her way to the wall and there crept along, as if a precipice lay on her other side.

At last she came to the narrow oak door which gave on to the staircase leading into the open air. The door was ajar ; it was from there that blew the current of air which caused those thin, fantastic flames to flare and gutter in the awful stillness.

She drew the door to, and went on her way, so round to the altar. In the now steadier light Catherine saw that the large missal lay open at the Office for the Dead.

She laid her hands with a blind instinct upon the altar, and felt a healing touch upon their palms. Henceforth—and Catherine Nagle was fated to live many long years—she remained persuaded that it was then there had come to her a shaft of divine light piercing the dark recesses of her soul. For it was at that moment that there came to her the conviction, and one which never faltered, that Charles Nagle had done no injury to James Mottram. And there also came to her then the swift understanding of what others would believe, were there to be found in the private chapel of Edgecombe Manor that which now lay on the ground behind her, close to her feet.

So understanding, Catherine suddenly saw the way open before her, and the dread thing which she must do if Charles were to be saved from a terrible suspicion—one which would undoubtedly lead to his being taken away from her and from all that his poor, atrophied heart held dear, to be asylumed.

With steps that did not falter, Catherine Nagle went behind the altar into the little sacristy, there to seek in the darkness an altar-cloth.

Holding the cloth up before her face she went back into the lighted chapel, and kneeling down, she uncovered her face and threw the cloth over what lay before her.

And then Catherine's teeth began to chatter, and a mortal chill overtook her. She was being faced by a new and to her a most dread enemy, for till to-night she and that base physical fear which is the coward's foe had never met. Pressing her hands together, she whispered the short, simple prayer for the Faithful Departed that she had said so often and, she now felt, so unmeaningly. Even as she uttered the familiar words, base fear slunk away, leaving in his place her soul's old companion, courage, and his attendant, peace.

She rose to her feet, and opening wide her eyes forced

herself to think out what must be done by her in order that no
trace of Charles's handiwork should remain in the chapel.

Snuffing out the wicks, Catherine lifted the candlesticks
from the ground and put them back in their accustomed place
upon the altar.   Then, stooping, she forced herself to wrap up
closely in the altar-cloth that which must be her burden till she
found James Mottram's headless body where Charles had left
it.   Placing that same precious burden within the ample
folds of her cloak, she held it with her left hand and arm closely
pressed to her bosom. . . .

With her right hand she gathered up the pile of stained
altar-linen from the ground, and going once more into the
sacristy she thrust it into the oak chest in which were kept the
Lenten furnishings of the altar.   Having done that, and walking
slowly lest she should trip and fall, she made her way to the
narrow door Charles had left open to the air.   Going down
the steep stairway she was soon out of doors in the dark and
windy night.

Charles had been right, the moon gave but little light ;
enough, however, so she told herself, for the accomplishment
of her task.

She sped swiftly along the terrace, keeping close under
the house, and then, more slowly she walked down the stone
steps where last time she trod them Mottram had been her
companion, his living lips as silent as were his dead lips now.

The orchard gate was wide open, and as she passed through
there came to Catherine Nagle the knowledge why Charles on
his way back from the wood had not even latched it ; he also,
when passing through it, had been bearing a burden. . . .

She walked down the field path ; and when she came to the
steep place where Mottram had told her that he was going
away, the tears for the first time began running down Catherine's face.   She felt again the sharp, poignant pain which his
then cold and measured words had dealt her, and the blow this
time fell on a bruised heart.   With a convulsive gesture she
pressed more closely that which she was holding to her desolate
breast.

At night the woodland is strangely, curiously alive.   Catherine shuddered as she heard the stuffless sounds, the tiny
rustlings and burrowings of those wild, shy creatures whose
solitude had lately been so rudely invaded, and who now of
man's night made their day.

Their myriad presence made her human loneliness more
intense than it had been in the open fields and, as she started

walking by the side of the iron rails, her eyes fixed on the dark drift of dead leaves which dimly marked the path, she felt solitary indeed, and beset with vague and fearsome terrors.

At last she found herself nearing the end of the wood. Soon would come the place where what remained of the ·cart-track struck sharply to the left, up the hill towards the Eype.

It was there, close to the open. that Catherine Nagle's quest ended, and that she was able to accomplish the task she had set herself, of making that which Charles had rendered incomplete, complete as men, considering the flesh, count completeness.

Within but a few yards of safety, James Mottram had met with death ; a swift, merciful death, due to the negligence of an engine-driver not only new to his work but made blindly merry by Mottram's gift of ale.

Charles Nagle woke late on the morning of St. Catherine's Day, and the pale November sun fell on the fully dressed figures of his wife and Mr. Dorriforth standing by his bedside.

But Charles, absorbed as always in himself, saw nothing untoward in their presence.

" I had a dream ! " he exclaimed. " A most horrible and gory dream this night. I thought I was in the wood over yonder, and James Mottram lay before me, done to death by that puffing devil we saw slithering by so fast. His head nearly severed—*à la guillotine*, you understand, my love ?—from his poor body."

There flashed a curious, secretive smile on Charles Nagle's pale, handsome face.

Catherine Nagle gave a cry, a stifled shriek of horror.

The priest caught her by the arm and led her to the couch which stood across the end of the bed.

" Charles," he said sternly, " this is no light matter. Your dream—there's not a doubt of it—was sent you in merciful preparation for the awful truth. Your kinsman, your almost brother, Charles, was found this morning in the wood, dead as you saw him in your dream."

The face of the man sitting up in bed stiffened—was it with fear, or grief ?

" They found James Mottram dead," he repeated, with an uneasy glance in the direction of the couch where crouched his wife. " And his head, most reverend sir—what of his head ? "

" James Mottram's body was terribly mangled. But his head," answered the priest solemnly, " was severed from his

body, as you saw it in your dream, Charles. A strangely clean
cut, it seems—— ”

" Ay," said Charles Nagle. " That was in my dream too ;
if I said nearly severed, I said wrong."

Catherine was now again standing by the priest's side.

" Charles," she said gravely, " you must now get up ; Mr.
Dorriforth is waiting for you to be up, and ready to serve the
Mass for James's soul."

She made the sign of the cross, and then, with her right
hand shading her sunken eyes, she went on, " My dear, I
entreat you to tell no one, not even faithful Collins, of this
awful dream. We want no such tale as that of your dream
spread about the place."

She looked at the old priest entreatingly, and he at once
responded. " Catherine is right, Charles. We of the Faith
should be more careful with regard to such matters than are
the ignorant and superstitious."

But he was surprised to hear the woman by his side say
insistently, " Charles, if only to please me, vow that you will
keep most secret your dreadful dream. Think if it should
come to your Aunt Felwake's ears ? "

" That I swear it shall not," said Charles sullenly.

And he kept his word.

THE SCREAMING SKULL

By

F. MARION CRAWFORD

I HAVE often heard it scream. No, I am not nervous, I am not imaginative, and I never believed in ghosts, unless that thing is one. Whatever it is, it hates me almost as much as it hated Luke Pratt, and it screams at me.

If I were you, I would never tell ugly stories about ingenious ways of killing people, for you never can tell but that someone at the table may be tired of his or her nearest and dearest. I have always blamed myself for Mrs. Pratt's death, and I suppose I was responsible for it in a way, though heaven knows I never wished her anything but long life and happiness. If I had not told that story she might be alive yet. That is why the thing screams at me, I fancy.

She was a good little woman, with a sweet temper, all things considered, and a nice gentle voice ; but I remember hearing her shriek once when she thought her little boy was killed by a pistol that went off, though everyone was sure that it was not loaded. It was the same scream ; exactly the same, with a sort of rising quaver at the end ; do you know what I mean ? Unmistakeable.

The truth is, I had not realised that the doctor and his wife were not on good terms. They used to bicker a bit now and then when I was here, and I often noticed that little Mrs. Pratt got very red and bit her lip hard to keep her temper, while Luke grew pale and said the most offensive things. He was that sort when he was in the nursery, I remember, and afterward at school. He was my cousin, you know ; that is how I came by this house ; after he died, and his boy Charley was killed in South Africa, there were no relations left. Yes, it's a pretty little property, just the sort of thing for an old sailor like me who has taken to gardening.

One always remembers one's mistakes much more vividly
than one's cleverest things, doesn't one ? I've often noticed it.
I was dining with the Pratts' one night, when I told them the
story that afterwards made so much difference. It was a wet
night in November, and the sea was moaning. Hush !—if you
don't speak you will hear it now. . . .

Do you hear the tide ? Gloomy sound, isn't it ? Sometimes, about this time of year—hallo !—there it is ! Don't
be frightened, man—it won't eat you—it's only a noise, after
all ! But I'm glad you've heard it, because there are always
people who think it's the wind, or my imagination, or something. You won't hear it again to-night, I fancy, for it doesn't
often come more than once. Yes—that's right. Put another
stick on the fire, and a little more stuff into that weak mixture
you're so fond of. Do you remember old Blauklot the car-
penter, on that German ship that picked us up when the
Clontarf went to the bottom ? We were hove to in a howling
gale one night, as snug as you please, with no land within five
hundred miles, and the ship coming up and falling off as
regularly as clockwork—" Biddy te boor beebles ashore tis
night, poys ! " old Blauklot sang out, as he went off to his
quarters with the sail-maker. I often think of that, now that
I'm ashore for good and all.

Yes, it was on a night like this, when I was at home for a
spell, waiting to take the *Olympia* out on her first trip—it was
on the next voyage that she broke the record, you remember—
but that dates it. Ninety-two was the year, early in November.

The weather was dirty, Pratt was out of temper, and the
dinner was bad, very bad indeed, which didn't improve
matters, and cold, which made it worse. The poor little lady
was very unhappy about it, and insisted on making a Welsh
rarebit on the table to counteract the raw turnips and the half-
boiled mutton. Pratt must have had a hard day. Perhaps he
had lost a patient. At all events, he was in a nasty temper.

" My wife is trying to poison me, you see ! " he said.
" She'll succeed some day." I saw that she was hurt, and I
made believe to laugh, and said that Mrs. Pratt was much
too clever to get rid of her husband in such a simple way ;
and then I began to tell them about Japanese tricks with spun
glass and chopped horsehair and the like.

Pratt was a doctor, and knew a lot more than I did about
such things, but that only put me on my mettle, and I told a
story about a woman in Ireland who did for three husbands
before anyone suspected foul play.

Did you never hear that tale ? The fourth husband managed to keep awake and caught her, and she was hanged. How did she do it ? She drugged them, and poured melted lead into their ears through a little horn funnel when they were asleep. . . . No—that's the wind whistling. It's backing up to the southward again. I can tell by the sound. Besides, the other thing doesn't often come more than once in an evening even at this time of year—when it happened. Yes, it was in November. Poor Mrs. Pratt died suddenly in her bed not long after I dined here. I can fix the date, because I got the news in New York by the steamer that followed the *Olympia* when I took her out on her first trip. You had the *Leofric* the same year ? Yes, I remember. What a pair of old buffers we are coming to be, you and I. Nearly fifty years since we were apprentices together on the *Clontarf*. Shall you ever forget old Blauklot ? " Biddy te boor beebles ashore, poys ! " Ha, ha ! Take a little more, with all that water. It's the old Hulstkamp I found in the cellar when this house came to me, the same I brought Luke from Amsterdam five-and-twenty years ago. He had never touched a drop of it. Perhaps he's sorry now, poor fellow.

Where did I leave off ? I told you that Mrs. Pratt died suddenly—yes. Luke must have been lonely here after she was dead, I should think ; I came to see him now and then, and he looked worn and nervous, and told me that his practice was growing too heavy for him, though he wouldn't take an assistant on any account. Years went on, and his son was killed in South Africa, and after that he began to be queer. There was something about him not like other people. I believe he kept his senses in his profession to the end ; there was no complaint of his having made bad mistakes in cases, or anything of that sort, but he had a look about him——

Luke was a red-headed man with a pale face when he was young, and he was never stout ; in middle age he turned a sandy grey, and after his son died he grew thinner and thinner, till his head looked like a skull with parchment stretched over it very tight, and his eyes had a sort of glare in them that was very disagreeable to look at.

He had an old dog that poor Mrs. Pratt had been fond of, and that used to follow her everywhere. He was a bull-dog, and the sweetest tempered beast you ever saw, though he had a way of hitching his upper lip behind one of his fangs that frightened strangers a good deal. Sometimes, of an evening, Pratt and Bumble—that was the dog's name—used to sit and look at each other a long time, thinking about old times, I suppose, when Luke's wife used to sit in that chair you've got. That was always her place, and this was the doctor's, where I'm sitting. Bumble used to climb up by the footstool—he was old and fat by that time, and could not jump much, and his teeth were getting shaky. He would look steadily at Luke, and Luke looked steadily at the dog, his face growing more and more like a skull with two little coals for eyes ; and after about five minutes or so, though it may have been less, old Bumble would suddenly begin to shake all over, and all on a sudden he would set up an awful howl, as if he had been shot, and tumble out of the easy-chair and trot away, and hide himself under the sideboard, and lie there making odd noises.

Considering Pratt's looks in those last months, the thing is not surprising, you know. I'm not nervous or imaginative, but I can quite believe he might have sent a sensitive woman into hysterics—his head looked so much like a skull in parchment.

At last I came down one day before Christmas, when my ship was in dock and I had three weeks off. Bumble was not about, and I said casually that I supposed the old dog was dead.

" Yes," Pratt answered, and I thought there was something odd in his tone even before he went on after a little pause. " I killed him," he said presently. " I could not stand it any longer."

I asked what it was that Luke could not stand, though I guessed well enough.

" He had a way of sitting in her chair and glaring at me, and then howling." Luke shivered a little. " He didn't suffer at all, poor old Bumble," he went on in a hurry, as if he thought I might imagine he had been cruel. " I put dionine into his drink to make him sleep soundly, and then I chloroformed him gradually, so that he could not have felt suffocated even if he was dreaming. It's been quieter since then."

I wondered what he meant, for the words slipped out as if he could not help saying them. I've understood since. He meant that he did not hear that noise so often after the dog was out of the way. Perhaps he thought at first that it was old Bumble in the yard howling at the moon, though it's not that kind of noise, is it ? Besides, I know what it is, if Luke didn't. It's only a noise, after all, and a noise never hurt anybody yet. But he was much more imaginative than I am. No doubt there really is something about this place that I don't understand ; but when I don't understand a thing, I call it a phenomenon, and I don't take it for granted that it's going to kill me, as he did. I don't understand everything, by long odds, nor do you, nor does any man who has been to sea. We used to talk of tidal waves, for instance, and we could not account for them ; now we account for them by calling them submarine earthquakes, and we branch off into fifty theories, any one of which might make earthquakes quite comprehensible if we only knew what they are. I fell in with one of them once, and the inkstand flew straight up from the table against the ceiling of my cabin. The same thing happened to Captain Lecky—I dare say you've read about it in his " Wrinkles." Very good If that sort of thing took place ashore, in this room for instance, a nervous person would talk about spirits and levitation and fifty things that mean nothing, instead of just quietly setting it down as a " phenomenon " that has not been explained yet. My view of that voice, you see.

Besides, what is there to prove that Luke killed his wife ? I would not even suggest such a thing to anyone but you. After all, there was nothing but the coincidence that poor little Mrs. Pratt died suddenly in her bed a few days after I told that story at dinner. She was not the only woman who ever died like that. Luke got the doctor over from the next parish, and they agreed that she had died of something the matter with her heart. Why not ? It's common enough.

Of course, there was the ladle. I never told anybody about that, and it made me start when I found it in the cupboard in the bedroom. It was new, too—a little tinned iron ladle that had not been in the fire more than once or twice, and there was some lead in it that had been melted, and stuck to the bottom of the bowl, all grey, with hardened dross on it. But that proves nothing. A country doctor is generally a handy man, who does everything for himself, and Luke may have had a dozen reasons for melting a little lead in a ladle. He was fond of sea-fishing, for instance, and he may have cast a sinker for a night-line ; perhaps it was a weight for the hall clock, or something like that. All the same, when I found it I had a rather queer sensation, because it looked so much like the thing I had described when I told them the story. Do you understand ? It affected me unpleasantly, and I threw it away ; it's at the bottom of the sea a mile from the Spit, and it will be jolly well rusted beyond recognising if it's ever washed up by the tide.

You see, Luke must have bought it in the village, years ago, for the man sells just such ladles still. I suppose they are used in cooking. In any case, there was no reason why an inquisitive housemaid should find such a thing lying about, with lead in it, and wonder what it was, and perhaps talk to the maid who heard me tell the story at dinner—for that girl married the plumber's son in the village, and may remember the whole thing.

You understand me, don't you? Now that Luke Pratt is dead and gone, and lies buried beside his wife, with an honest man's tombstone at his head, I should not care to stir up anything that could hurt his memory. They are both dead, and their son, too. There was trouble enough about Luke's death, as it was.

How? He was found dead on the beach one morning, and there was a coroner's inquest. There were marks on his throat, but he had not been robbed. The verdict was that he had come to his end " by the hands or teeth of some person or animal unknown," for half the jury thought it might have been a big dog that had thrown him down and gripped his windpipe, though the skin of his throat was not broken. No one knew at what time he had gone out, nor where he had been. He was found lying on his back above high-water mark, and an old cardboard bandbox that had belonged to his wife lay under his hand, open. The lid had fallen off. He seemed to have been carrying home a skull in the box—doctors are fond of collecting such things. It had rolled out and lay near his head, and it was a remarkably fine skull, rather small, beautifully shaped and very white, with perfect teeth. That is to say, the upper jaw was perfect, but there was no lower one at all, when I first saw it.

Yes, I found it here when I came. You see, it was very white, and polished like a thing meant to be kept under a glass case, and the people did not know where it came from, nor what to do with it; so they put it back into the bandbox and set it on the shelf of the cupboard in the best bedroom, and of course they showed it to me when I took possession. I was taken down to the beach, too, to be shown the place where Luke was found, and the old fisherman explained just how he was lying, and the skull beside him. The only point he could not explain was why the skull had rolled up the sloping sand towards Luke's head instead of rolling downhill to his feet. It did not seem odd to me at the time but I have often thought of it since, for the place is rather steep. I'll take you there to-morrow if you like—I made a sort of cairn of stones there afterward.

When he fell down, or was thrown down—whichever happened—the bandbox struck the sand, and the lid came off, and the thing came out and ought to have rolled down. But it didn't. It was close to his head, almost touching it, and turned with the face toward it. I say it didn't strike me as odd when the man told me ; but I could not help thinking about it afterward, again and again, till I saw a picture of it all when I closed my eyes ; and then I began to ask myself why the plaguy thing had rolled up instead of down, and why it had stopped near Luke's head, instead of anywhere else, a yard away, for instance.

You naturally want to know what conclusion I reached, don't you ? None that at all explained the rolling, at all events. But I got something else into my head, after a time, that made me feel downright uncomfortable.

Oh, I don't mean as to anything supernatural ! There may be ghosts, or there may not be. If there are, I'm not inclined to believe that they can hurt living people except by frightening them, and, for my part, I would rather face any shape of a ghost than a fog in the Channel when it's crowded. No. What bothered me was just a foolish idea, that's all, and I cannot tell how it began, nor what made it grow till it turned into a certainty.

I was thinking about Luke and his poor wife one evening over my pipe and a dull book, when it occurred to me that the skull might possibly be hers, and I have never got rid of the thought since. You'll tell me there's no sense in it, no doubt ; that Mrs. Pratt was buried like a Christian and is lying in the churchyard where they put her, and that it's perfectly monstrous to suppose her husband kept her skull in her old bandbox in his bedroom. All the same, in the face of reason, and common sense, and probability, I'm convinced that he did. Doctors do all sorts of queer things that would make men like you and me feel creepy, and those are just the things that don't seem probable, nor logical, nor sensible to us.

Then, don't you see ?—if it really was her skull, poor woman, the only way of accounting for his having it is that, he really killed her, and did it in that way, as the woman killed her husbands in the story, and that he was afraid there might be an examination some day which would betray him. You see, I told that too, and I believe it had really happened some fifty or sixty years ago. They dug up the three skulls, you know, and there was a small lump of lead rattling about in each one. That was what hanged the woman. Luke remembered that, I'm sure. I don't want to know what he did when he thought of it ; my taste never ran in the direction of horrors, and I don't fancy you care for them either, do you ? No. If you did you might supply what is wanting to the story.

It must have been rather grim, eh ? I wish I did not see the whole thing so distinctly, just as everything must have happened. He took it the night before she was buried, I'm sure, after the coffin had been shut, and when the servant girl was asleep. I would bet anything, that when he'd got it, he put something under the sheet in its place, to fill up and look like it. What do you suppose he put there, under the sheet ?

I don't wonder you take me up on what I'm saying ! First I tell you that I don't want to know what happened, and that I hate to think about horrors, and then I describe the whole thing to you as if I had seen it. I'm quite sure that it was her work-bag that he put there. I remember the bag very well, for she always used it of an evening ; it was made of brown plush, and when it was stuffed full it was about the size of—you understand. Yes, there I am, at it again ! You may laugh at me, but you don't live here alone, where it was done, and you didn't tell Luke the story about the melt d lead. I'm not nervous, I tell you, but sometimes I begin to feel that I understand why some people are. I dwell on all this when I'm alone, and I dream of it, and when that thing screams— well, frankly, I don't like the noise any more than you do, though I should be used to it by this time.

I ought not to be nervous. I've sailed in a haunted ship. There was a Man in the Top, and two-thirds of the crew died of the West Coast fever inside of ten days after we anchored; but I was all right, then and afterwards. I have seen some ugly sights, too, just as you have, and all the rest of us. But nothing ever stuck in my head in the way this does.

You see, I've tried to get rid of the thing, but it doesn't like that. It wants to be there in its place, in Mrs. Pratt's bandbox in the cupboard in the best bedroom. It's not happy anywhere else. How do I know that ? Because I've tried it. You don't suppose that I've not tried, do you ? As long as it's there it only screams now and then, generally at this time of year, but if I put it out of the house it goes on all night, and no servant will stay here twenty-four hours. As it is.

I've often been left alone and have been obliged to shift for myself for a fortnight at a time. No one from the village would ever pass a night under the roof now, and as for selling the place, or even letting it, that's out of the question. The old women say that if I stay here I shall come to a bad end myself before long.

I'm not afraid of that. You smile at the mere idea that any one could take such nonsense seriously. Quite right. It's utterly blatant nonsense, I agree with you. Didn't I tell you that it's only a noise after all when you started and looked round as if you expected to see a ghost standing behind your chair ?

I may be all wrong about the skull, and I like to think that I am—when I can. It may be just a fine specimen which Luke got somewhere long ago, and what rattles about inside when you shake it may be nothing but a pebble, or a bit of hard clay, or anything. Skulls that have lain long in the ground generally have something inside them that rattles, don't they ? No, I've never tried to get it out, whatever it is ; I'm afraid it might be lead, don't you see ? And if it is, I don't want to know the fact, for I'd much rather not be sure. If it really is lead, I killed her quite as much as if I had done the deed myself. Anybody must see that, I should think. As long as I don't know for certain, I have the consolation of saying that it's all utterly ridiculous nonsense, that Mrs. Pratt died a natural death and that the beautiful skull belonged to Luke when he was a student in London. But if I were quite sure, I believe I should have to leave the house ; indeed I do, most certainly. As it is, I had to give up trying to sleep in the best bedroom where the cupboard is.

You ask me why I don't throw it into the pond—yes, but please don't call it a " confounded bugbear "—it doesn't like being called names.

There ! Lord, what a shriek ! I told you so ! You're quite pale, man. Fill up your pipe and draw your chair nearer to the fire, and take some more drink. Old Hollands never hurt anybody yet. I've seen a Dutchman in Java drink half a jug of Hulstkamp in a morning without turning a hair. I don't take much rum myself, because it doesn't agree with my rheumatism, but you are not rheumatic and it won't damage you. Besides, it's a very damp night outside. The wind is howling again, and it will soon be in the south-west ; do you hear how the windows rattle ? The tide must have turned too, by the moaning.

We should not have heard the thing again if you had not said that. I'm pretty sure we should not. Oh yes, if you choose to describe it as a coincidence, you are quite welcome, but I would rather that you should not call the thing names again, if you don't mind. It may be that the poor little woman hears, and perhaps it hurts her, don't you know ? Ghost ? No ! You don't call anything a ghost that you can take in your hands and look at in broad daylight, and that rattles when you shake it. Do you now ? But it's something that hears and understands ; there's no doubt about that.

I tried sleeping in the best bedroom when I first came to the house, just because it was the best and the most comfortable, but I had to give it up. It was their room, and there's the big bed she died in, and the cupboard is in the thickness of the wall, near the head, on the left. That's where it likes to be kept, in its bandbox. I only used the room for a fortnight after I came, and then I turned out and took the little room downstairs, next to the surgery, where Luke used to sleep when he expected to be called to a patient during the night.

I was always a good sleeper ashore ; eight hours is my dose, eleven to seven when I'm alone, twelve to eight when I have a friend with me. But I could not sleep after three o'clock in the morning in that room—a quarter past, to be accurate—as a matter of fact, I timed it with my old pocket chronometer, which still keeps good time, and it was always at exactly seventeen minutes past three. I wonder whether that was the hour when she died ?

It was not what you have heard. If it had been that I could not have stood it two nights. It was just a start and a moan and hard breathing for a few seconds in the cupboard, and it could never have waked me under ordinary circumstances, I'm sure. I suppose you are like me in that, and we are just like other people who have been to sea. No natural sounds disturb us at all, not all the racket of a square-rigger hove to in a heavy gale, or rolling on her beam ends before the wind. But if a lead pencil gets adrift and rattles in the drawer of your cabin table you are awake in a moment. Just so—you always understand. Very well, the noise in the cupboard was no louder than that, but it waked me instantly.

I said it was like a " start." I know what I mean, but it's hard to explain without seeming to talk nonsense. Of course you cannot exactly " hear " a person " start ; " at the most, you might hear the quick drawing of the breath between the parted lips and closed teeth, and the almost imperceptible sound of clothing that moved suddenly though very slightly. It was like that.

You know how one feels what a sailing vessel is going to do, two or three seconds before she does it, when one has the wheel. Riders say the same of a horse, but that's less strange, because the horse is a live animal with feelings of its own, and only poets and landsmen talk about a ship being alive, and all that. But I have always felt somehow that besides being a steaming machine or a sailing machine for carrying weights, a vessel at sea is a sensitive instrument, and a means of communication between nature and man, and most particularly the man at the wheel, if she is steered by hand. She takes her impressions directly from wind and sea, tide and stream, and transmits them to the man's hand just as the wireless telegraph picks up the interrupted currents aloft and turns them out below in the form of a message.

You see what I am driving at ; I felt that something started in the cupboard, and I felt it so vividly that I heard it, though there may have been nothing to hear, and the sound inside my head waked me suddenly. But I really heard the other noise. It was as if it were muffled inside a box, as far away as if it came through a long-distance telephone ; and yet I knew that it was inside the cupboard near the head of my bed. My hair did not bristle and my blood did not run cold that time. I simply resented being waked up by something that had no business to make a noise, any more than a pencil should rattle in the drawer of my cabin table on board ship. For I did not understand ; I just supposed that the cupboard had some communication with the outside air, and that the wind had got in and was moaning through it with a sort of very faint screech. I struck a light and looked at my watch, and it was seventeen minutes past three. Then I turned over and went to sleep on my right ear. That's my good one ; I'm pretty deaf with the other, for I struck the water with it when I was a lad in diving from the foretopsail yard. Silly thing to do, it was, but the result is very convenient when I want to go to sleep when there's a noise.

That was the first night, and the same thing happened again and several times afterward, but not regularly, though it was always at the same time, to a second ; perhaps I was sometimes sleeping on my good ear, and sometimes not. I overhauled the cupboard and there was no way by which the wind could get in, or anything else, for the door makes a good fit, having been meant to keep out moths. I suppose Mrs.

Pratt must have kept her winter things in it, for it still smells of camphor and turpentine.

After about a fortnight I had had enough of the noises. So far I had said to myself that it would be silly to yield to it and take the skull out of the room. Things always look differently by daylight, don't they? But the voice grew louder —I suppose one may call it a voice—and it got inside my deaf ear, too, one night. I realised that when I was wide awake, for my good ear was jammed down on the pillow, and I ought not to have heard a fog-horn in that position. But I heard that, and it made me lose my temper, unless it scared me, for sometimes the two are not far apart. I struck a light and got up, and I opened the cupboard, grabbed the bandbox and three it out of the window, as far as I could.

Then my hair stood on end. The thing screamed in the air, like a shell from a twelve-inch gun. It fell on the other side of the road. The night was very dark, and I could not see it fall, but I know it fell beyond the road. The window is just over the front door, it's fifteen yards to the fence, more or less, and the road is ten yards wide. There's a quickset hedge beyond, along the glebe that belongs to the vicarage.

I did not sleep much more that night. It was not more than half an hour after I had thrown the bandbox out when I heard a shriek outside—like what we've heard to-night, but worse, more despairing, I should call it ; and it may have been my imagination, but I could have sworn that the screams came nearer and nearer each time. I lit my pipe, and walked up and down for a bit, and then took a book and sat up reading, but I'll be hanged if I can remember what I read nor even what the book was, for every now and then a shriek came up that would have made a dead man turn in his coffin.

A little before dawn some one knocked at the front door. There was no mistaking that for anything else, and I opened my window and looked down, for I guessed that some one wanted the doctor, supposing that the new man had taken Luke's house. It was rather a relief to hear a human knock after that awful noise.

You cannot see the door from above, owing to the little porch. The knocking came again, and I called out, asking who was there, but nobody answered, though the knock was repeated. I sang out again, and said that the doctor did not live here any longer. There was no answer, but it occurred to me that it might be some old countryman who was stone deaf. So I took my candle and went down to open the door.

Upon my word, I was not thinking of the thing yet, and I had almost forgotten the other noises. I went down convinced that I should find somebody outside, on the doorstep, with a message. I set the candle on the hall table, so that the wind should not blow it out when I opened the door. While I was drawing the old-fashioned bolt I heard the knocking again. It was not loud, and it had a queer, hollow sound, now that I was close to it, I remember, but I certainly thought it was made by some person who wanted to get in.

It wasn't. There was nobody there, but as I opened the door inward, standing a little on one side, so as to see out at once, something rolled across the threshold and stopped against my foot.

I drew back as I felt it, for I knew what it was before I looked down. I cannot tell you how I knew, and it seemed unreasonable, for I am still quite sure that I had thrown it across the road. It's a French window, that opens wide, and I got a good swing when I flung it out. Besides, when I went out early in the morning, I found the bandbox beyond the thickset hedge.

You may think it opened when I threw it, and that the skull dropped out ; but that's impossible, for nobody could throw an empty cardboard box so far. It's out of the question ; you might as well try to fling a ball of paper twenty-five yards, or a blown bird's egg.

To go back, I shut and bolted the hall door, picked the thing up carefully, and put it on the table beside the candle. I did that mechanically, as one instinctively does the right thing in danger without thinking at all—unless one does the opposite. It may seem odd, but I believe my first thought had been that somebody might come and find me there on the threshold while it was resting against my foot, lying a little on its side, and turning one hollow eye up at my face, as if it meant to accuse me. And the light and shadow from the candle played in the hollows of the eyes as it stood on the table, so that they seemed to open and shut at me. Then the candle went out quite unexpectedly, though the door was fastened and there was not the least draught ; and I used up at least half a dozen matches before it would burn again.

I sat down rather suddenly, without quite knowing why. Probably I had been badly frightened, and perhaps you will admit there was no great shame in being scared. The thing had come home, and it wanted to go upstairs, back to its cupboard. I sat still and stared at it for a bit, till I began to feel very cold ; then I took it and carried it up and set it in its place, and I remember that I spoke to it, and promised that it should have its bandbox again in the morning.

You want to know whether I stayed in the room till day-break ? Yes, but I kept a light burning, and sat up smoking and reading, most likely out of fright ; plain, undeniable fear, and you need not call it cowardice either, for that's not the same thing. I could not have stayed alone with that thing in the cupboard ; I should have been scared to death, though I'm not more timid than other people. Confound it all, man, it had crossed the road alone, and had got up the doorstep, and had knocked to be let in.

When the dawn came, I put on my boots and went out to find the bandbox. I had to go a good way round, by the gate near the highroad, and I found the box open and hanging on the other side of the hedge. It had caught on the twigs by the string, and the lid had fallen off and was lying on the ground below it. That shows that it did not open till it was well over ; and if it had not opened as soon as it left my hand, what was inside it must have gone beyond the road too.

That's all. I took the box upstairs to the cupboard, and put the skull back and locked it up. When the girl brought me my breakfast she said she was sorry, but that she must go, and she did not care if she lost her month's wages. I looked at her, and her face was a sort of greenish, yellowish, white. I pretended to be surprised, and asked what was the matter ; but that was of no use, for she just turned on me and wanted to know whether I meant to stay in a haunted house, and how long I expected to live if I did, for though she noticed I was sometimes a little hard of hearing, she did not believe that even I could sleep through those screams again—and if I could, why had I been moving about the house and opening and shutting the front door, between three and four in the morning ? There was no answering that since she had heard me, so off she went, and I was left to myself. I went down to the village during the morning and found a woman who was willing to come and do the little work there is and cook my dinner, on condition that she might go home every night. As for me, I moved downstairs that day, and I have never tried to sleep in the best bedroom since. After a little while I got a brace of middle-aged Scotch servants from London, and things were quiet enough for a long time. I began by telling them that the house was in a very exposed position, and that the wind whistled round it a good deal in

the autumn and winter, which had given it a bad name in
the village, the Cornish people being inclined to superstition
and telling ghost stories. The two hard-faced, sandy-haired
sisters almost smiled, and they answered with great contempt
that they had no great opinion of any Southern bogey whatever, having been in service in two English haunted houses,
where they had never seen so much as the Boy in Gray,
whom they reckoned no very particular rarity in Forfarshire.

They stayed with me several months, and while they were
in the house we had peace and quiet. One of them is here
again now, but she went away with her sister within the year.
This one—she was the cook—married the sexton, who works
in my garden. That's the way of it. It's a small village and
he has not much to do, and he knows enough about flowers
to help me nicely, besides doing most of the hard work ; for
though I'm fond of exercise, I'm getting a little stiff in the
hinges. He's a sober, silent sort of fellow, who minds his
own business, and he was a widower when I came here—
Trehearn is his name, James Trehearn. The Scotch sisters
would not admit that there was anything wrong about the
house, but when November came they gave me warning that
they were going, on the ground that the chapel was such a
long walk from here, being in the next parish, and that they
could not possibly go to our church. But the younger one
came back in the spring, and as soon as the banns could be
published she was married to James Trehearn by the vicar,
and she seems to have had no scruples about hearing him
preach since then. I'm quite satisfied, if she is ! The couple
live in a small cottage that looks over the churchyard.

I suppose you are wondering what all this has to do with
what I was talking about. I'm alone so much that when an
old friend comes to see me, I sometimes go on talking just
for the sake of hearing my own voice. But in this case there
is really a connection of ideas. It was James Trehearn who
buried poor Mrs. Pratt, and her husband after her in the same
grave, and it's not far from the back of his cottage. That's
the connection in my mind, you see. It's plain enough. He
knows something ; I'm quite sure that he does, by his manner,
though he's such a reticent beggar.

Yes, I'm alone in the house at night now, for Mrs. Trehearn
does everything herself, and when I have a friend the sexton's
niece comes in to wait on the table. He takes his wife home
every evening in winter, but in summer, when there's light,
she goes by herself. She's not a nervous woman, but she's

less sure than she used to be that there are no bogies in England
worth a Scotch-woman's notice. Isn't it amusing, the idea
that Scotland has a monopoly of the supernatural ? Odd sort
of national pride, I call that, don't you ?

That's a good fire, isn't it ? When drift-wood gets started
at last there's nothing like it, I think. Yes, we get lots of it,
for I'm sorry to say there are still a great many wrecks about
here. It's a lonely coast, and you may have all the wood you
want for the trouble of bringing it in. Trehearn and I borrow
a cart now and then, and load it between here and the Spit.
I hate a coal fire when I can get wood of any sort. A log is
company, even if it's only a piece of a deck-beam or timber
sawn off, and the salt in it makes pretty sparks. See how
they fly, like Japanese hand-fireworks ! Upon my word, with
an old friend and a good fire and a pipe, one forgets all about
that thing upstairs, especially now that the wind has moderated.
It's only a lull, though, and it will blow a gale before morning.

You think you would like to see the skull ? I've no objection. There's no reason why you shouldn't have a look at it,
and you never saw a more perfect one in your life, except
that there are two front teeth missing in the lower jaw.

Oh yes—I had not told you about the jaw yet. Trehearn
found it in the garden last spring when he was digging a
pit for a new asparagus bed. You know we make asparagus
beds six or eight feet deep here. Yes, yes—I had forgotten
to tell you that. He was digging straight down, just as he
digs a grave ; if you want a good asparagus bed made, I
advise you to get a sexton to make it for you. Those fellows
have a wonderful knack at that sort of digging.

Trehearn had got down about three feet when he cut into
a mass of white lime in the side of the trench. He had noticed
that the earth was a little looser there, though he says it had
not been disturbed for a number of years. I suppose he thought
that even old lime might not be good for asparagus, so he
broke it out and threw it up. It was pretty hard, he says, in
biggish lumps, and out of sheer force of habit he cracked the
lumps with his spade as they lay outside the pit beside him ;
the jawbone of a skull dropped out of one of the pieces. He
thinks he must have knocked out the two front teeth in
breaking up the lime, but he did not see them anywhere.
He's a very experienced man in such things, as you may
imagine, and he said at once that the jaw had probably belonged to a young woman, and that the teeth had been complete
when she died. He brought it to me, and asked me if I wanted

to keep it ; if I did not, he said he would drop it into the next grave he made in the churchyard, as he supposed it was a Christian jaw, and ought to have decent burial, wherever the rest of the body might be. I told him that doctors often put bones into quicklime to whiten them nicely, and that I supposed Dr. Pratt had once had a little lime pit in the garden for that purpose, and had forgotten the jaw. Trehearn looked at me quietly.

"Maybe it fitted that skull that used to be in the cupboard upstairs, sir," he said. "Maybe Dr. Pratt had put the skull into the lime to clean it, or something, and when he took it out he left the lower jaw behind. There's some human hair sticking in the lime, sir."

I saw there was, and that was what Trehearn said. If he did not suspect something, why in the world should he have suggested that the jaw might fit the skull ? Besides, it did. That's proof that he knows more than he cares to tell. Do you suppose he looked before she was buried ? Or perhaps— when he buried Luke in the same grave——

Well, well, it's of no use to go over that, is it ? I said I would keep the jaw with the skull, and I took it upstairs and fitted it into its place. There's not the slightest doubt about the two belonging together, and together they are.

Trehearn knows several things. We were talking about plastering the kitchen a while ago, and he happened to remember that it had not been done since the very week when Mrs. Pratt died. He did not say that the mason must have left some lime on the place, but he thought it, and that it was the very same lime he had found in the asparagus pit. He knows a lot. Trehearn is one of your silent beggars who can put two and two together. That grave is very near the back of his cottage, too, and he's one of the quickest men with a spade I ever saw. If he wanted to know the truth, he could, and no one else would ever be the wiser unless he chose to tell. In a quiet village like ours, people don't go and spend the night in the churchyard to see whether the sexton potters about by himself between ten o'clock and daylight.

What is awful to think of, is Luke's deliberation, if he did it ; his cool certainty that no one would find him out ; above all, his nerve, for that must have been extraordinary. I sometimes think it's bad enough to live in the place where it was done, if it really was done. I always put in the condition, you see, for the sake of his memory, and a little bit for my own sake, too.

I'll go upstairs and fetch the box in a minute. Let me light my pipe ; there's no hurry ! We had supper early, and it's only half-past nine o'clock. I never let a friend go to bed before twelve, or with less than three glasses—you may have as many more as you like, but you shan't have less, for the sake of old times.

It's breezing up again, do you hear ? That was only a lull just now, and we are going to have a bad night.

A thing happened that made me start a little when I found that the jaw fitted exactly. I'm not very easily startled in that way myself, but I have seen people make a quick movement, drawing their breath sharply, when they had thought they were alone and suddenly turned and saw some one very near them. Nobody can call that fear. You wouldn't, would you ? No. Well, just when I had set the jaw in its place under the skull, the teeth closed sharply on my finger. It felt exactly as if it were biting me hard, and I confess that I jumped before I realised that I had been pressing the jaw and the skull together with my other hand. I assure you I was not at all nervous. It was broad daylight, too, and a fine day, and the sun was streaming into the best bedroom. It would have been absurd to be nervous, and it was only a quick mistaken impression, but it really made me feel queer. Somehow it made me think of the funny verdict of the coroner's jury on Luke's death, " by the hand or teeth of some person or animal unknown." Ever since that I've wished I had seen those marks on his throat, though the lower jaw was missing then.

I have often seen a man do insane things with his hands that he does not realise at all. I once saw a man hanging on by an old awning stop with one hand, leaning backward, outboard, with all his weight on it, and he was just cutting the stop with the knife in his other hand when I got my arms round him. We were in mid-ocean, going twenty knots. He had not the smallest idea what he was doing ; neither had I when I managed to pinch my finger between the teeth of that thing. I can feel it now. It was exactly as if it were alive and were trying to bite me. It would if it could, for I know it hates me, poor thing ! Do you suppose that what rattles about inside is really a bit of lead ? Well, I'll get the box down presently, and if whatever it is happens to drop out into your hands that's your affair. If it's only a clod of earth or a pebble, the whole matter would be off my mind, and I don't believe I should ever think of the skull again ; but somehow I cannot bring myself to shake out the bit of hard stuff myself. The mere idea that it may be lead makes me confoundedly uncomfortable, yet I've got the conviction that I shall know before long. I shall certainly know. I'm sure Trehearn knows, but he's such a silent beggar.

I'll go upstairs now and get it. What ? You had better go with me ? Ha, ha ! do you think I'm afraid of a bandbox and a noise ? Nonsense !

Bother the candle, it won't light ! As if the ridiculous thing understood what it's wanted for ! Look at that—the third match. They light fast enough for my pipe. There, do you see ? It's a fresh box, just out of the tin safe where I keep the supply on account of the dampness. Oh, you think the wick of the candle may be damp, do you ? All right, I'll light the beastly thing in the fire. That won't go out, at all events. Yes, it sputters a bit, but it will keep lighted now. It burns just like any other candle, doesn't it ? The fact is, candles are not very good about here. I don't know where they come from, but they have a way of burning low occasionally, with a greenish flame that spits tiny sparks, and I'm often annoyed by their going out of themselves. It cannot be helped, for it will be long before we have electricity in our village. It really is rather a poor light, isn't it ?

You think I had better leave you the candle and take the lamp, do you ? I don't like to carry lamps about, that's the truth. I never dropped one in my life, but I have always thought I might, and it's so confoundedly dangerous if you do. Besides, I am pretty well used to these rotten candles by this time.

You may as well finish that glass while I'm getting it, for I don't mean to let you off with less than three before you go to bed. You won't have to go upstairs, either, for I've put you in the old study next to the surgery—that's where I live myself. The fact is, I never ask a friend to sleep upstairs now. The last man who did was Crackenthorpe, and he said he was kept awake all night. You remember old Crack, don't you ? He stuck to the Service, and they've just made him an admiral. Yes, I'm off now—unless the candle goes out. I couldn't help asking if you remembered Crackenthorpe. If any one had told us that the skinny little idiot he used to be was to turn out the most successful of the lot of us, we should have laughed at the idea, shouldn't we ? You and I did not do badly, it's true—but I'm really going now. I don't mean to let you think that I've been putting it off by talking ! As if there were anything to be afraid of ! If I were scared,

I should tell you so quite frankly, and get you to go upstairs with me.

*   *   *   *   *   *

Here's the box. I brought it down very carefully, so as not to disturb it, poor thing. You see, if it were shaken, the jaw might get separated from it again, and I'm sure it wouldn't like that. Yes, the candle went out as I was coming downstairs, but that was the draught from the leaky window on the landing. Did you hear anything ? Yes, there was another scream. Am I pale, do you say ? That's nothing. My heart is a little queer sometimes, and I went upstairs too fast. In fact, that's one reason why I really prefer to live altogether on the ground floor.

Wherever that shriek came from, it was not from the skull, for I had the box in my hand when I heard the noise, and here it is now ; so we have proved definitely that the screams are produced by something else. I've no doubt I shall find out some day what makes them. Some crevice in the wall, of course, or a crack in a chimney, or a chink in the frame of a window. That's the way all ghost stories end in real life. Do you know, I'm jolly glad I thought of going up and bringing it down for you to see, for that last shriek settles the question. To think that I should have been so weak as to fancy that the poor skull could really cry out like a living thing !

Now I'll open the box, and we'll take it out and look at it under the bright light. It's rather awful to think that the poor lady used to sit there, in your chair, evening after evening, in just the same light, isn't it ? But then—I've made up my mind that it's all rubbish from beginning to end, and that it's just an old skull that Luke had when he was a student ; and perhaps he put it into the lime merely to whiten it, and could not find the jaw.

I made a seal on the string, you see, after I had put the jaw in its place, and I wrote on the cover. There's the old white label on it still, from the milliner's, addressed to Mrs. Pratt when the hat was sent to her, and as there was room I wrote on the edge : " A skull, once the property of the late Luke Pratt, M.D." I don't quite know why I wrote that, unless it was with the idea of explaining how the thing happened to be in my possession. I cannot help wondering sometimes what sort of hat it was that came in the bandbox. What colour was it, do you think ? Was it a gay spring hat with a bobbing feather and pretty ribands ? Strange that the very same box should hold the head that wore the finery—perhaps. No—

we made up our minds that it just came from the hospital in London where Luke did his time. It's far better to look at it in that light, isn't it ? There's no more connection between that skull and poor Mrs. Pratt than there was between my story about the lead and——

Good Lord ! Take the lamp—don't let it go out, if you can help it—I'll have the window fastened again in a second— I say, what a gale ! There, it's out ! I told you so ! Never mind, there's the firelight—I've got the window shut—the bolt was only half down. Was the box blown off the table ? Where the deuce is it ? There ! That won't open again, for I've put up the bar. Good dodge, an old-fashioned bar—there's nothing like it. Now, you find the bandbox while I light the lamp. Confound those wretched matches ! Yes, a pipe spill is better —it must light in the fire—I hadn't thought of it—thank you —there we are again. Now, where's the box ? Yes, put it back on the table, and we'll open it.

That's the first time I have ever known the wind to burst that window open ; but it was partly carelessness on my part when I last shut it. Yes, of course I heard the scream. It seemed to go all round the house before it broke in at the window. That proves that it's always been the wind and nothing else, doesn't it ? When it was not the wind, it was my imagination. I've always been a very imaginative man : I must have been, though I did not know it. As we grow older we understand ourselves better, don't you know ?

I'll have a drop of the Hulstkamp neat, by way of an exception, since you are filling up your glass. That damp gust chilled me, and with my rheumatic tendency I'm very much afraid of a chill, for the cold sometimes seems to stick in my joints all winter when it once gets in.

By George, that's good stuff ! I'll just light a fresh pipe, now that everything is snug again, and then we'll open the box. I'm so glad we heard that last scream together, with the skull here on the table between us, for a thing cannot possibly be in two places at the same time, and the noise most certainly came from outside as any noise the wind makes must. You thought you heard it scream through the room after the window was burst open ? Oh yes, so did I, but that was natural enough when everything was open. Of course we heard the wind. What could one expect ?

Look here, please. I want you to see that the seal is intact before we open the box together. Will you take my glasses ? No, you have your own. All right. The seal is sound, you

see, and you can read the words of the motto easily. " Sweet
and low "—that's it—because the poem goes on " Wind of
the Western sea," and says, " blow him again to me," and
all that. Here is the seal on my watch-chain, where it's hung
for more than forty years. My poor little wife gave it to me
when I was courting, and I never had any other. It was just
like her to think of those words—she was always fond of
Tennyson.

It's of no use to cut the string, for it's fastened to the box,
so I'll just break the wax and untie the knot, and afterward
we'll seal it up again. You see, I like to feel that the thing
is safe in its place, and that nobody can take it out. Not that
I should suspect Trehearn of meddling with it, but I always
feel that he knows a lot more than he tells.

You see, I've managed it without breaking the string,
though when I fastened it I never expected to open the bandbox again. The lid comes off easily enough. There! Now
look !

What ? Nothing in it ? Empty ? It's gone, man, the skull
is gone !

*   *   *   *   *   *

No, there's nothing the matter with me. I'm only trying
to collect my thoughts. It's so strange. I'm positively certain
that it was inside when I put on the seal last spring. I can't
have imagined that : it's utterly impossible. If I ever took
a stiff glass with a friend now and then, I would admit that
I might have made some idiotic mistake when I had taken
too much. But I don't, and I never did. A pint of ale at
supper and half a go of rum at bedtime was the most I ever
took in my good days. I believe it's always we sober fellows
who get rheumatism and gout ! Yet there was my seal, and
there is the empty bandbox. That's plain enough.

I say, I don't half like this. It's not right. There's something wrong about it, in my opinion. You needn't talk to me
about supernatural manifestations, for I don't believe in them,
not a little bit ! Somebody must have tampered with the seal
and stolen the skull. Sometimes, when I go out to work in the
garden in summer, I leave my watch and chain on the table.
Trehearn must have taken the seal then, and used it, for he
would be quite sure that I should not come in for at least an
hour.

If it was not Trehearn—oh, don't talk to me about the
possibility that the thing has got out by itself ! If it has, it
must be somewhere about the house, in some out-of-the-way

corner, waiting. We may come upon it anywhere, waiting for us, don't you know ?—just waiting in the dark. Then it will scream at me ; it will shriek at me in the dark, for it hates me, I tell you !

The bandbox is quite empty. We are not dreaming, either of us. There, I turn it upside down.

What's that ? Something fell out as I turned it over. It's on the floor, it's near your feet, I know it is, and we must find it ! Help me to find it, man. Have you got it ? For God's sake, give it to me quickly !

Lead ! I knew it when I heard it fall ; I knew it couldn't be anything else by the little thud it made on the hearth-rug. So it was lead after all, and Luke did it.

I feel a little bit shaken up—not exactly nervous, you know but badly shaken up, that's the fact. Anybody would, I should think. After all, you cannot say that it's fear of the thing, for I went up and brought it down—at least, I believed I was bringing it down, and that's the same thing, and by George, rather than give in to such silly nonsense, I'll take the box upstairs again and put it back in its place. It's not that. It's the certainty that the poor little woman came to her end in that way, by my fault, because I told the story. That's what is so dreadful. Somehow, I had always hoped that I should never be quite sure of it, but there is no doubting it now. Look at that !

Look at it ! That little lump of lead with no particular shape. Think of what it did, man ! Doesn't it make you shiver ? He gave her something to make her sleep, of course, but there must have been one moment of awful agony. Think of having boiling lead poured into your brain. Think of it. She was dead before she could scream, but only think of—oh ! there it is again—it's just outside—I know it's just outside— I can't keep it out of my head !—oh !—oh !

* * * * * *

You thought I had fainted ? No, I wish I had, for it would have stopped sooner. It's all very well to say that it's only a noise, and that a noise never hurt anybody—you're as white as a shroud yourself. There's only one thing to be done, if we hope to close an eye to-night. We must find it and put it back into its bandbox and shut it up in the cupboard, where it likes to be. I don't know how it got out, but it wants to get in again. That's why it screams so awfully to-night— it was never so bad as this—never since I first . . .

Bury it ? Yes, if we can find it, we'll bury it, if it takes us all night. We'll bury it six feet deep and ram down the earth over it, so that it shall never get out again, and if it screams we shall hardly hear it so deep down. Quick, we'll get the lantern and look for it. It cannot be far away ; I'm sure it's just outside—it was coming in when I shut the window, I know it.

Yes, you're quite right. I'm losing my senses, and I must get hold of myself. Don't speak to me for a minute or two ; I'll sit quite still and keep my eyes shut and repeat something I know. That's the best way.

" Add together the altitude, the latitude, and the polar distance, divide by two and subtract the altitude from the half-sum ; then add the logarithm of the secant of the latitude, and cosecant of the polar distance, the cosine of the half-sum and the sine of the half-sum minus the altitude "—there ! Don't say that I'm out of my senses, for my memory is all right, isn't it ?

Of course, you may say that it's mechanical, and that we never forget the things we learned when we were boys and have used almost every day for a lifetime. But that's the very point. When a man is going crazy, it's the mechanical p rt of his mind that gets out of order and won't work right ; he remembers things that never happened, or he sees things that aren't real, or he hears noises when there is perfect silence. That's not what is the matter with either of us, is it ?

Come, we'll get the lantern and go round the house. It's not raining—only blowing like old boots, as we used to say. The lantern is in the cupboard under the stairs in the hall, and I always keep it trimmed in case of a wreck.

No use to look for the thing ? I don't see how you can say that. It was nonsense to talk of burying it, of course, for it doesn't want to be buried ; it wants to go back into its bandbox and be taken upstairs, poor thing ! Trehearn took it out, I know, and made the seal over again. Perhaps he took it to the churchyard, and he may have meant well. I daresay he thought that it would not scream any more if it were quietly laid in consecrated ground, near where it belonçs. But it has come home. Yes, that's it. He's not half a bad fellow, Trehearn, and rather religiously inclined, I think. Does not that sound natural, and reasonable, and well meant ? He supposed it screamed because it was not decently buried— with the rest. But he was wrong. How should he know that it screams at me because it hates me, and because it's my fault that there was that little lump of lead in it ?

No use to look for it, anyhow ? Nonsense ! I tell you it wants to be found—hark ! What's that knocking ? Do you hear it ? Knock—knock—knock—three times, then a pause, and then again. It has a hollow sound, hasn't it ?

It has come home. I've heard that knock before. It wants to come in and be taken upstairs, in its box. It's at the front door.

Will you come with me ? We'll take it in. Yes, I own that I don't like to go alone and open the door. The thing will roll in and stop against my foot, just as it did before, and the light will go out. I'm a good deal shaken by finding that bit of lead, and, besides, my heart isn't quite right—too much strong tobacco, perhaps. Besides, I'm quite willing to own that I'm a bit nervous to-night, if I never was before in my life.

That's right, come along ! I'll take the box with me, so as not to come back. Do you hear the knocking ? It's not like any other knocking I ever heard. If you will hold this door open, I can find the lantern under the stairs by the light from this room without bringing the lamp into the hall—it would only go out.

The thing knows we are coming—hark ! It's impatient to get in. Don't shut the door till the lantern is ready, whatever you do. There will be the usual trouble with the matches, I suppose—no, the first one, by Jove ! I tell you it wants to get in, so there's no trouble. All right with that door now ; shut it, please. Now come and hold the lantern, for it's blowing so hard outside that I shall have to use both hands. That's it, hold the light low. Do you hear the knocking still ? Here goes—I'll open just enough, with my foot against the bottom of the door—now !

Catch it ! it's only the wind that blows it across the floor, that's all—there's half a hurricane outside, I tell you ! Have you got it ? The bandbox is on the table. One minute, and I'll have the bar up. There !

Why did you throw it into the box so roughly ? It doesn't like that, you know.

What do you say ? Bitten your hand ? Nonsense, man ! You did just what I did. You pressed the jaws together with your other hand and pinched yourself. Let me see. You don't mean to say you have drawn blood ? You must have squeezed hard, by Jove, for the skin is certainly torn. I'll give you some carbolic solution for it before we go to bed, for they say a scratch from a skull's tooth may go bad and give trouble.

Come inside again and let me see it by the lamp. I'll bring the bandbox—never mind the lantern, it may just as well burn in the hall, for I shall need it presently when I go up the stairs. Yes, shut the door if you will ; it makes it more cheerful and bright. Is your finger still bleeding ? I'll get you the carbolic in an instant ; just let me see the thing.

Ugh ! There's a drop of blood on the upper jaw. It's on the eye-tooth. Ghastly, isn't it ? When I saw it running along the floor of the hall, the strength almost went out of my hands and I felt my knees bending ; then I understood that it was the gale, driving it over the smooth boards. You don't blame me ? No, I should think not ! We were boys together, and we've seen a thing or two, and we may just as well own to each other that we were both in a beastly funk when it slid across the floor at you. No wonder you pinched your finger picking it up, after that, if I did the same thing out of sheer nervousness in broad daylight, with the sun streaming in on me.

Strange that the jaw should stick to it so closely, isn't it ? I suppose it's the dampness, for it shuts like a vice—I have wiped off the drop of blood, for it was not nice to look at. I'm not going to try to open the jaws, don't be afraid ! I shall not play any tricks with the poor thing, but I'll just seal the box again, and we'll take it upstairs and put it away where it wants to be. The wax is on the writing-table by the window. Thank you. It will be long before I leave my seal lying about again, for Trehearn to use, I can tell you. Explain ? I don't explain natural phenomena, but if you choose to think that Trehearn had hidden it somewhere in the bushes, and that the gale blew it to the house against the door, and made it knock, as if it wanted to be let in, you're not thinking the impossible, and I'm quite ready to agree with you.

Do you see that ? You can swear that you've actually seen me seal it this time, in case anything of the kind should occur again. The wax fastens the strings to the lid, which cannot possibly be lifted, even enough to get in one finger. You're quite satisfied, aren't you ? Yes. Besides, I shall lock the cupboard and keep the key in my pocket hereafter.

Now we can take the lantern and go upstairs. Do you know ? I'm very much inclined to agree with your theory that the wind blew it against the house. I'll go ahead, for I know the stairs ; just hold the lantern near my feet as we go up. How the wind howls and whistles ! Did you feel the sand on the floor under your shoes as we crossed the hall ?

Yes—this is the door of the best bedroom. Hold up the

lantern, please. This side, by the head of the bed. I left the cupboard open when I got the box. Isn't it queer how the faint odour of women's dresses will hang about an old closet for years ? This is the shelf. You've seen me set the box there, and now you see me turn the key and put it into my pocket. So that's done !

* * * * * *

Good-night. Are you sure you're quite comfortable ? It's not much of a room, but I daresay you would as soon sleep here as upstairs to-night. If you want anything, sing out ; there's only a lath and plaster partition between us. There's not so much wind on this side by half. There's the Hollands on the table, if you'll have one more nightcap. No ? Well, do as you please. Good-night again, and don't dream about that thing if you can.

* * * * * *

The following paragraph appeared in the *Penradden News*, 23rd November, 1906 :

MYSTERIOUS DEATH OF A RETIRED SEA CAPTAIN

The village of Tredcombe is much disturbed by the strange death of Captain Charles Braddock, and all sorts of impossible stories are circulating with regard to the circumstances, which certainly seem difficult of explanation. The retired captain, who had successively commanded in his time the largest and fastest liners belonging to one of the principal transatlantic steamship companies, was found dead in his bed on Tuesday morning in his own cottage, a quarter of a mile from the village. An examination was made at once by the local practitioner, which revealed the horrible fact that the deceased had been bitten in the throat by a human assailant, with such amazing force as to crush the windpipe and cause death. The marks of the teeth of both jaws were so plainly visible on the skin that they could be counted, but the perpetrator of the deed had evidently lost the two lower middle incisors. It is hoped that this peculiarity may help to identify the murderer, who can only be a dangerous escaped maniac. The deceased, though over sixty-five years of age, is said to have been a hale man of considerable physical strength,

and it is remarkable that no signs of any struggle were
visible in the room, nor could it be ascertained how the
murderer had entered the house. Warning has been sent
to all the insane asylums in the United Kingdom, but as
yet no information has been received regarding the escape
of any dangerous patient.

The Coroner's jury returned the somewhat singular
verdict that Captain Braddock came to his death " by the
hands or teeth of some person unknown." The local
surgeon is said to have expressed privately the opinion
that the maniac is a woman, a view he deduces from the
small size of the jaws, as shown by the marks of the teeth.
The whole affair is shrouded in mystery. Captain
Braddock was a widower, and lived alone. He leaves no
children.

[*Note*—Students of ghost lore and haunted houses will
find the foundation of the foregoing story in the legends
about a skull which is still preserved in the farmhouse
called Bettiscombe Manor, situated, I believe, on the
Dorsetshire coast.]

THE IDIOTS

By

JOSEPH CONRAD

W E were driving along the road from Treguier to Ker-
vanda. We passed at a smart trot between the hedges
topping an earth wall on each side of the road ; then
at the foot of the steep ascent before Ploumar the horse dropped
into a walk, and the driver jumped down heavily from the box.
He flicked his whip and climbed the incline, stepping clumsily
uphill by the side of the carriage, one hand on the footboard,
his eyes on the ground. After a while he lifted his head, pointed
up the road with the end of the whip, and said—
" The idiot ! "
The sun was shining violently upon the undulating surface
of the land. The rises were topped by clumps of meagre trees,
with their branches showing high on the sky as if they had been
perched upon stilts. The small fields, cut up by hedges and
stone walls that zigzagged over the slopes, lay in rectangular
patches of vivid greens and yellows, resembling the unskilful
daubs of a naïve picture. And the landscape was divided in
two by the white streak of a road stretching in long loops far
away, like a river of dust crawling out of the hills on its way to
the sea.
" Here he is," said the driver, again.
In the long grass bordering the road a face glided past the
carriage at the level of the wheels as we drove slowly by. The
imbecile face was red, and the bullet head with close-cropped
hair seemed to lie alone, its chin in the dust. The body was
lost in the bushes growing thick along the bottom of the deep
ditch.
It was a boy's face. He might have been sixteen, judging
from the size—perhaps less, perhaps more. Such creatures are
forgotten by time, and live untouched by years till death gathers

them up into its compassionate bosom ; the faithful death that
never forgets in the press of work the most insignificant of its
children.

" Ah ! there's another," said the man, with a certain satisfaction in his tone, as if he had caught sight of something
expected.

There was another. That one stood nearly in the middle
of the road in the blaze of sunshine at the end of his own short
shadow. And he stood with hands pushed into the opposite
sleeves of his long coat, his head sunk between the shoulders,
all hunched up in the flood of heat. From a distance he had
the aspect of one suffering from intense cold.

" Those are twins," explained the driver.

The idiot shuffled two paces out of the way and looked at us
over his shoulder when we brushed past him. The glance was
unseeing and staring, a fascinated glance ; but he did not turn
to look after us. Probably the image passed before the eyes
without leaving any trace on the misshapen brain of the creature. When we had topped the ascent I looked over the hood.
He stood in the road just where we had left him.

The driver clambered into his seat, clicked his tongue, and
we went down hill. The brake squeaked horribly from time
to time. At the foot he eased off the noisy mechanism and said,
turning half round on his box—

" We shall see some more of them by-and-by."

" More idiots ?   How many of them are there, then ? " I
asked.

" There's four of them—children of a farmer near Ploumar
here. . . .   The parents are dead now," he added, after a while.
" The grandmother lives on the farm. In the daytime they
knock about on this road, and they come home at dusk along
with the cattle. . . .   It's a good farm." .

We saw the other two : a boy and a girl, as the driver said.
They were dressed exactly alike, in shapeless garments with
petticoat-like skirts. The imperfect thing that lived within
them moved those beings to howl at us from the top of the
bank, where they sprawled amongst the tough stalks of furze.
Their cropped black heads stuck out from the bright yellow
wall of countless small blossoms. The faces were purple with
the strain of yelling ; the voices sounded blank and cracked
like a mechanical imitation of old people's voices ; and suddenly
ceased when we turned into a lane.

I saw them many times in my wandering about the country.
They lived on that road, drifting along its length here and

there, according to the inexplicable impulses of their monstrous darkness. They were an offence to the sunshine, a reproach to empty heaven, a blight on the concentrated and purposeful vigour of the wild landscape. In time the story of their parents shaped itself before me out of the listless answers to my questions, out of the indifferent words heard in wayside inns or on the very road those idiots haunted. Some of it was told by an emaciated and sceptical old fellow with a tremendous whip, while we trudged together over the sands by the side of a two-wheeled cart loaded with dripping seaweed. Then at other times other people confirmed and completed the story : till it stood at last before me, a tale formidable and simple, as they always are, those disclosures of obscure trials endured by ignorant hearts.

When he returned from his military service Jean-Pierre Bacadou found the old people very much aged. He remarked with pain that the work of the farm was not satisfactorily done. The father had not the energy of old days. The hands did not feel over them the eye of the master. Jean-Pierre noted with sorrow that the heap of manure in the courtyard before the only entrance to the house was not so large as it should have been. The fences were out of repair, and the cattle suffered from neglect. At home the mother was practically bedridden, and the girls chattered loudly in the big kitchen, unrebuked, from morning to night. He said to himself : " We must change all this." He talked the matter over with his father one evening when the rays of the setting sun entering the yard between the outhouses ruled the heavy shadows with luminous streaks. Over the manure heap floated a mist, opal-tinted and odorous, and the marauding hens would stop in their scratching to examine with a sudden glance of their round eye the two men, both lean and tall, talking in hoarse tones. The old man, all twisted with rheumatism and bowed with years of work, the younger bony and straight, spoke without gestures in the indifferent manner of peasants, grave and slow. But before the sun had set the father had submitted to the sensible arguments of the son. " It is not for me that I am speaking," insisted Jean-Pierre. " It is for the land. It's a pity to see it badly used. I am not impatient for myself." The old fellow nodded over his stick. " I dare say ; I dare say," he muttered. " You may be right. Do what you like. It's the mother that will be pleased."

The mother was pleased with her daughter-in-law. Jeane-Pierre brought the two-wheeled spring-cart with a rush into

the yard. The grey horse galloped clumsily, and the bride
and bridegroom, sitting side by side, were jerked backwards
and forwards by the up and down motion of the shafts, in a
manner regular and brusque. On the road the distanced
wedding guests straggled in pairs and groups. The men
advanced with heavy steps, swinging their idle arms. They
were clad in town clothes : jackets cut with clumsy smartness,
hard black hats, immense boots, polished highly. Their
women all in simple black, with white caps and shawls of faded
tints folded triangularly on the back, strolled lightly by their
side. In front the violin sang a strident tune, and the biniou
snored and hummed, while the player capered solemnly, lifting
high his heavy clogs. The sombre procession drifted in and
out of the narrow lanes, through sunshine and through shade,
between fields and hedgerows, scaring the little birds that
darted away in troops right and left. In the yard of Bacadou's
farm the dark ribbon wound itself up into a mass of men and
women pushing at the door with cries and greetings. The
wedding dinner was remembered for months. It was a splendid
feast in the orchard. Farmers of considerable means and excellent repute were to be found sleeping in ditches, all along
the road to Treguier, even as late as the afternoon of the next
day. All the countryside participated in the happiness of
Jean-Pierre. He remained sober, and, together with his quiet
wife, kept out of the way, letting father and mother reap their
due of honour and thanks. But the next day he took hold
strongly, and the old folks felt a shadow—precursor of the grave
—fall upon them finally. The world is to the young.

When the twins were born there was plenty of room in the
house, for the mother of Jean-Pierre had gone away to dwell
under a heavy stone in the cemetery of Ploumar. On that day,
for the first time since his son's marriage, the elder Bacadou,
neglected by the cackling lot of strange women who thronged
the kitchen, left in the morning his seat under the mantel of the
fireplace, and went into the empty cow-house, shaking his
white locks dismally. Grandsons were all very well, but he
wanted his soup at midday. When shown the babies, he stared
at them with a fixed gaze, and muttered something like : " It's
too much." Whether he meant too much happiness, or simply
commented upon the number of his descendants, it is impossible to say. He looked offended—as far as his old wooden face
could express anything ; and for days afterwards could be seen,
almost any time of the day, sitting at the gate, with his nose
over his knees, a pipe between his gums, and gathered up into

a kind of raging concentrated sulkiness. Once he spoke to his son, alluding to the newcomers with a groan : " They will quarrel over the land." " Don't bother about that, father," answered Jean-Pierre, stolidly, and passed, bent double, towing a recalcitrant cow over his shoulder.

He was happy, and so was Susan, his wife. It was not an ethereal joy welcoming new souls to struggle, perchance to victory. In fourteen years both boys would be a help ; and, later on, Jean-Pierre pictured two big sons striding over the land from patch to patch, wringing tribute from the earth beloved and fruitful. Susan was happy too, for she did not want to be spoken of as the unfortunate woman, and now she had children no one could call her that. Both herself and her husband had seen something of the larger world—he during the time of his service ; while she had spent a year or so in Paris with a Breton family ; but had been too home-sick to remain longer away from the hilly and green country, set in a barren circle of rocks and sands, where she had been born. She thought that one of the boys ought perhaps to be a priest, but said nothing to her husband, who was a republican, and hated the " crows," as he called the ministers of religion. The christening was a splendid affair. All the commune came to it, for the Bacadous were rich and influential, and, now and then, did not mind the expense. The grandfather had a new coat.

Some months afterwards, one evening when the kitchen had been swept, and the door locked, Jean-Pierre, looking at the cot, asked his wife : " What's the matter with those children ? " And, as if these words, spoken calmly, had been the portent of misfortune, she answered with a loud wail that must have been heard across the yard in the pig-sty ; for the pigs (the Bacadous had the finest pigs in the country) stirred and grunted complainingly in the night. The husband went on grinding his bread and butter slowly, gazing at the wall, the soup-plate smoking under his chin. He had returned late from the market, where he had overheard (not for the first time) whispers behind his back. He revolved the words in his mind as he drove back. " Simple ! Both of them. . . . Never any use ! . . . Well ! May be, may be. One must see. Would ask his wife." This was her answer. He felt like a blow on his chest, but said only : " Go, draw me some cider. I am thirsty ! "

She went out moaning, an empty jug in her hand. Then he arose, took up the light, and moved slowly towards the cradle. They slept. He looked at them sideways, finished his mouthful there, went back heavily, and sat down before his plate. When his wife returned he never looked up, but swallowed a couple of spoonfuls noisily, and remarked, in a dull manner—

"When they sleep they are like other people's children."

She sat down suddenly on a stool near by, and shook with a silent tempest of sobs, unable to speak. He finished his meal, and remained idly thrown back in his chair, his eyes lost amongst the black rafters of the ceiling. Before him the tallow candle flared red and straight, sending up a slender thread of smoke. The light lay on the rough, sunburnt skin of his throat; the sunk cheeks were like patches of darkness, and his aspect was mournfully stolid, as if he had ruminated with difficulty endless ideas. Then he said, deliberately—

"We must see . . . consult people. Don't cry. . . . They won't be all like that . . . surely ! We must sleep now."

After the third child, also a boy, was born, Jean-Pierre went about his work with tense hopefulness. His lips seemed more narrow, more tightly compressed than before ; as if for fear of letting the earth he tilled hear the voice of hope that murmured within his breast. He watched the child, stepping up to the cot with a heavy clang of sabots on the stone floor, and glanced in, along his shoulder, with that indifference which is like a deformity of peasant humanity. Like the earth they master and serve, those men, slow of eye and speech, do not show the inner fire ; so that, at last, it becomes a question with them as with the earth, what there is in the core : heat, violence, a force mysterious and terrible—or nothing but a clod, a mass fertile and inert, cold and unfeeling, ready to bear a crop of plants that sustain life or give death.

The mother watched with other eyes ; listened with otherwise expectant ears. Under the high hanging shelves supporting great sides of bacon overhead, her body was busy by the great fireplace, attentive to the pot swinging on iron gallows, scrubbing the long table where the field hands would sit down directly to their evening meal. Her mind remained by the cradle, night and day on the watch, to hope and suffer. That child, like the other two, never smiled, never stretched its hands to her, never spoke ; never had a glance of recognition for her in its big black eyes, which could only stare fixedly at any glitter, but failed hopelessly to follow the brilliance of a sun-ray slipping slowly along the floor. When the men were at work she spent long days between her three idiot children and the childish grandfather, who sat grim, angular, and immovable, with his feet near the warm ashes of the fire. The feeble old fellow seemed to suspect that there was something wrong with his grandsons. Only once, moved either by affection or by the sense of proprieties, he attempted to nurse the youngest. He took the boy up from the floor, clicked his tongue at him, and essayed a shaky gallop of his bony knees. Then he looked closely with his misty eyes at the child's face and deposited him down gently on the floor again. And he sat, his lean shanks crossed, nodding at the steam escaping from the cooking-pot with a gaze senile and worried.

Then mute affliction dwelt in Bacadou's farmhouse, sharing the breath and the bread of its inhabitants ; and the priest of the Ploumar parish had great cause for congratulation. He called upon the rich landowner, the Marquis de Chavanes, on purpose to deliver himself with joyful unction of solemn platitudes about the inscrutable ways of Providence. In the vast dimness of the curtained drawing-room, the little man, resembling a black bolster, leaned towards a couch, his hat on his knees, and gesticulated with a fat hand at the elongated, gracefully-flowing lines of the clear Parisian toilette from within which the half-amused, half-bored marquise listened with gracious languor. He was exulting and humble, proud and awed. The impossible had come to pass. Jean-Pierre Bacadou, the enraged republican farmer, had been to mass last Sunday —had proposed to entertain the visiting priests at the next festival of Ploumar ! It was a triumph for the Church and for the good cause. " I thought I would come at once to tell Monsieur le Marquis. I know how anxious he is for the welfare of our country," declared the priest, wiping his face. He was asked to stay to dinner.

The Chavanes returning that evening, after seeing their guest to the main gate of the park, discussed the matter while they strolled in the moonlight, trailing their long shadows up the straight avenue of chestnuts. The marquis, a royalist of course, had been mayor of the commune which includes Ploumar, the scattered hamlets of the coast, and the stony islands that fringe the yellow flatness of the sands. He had felt his position insecure, for there was a strong republican element in that part of the country ; but now the conversion of Jean-Pierre made him safe. He was very pleased " You have no idea how influential those people are," he explained to his wife. " Now, I am sure, the next communal election will go all right. I shall be re-elected," " Your ambition is perfectly insatiable, Charles," exclaimed the marquise, gaily. " But, ma chère amie," argued the husband, seriously, " it's most important that the right man should be mayor this year, because of the elections to the Chamber. If you think it amuses me . . ."

Jean-Pierre had surrendered to his wife's mother. Madame Levaille was a woman of business, known and respected within a radius of at least fifteen miles. Thick-set and stout, she was seen about the country, on foot or in an acquaintance's cart, perpetually moving, in spite of her fifty-eight years, in steady pursuit of business. She had houses in all the hamlets, she worked quarries of granite, she freighted coasters with stone— even traded with the Channel Islands. She was broad-cheeked, wide-eyed, persuasive in speech : carrying her point with the placid and invincible obstinacy of an old woman who knows her own mind. She very seldom slept for two nights together in the same house ; and the wayside inns were the best places to inquire in as to her whereabouts. She had either passed, or was expected to pass there at six ; or somebody, coming in, had seen her in the morning, or expected to meet her that evening. After the inns that command the roads, the churches were the buildings she frequented most. Men of liberal opinions would induce small children to run into sacred edifices to see whether Madame Levaille was there, and to tell her that so-and-so was in the road waiting to speak to her—about potatoes, or flour, or stones, or houses ; and she would curtail her devotions, come out blinking and crossing herself into the sunshine ; ready to discuss business matters in a calm, sensible way across a table in the kitchen of the inn opposite. Latterly she had stayed for a few days several times with her son-in-law, arguing against sorrow and misfortune with composed face and gentle tones. Jean-Pierre felt the convictions imbibed in the regiment torn out of his breast—not by arguments, but by facts. Striding over his fields he thought it over. There were three of them. Three ! All alike ! Why ? Such things did not happen to everybody—to nobody he ever heard of. One yet—it might pass. But three ! All three. For ever useless, to be fed while he lived and . . . What would become of the land when he died ? This must be seen to. He would sacrifice his convictions. One day he told his wife—

" See what your God will do for us. Pay for some masses."

Susan embraced her man. He stood unbending, then turned on his heels and went out. But afterwards, when a black *soutane* darkened his doorway, he did not object ; even offered some cider himself to the priest. He listened to the talk meekly; went to mass between the two women ; accomplished what the priest called " his religious duties " at Easter. That morning he felt like a man who had sold his soul. In the afternoon he fought ferociously with an old friend and neighbour who had remarked that the priests had the best of it and were now going to eat the priest-eater. He came home dishevelled and bleeding, and happening to catch sight of his children (they were kept generally out of the way), cursed and swore incoherently, banging the table. Susan wept. Madame Levaille sat serenely unmoved. She assured her daughter that " It will pass " ; and taking up her thick umbrella, departed in haste to see after a schooner she was going to load with granite from her quarry.

A year or so afterwards the girl was born. A girl. Jean-Pierre heard of it in the fields, and was so upset by the news that he sat down on the boundary wall and remained there till the evening, instead of going home as he was urged to do. A girl ! He felt half cheated. However, when he got home he was partly reconciled to his fate. One could marry her to a good fellow—not to a good for nothing, but to a fellow with some understanding and a good pair of arms. Besides, the next may be a boy, he thought. Of course they would be all right. His new credulity knew of no doubt. The ill luck was broken. He spoke cheerily to his wife. She was also hopeful. Three priests came to that christening, and Madame Levaille was godmother. The child turned out an idiot too.

Then on market days Jean-Pierre was seen bargaining bitterly, quarrelsome and greedy ; then getting drunk with taciturn earnestness ; then driving home in the dusk at a rate fit for a wedding, but with a face gloomy enough for a funeral. Sometimes he would insist for his wife to come with him ; and they would drive in the early morning, shaking side by side on the narrow seat above the helpless pig, that, with tied legs, grunted a melancholy sigh at every rut. The morning drives were silent ; but in the evening, coming home, Jean-Pierre, tipsy, was viciously muttering, and growled at the confounded woman who could not rear children that were like anybody else's. Susan, holding on against the erratic swayings of the cart, pretended not to hear. Once, as they were driving through Ploumar, some obscure and drunken impulse caused him to pull up sharply opposite the church. The moon swam amongst light white clouds. The tombstones gleamed pale under the fretted shadows of the trees in the churchyard. Even the village dogs slept. Only the nightingales, awake, spun out the thrill of their song above the silence of graves. Jean-Pierre said thickly to his wife—

" What do you think is there ? "

He pointed his whip at the tower—in which the big dial of the clock appeared high in the moonlight like a pallid face without eyes—and getting out carefully, fell down at once by the wheel. He picked himself up and climbed one by one the few steps to the iron gate of the churchard. He put his face to the bars and called out indistinctly—

" Hey there ! Come out ! "

" Jean ! Return ! Return ! " entreated his wife in low tones.

He took no notice, and seemed to wait there. The song of nightingales beat on all sides against the high walls of the church, and flowed back between stone crosses and flat grey slabs, engraved with words of hope and sorrow.

" Hey ! Come out ! " shouted Jean-Pierre loudly.

The nightingales ceased to sing.

" Nobody ? " went on Jean-Pierre. " Nobody there. A swindle of the crows. That's what this is. Nobody anywhere. I despise it. Allez ! Houp ! "

He shook the gate with all his strength, and the iron bars rattled with a frightful clanging, like a chain dragged over stone steps. A dog near-by barked hurriedly. Jean-Pierre staggered back, and after three successive dashes got into his cart. Susan sat very quiet and still. He said to her with drunken severity—

" See ? Nobody. I've been made a fool ! Malheur ! Somebody will pay for it. The next one I see near the house I will lay my whip on . . . on the black spine . . . I will. I don't want him in there . . . he only helps the carrion crows to rob poor folk. I am a man. . . . We will see if I can't have children like anybody else . . . now you mind. . . . They won't be all . . . all . . . we see. . . ."

She burst out through the fingers that hid her face—

" Don't say that, Jean ; don't say that, my man ! "

He struck her a swinging blow on the head with the back of his hand and knocked her into the bottom of the cart, where she crouched, thrown about lamentably by every jolt. He drove furiously, standing up, brandishing his whip, shaking the reins over the grey horse that galloped ponderously, making the heavy harness leap upon his broad quarters. The country rang clamorous in the night with the irritated barking of farm dogs, that followed the rattle of wheels all along the road. A couple of belated wayfarers had only just time to step into the ditch. At his own gate he caught the post and was shot out of the cart head first. The horse went on slowly to the door. At Susan's piercing cries the farm hands rushed out. She thought him dead, but he was only sleeping where he fell, and cursed his men, who hastened to him, for disturbing his slumbers.

Autumn came. The clouded sky descended low upon the black contours of the hills ; and the dead leaves danced in spiral whirls under naked trees, till the wind, sighing profoundly, laid them to rest in the hollows of bare valleys. And from morning till night one could see all over the land black denuded boughs, the boughs gnarled and twisted, as if contorted with pain, swaying sadly between the wet clouds and the soaked earth. The clear and gentle streams of summer days rushed discoloured and raging at the stones that barred the way to the sea, with the fury of madness bent upon suicide. From horizon to horizon the great road to the sands lay between the hills in a dull glitter of empty curves, resembling an unnavigable river of mud.

Jean-Pierre went from field to field, moving blurred and tall in the drizzle, or striding on the crests of rises, lonely and high upon the grey curtain of drifting clouds, as if he had been pacing along the very edge of the universe. He looked at the black earth, at the earth mute and promising, at the mysterious earth doing its work of life in death-like stillness under the veiled sorrow of the sky. And it seemed to him that to a man worse than childless there was no promise in the fertility of fields, that from him the earth escaped, defied him, frowned at him like the clouds, sombre and hurried above his head. Having to face alone his own fields, he felt the inferiority of man who passes away before the clod that remains. Must he give up the hope of having by his side a son who would look at the turned-up sods with a master's eye ? A man that would think as he thought, that would feel as he felt ; a man who would be part of himself, and yet remain to trample masterfully on that earth when he was gone ! He thought of some distant relations, and felt savage enough to curse them aloud. They ! Never ! He turned homewards, going straight at the roof of his dwelling visible between the enlaced skeletons of trees. As he swung his legs over the stile a cawing flock of birds settled slowly on the field ; dropped down behind his back, noiseless and fluttering, like flakes of soot.

That day Madame Levaille had gone early in the afternoon to the house she had near Kervanion. She had to pay some of

the men who worked in her granite quarry there, and she went
in good time because her little house contained a shop where
the workmen could spend their wages without the trouble of
going to town.   The house stood alone amongst rocks.   A lane
of mud and stones ended at the door.   The sea-winds coming
ashore on Stonecutter's point, fresh from the fierce turmoil of
the waves, howled violently at the unmoved heaps of black
boulders holding up steadily short-armed, high crosses against
the tremendous rush of the invisible.   In the sweep of gales
the sheltered dwelling stood in a calm resonant and disquieting,
like the calm in the centre of a hurricane.   On stormy nights,
when the tide was out, the bay of Fougère, fifty feet below the
house, resembled an immense black pit, from which ascended
mutterings and sighs as if the sands down there had been alive
and complaining.   At high tide the returning water assaulted
the ledges of rock in short rushes, ending in bursts of livid light
and columns of spray, that flew inland, stinging to death the
grass of pastures.

The darkness came from the hills, flowed over the coast,
put out the red fires of sunset, and went on to seaward pursuing the retiring tide.   The wind dropped with the sun,
leaving a maddened sea and a devastated sky.   The heavens
above the house seemed to be draped in black rags, held up
here and there by pins of fire.   Madame Levaille, for this evening the servant of her own workmen, tried to induce them to
depart.   " An old woman like me ought to be in bed at this
late hour," she good-humouredly repeated.   The quarrymen
drank, asked for more.   They shouted over the table as if they
had been talking across a field.   At one end four of them played
cards, banging the wood with their hard knuckles, and swearing
at every lead.   One sat with a lost gaze, humming a bar of
some song, which he repeated endlessly.   Two others, in a
corner, were quarrelling confidentially and fiercely over some
woman, looking close into one another's eyes as if they had
wanted to tear them out, but speaking in whispers that promised violence and murder discreetly, in a venomous sibillation
of subdued words.   The atmosphere in there was thick enough
to slice with a knife.   Three candles burning about the long
room glowed red and dull like sparks expiring in ashes.

The slight click of the iron latch was at that late hour as
unexpected and startling as a thunder-clap.   Madame Levaille
put down a bottle she held above a liqueur glass ; the players
turned their heads ; the whispered quarrel ceased ; only the
singer, after darting a glance at the door, went on humming with

a stolid face. Susan appeared in the doorway, stepped in, flung the door to, and put her back against it, saying, half aloud—

"Mother!"

Madame Levaille, taking up the bottle again, said calmly : "Here you are, my girl. What a state you are in!" The neck of the bottle rang on the rim of the glass, for the old woman was startled, and the idea that the farm had caught fire had entered her head. She could think of no other cause for her daughter's appearance.

Susan, soaked and muddy, stared the whole length of the room towards the men at the far end. Her mother asked—

"What has happened? God guard us from misfortune!"

Susan moved her lips. No sound came. Madame Levaille stepped up to her daughter, took her by the arm, looked into her face.

"In God's name," she said shakily, "what's the matter? You have been rolling in mud. . . . Why did you come? . . . Where's Jean?"

The men had all got up and approached slowly, staring with dull surprise. Madame Levaille jerked her daughter away from the door, swung her round upon a seat close to the wall. Then she turned fiercely to the men—

"Enough of this! Out you go—you others! I close."

One of them observed, looking down at Susan collapsed on the seat : "She is—one may say—half dead."

Madame Levaille flung the door open.

"Get out! March!" she cried, shaking nervously.

They dropped out into the night, laughing stupidly. Outside, the two Lotharios broke out into loud shouts. The others tried to soothe them, all talking at once. The noise went away up the lane with the men, who staggered together in a tight knot, remonstrating with one another foolishly.

"Speak, Susan. What is it? Speak!" entreated Madame Levaille, as soon as the door was shut.

Susan pronounced some incomprehensible words, glaring at the table. The old woman clapped her hands above her head, let them drop, and stood looking at her daughter with disconsolate eyes. Her husband had been "deranged in his head" for a few years before he died, and now she began to suspect her daughter was going mad. She asked, pressingly—

"Does Jean know where you are? Where is Jean?"

Susan pronounced with difficulty—

"He knows . . . he is dead."

" What ! " cried the old woman. She came up near, and
peering at her daughter, repeated three times : " What do
you say ? What do you say ? What do you say ? "

Susan sat dry-eyed and stony before Madame Levaille,
who contemplated her, feeling a strange sense of inexplicable
horror creep into the silence of the house. She had hardly
realised the news, further than to understand that she had been
brought in one short moment face to face with something unexpected and final. It did not even occur to her to ask for any
explanation. She thought : accident—terrible accident—
blood to the head—fell down a trap door in the loft. . . . She
remained there, distracted and mute, blinking her old eyes.

Suddenly, Susan said—

" I have killed him."

For a moment the mother stood still, almost unbreathing,
but with composed face. The next second she burst out into
a shout—

" You miserable madwoman . . . they will cut your
neck. . . ."

She fancied the gendarmes entering the house, saying to
her : " We want your daughter ; give her up : " the gendarmes with the severe, hard faces of men on duty. She knew
the brigadier well—an old friend, familiar and respectful,
saying heartily, " To your good health, madame ! " before
lifting to his lips the small glass of cognac—out of the special
bottle she kept for friends. And now ! . . . She was losing
her head. She rushed here and there, as if looking for something urgently needed—gave that up, stood stock still in the
middle of the room, and screamed at her daughter—

" Why ? Say ! Say ! Why ? "

The other seemed to leap out of her strange apathy.

" Do you think I am made of stone ? " she shouted back,
striding towards her mother.

" No ! It's impossible . . ." said Madame Levaille, in a
convinced tone.

" You go and see, mother," retorted Susan, looking at her
with blazing eyes. " There's no mercy in heaven—no justice.
No ! . . . I did not know. . . . Do you think I have no heart ?
Do you think I have never heard people jeering at me, pitying
me, wondering at me ? Do you know how some of them were
calling me ? The mother of idiots—that was my nickname !
And my children never would know me, never speak to me.
They would know nothing ; neither men—nor God. Haven't
I prayed ! But the Mother of God herself would not hear me.

A mother ! . . . Who is accursed—I, or the man who is dead ?
Eh ? Tell me. I took care of myself. Do you think I would
defy the anger of God and have my house full of those things
—that are worse than animals who know the hand that feeds
them ? Who blasphemed in the night at the very church
door ? Was it I ? . . . I only wept and prayed for mercy . . .
and I feel the curse at every moment of the day—I see it round
me from morning to night . . . I've got to keep them alive—
to take care of my misfortune and shame. And he would come.
I begged him and Heaven for mercy. . . . No ! . . . Then we
shall see. . . . He came this evening. I thought to myself :
' Ah ! again ! ' . . . I had my long scissors. I heard him shouting. . . . I saw him near. . . . I must— must I ? . . . Then
take ! . . . And I struck him in the throat above the breast-
bone. . . . I never heard him even sigh. . . . I left him
standing. . . . It was a minute ago. How did I come here ? "
     Madame Levaille shivered. A wave of cold ran down her
back, down her fat arms under her tight sleeves, made her
stamp gently where she stood. Quivers ran over the broad
cheeks, across the thin lips, ran amongst the wrinkles at the
corners of her steady old eyes. She stammered—
     " You wicked woman—you disgrace me. But there !
You always resembled your father. What do you think will
become of you . . . in the other world ? In this . . . Oh
misery ! "
     She was very hot now. She felt burning inside. She
wrung her perspiring hands—and suddenly, starting in great
haste, began to look for her big shawl and umbrella, feverishly,
never once glancing at her daughter, who stood in the middle
of the room following her with a gaze distracted and cold.
     " Nothing worse than in this," said Susan.
     Her mother, umbrella in hand and trailing the shawl over
the floor, groaned profoundly.
     " I must go to the priest," she burst out passionately. " I
do not know whether you even speak the truth ! You are a
horrible woman. They will find you anywhere. You may
stay here—or go. There is no room for you in this world."
     Ready now to depart, she yet wandered aimlessly about the
room, putting the bottles on the shelf, trying to fit with trembling hands the covers on cardboard boxes. Whenever the real
sense of what she had heard emerged for a second from the
haze of her thoughts she would fancy that something had
exploded in her brain without, unfortunately, bursting her
head to pieces—which would have been a relief. She blew the

candles out one by one without knowing it, and was horribly
startled by the darkness. She fell on a bench and began to
whimper. After a while she ceased, and sat listening to the
breathing of her daughter, whom she could hardly see, still
and upright, giving no other sign of life. She was becoming
old rapidly at last, during those minutes. She spoke in tones
unsteady, cut about by the rattle of teeth, like one shaken by
a deadly cold fit of ague.

" I wish you had died little. I will never dare to show my
old head in the sunshine again. There are worse misfortunes
than idiot children. I wish you had been born to me simple—
like you own. . . ."

She saw the figure of her daughter pass before the faint and
livid clearness of a window. Then it appeared in the doorway
for a second, and the door swung to with a clang. Madame
Levaille, as if awakened by the noise from a long nightmare,
rushed out.

" Susan ! " she shouted from the doorstep.

She heard a stone roll a long time down the declivity of
the rocky beach above the sands. She stepped forward cautiously, one hand on the wall of the house, and peered down
into the smooth darkness of the empty bay. Once again she
cried—

" Susan ! You will kill yourself there."

The stone had taken its last leap in the dark, and she heard
nothing now. A sudden thought seemed to strangle her, and
she called no more. She turned her back upon the black silence
of the pit and went up the lane towards Ploumar, stumbling
along with sombre determination, as if she had started on a
desperate journey that would last, perhaps, to the end of her
life. A sullen and periodic clamour of waves rolling over reefs
followed her far inland between the high hedges sheltering the
gloomy solitude of the fields.

Susan had run out, swerving sharp to the left at the door, and
on the edge of the slope crouched down behind a boulder. A
dislodged stone went on downwards, rattling as it leaped.
When Madame Levaille called out, Susan could have, by
stretching her hand, touched her mother's skirt, had she had
the courage to move a limb. She saw the old woman go away,
and she remained still, closing her eyes and pressing her side
to the hard and rugged surface of the rock. After a while a
familiar face with fixed eyes and an open mouth became visible
in the intense obscurity amongst the boulders. She uttered a
low cry and stood up. The face vanished, leaving her to gasp

and shiver alone in the wilderness of stone heaps. But as soon as she had crouched down again to rest, with her head against the rock, the face returned, came very near, appeared eager to finish the speech that had been cut short by death, only a moment ago. She scrambled quickly to her feet and said : " Go away, or I will do it again." The thing wavered, swung to the right, to the left. She moved this way and that, stepped back, fancied herself screaming as it, and was appalled by the unbroken stillness of the night. She tottered on the brink, felt the steep declivity under her feet, and rushed down blindly to save herself from a headlong fall. The shingle seemed to wake up ; the pebbles began to roll before her, pursued her from above, raced down with her on both sides, rolling past with an increasing clatter. In the peace of the night the noise grew, deepening to a rumour, continuous and violent, as if the whole semicircle of the stony beach had started to tumble down into the bay. Susan's feet hardly touched the slope that seemed to run down with her. At the bottom she stumbled, shot forward, throwing her arms out, and fell heavily. She jumped up at once and turned swiftly to look back, her clenched hands full of sand she had clutched in her fall. The face was there, keeping its distance, visible in its own sheen that made a pale stain in the night. She shouted, " Go away "—she shouted at it with pain, with fear, with all the rage of that useless stab that could not keep him quiet, keep him out of her sight. What did he want now ? He was dead. Dead men have no children. Would he never leave her alone ? She shrieked at it—waved her outstretched hands. She seemed to feel the breath of parted lips, and, with a long cry of discouragement, fled across the level bottom of the bay.

She ran lightly, unaware of any effort of her body. High sharp rocks that, when the bay is full, show above the glittering plain of blue water like pointed towers of submerged churches, glided past her, rushing to the land at a tremendous pace. To the left, in the distance, she could see something shining : a broad disc of light in which narrow shadows pivoted round the centre like the spokes of a wheel. She heard a voice calling, " Hey ! There ! " and answered with a wild scream. So, he could call yet ! He was calling after her to stop. Never ! . . . She tore through the night, past the startled group of sea-weed-gatherers who stood round their lantern paralysed with fear at the unearthly screech coming from that fleeing shadow. The men leaned on their pitchforks staring fearfully. A woman fell on her knees, and, crossing herself, began to pray aloud. A little girl with her ragged skirt full of slimy seaweed began to sob despairingly, lugging her soaked burden close to the man who carried the light. Somebody said : " The thing ran out towards the sea." Another voice exclaimed : " And the sea is coming back ! Look at the spreading puddles. Do you hear —you woman—there ! Get up ! " Several voices cried together. " Yes, let us be off ! Let the accursed thing go to the sea ! " They moved on, keeping close round the light. Suddenly a man swore loudly. He would go and see what was the matter. It had been a woman's voice. He would go. There were shrill protests from women—but his high form detached itself from the group and went off running. They sent an unanimous call of scared voices after him. A word, insulting and mocking, came back, thrown at them through darkness. A woman moaned. An old man said gravely : " Such things ought to be left alone." They went on slower, shuffling in the yielding sand and whispering to one another that Millot feared nothing, having no religion, but that it would end badly some day.

Susan met the incoming tide by the Raven islet and stopped, panting, with her feet in the water. She heard the murmur and felt the cold caress of the sea, and, calmer now, could see the sombre and confused mass of the Raven on one side and on the other the long white streak of Molène sands that are left high above the dry bottom of Fougère Bay at every ebb. She turned round and saw far away, along the starred background of the sky, the ragged outline of the coast. Above it, nearly facing her, appeared the tower of Ploumar Church ; a slender and tall pyramid shooting up dark and pointed into the clustered glitter of the stars. She felt strangely calm. She knew where she was, and began to remember how she came there—and why. She peered into the smooth obscurity near her. She was alone. There was nothing there ; nothing near her, either living or dead.

The tide was creeping in quietly, putting out long impatient arms of strange rivulets that ran towards the land between ridges of sand. Under the night the pools grew bigger with mysterious rapidity, while the great sea, yet far off, thundered in a regular rhythm along the indistinct line of the horizon. Susan splashed her way back for a few yards without being able to get clear of the water that murmured tenderly all around and, suddenly, with a spiteful gurgle, nearly took her off her feet. Her heart thumped with fear. This place was too big and too empty to die in. To-morrow they would do with her

what they liked. But before she died she must tell them—tell
the gentlemen in black clothes that there are things no woman
can bear. She must explain how it happened. . . . She
splashed through a pool, getting wet to the waist, too preoccupied to care. . . . She must explain. " He came in the
same way as ever and said, just so : ' Do you think I am going
to leave the land to those people from Morbihan that I do not
know ? Do you ? We shall see ! Come along, you creature
of mischance ! ' And he put his arms out. Then, Messieurs,
I said : ' Before God—never ! ' And he said, striding at me
with open palms : ' There is no God to hold me ! Do you
understand, you useless carcase. I will do what I like.' And
he took me by the shoulders. Then I, Messieurs, called to
God for help, and next minute, while he was shaking me, I felt
my long scissors in my hand. His shirt was unbuttoned, and,
by the candle-light, I saw the hollow of his throat. I cried :
' Let go ! ' He was crushing my shoulders. He was strong,
my man was ! Then I thought : No ! . . . Must I ? . . .
Then take !—and I struck in the hollow place. I never saw
him fall. Never ! Never ! . . . Never saw him fall. . . . The
old father never turned his head. He is deaf and childish,
gentlemen. . . . Nobody saw him fall. I ran out. . . . Nobody
saw. . . ."

She had been scrambling amongst the boulders of the Raven
and now found herself, all out of breath, standing amongst the
heavy shadows of the rocky islet. The Raven is connected with
the main land by a natural pier of immense and slippery stones.
She intended to return home that way. Was he still standing
there ? At home. Home ! Four idiots and a corpse. She
must go back and explain. Anybody would understand. . . .

Below her the night or the sea seemed to pronounce
distinctly—

" Aha ! I see you at last ! "

She started, slipped, fell ; and without attempting to rise,
listened, terrified. She heard heavy breathing, a clatter of
wooden clogs. It stopped.

" Where the devil did you pass ? " said an invisible man,
hoarsely.

She held her breath. She recognised the voice. She had
not seen him fall. Was he pursuing her there dead, or perhaps
. . . alive ?

She lost her head. She cried from the crevice where she
lay huddled, " Never, never ! "

" Ah ! You are still there. You led me a fine dance. Wait,

my beauty, I must see how you look after all this. You wait. . . .

Millot was stumbling, laughing, swearing meaninglessly
out of pure satisfaction, pleased with himself for having run
down that fly-by-night. " As if there were such things as
ghosts ! Bah ! It took an old African soldier to show those
clodhoppers. . . . But it was curious. Who the devil was she ? "

Susan listened, crouching. He was coming for her, this
dead man. There was no escape. What a noise he made
amongst the stones. . . . She saw his head rise up, then the
shoulders. He was tall—her own man ! His long arms waved
about, and it was his own voice sounding a little strange . . .
because of the scissors. She scrambled out quickly, rushed to
the edge of the causeway, and turned round. The man stood
still on a high stone, detaching himself in dead black on the
glitter of the sky.

" Where are you going to ? " he called roughly.

She answered, " Home ! " and watched him intensely. He
made a striding, clumsy leap on to another boulder, and stopped
again, balancing himself, then said—

" Ha ! ha ! Well, I am going with you. It's the least I
can do. Ha ! ha ! ha ! "

She stared at him till her eyes seemed to become glowing
coals that burned deep into her brain, and yet she was in mortal
fear of making out the well-known features. Below her the
sea lapped softly against the rock with a splash, continuous and
gentle.

The man said, advancing another step—

" I am coming for you. What do you think ? "

She trembled. Coming for her ! There was no escape,
no peace, no hope. She looked round despairingly. Suddenly
the whole shadowy coast, the blurred islets, the heaven itself,
swayed about twice, then came to a rest. She closed her eyes
and shouted—

" Can't you wait till I am dead ! "

She was shaken by a furious hate for that shade that pursued her in this world, unappeased even by death in its longing
for an heir that would be like other people's children.

" Hey ! What ? " said Millot, keeping his distance prud-
ently. He was saying to himself : " Look out ! Some lunatic.
An accident happens soon."

She went on, wildly—

" I want to live. To live alone—for a week—for a day. I
must explain to them. . . . I would tear you to pieces, I would
kill you twenty times over rather than let you touch me while

*She had screamed " alive ! " and at once
vanished before his eyes.*

I live. How many times must I kill you—you blasphemer!
Satan sends you here. I am damned too!"

" Come," said Millot, alarmed and conciliating. " I am
perfectly alive!... Oh, my God!"

She had screamed, " Alive!" and at once vanished before
his eyes, as if the islet itself had swerved aside from under her
feet. Millot rushed forward, and fell flat with his chin over
the edge. Far below he saw the water whitened by her
struggles, and heard one shrill cry for help that seemed to dart
upwards along the perpendicular face of the rock, and soar past,
straight into the high and impassive heaven.

Madame Levaille sat, dry-eyed, on the short grass of the
hill side, with her thick legs stretched out, and her old feet
turned up in their black cloth shoes. Her clogs stood near by,
and further off the umbrella lay on the withered sward like a
weapon dropped from the grasp of a vanquished warrior. The
Marquis of Chavanes, on horseback, one gloved hand on thigh,
looked down at her as she got up laboriously, with groans. On
the narrow track of the seaweed-carts four men were carrying
inland Susan's body on a hand-barrow, while several others
straggled listlessly behind. Madame Levaille looked after the
procession. " Yes, Monsieur le Marquis," she said dispassionately, in her usual calm tone of a reasonable old woman.
" There are unfortunate people on this earth. I had only one
child. Only one! And they won't bury her in consecrated
ground!"

Her eyes filled suddenly, and a short shower of tears rolled
down the broad cheeks. She pulled the shawl close about her.
The Marquis leaned slightly over in his saddle, and said—

" It is very sad. You have all my sympathy. I shall speak
to the Curé. She was unquestionably insane, and the fall was
accidental. Millot says so distinctly. Good-day, Madame."

And he trotted off, thinking to himself : I must get this old
woman appointed guardian of those idiots, and administrator
of the farm. It would be much better than having here one of
those other Bacadous, probably a red republican, corrupting
my commune.

THE VAMPIRE

By

SYDNEY HORLER

UNTIL his death, quite recently, I used to visit at least once a week a Roman Catholic priest. The fact that I am a Protestant did nothing to shake our friendship. Father R—— was one of the finest characters I have ever known ; he was capable of the broadest sympathies, and was, in the best sense of that frequently-abused term, " a man of the world." He was good enough to take considerable interest in my work as a novelist, and I often discussed plots and situations with him.

The story I am about to relate occurred about eighteen months ago—ten months before his illness. I was then writing my novel " The Curse of Doone." In this story I made the villain take advantage of a ghastly legend attached to an old manor-house in Devonshire and use it for his own ends.

Father R—— listened while I outlined the plot I had in mind, and then said, to my great surprise : " Certain people may scoff because they will not allow themselves to believe that there is any credence in the vampire tradition."

" Yes, that is so," I parried ; " but, all the same, Bram Stoker stirred the public imagination with his ' Dracula '—one of the most horrible and yet fascinating books ever written— and I am hoping that my public will extend to me the customary ' author's licence.' "

My friend nodded.

" Quite," he replied. " As a matter of fact," he went on to say, " I believe in vampires myself."

" You do ? " I felt the hair on the back of my neck commence to irritate. It is one thing to write about a horror, but quite another to begin to see it assume definite shape.

" Yes," said Father R——. " I am forced to believe in vampires for the very good but terrible reason that I have met one ! "

I half-rose in my chair. There could be no questioning R——'s word, and yet——

" That, no doubt, my dear fellow," he continued, " may appear a very extraordinary statement to have made, and yet I assure you it is the truth. It happened many years ago and in another part of the country—exactly where I do not think I had better tell you."

" But this is amazing—you say you actually met a vampire face to face ? "

" And talked to him. Until now I have never mentioned the matter to a living soul apart from a brother priest."

It was clearly an invitation to listen ; I crammed tobacco into my pipe and leaned back in the chair on the opposite side of the crackling fire. I had heard that Truth was said to be stranger than fiction—but here I was about to have, it seemed, the strange experience of listening to my own most sensational imagining being hopelessly out-done by FACT !

The name of the small town does not matter (Father R—— started) ; let it suffice it was in the West of England and was inhabited by a good many people of superior means. There was a large city seventy-five miles away and business men, when they retired, often came to —— to wind up their lives. I was young and very happy there in my work until —— But I am a little previous.

I was on very friendly terms with a local doctor ; he often used to come in and have a chat when he could spare the time. We used to try to thresh out many problems which later experience has convinced me are insoluble—in this world, at least.

One night, he looked at me rather curiously I thought.

" What do you think of that man, Farington ? " he asked.

Now, it was a curious fact that he should have made that inquiry at that exact moment, for by some subconscious means I happened to be thinking of this very person myself.

The man who called himself " Joseph Farington " was a stranger who had recently come to settle in ——. That circumstance alone would have caused comment, but when I say that he had bought the largest house on the hill overlooking the town on the south side (representing the best residential quarter) and had had it furnished apparently regardless of cost by one of the famous London houses, that he sought to entertain a great deal but that no one seemed anxious to go twice to "The Gables."—— Well, there was " something funny " about Farington, it was whispered.

I knew this, of course—the smallest fragment of gossip comes to a priest's ears—and so I hesitated before replying to the doctor's direct question.

" Confess now, Father," said my companion, " you are like all the rest of us—you don't like the man ! He has made me his medical attendant, but I wish to goodness he had chosen someone else. There's ' something funny ' about him."

" Something funny "—there it was again. As the doctor's words sounded in my ears I remembered Farington as I had last seen him walking up the main street with every other eye half-turned in his direction. He was a big-framed man, the essence of maculinity. He looked so robust that the thought came instinctively : This man will never die. He had a florid complexion ; he walked with the elasticity of youth and his hair was jet-black. Yet from remarks he had made the impression in —— was that Farington must be at least sixty years of age.

" Well, there's one thing, Sanders," I replied ; " if appearances are anything to go by, Farington will not be giving you much trouble. The fellow looks as strong as an ox."

" You haven't answered my question," persisted the doctor. " Forget your cloth, Father, and tell me exactly what you think of Joseph Farington. Don't you agree that he is a man to give you the shudders ? "

" You—a doctor—talking about getting the shudders ! " I gently scoffed because I did not want to give my real opinion of Joseph Farington.

" I can't help it—I have an instinctive horror of the fellow. This afternoon I was called up to ' The Gables.' Farington, like ever so many of his ox-like kind, is really a bit of a hypochondriac. He thought there was something wrong with his heart, he said."

" And was there ? "

" The man ought to live to a hundred ! But, I tell you, Father, I hated having to be near the fellow, there's something uncanny about him. I felt frightened—yes, frightened—all the time I was in the house. I had to talk to someone about it and as you are the safest person in —— I dropped in. . . . You haven't said anything yourself, I notice."

" I prefer to wait," I replied. It seemed the safest answer.

Two months after that conversation with Sanders, not only —— but the whole of the country was startled and horrified by a terrible crime. A girl of eighteen, the belle of the district, was found dead in a field. Her face, in life so beautiful, was revolting in death because of the expression of dreadful horror it held.

The poor girl had been murdered—but in a manner which sent shudders of fear racing up and down people's spines. . . . There was a great hole in the throat, as though a beast of the jungle had attacked. . . .

It is not difficult to say how suspicion for this fiendish crime first started to fasten itself on Joseph Farington, preposterous as the statement may seem. Although he had gone out of his way to become sociable, the man had made no real friends. Sanders, although a clever doctor, was not the most tactful of men and there is no doubt that his refusal to visit Farington professionally—he had hinted as much on the night of his visit to me, you will remember—got noised about. In any case, public opinion was strongly roused ; without a shred of direct evidence to go upon, people began to talk of Farington as being the actual murderer. There was some talk among the wild young spirits of setting fire to " The Gables " one night, and burning Farington in his bed.

It was whilst this feeling was at its height that, very unwillingly, as you may imagine, I was brought into the affair. I received a note from Farington asking me to dine with him one night.

> " I have something on my mind which I wish to talk over with you ; so please do not fail me."

These were the concluding words of the letter.

Such an appeal could not be ignored by a man of religion and so I replied accepting.

Farington was a good host ; the food was excellent ; on the surface there was nothing wrong. But—and here is the curious part—from the moment I faced the man I knew there *was* something wrong. I had the same uneasiness as Sanders, the doctor : *I felt afraid.* The man had an aura of evil ; he was possessed of some devilish force or quality which chilled me to the marrow.

I did my best to hide my discomfiture, but when, after dinner, Farington began to speak about the murder of that poor, innocent girl, this feeling increased. And at once the terrible truth leaped into my mind : I knew it was Farington who had done this crime : the man was a monster !

Calling upon all my strength, I challenged him.

"You wished to see me to-night for the purpose of easing your soul of a terrible burden," I said ; "you cannot deny that it was you who killed that unfortunate girl."

"Yes," he replied slowly, "that is the truth. I killed the girl. The demon which possesses me forced me to do it. But you, as a priest, must hold this confession sacred—you must preserve it as a secret. Give me a few more hours ; then I will decide myself what to do."

I left shortly afterwards. The man would not say anything more.

"Give me a few hours," he repeated.

That night I had a horrible dream. I felt I was suffocating. Scarcely able to breathe, I rushed to the window, pulled it open —and then fell senseless to the floor. The next thing I remember was Dr. Sanders—who had been summoned by my faithful housekeeper—bending over me.

"What happened ?" he asked. "You had a look on your face as though you had been staring into hell."

"So I had," I replied.

"Had it anything to do with Farington ?" he asked bluntly.

"Sanders," and I clutched him by the arm in the intensity of my feeling, "does such a monstrosity as a vampire exist nowadays ? Tell me, I implore you !"

The good fellow forced me to take another nip of brandy before he would reply.

Then he put a question himself.

"Why do you ask that ?" he said.

"It sounds incredible—and I hope I really dreamed it— but I fainted to-night because I saw—or imagined I saw—the man Farington flying past the window that I had just opened."

"I am not surprised," he nodded. "Ever since I examined the mutilated body of that poor girl I came to the conclusion that she had come to her death through some terrible abnormality.

"Although we hear practically nothing about vampirism nowadays," he continued, "that is not to say that ghoulish spirits do not still take up their abode in a living man or woman, thus conferring upon them supernatural powers. What form was the shape you thought you saw ?"

"It was like a huge bat," I replied shuddering.

"To-morrow," said Sanders determinedly, "I'm going to London to see Scotland Yard. They may laugh at me at first, but——"

THE VAMPIRE

445

Scotland Yard did not laugh. But criminals with supernatural powers were rather out of their line, and, besides, as they told Sanders, they had to have *proof* before they could convict Farington. Even my testimony—had I dared to break my priestly pledge, which, of course, I couldn't in any circumstances do—would not have been sufficient.

Farington solved the terrible problem by committing suicide. He was found in bed with a bullet wound in his head.

But, according to Sanders, only the body is dead—the vile spirit is roaming free, looking for another human habitation.

God help its luckless victim.

THE INTERLOPERS

By

" SAKI " (H. H. MUNRO)

IN a forest of mixed growth somewhere on the eastern spurs
of the Carpathians, a man stood one winter night watching
and listening, as though he waited for some beast of the
woods to come within the range of his vision, and, later, of
his rifle. But the game for whose presence he kept so keen
an outlook was none that figured in the sportsman's calendar
as lawful and proper for the chase ; Ulrich von Gradwitz
patrolled the dark forest in quest of a human enemy.

The forest lands of Gradwitz were of wide extent and well
stocked with game ; the narrow strip of precipitous woodland
that lay on its outskirt was not remarkable for the game it
harboured or the shooting it afforded, but it was the most
jealously guarded of all its owner's territorial possessions. A
famous lawsuit, in the days of his grandfather, had wrested
it from the illegal possession of a neighbouring family of petty
landowners ; the dispossessed party had never acquiesced in
the judgment of the Courts, and a long series of poaching
affrays and similar scandals had embittered the relationships
between the families for three generations. The neighbour
feud had grown into a personal one since Ulrich had come
to be head of his family ; if there was a man in the world
whom he detested and wished ill to it was Georg Znaeym,
the inheritor of the quarrel and the tireless game-snatcher
and raider of the disputed border-forest. The feud might,
perhaps, have died down or been compromised if the personal
ill-will of the two men had not stood in the way ; as boys
they had thirsted for one another's blood, as men each prayed
that misfortune might fall on the other, and this wind-scourged
winter night Ulrich had banded together his foresters to watch
the dark forest, not in quest of four-footed quarry, but to keep

446

a look-out for the prowling thieves whom he suspected of being afoot from across the land boundary. The roebuck, which usually kept in the sheltered hollows during a storm-wind, were running like driven things to-night, and there was movement and unrest among the creatures that were wont to sleep through the dark hours. Assuredly there was a disturbing element in the forest, and Ulrich could guess the quarter from whence it came.

He strayed away by himself from the watchers whom he had placed in ambush on the crest of the hill, and wandered far down the steep slopes amid the wild tangle of undergrowth, peering through the tree-trunks and listening through the whistling and skirling of the wind and the restless beating of the branches for sight or sound of the marauders. If only on this wild night, in this dark, lone spot, he might come across Georg Znaeym, man to man, with none to witness—that was the wish that was uppermost in his thoughts. And as he stepped round the trunk of a huge beech he came face to face with the man he sought.

The two enemies stood glaring at one another for a long silent moment. Each had a rifle in his hand, each had hate in his heart and murder uppermost in his mind. The chance had come to give full play to the passions of a lifetime. But a man who has been brought up under the code of a restraining civilization cannot easily nerve himself to shoot down his neighbour in cold blood and without word spoken, except for an offence against his hearth and honour. And before the moment of hesitation had given way to action a deed of Nature's own violence overwhelmed them both. A fierce shriek of the storm had been answered by a splitting crash over their heads, and ere they could leap aside a mass of falling beech tree had thundered down on them. Ulrich von Gradwitz found himself stretched on the ground, one arm numb beneath him and the other held almost as helplessly in a tight tangle of forked branches, while both legs were pinned beneath the fallen mass. His heavy shooting-boots had saved his feet from being crushed to pieces, but if his fractures were not as serious as they might have been, at least it was evident that he could not move from his present position till some one came to release him. The descending twigs had slashed the skin of his face, and he had to wink away some drops of blood from his eyelashes before he could take in a general view of the disaster. At his side, so near that under ordinary circumstances he could almost have touched him, lay Georg Znaeym, alive and struggling, but obviously as helplessly pinioned down as himself. All round them lay a thick-strewn wreckage of splintered branches and broken twigs.

Relief at being alive and exasperation at his captive plight brought a strange medley of pious thank-offerings and sharp curses to Ulrich's lips. Georg, who was nearly blinded with the blood which trickled across his eyes, stopped his struggling for a moment to listen, and then gave a short, snarling laugh.

" So you're not killed, as you ought to be, but you're caught, anyway," he cried ; " caught fast. Ho, what a jest, Ulrich von Gradwitz snared in his stolen forest. There's real justice for you ! "

And he laughed again, mockingly and savagely.

" I'm caught in my own forest-land," retorted Ulrich. " When my men come to release us you will wish, perhaps, that you were in a better plight than caught poaching on a neighbour's land, shame on you."

Georg was silent for a moment ; then he answered quietly. " Are you sure that your men will find much to release ? I have men, too, in the forest to-night, close behind me, and *they* will be here first and do the releasing. When they drag me out from under these damned branches it won't need much clumsiness on their part to roll this mass of trunk right over on the top of you. Your men will find you dead under a fallen beech tree. For form's sake I shall send my condolences to your family."

" It is a useful hint," said Ulrich fiercely. " My men had orders to follow in ten minutes' time, seven of which must have gone by already, and when they get me out—I will remember the hint. Only as you will have met your death poaching on my lands I don't think I can decently send any message of condolence to your family."

" Good," snarled Georg, " good. We fight this quarrel out to the death, you and I and our foresters, with no cursed interlopers to come between us. Death and damnation to you, Ulrich von Gradwitz."

" The same you, Georg Znaeym, forest-thief, game-snatcher."

Both men spoke with the bitterness of possible defeat before them, for each knew that it might be long before his men would seek him out or find him ; it was a bare matter of chance which party would arrive first on the scene.

Both had now given up the useless struggle to free themselves from the mass of wood that held them down ; Ulrich limited his endeavours to an effort to bring his one partially free arm near enough to his outer coat-pocket to draw out his wine-flask. Even when he had accomplished that operation it was long before he could manage the unscrewing of the stopper or get any of the liquid down his throat. But what a Heaven-sent draught it seemed ! It was an open winter, and little snow had fallen as yet, hence the captives suffered less from the cold than might have been the case at that season of the year ; nevertheless, the wine was warming and reviving to the wounded man, and he looked across with something like a throb of pity to where his enemy lay, just keeping the groans of pain and weariness from crossing his lips.

" Could you reach this flask if I threw it over to you ? " asked Ulrich suddenly ; " there is good wine in it, and one may as well be as comfortable as one can. Let us drink, even if to-night one of us dies."

" No, I can scarcely see anything ; there is so much blood caked round my eyes," said Georg, " and in any case I don't drink wine with an enemy."

Ulrich was silent for a few minutes, and lay listening to the weary screeching of the wind. An idea was slowly form-ing and growing in his brain, an idea that gained strength every time that he looked across at the man who was fighting so grimly against pain and exhaustion. In the pain and languor that Ulrich himself was feeling the old fierce hatred seemed to be dying down.

" Neighbour," he said presently, " do as you please if your men come first. It was a fair compact. But as for me, I've changed my mind. If my men are the first to come you shall be the first to be helped, as though you were my guest. We have quarrelled like devils all our lives over this stupid strip of forest, where the trees can't even stand upright in a breath of wind. Lying here to-night, thinking, I've come to think we've been rather fools ; there are better things in life than getting the better of a boundary dispute. Neighbour, if you will help me to bury the old quarrel I—I will ask you to be my friend."

Georg Znaeym was silent for so long that Ulrich thought, perhaps, he had fainted with the pain of his injuries. Then he spoke slowly and in jerks.

" How the whole region would stare and gabble if we rode into the market-square together. No one living can remember seeing a Znaeym and a von Gradwitz talking to one another in friendship. And what peace there would be among the forester folk if we ended our feud to-night. And if we choose to make peace among our people there is none other to interfere, no interlopers from outside. . . . You would come and keep the Sylvester night beneath my roof, and I would come and feast on some high day at your castle. . . . I would never fire a shot on your land, save when you invited me as a guest ; and you should come and shoot with me down in the marshes where the wildfowl are. In all the countryside there are none that could hinder if we willed to make peace. I never thought to have wanted to do other than hate you all my life, but I think I have changed my mind about things too, this last half-hour. And you offered me your wine-flask. . . . Ulrich von Gradwitz, I will be your friend."

For a space both men were silent, turning over in their minds the wonderful changes that this dramatic reconciliation would bring about. In the cold, gloomy forest, with the wind tearing in fitful gusts through the naked branches and whistling round the tree-trunks, they lay and waited for the help that would now bring release and succour to both parties. And each prayed a private prayer that his men might be the first to arrive, so that he might be the first to show honourable attention to the enemy that had become a friend.

Presently, as the wind dropped for a moment, Ulrich broke silence.

" Let's shout for help," he said ; " in this lull our voices may carry a little way."

" They won't carry far through the trees and undergrowth," said Georg, " but we can try. Together, then."

The two raised their voices in a prolonged hunting call.

" Together again," said Ulrich a few minutes later, after listening in vain for an answering halloo.

" I heard something that time, I think," said Ulrich.

" I heard nothing but the pestilential wind," said Georg hoarsely.

There was silence again for some minutes, and then Ulrich gave a joyful cry.

" I can see figures coming through the wood. They are following in the way I came down the hillside."

Both men raised their voices in as loud a shout as they could muster.

" They hear us ! They've stopped. Now they see us. They're running down the hill towards us," cried Ulrich.

" How many of them are there ? " asked Georg.

" I can't see distinctly," said Ulrich ; " nine or ten."

" Then they are yours," said Georg ; " I had only seven out with me."

" They are making all the speed they can, brave lads," said Ulrich gladly.

" Are they your men ? " asked Georg. " Are they your men ? " he repeated impatiently as Ulrich did not answer.

" No," said Ulrich with a laugh, the idiotic chattering laugh of a man unstrung with hideous fear.

" Who are they ? " asked Georg quickly, straining his eyes to see what the other would gladly not have seen.

" *Wolves.*"

THE TRAVELLING GRAVE

By

L. P. HARTLEY

HUGH CURTIS was in two minds about accepting Dick
Munt's invitation to spend Sunday at Lowlands. He
knew little of Munt, who was supposed to be rich and
eccentric and, like many people of that kind, a collector.
Hugh dimly remembered having asked his friend Valentine
Ostrop what it was that Munt collected, but he could not
recall Valentine's answer. Hugh Curtis was a vague man
with an unretentive mind, and the mere thought of a collection,
with its many separate challenges to the memory, fatigued
him. What he required of a week-end party was to be left
alone as much as possible, and to spend the remainder of his
time in the society of agreeable women. Searching his mind,
though with distaste, for he hated to disturb it, he remembered
Ostrop telling him that parties at Lowlands were generally
composed entirely of men, and rarely exceeded four in number.
Valentine didn't know who the fourth was to be, but he begged
Hugh to come.
  " You will enjoy Munt," he said. " He really doesn't
pose at all. It's his nature to be like that."
  " Like what ? " his friend had enquired.
  " Oh, original and—and queer, if you like," answered
Valentine. " He's one of the exceptions—he's much odder
than he seems, whereas most people are more ordinary than
they seem."
  Hugh Curtis agreed. " But I like ordinary people," he
added. " So how shall I get on with Munt ? "
  " Oh," said his friend, " but you're just the type he likes.
He prefers ordinary—it's a stupid word—I mean normal
people, because their reactions are more valuable."

" Shall I be expected to react ? " asked Hugh with nervous facetiousness.

" Ha ! ha ! " laughed Valentine, poking him gently—" we never quite know what he'll be up to. But you will come, won't you ? "

Hugh Curtis had said he would.

All the same, when Saturday morning came he began to regret his decision and to wonder whether it might not honourably be reversed. He was a man in early middle life, rather set in his ideas, and, though not specially a snob, unable to help testing a new acquaintance by the standards of the circle to which he belonged. This circle had never warmly welcomed Valentine Ostrop ; he was the most unconventional of Hugh's friends. Hugh liked him when they were alone together, but directly Valentine fell in with kindred spirits he developed a kind of foppishness of manner that Hugh instinctively disliked. He had no curiosity about his friends, and thought it out of place in personal relationships, so he had never troubled to ask himself what this altered demeanour of Valentine's, when surrounded by his cronies, might denote. But he had a shrewd idea that Munt would bring out Valentine's less sympathetic side. Could he send a telegram saying he had been unexpectedly detained ? Hugh turned the idea over ; but partly from principle, partly from laziness (he hated the mental effort of inventing false circumstances to justify change of plans) he decided he couldn't. His letter of acceptance had been so unconditional. He also had the fleeting notion (a totally unreasonable one) that Munt would somehow find out and be nasty about it.

So he did the best he could for himself ; looked out the latest train that would get him to Lowlands in decent time for dinner, and telegraphed that he would come by that. He would arrive at the house, he calculated, soon after seven. " Even if dinner is as late as half-past eight," he thought to himself, " they won't be able to do me much harm in an hour and a quarter." This habit of mentally assuring to himself periods of comparative immunity from unknown perils had begun at school. " Whatever I've done," he used to say to himself, " they can't kill me." With the war, this saving reservation had to be dropped : they could kill him, that was what they were there for. But now that peace was here the little mental amulet once more diffused its healing properties ; Hugh had recourse to it more often than he would have admitted. Absurdly enough he invoked it now.

But it annoyed him that he would arrive in the dusk of the
September evening. He liked to get his first impression of a
new place by daylight.

*   *   *   *   *   *

Hugh Curtis' anxiety to come late had not been shared by
the other two guests. They arrived at Lowlands in time for
tea. Though they had not travelled together, Ostrop motoring
down, they met practically on the doorstep, and each privately
suspected the other of wanting to have his host for a few
moments to himself.

But it seemed unlikely that their wish would have been
gratified even if they had not both been struck by the same
idea.   Tea came in, the water bubbled in the urn, but still
Munt did not present himself, and at last Ostrop asked his
fellow-guest to make the tea.

" You must be deputy-host," he said ; " you know Dick
so well, better than I do."

This was true.   Ostrop had long wanted to meet Tony
Bettisher who, after the death of someone vaguely known to
Valentine as Squarchy, ranked as Munt's oldest and closest
friend. He was a short, dark, thick-set man, whose appearance
gave no clue to his character or pursuits. He had, Valentine
knew, a job at the British Museum, but, to look at, he might
easily have been a stockbroker.

" I suppose you know this place at every season of the
year," Valentine said. " This is the first time I've been here
in the autumn. How lovely everything looks."

He gazed out at the wooded valley and the horizon fringed
with trees. The scent of burning garden-refuse drifted in
through the windows.

" Yes, I'm a pretty frequent visitor," answered Bettisher,
busy with the teapot.

" I gather from his letter that Dick has just returned from
abroad," said Valentine. " Why does he leave England on
the rare occasions when it's tolerable ? Does he do it for fun,
or does he have to ? " He put his head on one side and contemplated Bettisher with a look of mock despair.

Bettisher handed him a cup of tea.

" I think he goes when the spirit moves him."

" Yes, but *what* spirit ? " cried Valentine with an affected
petulance of manner. " Of course, our Richard is a law unto
himself : we all know that. But he must have some motive.
I don't suppose he's *fond* of travelling. It's *so* uncomfortable.

Now Dick cares for his comforts. That's why he travels with so much luggage."

" Oh does he ? " enquired Bettisher. " Have you been with him ? "

" No, but the Sherlock Holmes in me discovered that," declared Valentine triumphantly. " The trusty Franklin hadn't time to put it away. Two large crates. Now would you call that *personal* luggage ? " His voice was for ever underlining : it pounced upon " personal " like a hawk on a dove.

" Perambulators, perhaps," suggested Bettisher laconically.

" Oh, do you think so ? Do you think he collects perambulators ? That would explain everything ! "

" What would it explain ? " asked Bettisher, stirring in his chair.

" Why, his collection, of course ! " exclaimed Valentine, jumping up and bending on Bettisher an intensely serious gaze. " It would explain why he doesn't invite us to see it, and why he's so shy of talking about it. Don't you see ? An unmarried man, a bachelor, *sine prole*, as far as we know with whole *attics-full* of perambulators ! It would be *too* fantastic. The world would laugh, and Richard, much as we love him, is terribly serious. Do you imagine it's a kind of vice ? "

" All collecting is a form of vice."

" Oh no, Bettisher, don't be hard, don't be cynical—a *substitute* for vice. But tell me before he comes—he *must* come soon, the laws of hospitality demand it—am I right in my surmise ? "

" Which ? You have made so many."

" I mean that what he goes abroad for, what he fills his house with, what he thinks about when we're not with him—in a word, what he collects, is perambulators ? "

Valentine paused dramatically.

Bettisher did not speak. His eyelids flickered and the skin about his eyes made a sharp movement inwards. He was beginning to open his mouth when Valentine broke in—

" Oh no, of course, you're in his confidence, your lips are sealed. Don't tell me, you mustn't, I forbid you to ! "

" What's that he's not to tell you ? " said a voice from the other end of the room.

" Oh, Dick ! " cried Valentine, " what a start you gave me ! You must learn to move a little less like a dome of silence, mustn't he, Bettisher ? "

Their host came forward to meet them, on silent feet and

laughing soundlessly. He was a small, thin, slightly built man, very well turned out and with a conscious elegance of carriage.

" But I thought you didn't know Bettisher ? " he said, when their greetings had been accomplished. " Yet when I come in I find you with difficulty stemming the flood of confidences pouring from his lips."

His voice was slightly ironical, it seemed at the same moment to ask a question and to make a statement.

" Oh, we've been together for hours," said Valentine airily, " and had the most enchanting conversation. Guess what we talked about."

" Not about me, I hope ? "

" Well, about something very dear to you."

" About you, then ? "

" Don't make fun of me. The objects I speak of are solid and useful."

" That does rather rule you out," said Munt meditatively. " What are they useful for ? "

" Carrying bodies."

Munt glanced across at Bettisher, who was staring into the grate.

" And what are they made of ? "

Valentine tittered, pulled a face, answered, " I've had little experience of them, but I should think chiefly of wood."

Munt got up and looked hard at Bettisher, who raised his eyebrows and said nothing.

" They perform at one time or another," said Valentine, enjoying himself enormously, " an essential service for us all."

There was a pause. Then Munt asked—

" Where do you generally come across them ? "

" Personally I always try to avoid them," said Valentine. " But one meets them every day in the street and—and here, of course."

" Why do you try to avoid them ? " asked Munt rather grimly.

" Since you think about them, and dote upon them, and collect them from all the corners of the earth, it pains me to have to say it," said Valentine with relish, " but I do not care to contemplate lumps of human flesh lacking the spirit that makes flesh tolerable."

He struck an oratorical attitude and breathed audibly through his nose. There was a prolonged silence. The dusk began to make itself felt in the room.

" Well," said Munt at last, in a hard voice. " You are the

first person to guess my little secret, if I can give it so grandiose a name. I congratulate you."

Valentine bowed.

" May I ask how you discovered it ? While I was detained upstairs, I suppose you—you—poked about ? " His voice had a disagreeable ring ; but Valentine, unaware of this, said loftily—

" It was unnecessary. They were in the hall, plain to be seen by anyone. My Sherlock Holmes sense (I have eight or nine) recognized them immediately."

Munt shrugged his shoulders, then said in a less constrained tone—

" At this stage of our acquaintance I did not really intend to enlighten you. But since you know already, tell me, as a matter of curiosity, were you horrified ? "

." Horrified ? " cried Valentine. " I think it a charming taste, so original, so—so human. It ravishes my æsthetic sense ; it slightly offends my moral principles."

" I was afraid it might," said Munt.

" I am a believer in Birth Control," Valentine prattled on. " Every night I burn a candle to Stopes."

Munt looked puzzled. " But then, how can you object ? " he began.

Valentine went on without heeding him.

" But of course by making a corner in the things, you do discourage the whole business. Being exhibits they have to stand idle, don't they ? You keep them empty ? "

Bettisher started up in his chair, but Munt held out a pallid hand and murmured in a stifled voice—

" Yes, that is, most of them are."

Valentine clapped his hands in ectasy.

" But some are not ? Oh, but that's too ingenious of you. To think of the darlings lying there quite still, not able to lift a finger, much less scream ! A sort of mannequin parade ! "

" They certainly seem more complete with an occupant," Munt observed.

" But who's to push them ? They can't go of themselves."

" Listen," said Munt slowly. " I've just come back from abroad, and I've brought with me a specimen that does go by itself, or nearly. It's outside there where you saw, waiting to be unpacked."

Valentine Ostrop had been the life and soul of many a party. No one knew better than he how to breathe new life into a flagging joke. Privately he felt that this one was played

out ; but he had a social conscience ; he realized his responsibility towards conversation, and summoning all the galvanic
enthusiasm at his command he cried out—

"Do you mean to say that it looks after itself, it doesn't
need a helping hand, and that a fond mother can entrust her
precious charge to it without a nursemaid and without a
tremor ? "

"She can," said Munt, " and without an undertaker and
without a sexton."

"Undertaker . . .? Sexton . . .? " echoed Valentine. " What
have they to do with perambulators ? "

There was a pause, during which the three figures, struck
in their respective attitudes, seemed to have lost relationship
with each other.

"So you didn't know," said Munt at length, " that it was
coffins I collected."

*   *   *   *   *   *

An hour later the three men were standing in an upper
room, looking down at a large oblong object that lay in the
middle of a heap of shavings and seemed, to Valentine's sick
fancy, to be burying its head among them. Munt had been
giving a demonstration.

"Doesn't it look funny now it's still ? " he remarked.
" Almost as though it had been killed." He touched it pensively with his foot and it slid towards Valentine, who edged
away. You couldn't quite tell where it was coming ; it seemed
to have no settled direction, and to move all ways at once,
like a crab. " Of course the chances are really against it,"
sighed Munt. " But it's very quick, and it has that funny
gift of anticipation. If it got a fellow up against a wall, I
don't think he'd stand much chance. I didn't show you here,
because I value my floors, but it can bury itself in wood in
three minutes and in newly turned earth, say a flower-bed,
in one. It has to be this squarish shape, or it couldn't dig.
It just doubles the man up, you see, directly it catches him—
backwards, so as to break the spine. The top of the head fits
in just below the heels. The soles of the feet come uppermost.
The spring sticks a bit." He bent down to adjust something.
" Isn't it a charming toy ? "

"Looking at it from the criminal's standpoint, not the
engineer's," said Bettisher, " I can't see that it would be
much use in a house. Have you tried it on a stone floor ? "

"Yes, it screams in agony and blunts the blades."

" Exactly. Like a mole on paving-stones. And even on an ordinary carpeted floor it could cut its way in, but there would be a nice hole left in the carpet to show where it had gone."

Munt conceded this point also. " But it's an odd thing," he added, " that in several of the rooms in this house it would really work, and baffle anyone but an expert detective. Below, of course, are the knives, but the top is inlaid with real parquet. The grave is so sensitive—you saw just now how it seemed to grope—that it can feel the ridges and adjust itself perfectly to the pattern of the parquet. But of course I agree with you. It's not an indoor game, really : it's a field sport. You go on, will you, and leave me to clear up this mess. I'll join you in a moment."

Valentine followed Bettisher down into the library. He was very much subdued.

" Well, that was the funniest scene," remarked Bettisher, chuckling.

" Do you mean just now ? I confess it gave me the creeps."

" Oh no, not that : when you and Dick were talking at cross-purposes."

" I'm afraid I made a fool of myself," said Valentine dejectedly. " I can't quite remember what we said. I know there was something I wanted to ask you."

" Ask away, but I can't promise to answer."

Valentine pondered a moment.

" Now I remember what it was."

" Spit it out."

" To tell you the truth, I hardly like to. It was something Dick said. I hardly noticed at the time. I expect he was just playing up to me."

" Well ? "

" About those coffins. Are they real ? "

" How do you mean ' real ' ? "

" I mean, could they be used as——? "

" My dear chap, they have been."

Valentine smiled, rather mirthlessly.

" Are they full-size—life-size, as it were ? "

" The two things aren't quite the same," said Bettisher with a grin. " But there's no harm in telling you this : Dick's like all collectors. He prefers rarities, odd shapes, dwarfs, and that sort of thing. Of course any anatomical peculiarity has to have allowance made for it in the coffin. On the whole his specimens tend to be smaller than the general run—shorter, anyhow. Is that what you wanted to know ? "

" You've told me a lot," said Valentine. " But there was another thing."

" Out with it."

" When I imagined we were talking about perambulators—— "

" Yes, yes."

" I said something about their being empty. Do you remember ? "

" I think so."

" Then I said something about them having mannequins inside, and he seemed to agree."

" Oh, yes."

" Well, he couldn't have meant that. It would be too—too realistic."

" Mannequins aren't very realistic."

" Well, then, any sort of dummy."

" There are dummies and dummies. A skeleton isn't very talkative."

Valentine stared.

" He's been away," said Bettisher hastily. " I don't know what his latest idea is. But here's the man himself."

Munt came into the room.

" Children," he called out, " have you observed the time ? It's nearly seven o'clock. And do you remember that we have another guest coming ? He must be almost due."

" Who is he ? " asked Bettisher.

" A friend of Valentine's. Valentine, you must be responsible for him. I asked him partly to please you. I scarcely know him. What shall we do to entertain him ? "

" What sort of man is he ? " Bettisher enquired.

" Describe him, Valentine. Is he tall or short ? I don't remember."

" Medium."

" Dark or fair ? "

" Mouse-coloured."

" Old or young ? "

" About thirty-five."

" Married or single ? "

" Single."

" What, has he no ties ? No one to take an interest in him or bother what becomes of him ? "

" He has no near relations."

" Do you mean to say that very likely nobody knows he is coming to spend Sunday here ? "

" Probably not. He has rooms in London, and he wouldn't trouble to leave his address."

" Extraordinary the casual way some people live. Is he brave or timid ? "

" Oh, come, what a question ! About as brave as I am."

" Is he clever or stupid ? "

" All my friends are clever," said Valentine, with a flicker of his old spirit. " He's not intellectual : he'd be afraid of difficult parlour games or brilliant conversation."

" He ought not to have come here. Does he play bridge ? "

" I don't think he has much head for cards."

" Could Tony induce him to play chess ? "

" Oh, no, chess needs too much concentration."

" Is he given to wool-gathering, then ? " Munt asked. " Does he forget to look where he's going ? "

" He's the sort of man," said Valentine, " who expects to find everything just so. He likes to be led by the hand. He is perfectly tame and confiding, like a nicely brought up child."

" In that case," said Munt, " we must find some childish pastime that won't tax him too much. Would he like Musical Chairs ? "

" I think that would embarrass him," said Valentine. He began to feel a tenderness for his absent friend, and a wish to stick up for him. " I should leave him to look after himself. He's rather shy. If you try to make him come out of his shell, you'll scare him. He'd rather take the initiative himself. He doesn't like being pursued, but in a mild way he likes to pursue."

" A child with hunting instincts," said Munt pensively. " How can we accommodate him ? I have it ! Let's play Hide and Seek. We will hide and he shall seek. Then he can't feel that we are forcing ourselves upon him. It will be the height of tact. He will be here in a few minutes. Let's go and hide now."

" But he doesn't know his way about the house."

" That will be all the more fun for him, since he likes to make discoveries on his own account."

" He might fall and hurt himself."

" Children never do. Now you run away and hide while I talk to Franklin," Munt continued quietly, " and mind you play fair, Valentine—don't let your natural affections lead you astray. Don't give yourself up because you're hungry for your dinner."

* * * * * *

462   L. P. HARTLEY

The motor that met Hugh Curtis was shiny and smart and glittered in the rays of the setting sun. The chauffeur was like an extension of it, and so quick in his movements that in the matter of stowing Hugh's luggage, putting him in and tucking the rug round him, he seemed to steal a march on Time. Hugh regretted this precipitancy, this interference with the rhythm of his thoughts. It was a foretaste of the effort of adaptability he would soon have to make ; the violent mental readjustment that every visit, and specially every visit among strangers entails : a surrender of the personality, the fanciful might call it a little death.

The car slowed down, left the main road, passed through white gate-posts and followed for two or three minutes a gravel drive shadowed by trees. In the dusk Hugh could not see how far to right and left these extended. But the house, when it appeared, was plain enough : a large, regular, early nineteenth century building, encased in cream-coloured stucco and pierced at generous intervals by large windows, some round-headed, some rectangular. It looked dignified and quiet, and in the twilight seemed to shine with a soft radiance of its own. Hugh's spirits began to rise. In his mind's ear he already heard the welcoming buzz of voices from a distant part of the house. He smiled at the man who opened the door. But the man didn't return his smile, and no sound came through the gloom that spread out behind him.

" Mr. Munt and his friends are playing ' Hide-and-Seek ' in the house, Sir," the man said, with a gravity that checked Hugh's impulse to laugh. " I was to tell you that the library is home, and you were to be ' He,' or I think he said, ' It,' Sir. This is the way to the library. Be careful, Sir, Mr. Munt did not want the lights turned on till the game was over."

" Am I to start now ? " asked Hugh, stumbling a little as he followed his guide—" or can I go to my room first ? "

The butler stopped and opened a door. " This is the library," he said. " I think it was Mr. Munt's wish that the game should begin immediately upon your arrival, Sir."

A faint coo-ee sounded through the house.

" Mr. Munt said you could go anywhere you liked," the man added as he went away.

*   *   *   *   *   *

Valentine's emotions were complex. The harmless frivolity of his mind had been thrown out of gear by its encounter with the harsher frivolity of his friend. Munt, he felt sure, had a heart of gold which he chose to hide beneath a slightly sinister exterior. With his travelling graves and charnel-talk he had hoped to get a rise out of his guest, and he had succeeded. Valentine still felt slightly unwell. But his nature was remarkably resilient, and the charming innocence of the pastime on which they were now engaged soothed and restored his spirits, gradually reaffirming his first impression of Munt as a man of fine mind and keen perceptions, a dilettante with the personal force of a man of action, a character with a vein of implacability, to be respected but not to be feared. He was conscious also of a growing desire to see Curtis ; he wanted to see Curtis and Munt together, confident that two people he liked could not fail to like each other. He pictured the pleasant encounter after the mimic warfare of Hide-and-Seek—the captor and the caught laughing a little breathlessly over the diverting circumstances of their reintroduction. With every passing moment his mood grew more sanguine.

Only one misgiving remained to trouble it. He felt he wanted to confide in Curtis, tell him something of what had happened during the day ; and this he could not do without being disloyal to his host. Try as he would to make light of Munt's behaviour about his collection, it was clear he wouldn't have given away the secret if it had not been surprised out of him. And Hugh would find his friend's bald statement of the facts difficult to swallow.

But what was he up to, letting his thoughts run on like this ? He must hide, and quickly too. His acquaintance with the lie of the house, the fruits of two visits, was scanty, and the darkness did not help him. The house was long and symmetrical ; its principal rooms lay on the first floor. Above were servants' rooms, attics, boxrooms, probably—plenty of natural hiding-places. The second storey was the obvious refuge.

He had been there only once, with Munt that afternoon, and he did not specially want to re-visit it ; but he must enter into the spirit of the game. He found the staircase and went up, then paused : there was really no light at all.

" This is absurd," thought Valentine. " I must cheat." He entered the first room to the left, and turned down the switch. Nothing happened : the current had been cut off at the main. But by the light of a match he made out that he was in a combined bed-and-bathroom. In one corner was a bed, and in the other a large rectangular object with a lid over it, obviously a bath. The bath was close to the door.

As he stood debating he heard footsteps coming along the corridor. It would never do to be caught like this, without a run for his money. Quick as thought he raised the lid of the bath, which was not heavy, and slipped inside, cautiously lowering the lid.

It was narrower than the outside suggested, and it did not feel like a bath, but Valentine's enquiries into the nature of his hiding-place were suddenly cut short. He heard voices in the room, so muffled that he did not know at first whose they were. But they were evidently in disagreement.

Valentine lifted the lid. There was no light, so he lifted it farther. Now he could hear clearly enough.

" But I don't know what you really want, Dick," Bettisher was saying. " With the safety-catch it would be pointless, and without it would be damned dangerous.. Why not wait a bit ? "

" I shall never have a better opportunity than this," said Munt, but in a voice so unfamiliar that Valentine scarcely recognized it.

" Opportunity for what ? " said Bettisher.

" To prove whether the Travelling Grave can do what Madrali claimed for it."

" You mean whether it can disappear ? We know it can."

" I mean whether it can effect somebody' else's disappearance."

There was a pause. Then Bettisher said—" Give it up. That's my advice."

" But he wouldn't leave a trace," said Munt half petulant, half pleading, like a thwarted child. " He has no relations. Nobody knows he's here. Perhaps he isn't here. We can tell Valentine he never turned up."

" We discussed all that," said Bettisher decisively, " and it won't wash."

There was another silence, disturbed by the distant hum of a motor-car.

" We must go," said Bettisher.

But Munt appeared to detain him. Half imploring, half whining, he said—

" Anyhow, you don't mind me having put it there with the safety-catch down."

" Where ? "

" By the china-cabinet. He's certain to run into it."

Bettisher's voice sounded impatiently from the passage.

" Well, if it pleases you. But it's quite pointless."

Munt lingered a moment, chanting to himself in a high voice, greedy with anticipation : " I wonder which is up and which is down."

When he had repeated this three times he scampered away, calling out peevishly : " You might have helped me, Tony. It's so heavy for me to manage."

* * * * * *

It was heavy indeed. Valentine, when he had fought down the hysteria that came upon him, had only one thought : to take the deadly object and put it somewhere out of Hugh Curtis' way. If he could drop it from a window, so much the better. In the darkness the vague outline of its bulk, placed just where one had to turn to avoid the china-cabinet, was dreadfully familiar. He tried to recollect the way it worked. Only one thing stuck in his mind. " The ends are dangerous, the sides are safe." Or should it be, " The sides are dangerous, the ends are safe ? " While the two sentences were getting mixed up in his mind, he heard the sound of " coo-ee," coming first from one part of the house, then from another. He could also hear footsteps in the hall below him.

Then he made up his mind, and with a confidence that surprised him put his arms round the wooden cube and lifted it into the air. He hardly noticed its weight as he ran with it down the corridor. Suddenly he realized that he must have passed through an open door. A ray of moonlight showed him that he was in a bedroom, standing directly in front of an old-fashioned wardrobe, a towering majestic piece of furniture with three doors, the middle one holding a mirror. Dimly he saw himself reflected there, his burden in his arms. He deposited it on the parquet without making a sound ; but on the way out he tripped over a footstool and nearly fell. He was relieved at making so much clatter, and the grating of the key, as he turned it in the lock, was music to his ears.

Automatically he put it in his pocket. But he paid the penalty for his clumsiness. He had not gone a step when a hand caught him by the elbow.

" Why, it's Valentine ! " Hugh Curtis cried. " Now come quietly, and take me to my host. I must have a drink."

" I should like one too," said Valentine, who was trembling all over. " Why can't we have some light ? "

" Turn it on, idiot," commanded his friend.

" I can't—it's cut off at the main. We must wait till Richard gives the word."

" Where is he ? "

" I expect he's tucked away somewhere. Richard ! " Valentine called out, " Dick ! " He was too self-conscious to be able to give a good shout. " Bettisher ! I'm caught ! The game's over ! "

There was silence a moment, then steps could be heard descending the stairs.

" Is that you, Dick ? " asked Valentine of the darkness.

" No, Bettisher." The gaiety of the voice did not ring quite true.

" I've been caught," said Valentine again, almost as Atalanta might have done, and as though it was a wonderful achievement reflecting great credit upon everybody. " Allow me to present you to my captor. No, this is me. We've been introduced already."

It was a moment or two before the mistake was corrected, the two hands groping vainly for each other in the darkness.

" I expect it will be a disappointment when you see me," said Hugh Curtis in the pleasant voice that made many people like him.

" I want to see you," declared Bettisher. " I will, too. Let's have some light."

" I suppose it's no good asking you if you've seen Dick ? " enquired Valentine facetiously. " He said we weren't to have any light till the game was finished. He's so strict with his servants ; they have to obey him to the letter. I daren't even ask for a candle. But *you* know the faithful Franklin well enough."

" Dick will be here in a moment surely," Bettisher said, for the first time that day appearing undecided.

They all stood listening.

" Perhaps he's gone to dress," Curtis suggested. " It's past eight o'clock."

" How can he dress in the dark ? " asked Bettisher.

Another pause.

" Oh, I'm tired of this," said Bettisher. " Franklin ! Franklin ! " His voice boomed through the house and a reply came almost at once from the hall, directly below them. " We think Mr. Munt must have gone to dress," said Bettisher. " Will you please turn on the light ? "

" Certainly, Sir, but I don't think Mr. Munt is in his room."

" Well, anyhow——"

" Very good, Sir."

At once the corridor was flooded with light, and to all of them, in greater or less degree according to their familiarity with their surroundings, it seemed amazing that they should have had so much difficulty, half an hour before, in finding their way about. Even Valentine's harassed emotions experienced a moment's relaxation. They chaffed Hugh Curtis a little about the false impression his darkling voice had given them. Valentine, as always the more loquacious, swore it seemed to proceed from a large gaunt man with a hair-lip. They were beginning to move towards their rooms, Valentine had almost reached his, when Hugh Curtis called after them :
" I say, may I be taken to my room ? "
" Of course," said Bettisher, turning back. " Franklin ! Franklin ! Franklin, show Mr. Curtis where his room is. I don't know myself." He disappeared and the butler came slowly up the stairs.
" It's quite near, Sir, at the end of the corridor," he said. " I'm sorry, with having no light we haven't got your things put out. But it'll only take a moment."
The door did not open when he turned the handle.
" Odd ! It's stuck," he remarked : but it did not yield to the pressure of his knee and shoulder. " I've never known it to be locked before," he muttered, thinking aloud, obviously put out by this flaw in the harmony of the domestic arrangements. " If you'll excuse me, Sir, I'll go and fetch my key."
In a minute or two he was back with it. So gingerly did he turn the key in the lock he evidently expected another rebuff ; but it gave a satisfactory click and the door swung open with the best will in the world.
" Now I'll go and fetch your suitcase," he said as Hugh Curtis entered.

*　　*　　*　　*　　*　　*

" No, it's absurd to stay," soliloquized Valentine, fumbling feverishly with his front stud, " after all these warnings, it would be insane. It's what they do in a ' shocker,' linger on and on, disregarding revolvers and other palpable hints, while one by one the villain picks them off, all except the hero, who is generally the stupidest of all, but the luckiest. No doubt by staying I should qualify to be the hero : I should survive ; but what about Hugh, and Bettisher, that close-mouthed rat-trap ? " He studied his face in the glass : it looked flushed. " I've had an alarming increase in blood-pressure : I am seriously unwell ; I must go away at once to a nursing home, and Hugh must accompany me." He gazed

round wretchedly at the charmingly furnished room, with its
chintz and polished furniture, so comfortable, safe and
unsensational. And for the hundredth time his thoughts
veered round and blew from the opposite quarter. It would
equally be madness to run away at a moment's notice, scared
by what was no doubt only an elaborate practical joke. Munt,
though not exactly a jovial man, would have his joke, as
witness the game of Hide-and-Seek. No doubt the Travelling
Grave itself was just a take-in, a test of his and Bettisher's
credulity. Munt was not popular, he had few friends, but
that did not make him a potential murderer. Valentine had
always liked him, and no one, to his knowledge, had ever
spoken a word against him. What sort of figure would he,
Valentine, cut, after this nocturnal flitting ? He would lose
at least two friends, Munt and Bettisher, and cover Hugh
Curtis and himself with ridicule.

Poor Valentine ! So perplexed was he that he changed
his mind five times on the way down to the library. He kept
repeating to himself the sentence, " I'm so sorry, Dick, I
find my blood-pressure rather high, and I think I ought to
go into a nursing home to-night—Hugh will see me safely
there——" until it became meaningless : even its absurdity
disappeared.

Hugh was in the library alone. It was now or never ;
but Valentine's opening words were swept aside by his friend
who came running across the room to him.

" Oh, Valentine, the funniest thing has happened."

" Funny ? Where ? What ? " Valentine asked.

" No, no, don't look as if you'd seen a ghost. It's not the
least serious. Only it's so *odd*. This is a house of surprises.
I'm glad I came."

" Tell me quickly."

" Don't look so alarmed. It's only very amusing. But I
must show it you, or you'll miss the funny side of it. Come
on up to my room ; we've got five minutes."

But before they crossed the threshold Valentine pulled up
with a start.

" Is *this* your room ? "

" Oh, yes. Don't look as if you had seen a ghost. It's a
perfectly ordinary room, I tell you, except for one thing.
No, stop a moment ; wait here while I arrange the scene."

He darted in, and after a moment summoned Valentine
to follow.

" Now, do you notice anything strange ? "

" I see the usual evidences of untidiness."

A coat was lying on the floor and various articles of clothing were scattered about.

" You do ? Well then—no deceit, gentlemen." With a gesture he snatched the coat up from the floor. " Now what do you see ? "

" I see a further proof of slovenly habits—a pair of shoes where the coat was."

" Look well at those shoes. There's nothing about them that strikes you as peculiar ? "

Valentine studied them. They were ordinary brown shoes, lying side by side, the soles uppermost, a short pace from the wardrobe. They looked as though someone had taken them off and forgotten to put them away, or taken them out, and forgotten to put them on.

" Well," pronounced Valentine at last, " I don't usually leave my shoes upside-down like that, but you might."

" Ah," said Hugh triumphantly, " your surmise is incorrect. They're *not* my shoes."

" Not yours ? Then they were left here by mistake. Franklin should have taken them away."

" Yes, but that's where the coat comes in. I'm reconstructing the scene, you see, hoping to impress you. While he was downstairs fetching my bag, to save time I began to undress ; I took my coat off and hurled it down there. After he had gone I picked it up. So he never saw the shoes."

" Well, why make such a fuss ? They won't be wanted till morning. Or would you rather ring for Franklin and tell him to take them away ? "

" Ah ! " cried Hugh, delighted by this. " At last you've come to the heart of the matter. He *couldn't* take them away."

" Why couldn't he ? "

" Because they're fixed to the floor ! "

" Oh, rubbish ! " said Valentine. " You must be dreaming."

He bent down, took hold of the shoes by the welts, and gave a little tug. They did not move.

" There you are ! " cried Hugh. " Apologize. Own that it is unusual to find in one's room a strange pair of shoes adhering to the floor."

Valentine's reply was to give another heave. Still the shoes did not budge.

" No good," commented his friend. " They're nailed down, or gummed down, or something."

" The dinner-bell hasn't rung ; we'll get Franklin to clear up the mystery."

The butler when he came looked uneasy, and surprised them by speaking first.

" Was it Mr. Munt you were wanting, Sir ? " he said to Valentine. " I don't know where he is. I've looked everywhere and can't find him."

" Are these his shoes by any chance ? " asked Valentine.

They couldn't deny themselves the mild entertainment of watching Franklin stoop down to pick up the shoes, and recoil in perplexity when he found them fast in the floor.

" These should be Mr. Munt's, Sir," he said doubtfully— " these should. But what's happened to them that they won't leave the floor ? "

The two friends laughed gaily.

" That's what *we* want to know," Hugh Curtis chuckled. " That's why we called you : we thought you could help us."

" They're Mr. Munt's right enough," muttered the butler. " They must have got something heavy inside."

" Damned heavy," said Valentine, playfully grim.

Fascinated, the three men stared at the upturned soles, so close together that there was no room between for two thumbs set side by side.

Rather gingerly the butler stooped again, and tried to feel the uppers. This was not as easy as it seemed, for the shoes were flattened against the floor, as if a weight had pressed them down.

His face was white as he stood up.

" There *is* something in them," he said in a frightened voice.

" And his shoes were full of feet," carolled Valentine flippantly. " Trees, perhaps."

" It was not as hard as wood," said the butler. " You can squeeze it a bit if you try."

They looked at each other, and a tension made itself felt in the room.

" There's only one way to find out," declared Hugh Curtis suddenly, in a determined tone one could never have expected from him.

" How ? "

" Take them off "

" Take what off ? "

" His shoes off, you idiot."

" Off what ? "

*."The foot's inside it all right," cried Curtis, and began tugging
at one of the shoes.*

" That's what I don't know yet, you bloody fool ! " Curtis almost screamed ; and kneeling down, he tore apart the laces and began tugging and wrenching at one of the shoes.

" It's coming, it's coming," he cried. " Valentine, put your arms round me and pull, that's a good fellow. It's the heel that's giving the trouble."

Suddenly the shoe slipped off.

" Why, it's only a sock," whispered Valentine ; " it's so thin."

" Yes, but the foot's inside it all right," cried Curtis in a loud strange voice, speaking very rapidly. " And here's the ankle, see, and here's where it begins to go down into the floor, see ; he must have been a very small man ; you see I never saw him, but it's all so crushed——"

The sound of a heavy fall made them turn.

Franklin had fainted.

THE TELL TALE HEART

By

EDGAR ALLAN POE

TRUE !—nervous—very, very dreadfully nervous I had been and am ; but why *will* you say that I am mad ? The disease had sharpened my senses—not destroyed—not dulled them. Above all was the sense of hearing acute. I heard all things in the heaven and in the earth. I heard many things in hell. How, then, am I mad ? Hearken ! and observe how healthily—how calmly I can tell you the whole story.

It is impossible to say how first the idea entered my brain ; but once conceived, it haunted me day and night. Object there was none. Passion there was none. I loved the old man. He had never wronged me. He had never given me insult. For his gold had no desire. I think it was his eye ! yes, it was this ! One of his eyes resembled that of a vulture—a pale blue eye, with a film over it. Whenever it fell upon me, my blood ran cold ; and so by degrees—very gradually—I made up my mind to take the life of the old man, and thus rid myself of the eye for ever.

Now this is the point. You fancy me mad. Madmen know nothing. But you should have seen *me*. You should have seen how wisely I proceeded—with what caution—with what fore-sight—with what dissimulation I went to work ! I was never kinder to the old man than during the whole week before I killed him. And every night, about midnight, I turned the latch of his door and opened it—oh, so gently ! And then when I had made an opening sufficient for my head, I put in a dark lantern, all closed, closed, so that no light shone out, and then I thrust in my head. Oh, you would have laughed to see how cunningly I thrust it in ! I moved it slowly—very, very slowly, so that I might not disturb the old man's sleep. It took me an hour to place my whole head within the opening so far that I

could see him as he lay upon his bed. Ha !—would a madman
have been so wise as this ? And then, when my head was well
in the room, I undid the lantern cautiously—oh, so cautiously
—cautiously (for the hinges creaked)—I undid it just so much
that a single thin ray fell upon the vulture eye. And this I did
for seven long nights—every night just at midnight—but I
found the eye always closed ; and so it was impossible to do
the work ; for it was not the old man who vexed me, but his
Evil Eye. And every morning, when the day broke, I went
boldly into the chamber, and spoke courageously to him, calling
him by name in a hearty tone, and inquiring how he had passed
the night. So you see he would have been a very profound
old man, indeed, to suspect that every night, just at twelve, I
looked in upon him while he slept.

Upon the eighth night I was more than usually cautious in
opening the door. A watch's minute hand moves more quickly
than did mine. Never before that night had I *felt* the extent
of my own powers—of my sagacity. I could scarcely contain
my feelings of triumph. To think that there I was, opening
the door, little by little, and he not even to dream of my secret
deeds or thoughts. I fairly chuckled at the idea ; and perhaps
he heard me ; for he moved on the bed suddenly, as if startled.
Now you may think that I drew back—but no. His room was
as black as pitch with the thick darkness (for the shutters were
close fastened, through fear of robbers), and so I knew that he
could not see the opening of the door, and I kept pushing it on
steadily, steadily.

I had my head in, and was about to open the lantern, when
my thumb slipped upon the tin fastening, and the old man
sprang up in the bed, crying out—" Who's there ? "

I kept quite still and said nothing. For a whole hour I did
not move a muscle, and in the meantime I did not hear him
lie down. He was still sitting up in the bed, listening ;—just
as I have done, night after night, hearkening to the death-
watches in the wall.

Presently I heard a slight groan, and I knew it was the groan
of mortal terror. It was not a groan of pain or of grief—oh,
no !—it was the low stifled sound that arises from the bottom
of the soul when overcharged with awe. I knew the sound
well. Many a night, just at midnight, when all the world slept,
it has welled up from my own bosom, deepening, with its
dreadful echo, the terrors that distracted me. I say I knew it
well. I knew what the old man felt, and pitied him, although
I chuckled at heart. I knew that he had been lying awake ever

since the first slight noise, when he had turned in the bed.
His fears had been ever since growing upon him.   He had been
trying to fancy them causeless, but could not.   He had been
saying to himself—" It is nothing but the wind in the chimney
—it is only a mouse crossing the floor," or, " it is merely a
cricket which has made a single chirp."   Yes, he has been
trying to comfort himself with these suppositions : but he had
found all in vain.   *All in vain ;* because Death, in approaching
him, had stalked with his black shadow before him, and
enveloped the victim.   And it was the mournful influence of
the unperceived shadow that caused him to feel,—although he
neither saw nor heard—to *feel* the presence of my head within
the room.

When I had waited a long time, very patiently, without
hearing him lie down, I resolved to open a little—a very, very
little crevice in the lantern.   So I opened it—you cannot
imagine how stealthily, stealthily—until, at length, a single
dim ray, like the thread of the spider, shot from out the crevice
and fell upon the vulture eye.

It was open—wide, wide open—and I grew furious as I
gazed upon it.   I saw it with perfect distinctness—all a dull
blue, with a hideous veil over it that chilled the very marrow
in my bones ; but I could see nothing else of the old man's
face or person : for I had directed the ray, as if by instinct,
precisely upon the damned spot.

And now have I not told you that what you mistake for
madness is but over acuteness of the senses ?—now, I say,
there came to my ears a low, dull, quick sound, such as a watch
makes when enveloped in cotton.   I knew *that* sound well, too.
It was the beating of the old man's heart.   It increased my
fury, as the beating of a drum stimulates the soldier into courage.

But even yet I refrained and kept still.   I scarcely breathed.
I held the lantern motionless.   I tried how steadily I could
maintain the ray upon the eye.   Meantime the hellish tatoo of
the heart increased.   It grew quicker and quicker, and louder
and louder every instant.   The old man's terror *must* have been
extreme !   It grew louder, I say, louder every moment !—do
you mark me well ?   I have told you that I am nervous : so I
am.   And now, at the dead hour of the night, amid the dreadful
silence of that old house, so strange a noise as this excited me
to uncontrollable terror.   Yet, for some minutes longer, I
refrained and stood still.   But the beating grew louder, louder !
I thought the heart must burst.   And now a new anxiety seized
me—the sound would be heard by a neighbour !   The old

man's hour had come ! With a loud yell I threw open the
lantern and leaped into the room. He shrieked once—once
only. In an instant I dragged him to the floor, and pulled the
heavy bed over him. I then smiled gaily, to find the deed so
far done. But, for many minutes, the heart beat on with a
muffled sound. This, however, did not vex me ; it would not
be heard through the wall. At length it ceased. The old man
was dead. I removed the bed and examined the corpse. Yes,
he was stone, stone dead. I placed my hand upon the heart
and held it there many minutes. There was no pulsation. He
was stone dead. His eye would trouble me no more.

If still you think me mad, you will think so no longer when
I describe the wise precautions I took for the concealment of
the body. The night waned, and I worked hastily, but in
silence. First of all I dismembered the corpse. I cut off the
head and the arms and the legs.

I then took up three planks from the flooring of the chamber
and deposited all between the scantlings. I then replaced the
boards so cleverly, so cunningly, that no human eye—not even
his—could have detected anything wrong. There was nothing
to wash out—no stain of any kind—no blood-spot whatever.
I had been too wary for that. A tub had caught all—ha ! ha !

When I had made an end of these labours, it was four
o'clock—still dark as midnight. As the bell sounded the hour,
there came a knocking at the street door. I went down to open
it with a light heart,—for what had I *now* to fear ? There
entered three men, who introduced themselves with perfect
suavity, as officers of the police. A shriek had been heard by
a neighbour during the night ; suspicion of foul play had been
aroused ; information had been lodged at the police office, and
they (the officers) had been deputed to search the premises.

I smiled—for *what* had I to fear ? I bade the gentlemen
welcome. The shriek, I said, was my own in a dream. The
old man, I mentioned, was absent in the country. I took my
visitors all over the house. I bade them search—search *well*.
I led them, at length, to *his* chamber. I showed them his
treasures, secure, undisturbed. In the enthusiasm of my
confidence, I brought chairs into the room, and desired them
here to rest from their fatigues, while I myself, in the wild
audacity of my perfect triumph, placed my own seat upon the
very spot beneath which reposed the corpse of the victim.

The officers were satisfied. My *manner* had convinced
them. I was singularly at ease. They sat, and while I answered cheerily, they chatted of familiar things. But, ere long.

I felt myself getting pale and wished them gone. My head ached, and I fancied a ringing in my ears : but still they sat and still chatted. The ringing became more distinct :—it continued and became more distinct : I talked more freely to get rid of the feeling : but it continued and gained definitiveness—until, at length, I found that the noise was *not* within my ears.

No doubt I now grew *very* pale :—but I talked more fluently, and with a heightened voice. Yet the sound increased —and what could I do ? It was *a low, dull, quick sound—much such a sound as a watch makes when enveloped in cotton*. I gasped for breath—and yet the officers heard it not. I talked more quickly—more vehemently ; but the noise steadily increased. I arose and argued about trifles, in a high key and with violent gesticulations ; but the noise steadily increased. Why *would* they not be gone ? I paced the floor to and fro with heavy strides, as if excited to fury by the observations of the men— but the noise steadily increased. Oh God ! what *could* I do ? I foamed—I raved—I swore ! I swung the chair upon which I had been sitting, and grated it upon the boards, but the noise arose over all and continually increased. It grew louder —louder—*louder* ! And still the men chatted pleasantly, and smiled. Was it possible they heard not ? Almighty God !— no, no ! They heard !—they suspected !—they *knew* !—they were making a mockery of my horror !—this I thought, and this I think. But anything was better than this agony ! Anything was more tolerable than this derision ! I could bear those hypocritical smiles no longer ! I felt that I must scream or die !—and now—again ! hark ! louder ! louder ! louder ! *louder* !—

" Villains ! " I shrieked, " dissemble no more ! I admit the deed !—tear up the planks !—here, here !—it is the beating of his hideous heart ! "

THE BIRD WOMAN

By

H. SPICER

THE events of this strange tale, though they actually occurred in England but a short while since would scarcely be out of place in a book of German dreams and fancies.

The narrator, a girl of the servant class, but of rather superior education and manners, had called on the writer's sister on the subject of a place to which she had been recommended, and in the course of conversation, related the following as a recent experience.

The advertisement in which she set forth her willingness to take charge of an invalid, infirm, or lunatic person, or to assume any office demanding unusual steadiness of nerve, was replied to by a lady whose letter was dated from a certain locality on the outskirts of a large commercial city, and who requested her attendance there at an appointed time.

The house proved to be a dingy, deserted looking mansion, and was not rendered more cheerful by the fact that the adjoining tenements on either side were unoccupied. It wore altogether a haunted and sinister aspect, and the girl, as she rang the bell, was sensible of a kind of misgiving for which she could not account. A timid person might have hesitated. This girl possessed unusual firmness and courage, and, in spite of the presentiment we have mentioned, she determined, at all events, to see *what* she would be called on to encounter.

A lady-like person, the mistress herself, opened the door, and conducting the applicant into a vacant apartment, informed her in a few words that the service that would be required of her was of a very peculiar nature imperatively demanding those precise qualities she conceived her to possess. It was right, she added, to mention that the family lived in great seclusion, partly from choice, partly from necessity, an impression having gone abroad that there existed something strange and evil in connection with the residence, which was, in reality, known in the vicinity by the title of the " haunted house."

With these preliminary warnings, the lady suggested that the applicant might wish to reconsider her purpose. The latter, however, having little fear of anything human, and none at all of apparitions, at once agreed to the terms proposed stipulating only that the cause of the strange reports affecting the mansion should be a little more clearly explained, and her own particular duties defined.

The mistress readily assented to both conditions, and, leading the way to a ground floor apartment at the back, unlocked the door and turned the handle as about to enter, but checking herself suddenly, warned her companion, without sinking her voice below its ordinary tone, that she was about to be brought face to face with a spectacle that might well try the strongest nerves ; nevertheless, there was nothing to fear so long as she retained her self-command. With this not very re-assuring preface, they entered the room.

It was rather dark, for the lower half of the windows were boarded up ; but in one corner, on the floor was plainly distinguishable what looked like a heap of clothes flung together in disorder. It appeared to be in motion, however, and the mistress of the house once more turning to her follower had just time to utter the mysterious words—

" Don't be frightened. If she likes you she'll hoot ; if she doesn't she'll scream."

When from the apex of the seeming heap of clothes there rose a head that made the stranger's blood run chill. It was human, indeed, in general structure, but exhibited, in place of a nose, a huge beak curved and pointed like that of an owl. Two large staring yellow eyes increased the bizarre resemblance, while numerous tufts of some feathery substance, sprouting from a hard skin and black as a parrot's tongue, completed this horrible intermingling of bird and woman.

As they approached, the unhappy being rose and sunk with the measured motion of a bird upon a perch, and presently, opening its mouth, gave utterance to a hideous and prolonged " tu-whoo."

" All right," said the lady quietly, " she likes you ! "

They were now standing as it were over the unfortunate freak of nature.

" Have you the courage to lift her ? " enquired the lady.
" Try."

The girl, though recoiling instinctively from the contact, nerved herself to the utmost, and, putting her arms beneath those of the still hooting creature, strove to raise it up. In doing so, the hands became disengaged from the clothes. They were black, and armed with long curved talons, like those of a bird of prey.

Even this new discovery might not have made the girl's courage quail, had she not, in raising the creature, observed that she was not, as had seemed to be the case, crouched on the ground, but balanced on an actual perch, or rail, round which her feet closed and clung by means of talons similar to those which adorned her hands.

So inexpressible was the feeling of horror that now overcame the visitor, that, after one desperate effort of self control, she was forced to let go of the thing she held. A wild, unearthly scream that rang through the house marked the creature's change of mood. The baleful eyes shot yellow fire, and scream after scream pursued her as she fairly fled from the apartment, followed at a steadier pace, by the lady.

The latter took her into another room, did all in her power to sooth her agitation, but expressed no surprise when the girl declared that ten times the liberal amount already offered, would not tempt her to undertake such a charge.

THE DABBLERS

By

WILLIAM FRYER HARVEY

I T was a wet July evening. The three friends sat around
the peat fire in Harborough's den, pleasantly weary after
their long tramp across the moors. Scott, the ironmaster,
had been declaiming against modern education. His partner's
son had recently entered the business with everything to learn,
and the business couldn't afford to teach him. " I suppose,"
he said, " that from preparatory school to University, Wilkins
must have spent the best part of three thousand pounds on
filling a suit of plus-fours with brawn. It's too much. My
boy is going to Steelborough grammar school. Then when
he's sixteen I shall send him to Germany so that he can learn
from our competitors. Then he'll put in a year in the office ;
afterwards, if he shows any ability, he can go up to Oxford.
Of course he'll be rusty and out of his stride, but he can mug
up his Latin in the evenings as my shop stewards do with their
industrial history and economics."

" Things aren't as bad as you make out," said Freeman,
the architect. " The trouble I find with schools is in choosing
the right one where so many are excellent. I've entered my
boy for one of those old country grammar schools that have
been completely re-modelled. Wells showed in the *Undying
Fire* what an enlightened headmaster can do when he is given
a free hand and isn't buried alive in mortar and tradition."

" You'll probably find," said Scott, " that it's mostly eye-
wash ; no discipline, and a lot of talk about self-expression
and education for service."

" There you're wrong. I should say the discipline is too
severe if anything. I heard only the other day from my young
nephew that two boys had been expelled for a raid on a hen-
roost or some such escapade ; but I suppose there was more

482

to it than met the eye. What are you smiling about, Harborough ? "

" It was something you said about headmasters and tradition. I was thinking about tradition and boys. Rum, secretive little beggars. It seems to me quite possible that there is a wealth of hidden lore passed on from one generation of schoolboys to another that it might be well worth while for a psychologist or an anthropologist to investigate. I remember at my first school writing some lines of doggerel in my books. They were really an imprecation against anyone who should steal them. I've seen practically the same words in old monkish manuscripts ; they go back to the time when books were of value. But it was on the fly-leaves of Abbott's *Via Latina* and Locke's *Arithmetic* that I wrote them. Nobody would want to steal those books. Why should boys start to spin tops at a certain season of the year ? The date is not fixed by shopkeepers, parents are not consulted, and though saints have been flogged to death I have found no connection between top whipping and the church calendar. The matter is decided for them by an unbroken tradition, handed down, not from father to son, but from boy to boy. Nursery rhymes are not perhaps a case in point, though they are stuffed with odd bits of folk lore. I remember being taught a game that was played with knotted handkerchiefs manipulated by the fingers to the accompaniment of a rhyme which began, ' Father Confessor, I've come to confess.' My instructor, aged eight, was the son of a High Church vicar. I don't know what would have happened if old Tomlinson had heard the last verse :—

> " ' Father Confessor, what shall I do ?'
> ' Go to Rome and kiss the Pope's toe.'
> ' Father Confessor, I'd rather kiss you.'
> ' Well, child, do.' "

" What was the origin of that little piece of doggerel ? " asked Freeman. " It's new to me."

" I don't know," Harborough replied. " I've never seen it in print. But behind the noddings of the knotted handkerchiefs and our childish giggles lurked something sinister. I seem to see the cloaked figure, cat-like and gliding, of one of those emissaries of the Church of Rome that creep into the pages of George Borrow—hatred and fear masked in ribaldry. I could give you other examples, the holly and ivy

carols, for instance, which used to be sung by boys and girls
to the accompaniment of a dance, and which, according to
some people, embody a crude form of nature worship."

" And the point of all this is what ? " asked Freeman.

" That there is a body of tradition, ignored by the ordinary
adult, handed down by one generation of children to another.
If you want a really good example—a really bad example I
should say, I'll tell you the story of the Dabblers." He waited
until Freeman and Scott had filled their pipes and then began.

" When I came down from Oxford and before I was
called to the Bar, I put in three miserable years at school
teaching."

Scott laughed.

" I don't envy the poor kids you cross-examined," he said.

" As a matter of fact, I was more afraid of them than they
of me. I got a job as usher at one of Freeman's old grammar
schools, only it had not been re-modelled and the headmaster
was a completely incompetent cleric. It was in the eastern
counties. The town was dead alive. The only thing that
seemed to warm the hearts of the people there was a dull
smouldering fire of gossip, and they all took turns in fanning
the flame. But I mustn't get away from the school. The
buildings were old ; the chapel had once been the choir of
a monastic church. There was a fine tithe barn, and a few
old stones and bases of pillars in the headmaster's garden,
but nothing more to show where monks had lived for centuries
except a dried-up fish pond.

" Late in June at the end of my first year, I was crossing the
playground at night on my way to my lodgings in the High
Street. It was after twelve. There wasn't a breath of air, and
the playing fields were covered with a thick mist from the
river. There was something rather weird about the whole
scene ; it was all so still and silent. The night smelt stuffy ;
and then suddenly I heard the sound of singing. I don't
know where the voices came from nor how many voices there
were, and not being musical I can't give you any idea of the
tune. It was very ragged with gaps in it, and there was something about it which I can only describe as disturbing. Anyhow I had no desire to investigate. I stood still for two or three
minutes listening and then let myself out by the lodge gate
into the deserted High Street. My bedroom above the
tobacconist's looked out on to a lane that led down to the
river. Through the open window I could still hear, very
faintly, the singing. Then a dog began to howl, and when

after a quarter of an hour it stopped, the June night was again still. Next morning in the master's common room I asked if anyone could account for the singing.

" ' It's the Dabblers,' said old Moneypenny, the science master, ' they usually appear about now.'

" Of course I asked who the Dabblers were.

" ' The Dabblers,' said Moneypenny, ' are carol singers born out of their due time. They are certain lads of the village who for reasons of their own, desire to remain anonymous ; probably choir boys with a grievance, who wish to pose as ghosts. And for goodness sake let sleeping dogs lie. We've thrashed out the Dabbler controversy so often that I'm heartily sick of it.'

" He was a cross-grained customer and I took him at his word. But later on in the week I got hold of one of the junior masters and asked him what it all meant. It seemed an established fact that the singing did occur at this particular time of the year. It was a sore point with Moneypenny, because on one occasion when somebody had suggested that it might be boys from the schoolhouse skylarking he had completely lost his temper.

" ' All the same,' said Atkinson, ' it might just as well be our boys as any others. If you are game next year we'll try to get to the bottom of it.'

" I agreed and there the matter stood. As a matter of fact when the anniversary came round I had forgotten all about the thing. I had been taking the lower school in prep. The boys had been unusually restless—we were less than a month from the end of term—and it was with a sigh of relief that I turned into Atkinson's study soon after eight to borrow an umbrella, for it was raining hard.

" ' By the by,' he said, ' to-night's the night the Dabblers are due to appear. What about it ? '

" I told him that if he imagined that I was going to spend the hours between then and midnight in patrolling the school precincts in the rain, he was greatly mistaken.

" ' That's not my idea at all,' he said. ' We won't set foot out of doors. I'll light the fire ; I can manage a mixed grill of sorts on the gas ring and there are a couple of bottles of beer in the cupboard. If we hear the Dabblers we'll quietly go the round of the dormitories and see if anyone is missing. If they are, we can await their return.'

" The long and short of it was that I fell in with his proposal. I had a lot of essays to correct on the Peasants'

Revolt—fancy kids of thirteen and fourteen being expected to write essays on anything—and I could go through them just as well by Atkinson's fire as in my own cheerless little sitting-room.

" It's wonderful how welcome a fire can be in a sodden June. We forgot our lost summer as we sat beside it smoking, warming our memories in the glow from the embers.

" ' Well,' said Atkinson at last, ' it's close on twelve. If the Dabblers are going to start, they are due about now.' He got up from his chair and drew aside the curtains.

" ' Listen ! " he said. Across the playground, from the direction of the playing-fields, came the sound of singing. The music—if it could be called such—lacked melody and rhythm and was broken by pauses ; it was veiled, too, by the drip, drip of the rain and the splashing of water from the gutter spouts. For one moment I thought I saw lights moving, but my eyes must have been deceived by reflections on the window pane.

" ' We'll see if any of our birds have flown,' said Atkinson. He picked up an electric torch and we went the rounds of the dormitories. Everything was as it should be. The beds were all occupied, the boys all seemed to be asleep. It was a quarter-past twelve by the time we got back to Atkinson's room. The music had ceased ; I borrowed a macintosh and ran home through the rain.

" That was the last time I heard the Dabblers, but I was to hear of them again. Act II was staged up at Scapa. I'd been transferred to a hospital ship, with a dislocated shoulder for X-ray, and as luck would have it the right-hand cot to mine was occupied by a lieutenant, R.N.V.R., a fellow called Holster, who had been at old Edmed's school a year or two before my time. From him I learned a little more about the Dabblers. It seemed that they were boys who for some reason or other kept up a school tradition. Holster thought that they got out of the house by means of the big wistaria outside B dormitory, after leaving carefully constructed dummies in their beds. On the night in June when the Dabblers were due to appear it was considered bad form to stay awake too long and very unhealthy to ask too many questions, so that the identity of the Dabblers remained a mystery. To the big and burly Holster there was nothing really mysterious about the thing ; it was a schoolboys' lark and nothing more. An unsatisfactory act, you will agree, and one which fails to carry the story forward. But with the third act the drama begins to move. You see I had the good luck to meet one of the Dabblers in the flesh.

" Burlingham was badly shell-shocked in the war ; a psycho-analyst took him in hand and he made a seemingly miraculous recovery. Then two years ago he had a partial relapse, and when I met him at Lady Byfleet's he was going up to Town three times a week for special treatment from some unqualified West-End practitioner, who seemed to be getting at the root of the trouble. There was something extra-ordinarily likeable about the man. He had a whimsical sense of humour that must have been his salvation, and with it was combined a capacity for intense indignation that one doesn't often meet with these days. We had a number of interesting talks together (part of his regime consisted of long cross-country walks, and he was glad enough of a companion) but the one I naturally remember was when in a tirade against English educational methods he mentioned Dr. Edmed's name,—' the head of a beastly little grammar school where I spent five of the most miserable years of my life.' "

" ' Three more than I did,' I replied.

" ' Good God ! ' he said, ' fancy you being a product of that place ! '

" ' I was one of the producers,' I answered. ' I'm not proud of the fact ; I usually keep it dark."

" ' There was a lot too much kept dark about that place,' said Burlingham. It was the second time he had used the words. As he uttered them, ' that place ' sounded almost the equivalent of an unnamable hell. We talked for a time about the school, of Edmed's pomposity, of old Jacobson the porter —a man whose patient good humour shone alike on the just and on the unjust—of the rat hunts in the tithe barn on the last afternoons of term.

" ' And now,' I said at last, ' tell me about the Dabblers.'

" He turned round on me like a flash and burst out laugh-ing, a high-pitched, nervous laugh that, remembering his condition, made me sorry I had introduced the subject. " How damnably funny ! " he said. " The man I go to in Town asked me the same question only a fortnight ago. I broke an oath in telling him, but I don't see why you shouldn't know as well. Not that there is anything to know ; it's all a queer boyish nightmare without rhyme or reason. You see I was one of the Dabblers myself."

" It was a curious disjointed story that I got out of Burling-ham. The Dabblers were a little society of five, sworn on solemn oath to secrecy. On a certain night in June, after warning had been given by their leader, they climbed out of the dormitories and met by the elm tree in old Edmed's garden. A raid was made on the doctor's poultry run, and, having secured a fowl, they retired to the tithe barn, cut its throat, plucked and cleaned it, and then roasted it over a fire in a brazier while the rats looked on. The leader of the Dabblers produced sticks of incense ; he lit his own from the fire, the others kindling theirs from his. Then all moved in slow procession to the summer-house in the corner of the doctor's garden, singing as they went. There was no sense in the words they sang. They weren't English and they weren't Latin. Burlingham described them as reminding him of the refrain in the old nursery rhyme :

> There were three brothers over the sea.
> *Peri meri dixi domine*
> They sent three presents unto me
> *Petrum partrum paradisi tempore*
> *Peri meri dixi domine.*

" ' And that was all ? ' I said to him.
" ' Yes,' he replied, ' that was all there was to it ; but—— '
" I expected the but.
" ' We were all of us frightened, horribly frightened. It was quite different from the ordinary schoolboy escapade. And yet there was fascination, too, in the fear. It was rather like,' and here he laughed, ' dragging a deep pool for the body of someone who had been drowned. You didn't know who it was, and you wondered what would turn up.'
" I asked him a lot of questions but he hadn't anything very definite to tell us. The Dabblers were boys in the lower and middle forms and with the exception of the leader their membership of the fraternity was limited to two years. Quite a number of boys, according to Burlingham, must have been Dabblers, but they never talked about it and no one, as far as he knew, had broken his oath. The leader in his time was called Tancred, the most unpopular boy in the school, despite the fact that he was their best athlete. He was expelled following an incident that took place in chapel. Burlingham didn't know what it was ; he was away in the sick-room at the time, and the accounts, I gather, varied considerably."
Harborough broke off to fill his pipe.
" Act IV will follow immediately," he said.
" All this is very interesting," observed Scott, " but I'm

A slow procession singing—but frightened, horribly frightened.

afraid that if it's your object to curdle our blood you haven't quite succeeded. And if you hope to spring a surprise on us in Act IV we must disillusion you." Freeman nodded assent.

" ' Scott who Edgar Wallace read,' " he began. " We're familiar nowadays with the whole bag of tricks. Black Mass is a certain winner ; I put my money on him. Go on, Harborough."

" You don't give a fellow half a chance, but I suppose you're right. Act IV takes place in the study of the Rev. Montague Cuttler, Vicar of St. Mary Parbeloe, a former senior mathematics master, but before Edmed's time—a dear old boy, blind as a bat, and a Fellow of the Society of Antiquaries. He knew nothing about the Dabblers. He wouldn't. But he knew a very great deal about the past history of the school, when it wasn't a school but a monastery. He used to do a little quiet excavating in the vacations and had discovered what he believed to be the stone that marked the tomb of Abbot Polegate. The man, it appeared, had a bad reputation for dabbling in forbidden mysteries.

" Hence the name Dabblers, I suppose," said Scott.

" I'm not so sure," Harborough answered. " I think that more probably it's derived from *diabolos*. But, anyhow, from old Cuttler I gathered that the Abbot's stone was where Edmed had placed his summer-house. Now doesn't it all illustrate my theory beautifully ? I admit that there are no thrills in the story. There's nothing really supernatural about it. Only it does show the power of oral tradition when you think of a bastard form of the black mass surviving like this for hundreds of years under the very noses of the pedagogues."

" It shows too," said Freeman, " what we have to suffer from incompetent headmasters. Now at the place I was telling you about where I've entered my boy—and I wish I could show you their workshops and art rooms—they've got a fellow who is—— "

" What was the name of the school ? " interrupted Harborough.

" Whitechurch Abbey."

" And a fortnight ago, you say, two boys were expelled for a raid on a hen roost ? "

" Yes."

" Well, it's the same place that I've been talking about. The Dabblers were out."

" Act V," said Scott, " and curtain. Harborough, you've got your thrill after all."

MARSYAS IN FLANDERS

By

VERNON LEE

"YOU are right. This is not the original crucifix at all.
Another one has been put instead. *Il y a eu substitution,*" and the little old Antiquary of Dunes
nodded mysteriously, fixing his ghostseer's eyes upon mine.

He said it in a scarce audible whisper. For it happened
to be the vigil of the Feast of the Crucifix, and the once famous
church was full of semi-clerical persons decorating it for the
morrow, and of old ladies in strange caps, clattering about
with pails and brooms. The Antiquary had brought me there
the very moment of my arrival, lest the crowd of faithful should
prevent his showing me everything next morning.

The famous crucifix was exhibited behind rows and rows
of unlit candles, and surrounded by strings of paper flowers
and coloured muslin, and garlands of sweet resinous maritime
pine ; and two lighted chandeliers illumined it.

"There has been an exchange," he repeated, looking
round that no one might hear him. " Il y a eu substitution."

For I had remarked, as anyone would have done, at the
first glance, that the crucifix had every appearance of French
work of the thirteenth century, boldly realistic, whereas the
crucifix of the legend, which was a work of St. Luke, which
had hung for centuries in the Holy Sepulchre at Jerusalem
and been miraculously cast ashore at Dunes in 1195, would
surely have been a more or less Byzantine image, like its
miraculous companion of Lucca.

"But why should there have been a substitution ? " I
inquired innocently.

"Hush, hush," answered the Antiquary, frowning, " not
here—later, later——"

He took me all over the church, once so famous for pilgrimages ; but from which, even like the sea which has left it

in a salt marsh beneath the cliffs, the tide of devotion has receded for centuries. It is a very dignified little church, of charmingly restrained and shapely Gothic, built of a delicate pale stone, which the sea damp has picked out, in bases and capitals and carved foliation, with stains of a lovely bright green. The Antiquary showed me where the transept and belfry had been left unfinished when the miracles had diminished in the fourteenth century. And he took me up to the curious warder's chamber, a large room up some steps in the triforium ; with a fireplace and stone seats for the men who guarded the precious crucifix day and night. There had even been beehives in the window, he told me, and he remembered seeing them still as a child.

" Was it usual, here in Flanders, to have a guardroom in churches containing important relics ? " I asked, for I could not remember having seen anything similar before.

" By no means," he answered, looking round to make sure we were alone, " but it was necessary here. You have never heard in what the chief miracles of this church consisted ? "

" No," I whispered back, gradually infected by his mysteriousness, " unless you allude to the legend that the figure of the Saviour broke all the crosses until the right one was cast up by the sea ? "

He shook his head but did not answer, and descended the steep stairs into the nave, while I lingered a moment looking down into it from the warder's chamber. I have never had so curious an impression of a church. The chandeliers on either side of the crucifix swirled slowly round, making great pools of light which were broken by the shadows of the clustered columns ; and among the pews of the nave moved the flicker of the sacristan's lamp. The place was full of the scent of resinous pine branches, evoking dunes and mountain-sides ; and from the busy groups below rose a subdued chatter of women's voices, and a splash of water and clatter of pattens. It vaguely suggested preparations for a witches' sabbath.

" What sort of miracles did they have in this church ? " I asked, when we had passed into the dusky square, " and what did you mean about their having exchanged the crucifix— about a *substitution* ? "

It seemed quite dark outside. The church rose black, a vague lopsided mass of buttresses and high-pitched roofs, against the watery, moonlit sky ; the big trees of the church-yard behind waving about in the seawind ; and the windows shone yellow, like flaming portals, in the darkness.

"Please remark the bold effect of the gargoyles," said the Antiquary pointing upwards.

They jutted out, vague wild beasts, from the roof-line ; and, what was positively frightening, you saw the moonlight, yellow and blue through the open jaws of some of them.   A gust swept through the trees, making the weathercock clatter and groan.

"Why, those gargoyle wolves seem positively to howl," I exclaimed.

The old Antiquary chuckled.   "Aha," he answered, " did I not tell you that this church has witnessed things like no other church in Christendom ?   And it still remembers them !   There—have you ever known such a wild, savage church before ? "

And as he spoke there suddenly mingled with the sough of the wind and the groans of the weather-vane, a shrill quavering sound as of pipers inside.

"The organist trying his vox humana for to-morrow," remarked the Antiquary.

II

NEXT day I bought one of the printed histories of the miraculous crucifix which they were hawking all round the church ; and next day also, my friend the Antiquary was good enough to tell me all that he knew of the matter. Between my two informants, the following may be said to be the true story.

In the autumn of 1195, after a night of frightful storm, a boat was found cast upon the shore of Dunes, which was at that time a fishing village at the mouth of the Nys, and exactly opposite a terrible sunken reef.

The boat was broken and upset ; and close to it, on the sand and bent grass, lay a stone figure of the crucified Saviour, without its cross and, as seems probable, also without its arms, which had been made of separate blocks.   A variety of persons immediately came forward to claim it ;   the little church of Dunes, on whose glebe it was found ;   the Barons of Croÿ, who had the right of jetsam on that coast, and also the great Abbey of St. Loup of Arras, as possessing the spiritual overlordship of the place.   But a holy man who lived close by in the cliffs, had a vision which settled the dispute.   St. Luke in person appeared and told him that he was the original maker of the figure ;   that it had been one of three which had hung round the Holy Sepulchre of Jerusalem ; that three knights, a Norman, a Tuscan, and a man of Arras, had with the permis- sion of Heaven stolen them from the Infidels and placed them on unmanned boats ; that one of the images had been cast upon the Norman coast near Salenelles ; that the second had run aground not far from the city of Lucca, in Italy ; and that this third was the one which had been embarked by the knight from Artois. As regarded its final resting place, the hermit, on the authority of St. Luke, recommended that the statue should be left to decide the matter itself. Accordingly, the crucified figure was solemnly cast back into the sea. The very next day it was found once more in the same spot, among the sand and bent grass at the mouth of the Nys. It was therefore deposited in the little church of Dunes ; and very soon indeed the flocks of pious persons who brought it offerings from all parts made it necessary and possible to rebuild the church thus sanctified by its presence.

The Holy Effigy of Dunes—Sacra Dunarum Effigies as it was called—did not work the ordinary sort of miracles. But its fame spread far and wide by the unexampled wonders which became the constant accompaniment of its existence. The Effigy, as above mentioned, had been discovered without the cross to which it had evidently been fastened, nor had any researches or any subsequent storms brought the missing blocks to light, despite the many prayers which were offered for the purpose. After some time therefore, and a deal of discussion, it was decided that a new cross should be provided for the effigy to hang upon. And certain skilful stonemasons of Arras were called to Dunes for this purpose. But behold ! the very day after the cross had been solemnly erected in the church, an unheard of and terrifying fact was discovered. The Effigy, which had been hanging perfectly straight the previous evening, had shifted its position, and was bent violently to the right, as if in an effort to break loose.

This was attested not merely by hundreds of laymen, but by the priests of the place, who notified the fact in a document, existing in the episcopal archives of Arras until 1790, to the Abbot of St. Loup their spiritual overlord.

This was the beginning of a series of mysterious occur- rences which spread the fame of the marve'lous crucifix all over Christendom. The Effigy did not remain in the position into which it had miraculously worked itself : it was found, at intervals of time, shifted in some other manner upon its cross, and always as if it had gone through violent contortions. And one day, about ten years after it had been cast up by the sea, the priests of the church and the burghers of Dunes discovered the Effigy hanging in its original outstretched, symmetrical attitude, but, O wonder ! with the cross, broken in three pieces, lying on the steps of its chapel.

Certain persons, who lived in the end of the town nearest the church, reported to have been roused in the middle of the night by what they had taken for a violent clap of thunder, but which was doubtless the crash of the cross falling down ; or perhaps, who knows ? the noise with which the terrible Effigy had broken loose and spurned the alien cross from it. For that was the secret : the Effigy, made by a saint and come to Dunes by miracle, had evidently found some trace of unholiness in the stone to which it had been fastened. Such was the ready explanation afforded by the Prior of the church, in answer to an angry summons of the Abbot of St. Loup, who expressed his disapproval of such unusual miracles. Indeed, it was discovered that the piece of marble had not been cleaned from sinful human touch with the necessary rites before the figure was fastened on ; a most grave, though excusable oversight. So a new cross was ordered, although it was noticed that much time was lost about it ; and the consecration took place only some years later.

Meanwhile the Prior had built the warder's chamber, with the fireplace and recess, and obtained permission from the Pope himself that a clerk in orders should watch day and night, on the score that so wonderful a relic might be stolen. For the relic had by this time entirely cut out all similar crucifixes, and the village of Dunes, through the concourse of pilgrims, had rapidly grown into a town, the property of the now fabulously wealthy Priory of the Holy Cross.

The Abbots of St. Loup, however, looked upon the matter with an unfavourable eye. Although nominally remaining their vassals, the Priors of Dunes had contrived to obtain gradually from the Pope privileges which rendered them virtually independent, and in particular, immunities which sent to the treasury of St. Loup only a small proportion of the tribute money brought by the pilgrims. Abbot Walterius in particular, showed himself actively hostile. He accused the Prior of Dunes of having employed his warders to trump up stories of strange movements and sounds on the part of the still crossless Effigy, and of suggesting, to the ignorant, changes in its attitude which were more credulously believed in now that there was no longer the straight line of the cross by which to verify. So finally the new cross was made, and consecrated, and on Holy Cross Day of the year, the Effigy was fastened to it in the presence of an immense concourse of clergy and laity. The Effigy, it was now supposed, would be satisfied, and no unusual occurrences would increase or perhaps fatally compromise its reputation for sanctity.

These expectations were violently dispelled. In November, 1293, after a year of strange rumours concerning the Effigy, the figure was again discovered to have moved, and continued moving, or rather (judging from the position on the cross) writhing ; and on Christmas Eve of the same year, the cross was a second time thrown down and dashed in pieces. The priest on duty was, at the same time, found, it was thought, dead, in his warder's chamber. Another cross was made and this time privately consecrated and put in place, and a hole in the roof made a pretext to close the church for a while, and to perform the rites of purification necessary after its pollution by workmen. Indeed, it was remarked that on this occasion the Prior of Dunes took as much trouble to diminish and if possible to hide away the miracles, as his predecessor had done his best to blazon the preceding ones abroad. The priest who had been on duty on the eventful Christmas Eve disappeared mysteriously, and it was thought by many persons that he had gone mad and was confined in the Prior's prison, for fear of the revelations he might make. For by this time, and not without some encouragement from the Abbots at Arras, extraordinary stories had begun to circulate about the goings-on in the church of Dunes. This church, be it remembered, stood a little above the town, isolated and surrounded by big trees. It was surrounded by the precincts of the Priory and, save on the water side, by high walls. Nevertheless, persons there were who affirmed that, the wind having been in that direction, they had heard strange noises come from the church of nights. During storms, particularly, sounds had been heard which were variously described as howls, groans, and the music of rustic dancing. A master mariner affirmed that one Hallow Even, as his boat approached the mouth of the Nys, he had seen the church of Dunes brilliantly lit up, its immense windows flaming. But he was suspected of being drunk and of having exaggerated the effect of the small light shining from the warder's chamber. The interest of the townfolk of Dunes coincided with that of the Priory, since they prospered greatly by the pilgrimages, so these tales were promptly hushed up. Yet they undoubtedly reached the ear of the Abbot of St. Loup. And at last there came an event which brought them all back to the surface.

For, on the Vigil of All Saints, 1299, the church was struck by lightning. The new warder was found dead in the middle of the nave, the cross broken in two ; and oh, horror ! the Effigy was missing. The indescribable fear which overcame every one was merely increased by the discovery of the Effigy lying behind the high altar, in an attitude of frightful convulsion, and, it was whispered, blackened by lightning.

This was the end of the strange doings at Dunes.

An ecclesiastical council was held at Arras, and the church shut once more for nearly a year. It was opened this time and re-consecrated by the Abbot of St. Loup, whom the Prior of Holy Cross served humbly at mass. A new chapel had been built, and in it the miraculous crucifix was displayed, dressed in more splendid brocade and gems than usual, and its head nearly hidden by one of the most gorgeous crowns ever seen before ; a gift, it was said, of the Duke of Burgundy.

All this new splendour, and the presence of the great Abbot himself, was presently explained to the faithful, when the Prior came forward to announce that a last and greatest miracle had now taken place. The original cross, on which the figure had hung in the Church of the Holy Sepulchre, and for which the Effigy had spurned all others made by less holy hands, had been cast on the shore of Dunes, on the very spot where, a hundred years before, the figure of the Saviour had been discovered in the sands. " This," said the Prior, " was the explanation of the terrible occurrences which had filled all hearts with anguish. The Holy Effigy was now satisfied, it would rest in peace and its miraculous powers would be engaged only in granting the prayers of the faithful."

One-half of the forecast came true : from that day forward the Effigy never shifted its position ; but from that day forward also, no considerable miracle was ever registered ; the devotion of Dunes diminished, other relics threw the Sacred Effigy into the shade ; and the pilgrimages dwindling to mere local gatherings, the church was never brought to completion.

What had happened ? No one ever knew, guessed, or perhaps even asked. But, when in 1790 the Archiepiscopal palace of Arras was sacked, a certain notary of the neighbourhood bought a large portion of the archives at the price of waste paper, either from historical curiosity, or expecting to obtain thereby facts which might gratify his aversion to the clergy. These documents lay unexamined for many years, till my friend the Antiquary bought them. Among them, taken helter skelter from the Archbishop's palace, were sundry papers referring to the suppressed Abbey of St. Loup of Arras, and among these latter, a series of notes concerning the affairs of the church of Dunes ; they were, so far as their fragmentary nature explained, the minutes of an inquest made in 1309, and contained the deposition of sundry witnesses. To understand their meaning it is necessary to remember that this was the time when witch trials had begun, and when the proceedings against the Templars had set the fashion of inquests which could help the finances of the country while furthering the interests of religion.

What appears to have happened is that after the catastrophe of the Vigil of All Saints, October, 1299, the Prior, Urbain de Luc, found himself suddenly threatened with a charge of sacrilege and witchcraft, of obtaining the miracles of the Effigy by devilish means, and of converting his church into a chapel of the Evil One.

Instead of appealing to high ecclesiastical tribunals, as the privileges obtained from the Holy See would have warranted, Prior Urbain guessed that this charge came originally from the wrathful Abbey of St. Loup, and, dropping all his pretensions in order to save himself, he threw himself upon the mercy of the Abbot whom he had hitherto flouted. The Abbot appears to have been satisfied by his submission, and the matter to have dropped after a few legal preliminaries, of which the notes found among the archiepiscopal archives of Arras represented a portion. Some of these notes my friend the Antiquary kindly allowed me to translate from the Latin, and I give them here, leaving the reader to make what he can of them.

" Item. The Abbot expresses himself satisfied that His Reverence the Prior has had no personal knowledge of or dealings with the Evil One (Diabolus). Nevertheless, the gravity of the charge requires . . ."—here the page is torn.

" Hugues Jacquot, Simon le Couvreur, Pierre Denis, burghers of Dunes, being interrogated, witness :

" That the noises from the Church of the Holy Cross always happened on nights of bad storms, and foreboded shipwrecks on the coast ; and were very various, such as terrible rattling, groans, howls as of wolves, and occasional flute playing. A certain Jehan, who has twice been branded and flogged for lighting fires on the coast and otherwise causing ships to wreck at the mouth of the Nys, being promised immunity, after two or three slight pulls on the rack, witnesses as follows : That the band of wreckers to which he belongs always knew when a dangerous storm was brewing, on account of the noises which issued from the church of Dunes. Witness has often climbed the walls and prowled round in the church-yard, waiting to hear such noises. He was not unfamiliar with the howlings and roarings mentioned by the previous witnesses. He has heard tell by a countryman who passed in the night that the howling was such that the countryman thought himself pursued by a pack of wolves, although it is well known that no wolf has been seen in these parts for thirty years. But the witness himself is of opinion that the most singular of all the noises, and the one which always accompanied or foretold the worst storms, was a noise of flutes and pipes (quod vulgo dicuntur flustes et musettes) so sweet that the King of France could not have sweeter at his Court. Being interrogated whether he had ever seen anything ? the witness answers : ' That he has seen the church brightly lit up from the sands ; but on approaching found all dark, save the light from the warder's chamber. That once, by moonlight, the piping and fluting and howling being uncommonly loud, he thought he had seen wolves, and a human figure on the roof, but that he ran away from fear, and cannot be sure.'

" Item. His Lordship the Abbot desires the Right Reverend Prior to answer truly, placing his hand on the Gospels, whether or not he had himself heard such noises.

" The Right Reverend Prior denies ever having heard anything similar. But, being threatened with further proceedings (the rack ?) acknowledges that he had frequently been told of these noises by the Warder on duty.

" *Query:* Whether the Right Reverend Prior was ever told anything else by the Warder ?

" *Answer:* Yes ; but under the seal of confession. The last Warder, moreover, the one killed by lightning, had been a reprobate priest, having committed the greatest crimes and obliged to take asylum, whom the Prior had kept there on account of the difficulty of finding a man sufficiently courageous for the office.

" *Query:* Whether the Prior has ever questioned previous Warders ?

" *Answer:* That the Warders were bound to reveal only in confession whatever they had heard ; that the Prior's predecessors had kept the seal of confession inviolate, and that though unworthy, the Prior himself desired to do alike.

" *Query:* What had become of the Warder who had been found in a swoon after the occurrences of Hallow Even ?

" *Answer:* That the Prior does not know. The Warder was crazy. The Prior believes he was secluded for that reason."

A disagreeable surprise had been, apparently, arranged for Prior Urbain de Luc. For the next entry states that :

" Item. By order of His Magnificence the Lord Abbot, certain servants of the Lord Abbot aforesaid introduce Robert Baudouin, priest, once Warder in the Church of the Holy Cross, who has been kept ten years in prison by His Reverence the Prior, as being of unsound mind. Witness manifests great terror on finding himself in the presence of their Lordships, and particularly of His Reverence the Prior. And refuses to speak, hiding his face in his hands and uttering shrieks. Being comforted with kind words by those present, nay even most graciously by My Lord the Abbot himself, *etiam* threatened with the rack if he continue obdurate, this witness deposes as follows, not without much lamentation, shrieking and senseless jabber after the manner of mad men.

" *Query:* Can he remember what happened on the Vigil of All Saints, in the church of Dunes, before he swooned on the floor of the church ?

" *Answer:* He cannot. It would be sin to speak of such things before great spiritual Lords. Moreover he is but an ignorant man, and also mad. Moreover his hunger is great.

" Being given white bread from the Lord Abbot's own table, witness is again cross-questioned.

" *Query:* What can he remember of the events of the Vigil of All Saints ?

"*Answer:* Thinks he was not always mad. Thinks he has not always been in prison. Thinks he once went in a boat on sea, etc.

" *Query:* Does witness think he has ever been in the church of Dunes ?

" *Answer:* Cannot remember. But is sure that he was not always in prison.

" *Query:* Has witness ever heard anything like that ? (My Lord the Abbot having secretly ordered that a certain fool in his service, an excellent musician, should suddenly play the pipes behind the Arras.)

" At which sound witness began to tremble and sob and fall on his knees, and catch hold of the robe even of My Lord the Abbot, hiding his head therein.

" *Query:* Wherefore does he feel such terror, being in the fatherly presence of so clement a prince as the Lord Abbot ?

" *Answer:* That witness cannot stand that piping any longer. That it freezes his blood. That he has told the Prior many times that he will not remain any longer in the warder's chamber. That he is afraid for his life. That he dare not make the sign of the Cross nor say his prayers for fear of the Great Wild Man. That the Great Wild Man took the Cross and broke it in two and played at quoits with it in the nave. That all the wolves trooped down from the roof howling, and danced on their hind legs while the Great Wild Man played the pipes on the high altar. That witness had surrounded himself with a hedge of little crosses, made of broken rye straw, to keep off the Great Wild Man from the warder's chamber. Ah—ah—ah ! He is piping again ! The wolves are howling ! He is raising the tempest.

" *Item:* That no further information can be extracted from witness, who falls on the floor like one possessed and has to be removed from the presence of His Lordship the Abbot and His Reverence the Prior."

III

HERE the minutes of the inquest break off. Did those great spiritual dignitaries ever get to learn more about the terrible doings in the church of Dunes ? Did they ever guess at their cause ?

" For there was a cause," said the Antiquary, folding his spectacles after reading me these notes, " or more strictly the cause still exists. And you will understand, though those learned priests of six centuries ago could not."

And rising, he fetched a key from a shelf and preceded me into the yard of his house, situated on the Nys, a mile below Dunes.

Between the low steadings one saw the salt marsh, lilac with sea lavender, the Island of Birds, a great sandbank at the mouth of the Nys, where every kind of sea fowl gathers ; and beyond, the angry white-crested sea under an angry orange afterglow. On the other side, inland, and appearing above the farm roofs, stood the church of Dunes, its pointed belfry and jagged outlines of gables and buttresses and gargoyles and wind-warped pines black against the easterly sky of ominous livid red.

" I told you," said the Antiquary, stopping with the key in the lock of a big outhouse, " that there had been a *substitution* ; that the crucifix at present at Dunes is not the one miraculously cast up by the storm of 1195. I believe the present one may be identified as a life-size statue, for which a receipt exists in the archives of Arras, furnished to the Abbot of St. Loup by Estienne Le Mas and Guillaume Pernel, stone masons, in the year 1299, that is to say the year of the inquest and of the cessation of all supernatural occurrences at Dunes. As to the original effigy, you shall see it and understand everything."

The Antiquary opened the door of a sloping, vaulted passage, lit a lantern and led the way. It was evidently the cellar of some mediæval building ; and a scent of wine, of damp wood, and of fir branches from innumerable stacked up faggots, filled the darkness among thickset columns.

" Here," said the Antiquary, raising his lantern, " he was buried beneath this vault, and they had run an iron stake through his middle, like a vampire, to prevent his rising."

The Effigy was erect against the dark wall, surrounded by brushwood. It was more than life-size, nude, the arms broken off at the shoulders, the head, with stubbly beard and clotted hair, drawn up with an effort, the face contracted with agony ; the muscles dragged as of one hanging crucified, the feet bound together with a rope. The figure was familiar to me in various galleries. I came forward to examine the ear : it was leaf-shaped.

" Ah, you have understood the whole mystery," said the Antiquary.

" I have understood," I answered, not knowing how far his thought really went, " that this supposed statue of Christ is an antique satyr, a Marsyas awaiting his punishment."

The Antiquary nodded. " Exactly," he said drily, " that is the whole explanation. Only I think the Abbot and the Prior were not so wrong to drive the iron stake through him when they removed him from the church."

THE ROOM

By

ELEANOR SCOTT

" Y OU all agree, then ? " asked Massingham, looking round at his guests.

" Quite, quite," said young Grindley of Brasenose.

" I am ready to fall in," said the Parson.

Vernon merely grunted. Really, after a dinner like that, it was a beastly shame to chatter.

" I'll do it, of course," said Reece, the tubby little curate whom Massingham had invited more out of cussedness than anything.

" All right, then. Mind, I don't guarantee that there is a ghost. I'm only going on local gossip and the fact that it's so damned hard to get any servants. And the house-agents, of course."

" You don't mean to say that *they* admit there's a ghost ? " asked Ladislaw.

" No," grinned Massingham ; " I'm going by what they didn't say . . . By the way, are you coming in, Mac ? "

Ladislaw flushed.

" I—of course I will, if that's part of the bargain," he said a little doubtfully.

" My dear chap," drawled Grindley, " surely—I mean, I know people who think there's something in it and that, but *surely*—— ? "

" I don't know," blurted Ladislaw. " Oh well, of course no one believes in the white-sheet-and-clanking-chains ghost ; but—no, perhaps there aren't any in England," he ended abruptly.

They shouted with laughter. Ladislaw had in him the blood of generations of Highlanders, fanatical in their isolation and pride. Ladislaw grinned shamefacedly. He knew—well, perhaps he knew more than the others.

" Well, since we're all agreed," said Massingham briskly, " the next thing to do is to draw lots as to the order we go in. And look here," he added, reddening a little, " If anyone feels, when it comes to the point, that—that he'd rather drop it, you know, we'd—well, nobody'd think the worse of him." He looked round a little shamefacedly. " I don't want any nervous wrecks on my conscience," he added with a half-laugh.

Everybody smiled in his own individual fashion—Grindley just a trifle superior, Ladislaw sympathetic, the Parson very kind and indulgent, Vernon bored, and Reece with the spontaneity of a child. Massingham, his duty done, looked relieved.

" Let's draw, then," he said. " I'll put all our names in this "—he tipped out the cigars from the box—" and numbers from one to—let's see—six, in this." He took a clean tumbler off the tray. Then he drew out his pocket-book and tore out two leaves which he again tore, each into six pieces. On one set he wrote numbers, on the other names. Then, folding up the scraps, he dropped one set into the box and the other into the tumbler.

" Now, let's see—Reece, you're the most transparently honest. You draw."

Reece jogged his chair up, his face beaming like a small boy at a conjuring show.

" What do I do ? " he asked eagerly.

" You take one paper out of the box and another out of the glass and open them."

Reece obeyed.

" Amory," he said, opening one—" three."

The Parson smiled, still indulgent. " So two of you experience the ghost before I do," he said.

Reece went on with the drawing.

" Ladislaw—four," he said. " Grindley—one."

" Good old Grindley ! " " Do down the spook, Grinders ! " " Leave some for me ! " vociferated the crowd, now thoroughly aroused.

" Reece—six. Oh, I did hope I'd be fairly early ! Never mind. Vernon—two. Massingham—five. That's all." Reece beamed round on the company, polishing his circular steel-rimmed spectacles, rosy with excitement.

" Then I take it the order is Grindley, Vernon, myself, Ladislaw, Massingham, Reece," said the Parson. " Upon my word, I hope something will come of it. I rather envy you, Grindley—and you, Reece." Then he drew Reece a little aside. " I mean to exorcise anything I see," he said in

a low voice. " Did you think of doing that ? I'm quite willing
to come last if—if the others really want to find out if they can
see anything."

" Just as you like," said Reece. " But won't your exorcism
have a better chance of proof if you try it on somewhere in the
middle ? I mean, say Grindley and Vernon—er—see something, and Ladislaw and Massingham and I don't——— "

" Yes, you're right," said Amory, with more animation
than usual. " It's best as it is. It's a clearer proof of the
truth. Yes, Reece, you're quite right. Thank you."

His eyes had a curious gleam—the light of the fanatic,
eager, bright and hard—in them.

" Lord ! I pity the poor ghost when Amory once gets
going," said Vernon with a short laugh. " I shouldn't like to
be up against you when you were really mad, old man."

" Oh, come ! " said Amory, flushing a little, with a rather
shamefaced laugh. " It's only when I'm sure that I'm face to
face with something really evil that I get angry. Then, I
admit, I'm—er——— "

" Implacable," put in Grindley. " It's most extraordinary,"
he went on, " how people seem to take a pride in certain of
their—well, faults. Look at Massingham, now : he's got an
absolute devil of a temper—I wouldn't answer for the safety
of anyone who roused him—but I don't mind betting that he'll
not only own to it, but be quite proud of it."

" Eh, what's that ? " asked Massingham from the sideboard. " What's that about me ? "

" Isn't it true that you're rather hot-tempered ? " drawled
Grindley.

" Got a brute of a temper," answered Massingham cheerfully. " 'Fact, when I do get going, I absolutely see red."
He turned back to the syphon.

Grindley smiled faintly.

" I believe anger and pride are deadly sins, aren't they,
Amory ?—and no one minds owning to 'em ; in fact, most
people rather like being accused of 'em. But if I were to say
that Vernon was a greedy sensualist, or that you, Amory, were
the most damnably narrow, uncharitable brute I'd ever met,
you'd be quite annoyed. Here's an example now," went on
the youthful moralist. " You know that pretty maid Lily who
used to wait at dinner ? What's become of her ? "

" Left," growled Massingham. " She—er—well, *you*
know. Pity, too, for I don't think she was a real bad 'un.
Pretty girls don't stand much chance in country villages."

"Exactly," said Grindley. "It wasn't, probably, her fault at all, if you can call it a fault to follow the dictates of Nature ; yet she gets kicked downhill by the likes of us."

"Really, Grindley," said Amory, his thin face pale, "I know its the fashion to be cynical about these things, but I consider it most immoral to take any but the strongest views on such a subject. If I had my way I should so deal with these cases as to prevent effectually their ever occurring again."

"Oh, come now, Amory!" broke in Vernon. "The cart-tail and whipping-post, eh? Damn it all, man, it's nature! Why, even in the Bible isn't there a woman—a real bad lot, too—who—er—got let off, don't you know?"

"If you mean the eighth chapter of St. John's Gospel," said Amory coldly, "most critics agree that it's not authentic. I believe the Romans admit it to be an interpolation. And in any case, there was no condoning of the crime : the woman was told to ' sin no more,' not that it was ' natural ' and therefore not worthy of blame."

"Oh, well," yawned Vernon, "we all know that it's you Christians who go in for whips and tortures and burnings alive. Poor degraded sensualists like myself believe in the motto ' Live and let live.' "

Amory opened his mouth for an indignant reply, but Massingham cut in.

"I suppose we all show up on a question of that kind," he said, philosophically. "Amory'd do anything—anything at all—to punish transgressors—eh, Amory?" The Parson nodded. "Old Vernon says ' Let 'em, if they want to. It don't hurt anyone else.' (Please stop me if I'm misjudging anyone.) Grindley says ' It's below me, of course, vulgar and that : but I believe it's natural, like over-eating or getting-drunk.' I—well, I dislike the whole thing thoroughly, but I can't help thinking it's a necessary evil. As for Ladislaw, I don't believe he even knows it exists, or if he does he's so disgusted he shuts it out of his existence. Reece— I'm blessed if I know what Reece thinks."

"I think," said Reece, very pink and hot, and stammering in his confusion, "that it's a horrible thing, like d-deformity, that we are responsible for, just as we are for c-consumption or drink. It's b-beastly, but it's our f-fault, and we've got to s-stop it. And I'm af-fraid I don't quite agree with you, Amory, that p-punishment stops it. It's d-decency in people's lives that *p-prevents* it. And we've got to see that they have a chance to—well, to live c-clean. I say, I'm sorry. I didn't mean to jaw like that." He collapsed into a deep arm-chair.

Grindley yawned.

" I'd no idea I'd uncork such deep vials of emotion and opinion," he said in his most irritating voice. " Shall we chuck it ? " He lit a cigarette. " By-the-way, Masser, I suppose the—er—experiment begins to-night ? "

" Just as you like," said Massingham. " It's your look-out, since you're the first on the list."

" Oh, well, I'll begin at once," said Grindley, rising. " I only hope they've made me up a decent bed. I believe that's really why people can't sleep in haunted rooms—maids won't take any trouble with the beds. Good-night, you men."

" 'Night, old chap." " Mind you have a good yarn for us to-morrow night." " Don't sleep right through the show, lazy swine," " Call out if you're frightened."

And so young Oxford went up to encounter the spirits of all time.

*   *   *   *   *   *

" If it wasn't that I'd promised," said Grindley next evening, with an abruptness strange to him, " I'd never say a word. And, mind, it isn't what you expect, any of you. I didn't see a thing."

His eyes, flickering and dark in his white face, glanced nervously round the group of men. He passed his tongue rapidly over his lips.

" But—something happened ? " asked Vernon.

" Yes—oh yes ! Something happened all right. But what it was I don't know—a dream, or a vision, or—an incarnation."

They looked at him intently. Could this nervous boy be the calm and slightly superior Grindley who had talked so fluently and well of the power of the trained intellect ?

" P'raps once I tell you I'll get over it a bit," he broke out at last. " I think—I'm—possessed . . . No, I mean it absolutely literally. I never guessed before what it meant. . . .

" I didn't take long over going to bed. It's a pleasant enough room, you know, and I was a bit sleepy after the warmth and the talking and that, and I never for a moment thought I'd be disturbed. If I'd known, nothing in this world—or the next—would ever have persuaded me to sleep in that cursed —yes, I mean it, *cursed*—room."

He paused a moment, trying to recover some of his wonted calm.

" Well, I went to bed, and, I suppose, to sleep   I never

before quite understood what Hamlet meant about the dreams that might come when you're lying in the grave, dead. I thought I did, but I didn't. And he only guessed what the dreams of death might be. I *know*. . . .

" I don't mean you to think that I just had a bad dream. I quite literally *became someone else*—in every nerve of my body, in every thought of my mind—yes, and in every secret wish of my heart. I knew myself intimately. I was myself in another incarnation, older, stronger, freer, nearer to elemental things, but still myself. . . . I wish I could make you understand ! "

He broke off abruptly, and as abruptly resumed :

" Of course you all know the story of Dr. Faustus. It's a fine, dramatic story, you think, and Marlowe made a glorious, marvellous poem of it. You don't know—thank God every day of your lives that you don't know—what a fearful story it is. I do know. Last night—and God only knows how long before—I *was* that man."

He gulped.

" I-I'd done it, you know. I'd abandoned all goodness : I'd made my intellect, *mine*, my God, and worshipped it. I'd blasphemed, and—I had sold my soul.

" I can't attempt to tell you what it was like. You couldn't ever imagine it if you hadn't felt it. I was terrified at what I'd done. I was the living home of everything evil—I tell you, I was evil through and through, as if some fearful vapour had surrounded and soaked me. And—I was *afraid*. I tried to pray, and I knew it was hopeless. How could I hope to be heard ? Oh, it's easy to talk of Despair—you don't know, you can never guess, what it is ! I fought and struggled. I began broken prayers, and abandoned them at the first word, knowing I couldn't pray. . . .

" I can't tell you how long it lasted. I lived a whole spiritual life through. No words can tell you what it was— it was a living hell, and it's—it's heaven to be awake."

" Grindley, old chap," said Reece softly, " it—it wasn't *you*, you know. It was some evil outside of you. It wasn't the real you."

Grindley turned a haggard face.

" It was—a possible me. I might have been—I nearly was—just that, blasphemous, hopeless. But—I know in time . . . . I'm going out," he added abruptly. " Reece, will you come ? "

Reece rose—Reece, on whom Grindley had often exercised

a pretty wit ; Reece the plain, the stupid, the comical and the
kindly ; and, without a word, they set out together.

The others lit pipes and cigarettes, poked the fire, mixed
drinks ; they breathed more freely.

" 'Pon my word," said Vernon between puffs, " I'd no
idea Grindley was such a kid. 'Xpect he was horribly jumpy
the whole time. Poor kid, he's beastly upset ! And all about
a dream ! "

" Well, but it must have been a horribly vivid and peculiarly
beastly dream," said Massingham. " He looks quite changed.
Poor old Grindley ! "

" Why ' poor ' ? " asked Ladislaw. " I call him lucky."

" *Lucky !* " exclaimed two or three of the others. And
" How d'you make that out ? " asked Vernon.

" Well—he knows in time. He's warned. It *was* in him,
you know—that ambition and pride of intellect. Well—he's
cured."

" Want to back out, Vernon ? " asked Massingham,
grinning. " Your shot to-night, you know. Don't think
there's much chance of your letting your ambition and intellect
sell *your* soul to the devil, you lazy swine. You'll sell it
another way."

Vernon grinned blandly.

" If the bed's warm and comfortable I'll be all right,
thanks," he yawned. " Don't mind how soon I get off,
either. Say good-night to the others for me, will you ? "

He rose, stretching his arms, a fine figure of a man, verging
on the corpulent, a little spoilt by good living, but handsome still.

It was very late when Grindley and Reece returned. They
went upstairs, still together.

*   *   *   *   *   *

Everyone noticed how odd Vernon looked at breakfast.
He did not look terrified and—yes, possessed—like Grindley ;
he looked like a man who has been brought face to face with
some disgusting sight—white and shaken and sick. He ate
nothing ; he sat and crumbled bread with trembling fingers,
and every now and then he would lift his eyes and look at one
or another of them in a queer appealing way, as if he were
guilty of some sin, and sorry for it, and his friends were his
judges.

Everybody was a little uncomfortable and ill at ease : it
was so odd to see Vernon, the debonair and confident Vernon,
so piteously shaken. Breakfast was a hasty meal, for everyone

was anxious to get it over and escape from those troubled questioning eyes

But as chairs were pushed back and pipes lighted, Vernon suddenly spoke.

" I'm not going to make any story for you chaps to-night," he said abruptly. " There isn't one—for you. Yes, I've seen something. And I shan't forget what I've seen, as long as I live." Sweat started out on his forehead. " I'm not going to try and tell you what it was," he went on jerkily. " I'd as soon try to describe the most loathsome surgical operation or the most indecent physical illness. And if I wanted to, I couldn't. Thank Heaven, we haven't made the words for what I saw."

Eyes met startled eyes over the untidy table. It was mad, the whole business—a ghost hinted at while the remains of breakfast still littered the table ; Vernon, of all people, confused ashamed, disgusted, and—yes—penitent.

" Grindley was right," said Vernon heavily ; " that place is cursed. And he's right, too, when he says that no one who hasn't tried can even guess what evil it puts into your mind, and how it brings out the vile things you have in your own soul. Only I'd rather have had his—dream, or incarnation, or whatever it was, than——"

There was silence in the room. Suddenly Vernon stood up. Involuntarily everyone looked at him—at the handsome face, now tormented with a kind of passion of disgust and remorse, at the haunted eyes that used to be so gay.

" I'm—I'm not so bad as that yet ! " he cried with a sound like a sob, and left them sitting there.

Grindley rose, and soon was seen passing the window, making for the stables. Ladislaw sat with bowed head, contemplating his plate. Reece and Amory murmured together, and Massingham caught the words " holy water." He got up and went across to them.

" I say, you men, shall we drop it ? " he asked. He was quite pale. " Grindley's collapse didn't altogether surprise me, but when poor old Vernon gets bowled over like this it's too much of a good thing. He looks ghastly. I didn't think he had it in him to feel like that."

The others glanced at one another.

" There must be some—well, influence or something—in that room," Massingham continued. " Something pretty awful, too. And I don't want anybody to go in there just out of bravado and get—well, damaged."

" I agree," said the Parson gravely, " that there must be
something evil in that room. It's not contrary to dogma to
believe that some places are soaked, as it were, in evil influence.
But that's all the more reason, Massingham, for me to spend
the night there. If exorcism and prayer can lay your ghost, I
promise you it shall be laid."

" I know you're not afraid," said Massingham. " I'll
admit that in a way it's your job. But, Amory, you know that
young Grindley wasn't just a frightened kid last night. Something *had* happened to him—something pretty awful. And
God only knows what it can have been that poor old Vernon
saw. He's horrified—and I should have said that no god or
devil could horrify Vernon."

" Whatever it is," said Amory steadily—" and I don't
think we can deny that there is something—it's not stronger,
nor half as strong, as the Powers that will be on my side. I
am going into that room to-night, Massingham, convinced
that there is in it some shocking evil, and equally convinced that
I shall overcome it. It cannot withstand the minister of God."

Massingham flushed, as some men do when asked to talk
familiarly of God. He preferred to speak of Providence.

" Well, Amory, you know best," he said. " Do as you think
right. Only, for Heaven's sake, if you feel the smallest
reluctance when it comes to the point, do chuck it ! Swear
you will."

" I am going to lay that spirit," said the Parson, steadily as
ever, with a set mouth and a light in his eyes that warned
Massingham that remonstrance was useless. He shrugged his
shoulders.

" It's a pity you weren't born in the days of martyrs,
Amory," he remarked. " You'd have enjoyed going to the
stake for your principles."

Amory said nothing. Perhaps it was as well.

*   *   *   *   *   *

There was an unusual silence in the smoking-room that
night. Grindley had been out in the wind and rain all day, and
looked more his normal self, though there was an odd hesitation
in his manner and dread still lurked in his eyes. He glanced
over his shoulder often, like a man who fears a horrible
presence at his elbow ; and he kept close to Reece. Vernon
sat, his head sunk between his shoulders, staring sombrely at
the fire. No one knew where he had been all that long and
dreary day. The Parson sat apart, reading with moving lips,

a look of exaltation on his face. Ladislaw and Massingham made an idle pretence at talk.

Suddenly Amory rose.

"Good-night, all of you," he said. "It will be all right in the morning."

Massingham got slowly to his feet.

"Amory," he began doubtfully; but the Parson's eyes were bright and his face transfigured.

"Hush, Massingham," he said. "Nothing you can say shall stop me. This is my duty, and I shall do it. I will crush this evil thing down into the everlasting fire of punishment——"

A quick cry broke in on him.

"Don't! Don't talk of everlasting punishment! You don't know what it means. God wouldn't—He *couldn't*——"

Amory smiled.

"Grindley, God is, before all, just. Evil must receive its reward. By God's grace, I hope to be His minister in dealing out that punishment."

Massingham looked at him heavily.

"Well—good luck," he said. Amory smiled, an odd smile of confidence, pity, and triumph. The door closed softly behind him.

For a few minutes there was silence. Then Grindley whispered:

"He can't *really* believe there's a God like that?"

No one answered; then Vernon, speaking for the first time that evening, muttered:

"Some evil deserves—anything."

He rose heavily and went out. A little later Grindley caught Reece's eye: the little curate laid down his book, and without a word the odd pair left the room together. Massingham and Ladislaw sat on and on in silence, Massingham smoking sombrely, Ladislaw nervously touching up the fire.

At last the Scotsman dropped the poker with a clatter.

"Massingham," he said in a queer strained voice, "I can't bear this. What do you imagine is going on in there?"

Massingham stirred.

"God only knows!" he said. Then he added suddenly:

"I'm going to listen. Don't you come, Mac. I'd rather you didn't."

He went out, and Ladislaw heard his steps mounting the stairs, going along the corridor, fading into silence. In the smoking-room the fire sank lower and the ashes fell softly.

In a few minutes Massingham returned, paler, and looking
a little apprehensive.

" Well ? " asked Ladislaw.

" There's—something awful going on in there," said
Massingham jerkily. " I don't know what. I heard Amory's
voice—and hard breathing, and a kind of ghastly muffled
moaning noise——"

Ladislaw sprang up.

" Moaning ? Amory ? "

Massingham shook his head.

" Amory's voice was steady enough," he said. " It was
like steel—ice—I don't know. . . . *He* wasn't the—thing—
that moaned."

Ladislaw shuddered.

" Could you hear what he said ? "

" Not entirely," said Massingham reluctantly. He wiped
his forehead, and Ladislaw saw that his hand shook.

The two men stared into each other's eyes.

" There was a smell like scorching," added Massingham
suddenly, " and a horrible sound, like something cracking very
slowly—or crushing, p'r'aps."

Again they stood in silence, straining their ears.

" Oh, for God's sake, let's go and stop it ! " cried Ladislaw
abruptly ; and both men turned on an impulse and ran up
the shallow wooden stairs.

At the top they came face to face with Amory himself.
He stood staring blindly before him, his skin stretched and
white over the bones of his face, his eyes wide and blank and
horrified.

" Amory ! Thank God you're here ! " cried Massingham.

Amory stared on silently. Then suddenly he spoke.

" *The tears ran down over my hands,*" he said in an odd,
strained voice. He held his hands, thin and dry and rigid,
a little before him. Massingham and Ladislaw looked at them
instinctively. Then Ladislaw touched Amory gently on the
shoulder.

" Come away, man," he said in his soft Highland voice.

The lids blinked rapidly once over Amory's blank staring
eyes. Otherwise he did not move. Ladislaw slipped his hand
through the rigid arm. Together he and Massingham got
Amory down the stairs.

The clock struck three as they passed through the hall,
and the sound seemed to rouse Amory from his stupor of
horror   He passed a hand rapidly over his face, and then

looked in an odd bewildered way at the concerned faces of his
two friends. He shuddered a little.

" Massingham—" he said in a troubled voice.

" Yes, Amory ; all right, old chap," said Massingham.

" Massingham—oh, Massingham, the tears ran down over
my hands. I went on, and the tears ran down over my hands."

They sat with him till day came, a watery yellow rim
between the wet earth and the weeping sky. They could hear
the little sound as he passed his tongue over his dry lips.

*   *   *   *   *   *

The next day was Sunday. When Massingham's guests
first came, there had been some talk of Amory's preaching in
the village church to relieve the vicar, an old man in feeble
health ; but Massingham hardly liked to broach the subject
to a man so utterly broken as Amory. But it seemed that he
himself had not forgotten. He appeared at the breakfast-table,
exhausted and livid, but composed ; and at the end of the meal
—through which he sat, silent and nervous, looking like a man
who has passed through an agony—he spoke.

" What time is the service, Massingham ? "

" Eleven. But, I say, Amory, you're not fit to preach."

" I know. I'm utterly unfit. But I must preach to-day,
if I never enter a pulpit again."

" But, Amory, you're ill—done in. You ought to rest."

" Rest ! " said Amory, raising his head for the first time ; and
at the look in his tortured eyes Massingham dropped his own.

It was an odd sermon, prefaced not by a single text, but
by a reading from St. Paul's Epistle to the Corinthians—
that famous passage that deals with charity. And Amory spoke
in a voice strained to the point of quivering of the guilt of
those who condemn their brothers. His usual beautiful style
was gone. His sentences were harsh, abrupt, and broken.
There was one strange passage, which he delivered as if under
appalling physical stress, his white-knuckled hands clutching
the pulpit, sweat beading his brow and lips.

" Years ago," he said, " men tried to convert their op-
ponents by torture. They showed them the human version
of hell. They ground their bones, scorched their flesh, tore
their eyes." (Here he turned ashy white to the lips.) " The
tears of their victims wetted their hands, and they lifted those
hands, wet with tears and blood, to God, the merciful God,
to ask His blessing and His help. We torture souls in the same
Name. We condemn them to a lingering death of torture by

despair. I have tortured a soul to death—crushed it, broken—"
He stopped, gasped audibly, opened his mouth once or twice,
and then added abruptly, " Be merciful. You don't know—
you can't judge other souls. Have mercy, always." He paused
again, and then, in the astonished silence of the country
church, abruptly left the puplit.

That was the only reference he made to the appalling
happenings of that night.

*   *   *   *   *   *

In the afternoon Ladislaw, Massingham and Vernon sat
together at one end of the long library. Reece and Grindley,
at the far end, talked together ; Amory alone was absent.

" I say," said Massingham a little awkwardly, " don't you
chaps think we've gone far enough ? I mean, there's not much
point in crocking ourselves over this confounded business, is
there ? Look at Reece, for instance ; we don't want to push
a simple-minded kid like that into this hell-hole. What do
you think ? "

" Reece won't hurt." said Vernon heavily.

" Oh, I don't know," said Massingham. " He's more
sensitive than you'd think. Look what he's done for poor old
Grindley. What do you say, Mac ? "

" No one ought to go near that room," cried Ladislaw
fiercely. " You're right, Massingham—hell-hole's the word
for it."

Vernon opened his mouth and closed it without speaking.

" *I'm* not going ! " said Ladislaw. " It's my turn to-night,
isn't it ? Well, I've got pluck enough not to go."

Vernon looked up at him with an odd questioning glance,
and their eyes met.

" You know ? " asked Vernon.

Ladislaw nodded. " Enough," he said. " I've seen things
—at home. I know what might—anyway, I'm not going."

He rose and went towards the door ; then he turned back.

" What about you, Massingham ? Will you be wise in
time and chuck it too ? "

Massingham flushed a little.

" No, I don't think I'll chuck it," he said slowly. " Oh,
I'm in a funk all right ! But I can't exactly ask people here,
and make them face—whatever's in that room—and not go
myself, can I ? "

Vernon suddenly broke in.

" Massingham—don't," he said, laying his hand on the

other man's arm. " We, who've been—we'll understand.
And Ladislaw will."

Massingham looked at him intently.

" I think I must go, Vernon," he said very quietly.
" Besides, if Reece, why not me ? "

Vernon got rather red.

" Look here," he said, " I've been, and I know what I'm
talking about. Reece will be all right ; but you——! Don't
ask why, Dick, but don't—don't go into that damned place."

Massingham looked gravely at Vernon's pleading face, and
shook his head.

" I'm sorry, Bill," he said. Vernon stared with a kind of
hopeless entreaty into his face, then turned away with a half-
groan.

At eleven that night Massingham went to face his ordeal.

*   *   *   *   *   *

Massingham said nothing of his experiences when he
joined his friends next day. Like those who had already met
Fate in that room of his, he was very pale, and his eyes had
that same piteous look—the look of one who has sinned past
hope of forgiveness, and yet hopes, however faintly, that his
friends may not cast him out. He spoke very little, and not at
all of the subject that lay uppermost in all their minds. Only,
when dusk was falling, and they all sat together in the long
library, he said suddenly, breaking into the conversation with
the manner of a man who has been totally abstracted :

" Reece, I want to ask something of you."

" Yes ? " said Reece in his commonplace tone of cheerful
willingness.

" Don't go into that ghastly room to-night."

The other voices had all died away, as does ordinary talk
when the speakers hear the voice of a dying man. But Massingham's request was like the releasing of a spring—as if they
had been waiting for a signal.

Amory spoke first.

" Reece, he's right," he said in a very gentle voice. " It's
not necessary, and it's——" He gulped.

" Yes, Reece," chimed in Ladislaw, " don't go. Let me
have a companion in my cowardice ! " he added, with a half-
laugh.

Grindley said nothing, but he looked at the little curate
with a glance oddly compounded of confidence and entreaty,
admiration and fear.

Reece looked at Vernon.

" What do you think, Vernon ? " he asked.

Vernon hesitated : then :

" Go, if you like, I say," he said. " It's not as if you were—
like the rest of us."

" *Vernon !* " broke in Massingham sharply. He knew
that the two were utterly opposed, but really. . . . ! " Don't
listen to him, Reece. Don't go. I tell you it's ghastly. No
one can imagine it." He became very pale. " Don't go," he
urged again.

Reece was still looking steadily into Vernon's eyes ; neither
wavered. Then the little curate turned to Massingham.

" I'm sorry, Massingham," he said, " but if you don't
mind, I'd like to go. All the rest of you have been."

" Oh, if that's the way you look at it ! " exclaimed Massingham bitterly. Then his voice dropped and sounded weary.
" Have it your own way," he muttered. " I suppose it's your
own look-out. You've been warned." He walked away.

The others glanced at each other. Was it of any use to
say any more ? Then they gave it up. After all, simple as he
was, Reece was not a child.

Still, they all felt horribly uncomfortable when, shortly
before eleven, Reece laid down the copy of *Punch* over which
he had been chuckling for nearly an hour, and rose.

" Good-night, you chaps," he said. " See you in the
morning."

Grindley half rose ; Reece caught his eye and grinned.

" 'Night," he said again and, went out.

The others with one accord drew together round the fire.
For a few minutes no one spoke.

" Good lord ! " said Massingham suddenly. " I think
this is the most horrible thing that's happened yet. He's
such an utter kid to go into that pit of evil. He doesn't know—
anything."

" If you come to that," said Amory, " I don't think any of
us really knew what evil was. There's something in that
room—God only knows what—some loathsome spirit of
evil—that fills you until you become evil incarnate."

" There is—you're right ! " cried Grindley excitedly.
" You are—cut off. It's appalling——"

" It is appalling," said Massingham slowly, " to know
that one is cut off oneself from hope of mercy or forgiveness.
It is worse to cut off someone else."

They looked at him attentively.

"When one lets go the reins—allows blind fury to possess one utterly," said Massingham, still in that slow, almost detached voice, "one does not only kill one's own soul. There's the other soul. It's let out of the dead, heavy body— a damned soul, reproaching you for its damnation. And you can do nothing—nothing! It's—oh, I can't tell you! There aren't human words for a thing like that, which is inhuman."

The others remained silent.

"Have you ever thought," added Massingham abruptly, "how terrible it must be to be God? To know things like that, and let them be, because they're just?"

"God is merciful first and just afterwards," said Amory. "I know I used to say the reverse, but now I know better."

"You may be right," said Massingham. "There must be an amazing amount of goodness somewhere when there is such a quantity of unspeakable evil in men like us, who thought ourselves decent fellows enough."

Grindley moved impatiently.

"There is," he said; "I know there is. But I can't bear to think of that horror of evil, which we all know of, let loose on Reece. He knows all I could tell him, but you can't *tell* about——"

"No, you can't," agreed Amory.

"What I can't understand," said Massingham, "was why you were so—well, so callous—about it, Vernon. You had as ghastly a time as any of us, and yet, when you could have dissuaded that kid—(for you could have dissuaded him, only you could)—you let him go on."

"It's like this," said Vernon, and the others were astonished at the gentleness of his voice. "Since—that night—I've felt the most tremendous reverence for innocence—purity of mind and thought. It seems to me that evil can't touch it, but it might touch evil. Do you see what I mean?—You do, Amory."

"Y-Yes, I do," admitted the Parson; "but—oh, Vernon, it's the ghastly risk! None of us ever guessed what would happen to the others, and we were more or less intimate with them. Now we know—(a little: we shall never know really)— what each has gone through; we can see how it worked. That room is so evil that when a man goes into it all the worst in him is drawn out. He is himself still, but filled and soaked with evil passions. He becomes vice incarnate——"

"Yes!" cried Vernon; "that's it!"

"What evil is in Reece?" asked Ladislaw.

They were silent a little, and then Grindley said apologetically :

" You see, one knows him so little. As Amory said, we aren't intimate with him, any of us. We've only been in close contact with him just lately, when we're all abnormal. I don't know—I hate to think of him alone up there, unsuspecting——"

They fell silent again, like men who anxiously await news. Suddenly Ladislaw rose and went and opened the door. They all listened intently. The house was utterly still.

Ladislaw came back, but he left the door open. " Just in case," he murmured, half-apologetically.

The night wore on. Somehow no one cared to go to bed. With the others it had been different—they could look after themselves ; but they all felt a queer responsibility for Reece. He was such a kid, they kept saying, and the danger was so horrible. The dead silence of the house, dark and brooding beyond the open door of the warm and well-lit smoking-room, was terrible. Reece was out there, alone. . . .

Dawn showed grey at last, and slowly the night lifted. The five men had been silent for the last hour or more. Now they looked dully, almost hopelessly, at each other's faces, grey in the early light, and silently they rose. It was over. Whatever had happened was ended.

They all felt a shock of surprise, relief—yes, and delight— when Reece came into the dining-room. He looked round at their drawn faces with concern.

" I say—is anything wrong ? " he asked.

" No," said Massingham, with a half-laugh. " No ; not if you're all right."

" Oh, *I'm* all right," said the little curate cheerfully. " Never slept better in my life, and that's saying a lot."

" Then, you saw—— ? " began Grindley.

" I didn't see a thing," said Reece half-regretfully. " Something missing in my make-up, I expect. It *is* a pity ! However, I've had my chance."

And he fell hungrily on his breakfast.

FLORENCE FLANNERY

By

MARJORIE BOWEN

SHE who had been Florence Flannery noted with a careless
eye the stains of wet on the dusty stairs, and with a glance
ill used to observance of domesticities looked up for damp
or dripping ceilings. The dim-walled staircase revealed
nothing but more dust, yet this would serve as a peg for ill-
humour to hang on, so Florence pouted.

"An ill, muddy place," said she, who loved gilding and
gimcracks and mirrors reflecting velvet chairs, and flounced
away to the upper chamber, lifting frilled skirts contemptuously
high.

Her husband followed ; they had been married a week
and there had never been any happiness in their wilful passion.
Daniel Shute did not now look for any ; in the disgust of this
draggled homecoming he wondered what had induced him to
marry the woman and how soon he would come to hate her.

As she stood in the big bedroom he watched her with
dislike ; her tawdry charms of vulgar prettiness had once
been delightful to his dazed senses and muddled wits, but
here, in his old home, washed by the fine Devon air, his sight
was clearer and she appeared coarse as a poppy at the far end
of August.

"Of course you hate it," he said cynically, lounging with
his big shoulders against one of the bedposts, his big hands
in the pockets of his tight nankeen trousers, and his fair hair,
tousled from the journey, hanging over his mottled face.

"It is not the place you boasted to have," replied Florence,
but idly, for she stood by the window and looked at the tiny
leaded panes ; the autumn sun gleaming sideways on this
glass, picked out a name scratched there :

Florence Flannerye. Born 1500.

"Look here," cried the woman, excited, "this should be my ancestress!"

She slipped off a huge diamond ring she wore and scratched underneath the writing the present year, "1800."

Daniel Shute came and looked over her shoulder.

"That reads strange—'Born 1500'—as if you would say died 1800," he remarked. "Well, I don't suppose she had anything to do with you, my charmer, yet she brought you luck, for it was remembering this name here made me notice you when I heard what you were called."

He spoke uncivilly, and she responded in the same tone.

"Undervalue what is your own, Mr. Shute. There was enough for me to choose from, I can swear!"

"Enough likely gallants," he grinned, "not so many likely husbands, eh?"

He slouched away, for, fallen as he was, it stung him that he had married a corybante of the opera, an unplaced, homeless, nameless creature for all he knew, for he could never quite believe that "Florence Flannery" was her real name.

Yet that name had always attracted him; it was so queer that he should meet a real woman called Florence Flannery when one of the earliest of his recollections was tracing that name over with a curious finger in the old diamond pane.

"You have never told me who she was," said Mrs. Shute.

"Who knows? Three hundred years ago, m'dear. There are some old wives' tales, of course."

He left the great bedroom and she followed him doggedly downstairs.

"Is this your fine manor, Mr. Shute? And these your noble grounds? And how am I to live here, Mr. Shute, who left the gaieties of London for you?"

Her voice, shrill and edged, followed him down the stairs and into the vast dismantled drawing-room where they paused, facing each other like things caught in a trap, which is what they were.

For he had married her because he was a ruined man, driven from London by duns, and a drunken man who dreaded lonely hours and needed a boon companion to pledge him glass for glass, and a man of coarse desires who had bought with marriage what he was not rich enough to buy with money, and she had married him because she was past her meridian and saw no more conquests ahead and also was in love with the idea of being a gentlewoman and ruling in the great grand house by the sea—which was how she had thought of Shute Manor.

And a great grand house it had been, but for twenty years it had been abandoned by Daniel Shute, and stripped and mortgaged to pay for his vices, so that now it stood barren and desolate, empty and tarnished, and only a woman with love in her heart could have made a home of it ; never had there been love in Florence Flannery's heart, only greed and meanness.

Thus these two faced each other in the gaunt room with the monstrous chandelier hanging above them wrapped in a dusty brown holland bag, the walls festooned with cobwebs, the pale wintry sunshine showing the thick dust on the unpolished boards.

" I never can live here ! " cried Mrs. Shute. There was a touch of panic in her voice and she lifted her hands to her heart with a womanly gesture of grief.

The man was touched by a throb of pity ; he did not himself expect the place to be so dilapidated. Some kind of a rascally agent had been looking after it for him, and he supposed some effort would have been made for his reception.

Florence saw his look of half-sullen shame and urged her point.

" We can go back, cannot we ? " she said, with the rich drop in her voice, so useful for coaxing ; " back to London and the house in Baker Street ? All the old friends and old pleasures, Mr. Shute, and a dashing little cabriolet to go round the park ? "

" Curse it ! " he answered, chagrined. " I haven't the money. Flo ; I haven't the damned money ! " She heard the ring of bitter truth in his voice and the atrocious nature of the deception he had practised on her overwhelmed her shallow understanding.

" You mean you've got no money, Mr. Shute ? " she screamed.

" Not enough for London, m'dear."

" And I've to live in this filthy barn ? "

" It has been good enough for my people, Mrs. Shute," he answered grimly. " For all the women of my family, gentlewomen, all of 'em with quarterings, and it will be good enough for you, m'dear, so none of your Bartholomew Fair airs and graces."

She was cornered, and a little afraid of him ; he had been drinking at the last place where they stopped to water the horses and she knew how he could be when he was drunk ; she remembered that she was alone with him and what a huge man he was.

So she crept away and went down into the vast kitchens where an old woman and a girl were preparing a meal.

The sight of this a little heartened Mrs. Shute ; in her frilled taffetas and long ringlets she sat down by the great open hearth, moving her hands to show the firelight flashing in her rings and shifting her petticoats so that the girl might admire her kid shoes.

" I'll take a cordial to stay my strength," she said, " for I've come a long way and find a sour welcome at the end of it, and that'll turn any woman's blood."

The old dame smiled, knowing her type well enough ; for even in a village you may find women like this.

So she brought Mrs. Shute some damson wine and a plate of biscuits, and the two women became friendly enough and gossiped in the dim candle-lit kitchen while Daniel Shute wandered about his old home, even his corrupt heart feeling many a pang to see the places of his childhood desolate, the walks overgrown, the trees felled, the arbours closed, the fountains dried, and all the spreading fields about fenced by strangers.

The November moon was high in a misted space of open heaven by the time he reached the old carp pond.

Dead weeds tangled over the crumbling, moss-grown stone, trumpery and slime coated the dark waters.

" I suppose the carp are all dead ? " said Mr. Shute.

He had not been aware that he spoke aloud, and was surprised to hear himself answered.

" I believe there are some left, esquire."

Mr. Shute turned sharply and could faintly discern the figure of a man sitting on the edge of the pond so that it seemed as if his legs half danged in the black water.

" Who are you ? " asked Daniel Shute quickly.

" I'm Paley, sir, who looks after the grounds."

" You do your work damned badly," replied the other, irritated.

" It is a big place, esquire, for one man to work."

He seemed to stoop lower and lower as if at any moment he would slip into the pond ; indeed, in the half dark, it seemed to Mr. Shute as if he was already half in the water ; yet, on this speech, he moved and showed that he was but bending over the sombre depths of the carp pond.

The moonlight displayed him as a drab man of middling proportions with slow movements and a large languid eye which glittered feebly in the pale light ; Mr. Shute had an impression that this eye looked at him sideways as if it was set at the side of the man's head, but soon saw that this was an illusion.

" Who engaged you ? " he asked acidly, hating the creature.

" Mr. Tregaskis, the agent," replied the man in what appeared to be a thick foreign accent or with some defect of speech, and walked away into the wintry undergrowth.

Mr. Shute returned home grumbling ; in the grim parlour Mr. Tregaskis was waiting for him—a red Cornishman, who grinned at his employer's railings. He knew the vices of Mr. Shute, and the difficulties of Mr. Shute, and he had seen Mrs. Shute in the kitchen deep in maudlin gossip with old Dame Chase and the idiot-faced girl, drinking the alcoholic country wine till it spilled from her shaking fingers on to her taffeta skirt.

So he assumed a tone of noisy familiarity that Mr. Shute was too sunken to resent ; the last of the old squire's Oporto was sent for and the men drank themselves on to terms of easy good-fellowship.

At the last, when the candles were guttering, the bottles empty, and the last log's ashes on the hearth, Mr. Shute asked who was the creature Paley he had found hanging over the carp pond.

Mr. Tregaskis told him, but the next morning Mr. Shute could not recollect what he had said ; the whole evening had, in his recollection, an atmosphere of phantasmagoria ; but he thought that the agent had said that Paley was a deserted sailor who had wandered up from Plymouth and taken the work without pay, a peculiar individual who lived in a wattled hut that he had made himself, and on food he caught with his own hands.

His sole explanation of himself was that he had waited for something a long time and was still waiting for it ; useful he was, Mr. Tregaskis had said, and it was better to leave him alone.

All this Mr. Shute remembered vaguely, lying in the great bed staring at the pale sun glittering on the name " Florence Flannery " scratched on the window with the two dates.

It was late in the autumnal morning, but his wife still lay beside him, heavily asleep, with her thick heavy chestnut hair tossed over the pillow and her full bosom panting, the carnation of her rounded face flushed and stained the coarse diamonds glowing on her plump hands, the false pearls slipping round her curved throat.

Daniel Shute sat up in bed and looked down at her prone sleep.

"Who is she ? And where does she come from ? " he wondered. He had never cared to find out, but now his ignorance of all appertaining to his wife annoyed him.

He shook her bare shoulder till she yawned out of her heavy sleep.

"Who are you, Flo ? " he asked. "You must know something about yourself."

The woman blinked up at him, drawing her satin bedgown round her breast.

"I was in the opera, wasn't I ? " she answered lazily. " I never knew my people."

"Came out of an orphanage or the gutter, I suppose ? " he returned bitterly.

"Maybe."

"But your name ? " he insisted. " That is never your name, ' Florence Flannery ' ? "

"I've never known another," she responded indifferently.

"You're not Irish."

"I don't know, Mr. Shute. I've been in many countries and seen many strange things."

He laughed ; he had heard some of her experiences.

"You've seen so much and been in so many places I don't know how you've ever got it all into one life."

"I don't know myself. It's all rather like a dream and the most dreamlike of all is to be lying here looking at my own name written three hundred years ago."

She moved restlessly and slipped from the bed, a handsome woman with troubled eyes.

" 'Tis the drink brings the dreams, m'dear," said Mr. Shute. " I had some dreams last night of a fellow named Paley I met by the carp pond."

"You were drinking in the parlour," she retorted scornfully.

"And you in the kitchen, m'dear."

Mrs. Shute flung a fringed silk shawl, the gift of an Indian nabob, round her warm body and dropped, shivering and yawning, into one of the warm tapestry chairs.

"Who was this Florence Flannery ? " she asked idly.

"I told you no one knows. An Irish girl born in Florence, they said, when I was a child and listened to beldam's gossip.

Her mother a Medici, m'dear, and he a groom! And she came here, the trollop, with some young Shute who had been travelling in Italy—picked her up and brought her home, like I've brought you!"

"He didn't marry her?" asked Mrs. Shute indifferently.

"More sense," said her husband coarsely. "I'm the first fool of me family. She was a proper vixen. John Shute took her on his voyages; he'd a ship and went discovering. They talk yet at Plymouth of how she would sit among the parrots and the spices and the silks when the ship came into Plymouth Hoe."

"Ah, the good times!" sighed Mrs. Shute, "when men were men and paid a good price for their pleasures!"

"You've fetched your full market value, Mrs. Shute," he answered, yawning in the big bed.

"I'd rather be John Shute's woman than your wife," she returned.

"What do you know of him?"

"I saw his portrait on the back stairs last night. Goody Chase showed me. A noble man with a clear eye and great arms to fight and love with."

"He used 'em to push Florence Flannery out with," grinned Mr. Shute, "if half the tales are true. On one of their voyages they picked up a young Portuguese who took the lady's fancy and she brought him back to Shute Court."

"And what was the end of it?"

"I know no more, save that she was flung out, as I'd like to fling you out, my beauty!" foamed Mr. Shute with gusty violence.

His wife laughed loud and discordantly.

"I'll tell the rest of the tale. She got tired of her new love, and he wasn't a Portuguese, but an Indian, or partly, and his name was D'Ailey, Daly the people called it here. On one voyage she told John Shute about him and he marooned him on a lonely island in the South Seas—tied up to a great, great stone image of a god, burning hot in the tropic sun. He must have been a god of fishes for there was nothing else near that island but monstrous fish."

"Who told you this?" demanded Mr. Shute. "Old Dame Chase, with her lies? I never heard of this before."

"'Tis the story," resumed his wife. "The last she saw of him was his bound figure tied tight, tight, to the gaping, grinning idol while she sat on the poop as the ship—the *Phœnix*—sailed away. He cursed her and called on the idol to let her

live till he was avenged on her—he was of the breed, or partly of
the breed, that these gods love, and Florence Flannery was
afraid, afraid, as she sailed away—— "

" Goody Chase in her cups ! " sneered Mr. Shute. " And
what's the end of your story ? "

" There's no end," said the woman sullenly. " John Shute
cast her off, for the bad luck that dogged him, and what became
of her I don't know."

" It's an ugly tale and a stupid tale," grumbled Daniel
Shute with a groan as he surveyed the bleak chill weather
beyond the lattice panes. " Get down and see what's to eat in
the house and what's to drink in the cellar, and if that rogue
Tregaskis is there send him up to me."

Mrs. Shute rose and pulled fiercely at the long wool-
embroidered bell-rope so that the rusty bell jangled violently.

" What'll you do when the wine is all drunk and the boon
companions have cleared out your pockets ? " she asked wildly.
" Do your own errands, Mr. Shute."

He flung out of bed with a pretty London oath, and she
remained huddled in the chair while he dressed and after he
had left her, wringing her hands now and then and wailing
under her breath, till Dame Chase came up with a posset and
helped her to dress. The sight of her dishevelled trunks restored some of Mrs. Shute's spirits ; she pulled out with relish
her furbelows and flounces, displaying to Goody Chase's
amazed admiration the last fashions of Paris and London, ming-
ling her display with fond reminiscences of gilded triumphs.

" Maybe you'd be surprised to learn that Mr. Shute isn't
my first husband," she said, tossing her head.

The fat old woman winked.

" I'd be more surprised, m'lady, to learn he was your last."

Mrs. Shute laughed grossly, but her spirits soon fell ;
kneeling on the floor with her tumbled finery in her lap, she
stared out through the window on which her name was written
at the tossing bare boughs, the chill sky, the dry flutter of the
last leaves.

" I'll never get away," she said mournfully, " the place
bodes me no good. I've had the malaria in me time, Mrs.
Chase, in one of those cursed Italian swamps and it affected
me memory ; there's much I can't place together and much I
recall brokenly—dreams and fevers, Mrs. Chase."

" The drink, m'lady."

" No," returned the kneeling woman fiercely. " Wasn't
the drink taken to drown those dreams and fevers ? I wish I

could tell you half I know—there's many a fine tale in me head,
but when I begin to speak it goes ! "

She began to rock to and fro, lamenting.

" To think of the fine times I've had with likely young men
drinking me health in me slipper and the little cabriolet in
Paris and the walks in the Prater outside Vienna. So pleasant
you would hardly believe ! "

" You'll settle down, m'lady, like women do."

Indeed, Mrs. Shute seemed to make some attempt at
" settling down " ; there was something piteous in the despairing energy with which she set to work to make her life tolerable ;
there was a suite of rooms lined with faded watered green silk
that she took for her own and had cleaned and furnished with
what she could gather from the rest of the house—old gilt
commodes and rococo chairs and threadbare panels of tapestries
and chipped vases of Saxe or Lunéville, one or two pastel
portraits that the damp had stained, together with some tawdry
trifles she had brought in her own baggage.

She employed Mr. Tregaskis to sell her big diamond in
Plymouth and bought pale blue satin hangings for her bedroom
and spotted muslin for her bed, a carpet wreathed with roses,
a gaudy dressing-table and phials of perfume, opopanax,
frangipane, musk, potent, searing, to dissipate, she said, the
odours of must and mildew.

Arranging these crude splendours was her sole occupation.
There were no neighbours in the lonely valley and Mr. Shute
fell into melancholy and solitary drinking ; he hung on to this
existence as just more tolerable than a debtor's prison, but the
fury with which he met his fate expressed itself in curses awful
to hear. Such part of the estate as still belonged to him he
treated with complex contempt ; Mr. Tregaskis continued to
supervise some rough farming and the man Paley worked in
the garden ; taciturn, solitary and sullen, he made an ill impression on Mr. Shute, yet he cost nothing and did some labour,
as carrying up the firewood to the house and clearing away some
of the thickets and dying weeds and vast clumps of nettles
and docks.

Mrs. Shute met him for the first time by the carp pond ;
she was tricked out in a white satin pelisse edged with fur and
a big bonnet, and wandered forlornly in the neglected paths.
Paley was sitting on the edge of the carp pond, looking intently
into the murky depths.

" I'm the new mistress," said Mrs. Shute, " and I'll thank
you to keep better order in the place."

Paley looked up at her with his pale eyes.

" Shute Court isn't what it was," he said, " there is a lot of work to do."

" You seem to spend a power of time by the pond," she replied. " What are you here for ? "

" I'm waiting for something," he said. " I'm putting in time, Mrs. Shute."

" A sailor, I hear ? " she said curiously, for the draggled nondescript man in his greenish-black clothes was difficult to place ; he had a peculiar look of being boneless, without shoulders or hips, one slope slipping into another as if there was no framework under his flabby flesh.

" I've been at sea," he answered, " like yourself, Mrs. Shute."

She laughed coarsely.

" I would I were at sea again," she replied ; " this is horror to me."

" Why do you stay ? "

" I'm wondering. It seems that I can't get away, the same as I couldn't help coming," a wail came into her voice. " Must I wait till Mr. Shute has drunk himself to death ? "

The wind blew sharp across the pond, cutting little waves in the placid surface, and she who had been Florence Flannery shuddered in the bite of it and turned away and went muttering up the path to the desolate house.

Her husband was in the dirty parlour playing at bezique with Mr. Tregaskis and she flared in upon them.

" Why don't you get rid of that man Paley ? I hate him. He does no work—Mrs. Chase told me that he always sits by the carp pond and to-day I saw him—ugh ! "

" Paley's all right, Mrs. Shute," replied Tregaskis, " he does more work than you think."

" Why does he stay ? "

" He's waiting for a ship that's soon due in Plymouth."

" Send him off," insisted Mrs. Shute. " Isn't the place melancholic enough without you having that sitting about ? "

Her distaste and disgust of the man seemed to amount to a panic, and her husband, whose courage was snapped by the drink, was infected by her fear.

" When did this fellow come ? " he demanded.

" About a week before you did. He'd tramped up from Plymouth."

" We've only his word for that," replied Mr. Shute with drunken cunning ; " maybe he's a Bow Street runner sent by one of those damned creditors ! You're right, Flo, I don't like the wretch—he's watching me, split him ! I'll send him off."

Mr. Tregaskis shrugged as Daniel Shute staggered from his chair.

" The man's harmless, sir ; half-witted if you like, but useful."

Still Mr. Shute dragged on his greatcoat with the capes and followed his wife out into the grey garden.

The carp pond was not near the house, and by the time that they had reached it a dull twilight had fallen in the cold heavy air.

The great trees were quite bare now and flung a black tracing of forlorn branches against the bleak evening sky ; patches and clumps of dead weeds obstructed every path and alley ; by the carp pond showed the faint outline of a blind statue crumbling beneath the weight of dead mosses.

Paley was not there.

" He'll be in his hut," said Mr. Shute, " sleeping or spying —the ugly old devil. I'll send him off."

The dead oyster white of Mrs. Shute's pelisse gleamed oddly as she followed her husband through the crackling undergrowth.

There, in the thickening twilight, they found the hut, a queer arrangement of wattles cunningly interwoven in which there was no furniture whatever, nothing but a bare protection from the wind and weather.

Paley was not there.

" I'll find him," muttered Mr. Shute, " if I have to stay out all night."

For his half-intoxicated mind had fixed on this stranger as the symbol of all his misfortunes and perhaps the avenger of all his vices.

His wife turned back, for her pelisse was being caught on the undergrowth ; she went moodily towards the carp pond.

A moment later a sharp shriek from her brought Mr. Shute plunging back to her side. She was standing in a queer bent attitude, pointing with a shaking plump hand to the murky depths of the pond.

" The wretch ! He's drowned himself ! " she screamed.

Mr. Shute's worn-out nerves reacted to her ignoble panic ; he clutched her arm as he gazed in the direction of her finger ; there was something dark in the shallower side of the pond, something large and dark, with pale flat eyes that glittered malevolently.

" Paley ! " gasped Mr. Shute.

He bent closer in amazed horror, then broke into tremulous laughter.

" 'Tis a fish," he declared ; " one of the old carp."

Mrs. Shute indeed now perceived that the monstrous creature in the water was a fish ; she could make out the wide gaping jaw, tall spines shadowing in the murk, and a mottled skin of deadly yellow and dingy white.

" It's looking at me," she gasped.   " Kill it, kill it, the loathsome wretch ! "

" It's—it's—too big," stammered Mr. Shute, but he picked up a stone to hurl ; the huge fish, as if aware of his intentions, slipped away into the murky depths of the pond, leaving a sluggish ripple on the surface.

Daniel Shute now found his courage.

" Nothing but an old carp," he repeated.   " I'll have the thing caught."

Mrs. Shute began to weep and wring her hands.   Her husband dragged her roughly towards the house, left her there, took a lantern, and accompanied now by Mr. Tregaskis returned in search of Paley.

This time they found him sitting in his usual place by the side of the pond.   Mr. Shute had now changed his mind about sending him away ; he had a muddled idea that he would like the pond watched, and who was to do this if not Paley ?

" Look here, my man," he said, " there's a great carp in this pond—a very big, black old carp."

" They live for hundreds of years," said Paley.   " But this isn't a carp."

" You know about it, then ? " demanded Mr. Shute.

" I know about it."

" Well, I want you to catch it—kill it.   Watch till you do. I loathe it—ugh ! "

" Watch the pond ? " protested Mr. Tregaskis, who held the lantern and was chilled and irritable.   " Damme, esquire, what can the thing do ?   It can't leave the water."

" I wouldn't," muttered Mr. Shute, " promise you that."

" You're drunk," said the other coarsely.

But Mr. Shute insisted on his point.

" Watch the pond, Paley, watch it day and night till you get that fish."

" I'll watch," answered Paley, never moving from his huddled position.

The two men went back to the desolate house.   When Mr.

Shute at last staggered upstairs he found his wife with half a dozen candles lit, crouching under the tawdry muslin curtains with which she had disfigured the big bed.

She clutched a rosary that she was constantly raising to her lips as she muttered ejaculations.

Mr. Shute lurched to the bedside.

" I didn't know that you were a Papist, Flo," he sneered.

She looked up at him.

" That story's got me," she whispered, " the man tied up to the fish god—the curse—and he following her—tracking her down—for three hundred years, till she was hounded back to the old place where they'd loved."

Daniel Shute perceived that she had been drinking, and sank into a chair.

" Goody Chase's gossip," he answered, yawning, " and that damned ugly fish. I've set Paley to catch him—to watch the pond till he does."

She looked at him sharply, and appeared relieved.

" Anyhow, what's it to do with you ? " he continued. " You ain't the jade who left the man on the island ! " He laughed crudely.

Mrs. Shute sank down on her pillows.

" As long as the pond is watched," she murmured, " I don't mind."

But during the night she tossed and panted in a delirium, talking of great ships with strange merchandise, of lonely islands amid blazing seas, of mighty stone gods rearing up to the heavens, of a man in torture and a curse following a woman who sailed away, till her husband shook her and left her alone, sleeping on a couch in the dreary parlour.

The next day he spoke to Mrs. Chase.

" Between your news and your lies you've turned your mistress's head. Good God ! she is like a maniac with your parcel of follies ! "

But Goody Chase protested that she had told her nothing.

" She told me that story, esquire, and said she had found it in an old book. What did I know of Florence Flannery ? Many a time you've asked me about her when you were a child and I've had no answer to give you—what did I know save she was a hussy who disgraced Shute Court ? "

At this Daniel Shute vehemently demanded of his wife where she had got the tales which she babbled about, but the woman was sullen and heavy and would tell him nothing ; all the day she remained thus, but when the few hours of wintry light were over she fell again into unbridled terror, gibbering like a creature deprived of reason, beating her breast, kissing the rosary, and muttering, " *Mea culpâ, mea culpâ, mea maximâ culpâ !* "

Mr. Shute was not himself in any state to endure this ; he left his wife to herself and made Tregaskis sleep with him for company in another room.

Winter froze the bleak countryside ; Paley kept guard by the pond and the Shutes somehow dragged on an intolerable existence in the deserted house.

In the daytime Mrs. Shute revived a little and would even prink herself out in her finery and gossip with Mrs. Chase over the vast log fire, but the nights always found her smitten with terror, shivering with cowardly apprehension ; and the object of all her nightmare dread was the fish she had seen in the pond.

" It can't leave the water," they told her, and she always answered :

" The first night I was here I saw wet on the stairs."

" My God, my God ! " Daniel Shute would say, " this is like living with some one sentenced to death."

" Get a doctor over from Plymouth," suggested Mr. Tregaskis.

But Mr. Shute would not, for fear of being betrayed to his creditors.

" Better rot here than in the Fleet," he swore.

" Then take her away—and keep her from the bottle."

The wretched husband could do neither of these things ; he had no money and no influence over Mrs. Shute. He was indeed indifferent to her sufferings save in so far as they reacted on him and ever accustomed him to the spectacle of her breakdown ; he knew it was not really strange that a woman such as she was should collapse under conditions such as these, and his life was already so wretched that he cared little for added horrors.

He began to find a strange comfort in the man Paley, who, taciturn, slow and queer, yet did his work and watched the pond with an admirable diligence.

One night in the blackest time of the year, the bitter dark nights before Christmas, the shrieks of Mrs. Shute brought her husband cursing up the stairs.

Her door was unbolted and she sat up in bed, displaying, in the light of his snatched-up taper, some red marks on her arm.

" Let him kill me and done with it," she jabbered.

"*He came flopping up the stairs, he broke the bolts ;
he jumped on the bed.*"

Mr. Tregaskis came pushing in and caught rudely hold of her arm.

" She's done it herself," he cried ; " those are the marks of her own teeth."

But Mrs. Shute cried piteously :

" He came flopping up the stairs, he broke the bolts ; he jumped on the bed ! Oh ! oh ! oh ! Isn't this the bed, the very bed I slept in then—and didn't he used to creep into this room when John Shute was away ? "

" Still thinking of that damned fish," said Mr. Tregaskis, " and it's my belief you neither of you saw it at all, esquire— that man Paley has been watching, and he's seen nothing."

Mr. Shute bit his finger-nails, looking down on the writhing figure of his wife.

" Light all the candles, can't you ? " he said. " I'll stay with the poor fool to-night."

While Mr. Tregaskis obeyed he went to the door and looked out, holding his taper high.

There were pools of wet and a long trail of slime down the dusty, neglected stairs.

He called Mr. Tregaskis.

" Ugh ! " cried the Cornishman, then, " It's from Goody Chase's water crock."

On the following windy morning Mr. Shute went out, shivering in the nipping air, to the carp pond.

" I don't want another night like last," he said. " You'll sleep across my wife's door—she thinks that cursed carp is after her—— "

Then, at the gross absurdity of what he said, he laughed miserably.

" This is a pretty pantomime I'm playing," he muttered.

A horrid curiosity drove him up to look at his wife.

She sat between the draggled muslin curtains hugging her knees in the tumbled bed ; a wretched fire flickered wanly in the chill depths of the vast room ; a wind blew swift and remote round the window on which was scratched the name of Florence Flannery.

Mr. Shute shivered.

" I must get you away," he said, stirred above his fears for himself ; " this is a damned place—the Fleet would be better, after all."

She turned lustreless eyes on him.

" I can't get away," she said dully. " I've come here to die —don't you see it on that window—' Died 1800 ' ? "

MARJORIE BOWEN

He crossed the floor and peered at the scratching on the glass. Some one had indeed added the word " died " before the last date.

" These are the tricks of a Bedlamite," he said nervously. " Do you think there was only one Florence Flannery ? "

" And do you think," she returned harshly, " that there were two ? "

She looked so awful crouched up in bed with her hanging hair, her once plump face fallen in the cheeks, her soiled satin gown open over her labouring breast, her whole air and expression so agonized, so malevolent, so dreadful, that Daniel Shute passed his hand over his eyes as if to brush away a vision of unsubstantial horror.

He was shaken by an hallucination of light-headedness ; he appeared to enter another world, in which many queer things were possible.

" What are you ? " he asked uneasily. " He's been after you for nearly three hundred years ? Aren't you punished enough ? "

" Oh, oh ! " moaned the woman. " Keep him out ! Keep him out ! "

" I'll put Paley at the door to-night," muttered Mr. Shute.

He crept out of the horrible chamber ; he now detested his wife beyond all reason, yet somehow he felt impelled to save her from the invincible furies who were pursuing her in so gruesome a fashion.

" She's a lunatic," said Mr. Tregaskis brusquely. " You'll have to keep her shut up in that room—it's not difficult to account for—with the life she's led and this place and the coincidence of the names."

The first snow of the year began to fall that night, sullen flakes struggling in the coils of the leaping wind that circled round Shute Court.

In the last glimmer of daylight Paley came to take up his post.

Drab, silent, with his sloping shoulders and nondescript clothes, he went slowly upstairs and sat down outside Mrs. Shute's door.

" He seems to know the way," remarked Daniel Shute.

" Don't you know he works in the house ? " retorted Mr. Tregaskis.

The two men slept, as usual, in the parlour, on stiff horse-hair couches bundled up with pillows and blankets ; the litter of their supper was left on the table and they piled the fire up with logs before going to sleep. Mr. Shute's nerves were in no state to permit him to risk waking up in the dark.

The wind dropped and the steady downdrift of the soft snow filled the blackness of the bitter night.

As the grandfather clock struck three Daniel Shute sat up and called to his companion.

" I've been thinking in my dreams," he said, with chattering teeth. " Is it Paley, or Daley ? You know the name was D'Ailey."

" Shut up, you fool," returned the agent fiercely ; but he then raised himself on his elbow, for a hoarse, bitter scream, followed by some yelled words in a foreign language tore through the stillness.

" The mad woman," said Mr. Tregaskis ; but Daniel Shute dragged the clothes up to his chattering teeth.

" I'm not going up," he muttered. " I'm not going up ! "

Mr. Tregaskis dragged on his trousers and flung a blanket over his shoulders and so, lighting a taper at the big fire, went up the gaunt stairs to Mrs. Shute's room. The glimmering beams of the rushlight showed him tracks of wet again on the dirty boards.

" Goody Chase with her crocks and possets," he murmured ; then louder, " Paley ! Paley ! "

There was no one outside Mrs. Shute's door, which hung open. Mr. Tregaskis entered.

She who had been Florence Flannery lay prone on her tawdry couch ; the deep wounds that had slain her appeared to have been torn by savage teeth : she looked infinitely old, shrivelled and detestable.

Mr. Tregaskis backed on to the stairs, the light lurching round him from the shaking of his taper, when Mr. Shute came bustling up out of the darkness.

" Paley's gone," whispered Mr. Tregaskis dully.

" I saw him go," gibbered Mr. Shute, " as I ventured to the door—by the firelight ; a great fish slithering away with blood on his jaws."

THE GHOST AT
MASSINGHAM MANSIONS

By

ERNEST BRAMAH

"Do you believe in ghosts, Max ? " inquired Mr. Carlyle.
"Only as ghosts," replied Carrados with decision.
"Quite so," assented the private detective with the
air of acquiescence with which he was wont to cloak his
moments of obfuscation. Then he added cautiously : " And
how don't you believe in them, pray ? "

"As public nuisances—or private ones for that matter,"
replied his friend. " So long as they are content to behave as
ghosts I am with them. When they begin to meddle with a
state of existence that is outside their province—to interfere in
business matters and depreciate property—to rattle chains,
bang doors, ring bells, predict winners, and to edit magazines
—and to attract attention instead of shunning it, I cease to
believe. My sympathies are entirely with the sensible old fellow
who was awakened in the middle of the night to find a shadowy
form standing by the side of his bed and silently regarding him.
For a few minutes the disturbed man waited patiently, expecting
some awful communication, but the same profound silence was
maintained. ' Well,' he remarked at length, ' if you have
nothing to do, I have,' and turning over went to sleep again."

"I have been asked to take up a ghost," Carlyle began to
explain.

"Then I don't believe in it," declared Carrados.

"Why not ? "

"Because it is a pushful, notoriety-loving ghost, or it would
not have gone so far. Probably it wants to get into the *Daily
Mail*. The other people, whoever they are, don't believe in it,
either, Louis, or they wouldn't have called you in. They would
have gone to Sir Oliver Lodge for an explanation, or to the
nearest priest for a stoup of holy water."

"I admit that I shall direct my researches towards the forces
of this world before I begin to investigate any other," conceded

Louis Carlyle. " And I don't doubt," he added, with his usual bland complacence, " that I shall hale up some mischievous or aggrieved individual before the ghost is many days older. Now that you have brought me so far, do you care to go on round to the place with me, Max, to hear what they have to say about it?"

Carrados agreed with his usual good nature. He rarely met his friend without hearing the details of some new case, for Carlyle's practice had increased vastly since the night when chance had led him into the blind man's study. They discussed the cases according to their interest, and there the matter generally ended so far as Max Carrados was concerned, until he casually heard the result subsequently from Carlyle's lips or learned the sequel from the newspaper. But these pages are primarily a record of the methods of the one man whose name they bear and therefore for the occasional case that Carrados completed for his friend there must be assumed the unchronicled scores which the inquiry agent dealt capably with himself. This reminder is perhaps necessary to dissipate the impression that Louis Carlyle was a pretentious humbug. He was, as a matter of fact, in spite of his amiable foibles and the self-assurance that was, after all, merely an asset of his trade, a shrewd and capable business man of his world, and behind his office manner nothing concerned him more than to pocket fees for which he felt that he had failed to render value.

Massingham Mansions proved to be a single block of residential flats overlooking a recreation ground. It was, as they afterwards found, an adjunct to a larger estate of similar property situated down another road. A porter, residing in the basement, looked after the interests of Massingham Mansions ; the business office was placed among the other flats. On that morning it presented the appearance of a well-kept, prosperous enough place, a little dull, a little unfinished, a little depressing perhaps ; in fact faintly reminiscent of the superfluous mansions that stand among broad, weedy roads on the outskirts of overgrown seaside resorts ; but it was persistently raining at the time when Mr. Carlyle had his first view of it.

" It is early to judge," he remarked, after stopping the car in order to verify the name on the brass plate, " but, upon my word, Max, I really think that our ghost might have discovered more appropriate quarters."

At the office, to which the porter had directed them, they found a managing clerk and two coltish youths in charge. Mr. Carlyle's name produced an appreciable flutter.

" The governor isn't here just now, but I have this matter

in hand," said the clerk with an easy air of responsibility—an effect unfortunately marred by a sudden irrepressible giggle from the least overawed of the colts. " Will you kindly step into our private room ? " He turned at the door of the inner office and dropped a freezing eye on the offender. " Get those letters copied before you go out to lunch, Binns," he remarked in a sufficiently loud voice. Then he closed the door quickly, before Binns could find a suitable retort.

So far it had been plain sailing, but now, brought face to face with the necessity of explaining, the clerk began to develop some hesitancy in beginning.

" It's a funny sort of business," he remarked, skirting the difficulty.

" Perhaps," admitted Mr. Carlyle ; " but that will not embarrass us. Many of the cases that pass through my hands are what you would call ' funny sorts of business.' "

" I suppose so," responded the young man, " but not through ours. Well, this is at 11 Massingham. A few nights ago—I suppose it must be more than a week now—Willett, the estate porter, was taking up some luggage to 75 Northanger for the people there when he noticed a light in one of the rooms at 11 Massingham. The backs face, though about twenty or thirty yards away. It struck him as curious, because 11 Massingham is empty and locked up. Naturally he thought at first that the porter at Massingham or one of us from the office had gone up for something. Still it was so unusual—being late at night—that it was his business to look into it. On his way round—you know where Massingham Mansions are ?—he had to pass here. It was dark, for we'd all been gone hours, but Willett has duplicate keys and he let himself in. Then he began to think that something must be wrong, for here, hanging up against their number on the board, were the only two keys of 11 Massingham that there are supposed to be. He put the keys in his pocket and went on to Massingham. Green, the resident porter there, told him that he hadn't been into No. 11 for a week. What was more, no one had passed the outer door, in or out, for a good half-hour. He knew that, because the door ' springs' with a noise when it is opened, no matter how carefully. So the two of them went up. The door of No. 11 was locked and inside everything was as it should be. There was no light then, and after looking well round with the lanterns that they carried they were satisfied that no one was concealed there."

" You say lanterns," interrupted Mr. Carlyle. " I suppose they lit the gas, or whatever it is there, as well ? "

" It is gas, but they could not light it because it was cut off at the meter. We always cut it off when a flat becomes vacant."

" What sort of a light was it, then, that Willet saw ? "

" It was gas, Mr. Carlyle. It is possible to see the bracket in that room from 75 Northanger. He saw it burning "

" Then the meter had been put on again ? "

" It is a locked cupboard in the basement. Only the office and the porters have keys. They tried the gas in the room and it was dead out ; they looked at the meter in the basement afterwards and it was dead off."

" Very good," observed Mr. Carlyle, noting the facts in his pocket-book. " What next ? "

" The next," continued the clerk, " was something that had really happened before. When they got down again—Green and Willet—Green was rather chipping Willet about seeing the light, you know, when he stopped suddenly. He'd remembered something. The day before the servant at 12 Massingham had asked him who it was that was using the bathroom at No. 11— she of course knowing that it was empty. He told her that no one used the bathroom. ' Well,' she said, ' we hear the water running and splashing almost every night and it's funny with no one there.' He had thought nothing of it at the time, concluding —as he told her—that it must be the water in the bathroom of one of the underneath flats that they heard. Of course he told Willett then and they went up again and examined the bathroom more closely. Water had certainly been run there, for the sides of the bath were still wet. They tried the taps and not a drop came. When a flat is empty we cut off the water like the gas."

" At the same place—the cupboard in the basement ? " inquired Carlyle.

" No ; at the cistern in the roof. The trap is at the top of the stairs and you need a longish ladder to get there. The next morning Willet reported what he'd seen and the governor told me to look into it. We didn't think much of it so far. That night I happened to be seeing some friends to the station here —I live not so far off—and I thought I might as well take a turn round here on my way home. I knew that if a light was burning I should be able to see the window lit up from the yard at the back, although the gas itself would be out of sight. And, sure enough, there was the light blazing out of one of the windows of No. 11. I won't say that I didn't feel a bit home-sick then, but I'd made up my mind to go up."

" Good man," murmured Mr. Carlyle approvingly.

" Wait a bit," recommended the clerk, with a shame-faced

laugh. " So far I had only had to make my mind up. It was then close on midnight and not a soul about. I came here for the keys, and I also had the luck to remember an old revolver that had been lying about in a drawer of the office for years. It wasn't loaded, but it didn't seem quite so lonely with it. I put it in my pocket and went on to Massingham, taking another turn into the yard to see that the light was still on. Then I went up the stairs as quietly as I could and let myself into No. 11."

" You didn't take Willett or Green with you ? "

The clerk gave Mr. Carlyle a knowing look, as of one smart man who will be appreciated by another.

" Willett's a very trustworthy chap," he replied, " and we have every confidence in him. Green also, although he has not been with us so long. But I thought it just as well to do it on my own, you understand, Mr. Carlyle. You didn't look in at Massingham on your way ? Well, if you had you would have seen that there is a pane of glass above every door, frosted glass to the hall doors and plain over each of those inside. It's to light the halls and passages, you know. Each flat has a small square hall and a longish passage leading off it. As soon as I opened the door I could tell that one of the rooms down the passage was lit up, though I could not see the door of it from there. Then I crept very quietly through the hall into the passage. A regular stream of light was shining from above the end door on the left. The room, I knew, was the smallest in the flat—it's generally used for a servant's bedroom or sometimes for a box-room. It was a bit thick, you'll admit—right at the end of a long passage and midnight, and after what the others had said."

" Yes, yes," assented the inquiry agent. " But you went on ? "

" I went on, tiptoeing without a sound. I got to the door, took out my pistol, put my hand almost on the handle and then——"

" Well, well," prompted Mr. Carlyle, as the narrator paused provokingly, with the dramatic instinct of an expert raconteur, " what then ? "

" Then the light went out ; while my hand was within an inch of the handle the light went out, as clean as if I had been watched all along and the thing timed. It went out all at once, without any warning and without the slightest sound from the beastly room beyond. And then it was as black as hell in the passage and something seemed to be going to happen."

" What did you do ? "

" I did a slope," acknowledged the clerk frankly. " I broke all the records down that passage, I bet you. You'll laugh, I dare say, and think you would have stood, but you don't know what it was like. I'd been screwing myself up, wondering what I should see in that lighted room when I opened the door, and then the light went out like a knife, and for all I knew the next second the door would open on me in the dark and Christ only knows what come out."

" Probably I should have run also," conceded Mr. Carlyle tactfully. " And you, Max ? "

" You see, I always feel at home in the dark," apologised the blind man. " At all events, you got safely away, Mr. ——?"

" My name's Elliott," responded the clerk. " Yes, you may bet I did. Whether the door opened and anybody or anything came out or nor I can't say. I didn't look. I certainly did get an idea that I heard the bath water running and swishing as I snatched at the hall door, but I didn't stop to consider that either, and if it was, the noise was lost in the slam of the door and my clatter as I took about twelve flights of stairs six steps at a time. Then when I was safely out I did venture to go round to look up again, and there was that damned light full on again."

" Really ? " commented Mr. Carlyle. " That was very audacious of him."

" Him ? Oh, well, yes, I suppose so. That's what the governor insists, but he hasn't been up there himself in the dark."

" Is that as far as you have got ? "

" It's as far as we can get. The bally thing goes on just as it likes. The very next day we tied up the taps of the gasmeter and the water cistern and sealed the string. Bless you, it didn't make a ha'peth of difference. Scarcely a night passes without the light showing, and there's no doubt that the water runs. We've put copying ink on the door handles and the taps and got into it ourselves until there isn't a man about the place that you couldn't implicate."

"' Has anyone watched up there ? "

" Willet and Green together did one night. They shut themselves up in the room opposite from ten till twelve and nothing happened. I was watching the window with a pair of opera-glasses from an empty flat here—85 Northanger. Then they chucked it, and before they could have been down the steps the light was there—I could see the gas as plain as I can see this ink-stand. I ran down and met them coming to tell me that nothing had happened. The three of us sprinted up again and the light was out and the flat as deserted as a churchyard. What do you make of that ? "

" It certainly requires looking into," replied Mr. Carlyle diplomatically.

"Looking into! Well, you're welcome to look all day and all night too, Mr. Carlyle. It isn't as though it was an old baronial mansion, you see, with sliding panels and secret passages. The place has the date over the front door, 1882— 1882 and haunted, by gosh! It was built for what it is, and there isn't an inch unaccounted for between the slates and the foundation."

"These two things—the light and the water running—are the only indications there have been?" asked Mr. Carlyle.

"So far as we ourselves have seen or heard. I ought perhaps to tell you of something else, however. When this business first started I made a few casual inquiries here and there among the tenants. Among others I saw Mr. Belting, who occupies 9 Massingham—the flat directly beneath No. 11. It didn't seem any good making up a cock-and-bull story, so I put it to him plainly—had he been annoyed by anything unusual going on at the empty flat above?

"'If you mean your confounded ghost up there, I have not been particularly annoyed,' he said at once, 'but Mrs. Belting has, and I should advise you to keep out of her way, at least until she gets another servant.' Then he told me that their girl, who slept in the bedroom underneath the little one at No. 11, had been going on about noises in the room above— footsteps and tramping and a bump on the floor—for some time before we heard anything of it. Then one day she suddenly said that she'd had enough of it and bolted. That was just before Willett first saw the light."

"It is being talked about, then—among the tenants?"

"You bet!" assented Mr. Elliott pungently. "That's what gets the governor. He wouldn't give a continental if no one knew, but you can't tell where it will end. The people at Northanger don't half like it either. All the children are scared out of their little wits and none of the slaveys will run errands after dark. It'll give the estate a bad name for the next three years if it isn't stopped."

"It shall be stopped," declared Mr. Carlyle impressively. "Of course we have our methods for dealing with this sort of thing, but in order to make a clean sweep it is desirable to put our hands on the offender *in flagranti delicto*. Tell your—er— principal not to have any further concern in the matter. One of my people will call here for any further details that he may require during the day. Just leave everything as it is in the meanwhile. Good-morning, Mr. Elliott, good-morning. . . . A fairly obvious game, I imagine, Max," he commented as they got into the car, " although the details are original and the motive not disclosed as yet. I wonder how many of them are in it ? "

" Let me know when you find out," said Carrados, and Mr. Carlyle promised.

Nearly a week passed and the expected revelation failed to make its appearance. Then, instead, quite a different note arrived :

> " MY DEAR MAX,—I wonder if you formed any conclusion of that Massingham Mansions affair from Mr. Elliott's refined narrative of the circumstances ?
>
> " I begin to suspect that Trigget, whom I put on, is somewhat of an ass, though a very remarkable circumstance has come to light which might—if it wasn't a matter of business—offer an explanation of the whole business by stamping it as inexplicable.
>
> " You know how I value your suggestions. If you happen to be in the neighbourhood—not otherwise, Max, I protest—I should be glad if you would drop in for a chat.
>
> > " Yours sincerely,
> > " LOUIS CARLYLE."

Carrados smiled at the ingenuous transparency of the note. He had thought several times of the case since the interview with Elliott, chiefly because he was struck by certain details of the manifestation that divided it from the ordinary methods of the bogy-raiser, an aspect that had apparently made no particular impression on his friend. He was sufficiently interested not to let the day pass without " happening " to be in the neighbourhood of Bampton Street.

" Max," exclaimed Mr. Carlyle, raising an accusing forefinger, " you have come on purpose."

" If I have," replied the visitor, " you can reward me with a cup of that excellent beverage that you were able to conjure up from somewhere down in the basement on a former occasion. As a matter of fact, I have."

Mr. Carlyle transmitted the order and then demanded his friend's serious attention.

" That ghost at Massingham Mansions—— "

" I still don't believe in that particular ghost, Louis," commented Carrados in mild speculation.

" I never did, of course," replied Carlyle, " but upon my word, Max, I shall have to very soon as a precautionary measure.

Trigget has been able to do nothing and now he has as good
as gone on strike."

"Downed—now what on earth can an inquiry man down
to go on strike, Louis? Note-books? So Trigget has got a
chill, like our candid friend Elliott, eh?"

"He started all right—said that he didn't mind spending a
night or a week in a haunted flat, and, to do him justice, I don't
believe he did at first. Then he came across a very curious
piece of forgotten local history, a very remarkable—er—coincidence in the circumstances, Max."

"I was wondering," said Carrados, "when we should
come up against that story, Louis."

"Then you know of it?" exclaimed the inquiry agent in
surprise.

"Not at all. Only I guessed it must exist. Here you have
the manifestation associated with two things which in themselves are neither usual nor awe-inspiring—the gas and the
water. It requires some association to connect them up, to
give them point and force. That is the story."

"Yes," assented his friend, "that is the story, and, upon
my soul, in the circumstances—well, you shall hear it. It
comes partly from the newspapers of many years ago, but only
partly, for the circumstances were successfully hushed up in a
large measure and it required the stimulated memories of
ancient scandalmongers to fill in the details. Oh yes, it was a
scandal, Max, and would have been a great sensation too, I do
not doubt, only they had no proper pictorial Press in those
days, poor beggars. It was very soon after Massingham Mansions had been erected—they were called Enderby House in
those days, by the way, for the name was changed on account
of this very business. The household at No. 11 consisted of a
comfortable, middle-aged married couple and one servant, a
quiet and attractive young creature, one is led to understand.
As a matter of fact, I think they were the first tenants of that
flat."

"The first occupants give the soul to a new house," remarked the blind man gravely. "That is why empty houses
have their different characters."

"I don't doubt it for a moment," assented Mr. Carlyle in
his incisive way, "but none of our authorities on this case made
any reference to the fact. They did say, however, that the
man held a good and responsible position—a position for which
high personal character and strict morality were essential. He
was also well known and regarded in quiet but substantial local

circles where serious views prevailed. He was, in short, a man of notorious ' respectability.'

" The first chapter of the tragedy opened with the painful death of the prepossessing handmaiden—suicide, poor creature. She didn't appear one morning and the flat was full of the reek of gas. With great promptitude the master threw all the windows open and called up the porter. They burst open the door of the little bedroom at the end of the passage, and there was the thing as clear as daylight for any coroner's jury to see. The door was locked on the inside and the extinguished gas was turned full on. It was only a tiny room, with no fireplace, and the ventilation of a closed well-fitting door and window was negligible in the circumstances. At all events the girl was proved to have been dead for several hours when they reached her, and the doctor who conducted the autopsy crowned the convincing fabric of circumstances when he mentioned as delicately as possible that the girl had a very pressing reason for dreading an inevitable misfortune that would shortly overtake her. The jury returned the obvious verdict.

" There have been many undiscovered crimes in the history of mankind, Max, but it is by no means every ingenious plot that carries. After the inquest, at which our gentleman doubtless cut a very proper and impressive figure, the barbed whisper began to insinuate and to grow in freedom. It is sheerly impossible to judge how these things start, but we know that when once they have been begun they gather material like an avalanche. It was remembered by someone at the flat underneath that late on the fatal night a window in the principal bedroom above had been heard to open, top and bottom, very quietly. Certain other sounds of movement in the night did not tally with the tale of sleep-wrapped innocence. Sceptical busybodies were anxious to demonstrate practically to those who differed from them on this question that it was quite easy to extinguish a gas-jet in one room by blowing down the gas-pipe in another ; and in this connection there was evidence that the lady of the flat had spoken to her friends more than once of her sentimental young servant's extravagant habit of reading herself to sleep occasionally with the light full on. Why was nothing heard at the inquest, they demanded, of the curious fact that an open novelette lay on the counterpane when the room was broken into ? A hundred trifling circumstances were adduced—arrangements that the girl had been making for the future down to the last evening of her life—interpretable hints that she had dropped to her acquaintances—her views on suicide and the best means to that end : a favourite topic, it would seem, among her class—her possession of certain comparatively expensive trinkets on a salary of a very few shillings a week, and so on. Finally, some rather more definite and important piece of evidence must have been conveyed to the authorities, for we know now that one fine day a warrant was issued. Somehow rumour preceded its execution. The eminently respectable gentleman with whom it was concerned did not wait to argue out the merits of the case. He locked himself in the bathroom, and when the police arrived they found that instead of an arrest they had to arrange the details for another inquest."

" A very convincing episode," conceded Carrados in response to his friend's expectant air. " And now her spirit passes the long winter evenings turning the gas on and off, and the one amusement of his consists in doing the same with the bath-water—or the other way, the other way about, Louis. Truly, one half the world knows not how the other half lives ! "

" All your cheap humour won't induce Trigget to spend another night in that flat, Max," retorted Mr. Carlyle. " Nor, I am afraid, will it help me through this business in any other way."

" Then I'll give you a hint that may," said Carrados. " Try your respectable gentleman's way of settling difficulties."

" What is that ? " demanded his friend.

" Blow down the pipes, Louis."

" Blow down the pipes ? " repeated Carlyle.

" At all events try it. I infer that Mr. Trigget has not experimented in that direction."

" But what will it do, Max ? "

" Possibly it will demonstrate where the other end goes to."

" But the other end goes to the meter."

" I suggest not—not without some interference with its progress. I have already met your Mr. Trigget, you know, Louis. An excellent and reliable man within his limits, but he is at his ꞁ..t posted outside the door of a hotel waiting to see the co-respondent go in. He hasn't enough imagination for this case—not enough to carry him away from what would be his own obvious method of doing it to what is someone else's equally obvious but quite different method. Unless I am doing him an injustice, he will have spent most of his time trying to catch someone getting into the flat to turn the gas and water on and off, whereas I conjecture that no one does go into the flat because it is perfectly simple—ingenious but simple—to produce these phenomena without. Then when Mr. Trigget has satisfied himself that it is physically impossible for anyone to be going in and out, and when, on the top of it, he comes across this romantic tragedy—a tale that might psychologically explain the ghost, simply because the ghost is moulded on the tragedy—then, of course, Mr. Trigget's mental process is swept away from its moorings and his feet begin to get cold."

"This is very curious and suggestive," said Mr. Carlyle. "I certainly assumed—— But shall we have Trigget up and question him on the point ? I think he ought to be here now— if he isn't detained at the Bull."

Carrados assented, and in a few minutes Mr. Trigget presented himself at the door of the private office. He was a melancholy-looking middle-aged little man, with an ineradicable air of being exactly what he was, and the searcher for deeper or subtler indications of character would only be rewarded by a latent pessimism grounded on the depressing probability that he would never be anything else.

"Come in, Trigget," called out Mr. Carlyle when his employee diffidently appeared. "Come in. Mr. Carrados would like to hear some of the details of the Massingham Mansions case."

"Not the first time I have availed myself of the benefit of your inquiries, Mr. Trigget," nodded the blind man. "Good-afternoon."

"Good-afternoon, sir," replied Trigget with gloomy deference. "It's very handsome of you to put it in that way, Mr. Carrados, sir. But this isn't another Tarporley-Templeton case, if I may say so, sir. That was as plain as a pikestaff after all, sir."

"When we saw the pikestaff, Mr. Trigget ; yes, it was," admitted Carrados, with a smile. "But this is insoluble ? Ah, well. When I was a boy I used to be extraordinarily fond of ghost stories, I remember, but even while reading them I always had an uneasy suspicion that when it came to the necessary detail of explaining the mystery I should be defrauded with some subterfuge as ' by an ingenious arrangement of hidden wires the artful Muggles had contrived,' etc., or ' an optical illusion effected by means of concealed mirrors revealed the *modus operandi* of the apparition.' I thought that I had been swindled. I think so still. I hope there are no ingenious wires or concealed mirrors here, Mr. Trigget ? "

Mr. Trigget looked mildly sagacious but hopelessly puzzled. It was his misfortune that in him the necessities of his business and the proclivities of his nature were at variance, so that he ordinarily presented the curious anomaly of looking equally alert and tired.

" Wires, sir ? " he began, with faint amusement.

" Not only wires, but anything that might account for what is going on," interposed Mr. Carlyle. " Mr. Carrados means this, Trigget : you have reported that it is impossible for anyone to be concealed in the flat or to have secret access to it—— "

" I have tested every inch of space in all the rooms, Mr. Carrados, sir," protested the hurt Trigget. " I have examined every board and, you may say, every nail in the floor, the skirting-boards, the window frames and in fact wherever a board or a nail exists. There are no secret ways in or out. Then I have taken the most elaborate precautions against the doors and windows being used for surreptitious ingress and egress. They have not been used, sir. For the past week I am the only person who has been in and out of the flat, Mr. Carrados, and yet night after night the gas that is cut off at the meter is lit and turned out again, and the water that is cut off at the cistern splashes about in the bath up to the second I let myself in. Then it's as quiet as the grave and everything is exactly as I left it. It isn't human, Mr. Carrados, sir, and flesh and blood can't stand it—not in the middle of the night, that is to say."

" You see nothing further, Mr. Trigget ? "

" I don't indeed, Mr. Carrados. I would suggest doing away with the gas in that room altogether. As a box-room it wouldn't need one."

" And the bathroom ? "

" That might be turned into a small bedroom and all the water fittings removed. Then to provide a bathroom—— "

" Yes, yes," interrupted Mr. Carlyle impatiently, " but we are retained to discover who is causing this annoyance and to detect the means, not to suggest structural alterations in the flat, Trigget. The fact is that after having put in a week on this job you have failed to bring us an inch nearer its solution. Now Mr. Carrados has suggested "—Mr. Carlyle was not usually detained among the finer shades of humour, but some appreciation of the grotesqueness of the advice required him to control his voice as he put the matter in its baldest form— " Mr. Carrados has suggested that instead of spending the time measuring the chimneys and listening to the wall-paper, if you had simply blown down the gas-pipe—— "

Carrados was inclined to laugh, although he thought it rather too bad of Louis.

" Not quite in those terms, Mr. Trigget," he interposed.

" Blow down the gas-pipe, sir ? " repeated the amazed man.
" What for ? "

" To ascertain where the other end comes out," replied
Carlyle.

" But don't you see, sir, that that is a detail until you
ascertain how it is being done ? The pipe may be tapped
between the bath and the cistern. Naturally, I considered that.
As a matter of fact, the water-pipe isn't tapped. It goes straight
up from the bath to the cistern in the attic above, a distance of
only a few feet, and I have examined it. The gas-pipe, it is
true, passes through a number of flats, and without pulling
up all the floors it isn't practicable to trace it. But how does
that help us, Mr. Carrados ? The gas-tap has to be turned on
and off ; you can't do that with these hidden wires. It has to
be lit. I've never heard of lighting gas by optical illusions, sir.
Somebody must get in and out of the flat or else it isn't human.
I've spent a week, a very trying week, sir, in endeavouring to
ascertain how it could be done. I haven't shirked cold and
wet and solitude, sir, in the discharge of my duty. I've freely
placed my poor gifts of observation and intelligence, such as
they are, sir, at the service—— "

" Not ' freely,' Trigget," interposed his employer with
decision.

" I am speaking under a deep sense of injury, Mr. Carlyle,"
retorted Mr. Trigget, who, having had time to think it over,
had now come to the conclusion that he was not appreciated.
" I am alluding to a moral attitude such as we all possess. I
am very grieved by what has been suggested. I didn't expect
it of you, Mr. Carlyle, sir ; indeed I did not. For a week I
have done everything that it has been possible to do, everything
that a long experience could suggest, and now, as I understand
it, sir, you complain that I didn't blow down the gas-pipe, sir.
It's hard, sir ; it's very hard."

" Oh, well, for heaven's sake don't cry about it, Trigget,"
exclaimed Mr. Carlyle. " You're always sobbing about the
place over something or other. We know you did your best—
God help you ! " he added aside.

" I did, Mr. Carlyle ; indeed I did, sir. And I thank you
for that appreciative tribute to my services. I value it highly,
very highly indeed, sir." A tremulous note in the rather im-
passioned delivery made it increasingly plain that Mr. Trigget's
regiment had not been confined entirely to solid food that day.
His wrongs were forgotten and he approached Mr. Carrados
with an engaging air of secrecy.

" What is this tip about blowing down the gas-pipe, sir ? "
he whispered confidently. " The old dog's always willing to
learn something new."

" Max," said Mr. Carlyle curtly, " is there anything more
that we need detain Trigget for ? "

" Just this," replied Carrados after a moment's thought.
" The gas-bracket—it has a mantle attachment on ? "

" Oh no, Mr. Carrados," confided the old dog with the
affectation of imparting rather valuable information, " not a
mantle on. Oh, certainly no mantle. Indeed—indeed, not a
mantle at all."

Mr. Carlyle looked at his friend curiously. It was half
evident that something might have miscarried. Furthermore,
it was obvious that the warmth of the room and the stress of
emotion were beginning to have a disastrous effect on the level
of Mr. Trigget's ideas and speech.

" A globe ? " suggested Carrados.

" A globe ? No, sir, not even a globe, in the strict sense of
the word. No globe, that is to say, Mr. Carrados. In fact
nothing like a globe."

" What is there, then ? " demanded the blind man without
any break in his unruffled patience. " There may be another
way—but surely—surely there must be some attachment ? "

" No," said Mr. Trigget with precision, " no attachment at
all ; nothing at all ; nothing whatsoever. Just the ordinary or
common or penny plain gas-jet, and above it the whayoumay-
callit thingamabob."

" The shade—gas consumer—of course ! " exclaimed
Carrados. " That is it."

" The tin thingamabob," insisted Mr. Trigget with slow
dignity. " Call it what you will. Its purpose is self-evident.
It acts as a dispirator—a distributor, that is to say—— "

" Louis," struck in Carrados joyously, " are you good for
settling it to-night ? "

" Certainly, my dear fellow, if you can really give the
time."

" Good ; it's years since I last tackled a ghost. What
about—— ? " His look indicated the other member of the
council.

" Would he be of any assistance ? "

" Perhaps—then."

" What time ? "

" Say eleven-thirty."

" Trigget," rapped out his employer sharply, " meet us at

the corner of Middlewood and Enderby Roads at half-past eleven sharp to-night. If you can't manage it I shall not require your services again."

"Certainly, sir ; I shall not fail to be punctual," replied Trigget without a tremor. The appearance of an almost incredible sobriety had possessed him in the face of warning, and both in speech and manner he was again exactly the man as he had entered the room. "I regard it as a great honour, Mr. Carrados, to be associated with you in this business, sir."

"In the meanwhile," remarked Carrados, "if you find the time hang heavy on your hands you might look up the subject of ' platinum black.' It may be the new tip you want."

"Certainly, sir. But do you mind giving me a hint as to what ' platinum black ' is ? "

"It is a chemical that has the remarkable property of igniting hydrogen or coal gas by mere contact," replied Carrados. "Think how useful that may be if you haven't got a match ! "

To mark the happy occasion Mr. Carlyle had insisted on taking his friend off to witness a popular musical comedy. Carrados had a few preparations to make, a few accessories to procure for the night's work, but the whole business had come within the compass of an hour and the theatre spanned the interval between dinner at the Palm Tree and the time when they left the car at the appointed meeting-place. Mr. Trigget was already there, in an irreproachable state of normal dejection. Parkinson accompanied the party, bringing with him the baggage of the expedition.

"Anything going on, Trigget ? " inquired Mr. Carlyle.

"I've made a turn round the place, sir, and the light was on," was the reply. "I didn't go up for fear of disturbing the conditions before you saw them. That was about ten minutes ago. Are you going into the yard to look again ? I have all the keys, of course."

"Do we, Max ? " queried Mr. Carlyle.

"Mr. Trigget might. We need not all go. He can catch us up again."

He caught them up again before they had reached the outer door.

"It's still on, sir," he reported.

"Do we use any special caution, Max ? " asked Carlyle.

"Oh, no. Just as though we were friends of the ghost, calling in the ordinary way."

Trigget, who retained the keys, preceded the party up the

stairs till the top was reached. He stood a moment at the door
of No. 11 examining, by the light of the electric lamp he
carried, his private marks there and pointing out to the others
in a whisper that they had not been tampered with. All at
once a most dismal wail, lingering, piercing, and ending in
something like a sob that died away because the life that gave
it utterance had died with it, drawled forebodingly through
the echoing emptiness of the deserted flat. Trigget had just
snapped off his light and in the darkness a startled exclamation
sprang from Mr. Carlyle's lips.

" It's all right," said the little man, with a private satisfaction that he had the diplomacy to conceal. " Bit creepy, isn't
it ? Especially when you hear it by yourself up here for the
first time. It's only the end of the bath-water running out."

He had opened the door and was conducting them to the
room at the end of the passage. A faint aurora had been
visible from that direction when they first entered the hall, but
it was cut off before they could identify its source.

" That's what happens," muttered Trigget.

He threw open the bedroom door without waiting to
examine his marks there and they crowded into the tiny
chamber. Under the beams of the lamps they carried it was
brilliantly though erratically illuminated. All turned towards
the central object of their quest, a tarnished gas-bracket of the
plainest description. A few inches above it hung the metal
disc that Trigget had alluded to, for the ceiling was low and
at that point it was brought even nearer to the gas by corresponding with the slant of the roof outside.

With the prescience so habitual with him that it had ceased
to cause remark among his associates Carrados walked straight
to the gas-bracket and touched the burner.

" Still warm," he remarked. " And so are we getting now.
A thoroughly material ghost, you perceive, Louis."

" But still turned off, don't you see, Mr. Carrados, sir,"
put in Trigget eagerly. " And yet no one's passed out."

" Still turned off—and still turned on," commented the
blind man.

" What do you mean, Max ? "

" The small screwdriver, Parkinson," requested Carrados.

" Well, upon my word ! " dropped Mr. Carlyle expres-
sively. For in no longer time than it takes to record the fact
Max Carrados had removed a screw and then knocked out the
tap. He held it up towards them and they all at once saw that
so much of the metal had been filed away that the gas passed

through no matter how the tap stood. " How on earth did you know of that ? "

" Because it wasn't practicable to do the thing in any other way. Now unhook the shade, Parkinson—carefully."

The warning was not altogether unnecessary, for the man had to stand on tiptoes before he could comply. Carrados received the dingy metal cone and lightly touched its inner surface.

" Ah, here, at the apex, to be sure," he remarked. " The gas is bound to get there. And there, Louis, you have an ever-lit and yet a truly ' safety ' match—so far as gas is concerned. You can buy the thing for a shilling, I believe."

Mr. Carlyle was examining the tiny apparatus with interest. So small that it might have passed for the mummy of a midget hanging from a cobweb, it appeared to consist of an insignificant black pellet and an inch of the finest wire.

" Um, I've never heard of it. And this will really light the gas ? "

" As often as you like. That is the whole bag of tricks."

Mr. Carlyle turned a censorious eye upon his lieutenant, but Trigget was equal to the occasion and met it without embarrassment.

" I hadn't heard of it either, sir," he remarked conversationally. " Gracious, what won't they be getting out next, Mr. Carlyle ! "

" Now for the mystery of the water." Carrados was finding his way to the bathroom and they followed him down the passage and across the hall. " In its way I think that this is really more ingenious than the gas, for, as Mr. Trigget has proved for us, the water does not come from the cistern. The taps, you perceive, are absolutely dry."

" It is forced up ? " suggested Mr. Carlyle, nodding towards the outlet.

" That is the obvious alternative. We will test it presently." The blind man was down on his hands and knees following the lines of the different pipes. " Two degrees more cold are not conclusive, because in any case the water has gone out that way. Mr. Trigget, you know the ropes, will you be so obliging as to go up to the cistern and turn the water on."

" I shall need a ladder, sir."

" Parkinson."

" We have a folding ladder out here," said Parkinson, touching Mr. Trigget's arm.

" One moment," interposed Carrados, rising from his

ERNEST BRAMAH

investigation among the pipes ; "this requires some care.
I want you to do it without making a sound or showing a light,
if that is possible. Parkinson will help you. Wait until you hear
us raising a diversion at the other end of the flat. Come, Louis."

The diversion took the form of tapping the wall and
skirting-board in the other haunted room. When Trigget
presented himself to report that the water was now on Carrados
put him to continue the singular exercise with Mr. Carlyle
while he himself slipped back to the bathroom.

"The pump, Parkinson," he commanded in a brisk whisper
to his man, who was waiting in the hall.

The appliance was not unlike a powerful tyre pump with
some modifications. One tube from it was quickly fitted to the
outlet pipe of the bath, another trailed a loose end into the
bath itself, ready to take up the water. There were a few other
details, the work of moments. Then Carrados turned on the
tap, silencing the inflow by the attachment of a short length
of rubber tube. When the water had risen a few inches he
slipped off to the other room, told his rather mystified confederates there that he wanted a little more noise and bustle
put into their performance, and was back again in the bathroom.

"Now, Parkinson," he directed, and turned off the tap.
There was about a foot of water in the bath.

Parkinson stood on the broad base of the pump and tried to
drive down the handle. It scarcely moved.

"Harder," urged Carrados, interpreting every detail of
sound with perfect accuracy.

Parkinson set his teeth and lunged again. Again he seemed
to come up against a solid wall of resistance.

"Keep trying ; something must give," said his master
encouragingly. "Here, let me——" He threw his weight
into the balance and for a moment they hung like a group
poised before action. Then, somewhere, something did give
and the sheathing plunger "drew."

"Now like blazes till the bath is empty. Then you can
tell the others to stop hammering." Parkinson, looking round
to acquiesce, found himself alone, for with silent step and
quickened senses Carrados was already passing down the dark
flights of the broad stone stairway.

It was perhaps three minutes later when an excited gentleman in the state of disrobement that is tacitly regarded as
falling upon the *punctum cœcum* in times of fire, flood, and
nocturnal emergency shot out of the door of No. 7 and bounding
up the intervening flights of steps pounded with the knocker

on the door of No. 9. As someone did not appear with the instantaneity of a jack-in-the-box, he proceeded to repeat the summons, interspersing it with an occasional " I say ! " shouted through the letter-box.

The light above the door made it unconvincing to affect that no one was at home. The gentleman at the door trumpeted the fact through his channel of communication and demanded instant attention. So immersed was he with his own grievance, in fact, that he failed to notice the approach of someone on the other side, and the sudden opening of the door, when it did take place, surprised him on his knees at his neighbour's door-step, a large and consequential-looking personage as revealed in the light from the hall, wearing the silk hat that he had instinctively snatched up, but with his braces hanging down.

" Mr. Tupworthy of No. 7, isn't it ? " quickly interposed the new man before his visitor could speak. " But why this—homage ? Permit me to raise you, sir."

" Confound it all," snorted Mr. Tupworthy indignantly, " you're flooding my flat. The water's coming through my bathroom ceiling in bucketfuls. The plaster'll fall next. Can't you stop it. Has a pipe burst or something ? "

" Something, I imagine," replied No. 9 with serene detach-ment. " At all events it appears to be over now."

" So I should hope," was the irate retort. " It's bad enough as it is. I shall go round to the office and complain. I'll tell you what it is, Mr. Belting : these mansions are becom-ing a pandemonium, sir, a veritable pandemonium."

" Capital idea ; we'll go together and complain : two will be more effective," suggested Mr. Belting. " But not to-night, Mr. Tupworthy. We should not find anyone there. The office will be closed. Say to-morrow—— "

" I had no intention of anything so preposterous as going there to-night. I am in no condition to go. If I don't get my feet into hot water at once I shall be laid up with a severe cold. Doubtless you haven't noticed it, but I am wet through to the skin, saturated, sir."

Mr. Belting shook his head sagely.

" Always a mistake to try to stop water coming through the ceiling," he remarked. " It will come, you know. Finds its own level and all that."

" I did not try to stop it—at least not voluntarily. A tem-porary emergency necessitated a slight rearrangement of our accommodation. I—I tell you this in confidence—I was sleeping in the bathroom."

At the revelation of so notable a catastrophe Mr. Belting actually seemed to stagger. Possibly his eyes filled with tears ; certainly he had to turn and wipe away his emotion before he could proceed.

"Not—not right under it ? " he whispered.

"I imagine so," replied Mr. Tupworthy. "I do not conceive that I could have been placed more centrally. I received the full cataract in the region of the ear. Well, if I may rely on you that it has stopped, I will terminate our interview for the present."

"Good-night," responded the still tremulous Belting. "Good-night—or good-morning, to be exact." He waited with the door open to light the first flight of stairs for Mr. Tupworthy's descent. Before the door was closed another figure stepped down quietly from the obscurity of the steps leading upwards.

"Mr. Belting, I believe ? " said the stranger. "My name is Carrados. I have been looking over the flat above. Can you spare me a few minutes ? "

"What, Mr. Max Carrados ? "

"The same," smiled the owner of the name.

"Come in, Mr. Carrados," exclaimed Belting, not only without embarrassment, but with positive affection in his voice. "Come in by all means. I've heard of you more than once. Delighted to meet you. This way. I know—I know." He put a hand on his guest's arm and insisted on steering his course until he deposited him in an easy-chair before a fire. "This looks like being a great night. What will you have ? "

Carrados put the suggestion aside and raised a corner of the situation.

"I'm afraid that I don't come altogether as a friend," he hinted.

"It's no good," replied his host. "I can't regard you in any other light after this. You heard Tupworthy ? But you haven't seen the man, Mr. Carrados. I know—I've heard— but no wealth of the imagination can ever really quite reconstruct Tupworthy, the shoddy magnifico, in his immense porcine complacency, his monumental self-importance. And sleeping right underneath ! Gods, but we have lived to-night ! Why—why ever did you stop ? "

"You associate me with this business ? "

"Associate you ! My dear Mr. Carrados, I give you the full glorious credit for the one entirely successful piece of low comedy humour in real life that I have ever encountered.

Indeed, in a legal and pecuniary sense, I hold you absolutely responsible."

" Oh ! " exclaimed Carrados, beginning to laugh quietly. Then he continued : " I think that I shall come through that all right. I shall refer you to Mr. Carlyle, the private inquiry agent, and he will doubtless pass you on to your landlord, for whom he is acting, and I imagine that he in turn will throw all the responsibility on the ingenious gentleman who has put them to so much trouble. Can you guess the result of my investigation in the flat above ? "

" Guess, Mr. Carrados ? I don't need to guess : I *know*. You don't suppose I thought for a moment that such transparent devices as two intercepted pipes and an automatic gaslighter would impose on a man of intelligence ? They were only contrived to mystify the credulous imagination of clerks and porters."

" You admit it, then ? "

" Admit ! Good gracious, of course I admit it, Mr. Carrados. What's the use of denying it ? "

" Precisely. I am glad you see that. And yet you seem far from being a mere practical joker. Does your confidence extend to the length of letting me into your object ? "

" Between ourselves," replied Mr. Belting, " I haven't the least objection. But I wish that you would have—say a cup of coffee. Mrs. Belting is still up, I believe. She would be charmed to have the opportunity——. No ? Well, just as you like. Now, my object ? You must understand, Mr. Carrados, that I am a man of sufficient leisure and adequate means for the small position we maintain. But I am not unoccupied—not idle. On the contrary, I am always busy. I don't approve of any man passing his time aimlessly. I have a number of interests in life—hobbies, if you like. You should appreciate that, as you are a private criminologist. I am— among other things which don't concern us now—a private retributionist. On every side people are becoming far too careless and negligent. An era of irresponsibility has set in. Nobody troubles to keep his word, to carry out literally his undertakings. In my small way I try to set that right by showing them the logical development of their ways. I am, in fact, the sworn enemy of anything approaching sloppiness. You smile at that ? "

" It is a point of view," replied Carrados. " I was wondering how the phrase at this moment would convey itself, say, to Mr. Tupworthy's ear."

Mr. Belting doubled up.

" But don't remind me of Tupworthy or I can't get on," he said. " In my method I follow the system of Herbert Spencer towards children. Of course you are familiar with his treatise on ' Education ' ? If a rough boy persists, after warnings, in tearing or soiling all his clothes, don't scold him for what, after all, is only a natural and healthy instinct overdone. But equally, of course, don't punish yourself by buying him other clothes. When the time comes for the children to be taken to an entertainment little Tommy cannot go with them. It would not be seemly, and he is too ashamed, to go in rags. He begins to see the force of practical logic. Very well. If a tradesman promises—promises explicitly—delivery of his goods by a certain time and he fails, he finds that he is then unable to leave them. I pay on delivery, by the way. If a man under-takes to make me an article like another—I am painstaking, Mr. Carrados : I point out at the time how exactly like I want it—and it is (as it generally is) on completion something quite different, I decline to be easy-going and to be put off with it. I take the simplest and most obvious instances ; I could multiply indefinitely. It is, of course, frequently inconvenient to me, but it establishes a standard."

" I see that you are a dangerous man, Mr. Belting," re-marked Carrados. " If most men were like you our national character would be undermined. People would have to behave properly."

" If most men were like me we should constitute an intoler-able nuisance," replied Belting seriously. " A necessary reaction towards sloppiness would set in and find me at its head. I am always with minorities."

" And the case in point ? "

" The present trouble centres round the kitchen sink. It is cracked and leaks. A trivial cause for so elaborate an out-come, you may say, but you will doubtless remember that two men quarrelling once at a spring as to who should use it first involved half Europe in a war, and the whole tragedy of *Lear* sprang from a silly business round a word. I hadn't noticed the sink when we took this flat, but the landlord had solemnly sworn to do everything that was necessary. Is a new sink necessary to replace a cracked one ? Obviously. Well, you know what landlords are : possibly you are one yourself. They promise you heaven until you have signed the agreement and then they tell you to go to hell. Suggested that we'd probably broken the sink ourselves and would certainly be looked to to replace it. An excellent servant caught a cold standing in the drip and left. Was I to be driven into paying for a new sink myself ? Very well, I thought, if the reasonable complaint of one tenant is nothing to you, see how you like the unreasonable complaints of fifty. The method served a useful purpose too. When Mrs. Belting heard that old tale about the tragedy at No. 11 she was terribly upset ; vowed that she couldn't stay alone in here at night on any consideration.

" ' My dear,' I said, ' don't worry yourself about ghosts. I'll make as good a one as ever lived, and then when you see how it takes other people in, just remember next time you hear of another that someone's pulling the string.' And I really don't think that she'll ever be afraid of ghosts again."

" Thank you," said Carrados, rising. " Altogether I have spent a very entertaining evening, Mr. Belting. I hope your retaliatory method won't get you into serious trouble this time."

" Why should it ? " demanded Belting quickly.

" Oh, well, tenants are complaining, the property is being depreciated. The landlord may think that he has legal redress against you."

" But surely I am at liberty to light the gas or use the bath in my own flat when and how I like ? "

A curious look had come into Mr. Belting's smiling face ; a curious note must have sounded in his voice. Carrados was warned and, being warned, guessed.

" You are a wonderful man," he said with upraised hand. " I capitulate. Tell me how it is, won't you ? "

" I knew the man at No. 11. His tenancy isn't really up till March, but he got an appointment in the north and had to go. His two unexpired months weren't worth troubling about, so I got him to sublet the flat to me—all quite regularly—for a nominal consideration, and not to mention it."

" But he gave up the keys ? "

" No. He left them in the door and the porter took them away. Very unwarrantable of him ; surely I can keep my keys where I like ? However, as I had another. . . . Really, Mr. Carrados, you hardly imagine that unless I had an absolute right to be there I should penetrate into a flat, tamper with the gas and water, knock the place about, tramp up and down——"

" I go," said Carrados, " to get our people out in haste. Good-night."

" Good-night, Mr. Carrados. It's been a great privilege to meet you. Sorry I can't persuade you . . ."

THE HOUSE ON BIG FARAWAY

By

NORMAN MATSON

SURELY the old woman told you she was *going* toward the Partelo farm, or had passed by there, something of that sort, rather than that she was stayir g there," Dr. Greerson said, gently correcting his host.

Bunny Brooks was positive. " ' *Staying* ' was the word she used."

Dr. Greerson hesitated, seemed to decide not to argue. He was a stout man with a brown beard. He turned toward Bunny's sister. " What did you think of her, Natalie ? "

Only her grey eyes moved, meeting his. " I did not see her."

Young Kenneth Durham, the Doctor's nephew, laughed in his nose. He was sprawled out for six feet on the grass. The Doctor owned a farm fifteen miles away. They were, the four of them, on the newly-cut lawn of Bunny's discovery, an old farm house with a stone chimney, small window panes and clapboards black with weather. It had been unoccupied for years, standing blind and empty on its round hill. Now that all its windows looked again they saw a scene that had greatly changed. The horizon was green woods.

The only meadow left—it sloped down to the glinting pond—was covered with sumac and young birch trees, its high stone walls lost under a tangle of grape vines, elderberry and poison ivy. And there was not in all the landscape one house visible, though thirty years before all this abandoned land was farmed.

Bunny was a small, rather dapper, city man with grey hair parted neatly in the middle, a neat round face. On either side of his nose was a red mark from the grip of the glasses that usually rode there, slanted forward, gleaming. He swung the glasses now at the end of their ribbon, nervously, his forehead puckered as with some irritating thought.

"Doctor, where is this Partelo farm?"

"Half a mile that way—it's on the Big Faraway Road, too."

"Who are they—the Partelos."

"There aren't any Partelos."

"Who lives there?"

"Nobody lives there."

Young Kenneth rolled half over and looked at the reddening afternoon sky, laughed with his big mouth. He had known that was coming.

"The house is empty?"

"There isn't any house. There's nothing there but a heap of chimney stones."

"And lilacs," Kenneth said. "Haw, haw."

Bunny tucked his glasses away. He looked quite dashed.

Natalie said : "If you're making it up, Bunny, do leave off now." She was pretty in a frail way, nostrils waxy and her ears small. Her hair was pale gold.

"No, I didn't see her, Doctor," she said. "I was in the back of the house. When I heard Bunny's voice I was frightened."

"At your brother's voice?" Dr. Greerson looked at her curiously.

"We've been alone here for three days. No one comes by on the road, you know, it goes nowhere but here : beyond it is quite impassable. I called out : 'Bunny, are you talking to yourself?' Then I went out into the front hall and . . ."

"I'll tell it," her brother said. "I had gone upstairs to get a coil of wire I remembered having seen in the bedroom (there's only one finished room up there ; the rest is attic, you know). The door wouldn't open at first. The latch must have fallen. I had to shove hard to get in. I picked up the wire—it was rusty and quite useless I found out later—and started down again. Someone had closed the door at the bottom of the stairway."

"I am sure I didn't," Natalie put in quietly. She had evidently said this before as it angered her brother. He spoke loudly, turning on her : "Very well. It was the cook we haven't got. It was a ghost. What the devil difference does it make what it was?"

"Oh, come," Dr. Greerson said reasonably. "It was the wind."

Kenneth winked at Natalie.

"Anyway," Bunny went on, "it was damned dark on that stairway. I had to grope for the catch and I came out blinking against the bright square of light from the window in the front door. When I could see clearly I was looking at *her*."

"Who ?" Kenneth asked.

"An old woman in a bonnet. Her face was close to the pane, her mouth slightly open. One tooth here at the side was gone. She was screwing up her eyes to see in, shading them with one hand. The hand had a black, fingerless mitten on it. She was looking at the air in front of me. Her eyes lifted slowly, focussed into mine. They opened wide. We stared at each other through the glass. I was frightened, I'll admit, but I managed to open the door and I said : ' How d'you do ? '

"She said slowly in a whisper, ' I don't know who you are.' I didn't say anything. For a moment I wasn't sure myself who I was. She whispered : ' I'm staying at the Partelo's.' Then, ' If you see my sister say I went to church.'

"Who was her sister ? Someone who had lived in this house before us ? I didn't know. I realised I was rudely gaping at her, our first visitor. I said ' Come in, won't you ? ' but she shook her black bonnet. ' I'll be back,' she whispered, and that was all. She went away. I watched her go along the road. She had scarlet stockings on and shiny black shoes."

Natalie looked to Dr. Greerson, wanting to know what he thought. She said : " So I called out : ' Are you talking to yourself, Bunny ? ' He didn't answer. I found him staring at the empty road. I ran out the back way, ran round the other side of the corncrib, my eyes all ready to see his old woman ; but the air was empty. She had evaporated."

"There's a footpath into the woods there," Dr. Greerson said. He repeated this as if he thought it important.

"You ran after her !" Bunny exclaimed. "That was a damned funny thing to do."

Kenneth sat up. His eyes were bright with mischief. He picked a blade of grass, said thoughtfully : " Scarlet stockings !

Bunny turned as if he had been slapped. "Yes. I saw them. I saw her and I talked with her."

"Man, man, we believe you," Dr. Greerson said.

"But you don't. Kenneth doesn't. Natalie doesn't. Hell, I've got feelings ! Doctor, you tell me, you're supposed to know something about the mind, you tell me why I should imagine that old woman."

"You didn't imagine her. You saw her, actually in the

flesh. We all know that. But you were going to show me the old mill dam, where you plan the swimming pool. Come on, the afternoon's already gone."

" Sorry." Bunny got up, looked at Kenneth.

Kenneth shook his head. " I've seen your dam."

Bunny and the Doctor started down through the timothy grass toward the pond.

They were soon out of sight. A Bob White called, sudden as a pistol shot, and that seemed to mark the end of the day, though it was still broad light. A chill breath ran across the yard.

" Who was she ? " Natalie reached for Kenneth and his hand met hers, held it. They were to be married, or at least so they had planned for two years. Her expression made him laugh.

" Who was she ? Nobody, darling." He tapped his forehead. " Is Bunny often followed by funny old women ? Are you ? "

" No. Or," she smiled, parting her red lips slowly, " or generally I'm not. I do feel strange upstairs. In the bedroom —my room now—whoever was there before me and who is gone now, is still there, in a way. For years this house waited. Now we come. Still the house waits. I don't know what for. I wish I did." He noticed goose-flesh on her arm. An actual shudder had run through her even while she smiled.

Saying how soon she would get over such notions, he put an arm around her waist, and she relaxed, pleased. All the green wood was still. It was evening.

" People walk about upstairs in these old houses, creak-creak, back and forth." He smiled down on her, feeling superior " Know why ? Because the wide floor-boards expand and contract with temperature changes. That's all. Bertha Bliven's no more than a thermal crack. Haw. Haw."

" Who's Bertha Bliven ? "

" She opens doors. She's in the bedroom upstairs."

" My room ! "

" Yes, and if I tell you about her you'll begin to imagine that you see her with her legs all limp, so I won't tell you."

" Please."

He was eager to tell, really ; and he quickly made her see Bertha Bliven, a thin woman of thirty-something, of extra-ordinary vitality and a bitterness toward Farmer Bliven. Neither one of their two babies had lived long, and she grieved for them. Perhaps he was weary of her grief. Once he thrashed her with a bridle. Bertha's sister Matilda, who was thirteen or fourteen, would walk down the road and visit. She came one Sunday on her way to church. Bertha wouldn't go. " I'll stay here alone," she said.

Matilda had gone on for a mile. There she stopped. For thinking of her sister's strange expression she could not go on nor turn back. In the end she turned back, retraced her steps, passed the smithy, over the little bridge, the long bridge where the Bonacutt rushes over big stones, under the chestnuts by the white school-house. When she came to the lower barn she stopped. Here one had the first glimpse of her sister's house. It had changed. Shutters upstairs and down were tight closed, all of them.

She crept in the back door, called " Bertha ! " in the darkness. No one answered. She dared at last to call at the stair door. She went up, one step at a time, and knocked.

In the attic darkness she remembered the still clear noon-day that surrounded the house. She heard her heart.

From inside the bedroom began another pounding, rapid and irregular, growing louder. It thundered through the house. Matilda ran down and hid in the cupboard under the stairs.

When Bliven returned from church Matilda was lying on the floor, hands to her ears. To prove to her that there was nothing to be afraid of, that Bertha had merely gone back to their mother's, as she had often threatened, he forced Matilda to go back upstairs with him.

Of course, Bertha was there in the bedroom. The wire she had used had cut into her neck ; blood lay long and thick down her Sunday white, and her stockinged heels had struck great holes in the plaster. In the candle-light her face seemed quite black.

" I suppose, it was," Kenneth added. " One has to fill it here and there."

Natalie played with her thin white hands, looking at them. She nodded slowly.

" Good story ? "

" Yes, a good, dreadful story. What a dreadful thing to do to that girl. What happened to her ? "

" There history is silent."

As soon as the others returned Kenneth and Dr. Greerson prepared to leave. The Doctor asked Natalie, holding her hands. " What has he been telling you ? "

" Stories." She stood very straight like a little girl. " Good night, Doctor. Good night, Kenneth."

"And you, Bunny, get a lot of sunlight into that house of yours. And fires going ! I'm afraid it's still damp."

Night had fallen. They inched along in second gear to the old Providence turnpike, a mile away, fearful lest tie-rod or differential strike against a stone. On asphalt at last and rolling smoothly, Kenneth said : " He ought to be psycho-analysed."

Dr. Greerson said : " Bosh."

" Well, he sees things, doesn't he ? He almost had Natalie believing in that old woman. I told her there never was such a person, that she was a figment of Bunny's disordered imagination."

" You did ! "

" I certainly did ! "

The Doctor found he had to think about that. He slowed down. He stopped and pulled the brake back.

" What's the matter ? "

" What else did you tell her ? "

The young man's voice rose. " What else ! My dear Uncle, she is my—— " He broke off, with a gasp. The headlights made a clear-edged cavern in the black dark. Someone had stepped into that radiance. An old woman. A stooping old woman with a bonnet on, who grinned and showed where one tooth was gone.

In a harsh whisper, peering blindly, she asked : " Who's that behind those glary lights ? "

" Dr. Greerson."

" Good evening to you, Doctor." She had gone back into the darkness, was walking away.

The Doctor started the car. After a minute : " That's Matilda," he said, " Matilda Morris, sister to Bertha Bliven who hanged herself. Matilda's the little girl or was. She's quite all right in the mind save for that one memory. Hello, there's a drop of rain." He started the windshield wiper. " She often walks this road. Walks like a man. She's strong.

" I'd have offered her a lift but she always refuses. They say she used to go running to that house, trying to be on time, you know, over and over again. The house was boarded up, of course, and the first sight of it often would straighten her out. She'd snap back to normal, but not always ; she has been seen trying to open the front door, whimpering, calling out to her sister that she was coming."

Kenneth's dry mouth finally made words. " So you knew it was she all the time Bunny was telling us ? "

" Of course."

"And you said nothing. Explained nothing to him."

"He's high-strung, though not as high-strung as his sister.
I didn't want to feed their imaginations any more than they
had already been fed."

Here was the Greerson driveway. They left the car in an
open carriage-shed and ran through pelting rain for a side door.

A gusty wind staggered against the window-panes. Greerson sat down before his fire. Kenneth paced the long room.
He said :

"Which direction was she going ? "

"Up the road, home—I suppose."

"Sure ? "

Dr. Greerson slowly shook his head. "Come to think of
it, maybe she wasn't."

"Maybe she was going back."

"Back where ? "

"To her sister's. To Bunny's house. For the first time she
finds somebody to open the door for her. You know, I think
we'd better go back there, too."

"In this downpour ? Over that road ? "

"We'll say that we've actually seen the old woman, that
we know who she is, that she's . . . Do come, for God's sake."

"They'll be in bed, my boy."

"Yes. But you see, I did another wrong thing. I told
Natalie about Bertha Bliven and how her little sister came
calling her, too late."

"You're a donkey," Dr. Greerson said.

Kenneth did not deny that. "All right. But I must get
there, and quickly."

"Go ahead."

"But you must come, we might need you."

II

WITH lamps and candles darkness is always near ; rooms
are not filled tanks of light as with electricity. Natalie,
putting dishes away in the new lean-to kitchen, walked from
darkness to darkness. A whip-poor-will began loudly its witless
reiteration outside the window and bending down she looked
out, saw in silhouette a large bird on the stone wall, ugly in
a nameless fashion, saw how it raised its head and fluttered
its wing each time it whistled, heard the slight smacking sound
after. She wished it would go away.

In the big room that had been the kitchen, within the outer radiance of the fire in the huge fireplace, Bunny sat at a trestle table, as usual writing down and diagramming further plans for the farm. He did not speak as she came in from the kitchen and sat down opposite him, started to sew on pink silk. The light was on her chin and under her eyes, which were all shadow save when she looked this way and that. Then they flashed. . . . It was too quiet. She wanted Bunny to say something. She did not believe in his old woman. Was he, she wondered, really a little queer despite his precise words, his neat diagrams ?

Into the silence, spreading out, filling it like a quick torrent, like the rising spreading sound heard under ether, she heard one word, one straining whisper :

" Bertha ! "

Natalie looked at her sewing. Bunny made another mark on his paper.

There were many other sounds, sounds in the walls. She even heard the latch of the front door click, and click again, as if it had been closed after someone entering. Her imagination was running wild. She looked across without raising her eyes, stealthily, at Bunny's hand, the one holding the pencil. Was it trembling ? Was he too concealing his fears ? She would have to say something.

" It's getting late." Her voice seemed loud.

He looked up, smiled. " Must be all of nine o'clock. How sleepy we get out here ! "

" Let's go to bed."

He yawned and agreed ; went out into the front hall and locked the door. He called from there : " Why did you lock the cupboard under the stairs ? "

" I didn't lock it."

He came back. " Perhaps I did," he said. " It's no matter."

They went upstairs, he first, said good-night at the head of the stairway.

" Sleep well."

" I'll try," she said. His expression in the lamplight was strange ; his eyes moved too quickly. Was he terrified, as she was ; or was this again her imagination ?

From his bed in a far corner of the great attic he called cheerfully to her. For a long time she combed her hair in the lamplight, watching herself in the mirror. Behind her on that square beam was an iron hook. Was that the one

Bertha had used ? Possibly. She combed very slowly. If she could only lock the door, perhaps that would make her feel better. But there was no lock, the latch was broken.

She heard, or seemed to hear, a door open downstairs in the hall. The cupboard door. One hand up with the comb she waited. It was nothing. It was the wind. . . . A stair creaked, quite plainly. After a long time another creaked. She heard someone breathing out there, just outside her door.

The latch began to move.

The door opened. She, the old woman, stood in the doorway, black bonnet and shawl gleaming with rain. She was terrified, her white hands shaking as she raised them and came into the room.

Natalie moved back. The lamp went over with an outburst of brittle little sounds. For a moment it was dark, black dark. In that blindness she felt the old woman's arms tight around her.

III

MIDWAY between highway and farm the car hit something with a clang. For a moment they sat in silence. The rain had stopped. Kenneth climbed out, flashlight in hand. Presently he said : " Tie-rod's bent almost double. We'll have to leave her here."

They splashed and stumbled on. At the first stone gate there was the house, and a light upstairs, reflecting on the wet leaves of an elm. They went on through the orchard. Kenneth whispered : " Wait ! " and pointed.

Under an apple tree near the house stood Matilda. She did not move.

" Good thing we came," Kenneth whispered.

The light upstairs was brighter. Lights flickered in the downstairs windows.

Bunny's voice, high strangled, called : " Who's that ? "

" Dr. Greerson and I," Kenneth shouted. " We came back. The car—— "

" For God's sake come quickly. Natalie's gone."

They found him crawling in the long grass. He looked up at them. " Natalie's gone."

He tried to tell how he had heard her screams, had found her room ablaze, had tried in vain to smother the fire.

All the windows were broadly lighted now. From the rain-soaked shingles of the great roof rose clouds of steam and smoke, and within a multitude of voices were started, crackling, whistling, whispering. The green woods stared. As flames filled the kitchen wing a dish fell. A small, deliberate crash, then another and another.

They looked over the ground for Natalie, called her name. The Doctor found her lying at Matilda's feet.

" What have you done ? "

The old woman looked above his head at the glare of the fire. She was smiling. The roof-tree pitched down with a rending final cry.

" I carried her out—in time, in time," Matilda said. Her head was filled with a weary confusion of madness and actual memories. How many times through the years she had come back here ! She sighed : " At last. At last."

Dr. Greerson on his knees listened for life. Terror, he thought. How would he tell those others. He pretended to listen.

MADAM JULIA'S TALE

By

NAOMI ROYDE-SMITH

THE tumult and the shouting were not ended when the two women left the hall by the small private staircase to the use of which Madam Julia had a prescriptive right. Outside, already at the door, the English chauffeur stood waiting, a little anxiously. He was never quite happy on such occasions as this until his mistress had been delivered again into the hands of the excellant Clara who, at this very instant, would be setting the silver thermos flask of bouillon and the dishes of caviare sandwiches on their tray ready to carry across the hall into the boudoir as soon as he pressed the button of the special bell in the entrance lobby that always rang on the ninth floor before Madam Julia so much as set foot on the ground descending from her car. He knew—Clara had told him so often enough this winter—that it was as much as Madam Julia's life was worth thus to venture out of the close warmth and stillness of her flat into the icy peril of a New York winter evening, to risk its breath-catching impact twice —and the second time after the heat and excitement of a concert-hall : and he knew her answer. When they had told her she had said " It is more than my life is worth to do without music." They had to let her go. Often she went alone : but this evening there had been a small dinner party, and one of the guests had gone on to the concert with her hostess. This was an Englishwoman, the murmur of whose voice had made the young chauffeur feel a little homesick as he overheard her talking with his mistress when the car came to its regular standstills in the traffic blocks on the way across from Park Avenue to Carnegie Hall.

Neither Madam Julia nor the stranger was talking as they came down the stair As they appeared at the open doorway the man recognised the familiar look in the elder woman's face, the rapt and starry gaze which, sometimes, when the concert had been particularly fine, had not left her eyes by the time he had worked his way across Fifth Avenue and round the Grand Central Terminal to the apartment tower at the corner of Thirty-ninth Street and had seen the sliding doors of the elevator in the lobby close on her tall figure multiplied in the mirrors of its panels so that she seemed to be carried upward in a company of the blessed as dignified and ecstatic as herself. " You couldn't take it harder if you'd been with her since young Mr. Carteret married, same as me," Clara had said, not without jealousy, on the night after a Bach concert when he had rung up to know if Madam had arrived safely on the ninth floor. That was in the autumn. He had been new then to the fierce efficiency of the city's traffic and still unused to the sense of risk that was taken by the frail, indomitable woman who had learnt to trust him as he drove her along the wide smooth highways and through the quiet lanes of the Wye Valley where she had spent the spring and summer. She had brought him back to the States with her because of this very thing : sensing the stolid-looking young man's understanding of her need to refresh the sources of her fluctuating spirit in her own way. Not that Mrs. Carteret Wenham ever spoke to her chauffeur of anything outside the routine of his work for her ; or that she had any idea that he knew, and in his unspoken thought of her used, the sobriquet he had caught from scraps of the overheard chatter of her grandchildren's friends. " Madam Julia " they called her, reviving the title of the famous eighteenth century beauty from whom she had inherited her given name. She was, of course, aware that the young man knew of the doctors' orders : knew that they insisted that she must be spared exertion and excitement. Most, if not all, of her excursions, even in the smooth security of the car it was his pride to keep in the most supple sparkling condition, were acts of a disobedience that might at any moment meet its threatened punishment. These escapes had, more than once during the year he had been driving her, resulted in a collapse that kept her indoors and abed for several days. The knowledge added to his sense of power over the car itself ; gratified his self-esteem, and gave him countenance in the face of Clara's amply supported sus- picion that he considered himself entitled to feel a personal devotion to his mistress as great and as well recognised as her own. He never argued this point with Clara. He bore her

snubs and superior airs with good humour. He forbore to
retort that, whereas Clara hedged her lady about with precautions and allowed herself the liberty of scolding her sometimes and often of frustrating the eager spirit that still would
be abroad in the world she loved so much, he was the aider
and abettor of her escapes, the servant on whom she depended
for access to the things that really kept her alive whatever her
family and the doctors might say. This knowledge kept him
from being overpowered by loneliness in the alien city with
its swarming polyglot, polychrome crowds moving slowly from
block to block of the vast, bleak, rectangular immensity of its
avenues ; eating its soft, sweet fish-foods and cereals in its
myriad restaurants ; thrusting its white-tiled bathrooms into
the private life of a decent fellow who wanted no more than
bed and breakfast and a can of hot water when he went to an
hotel.

To-night in particular, as he stood at the side door ten
minutes before the time he had been told to have the car waiting there, he felt the glow proper to a man who, trusted with
a grave responsibility, has it well within his power to meet
and discharge it in every particular. He had spent fifty cents
in an Automat after parking his car, slipping his nickels into
the slots under the glass doors of the shelves that yielded clam-
chowder and a roll and butter when released, and receiving a
cupful of hot milk-coffee from the silver plated spout that
never poured a drop too much or too little to fill the cup held
to its automatic gush. The food was good, and he was by this
time inured to the silent company that arrived singly and
waited, each on himself alone, in the glittering, efficient, lonely
vistas of the hall. After that he had turned into the Roxy for
half an hour. Quickly bored by the picture that flickered, small
and foolish on the screen below him in the pit of the vast dome,
he had waded to its highest gallery, striding ankle-deep in the
pile of the carpets that lapped its wide, unused staircases.
He had sat for ten minutes there, smoking a cigarette, still in
solitude, gazing through the arches of a replica of one of the
courts of the Alhambra lit with hanging Moorish lamps. It
had not occurred to him to try for a seat in one of the upper
galleries of the concert hall where his mistress had gone to
hear a very young violinist play Beethoven's Concerto with
the famous orchestra of which Clara boasted so much though
she had never heard it perform. He would, indeed, have
regarded it as rather a presumption to be listening to the same
performance as the lady he had driven to hear it. The Roxy,

for all its splendour, was a different matter and, once you had
admitted the over-powering magnificence of its furnishings,
not nearly so good a place of entertainment as the bar-room
of the George and Dragon at Ludlow.   There was a little
nostalgia in the comparison, but no real lack of cheerfulness.
He had work that he could do well : his pay was beyond
anything he dare admit in his letters home, lest he should be
classed with the open-mouthed liar or the brainless spendthrift
when he returned, after Easter, very little richer than when
he had left.   He had seen skyscrapers at their topmost impro-
bability—and . . . here his thoughts grew confused : he was
unable to explain to himself the underlying satisfaction that,
this evening, was more clearly present to his consciousness
than it had ever been.   He was a simple-minded mechanic, not
capable of self-analysis, too healthy and normal for introspec-
tion : but he knew that he was, not so much happy, as justified
in his way of life.   He had not merely the comfort and safety
of his employer in his control when he drove her : he was,
however remotely, the confederate of a rebel who placed her
life in his care every time she risked it for the sake of pleasures
he himself might consider empty in themselves though necessary to her.   He did not mind standing, the soft chinchilla rug
heaped on his arm, for an extra five minutes in the keen night
frost for the sake of getting the car exactly in front of the
exit so that she might have no more than a couple of steps
to take before he could close the door of the car on her, safe
and warm and in his care again.   This evening he had arrived
just in time to slide in before an enormous Hispano-Suisa ;
a rather fussy little Buick manœuvred into position immediately
in front of him before he could dismount.   His command of
the Manhattan vernacular was by this time rich enough to
enable him to take part very comfortably in the ensuing
dialogue.   All three chauffeurs were soon engaged in a remarkably free, and most un-English exchange of personalities that
ceased abruptly as Mrs. Carteret Wenham and her companion
appeared on the threshold.

II

THE hooded signal lamps at the far end of the block ran
quickly down from green to yellow, and halted steadying
into one round red eye that glared through the black and white
criss-cross of street standards and the headlights of the traffic
pouring down the Avenue.

"We're caught," said Madam Julia. "By the time the block is free again the concert will be out and there'll be a long jam. We may as well resign ourselves."

The light above her head, which would not be put out until the car started, shone down on her as she sat erect above the silvery folds of the rug that covered the knees of both women and heaped itself around their feet : its suggestion of hoar frost on a deep black velvet pile was repeated in the feathery waves of Madam Julia's once dark hair, brushed upward from her neck and lying, like the folded crest of a bird, from crown to brow of her delicate narrow head. If she had been a small woman Madam Julia would have been called bird-like. The woman at her side, looking at the aquiline profile and the round full eyes with their heavy lids, let the image of an eagle flit through her mind to vanish as Madam Julia turned towards her and the soft, diffused light gleamed on the double row of pearls that showed through the opening of her ermine coat, white against the dull white lace and satin of her dress. It was her way to smile before she spoke.

"That boy !" she said. "His playing of the cadenza was like a dream come true."

"One of our critics said the same thing when he played the Beethoven in London last winter," said the Englishwoman.

Madam Julia gave a little chuckle.

"Too bad I'm not original. But I don't see how anything else can be said of it. It's just pure music—it's youth in love with Art—no putting of a human personality between us and the divine, essential thing."

"I thought Toscanini pretty wonderful too," the other ventured. She was not a particularly musical woman.

"Oh." Madam Julia accepted Toscanini. "He's a master. He has a lifetime behind him. He does not *rise* to an occasion : he is equal to any—even to this."

"It must be a little disconcerting—not like an infant prodigy."

"My dear," said Madam Julia. "Don't let me hear *any*body use that dreadful term anywhere near such an experience as the one we have just enjoyed. I can't bear it."

"I'm sorry. I didn't mean . . ."

"I know. Forgive me. But there is something you cannot understand about it—something peculiar to me—part of my own life that has been recalled to me this evening. I have come to understand more about a very beautiful thing that once happened to me—to realise that it is not over and done with as I had been content to think it until to-night."

" Could you possibly . . ."

" Why I think I might. It looks as if we should sit here for hours."

She stretched out her hand and snapped off the light. Now we may talk," she said.

The two women settled themselves more comfortably in their seats, leaning back into the shadow, pulling gently at the soft masses of the fur that covered them both and gave them the sense of a warm, safe intimacy their short friendship had not reached until now.

" I haven't spoken of it for years," Madam Julia began. " It's been, not forgotten, but put away in my mind as we put our grandmother's lace away in lavender—ready for some special occasion. I don't quite know why I should be speaking of it now, unless it is that that boy to-night was more like an angel than a human being in spite of being so clearly *strong* flesh and blood."

The English woman was conscious of another shade of meaning when " strong " was pronounced " strawng " slowly, trailingly, almost as a dissyllable. Spoken thus the word conjured up the delicate ruddiness of the boy violinist's cheeks ; the thick young gold of his hair ; the sturdy figure ; the grave almost stolid composure of his mouth ; the miraculous, beautiful hand she had watched, its fingers curling and lifting over the strings as he played, his eyes half-closed, his side-long face pressed to listen against the chestnut-red wood of the violin.

" Perhaps," she heard herself saying rather foolishly, " he is an angel and that explains it—explains his perfect music— the thing that puzzles everybody—I mean."

Madam Julia took this calmly.

" I shouldn't be surprised," she said. " That's what makes me want to tell you what Carteret calls my ghost story —my husband I mean—I don't think my son knows about it. You believe in ghosts ? "

" Well . . ."

The younger woman was about to find words for the long and qualified answer to so provocative a question when the sporadic hooting that had already announced the impatience of such taxi-drivers as had wedged themselves in among the private cars in the block suddenly became general. Horns, brazen and silver, hooters and chiming bells all joined together in a din of protest that gathered purpose and rhythm as it increased in volume. Conversation was impossible while it lasted. Madam Julia laid a reassuring hand on her companion's arm.

" It's all right," her low voice made itself audible under the tumult. " They always do it when the regulation three minutes is exceeded."

The Englishwoman recovered her shaken composure.

" It's like the climax of *Belshazzar's Feast*," she shouted.

Madam Julia shook her head.

"Never heard it."

The din ceased as suddenly as it had begun : but Madam Julia did not immediately launch on her promised tale. She was watching, through the glass, the faces of her own chauffeur and of the driver of the empty car that stood next her own. They were engaged in an animated conversation, leaning out over the doors of their driving seats and evidently puzzled or concerned about something invisible to the two women inside the car. Madam Julia said nothing, but her silence conveyed that she was only suspending judgment on this breach of decorum until some explanation or excuse for it should be made plain. She had not long to wait. Some other sound had clearly made itself heard to the two men. They broke off their converse and each straightened himself to attention.

" The block is free," declared Madam Julia. " Why doesn't he start the engine ? "

A moment later the young man slid back the glass partition and with his arm along the window ledge turned in his seat to speak to his mistress. As he did so a sound like the crackle of a fire of dry sticks freshly lighted leaped distantly above the hum of the street.

" I thought I had better tell you, Madam," he said, " that we're likely to be here for some little time longer. The police are holding up all traffic above Forty-ninth Street. Would you like me to get out and find a call-office ? I daresay they'd let me ring up Mr. Wenham from one of the bureaux inside there," he nodded sideways towards the hall, knowing that Carteret Wenham was one of the directors.

" Why no," said Madam Julia smiling, " I think you had better stay where you are. And close that window. I don't feel that any down-town trouble is going to do me the harm a chill might while we are talking about it."

" Excuse me, Madam, but wouldn't it be better to fasten your coat ? "

"It might," said Madam Julia, "but I don't know that I feel like doing so yet."

The distant crackling had grown louder as they spoke. Even when the chauffeur had pushed the glass back into place again it still prickled in the ears of the two women, though neither of them referred to it. It was not the first time since she had arrived in New York that the Englishwoman had heard that spluttering noise. Sometimes it had waked her during the small hours, crackling through the streets below her window at the famous old-fashioned hotel to which she had been recommended on her first arrival in New York. Because of it, partly, she had moved that very afternoon to the bleak magnificence of one of the honeycombed towers above the Grand Central Railway.

"Oh, nuthing'. Just one tough beating up another," the desiccated floor-waiter who wheeled in her breakfast table had answered when she had, after the first occasion, enquired if it were really machine guns she had heard. Now, hearing that sound again, she recognised it for what it was and wondered if there were really no cause for alarm. She glanced quietly at her hostess but did not speak. There was something in the poise of the grey head, something grave and withheld in the downcast eyelids and faintly smiling mouth that made it impossible, a rudeness even, to dream of saying, however lightly, "Machine guns, I suppose."

The pause between the closing of the window and Madam Julia's next sentence was short but perceptible. While it lasted some fresh commotion evidently made itself known in the street. For a moment the anxious face of the chauffeur turned their way again and looked, pale and questioning, through the glass. But, if she saw it, Madam Julia took no notice. She remained sitting erect, away from her cushions, still looking down at her gloved hands clasping a little gold and ivory opera-glass in the folds of the rug over her lap.

"Why," she exclaimed at last. "Isn't it just splendid! We are held up and it becomes my duty to entertain you with the very story I've been longing to tell you for quite a time."

As she spoke she moved her shoulder slightly so that her white coat fell open displaying the lace and satin of her gown and the pearls around her neck. But whether she did so because of the increasing warmth of the heated car, or in some instinctive rejection of the caution implicit in her servant's warning request, was not clear; nor had her companion time to speculate about it before she began her tale.

III

"I BEGAN to see him for the first time," said Madam Julia, " during the summer after my daughter-in-law, Miranda, was so very ill. She had had a fall, soon after Easter that year —and her baby was born dead. It was the child that should have come between Vernon and Frances. You've seen them. Vernon was always his mother's child. I never had any child but Carteret, and, of course, I'd lost him to her from the beginning. Carteret is like his father, born to be a husband— and Miranda was a very lovely girl, lovely enough to make any young man forget everything and everybody but herself. Why, Carteret almost disliked his own child because it took off some of Miranda's attention from himself. And Vernon took after his father. From the very first, just as soon as he was old enough to show any signs of knowing anybody at all, that baby adored his mother. And there was I, still astonished at being a grandmother and hardly reconciled to losing my only son out of the house, with no one to take any notice of me. My husband was away in the Philippines that year—he was the Government architect, working at the new State House. So when Carteret told me that Miranda was going to have a second child I just beamed with joy. 'Carteret,' I said. " This new baby is going to be mine.' He wasn't the least bit astonished. ' Why, Mamma,' he said. ' That's just how Miranda feels about it.' So there it was, settled from the beginning : it was to be a boy and we were to call it John Van Muyden after my father. The baby was due for the first week in August and Miranda was to travel with me up to the Van Muyden house in Maine as soon as the hot weather set in, so that it could be born there. And then, as I told you, Miranda slipped and fell as she was getting out of her car, just after Easter, and everything was over. It was June before we could take her away from the Clinic, and mid-July before I got her safely up to the coast. She came with little Vernon, who was just over his third birthday. The sea air and the scent of the pine-woods began to do her good almost the moment she arrived. But she was very weak and listless and had to be carried up and down stairs for a long time. The house stands halfway up the hillside above a little creek with the pine-woods coming down to the very edge of the lawn. It has a wide verandah all along the front and the parlour gives on to it with three French windows : they stood open all day long that summer. It was the finest, stillest weather there has ever been, that year : the sea hardly ruffled more than lake water, even when the tide was flowing, and the sun so strong on the pine-woods that every room in the house was filled with their scent. Miranda would lie all day long in her chair, with a three-legged stool by her knee for little Vernon, who trotted in and out from the garden and the shore bringing his mother a shell he had picked up or a flower he had gathered. I read aloud to her a good deal. She was too weak to hold a book ; but sometimes she did a little sewing. She had with her some of the unfinished garments she had been making for the baby, and it seemed to comfort her somehow to try to go on with them. There were days when I could hardly bear the sight of those bits of cambric and fine flannel that should have clothed my grandchild who had died before he was born. There were days when I didn't dare to look at her or to speak for quite a time because I wanted to say ' killed ' not ' died.' And when I found out that Miranda was actually sewing on those baby clothes so that she could give them to Hattie Drew who was having her first baby in the fall, I felt I just could not understand her mentality. I had to keep on telling myself that Miranda had been through so much physical pain and danger that it was only fair she should have peace of mind now ; and that I ought to be glad I was suffering the un- happiness of the loss and was doing all the mourning over the child she did not seem to miss. She was able to find her comfort in little Vernon, who just lived for her all through that summer.

" Well, on the afternoon I am going to tell you about, I had been reading to her from a volume of Flecker's poetry someone had sent me. It was a very warm afternoon and Vernon had come in and was sitting close to his mother's knee listening to the reading as gravely as if he understood every word of it. After a time I saw Miranda had dropped her sewing and let her head lean back among the pillows of her chair. She had fallen asleep. So I stopped reading the *Golden Journey* aloud and turned over the pages for a new poem. And—it was the queerest thing—I've never forgotten it, I came on a poem I should never have noticed in the ordinary way, but my eye lighted on it, and just as I'd come to the lines,

> And I have heard a voice of broken seas
> And from the cliffs a cry,

little Vernon looked up and out to the woods along the bay and said : ' Look, Granny, an angel.'

"And I looked, and sure enough, there was a perfectly ordinary young man walking down the footpath through the pine-trees towards the wicket in our fence. He was walking quickly and as though he knew where he was, so I guessed he was no stranger. But as he passed along between the pine-trees it was difficult for me to be sure whether I'd seen him before, particularly as I'd not got my long distance glasses with me. He was wearing a blue serge suit over a grey tennis-shirt, so far as I could make out. Anything less like an angel you couldn't imagine : just a tall good-looking boy of eighteen or nineteen.

"'No, Vernon,' I said, 'that's not an angel, it's just a young man. One of the summer boarders from the guest-house down on the creek may be. He's lost his way in our woods.'

"But I was wrong : when he came to the wicket in the fence he didn't keep on alongside but just opened it and walked in. The path comes down the bank in a zig-zag and I lost sight of him at the first turning. And then Miranda's sewing fell out of her hands and the ball of silk rolled on the floor and Vernon's kitten began to play with it and we had to rescue it and be very quiet so as not to wake Miranda. So it was quite a little time before we could look out at the stranger again. At first we did not see him at all, and then, there he was at the window, standing outside on the verandah, looking in on us. He wore no hat, and I remember his hair was thick and tumbled, fair, almost golden.

"'Go out and see what he wants,' I said to Vernon who was by this time behind my chair on all fours playing with the kitten, so I had to turn round and speak over my back to the child. The little fellow scrambled to his feet and trotted off to the windows. But the stranger had gone. Vernon ran out and I saw him pass backwards and forwards outside all three windows as he ran from end to end of the verandah.

"Presently he came back.

"'I can't see him,' he said.

"'I guess he's gone round the house to the back door. Maybe he is some friend of one of the servants,' I said.

"And then Miranda woke and we forgot all about it. The next time I saw him I was alone. It was a week or ten days later by then, and Carteret had come down ; he and Miranda were out driving. I was sitting in the same place, reading quietly and just looked up from my book, and there he was ! He stood leaning against the window post, half smiling at me. I wanted to call to him, to come right in ; but before I had time to speak he had gone and I couldn't be sure I hadn't been dreaming.

"A day or two later I met little Vernon on the stairs : he was coming up to find me.

"'Granny,' he said, 'that big boy was on the verandah. I saw him. And I ran after him, but he was gone.'

"I told my maid to find out if any of the servants had a young man ; but she said no one at all answering to the description of this youth ever came to the kitchen. And I don't mind telling you, my dear, that I was very pleased to hear it.

"And then Miranda saw him.

"I was reading to her, just as usual, and she was very busy with her sewing because she wanted to get it finished. She was very much better by that time, more like her own self than she had been since her illness. I don't remember what it was we were reading, not that it matters, though I've never forgotten those Flecker poems. However, just as I was turning a page Miranda gave a start.

"'Oh,' she said, ' who is it ? '

"I looked up—but I saw nobody. Miranda was staring out to the path down through the wood. ' He's coming here,' she said. And then she began to cry.

"I knew she'd seen the same boy, and when, this time, I didn't see him I knew who it was : but I said nothing to her except to ask her how he looked. Then, just as it had been the other times, he came on to the verandah, looked through the door and vanished.

"She said it was a boy of eighteen with fair hair wearing a serge suit and a tennis-shirt open at the neck, and she begged me not to tell Carteret, which was about the last thing I should ever have wanted to do. I knew that if Carteret thought any strange young man was hanging about the place he'd go right off to the sheriff about it. I promised Miranda and told her she'd been having a dream. We never spoke of it again through the summer, and when I remembered that this was the week in which, if the child had lived, it would have been born, I could only wonder what Miranda made of it. But one day, after we'd been back in New York some little time, my maid told me that a young man, a stranger, had been drowned in the creek while we were there. Nobody knew who he was. They hadn't said anything about it at the time, so as not to upset Miranda or me : it just came up as Clara was talking

about the summer holiday while she brushed my hair. I had
come back from hearing Mischa Elmann play—his first appearance in New York. Perhaps that is why I've been reminded
of it again to-night."

Madam Julia broke off. There was some disturbance in
the street ; a hooting of cars and the sound of starting engines.
The car beside them began to back slowly and the white face
of the young chauffeur showed once more against the glass of
the partition. Then, the car itself moved, backing cautiously.

" I think," said the Englishwoman, " I can see a car coming
down towards us. It must have turned into the wrong street."

It was true. A string of cars was making its way against
the stream of the now moving block to the accompaniment of
shouting and hooting from the cars that were striving to make
way for the invading procession.

" Mercy ! " exclaimed Madam Julia.   " There's been a
breakdown somewhere. The police must be trying to clear
Fifth Avenue."

There was a just perceptible sharpening of tone in her
voice, but she did not otherwise betray agitation.

The car backed itself to a standstill as the moving block
slowed down to an absolute jam.

" It looks as if we should be here all night. I've never had
so good an excuse for making the best of my tale."

" Please go on. You saw him again ? "

" Not for three years. After what my maid had told me
I persuaded myself that our apparition and the stranger were
the same person, and that his being strange, and also a bit
queer, accounted for his wandering round our house, and also,
perhaps, for his being drowned. I just told myself not to be
fanciful about a thing that was quite natural : anyway, it was
over. Well, one morning in April, soon after Miranda's fine
little girl had been born and we were all feeling so happy
about it, I drove out to New Rochelle to see the mansion my
husband was building for the Morrisons in their park. I'd
only just gotten a car of my own and my chauffeur was pretty
bad about finding his way. I was giving a little luncheon party
at Delmonico's—this was all before the War you understand.
It was for Miranda, her first real day out since the baby came,
and, of course, I couldn't be late for it ; so I told the man to
take what I thought would be a short cut, not knowing that
they'd begun to excavate a new location right across one of
the roads. They'd stretched a chain alongside the pit they'd
made and usually, I believe, there was a man posted to warn

people about it. But it was after twelve when we started home, and the workmen were all at their dinner. Anyhow, before I'd realised that the way was barred we were well into it and the front wheels of the car were over the edge of the excavation. I don't mind telling you now that I thought my last hour had come. The chauffeur put on the brakes and reversed the engine and the car hung there grinding and throbbing as cars did in 1912. And then the door on my right was opened and a tall young man without a hat, wearing a blue serge suit, helped me out and took me across to a block of stone on the further side of the road, where I sat down to recover my wits. The young man went back to the car and began to haul away at the luggage rack at the rear, and that seemed to do what was needed. In a few moments my car was all on firm ground again and the chauffeur was getting her turned in the narrow space between the fence. The broken chain hanging over the edge of the pit made me realise what an escape I'd had. As soon as the car was at a standstill again I rose to thank the young man : but he was gone. There wasn't anywhere for him to go to and the chauffeur hadn't seen him at all. That wasn't so very unnatural, seeing how quickly it had all happened and considering how engrossed he had been with his own part in it. I went to the edge of the pit myself to see if my rescuer had fallen over, but there was no sign of him. So I told the man not to say a word about it to a living soul, because both the Carterets were getting nervous enough about my driving alone as it was, and the poor man was not to blame. I had told him to drive as hard as he could, and this was what had come of it.

" Well, this may have been a coincidence, but, next morning when I opened my newspaper, I saw that the body of an unidentified young man had been found in New Rochelle killed by a block of stone that had fallen from a crane. The report said that he had fair hair and was five feet eleven inches in height. That was all."

" I suppose," said the Englishwoman, " that he would have been killed in any case. Saving your life was fortunate for him, as it was for you. If there is a life hereafter it must be a good thing to leave this one just after a fine action."

" I don't know," said Madam Julia drily, " that I ever took credit to myself for his eternal welfare. The debt seems to me to be all on my side."

" Of course—on *this* side."

"Maybe this is the only side, my dear. It's the only side we know about."

"Then how do you explain . . ."

"There are times when I don't explain at all. I can't expect people like my husband and my son to believe such a thing unless there is an explanation. But I *have* thought— it seems clear énough to me, though you mayn't think so, that the life I'd longed for so much, the boy who was to be born and wasn't, keeps on coming back—and for a moment, to me, and that, perhaps it is his fate never to be a fully grown man. From the first, I realise now, I used to think of him, not as a babe in arms at all, but as a youth who would be my friend and protector, just as young Carteret was before he married Miranda, and as his father was when I first began to fall in love with him. It may be that I meet him often without knowing it. There was a look of him in the boy we have heard playing to-night. I thought of it suddenly in the interval and remembered how little Vernon had said ' an angel ' when he first saw him. And this boy—why he's more of a seraph than a human child—had the same look. His playing—in a way—has saved my life a little—given me back something I thought quite dead in me—the belief in the return of musical genius to a world I had thought too clever and too deafened to have any place for it again."

The Englishwoman nodded.

"It is wonderful to be there when these visitations come," she said. "People talk of Mozart when they discuss this child ; not a prodigy they say, a miracle, without explanation, just a divine fact—like your apparition."

Madam Julia did not reply at once—she was watching the red eye of the traffic signals high against the blackness at the end of the short street.

"I thought I saw it flicker," she said at last, "but it's steady again. The machine guns stopped a good five minutes ago." It was her first admission of having recognised the origin of the crackling sound.

"People seem to be getting out of their cars," observed the Englishwoman.

"It will be quicker for those who live in the Sixties to walk home than to wait while their cars get unjammed. We cannot do that. My heart would not carry me to my own door. There—the green light at last. I am so glad you have moved up to the Biltmore, my dear. It would be too late, and possibly not very safe for you to go down to the other

end of the city to-night. And I must get right home as soon
as possible for my old man's sake. Luckily he believes I am
to drive you down town before I go home, so he won't have
very long to be anxious about me."

There was already movement ahead of them. The stream
of invading cars was backing out to regain its proper direction.
One or two of the cars ahead of theirs hooted their warning
of a speedy advance. The two women were engrossed in
watching the signs of their coming release ; each, too, a little
careful to conceal the anxiety neither could help feeling. A
mutual reserve forbade them to discuss the possible cause of
the disturbance : the one, as guest, affecting to accept it as
nothing unusual or alarming ; the other as hostess, determined
to admit nothing that should cause uneasiness to the stranger
she entertained, and above all, to avoid any sign that might
give rise to fears for her own power of resistance under the
strain.

"We shall be moving in another minute or so," she
announced. "It will be a real joy to me to have left you safe
and near at hand while I drink hot soup and tell Carteret
about the music. We shall see the reasons for this delay in
the papers to-morrow, but I'm afraid they will give us nothing
more interesting than the capture of some gangsters. What
was it we were saying about Mozart ? "

" It was something the boy we have been hearing reminded
me of—an uncle of mine who collected violins once wrote a
sonnet to Mozart. I can't remember it all—but lines of it
came back to me to-night as I listened :

> For a brief space in a child's heart he dwelt. . .
> Untaught of earth, bearing the inner sense
> Of all celestial melody. . .

I suppose it does happen—the return of the divine. It has
happened to you. I know you believe this."

The elder woman leaned forward. They were moving
now, gaining speed as they left the side street and drove along
Fifth Avenue. The light from the tall street standards ; the
glow from the thousand beams illuminating the towers of the
Babylonish night, lit her fine-cut profile and sparkled in her
frosty hair. All at once her control left her. She had spoken
till now smoothly, almost lightly, offering her tale with a half-
whimsical deprecation as though courtesy compelled her to
allow her hearer the possibility of rejecting it without rudeness.

There had been more than a threat of danger in the situation from which they were now emerging. Into the task of relieving its strain, not only for her guest but for herself as well, she had thrown something very vital and sacred to her. Now that strain was ended she could not recover what she had given away. Her instinct had not betrayed her : her hearer had shared her experience as she listened ; now she found herself obliged to yield it with a completeness she had not supposed possible when she began to tell the old adventure. In bringing it back to clothe it with words once more she had found it grown and new to her comprehension.

"Why," she exclaimed, and there was the roughness of passion in her voice, "here am I, alive after years of being told by doctors that my life hung on by a thread which might snap at any moment, while that boy, who never lived, has died again and again. What for ? Why should it be just me who am old and useless and ill, and not that other life—it might be so strong and rich—that continues ? He dies that I may be saved—perhaps—or perhaps he lives again and again because of my desire that he should live at all. I desired a life, and it has been given to me so that I do not die, though its separate life has been broken from the beginning. It doesn't seem sensible to me. I used to feel like this when I was a little girl listening to the story of the Crucifixion. I just couldn't bear it : it seemed such a waste. I was angry with God for letting His beautiful son be hurt and broken. I could not understand what good it did to *any*body. I don't understand now, the price is so heavy—and the gain—why it isn't a gain, it's just a worthless consequence. And yet they hang together. He died that we might live—and we *do* live—we can't help it."

She drew her cloak about her, shivering in the heated car.

The younger woman took her friend's ice-cold hand and held it for a moment.

"It's no use flinging ourselves against these mysteries," she comforted. "We've only got our own experience to test them by. Perhaps they came out of a scheme of things no one has ever comprehended. When they cannot be evaded— when we are forced to recognise the existence of irreconcilable events, we either deny or dispute the evidence. Some people say that there is no purpose in the scheme of things. They look on everything inexplicable that happens as meaningless chance, grotesque coincidence. They are spiritual Philistines. They tar and feather the eccentric experience of a human soul just as the ordinary Philistine tarred and feathered Epstein's Rima in Hyde Park. But you, who have been part of such an experience, you cannot question its validity. Even though it puzzles you, you should be able to trust to an ultimate justification. You must allow for some scale too vast for our mortal recognition."

She paused, a little abashed by her own hasty utterance.

" Forgive me," she said. " I have no right to dogmatise like this. But your story has made me want it to be all happiness for you. I cannot bear it to make you sad."

Madam Julia withdrew her hand from her companion's clasp, and, as if to compensate for the gesture, turned and kissed her lightly on the cheek.

" Isn't this just too bad ? " she said with a smile. " Here am I talking to amuse us both during our delay, and all I can do is to stir you up to console me for being alive in a very, very pleasant world. All I really mean is that I can't help feeling that I have had my good time, and he has missed it, a great deal of it, and it doesn't seem altogether fair."

The car had driven under the cavernous approaches of the Grand Central Building, and was now drawn up before the flicker of one of the low revolving doors that seem so small in comparison with the height of the towers to which they give access. The chauffeur got down from his seat and stood waiting till the farewells between his mistress and her guest were completed before opening the door.

" Your chauffeur takes no risks," said the Englishwoman. " I was out in Long Island on Friday and caught a slight chill in a car while the people were saying good-bye with the door open."

Madam Julia smiled.

" He's almost too good to be true," she said. " Even Clara cannot find anything to grumble at in the way he takes care of me. I sometimes think she'd like him better if she trusted him less."

IV

THERE was a hold-up in the traffic at Forty-second Street before the young English chauffeur could get his car from the hotel door into Park Avenue. He sat at the wheel listening intently. Above the roar of the city, not very far away, the crackle of guns—police guns this time—spurted once more, like the striking of matches by angry giants who could not get

them alight. The shouted news of the drivers whose cars had
been forced through the jam outside Carnegie Hall had told
of trouble surging unexpectedly from the East Side, along
Second Avenue, and either timed or fated to synchronise with
a rush of the unemployed round the Opera House. This had
created a panic amongst the audience coming away from the
performance there and had driven all traffic westward and
northward for half an hour. It had been a far more serious
business than anything the young man had heard of yet.
Stories of gangsters ; occasional glimpses of an arrest ; the
dispersal of a mass meeting of Reds in Union Square, had
come into his adventure in the City of Towers. They had all
seemed part of a spectacle in which he had no more than a
spectator's concern. Now he was a participant ; his business
to get his car and its occupants safely through a danger that
had once more raised itself across his way. One of his charges
was already safe, as safe as shelter and the innumerable multi-
plicity of numbered anonymous hotel corridors could make
her ; the other, the infinitely frailer and, to him, more important being, had given no sign that she realised his position—
or her own. Women, he said to himself, with the gloomy
cynicism of the young, women were all alike ; ladies or mere
everyday girls, once they got together they'd talk and talk and
talk and never notice what was happening, even if it were the
Day of Judgment. Not that his own lady was as a rule
inattentive to what happened around her. But she had been
talking a great deal as they waited and had not seemed to be
in the least concerned when those cars forced themselves into
the street, all pushing in the wrong direction. Perhaps with
the windows of the car up she had not heard the guns. Perhaps,
even if she had heard them, she had not recognised or understood what the rattle signified. After all, she had not heard
the chauffeur of the Buick telling him what one of the invading
taxi-drivers had said. He must not judge her too harshly.
For a lady, and a rich one, and an American, she was a marvel.
Clara had often complained to him that Madam was not one
to be stopped by anything. How did he know that she didn't
know as much as he did about the row that was still going
on ? Perhaps Senator Wenham actually had had some warning ; he might have tried to keep his wife at home. . . .
    There was a movement ahead—the guns had ceased for
the past minute : the traffic began to flow once more.
    A quick glance behind him as he started the car showed
him Madam Julia's white figure gleaming erect against the

*A second before the lift took her out of his sight,
her eyes met his.*

darkness. She was alert, aware, a little anxious now. The
knowledge that she knew, at last, that she had probably known
all along, filled him with pride. He dismissed his recent
thought of her as unworthy, almost disloyal, and drove down
Park Avenue, avoiding the familiar uneven patches in its
surface with the skill on which he always prided himself.

In two minutes they were at the door : the janitor came
to help Mrs. Wenham to alight, giving her his arm for the
twenty paces from the street to the entrance of the lift at the
far end of the lobby.

The young chauffeur followed them, carrying Madam
Julia's rug and the footwarmer and cushions Clara would
never allow him to take down to the garage on the East Side.

When she was seated in the corner of the lift on the high
stool that was always placed there for her, she bade him good-
night, adding :

" Please ring up Clara when you get down to the garage.
I shall be glad to know that you have got there in safety."

So she did know ! The boy flushed and raised his hand
to touch his cap as he answered : " Thank you, Madam, I
will certainly."

As he did so, the janitor, turning to take the rugs and
cushions from him, jerked his elbow upwards so that his
peaked cap caught on his wrist and was pushed off his head,
to the ground. A lock of his blond hair fell across his forehead
and he shook it back as the lattice closed across the entrance
and the lift began to rise. A little confused by this mishap,
a little shaken by the kindness and recognition her words had
conveyed, the boy stood bareheaded, gazing up at his mistress
where she sat reflected by the mirrors of the lift. In the
second before it took her out of his sight, her eyes met his,
and he saw the whole expression of her face alter. She had
looked old and tired ; a little indifferent ; intent only on
reaching the end of her evening's effort when he had seen
her in the bright light of the lobby. Now, in the swiftness
of a glance, her face had become radiant and smiling and yet
a little awed—even alarmed, as though fear had met delight
in her response to what she saw. She had often smiled when
speaking to him ; always gently, sometimes with real kindness
and friendliness : but this was an altogether different look.
He stood at the bottom of the dark shaft listening to the long
ascending sigh of the elevator, until the clash of the gates,
faint and far overhead, told him that she had reached the
ninth floor and was safe in Clara's waiting care.

Then, before the janitor could descend to engage in the interchange of views and gossip that usually closed the evenings when Mrs. Wenham drove out, he turned and went out to his car. He did not want to talk to anyone after what he had seen. Coming at the end of an hour of a greater strain than he had in the least known himself to be feeling, Madam Julia's queer ecstatic smile had moved him to an extent he did not understand. He whistled a few bars of the *March of the Men of Harlech*, the only tune he knew, as he swung himself into the driving seat and restarted the car.

" Crikey," he said aloud. " She might have taken me for an angel."

At the corner of Forty-second Street and Second Avenue there was a sudden rush from the dark cavern of a tenement house and a fresh crackle of firing. The big car jerked to a standstill against the kerb, its driver bent double over the wheel.

*   *   *   *   *   *

The telephone bell in the Wenhams' garage rang and rang until long after midnight, but Clara, sitting pale and exasperated in the little boudoir outside Madam Julia's bedroom, could not get any reply.

THE CIGARETTE CASE

By

OLIVER ONIONS

" A CIGARETTE, Loder ? " I said, offering my case. For the moment Loder was not smoking ; for long enough he had not been talking.

" Thanks," he replied, taking not only the cigarette, but the case also. The others went on talking ; Loder became silent again ; but I noticed that he kept my cigarette case in his hand, and looked at it from time to time with an interest that neither its design nor its costliness seemed to explain. Presently I caught his eye.

" A pretty case," he remarked, putting it down on the table. " I once had one exactly like it."

I answered that they were in every shop window.

" Oh yes," he said, putting aside any question of rarity. . . . " I lost mine."

" Oh ? . . ."

He laughed. " Oh, that's all right—I got it back again—don't be afraid I'm going to claim yours. But the way I lost it—found it—the whole thing—was rather curious. I've never been able to explain it. I wonder if you could ? "

I answered that I certainly couldn't till I'd heard it, whereupon Loder, taking up the silver case again and holding it in his hand as he talked, began :

" This happened in Provence, when I was about as old as Marsham there—and every bit as romantic. I was there with Carroll—you remember poor old Carroll and what a blade of a boy he was—as romantic as four Marshams rolled into one. (Excuse me, Marsham, won't you ? It's a romantic tale, you see, or at least the setting is.) . . . We were in Provence, Carroll and I ; twenty-four or thereabouts ; romantic, as I say ; and—and this happened.

" And it happened on the top of a whole lot of other things,
you must understand, the things that do happen when you're
twenty-four. If it hadn't been Provence, it would have been
somewhere else, I suppose, nearly, if not quite as good ; but
this was Provence, that smells (as you might say) of twenty-four
as it smells of argelasse and wild lavender and broom. . . .

" We'd had the dickens of a walk of it, just with knapsacks
—had started somewhere in the Ardèche and tramped south
through the vines and almonds and olives—Montélimar,
Orange, Avignon, and a fortnight at that blanched skeleton of
a town, Les Baux. We'd nothing to do, and had gone just
where we liked, or rather just where Carroll had liked ; and
Carroll had had the *De Bello Gallico* in his pocket, and had had
a notion, I fancy, of taking in the whole ground of the Roman
conquest—I remember he lugged me off to some place or
other, Pourrières I believe its name was, because—I forget
how many thousands—were killed in a river-bed there, and
they stove in the water-casks so that if the men wanted water
they'd have to go forward and fight for it. And then we'd gone
on to Arles, where Carroll had fallen in love with everything
that had a bow of black velvet in her hair, and after that
Tarascon, Nîmes, and so on, the usual round—I won't bother
you with that. In a word, we'd had two months of it, eating
almonds and apricots from the trees, watching the women at
the communal washing-fountains under the dark plane-trees,
singing *Magali* and the *Qué Cantes*, and Carroll yarning away
all the time about Cæsar and Vercingetorix and Dante, and
trying to learn Provençal so that he could read the stuff in the
Journal des Félibriges that he'd never have looked at if it had
been in English. . . .

" Well, we got to Darbisson. We'd run across some young
chap or other—Rangon his name was—who was a vine-planter
in those parts, and Rangon had asked us to spend a couple of
days with him, with him and his mother, if we happened to be
in the neighbourhood. So as we might as well happen to be
there as anywhere else, we sent him a post-card and went. This
would be in June or early in July. All day we walked across a
plain of vines, past hurdles of wattled *cannes* and great windscreens of velvety cypresses, sixty feet high, all white with dust
on the north side of 'em, for the mistral was having its three-
days' revel, and it whistled and roared through the *cannes* till
scores of yards of 'em at a time were bowed nearly to the earth.
A roaring day it was, I remember. . . . But the wind fell a
little late in the afternoon, and we were poring over what it

had left of our Ordnance Survey—like fools, we'd got the un-
mounted maps instead of the linen ones—when Rangon himself
found us, coming out to meet us in a very badly turned-out trap.
He drove us back himself, through Darbisson, to the house, a
mile and a half beyond it, where he lived with his mother.

" He spoke no English, Rangon didn't, though, of course,
both French and Provençal ; and as he drove us, there was
Carroll, using him as a Franco-Provençal dictionary, peppering
him with questions about the names of things in the patois—
I beg its pardon, the language—though there's a good deal of
my eye and Betty Martin about that, and I fancy this Félibrige
business will be in a good many pieces when Frédéric Mistral
is under that Court-of-Love pavilion arrangement he's had
put up for himself in the graveyard at Maillanne. If the language has got to go, well, it's got to go, I suppose ; and while
I personally don't want to give it a kick, I rather sympathise
with the Government. Those jaunts of a Sunday out to Les
Baux, for instance, with paper lanterns and Bengal fire and a
fellow spouting *O blanche Venus d'Arles*—they're well enough,
and compare favourably with our Bank Holidays and Sunday
League picnics, but . . . but that's nothing to do with my tale
after all. . . . So he drove on, and by the time we got to Rangon's
house Carroll had learned the greater part of *Magali*. . . .

" As you, no doubt, know, it's a restricted sort of life in
some respects that a young *vigneron* lives in those parts, and it
was as we reached the house that Rangon remembered something—or he might have been trying to tell us as we came along
for all I know, and not been able to get a word in edgeways for
Carroll and his Provençal. It seemed that his mother was away
from home for some days—apologies of the most profound, of
course ; our host was the soul of courtesy, though he did try
to get at us a bit later. . . . We expressed our polite regrets,
naturally ; but I didn't quite see at first what difference it
made. I only began to see when Rangon, with more apologies,
told us that we should have to go back to Darbisson for dinner.
It appeared that when Madame Rangon went away for a few
days she dispersed the whole of the female side of her establishment also, and she'd left her son with nobody to look after him
except an old man we'd seen in the yard mending one of these
double-cylindered sulphur-sprinklers they clap across the
horse's back and drive between the rows of vines. . . . Rangon
explained all this as we stood in the hall drinking an *apéritif*—
a hall crowded with oak furniture and photographs and a
cradle-like bread-crib and doors opening to right and left to

the other rooms of the ground floor. He had also, it seemed, to ask us to be so infinitely obliging as to excuse him for one hour after dinner—our post-card had come unexpectedly, he said, and already he had made an appointment with his agent about the *vendange* for the coming autumn. . . . We begged him, of course, not to allow us to interfere with his business in the slightest degree. He thanked us a thousand times.

" ' But though we dine in the village, we will take our own wine with us,' he said, ' a wine *surfin*—one of my wines—you shall see——'

" Then he showed us round his place—I forget how many hundreds of acres of vines, and into the great building with the presses and pumps and casks and the huge barrel they call the thunderbolt—and about seven o'clock we walked back to Darbisson to dinner, carrying our wine with us. I think the restaurant we dined in was the only one in the place, and our gaillard of a host—he was a straight-backed, well-set-up chap, with rather fine eyes—did us on the whole pretty well. His wine certainly was good stuff, and set our tongues going. . . .

" A moment ago I said a fellow like Rangon leads a restricted sort of life in those parts. I saw this more clearly as dinner went on. We dined by an open window, from which we could see the stream with the planks across it where the women washed clothes during the day and assembled in the evening for gossip. There were a dozen or so of them there as we dined, laughing and chatting in low tones—they all seemed pretty— it was quickly falling dusk—all the girls are pretty then, and are quite conscious of it—*you* know, Marsham. Behind them, at the end of the street, one of these great cypress windscreens showed black against the sky, a ragged edge something like the line the needle draws on a rainfall chart ; and you could only tell whether they were men or women under the plaintains by their voices rippling and chattering and suddenly a deeper note. . . . Once I heard a muffled scuffle and a sound like a kiss. . . . It was then that Rangon's little trouble came out. . . .

" It seemed that he didn't know any girls—wasn't allowed to know any girls. The girls of the village were pretty enough, but you see how it was—he'd a position to keep up—appearances to maintain—couldn't be familiar during the year with the girls who gathered his grapes for him in the autumn. . . . And as soon as Carroll gave him a chance, *he* began to ask *us* questions, about England, English girls, the liberty they had, and so on.

" Of course, we couldn't tell him much he hadn't heard already, but that made no difference ; he could stand any

amount of that, our strapping young *vigneron* ; and he asked
us questions by the dozen, that we both tried to answer at once.
And his delight and envy ! . . . What ! In England did the
young men see the young women of their own class without
restraint—the sisters of their friends *même*—even at the house ?
Was it permitted that they drank tea with them in the afternoon,
or went without invitation to pass the *soirée* ? . . . He had all the
later Prévosts in his room, he told us (I don't doubt he had the
earlier ones also) ; Prévost and the Disestablishment between
them must be playing the mischief with the convent system of
education for young girls ; and our young man was—what d'you
call it ?—' Co-ed '—co-educationalist—by Jove, yes ! . . . He
seemed to marvel that we should have left a country so blessed
as England to visit his dusty, wild-lavender-smelling, girl-less
Provence. . . . You don't know half your luck, Marsham. . . .

" Well, we talked after this fashion—we'd left the dining-
room of the restaurant and had planted ourselves on a bench
outside with Rangon between us—when Rangon suddenly
looked at his watch and said it was time he was off to see this
agent of his. Would we take a walk, he asked us, and meet
him again there ? he said. . . . But as his agent lived in the
direction of his own home, we said we'd meet him at the house
in an hour or so. Off he went, envying every Englishman who
stepped, I don't doubt. . . . I told you how old—how young
—we were. . . . Heigho ! . . .

" Well, off goes Rangon, and Carroll and I got up, stretched
ourselves, and took a walk. We walked a mile or so, until it
began to get pretty dark, and then turned ; and it was as we
came into the blackness of one of these cypress hedges that
the thing I'm telling you of happened. The hedge took a sharp
turn at that point ; as we came round the angle we
saw a couple of women's figures hardly more than twenty yards
ahead—don't know how they got there so suddenly, I'm sure ;
and that same moment I found my foot on something white and
small and glimmering on the grass.

" I picked it up. It was a handkerchief—a woman's—
embroidered——

" The two figures ahead of us were walking in our direction;
there was every probability that the handkerchief belonged to
one of them ; so we stepped out. . . .

" At my ' Pardon, madame,' and lifted hat one of the figures
turned her head ; then, to my surprise, she spoke in English—
cultivated English. I held out the handkerchief. It belonged
to the elder lady of the two, the one who had spoken, a very

gentle-voiced old lady, older by very many years than her companion. She took the handkerchief and thanked me. . . .

"Somebody—Sterne, isn't it ?—says that Englishmen don't travel to see Englishmen. I don't know whether he'd stand to that in the case of Englishwomen ; Carroll and I didn't. . . . We were walking rather slowly along, four abreast across the road ; we asked permission to introduce ourselves, did so, and received some name in return which, strangely enough, I've entirely forgotten—I only remember that the ladies were aunt and niece, and lived at Darbisson. They shook their heads when I mentioned M. Rangon's name and said we were visiting him. They didn't know him. . . .

"I'd never been in Darbisson before, and I haven't been since, so I don't know the map of the village very well. But the place isn't very big, and the house at which we stopped in twenty minutes or so is probably there yet. It had a large double door—a double door in two senses, for it was a big *porte-cochère* with a smaller door inside it, and an iron grille shutting in the whole. The gentle-voiced old lady had already taken a key from her reticule and was thanking us again for the little service of the handkerchief ; then, with the little gesture one makes when one has found oneself on the point of omitting a courtesy, she gave a little musical laugh.

"' But,' she said with a little movement of invitation, ' one sees so few compatriots here—if you have the time to come in and smoke a cigarette . . . also the cigarette,' she added, with another rippling laugh, ' for we have few callers, and live alone—— '

"Hastily as I was about to accept, Carroll was before me, professing a nostalgia for the sound of the English tongue that made his recent protestations about Provençal a shameless hypocrisy. Persuasive young rascal, Carroll was—poor chap. . . . So the elder lady opened the grille and the wooden door beyond it, and we entered.

"By the light of the candle which the younger lady took from a bracket just within the door we saw that we were in a handsome hall or vestibule ; and my wonder that Rangon had made no mention of what was apparently a considerable establishment was increased by the fact that its tenants must be known to be English and could be seen to be entirely charming. I couldn't understand it, and I'm afraid hypotheses rushed into my head that cast doubts on the Rangons—you know— whether *they* were all right. We knew nothing about our young planter, you see. . . .

"I looked about me. There were tubs here and there

against the walls, gaily painted, with glossy-leaved aloes and palms in them—one of the aloes, I remember, was flowering ; a little fountain in the middle made a tinkling noise ; we put our caps on a carved and gilt console table ; and before us rose a broad staircase with shallow steps of spotless stone and a beautiful wrought-iron hand-rail. At the top of the staircase were more palms and aloes, and double doors painted in a clear grey.

" We followed our hostesses up the staircase. I can hear yet the sharp clean click our boots made on that hard shiny stone—see the lights of the candle gleaming on the handrail. . . . The young girl—she was not much more than a girl—pushed at the doors, and we went in.

" The room we entered was all of a piece with the rest for rather old-fashioned fineness. It was large, lofty, beautifully kept. Carroll went round for Miss . . . whatever her name was . . . lighting candles in sconces ; and as the flames crept up they glimmered on a beautifully polished floor, which was bare except for an Eastern rug here and there. The elder lady had sat down in a gilt chair, Louis Fourteenth I should say, with a striped rep of the colour of a petunia ; and I really don't know—don't smile, Smith—what induced me to lead her to it by the finger-tips, bending over her hand for a moment as she sat down. There was an old tambour-frame behind her chair, I remember, and a vast oval mirror with clustered candle-brackets filled the greater part of the farther wall, the brightest and clearest glass I've ever seen. . . ."

He paused, looking at my cigarette case, which he had taken into his hand again. He smiled at some recollection or other, and it was a minute or so before he continued.

" I must admit that I found it a little annoying, after what we'd been talking about at dinner an hour before, that Rangon wasn't with us. I still couldn't understand how he could have neighbours so charming without knowing about them, but I didn't care to insist on this to the old lady, who for all I knew might have her own reasons for keeping to herself. And, after all, it was our place to return Rangon's hospitality in London if he ever came there, not, so to speak, on his own doorstep. . . . So presently I forgot all about Rangon, and I'm pretty sure that Carroll, who was talking to his companion of some Félibrige junketing or other and having the air of Gounod's *Mireille* hummed softly over to him, didn't waste a thought on him either. Soon Carroll—you remember what a pretty crooning, humming voice he had—soon Carroll was murmuring what they call ' seconds,' but so low that the sound hardly came across the room ; and I came in with a soft bass note from time to time. No instrument, you know ; just an unaccompanied murmur no louder than an Æolian harp ; and it sounded infinitely sweet and plaintive and—what shall I say ?—weak— attenuated—faint—' pale ' you might almost say—in that formal, rather old-fashioned *salon*, with that great clear oval mirror throwing back the still flames of the candles in the sconces on the walls. Outside the wind had now fallen completely ; all was very quiet ; and suddenly in a voice not much louder than a sigh, Carroll's companion was singing *Oft in the Stilly Night* —you know it. . . ."

He broke off again to murmur the beginning of the air. Then, with a little laugh for which we saw no reason, he went on again :

" Well, I'm not going to try to convince you of such a special and delicate thing as the charm of that hour—it wasn't more than an hour—it would be all about an hour we stayed. Things like that just have to be said and left ; you destroy them the moment you begin to insist on them ; we've every one of us had experiences like that, and don't say much about them. I was as much in love with my old lady as Carroll evidently was with his young one—I can't tell you why—being in love has just to be taken for granted too, I suppose . . . Marsham understands. . . . We smoked our cigarettes, and sang again, once more filling that clear-painted, quiet apartment with a murmuring no louder than if a light breeze found that the bells of a bed of flowers were really bells and played on 'em. The old lady moved her fingers gently on the round table by the side of her chair . . . oh, infinitely pretty it was. . . . Then Carroll wandered off into the *Qué Cantes*—awfully pretty—' It is not for myself I sing, but for my friend who is near me '—and I can't tell you how like four old friends we were, those two so oddly met ladies and Carroll and myself. . . . And so to *Oft in the Stilly Night* again. . . .

" But for all the sweetness and the glamour of it, we couldn't stay on indefinitely, and I wondered what time it was, but didn't ask—anything to do with clocks and watches would have seemed a cold and mechanical sort of thing just then. . . . And when presently we both got up neither Carroll nor I asked to be allowed to call again in the morning to thank them for a charming hour. . . . And they seemed to feel the same as we did about it. There was no ' hoping that we should meet again in London '—neither an au revoir nor a good-bye—just a tacit understanding that that hour should remain isolated, accepted like a good gift without looking the gift-horse in the mouth, single, unattached to any hours before or after—I don't know whether you see what I mean. . . . Give me a match somebody. . . .

" And so we left, with no more than looks exchanged and finger-tips resting between the back of our hands and our lips for a moment. We found our way out by ourselves, down that shallow-stepped staircase with the handsome handrail, and let ourselves out of the double door and grille, closing it softly. We made for the village without speaking a word. . Heigho ! . . ."

Loder had picked up the cigarette case again, but for all the way his eyes rested on it I doubt whether he really saw it. I'm pretty sure he didn't ; I knew when he did by the glance he shot at me, as much as to say " I see you're wondering where the cigarette case comes in." . . . He resumed with another little laugh.

" Well," he continued, " we got back to Rangon's house. I really don't blame Rangon for the way he took it when we told him, you know—he thought we were pulling his leg, of course, and he wasn't having any ; not he ! There were no English ladies in Darbisson, he said. . . . We told him as nearly as we could just where the house was—we weren't very precise, I'm afraid, for the village had been in darkness as we had come through it, and I had to admit that the cypress hedge I tried to describe where we'd met our friends was a good deal like other cypress hedges—and, as I say, Rangon wasn't taking any. I myself was rather annoyed that he should think we were returning his hospitality by trying to get at him, and it wasn't very easy either to explain in my French and Carroll's Provençal that we were going to let the thing stand as it was and weren't going to call on our charming friends again. . . . The end of it was that Rangon just laughed and yawned. . . .

" ' I knew it was good, my wine,' he said, ' but—— a shrug said the rest. ' Not so good as all that,' he meant. . . .

" Then he gave us our candles, showed us to our rooms, shook hands, and marched off to his own room and the Prévosts.

" I dreamed of my old lady half the night.

" After coffee the next morning I put my hand into my pocket for my cigarette case and didn't find it. I went through all my pockets, and then I asked Carroll if he'd got it.

" ' No,' he replied. . . . ' Think you left it behind at that place last night ? '

" ' Yes ; did you ? ' Rangon popped in with a twinkle.

" I went through all my pockets again. No cigarette case. . . .

"Of course, it was possible that I'd left it behind, and I was annoyed again. I didn't want to go back, you see.
But, on the other hand, I didn't want to lose the case—it was a present—and Rangon's smile nettled me a good deal, too. It was both a challenge to our truthfulness and a testimonial to that very good wine of his. . . .

"'Might have done,' I grunted. . . 'Well, in that case we'll go and get it.'

"'If one tried the restaurant first—— ?' Rangon suggested, smiling again.

"'By all means,' said I stuffily, though I remembered having the case after we'd left the restaurant.

"We were round at the restaurant by half-past nine. The case wasn't there. I'd known jolly well beforehand it wasn't, and I saw Rangon's mouth twitching with amusement.

"'So we now seek the abode of these English ladies, *hein* ?' he said.

"'Yes,' said I ; and we left the restaurant and strode through the village by the way we'd taken the evening before.

"That *vigneron's* smile became more and more irritating to me. . . . 'It is then the *next* village ?' he said presently, as we left the last house and came out into the open plain.

"We went back. . . .

"I was irritated because we were two to one, you see, and Carroll backed me up. 'A double door, with a grille in front of it,' he repeated for the fiftieth time. . . . Rangon merely replied that it wasn't our good faith he doubted. He didn't actually use the word 'drunk.' . . .

"'*Mais tiens,*' he said suddenly, trying to conceal his mirth. '*Si c'est possible . . . si c'est possible . . .* a double door with a grille ? But perhaps that I know it, the domicile of these so elusive ladies. . . . Come this way.'

"He took us back along a plantain-groved street, and suddenly turned up an alley that was little more than two gutters and a crack of sky overhead between two broken-tiled roofs. It was a dilapidated, deserted *ruelle*, and I was positively angry when Rangon pointed to a blistered old *porte-cochère* with a half-unhinged railing in front of it.

"'Is it that, your house ?' he asked.

"'No,' says I, and 'No,' says Carroll . . . and off we started again. . . .

"But another half-hour brought us back to the same place, and Carroll scratched his head.

" ' Who lives there, anyway ? ' he said, glowering at the *porte-cochère*, chin forward, hands in pockets.

" ' Nobody,' says Rangon, as much as to say ' look at it ! ' ' M'sieu then meditates taking it ? ' . . .

" Then I struck in, quite out of temper by this time.

" ' How much would the rent be ? ' I asked, as if I really thought of taking the place just to get back at him.

" He mentioned something ridiculously small in the way of francs.

" ' One might at least see the place,' says I. ' Can the key be got ? '

" He bowed. The key was at the baker's, not a hundred yards away, he said. . . .

" We got the key. It was the key of the inner wooden door—that grid of rusty iron didn't need one—it came clean off its single hinge when Carroll touched it. Carroll opened, and we stood for a moment motioning to one another to step in. Then Rangon went in first, and I heard him murmur ' Pardon, Mesdames.' . . .

" Now this is the odd part. We passed into a sort of, vestibule or hall, with a burst lead pipe in the middle of a dry tank in the centre of it. There was a broad staircase rising in front of us to the first floor, and double doors just seen in the half-light at the head of the stairs. Old tubs stood against the walls, but the palms and aloes in them were dead—only a cabbage-stalk or two—and the rusty hoops lay on the ground about them. One tub had come to pieces entirely and was no more than a heap of staves on a pile of spilt earth. And everywhere, everywhere, was dust—the floor was an inch deep in dust and old plaster that muffled our footsteps, cobwebs hung like old dusters on the walls, a regular goblin's tatter of cobwebs draped the little bracket inside the door, and the wrought-iron of the hand-rail was closed up with webs in which not even a spider moved. The whole thing was preposterous. . . .

" ' It is possible that for even a less rental—— ' Rangon murmured, dragging his forefinger across the hand-rail and leaving an inch-deep furrow. . . .

" ' Come upstairs,' said I suddenly. . . .

" Up we went. All was in the same state there. A clutter of stuff came down as I pushed at the double doors of the *salon*, and I had to strike a stinking French sulphur match to see into the room at all. Underfoot was like walking on thicknesses of flannel, and except where we put our feet the place was as printless as a snowfield—dust, dust, unbroken grey dust. My match burned down. . . .

" ' Wait a minute—I've a *bougie*,' said Carroll, and struck the wax match. . . .

" There were the old sconces, with never a candle-end in them. There was the large oval mirror, but hardly reflecting Carroll's match for the dust on it. And the broken chairs were there, all giltless, and the rickety old round table. . . .

" But suddenly I darted forward. Something new and bright on the table twinkled with the light of Carroll's match. The match went out, and by the time Carroll had lighted another I had stopped. I wanted Rangon to see what was on the table. . . .

" ' You'll see by my footprints how far from that table *I've* been,' I said. ' Will you pick it up ? '

" And Rangon, stepping forward, picked up from the middle of the table—my cigarette case."

Loder had finished. Nobody spoke. For quite a minute nobody spoke, and then Loder himself broke the silence turning to me.

" Make anything of it ? " he said.

I lifted my eyebrows. " Only your *vigneron's* explanation —— " I began, but stopped again, seeing that wouldn't do.

" *Any*body make anything of it ? " said Loder, turning from one to another.

I gathered from Smith's face that he thought *one* thing might be made of it—namely, that Loder had invented the whole tale. But even Smith didn't speak.

" Were any English ladies ever found to have lived in the place—murdered, you know—bodies found and all that ? " young Marsham asked diffidently, yearning for an obvious completeness.

" Not that we could ever learn," Loder replied. " We made inquiries too. . . . So you all give it up ? Well, so do I. . . ."

And he rose. As he walked to the door, myself following him to get his hat and stick, I heard him humming softly the lines—they are from *Oft in the Stilly Night*—

> " I seem like one who treads alone
> Some banquet-hall deserted,
> Whose guests are fled, whose garlands dead,
> And all but he—departed ! "

A PAIR OF HANDS

By

A. T. QUILLER-COUCH

"YES," said Miss Le Petyt, gazing into the deep fireplace and letting her hands and her knitting lie for the moment idle in her lap. "Oh, yes, I have seen a ghost. In fact I have lived in a house with one for quite a long time."

"How you *could*——!" began one of my host's daughters ; and "*You*, Aunt Emily ?" cried the other at the same moment.

Miss Le Petyt, gentle soul, withdrew her eyes from the fireplace and protested with a gay little smile. "Well, my dears, I am not quite the coward you take me for. And, as it happens, mine was the most harmless ghost in the world. In fact "—and here she looked at the fire again—" I was quite sorry to lose her."

"It was a woman, then ? Now *I* think," said Miss Blanche, " that female ghosts are the horridest of all. They wear little shoes with high red heels, and go about *tap*, *tap*, wringing their hands."

"This one wrung her hands, certainly. But I don't know about the high red heels, for I never saw her feet. Perhaps she was like the Queen of Spain, and hadn't any. And as for the hands, it all depends *how* you wring them. There's an elderly shopwalker at Knightsbridge, for instance——"

"Don't be prosy, dear, when you know that we're just dying to hear the story."

Miss Le Petyt turned to me with a small deprecating laugh. "It's such a little one."

"The story, or the ghost ?"

"Both."

And this was Miss Le Petyt's story :—

"It happened when I lived down in Cornwall, at Tresillack

609

on the south coast. Tresillack was the name of the house, which stood quite alone at the head of a coombe, within sound of the sea but without sight of it ; for though the coombe led down to a wide open beach, it wound and twisted half a dozen times on its way, and its overlapping sides closed the view from the house, which was advertised as ' secluded.' I was very poor in those days. Your father and all of us were poor then, as I trust, my dears, you will never be ; but I was young enough to be romantic and wise enough to like independence, and this word ' secluded ' took my fancy.

" The misfortune was that it had taken the fancy, or just suited the requirements, of several previous tenants. You know, I dare say, the kind of person who rents a secluded house in the country ? Well, yes, there are several kinds ; but they seem to agree in being odious. No one knows where they come from, though they soon remove all doubt about where they're ' going to,' as the children say. ' Shady ' is the word, is it not ? Well, the previous tenants of Tresillack (from first to last a bewildering series) had been shady with a vengeance.

" I knew nothing of this when I first made application to the landlord, a solid yeoman inhabiting a farm at the foot of the coombe, on a cliff overlooking the beach. To him I presented myself fearlessly as a spinster of decent family and small but assured income, intending a rural life of combined seemliness and economy. He met my advances politely enough but with an air of suspicion which offended me. I began by disliking him for it : afterwards I set it down as an unpleasant feature in the local character. I was doubly mistaken. Farmer Hosking was slow-witted, but as honest a man as ever stood up against hard times ; and a more open and hospitable race than the people on that coast I never wish to meet. It was the caution of a child who had burnt his fingers, not once but many times. Had I known what I afterwards learned of Farmer Hosking's tribulations as landlord of a ' secluded country residence,' I should have approached him with the bashfulness proper to my suit and faltered as I undertook to prove the bright exception in a long line of painful experiences. He had bought the Tresillack estate twenty years before— on mortgage, I fancy—because the land adjoined his own and would pay him for tillage. But the house was a nuisance, an incubus ; and had been so from the beginning.

" ' Well, miss,' he said, ' you're welcome to look over it ; a pretty enough place, inside and out. There's no trouble about keys, because I've put in a house-keeper, a widow-woman, and she'll show you round. With your leave I'll step up the coombe so far with you, and put you in your way.' As I thanked him he paused and rubbed his chin. ' There's one thing I must tell you, though. Whoever takes the house must take Mrs. Carkeek along with it.'

" ' Mrs. Carkeek ? ' I echoed dolefully. ' Is that the housekeeper ? '

" ' Yes : she was wife to my late hind. I'm sorry, miss,' he added, my face telling him no doubt what sort of woman I expected Mrs. Carkeek to be ; ' but I had to make it a rule after—after some things had happened. And I dare say you won't find her so bad. Mary Carkeek's a sensible comfortable woman, and knows the place. She was in service there to Squire Kendall when he sold up and went : her first place it was.'

" ' I may as well see the house, anyhow,' said I dejectedly. So we started to walk up the coombe. The path, which ran beside a little chattering stream, was narrow for the most part, and Farmer Hosking, with an apology, strode on ahead to beat aside the brambles. But whenever its width allowed us to walk side by side I caught him from time to time stealing a shy inquisitive glance under his rough eyebrows. Courteously though he bore himself, it was clear that he could not sum me up to his satisfaction or bring me square with his notion of a tenant for his ' secluded country residence.'

" I don't know what foolish fancy prompted it, but about halfway up the coombe I stopped short and asked :

" ' There are no ghosts, I suppose ? '

" It struck me, a moment after I had uttered it, as a supremely silly question ; but he took it quite seriously. ' No ; I never heard tell of any *ghosts*.' He laid a queer sort of stress on the word. ' There's always been trouble with servants, and maids' tongues will be runnin'. But Mary Carkeek lives up there alone, and she seems comfortable enough.'

" We walked on. By-and-by he pointed with his stick. ' It don't look like a place for ghosts, now, do it ? '

" Certainly it did not. Above an untrimmed orchard rose a terrace of turf scattered with thorn bushes, and above this a terrace of stone, upon which stood the prettiest cottage I had ever seen. It was long and low and thatched ; a deep verandah ran from end to end. Clematis, Banksia roses and honeysuckle climbed the posts of this verandah, and big blooms of the Maréchal Niel were clustered along its roof, beneath the lattices of the bedroom windows. The house was small enough to be called a cottage, and rare enough in features and in situation to confer distinction on any tenant. It suggested what in those days we should have called ' elegant ' living. And I could have clapped my hands for joy.

" My spirits mounted still higher when Mrs. Carkeek opened the door to us. I had looked for a Mrs. Gummidge, and I found a healthy middle-aged woman with a thoughtful but contented face, and a smile which, without a trace of obsequiousness, quite bore out the farmer's description of her. She was a comfortable woman ; and while we walked through the rooms together (for Mr. Hosking waited outside) I ' took to ' Mrs. Carkeek. Her speech was direct and practical; the rooms, in spite of their faded furniture, were bright and exquisitely clean ; and somehow the very atmosphere of the house gave me a sense of well-being, of feeling at home and cared for ; yes, *of being loved*. Don't laugh, my dears ; for when I've done you may not think this fancy altogether foolish.

" I stepped out into the verandah, and Farmer Hosking pocketed the pruning-knife which he had been using on a bush of jasmine.

" ' This is better than anything I had dreamed of,' said I.

" ' Well, miss, that's not a wise way of beginning a bargain, if you'll excuse me.'

" He took no advantage, however, of my admission ; and we struck the bargain as we returned down the coombe to his farm, where the hired chaise waited to convey me back to the market town. I had meant to engage a maid of my own, but now it occurred to me that I might do very well with Mrs. Carkeek. This, too, was settled in the course of the next day or two, and within the week I had moved into my new home.

" I can hardly describe to you the happiness of my first month at Tresillack ; because (as I now believe) if I take the reasons which I had for being happy, one by one, there remains over something which I cannot account for. I was moderately young, entirely healthy ; I felt myself independent and adventurous ; the season was high summer, the weather glorious, the garden in all the pomp of June, yet sufficiently unkempt to keep me busy, give me a sharp appetite for meals, and send me to bed in that drowsy stupor which comes of the odours of earth. I spent the most of my time out of doors.

winding up the day's work as a rule with a walk down the cool valley, along the beach and back.

"I soon found that all housework could be safely left to Mrs. Carkeek. She did not talk much ; indeed her only fault (a rare one in housekeepers) was that she talked too little, and even when I addressed her seemed at times unable to give me her attention. It was as though her mind strayed off to some small job she had forgotten, and her eyes wore a listening look, as though she waited for the neglected task to speak and remind her. But as a matter of fact she forgot nothing. Indeed, my dears, I was never so well attended to in my life.

"Well, that is what I'm coming to. That, so to say, is just *it*. The woman not only had the rooms swept and dusted, and my meals prepared to the moment. In a hundred odd little ways this orderliness, these preparations, seemed to read my desires. Did I wish the roses renewed in a bowl upon the dining-table, sure enough at the next meal they would be replaced by fresh ones. Mrs. Carkeek (I told myself) must have surprised and interpreted a glance of mine. And yet I could not remember having glanced at the bowl in her presence. And how on earth had she guessed the very roses, the very shapes and colours I had lightly wished for ? This is only an instance, you understand. Every day, and from morning to night, I happened on others, each slight enough, but all together bearing witness to a ministering intelligence as subtle as it was untiring.

"I am a light sleeper, as you know, with an uncomfortable knack of waking with the sun and roaming early. No matter how early I rose at Tresillack, Mrs. Carkeek seemed to have preceded me. Finally I had to conclude that she arose and dusted and tidied as soon as she judged me safely a-bed. For once, finding the drawing-room (where I had been sitting late) ' redded up ' at four in the morning, and no trace of a plate of raspberries which I had carried thither after dinner and left overnight, I determined to test her, and walked through to the kitchen, calling her by name. I found the kitchen as clean as a pin, and the fire laid, but no trace of Mrs. Carkeek. I walked upstairs and knocked at her door. At the second knock a sleepy voice cried out, and presently the good woman stood before me in her nightgown, looking (I thought) very badly scared.

"' No,' I said, ' it's not a burglar. But I've found out what I wanted, that you do your morning's work over night.

But you mustn't wait for me when I choose to sit up. And now go back to your bed like a good soul, whilst I take a run down to the beach.'

" She stood blinking in the dawn. Her face was still white.

" ' Oh, miss,' she gasped, ' I made sure you must have seen something ! '

" ' And so I have,' I answered, ' but it was neither burglars nor ghosts.'

" ' Thank God ! ' I heard her say as she turned her back to me in her grey bedroom—which faced the north. And I took this for a carelessly pious expression and ran downstairs, thinking no more of it.

" A few days later I began to understand.

" The plan of Tresillack house (I must explain) was simplicity itself. To the left of the hall as you entered was the dining-room ; to the right the drawing-room, with a boudoir beyond. The foot of the stairs faced the front door, and beside it, passing a glazed inner door, you found two others right and left, the left opening on the kitchen, the right on a passage which ran by a store-cupboard under the bend of the stairs to a neat pantry with the usual shelves and linen-press, and under the window (which faced north) a porcelain basin and brass tap. On the first morning of my tenancy I had visited this pantry and turned the tap ; but no water ran. I supposed this to be accidental. Mrs. Carkeek had to wash up glass ware and crockery, and no doubt Mrs. Carkeek would complain of any failure in the water supply.

" But the day after my surprise visit (as I called it) I had picked a basketful of roses, and carried them into the pantry as a handy place to arrange them in. I chose a china bowl and went to fill it at the tap. Again the water would not run.

" I called Mrs. Carkeek. ' What is wrong with this tap ? ' I asked. ' The rest of the house is well enough supplied.'

" ' I don't know, miss. I never use it.'

" ' But there must be a reason ; and you must find it a great nuisance washing up the plate and glasses in the kitchen. Come around to the back with me, and we'll have a look at the cisterns.'

" ' The cisterns 'll be all right, miss. I assure you I don't find it a trouble.'

" But I was not to be put off. The back of the house stood but ten feet from a wall which was really but a stone face built against the cliff cut away by the architect. Above the cliff rose the kitchen garden, and from its lower path we looked over the wall's parapet upon the cisterns. There were two— a very large one, supplying the kitchen and the bathroom above the kitchen ; and a small one, obviously fed by the other, and as obviously leading, by a pipe which I could trace, to the pantry. Now the big cistern stood almost full, and yet the small one, though on a lower level, was empty.

" ' It's as plain as daylight,' said I. ' The pipe between the two is choked.' And I clambered on to the parapet.

" ' I wouldn't, miss. The pantry tap is only cold water, and no use to me. From the kitchen boiler I gets it hot, you see.'

" ' But I want the pantry water for my flowers.' I bent over and groped. ' I thought as much ! ' said I, as I wrenched out a thick plug of cork and immediately the water began to flow. I turned triumphantly on Mrs Carkeek, who had grown suddenly red in the face. Her eyes were fixed on the cork in my hand. To keep it more firmly wedged in its place somebody had wrapped it round with a rag of calico print ; and, discoloured though the rag was, I seemed to recall the pattern (a lilac sprig). Then, as our eyes met, it occurred to me that only two mornings before Mrs. Carkeek had worn a print gown of the same sprigged pattern.

" I had the presence of mind to hide this very small discovery, sliding over it some quite trivial remark ; and presently Mrs. Carkeek regained her composure. But I own I felt disappointed in her. It seemed such a paltry thing to be disingenuous over. She had deliberately acted a fib before me ; and why ? Merely because she preferred the kitchen to the pantry tap. It was childish. ' But servants are all the same,' I told myself. ' I must take Mrs. Carkeek as she is ; and, after all, she is a treasure.'

" On the second night after this, and between eleven and twelve o'clock, I was lying in bed and reading myself sleepy over a novel of Lord Lytton's, when a small sound disturbed me. I listened. The sound was clearly that of water trickling ; and I set it down to rain. A shower (I told myself) had filled the water-pipes which drained the roof. Somehow I could not fix the sound. There was a water pipe against the wall just outside my window. I rose and drew up the blind.

" To my astonishment no rain was falling ; no rain had fallen. I felt the slate window-sill ; some dew had gathered there—no more. There was no wind, no cloud : only a still moon high over the eastern slope of the coombe, the distant

plash of waves, and the fragrance of many roses. I went back
to bed and listened again. Yes, the trickling sound continued,
quite distinct in the silence of the house, not to be confused
for a moment with the dull murmur of the beach. After a
while it began to grate on my nerves. I caught up my candle,
flung my dressing-gown about me, and stole softly downstairs.

"Then it was simple. I traced the sound to the pantry.
'Mrs. Carkeek has left the tap running,' said I : and, sure
enough, I found it so—a thin trickle steadily running to waste
in the porcelain basin. I turned off the tap, went contentedly
back to my bed, and slept.

"—— for some hours. I opened my eyes in darkness,
and at once knew what had awakened me. The tap was
running again. Now it had shut easily in my hand, but not
so easily that I could believe it had slipped open again of its
own accord. 'This is Mrs. Carkeek's doing,' said I ; and am
afraid I added 'Bother Mrs. Carkeek!'

"Well, there was no help for it : so I struck a light, looked
at my watch, saw that the hour was just three o'clock, and
descended the stairs again. At the pantry door I paused. I
was not afraid—not one little bit. In fact the notion that
anything might be wrong had never crossed my mind. But I
remember thinking, with my hand on the door, that if Mrs.
Carkeek were in the pantry I might happen to give her a
severe fright.

"I pushed the door open briskly. Mrs. Carkeek was not
there. But something *was* there, by the porcelain basin—
something which might have sent me scurrying upstairs two
steps at a time, but which as a matter of fact held me to the spot.
My heart seemed to stand still—so still ! And in the stillness
I remember setting down the brass candlestick on a tall nest
of drawers beside me.

"Over the porcelain basin and beneath the water trickling
from the tap I saw two hands.

"That was all—two small hands, a child's hands. I
cannot tell you how they ended.

"No : they were not cut off. I saw them quite distinctly :
just a pair of small hands and the wrists, and after that—
nothing. They were moving briskly—washing themselves
clean. I saw the water trickle and splash over them—not
through them—but just as it would be on real hands. They
were the hands of a little girl, too. Oh, yes, I was sure of that
at once. Boys and girls wash their hands differently. I can't
just tell you what the difference is, but it's unmistakable.

" I saw all this before my candle slipped and fell with a crash. I had set it down without looking—for my eyes were fixed on the basin—and had balanced it on the edge of the nest of drawers. After the crash, in the darkness there, with the water running, I suffered some bad moments. Oddly enough, the thought uppermost with me was that I *must* shut off that tap before escaping. I *had* to And after a while I picked up all my courage, so to say, between my teeth, and with a little sob thrust out my hand and did it. Then I fled.

" The dawn was close upon me : and as soon as the sky reddened I took my bath, dressed and went downstairs. And there at the pantry door I found Mrs. Carkeek, also dressed, with my candlestick in her hand.

" ' Ah ! ' said I, ' you picked it up.'

" Our eyes met. Clearly Mrs. Carkeek wished me to begin, and I determined at once to have it out with her.

" ' And you knew all about it. That's what accounts for your plugging up the cistern.'

" ' You saw . . . ? ' she began.

" ' Yes, yes. And you must tell me all about it—never mind how bad. Is——is it—murder ? '

" ' Law bless you, miss, whatever put such horrors in your head ? '

" ' She was washing her hands.'

" ' Ah, so she does, poor dear ! But—murder ! And dear little Miss Margaret, that wouldn't go to hurt a fly ! '

" ' Miss Margaret ? '

" ' Eh, she died at seven year. Squire Kendall's only daughter ; and that's over twenty year ago. I was her nurse, miss, and I know—diphtheria it was ; she took it down in the village.'

" ' But how do you know it is Margaret ? '

" ' Those hands—why, how could I mistake, that used to be her nurse ? '

" ' But why does she wash them ? '

" ' Well, miss, being always a dainty child—and the house-work, you see——'

" I took a long breath. ' Do you mean to tell me that all this tidying and dusting——' I broke off. ' Is *she* who has been taking this care of me ? '

" Mrs. Carkeek met my look steadily.

" ' Who else, miss ? '

" ' Poor little soul ! '

" ' Well now '—Mrs. Carkeek rubbed my candlestick with

the edge of her apron—' I'm so glad you take it like this. For there isn't really nothing to be afraid of—is there ? ' She eyed me wistfully. ' It's my belief she loves you, miss. But only to think what a time she must have had with the others ! '

" ' The others ? ' I echoed.

" ' The other tenants, miss : the ones afore you.'

" ' Were they bad ? '

" ' They was awful. Didn't Farmer Hosking tell you ? They carried on fearful—one after another, and each one worse than the last.'

" ' What was the matter with them ? Drink ? '

" ' Drink, miss, with some of 'em. There was the Major— he used to go mad with it, and run about the coombe in his nightshirt. Oh, scandalous ! And his wife drank too—that is, if she ever *was* his wife. Just think of that tender child washing up after their nasty doings ! '

" I shivered.

" ' But that wasn't the worst, miss—not by a long way. There was a pair here—from the colonies, or so they gave out—with two children, a boy and gel, the eldest scarce six. Poor mites ! '

" ' Why, what happened ? '

" ' They beat those children, miss—your blood would boil !—*and* starved, *and* tortured 'em, it's my belief. You could hear their screams, I've been told, away back in the high-road, and that's the best part of half a mile. Sometimes they was locked up without food for days together. But it's my belief that little Miss Margaret managed to feed them somehow. Oh, I can see her, creeping to the door and comforting ! '

" ' But perhaps she never showed herself when these awful people were here, but took to flight until they left.'

" ' You didn't never know her, miss. The brave she was ! She'd have stood up to lions. She've been here all the while : and only to think what her innocent eyes and ears must have took in ! There was another couple——' Mrs. Carkeek sunk her voice.

" ' Oh, hush ! ' said I, ' if I'm to have any peace of mind in this house ! '

" ' But you won't go, miss ? She loves you, I know she do. And think what you might be leaving her to—what sort of tenant might come next. For she can't go. She've been here ever since her father sold the place. He died soon after. You musn't go ! '

" Now I had resolved to go, but all of a sudden I felt how mean this resolution was .

" ' After all,' said I, ' there's nothing to be afraid of.'

" ' That's it, miss ; nothing at all. I don't even believe it's so very uncommon. Why, I've heard my mother tell of farmhouses where the rooms were swept every night as regular as clockwork, and the floors sanded, and the pots and pans scoured, and all while the maids slept. They put it down to the piskies ; but we know better, miss, and now we've got the secret between us we can lie easy in our beds, and if we hear anything, say " God bless the child ! " and go to sleep.'

" ' Mrs. Carkeek,' said I, ' there's only one condition I have to make.'

" ' What's that ? '

" ' Why, that you let me kiss you.

" ' Oh, you dear ! ' said Mrs. Carkeek as we embraced : and this was as close to familiarity as she allowed herself to go in the whole course of my acquaintance with her.

" I spent three years at Tresillack, and all that while Mrs. Carkeek lived with me and shared the secret. Few women, I dare to say, were ever so completely wrapped around with love as we were during those three years. It ran through my waking life like a song : it smoothed my pillow, touched and made my table comely, in summer lifted the heads of the flowers as I passed, and in winter watched the fire with me and kept it bright.

" ' Why did I ever leave Tresillack ? ' Because one day, at the end of five years, Farmer Hosking brought me word that he had sold the house—or was about to sell it ; I forget which. There was no avoiding it, at any rate ; the purchaser being a Colonel Kendall, a brother of the old Squire.'

" ' A married man ? ' I asked.

" ' Yes, miss ; with a family of eight. As pretty children as ever you see, and the mother a good lady. It's the old home to Colonel Kendall.'

" ' I see. And that is why you feel bound to sell.'

" ' It's a good price, too, that he offers. You mustn't think but I'm sorry enough——'

" ' To turn me out ? I thank you, Mr. Hosking ; but you are doing the right thing.'

" Since Mrs. Carkeek was to stay, the arrangement lacked nothing of absolute perfection—except, perhaps, that it found no room for me

" ' *She*—Margaret—will be happy,' I said ; ' with her cousins, you know.'

" ' Oh yes, miss, she will be happy, sure enough.' Mrs. Carkeek agreed.

" So when the time came I packed up my boxes, and tried to be cheerful. But on the last morning, when they stood corded in the hall, I sent Mrs. Carkeek upstairs upon some poor excuse, and stepped alone into the pantry

" ' Margaret ! ' I whispered.

" There was no answer at all. I had scarcely dared to hope for one. Yet I tried again, and, shutting my eyes this time stretched out both hands and whispered :

" ' Margaret ! '

" And I will swear to my dying day that two little hands stole and rested—for a moment only—in mine."